Scrubs

L.M. NELSON

Scrubs
Copyright © 2015 L.M. Nelson

Edited by Bonnye Cavazos
Cover Art courtesy of:
Rich Niewiroski Jr (bridge) CC2.5
Sprinno CC1.0
pixabay.com alles CC0

ISBN-10: 0-9985135-0-4
ISBN-13: 978-0-9985135-0-8

2 3 4 5 6 7 8 9 10

PRINTED IN THE UNITED STATES OF AMERICA

This is a work of fiction. The events and characters
described herein are imaginary and are not intended to refer
to specific places or living persons. The opinions expressed
in this manuscript are solely the opinions of the author. The
author has represented and warranted full ownership
and/or legal right to publish all the materials in this book.

Acknowledgements

Special thanks to Kaylie, Lana, and Bonnye for their contributions to this book, and to my family for their patience through this process.

Chapter One

"Alright!" Randy cheered as he high-fived his best friend, Jim Ryan.

"And another one down. That's kickass, Bro." After their third consecutive volleyball game win, Jim spun the ball on his finger and set it down in the sand.

The warm summer sun beat down on the beaches of Santa Cruz where several college students gathered for their last big beach blowout before the start of a new academic year. Randy and Jim had played several games now and were taking a break before meeting their next opponents. Hot sand permeated his bare toes as Randy took off his shirt, exposing his muscularly toned chest and abs. He tossed the shirt onto a pile of sand beside his sandals then reached into the cooler on the side of the makeshift volleyball court and grabbed a blue, berry-flavored Gatorade. Dressed in his tropical print red and orange swimming shorts, he took a big swig before he sat down in the sand to take a breather while contemplating the upcoming year. The slightest drop of sweat fell from his brow, and his chest was moist with perspiration, causing him to glisten in the hot summer sun. He held the Gatorade bottle in his hand with his forearms rested on his bent knees.

"Yo, Randy!" Jim hollered. "I'm gonna grab the sunscreen out of the car. I'll be right back."

Randy flashed his hand in acknowledgment, and Jim headed toward the parked car. Girls all over UC Berkeley knew Randal Hanson, or Randy as all of his friends called him, and they adored him. He was charming, witty, and intelligent. At six feet tall, he was good looking, muscular, and athletically built with a firm body and broad, strong shoulders. His brown wavy hair, with bangs slightly dangling over his forehead, deep brown eyes, and sexy smile gave him the power of seduction, which always made the women swoon. He prided himself with the fact that he was a ladies' man. He had the reputation of being romantic, and rumor had it he was an exceptional lover. Besides enticing the ladies, his undeniable boyish charm also won him many friends. Everyone he ran into seemed to like him.

While Randy gulped down his Gatorade, out of the corner of his eye something captured his undivided attention. Looking up from his drink, he caught glance of a thin, femininely curved woman with long, flowing, light brown hair. She had on very short denim shorts and a bright yellow bikini top that tied behind her neck. She was staring at him, but he didn't mind. He was staring at her too. Then the young woman made her way toward him. She walked with a delicate, yet confident gait. Rounded hips, slender waistline, silky legs, toned muscles, sun-tanned skin—she had a perfect figure. As she got closer to him, Randy was more able to see the appealing facial features she had. Her eyes were a beautiful shade of emerald green and her full rounded lips were luscious and very kissable. She had sexy hands, soft and feminine, with her long fingernails painted in a French manicure. Her estimated C cup-sized breasts filled out her bikini top perfectly, and with those sexy feminine curves, he couldn't keep his eyes off her.

Jim came back with a bottle of sunscreen in his hand just as this woman stood crosscourt in front of them with her hands on her hips and looked Randy straight in the eye. Randy ogled over her with a devilish grin. Jim knew that look. "Oh, Jesus. Here we go again," he said, knowing Randy was sitting right there and could hear every word. But Jim Ryan knew his friend well. Randy was a sweet talker and knew exactly how to get what he wanted out of women.

This poor girl was tempting his friend's exceedingly hungry appetite.

Randy flashed her a friendly, charming smile.

She returned the gesture, with what Randy thought was the most beautiful smile he'd ever seen. Then, to Randy's surprise, she offered a challenge. "You guys up for a match or what?" she asked.

She was sassy and had a bit of feistiness in her tone. Randy liked it. He stood up, put his empty bottle back in the cooler, and confidently replied, "Why, you have something to prove?"

"Maybe." Again, she challenged him. "You game or not?"

Randy peered over at Jim, wanting his opinion. Jim shrugged, not really caring what Randy decided to do. All attention turned back to this woman, who now had a pretty blonde girl standing next to her. Randy glanced at the blonde, then drew his eyes back to the brunette. "Alright. If you think you can handle us, you're on."

She smiled again, picked the volleyball up from the sand, and took her side of the court with her friend. Randy stared at her butt as she walked. It was round and firm, and her tight shorts accentuated every curve of it.

Jim chuckled as he watched his friend lusting over her. "Why does this not surprise me?" he questioned in his usual smartass manner.

"What?" Randy pulled his eyes away from her.

"You know exactly what I'm talkin' about, Bro. Two babes?"

Randy flashed that devilish grin of his. "Oh, yeah. Pretty girls in bikinis." His head turned to the brunette again, staring in lustful delight. "Jim, do you see her?"

"Yeah, I see her."

"She…" Randy checked her out from head to toe, "is amazingly hot. Wow," he added, trying to contain his uncontrollable desire for this girl. "Oh, man, this is gonna be fun."

"Should be an easy win."

But Randy had other thoughts. He stared at the beautiful brunette with ravenous eyes. "Winning isn't what I was thinking," he said, raising his eyebrows lustfully.

"That's what I'm afraid of." Jim saw the look on Randy's face and knew what he wanted. That's all Randy ever wanted.

Randy confidently approached the court. "Whenever you are ready, ladies."

And the game was on.

He intended to prolong the game as long as possible so he could watch these women in bikinis play in the sand. He took it easy on the women at first, missing the ball on purpose several times to get the score up to 14-13 with the girls in the lead. He figured he'd pour it on at the last minute.

However, despite his very careful planning, things did not go as he anticipated. Jim served the ball, and it volleyed a few times. Then, unexpectedly, this dark-haired, green-eyed, luscious-lipped, gorgeous girl jumped up and spiked the ball right at Randy's face. Randy dove face first but landed flat on his side, throwing sand all over himself. He completely missed. In fact, the ball hit him smack in the head.

The brunette grinned smugly then turned and gave her friend a high five.

Jim strolled over to Randy, trying not to laugh. "Happy, Hotshot?"

Randy got up and dusted the sand off himself. "Damn."

"Is that what you were thinkin'? Gettin' wiped out by bodacious babes?"

Randy glared at him. "No."

Jim peered over at the girls who were staring at them, giggling. "Guess you really impressed them. Nice job, Romeo."

Randy smiled sheepishly.

Jim checked the time on his watch. "Man, I better go. Trina will go postal on my ass if I hang out here all day."

Katrina Rogers had been Jim's girlfriend for many years and was rather possessive of his time. She had a bit of a temper when she didn't get her way and blamed many things on Jim, even though most of the time he had nothing to do with them. Randy hated that Trina treated Jim that way, and the sad thing was Jim did nothing about it. Randy didn't understand why his best friend put up with that. He wouldn't. But it was Jim's life, so he didn't interfere. "I'll catch up with you on Monday," he said to his friend.

"See you in class, Dude." Before Jim headed to his car, he gave Randy a fist wave with his pinky and thumb sticking out, better known as the shaka sign. A shaka sign was the ultimate symbol of aloha in the local surfing culture of Hawaii. Interpreted to mean 'hang loose' or 'right on', the shaka was a constant reminder that it was not the norm to worry or rush. Although Jim was not a native of Hawaii, the shaka salute was used as a standard greeting for him.

After Jim left, Randy began to clean up. When he leaned over to pick up the ball, he heard a sweet voice behind him say, "Impressive."

He turned around to find the brunette staring at him. "You talkin' to me?" he asked.

"Yes."

"Nice move, but warn me the next time you try to take my head off."

"Oh, I don't know. I thought you looked kind of cute down in the sand like that," she quipped, trying to hold back a laugh.

This woman was a bit of a tease and seemed to find great joy in poking fun at him. Yet, he found her bantering adorable. He returned a smile and held out his hand in greeting. "I'm Randy."

She shook his hand. "Nice to meet you, Randy. I'm Jane."

Turning away from her, he walked over to the pile of sand to grab his shirt. "You're a good player. Do you play a lot?"

"I play a little."

5

He hesitated for a minute as he slipped his shirt over his head. "You live around here?"

She shook her head. "No. I'm just down here for the weekend enjoying the weather with my friends."

"Me too." He sat down, wiped the sand off his feet, and slipped on his sandals. "Where you from?"

"San Francisco. I'm a student at Cal." She sat down cross-legged by the cooler and made figure eights in the sand with her finger.

"Cal Berkeley?"

"Yup."

This sparked his interest. "I'm a student at Berkeley too. How long you been going there?"

"This is my third year. I'm an Alpha Phi." She beamed with pride.

Randy's eyebrows rose to this statement. "An Alpha girl, huh?"

"You have a problem with sorority girls?"

"No, not at all. I love sorority girls." He was even more intrigued by her now, so he probed further. "What are you studying?"

"Psychology," she answered.

He pondered this for a second. Psychology—the study of the brain, seekers of deep thoughts and feelings. Captivating topic. "Interesting," he mused. "You're a brain analyzer."

She was quick to correct. "Not exactly."

This woman was energetic, she was amazingly beautiful, she had the most incredible body Randy had ever laid eyes on, and he enjoyed carrying on a conversation with her. He found her fascinating. Even though he was interested in what she had to say, he tried to appear nonchalant by packing things into his grey athletic bag.

"What about you?" she asked curiously as she watched him.

"What about me?"

"What is your major?"

Uh oh. There it was. The question Randy hated women to ask him. The question he always hesitated to answer when they did ask. Every woman that ever asked him that tried to get him to commit to something serious. Even though he loved the attention this gave him, the prospect of having to settle with one woman made him want to run away screaming. He thoroughly enjoyed the company of women, but avoided love, relationships, and commitment of any kind at all costs. He liked having women around at his convenience, when it served his purposes. He was dedicated and hard-working and would let nothing, especially a woman, stand in the way of accomplishing his goals.

There was no doubt he was proud of the education he was receiving at University of California, Berkeley. Throughout his five years at Cal, he had taken pre-med classes as an undergrad while he worked toward his Bachelor's Degree in Public Health. He graduated summa cum laude. He continued his 4.0 grade point average throughout his first year of medical school. Now, excited and ambitious as ever, he was ready to begin his second year. However, medical school and relationships did not mix, in his opinion.

After some thought, he decided to tell her the truth. "I'm a medical student."

This girl's reaction was different than any other he had ever encountered. She didn't seem that interested in what he did and didn't give him the flirty eye he usually received when a woman found out he was studying medicine. She simply said, "Oh, I see how it is. You call me a brain analyzer when all along you are a brain dissector. Wow, there's a combination. Think of the damage we could do."

This comment made him laugh. Randy was awestruck by this woman—this beautiful, witty woman with an attitude unlike any he had ever witnessed.

She curled her lip in disgust. "You don't dissect dead bodies and rip apart tissues and stuff like that, do you?"

"They're called cadavers, and no, I don't rip apart tissues. We analyze them, examine them. It takes a very steady and gentle hand to…"

Her mind momentarily drifted. "Mmm, chicken," she blurted out. "I'm hungry. Are you hungry?"

Where did that random comment come from? How did this conversation turn from tissue ripping to food? He raised one eyebrow. "What?"

"Aren't you hungry?" She stood up and dusted the sand off her legs. "I don't know about you, but playing volleyball in the heat makes me hungry, and chicken sounds really good."

Ok. Maybe he was hungry. Chicken actually did sound good. Her mind was drifty; she was spontaneous and fun, and he loved it. The more this woman spoke, the more enthralled by her he became. Every word that came out of her pretty mouth intrigued him.

Just then they heard, "JANE!" She pivoted her head to find her friends signaling her to join them. "Let's go!"

"I'm coming!" She turned to Randy and said, "I have to go."

"I heard," he replied. "Maybe I'll see you on campus sometime."

"Maybe." She stared at him for a minute before she said, "It was nice meeting you, Randy."

"You too, Jane."

She flashed a beautiful smile then waved at him and ran to join her friends.

He laughed under his breath. Where did she come from? Even though it had no intellectual content whatsoever, he found their conversation more stimulating than any he'd had in a while. What a fascinating girl. Beautiful, fun-loving, sexy, conversation that held his attention, which wasn't easy to do, and the most amazing smile he had ever seen. He would definitely have to track her down. As he packed up his car to head back to Berkeley, he whistled a cheery tune.

Chapter Two

Classes for the new semester began Monday morning. Randy, Jim, and some of their friends from medical school gathered for their orientation to year two. Excitement and anticipation flooded the lecture hall.

All of the friends in Randy's circle had worked together in Anatomy lab as first year students. Together, they started a study group which met weekly to work on projects, analyze clinical data, and study for practicals and written exams. They planned to keep the group intact this year.

The first of Randy's friends was Amanda Stevens, Mandy to those close to her. She was the spontaneous one of the group, unpredictable and eccentric. A pretty blonde who was overly feminine with her pink lacy attire and flowery accessories, Mandy came across as slightly ditzy, although she was quite intelligent. She was scatter-brained most of the time and was dreadfully unorganized. She was impulsive and had no qualms about blurting out whatever was on her mind, regardless of who was around to hear it— never in a rude or disrespectful way, but she definitely expressed her opinion.

Steve Hall was the goof-off who never really seemed to take any of the work they did seriously. He coasted along, relying on others to get him by. He rarely had the appropriate equipment he needed and always lost pens and forgot paper. When a deadline came up, even though it was clearly written on the syllabus, Steve surprisingly knew nothing about it. He was arrogant and always wore a smartass grin on his face to go along with his laissez faire attitude. When he wasn't required to dress for professional purposes, he lived in high top tennis shoes, baggy jeans, and concert tee-shirts. His hair was purposefully messy, and he often appeared as if he just rolled out of bed, slapping himself together without ever looking into a mirror.

Bruce Buckman, the incredulous one, was the inquisitor and the one who paid attention to minute details. He was overly neat, incredibly organized, and private to an almost eerie degree. No one knew much about him because he didn't share personal information. He often had an intensely solemn expression on his face, and everyone always wondered what he was thinking. His eyebrows seemed to be permanently arched in a menacing downward position. That, along with the mustache and dark, flawless haircut he possessed, added to his mysteriousness.

Sarah Chan was a petite Chinese American who stood at only five feet tall. She was the introvert of the group. She didn't talk much unless she had a strong opinion about something. She was shy around unfamiliar people, yet very fluent and vocal in both Chinese and English. She spoke favorably of her heritage, but was a typical American college girl in her jeans and hooded sweatshirts.

Jim was the mediator of the group, the one who kept everyone content and happy. He was the peacekeeper of the clan, and he was a chronic joker. His spiky dishpan blonde hair, brightly colored tropical print Hawaiian shirts, baggy shorts, shark tooth necklace, and flip flops accentuated his class clown personality. His sunglasses sat on the top of his head when he wasn't out in the sun wearing them, and his cheery disposition made people smile. The way he dressed and the surfer slang he used led everyone to believe he was a surfer, yet he had never been on a surfboard in his life.

And Randy…he was the smart one of the group, the logical one, the organizer, the initiator, the one who guaranteed everyone was on task and serious. He was the ring leader and made sure the job was complete and done right. He made it very clear that he took their sessions seriously and was not in medical school to play around. He was a dedicated student, a diligent researcher, and in many ways a perfectionist and an overachiever. Randy was poised and confident—stress and pressure seemed to make him thrive rather than wear him down. And the high expectations he set for himself made him push the others right along with him. The group knew him well, as he was a pretty social guy. His friends teased him all the time because he drank too much coffee and had been with so many women they all lost count a long time ago. As his clothing and high priced watch indicated, he was from a wealthy family. He was well liked by everyone who knew him and was damn good when it came to medicine, one of the best.

Jim and Randy's friendship was well known among their circle of friends. Although they seemed quite different from each other on the outside, those two men had a connection the others didn't fully understand. Their playful, carefree relationship gave the study sessions a lighter, more relaxed feel.

After a busy day of introductory lectures, the six friends decided to meet at the Student Union Building for lunch to catch up on happenings that occurred over summer vacation. As Randy filled his tray with food, he turned to Jim and asked, "What do you know about the Greeks?"

Jim pondered over this unusual question. "Like Socrates? He's the one who said," his voice deepened as he quoted, "I know nothing except the fact of my own ignorance."

"No, not Philosophy, Jackass. Greeks," Randy corrected. "Fraternities and sororities."

"Since when do you care about Greeks?"

"You ever heard of the Alpha Phis?" Randy asked.

"Yes I have. The Phis are the ones who do all that philanthropy work for Women's Cardiac Care. You know, the ones who pass out those red dress pins and *TAKE HEART* wristbands. The red chicks."

Oh yes. Randy knew who they were. Those women were all over campus promoting their causes. "Those are the Alpha Phis?"

"Yeah."

"Aren't they the ones who do that cardiac care benefit run through the Berkeley campus every fall? The Bear Run I think it's called."

"Yup. That's them," Jim confirmed.

"So they support medical efforts," Randy said. "Good to know."

Jim didn't understand why Randy cared so much. He'd never shown an interest in any of the sororities before. "Why you hung up on the Phis?"

"Just wondering. Isn't the Alpha Phi house over by the…" In mid-thought, as Randy was about to sit down and eat his lunch, something caught his eye that made him look twice.

The grin on Randy's face made Jim inquire, "What?"

"I'll be damned." Randy stared off to another part of the room.

Jim peeked that direction but didn't see anything unusual. "What is it?"

"There she is." Randy stared in a daze, admiring the beauty before him.

Jim squinted his eyes to get a better look. "Who?"

"Jane."

Jane? Who the hell was Jane? Jim had never heard that name before. "Who's Jane?"

"The girl from the beach the other day. Remember?"

Jim laughed out loud. "Oh, you mean the bodacious wahine in the yellow bikini top who tried to squash your cojones with a volleyball?"

Randy continued to stare at her, almost in a hypnotic trance. "Yup."

Jim knew Randy better than anyone else alive, and he knew what he was thinking. Randy wanted to sweet talk this girl, romance her for a night, and hopefully get a one night stand out of it. That's always what Randy did. "So, Casanova, how you gonna reel this one in?"

Randy sniggered, "I'm just gonna talk to her."

"Yeah, right."

Randy glared at Jim, not impressed with his comment, true or not. After all, Randy did have the reputation of dating several women at once, but never committing to any. And Jim was right. Randy was a bed hopper and was definitely hoping to add this one to his list. He looked over at Jane again and said, "Now, if you'll excuse me. I have some business to attend to."

Jim had to laugh. "Go get 'em, Tiger."

Randy sauntered over to Jane's table with his lunch tray in his hands and his book bag over his shoulder. He cleared his throat to get her attention.

She glanced up from her reading and saw a handsome man with a charming smile looking down at her. She smiled when she recognized who he was.

That smile. Randy loved her smile. And he remembered those green eyes of hers as he looked into them again. "Is this seat taken?"

She moved an immense pile of books over to the side of the table to make room for him. "No. Go ahead."

He set his tray on the table, removed his backpack and placed it on the floor next to him, then sat down across from her. She had a chicken sandwich on her tray, which made him think back to the conversation he had with her out on the beach a few days earlier. "I see you got that chicken you wanted."

"Oh." She stared at his tray, repulsed. "How can you eat that?"

"Eat what?"

"That. Do you have any idea the amount of salt content, cholesterol, and fat that are in that hamburger you are about to put into your body? How can you eat fried food?"

He took a big bite.

She curled her lip. "Gross."

He chewed, swallowed, and let her reflect on that for a while. Then he picked up a licorice stick from her tray.

She tried to snatch it back. "Hey!"

"And what about this?" he said, dangling it in front of her. "What is this? This can't be good for you."

"That happens to have no calories and no fat and isn't infested with grease. And besides, it's sweet. And you know what they say, you are what you eat. So I'm sweet. But what does your food say about you, Sir?"

With a look of enthrallment on his face, Randy asked, "Do you psychoanalyze everything on purpose or is that just a happy coincidence?" They both stared at each other for a moment then laughed. Jane was outgoing, inquisitive, and intelligent. Randy found her easy to talk to and very much enjoyed her company. "We never did finish our conversation the other day."

Her cheeks flushed a bit. "I'm sorry about that. My stomach took over my brain, I'm afraid."

"Does that happen to you a lot?"

"From time to time."

He gazed at her pretty face, completely engrossed.

"Tell me," she said. "What do medical students do besides study all the time?"

"We don't study all the time." He took another sip of coffee. "See, I'm polluting my body with caffeine as we speak."

"I can see that." Her eyes turned back to her book.

Randy lifted up the front cover to see what she was reading. "Cognitive Neuroscience?"

"Yup."

He skimmed through the titles of the other books she had. One caught his attention. "Hey! Molecular Biology. I took that class. If you ever need help with that one, let me know."

"I'll keep that in mind."

"Why do you have all these books? Isn't it heavy carrying all of these around?"

She lifted her chin. "Yes it is. But I just got back from the bookstore."

He nodded knowingly. The textbook shopping excursion, dreaded by every college student.

A short, humorless laugh left her lips. "Can you believe how much they charge for all of this?"

"Tell me about it. The average medical book costs over three-hundred bucks."

Ok. She now officially had no reason to complain. "Ouch."

"Yeah, and try paying medical school tuition sometime."

"I hope you don't have to pay for that all by yourself." She closed her book and put it in the pile with the others.

"I have a few scholarships. My parents pay for books, lab fees, and any tuition that isn't covered through financial aid, but living expenses are all mine, which is why I have a job."

"What kind of job?"

"Over at the student clinic. I stock shelves and help the doctor three nights a week and on Saturdays. It's not very glamorous work, but it pays the bills. And sometimes, if I'm a good boy," he joked, "I get to work with real patients."

Jane giggled at his self-mockery.

"The experience will be helpful when I join my dad's clinic."

"Is your dad a doctor?"

"Yes. He has his own practice."

"Doing what?"

"He's an obstetrician."

"Delivering babies," she clarified with a smile.

"Yes, among other things."

"Aw. How cute." Their conversation turned when her eyes drifted to a picture on the wall. "Is that Van Gogh?" she asked.

There she was, getting sidetracked again. Her mind moved around a lot, but he found her randomness delightful. Randy turned his head to look. "You like Van Gogh?"

"Yes. He is incredible. I love his Starry Night painting. One of my favorites."

Well, here was an opportunity. Evidently she liked art, Van Gogh in particular. He used this to his advantage. "You know, there's a Van Gogh exhibit over at the museum this weekend. We could go on Saturday if you'd like."

She shook her head. "Can't. Pledge weekend."

"That's right. Sorority girl." His eyes met hers, and his heart raced. As much as he didn't want to admit it, he was starting to genuinely like this girl. "Ok, let me try this another way. Is there a time this week when you are available? Maybe we could have dinner together."

She tilted her head intuitively. "You're trying to ask me out, aren't you?"

Bingo! She nailed it. "You're observant."

"I'm not doing anything Thursday night. Will that work?"

"Perfect." He stared at her for a second, finding himself hypnotized by her eyes. "6:30?"

"6:30 is fine," she agreed.

He pulled out a small notebook where he kept phone numbers of potentials. Clicking open a ball point pen, he asked, "Can I have your number, just in case?"

"In case of what?"

"I don't know, I get a flat tire or something. Better to call than to have you think I didn't show up."

That made sense, now that she thought about it. So she gave him her number.

"Thursday at 6:30. I'll pick you up." He closed his pen and returned it and the notebook to his backpack. "You said Alpha Phi, right?"

"Yes." She reached into her backpack and pulled out a red dress pin. "Here. Since you're a medical student, I'm sure you'll support our cause."

He looked at the pin and proudly stated, "Women's heart disease."

She couldn't believe he actually knew the significance of the pin. "You know what it represents."

"Of course I do."

"That's impressive. Most people have to ask." She glanced down at her watch and started to panic. "Oh crap!"

"What's wrong?"

"Oh my god, I'm going to be late." She frantically packed up her books and shoved them into her bag.

Randy grabbed a few and helped her zip it. When he picked up her backpack, he almost fell over. "Damn. That is heavy. You gonna be able to carry that?"

"Yeah, I got it." She took it from him and put it over her shoulder. "It was good to see you again, Randy."

"The pleasure is all mine." As she walked away, he called out, "Bye, Jane."

She smiled and waved on her way out the door.

Randy pinned the red dress pin on his backpack then picked up his tray and his bag and moseyed over to the table to join his friends. As he approached, they all stared at him. Uncomfortable with their gawking eyes, he asked, "What?"

"'Bout time you decided to join us." Jim moved over to make room for him.

"I had to take care of something." Randy set his things down then leaned over and whispered, "I got her number."

Jim shook his head. "Sucker."

"Who? Me?"

"No. Her. She has no idea what she's gotten herself into."

Randy didn't like Jim's tone. "What is that supposed to mean?"

"Come on, Randy. You and I both know what you're after."

"I was just talking to her."

"And now you have her number, and I bet you asked her out too."

"So?"

"You are so predictable," Jim said. "You find an uber hot babe, ask her out, get her number, then romance her all night. And somehow you manage to smooth talk her into your bed. I still don't know how you do that. You are primo slick with that, Dude. The Kahuna."

Randy rolled his eyes. "Jim, please."

But Jim continued, "But when she tries to get more serious, which of course you aren't interested in 'cause it makes you feel choked like you're suckin' down kelp, you bail for a new chick. And this one is no different. She took the bait and you reeled her in just like all the others. You wrote her name in your book, didn't you?"

Although Jim was right, something about this girl was different. Randy just couldn't put his finger on it. "I want to keep my options open."

With an extremely sarcastic timbre in his voice, Jim replied, "That is your choice, Dude. Commitment is mine." Jim poked at the red dress pin on Randy's bag making it all crooked. "Did she give that to you?"

Randy pushed Jim's hand away then carefully straightened it. "Leave it alone."

"Oh my god," Jim snickered, watching his friend obsessing over a pin. "That's why you were askin' about the Phis. She's a damn Phi, isn't she?"

"Why do you care?"

"She is," Jim teased. "Oh, this is classic. A sorority chick. And a damn red dress Phi." He couldn't stop laughing.

Annoyed by Jim's bantering, Randy ignored him and finished his cup of coffee.

After work that day, Randy studied alone in his apartment for a few hours. Unable to concentrate any longer, he looked up from his book and combed his bangs off his forehead. For some strange reason Jane's face kept popping into his head. Flustered by this, he stood up and walked into the living room.

"Hello," said a voice from a cage.

Randy owned an African Grey parrot. He had spent countless hours training this bird to say many different phrases. "Well, hello, Mr. Fingers. How are you today?"

"Happy day," replied the bird.

"Yes it is." He opened the cage door and reached inside, allowing the bird to perch onto his arm. "I met this girl."

"Pretty girl," squawked the bird.

Randy laughed. "Yes she is. Very pretty. She's sweet and fun and easy to talk to. She has beautiful eyes, a gorgeous smile…"

The bird wolf whistled.

Laughing, Randy replied, "Mr. Fingers. Shame on you." His book of names sat on the coffee table next to his phone. He stared at it in deep thought. "Hmm, I wonder if I should call her."

The bird imitated the sound of Randy's ringtone. "Pretty girl."

"You're right. I should call her." He placed the bird on top of the cage and picked up his cellphone. But he didn't dial her number right away. Instead, he blankly stared at his phone. Never before had he hesitated to call a woman he was attracted to. Any other girl and he would have jumped at the opportunity to find a way to coax her or butter her up. But Jane was different. Why did she have this strange effect on him? He reflected on this for a minute before he dialed her number.

Three rings later, a sweet voice answered, "Hello?"

For a second or two, Randy didn't say anything.

"Hello?" she said again. "Is anyone there?"

He took a few seconds to compose himself. "Hi, Jane. This is Randy."

"Oh, hello. Canceling already?"

Of course he wasn't canceling. Why would she think that? "No. Just called to say hello."

Men didn't call Jane just to say hello. Men called her because they wanted something from her. She wondered what he was up to. "Why?"

He didn't have an answer to that, so he quickly made something up. "Actually, I was wondering what kind of food you like." There. That sounded purposeful. She should be satisfied with that.

"I don't know. I'm not picky."

"Ok. In that case, wear something nice on Thursday."

"You didn't think I was wearing something nice today?"

Flustered, Randy sputtered, "I didn't say that. I'm just saying…"

She giggled. "I know. I'm messing with you."

Jane was witty and loved to tease him. Randy found this characteristic alluring. "So, how was your day?"

Why was he so interested in her day? Guys were never interested in her day. But she humored him and told him anyway. "It was ok. We went to the mall this afternoon and picked up some things for the recruitment party this weekend."

"You expecting a big turnout?"

"Probably thirty or so."

She was making conversation. This was good. He found that the more they talked, the more they had to say to each other. Time seemed to fly by, and before he knew it, two hours passed. Realizing he needed to return to his studies, Randy stated, "As much as I'm enjoying this conversation, I need to get some studying done."

"Ok. I'll see you on Thursday then."

"Yup," he replied. "6:30. I'll be there."

"Great! I'll see you then."

"I'm looking forward to it." He hung up and sat on the couch in quiet contemplation. This woman was amazing. She had the power to keep him entertained on the phone for hours, something no one had ever been able to do before. They had many things to talk about, and the conversation between them flowed smoothly. No struggling for words, no awkwardness. Just friendly, fun conversation.

The bird broke the silence by squawking, "Pretty girl."

"Yes, Mr. Fingers. Yes she is."

Chapter Three

Thursday evening finally rolled around, much to Randy's enjoyment. Hoping to make a good impression, he washed and vacuumed his car and even wiped down the dash with Armor All. Upon returning home, he showered, shaved, and dressed in a pair of khaki dress pants, a navy blue polo shirt, and a pair of brown loafers. He neatly combed his hair and brushed his teeth then grabbed his keys, his phone, his wallet, and his brown leather jacket and headed out the door. Before he picked up Jane, he stopped at the flower shop to buy a dozen roses.

Meanwhile, at the Alpha house, Jane dug through her closet searching for something appropriate to wear.

"Who is this guy?" her best friend and fellow sorority sister, Lisa, asked.

"I told you. He's that guy I met in Santa Cruz."

"What fraternity is he in?"

"He's not in a frat," Jane clarified. "He's a medical student here at Cal."

"What do you know about him? How do you know he's not some psycho?"

Jane pulled out a red, knee-length, spaghetti strap dress with a small slit up the side. "Would you stop worrying?"

"Do you even know where he lives?"

"No."

"What's his last name?" Lisa insisted on knowing.

"I don't know. I never asked him." She took the dress off the hanger and slipped it over her head then straightened the fabric and shaped it around her figure.

"So if something happens, we don't know who he is or where he lives."

"Lisa, please." Jane walked over to the other side of the room to grab a necklace from her jewelry box.

Lisa followed her. "Where is he taking you?"

"He didn't say."

Lisa grew anxious about this entire situation. "You don't know anything about him."

"And how am I supposed to get to know anything about him if I don't go out with him?" She clipped a solid gold chain around her neck and put on a pair of gold hoop earrings. "He's a nice guy."

Lisa was not convinced. "Do you have your phone?"

"Yes."

"And you promise you'll call if anything weird happens?"

"I'll be fine." Jane slipped on her black strapped, open-toed heels and fastened them over her ankles. Then she stood in front of the mirror and piled her hair on top of her head, holding it in place with hair pins. When she was finished, she turned to her friend and asked, "How do I look?"

Lisa dodged the question, still concerned over the fact that she did not know the man Jane was going out with. "Why are you getting all dressed up for some guy you hardly know?"

"Because he said to wear something nice. What are you worried about?"

"You," Lisa admitted. "What if he tries something?"

"You have never been this concerned about anyone else I've ever dated."

"That's because I knew all those other guys."

"Oh, and they were real winners too, weren't they?" Jane scorned.

Lisa ignored that remark.

"Stop worrying. I'll be fine." Jane grabbed a lightweight black cardigan and her black clutch bag. "I've met a nice guy who wants to talk to me and isn't a jerk. Can you let me enjoy this please?"

Not wanting to upset her friend, Lisa dropped the subject. "Turn around."

Jane spun around in a circle and posed.

Lisa eyed her from head to toe. She looked absolutely stunning, and that dress accentuated her curves perfectly. "You look great," Lisa complimented.

"Do you think he'll like it?"

"If he doesn't, he's a fool and doesn't deserve to go out with you. I don't think he deserves to go out with you anyway."

Jane gave Lisa a hug. "You're a good friend, but you need to stop worrying. I'll leave my phone on if that will make you feel better."

Randy pulled up in front of the Alpha Phi house in his shiny, freshly washed red Camaro convertible. He had the top down. After taking one last glance in the rearview mirror to make sure his hair was in place, he grabbed the roses off the passenger seat, removed his keys from the ignition, and stepped out of the car. He beeped the alarm before he walked up to the door, whistling happily.

When he knocked, a young woman in shorts and a tee-shirt gave him a funny look. "May I help you?"

"Yes. Is Jane here?"

She sneered at him. "Who are you?"

Maybe he went to the wrong sorority house. "This is the Alpha Phi house, right?"

"Yes. What do you want?"

Geez. She was kind of rude. "I have a date with Jane. Is she here?"

"Yeah." She stood staring at him with her hands on her hips.

Randy tightened his stance, wondering why this woman appeared to be so offended by him. "Are you going to let me in?"

"What did you say your name was?"

"Randy. I have a date with Jane. Could you tell her I'm here please?"

The woman opened the door and showed him inside. "Wait here. I'll go get her."

He did as she asked. While he waited in the main gathering room, he looked at the group sorority pictures on the wall and skimmed over the book titles on the shelves. When he faced the opposite direction, a gorgeous young woman in a red dress descended the stairs.

She flashed a tantalizing smile. "Hey."

He ogled her from head to toe. She was absolutely gorgeous, truly a work of art. "Wow! You look incredible."

"Thank you."

He handed her the roses. "These are for you."

She sniffed them and bit her lower lip, which Randy found adorable. "These are beautiful. Thank you."

"My pleasure."

"Let me put these in water then we can go." Jane headed to the kitchen to retrieve a vase.

Lisa entered the room and shot Randy a wicked glare. "She's my best friend, and we look out for our sisters, you know."

This woman had a harsh tone. In fact, every woman in this sorority appeared to hold some sort of negativity toward him. "Excuse me?"

"If you try anything funny or do anything to hurt her…"

What was wrong with these women? And what was with the incriminating stares? They must have thought he was some sort of evil psychotic freak to be subjected to these kinds of reactions. "What?" he asked, offended by her negativity.

"We're all watching you. You can be assured of that."

Randy was unaware that he was on trial for anything, although being here made him feel like he was, with all the interrogating going on. These women made him uncomfortable. He wanted to leave. Where the hell was Jane?

Jane emerged from the kitchen. "I'm ready," she declared with a friendly smile.

Thank god. Now he could get the hell out of here. He gently grazed his hand across her back and escorted her out the door.

When Jane saw the top down on the shiny red convertible with black leather interior, she gasped. "Oh my god."

"What's the matter?" he wondered, a bit surprised by her reaction.

"Is that your car?"

Clearly she was impressed. "Yes it is."

She stroked the side of it with her finger and rubbed her hand across the leather seats. "I have never in my life ridden in a sports car."

Well, this was a great opportunity to show her something new. "Maybe we can go for a ride after dinner."

"Really?"

"Sure." He opened the passenger door. She stepped inside and sat down, grinning widely. Once she was situated, Randy circled around the car and took position behind the wheel. The engine revved when he started it up. The smile on Jane's face told him that he had scored.

As he pulled away from the curb, she asked, "Where are we going?"

"The Fleur de Lys in San Francisco. I hope you like French cuisine."

"French?"

Using his best French accent, he replied, "Oui, mon chéri."

"Ooh, and you speak French too," she giggled.

"A little."

She sighed contently and leaned back in her seat, enjoying the ride and the wind in her hair.

"No offense to you or anything, but what is up with your sorority sisters?"

Jane didn't know what he was talking about. "What do you mean?"

"One of them got all snarky with me at the door, and another one gave me an ice-piercing glare and snarled at me. Did I do something to offend them?"

"They just don't know you, that's all. Which reminds me." She sat up a little and turned to face him. "You never did tell me your last name."

"It's Hanson. Randy Hanson."

"That's a very dignified name."

Randy laughed, not so sure he agreed with her. "You think so? That's the first time anyone has ever said that to me."

"It is. It sounds so prominent." She used a deeper tone to make her voice sound like an intercom system. "Paging Dr. Hanson."

"Dr. Hanson is my dad."

"That will be you too, when you finish medical school," she reminded him.

Now that she mentioned it, that would be his title one of these days. "Oh man, I still have four years of this crap left before that happens."

"But you'll get there."

He stopped at a red light and gazed at her. "What's your last name? And if you say Doe, I'm turning this car around."

A small chitter left her lips. "It's Davine."

"Jane Davine." The corner of his mouth drew upward. "That's a pretty name."

They crossed the Bay Bridge into San Francisco. The air was warm, the sky was clear, and the sun was just starting to go down. San Francisco was picturesque when the sun set. The city sparkled, showing off its spectacular views of the city lights. It was a beautiful sight. The aromas from North Beach—San Francisco's Little Italy—tempted the senses, adding to the joy of the ride. Jane could not remember a time when she had so much fun cruising through the city.

"I grew up here, you know," she remarked.

"Did you?"

"Uh huh. Lived here my whole life. I love this city."

Expressing his thoughts on the topic, Randy replied, "The weather's nice. I like the beaches, and I've met some cool people. I miss home though."

"And where's that?" she asked.

"Seattle," he clarified. "Came to California to go to school. Berkeley has a good Public Health program, and I was able to get all of my pre-med requirements out of the way. Once I'm finished with med school, I'm hoping to go back home to complete my residency. UW has one of the best obstetrical programs in the country, but until I reach that phase of my training, here I am."

Randy pulled into the parking lot, put the top up on the car, and turned off the engine. Then, being chivalrous, he walked around to the passenger's side to open the door for Jane. She placed her hand in his and he helped her step out of the car. "Here we are," he said. "You hungry?"

"Starved."

"Good." He closed the door, locked the car, and escorted her inside.

This elegant restaurant was considered the most romantic dining experience in San Francisco and had played host to the city's finest for over forty-five years. The opulent dining room had ceilings tented with heavy swaths of fabric, high-backed chairs, plush carpeting, and curtained walls. The atmosphere was dramatic with its dim lighting and large vases full of flowers, scented with juniper berry and orange essence.

Jane was in awe. "Wow," she said as she looked around, admiring the ambience. "This place is incredible."

"You ever been here before?" Randy asked.

"No."

And again she was impressed. He was batting a thousand tonight. Winning her over was going to be easy. "You're in for a treat then. Wait 'til you taste the food."

Once inside, the maître de confirmed their reservations and led them to a cozy table in the corner. Randy pulled out Jane's chair then took his own seat. The maître de handed out the menus. "Can we get you anything while you wait, Sir?"

"Yes," Randy replied. "Can we get a bottle of Dom Pérignon, please?"

"Right away, Sir."

Flowers, fine dining, and French champagne? Jane had never been on a date like this before. She set her handbag on the table then took off her sweater and draped it over the back of her chair. Her soft, delicate shoulders were now completely exposed. The soft light hit her face and gave her an almost angelic aura.

Randy couldn't help but notice. "You look beautiful tonight. I love that dress. Red's my favorite color."

"Thank you." Leaning forward a little, she said, "And thank you for this. This is the most fun I've had in a long time."

To go with their champagne, Randy ordered a three course meal of Avocado and Frisée Salad, Muscovy Duck Breast with eggplant and purple olive jus, and a chocolate soufflé with cherry and Kirsch ice cream.

All through dinner, they laughed together, shared funny stories, and got to know each other. They learned that they were both Indiana Jones fans, both loved to dance, and neither one of them liked lima beans. Water was Randy's home away from home. Jane loved the water too. Likewise, both of them were into water sports and enjoyed the beach. Randy had always been a serious scholar who earned many honors and scholarships because of his grades and test scores. He came to find out that Jane had recently been inducted into the Order of Omega, the Greek honor society on campus, which implied that she took school seriously—a characteristic he very much admired in a woman.

Like him, she was an active participant in many charitable organizations. She told him all about the Alpha Phi foundation, which focused on heart disease and cardiac care for women. Many fundraising efforts took place during the school year to aid in this campaign, part of which was the 5K Bear Run. Randy had participated in a few of these runs over the years. Jane and some of her sorority sisters had also done fundraising for the American Cancer Society and UNICEF, and she volunteered at the local Children's Hospital. She was very supportive of health and medical efforts, which Randy found fascinating, since medicine was his passion in life. Randy had never been out with a girl he had so many things in common with. He thoroughly enjoyed the conversation they had and loved the similarities they shared.

After the waiter cleared their plates, Jane commented, "That was really good, Randy."

"Told you. I love this place."

"You come here a lot?"

"Not really. I come here once in a while. But I love French cuisine," he stated.

"I like French, but Chinese is my favorite."

"I like Chinese food too. In fact, I like to sample all types of culinary cookery. Experiencing different cultures has always been something I've enjoyed." The waiter brought the bill, and Randy pulled out his credit card.

Out of the corner of her eye, Jane saw the name on the card—*J. Randal Hanson.* "So Randy is short for Randal?" she asked.

"Yes it is."

"What's the J stand for?"

"Jonathan," he replied. "My birth name is Jonathan Randal Hanson, but everyone has always called me Randy."

"I like it," she said with a smile.

Randy paid the bill then stood up and carefully slipped Jane's sweater over her shoulders before he escorted her out to the car. When they were both buckled up, he turned to her and asked, "You ever been to the Berkeley Marina?"

"Yes. We've done some beach cleanup down there. Why?"

"There's a beautiful view from there, and it would be a nice drive with the top down if you're interested. You said you wanted to go for a ride after dinner."

"Sounds great."

"Cool." He revved up the engine and headed that direction.

They strolled around the marina for a while before Randy took her to a spot where all three bay bridges were in view. The moonlight reflected off the rippled water in the bay. It was a breathtaking sight.

"This is beautiful," she remarked.

"Yes it is. When the moon mirrors off the bay like this, it reminds me of the lake back home," he stated. "I love the Seattle skyline at night. And when the scent of pine permeates the air as a breeze blows through…ultimate sensory splendor."

"Sounds like a beautiful place."

"It is." Randy glanced at his watch. It was well after midnight. He didn't want to end the evening but knew he had to get some sleep if he was going to function at a rational level tomorrow. "Oh man. Where did the time go? I didn't realize how late it was. We should probably head back."

She nodded in agreement, although she really didn't want to go home. She was having too much fun.

At the end of their date, Randy escorted Jane up to the door of the Alpha house. They both stood on the porch staring at each other for a moment before Jane finally said, "I really had a good time tonight, Randy."

"I did too, but I need to get some sleep. Have fun recruiting this weekend." Usually at this point in a date, Randy used his charismatic charm to coax a woman back to his apartment and try to find a way to get her clothes off. At the least, he would be knee deep in a fiery kiss by now. But somehow, tonight with Jane, none of that seemed appropriate. Even though he wanted to kiss her, he ended the evening with an affectionate hug instead. He couldn't understand why, but Jane had some kind of strange effect on him that he couldn't be au fait with. He tried not to let it get to him. "Goodnight, Jane Davine."

"Goodnight, Randy." She opened the door and slowly slipped inside.

Immediately after hearing Jane come in, Lisa and three other sorority sisters rushed to her side to make sure everything was alright. "Well? How'd it go?"

Dreamy-eyed, with a blissful smile on her face, Jane leaned against the door. "Oh my god. He is amazing."

"Where did he take you?"

"The Fleur de Lys." Jane sat on the couch with her sisters gathered around her.

Lisa seemed particularly impressed by this. Her curiosity was piqued now. "And?" she probed further.

"And we ate French cuisine, he ordered champagne, then we went for a ride in his car."

"The convertible that was parked out front?"

"Yes." Jane was floating on the clouds. She couldn't stop smiling.

"Then what happened?"

"We held hands and went for a walk down at the marina," Jane explained. "Then he took me home."

With no juicy story to tell, Lisa lost interest. To her, this sounded suspicious. "That's it? He didn't even try to kiss you?"

"No."

"Weird guy."

Jane wondered the same thing as Lisa. Why didn't he try to kiss her? Why didn't he try anything at all? Why did he go through all of the trouble of such an elaborate evening if he had no objective? His intentions were unclear, which left her confused.

Randy awoke the next morning in an exceptional mood. Jane was on his mind. He wanted to see her again, so he sent her a text message referring back to the conversation they had over dinner. *You and I need have an Indiana Jones marathon. Name the time and place and I'll bring the DVDs.* He hoped that would intrigue her and get her to respond. She did respond, which led to a day of text messaging conversation between them.

After class, Randy met Jim at the recreation center to shoot some hoops. Midway through the game, Jim grabbed the ball and stood in the middle of the court staring at Randy.

"Come on. You gonna run and shoot the damn ball or just stand there looking like an idiot? Dribble," Randy commanded.

"Why haven't you mentioned one damn thing about your date last night?" Jim asked.

"I thought we were playing basketball?"

But Jim didn't let up. "I want to know what happened."

Randy moved over to the side of the court and leaned against the wall. "Why are you so interested?"

"Because you have done nothin' but talk about this chick all week, you finally go out with her then don't say a word about it afterwards."

"Nothing happened."

Jim found this hard to believe. He carried the ball over to the side of the court and sat down next to Randy. "What do you mean nothin' happened? Did you wipeout?"

"No, it's not that."

"Then what is it?" Jim wanted to know.

"We shared a nice dinner together, had great conversation, went for a walk, then I took her home. There's nothing to tell. What more do you want me to say?"

Jim knew Randy wasn't telling the whole story. "Bullshit. Come on, man. What happened?"

"Jim, when have I ever lied to you?"

"Never."

"Ok then. Enough said." He stood up and grabbed the ball, dribbling it onto the court. "Can we play now?"

Jim rose to his feet. "Wait a minute. You're serious, aren't you?"

"Yeah."

"Are you feeling ok?" Jim teased.

"I feel fine." He held the ball under his arm wishing Jim would hurry up and make his point. "What is the big deal?"

"You didn't take her to your apartment?"

"No. We weren't anywhere near my apartment."

This was not typical behavior from Randy. Something was up. "Did you at least kiss her?"

"No, I didn't kiss her, if you really must know. Why are you grilling me on this?"

"Because this doesn't sound like you at all. I expected you to brag about a night of hot sex with this girl, and you're tellin' me that you didn't even make a move?"

"No, I didn't."

"What, are you not attracted to her?"

"Hell yeah, I'm attracted to her. I'm extremely attracted to her. She is the sexiest woman I have ever seen."

"Then what's the problem?"

"There isn't a problem, dammit. It just didn't seem right."

"Didn't seem right?" Jim chortled. "When has that ever stopped you before?"

"Never, but this is different."

"How?"

"I don't know."

Jim was laughing so hard his sides hurt.

"What is so damn funny?"

"I see how it is."

"Oh, really?" Randy said. "Why don't you enlighten me then, Mr. Wizard."

"You like her, don't you?"

Of course he didn't like her. What a ludicrous thing to say. "That's crazy."

"Admit it."

"Look, I just didn't feel like it, okay."

This made Jim laugh even more.

"What is your problem?" Randy asked, annoyed by Jim's behavior.

Jim tried to be understanding but this was far too amusing. "Think about it, Dude. You have called her every day since you got her number. You talk about her all the damn time. You've been fiddlin' with your phone all day, and I know damn well it's because you've been texting her. And let me ask you somethin'."

Randy did not want to hear anything Jim had to say, but he humored him anyway. "What?"

"How many girls have you been with since you met her?"

Randy didn't answer. He didn't see the relevance of that question.

"Since that day at the beach, how many girls have you dicked?"

He rolled his eyes. "Dammit, Jim."

"Answer the damn question."

"None, ok. You happy now?" Frustrated, Randy let the ball drop and sat against the wall with his head buried in his hands.

Jim didn't mean to upset his friend, he was just trying to make a point. "I'm sorry, man."

Randy snapped, "Why do you do that?"

"Do what?"

"Make everything into a joke."

"I can't believe you don't see it."

"I have no idea what you're talking about." Randy knew exactly what Jim was talking about, but wasn't about to admit it.

"Why are you so afraid to admit that you like her?"

Randy glowered at his friend and huffed, "Can we drop this, please?"

But Jim remained persistent. "Admit it."

The glare Randy shot him could have chilled lava. He didn't find Jim's mockery amusing and didn't feel like playing basketball anymore. He stood up, ready to leave. "I have a paper to write and really do not wish to continue this conversation with you."

"C'mon, man," Jim said. "Don't be pissed."

"I'm not pissed. I'm just tired of your philosophical insights and psychological ramblings. You don't know as much as you think." He picked up his ball and dribbled toward the door.

Jim shook his head. He knew damn well his friend liked the girl, but Randy, in his pride, would never admit something like that. That would show he had weaknesses and human emotion like everyone else. Jim didn't understand, even though he tried to, why Randy Hanson wouldn't let a woman get close to his heart. Randy always tried to rationalize things, to find logical medical or scientific explanations for everything. But this had no explanation, no scientific backing. Randy liked this girl, plain and simple. Why was he so afraid of relationships and commitment and love? Jim knew all the inner workings of Randal Hanson, but for the life of him he did not understand that aspect of him. "Blind and stubborn," he muttered, feeling a bit of pity for his best friend.

After a shower, Randy decided to go to the library to do some research for a while. He was about to sit down when he noticed Jane studying alone at a table. He smiled when he saw her and immediately took advantage of this opportunity. Undetected, he snuck up behind her and whispered into her ear, "Hello."

She jumped slightly and turned her head. "Don't do that. You scared me."

He playfully grinned then took a seat across from her. "What are you doing here? I thought you had initiations this weekend?"

"We do, but I've only been in this class for a week and I'm already failing. I do not understand this."

He could tell she was thoroughly confused. "What's the problem?"

"This stupid class," she bellowed in aggravation.

Randy eyed the book she was reading. It was Molecular Biology. "I told you to let me know if you needed help with that."

"I know, but you're busy."

"I'm not that busy," he clarified. "What do you need help with?"

She explained her dilemma and he did his best to clarify it for her. He drew diagrams, highlighted important parts, and broke the content down so she could understand it.

When he was finished, she gave him a blank stare. "How do you do that?"

With a shrug, he asked, "Do what?"

"You make it sound so easy."

He didn't see why she didn't get it. To him, it was easy. "It's really not that complicated. You'll get the hang of it."

She took a deep breath, not as convinced.

"It'll be ok. I'll help you."

She just sat there with her forehead all crinkled up.

The expression on her face made Randy laugh. "What's wrong?"

"My professor tried to explain this and I didn't understand a word he said. Yet you open this book right up and spit it out, no problem."

Randy wondered where she was going with this. "So?"

"I don't get it."

Neither did he. "Don't get what?"

"Do you do that all the time?"

"Do what?"

"Throw out complicated information like it's Kindergarten curriculum."

"Does that bother you?"

"No. I find it fascinating that you can do that. I can't do that."

Ok. She liked it. More bonus points he had earned in her favor. Smiling smugly, he replied, "I'm sure there are many things that you're good at."

"Well, Molecular Biology isn't one of them." Frustrated, she closed her book and put it in her backpack. "So," she said with a smile as she rested her chin on her hand. "What are you doing here?"

Randy reached into his backpack to pull out his laptop. "Doing some research for a thesis I'm working on."

"Thesis about what?"

"How various biological, environmental, and chemical elements affect prenatal health."

Her eyebrows raised in curiosity. "And you find that interesting?"

"Oh, extremely." Enough about him. He wanted to hear about her, so he changed the subject. "What are you interested in, Ms. Davine?"

"I like to read, as long as it's not for my Biology class," she replied derisively.

Randy laughed at her response.

They talked for a while before Jane had to leave to help her sorority sisters prepare for the big pledge weekend. "We have a lot to do to get ready," she told Randy.

"Will you be available at all this weekend?"

"Doubtful."

Disappointed, his face drooped.

"Why? Did you need something?"

"Not exactly." Hoping to entice her, he said, "I had an amazing time last night and was hoping you'd be willing to spend another evening with me."

She seemed surprised that he suggested that. "Really?"

"Of course. So what do you say?"

She smiled sweetly. "I would love to."

"Cool. What about next Friday?"

"Friday is fine."

"Great! I'll give you a call later to make plans."

She checked the time on her phone. She was now officially late. "I really have to go," she said.

"I'll see you later, Jane."

"Bye, Randy." She stood up and waved as she snuck out the door.

He watched her adoringly until she was out of sight.

Chapter Four

Randy met his study group, as he always did on Sunday morning, hopeful that this session would go smoothly and he wouldn't have to deal with Steve deciding to be an asshole again. Steve Hall was Randy's least favorite person, but he felt obligated to put up with him for the sake of the group. Randy didn't like to cause problems and didn't like being in the middle of one, but somehow, when Steve was around, a problem always seemed to arise.

"Would you shut up, please," Randy heard Amanda fume as he walked into the room. "I swear, twelve year olds are more mature than you are."

Great, Steve was at it again. What was it this time? "Is everything alright?" He put his bag on the table and began to pull out his study materials.

Steve sat with a smug grin on his face. Condescendingly, he replied, "Mandy was just saying how she wishes she could give me a hard on."

Steve was the biggest loudmouth in all of California and thought he was God's gift to women. He bragged about his so-called sexual experiences he always seemed to have, but in reality, none of it was true. He made up stories in an attempt to make himself look good. Who he was trying to impress no one could say. Randy certainly didn't offer him any standing ovations.

Mandy growled in aggravation. "You are such an asshole!"

"That's not what you said last night," Steve taunted.

Of course he wasn't serious. There was no way, not in a million years, that Mandy would be caught dead with that son-of-a-bitch, and Randy knew it. He glared at Steve. The repugnance he felt for this man made him sneer. "Why do you treat women like crap?" Randy asked.

"The same reason you do. They are only good for one thing." He stuck his tongue out and slithered like a snake while he gave obscene pelvic thrusts.

Disgusted, Mandy picked up a book and held it above her head, fully prepared to throw it at Steve.

Randy interjected, "I happen to have the utmost respect for women."

Steve leaned back on his chair and put his feet on the table. "Bullshit, Hanson. How many women did you fuck last week?"

Randy found this comment offensive and unnecessary. "Who I decide to bring into my bed and when is none of your damn business."

"Boy, you are a hypocritical grouch today, aren't you?"

Not only was this rude and uncalled for, it was also untrue. Randy was in a great mood, until he saw Steve. He really hated Steve. He was obnoxious, vociferous, offensive, full of more shit than a cow pasture, and overall cacophonous. Randy wished he could somehow erase him from the world and do everyone a favor. "Hypocritical?" Randy retorted, "Such a big word for you. Do you even know what that means?"

The others got a laugh at Randy's quick comeback.

Steve, however, didn't think it was funny. "You know damn well that if Sarah and Mandy took their clothes off and did a little pole dance for us that you would disrespect them both right here, right now."

Sarah, who was usually pretty composed, lashed out, "Damn you, Steve!"

Jim had enough of this crap. He stared Steve down with a vile glare. "Will you shut the hell up? Jesus! You never know when to quit."

Randy sat in his chair and opened a textbook. "Can we get started, please? We have managed to waste a good seven minutes now. And I don't know about you, but I do not have time for this infantile psychobabble bullshit. I have better things to do."

The others agreed. Steve simply snorted under his breath.

"And get your feet off the table," Randy demanded.

Every time Steve was around, Randy felt like he was babysitting. Steve never contributed to the group, only seemed to drain the life and energy out of everyone. He was lazy and unmotivated and never did his share of the work. Randy wasn't one-hundred percent sure why the group kept him around. No one seemed to like him very much.

While Randy studied with his friends and attempted to ignore the annoyances of Steve Hall, Jane was out with Lisa picking up a few things for the sorority. When the girls were about to head home, Lisa tried to start her car. *Click, click, click*. Nothing. The engine did not turn over. She tried again. *Click, click, click*. "Ugh! I swear, I hate this car."

Jane took her phone out of her purse. "I know someone we can call."

Lisa knew who Jane was thinking of, and she did not approve. She grabbed Jane's phone right out of her hand. "Don't call him."

Jane gawked at Lisa and snatched her phone back. "Why not?" She searched through her contacts and found Randy's name.

"Because any guy who takes a girl out and doesn't try to kiss her…"

"Before I went out with him, you were worried he would try something. Now you're upset because he didn't. That is totally contradictory."

"I don't trust him," Lisa firmly stated.

"Well, I do." She dialed Randy's number and let it ring. "He's a nice guy, Lisa. He'll help." She put the phone up to her ear and waited.

The three-hour study session was about to wrap up when Randy's cellphone rang. When he saw Jane's name as the incoming number, he excused himself and walked over to a corner of the room and answered, "Well, hello."

"Oh, good. You had your phone on," she stated when she heard his voice.

"Unless I'm at the hospital, I always have my phone on. What's up?"

"I'm really sorry to bother you, but…"

Randy heard the distraught tone in her voice right away. "What's wrong?"

"Well," she tried not to sound like the damsel in distress. "Lisa and I are sort of stuck here. Her car broke down again."

"Do you need me to come get you?"

She hated that she probably sounded desperate. "If it wouldn't be too much trouble."

"Not at all," he said with a grin. "Where are you?" She told him where they were, and he said he would be there in about fifteen minutes. He hung up his phone, returned to the table, and began to pack up his belongings.

Randy was awfully quick to dismiss the session. Jim questioned this decision right away. "Everything alright?"

"Everything's fine." He zipped up his backpack and threw it over his shoulder. "I have to go."

Jim followed him toward the door. When he caught up with him, he asked, "Where you goin'?"

"Jane and her friend need me to pick them up. Their car broke down."

There was that name again—Jane. All Randy ever talked about anymore was that girl. And now he was dropping everything to go rescue her. Why couldn't Randy get it through his thick head that he liked the girl? Was he really that dense? Did he really not see it? Or was he just too pigheaded to admit it? "Prince Charming to the rescue, huh?"

Randy stuck his middle finger in the air and walked out the door.

About thirty minutes later, he dropped the girls off at the Alpha house and helped them carry their bags up to the porch.

"Thank you," Lisa said, wishing she hadn't been so coarse with him the other day. "That was really nice of you to go out of your way to help us."

Randy responded with a smile. "No problem."

Lisa walked inside, leaving Jane alone on the porch with Randy.

Jane sat on the front step and turned her eyes Randy's direction. "Thank you so much for picking us up."

He joined her on the steps, sitting close but not touching. "My pleasure. Anytime you run into a bind, just call and I'll do what I can." With his car keys dangling from his index finger, he stared down at the ground. "You busy right now?"

"Actually, I am. We have our big initiation dinner tonight, and we still need to get things ready for that."

"This sorority occupies a lot of your time, doesn't it?"

"Not normally. It's just this weekend, with pledges and initiations and everything, it's been kind of crazy. It's not usually like this."

"It's alright." Although he was disappointed, he did understand. His class schedule was just as chaotic, not to mention the hours he spent studying. All the same, he missed her company and didn't realize how much until he saw her again today. Throughout the day, they sent text messages to each other. He called her every night, and they talked for hours. The conversations they had stimulated him, and he felt like he could tell her anything. As much as he loved the sound of her voice when they would talk on the phone, nothing compared to face-to-face contact and being in the physical presence of her company. He'd only known her for a short time, but something about Jane made him come back for more. "Are you available to meet me between classes tomorrow so we can hang out and talk?"

She had a break in her schedule in the afternoon, so this plan was definitely doable. "I can do that."

This perked him up a bit. "What time?"

"Around noon. But I only have about thirty minutes."

Not exactly quality time, but it would have to do. "Wanna meet at the esplanade?"

"Sounds good."

She stood up, and his eyes followed her. Confirming their plans, he said, "I'll see you tomorrow then."

"I'll be there. Thanks again, Randy."

"Anytime."

Randy skipped lunch the next day, which was unusual. He rarely skipped lunch unless he had some school-oriented event to attend to. Wanting to gain insights into this peculiar behavior, Jim caught up with him after class. "What did you do this weekend?"

"Nothin'."

"Why not?"

Randy lifted a shoulder. "I don't know. Didn't feel like it."

It wasn't often Randy spent a weekend alone, and even rarer when he had nothing to say, yet he was awfully quiet today. "We missed you at lunch."

Randy wasn't in the mood to explain himself. "I had some things to do."

"What kind of things?"

Randy shrugged off the question.

The man was in complete denial. He might have been good at fooling women, but he couldn't fool Jim. Despite trying to dodge his emotions and pretend they didn't exist, Jim saw right through him. "You met with Jane, didn't you?"

Randy didn't see why that mattered. "So?"

"You are the most stubborn person I know."

Randy stopped mid-stride, wondering where that comment came from. "Why do you say that?"

"You really don't see it, do you?"

"See what?"

Randy was certainly dense. So dense, Jim couldn't believe he had to spell it out for him. "When are you going to admit that you like this chick?"

"What makes you think I like her?"

"Gee, let me think," he mocked. "You call her all the time, you sneak off between classes to meet with her, and you talk about her constantly. You left our study session to rescue her, and you have one of her damn red dress pins on your backpack. Hellacious signs you like the chick, Randy."

"Jim, come on. I'm not in the mood." What he really wasn't in the mood for was Jim's bantering. "And so what if I do?"

"Ha!" Jim finally got him to say it. He knew with a little perseverance and persuasion he would get Randy to admit it. "I knew it."

"I don't see how this has any relevance on anything. And I certainly don't see why you care so much," Randy added.

"Because you're my best friend." They continued their stroll down the sidewalk. "What's goin' on?"

"Nothing."

Jim didn't buy it. "What do you mean nothin'? I know you better than that. Somethin' is goin' down between you two. You've been spendin' a helluva lot of time with her. Don't tell me nothin' is goin' on."

"We like to hang out together and we have a lot to talk about. I see nothing wrong with that."

"Are you goin' out with her again?"

"Yup. Friday night." Randy grinned.

"Two dates with the same girl," Jim teased. "I think that's a record for you."

"Shut up."

The defensive tone in Randy's voice made Jim laugh.

Randy didn't find any of this amusing. "See, there you go again. I hate it when you do that."

"I'm just messin' with ya."

And Randy knew that. Jim was his best friend—the most trusted person he could confide in, the one who had seen him at his worst and was always there when he needed a friend to lean on. If anyone would understand what he was going through, it was James Ryan. "I don't know what it is. There's just something about her. Whenever I'm around her, I can't stop smiling." Randy drifted into a dreamy state as he spoke of Jane. "Those tantalizing green eyes of hers drive me crazy. She has an incredible smile, soft hands, a cute laugh, and she and I have the most stimulating conversation I've ever had. Her hair smells incredible. And I don't know what that body spray is she uses, but damn."

Jim completely understood. Jane was one of the hottest chicks he had ever seen. She could easily be the Kaha Huna, or any other goddess for that matter. "She's off the Richter, man."

"Yeah, she is. And her lips…Man, I would love to kiss her."

"So why don't you?"

Randy snapped out of his daze and stared at Jim with his dark eyes. "I can't kiss her."

"Why not?"

"I just can't."

"But you said…"

"I know what I said."

Jim knew what it was. Randy was scared to death about the feelings he had for Jane. He was dead-solid head over heels about this woman, and that must have terrified the hell out of him. Jim could have teased his best friend about this, but he sensed Randy was frustrated about the entire situation, so he dropped the subject instead. "You feel like catchin' the game tonight?"

Monday night football. A great way to spend an evening. "Sure. Your place?"

"Yup."

"I'll pick up some pizza on the way over."

The next day, while walking across the esplanade, Randy ran into Jane. He jogged to catch up with her. "Where you running off to?"

She turned to his voice. "The library. I need to find a quiet place to study. With all these initiates running around and the excitement going on at Alpha this week, I can't concentrate."

"Care if I join ya?"

With an arch of her lips, she said, "Sure."

They found a table together and each tended to their own work for a while. Randy read a chapter and typed some notes on his laptop, but it didn't take long before he became completely distracted. He kept glancing up at Jane and eventually neglected studying altogether to watch her.

His gawking eyes kind of creeped her out. "What?"

With his hands folded under his chin, he gazed at her with a devilish grin. "Nothing. Just looking at you."

Jane bowed her eyebrows. "Why?"

"No reason." He thought she was beautiful and couldn't get enough of her pretty facial features. Desperately wanting to touch her, he reached down and rubbed the back of her hand. Her hands were warm, soft, delicate, feminine. Touching her brought tingles. He couldn't believe how a single touch from her had this kind of effect on him. Her glance met his. Instinctively, he turned his eyes to her lips then back to her eyes again. He wanted to kiss her.

Forcing himself to turn away, he returned to his textbook and carried on with studying.

Chapter Five

During the week, Randy and Jane managed to sneak in a few meetings on the esplanade. He was even able to pull her away from her sorority long enough to share lunch with her. They talked every day, several times a day, and communicated via text message. In the process, they learned many things about each other.

Friday after class, they decided to spend the afternoon at Six Flags. They strolled through the park holding hands while they enjoyed carnival games and rode on every rollercoaster, log flume, and rapids ride they could until the 9:00 P.M. laser and fireworks show started. When the park closed, Jane walked out with a huge stuffed bear in her arms, which Randy had won from a dart game and given to her. Before heading back to Berkeley, they stopped at a late night Mexican restaurant to grab some food.

Jane was curious about Randy's schooling. She had never known any doctors or anyone who attended medical school before, so she found Randy's experience with it intriguing. He talked about medicine with so much enthusiasm that Jane was eager to learn as much about it as she could. "Last night on the phone you mentioned a Pathology class you had. What is that exactly?"

"Pathology deals with cells, molecules, and tissue differentiation," he answered.

"What do you do in a class like that?"

"Study blood and bodily fluids, infections of the blood, DNA, hereditary aspects of cell formation. It's basically the study of disease."

Sounded complicated and boring to her. Yet somehow he found excitement in it. "That sounds hard."

"It's challenging, but I love it. It's all inclusive with exams, labs, and practical applications. A good majority of what I do requires writing detailed lab reports."

"And you say I'm busy?" she teased.

Randy remembered when he accused her of that exact same thing. "My schedule is crazy, but it's worth it to me."

From their many conversations, Jane learned that medical school was Randy's passion in life. He wanted to become a doctor more than anything. She knew he worked hard, and that he would settle for nothing but the best from himself. But how he managed to do all of that and maintain his sanity was beyond her comprehension.

When they returned to Berkeley, Jane invited Randy into the Alpha house. She offered him a drink, and they sat on the sofa to chat. Jane kicked off her shoes and bent one leg underneath her. "You mentioned your dad is a doctor. What about the rest of your family?"

He rested his arm on the back of the sofa and turned to face her. "My parents and I have a good relationship. They support me and push me to do my best. Dad and I have great conversations and we enjoy each other's company. Spending time with him always helps me unwind. And Mom's really good at lending a listening ear. She offers good advice when I need it."

Family was a topic he enjoyed talking about, so Jane probed for more information. "Any brothers or sisters?"

"One of each, actually," he answered with a smile. "My sister, Stephanie, is a sophomore at Washington State. She doesn't take school seriously though. She's much more interested in the social aspects of college rather than the academics. Men in particular."

This made Jane giggle. "Oh, I see."

"She's a bit eccentric, but I love her dearly. And my little brother…well let me put it this way," Randy chuckled. "Robby's sixteen and full of hormonal teenage angst. He always seems to be getting into trouble. He's a pest."

"Isn't that a little brother's job, to pester his older siblings?"

Randy laughed. "Robby seems to excel at it."

"I have a little brother too," she said. "Let me rephrase that. He's younger than me but much bigger than I am. He plays linebacker on the football team. He made the district all-stars last year."

"Is that right? You a football fan?" he asked.

"Not really. I only watch when my brother plays. Basketball is my game."

How convenient was this? Jane liked basketball, Randy's favorite sport both to spectate and play in his free time. Basketball was his second love in life, second only to medicine. He couldn't believe his luck to find a girl who liked the sport as much as he did. "I love basketball."

She perked up at his response. "Who's your favorite team?"

"Lakers all the way, Baby. You ever play basketball?"

"I used to." The spark she had suddenly left, and her smile disappeared. With tears welling in her eyes, she said, "But I don't anymore."

When Randy saw she was crying, he grew concerned. He thought he had said something that upset her, so he offered her an apology, although he wasn't sure what he was apologizing for. "I'm sorry if I said something that…"

She interrupted, "Randy, don't. It's nothing you did."

Obviously basketball was a touchy subject. Had he known, he wouldn't have pushed the topic. With a soft, caring voice, he asked, "You okay?"

"It's just…" A tear rolled down her cheek. She felt foolish for sniveling like a baby in front of him, and believed she owed him an explanation for her sudden emotional breakdown. "My mom used to come to all my games. She was diagnosed with cancer a few years ago, and I quit school for a while to stay home and take care of her. We lost her last summer."

Randy now understood why Jane never mentioned anything about her mother. What a horrible thing for her and her family to endure. He scooted closer and gave her a hug, trying to sympathize with her, although he really couldn't fathom the hell she must have been through. "I am so sorry."

With misty eyes, she sniffled. "Mom was my inspiration, and she was always there cheering me on. After she was gone, I lost my drive to play."

He offered comfort by gently kissing the top of her head. The flowery scent of her hair, the warmth of her touch, and the feel of her breath on his skin made his heart race. He closed his eyes and absorbed it all. "I didn't mean to upset you."

"It's ok. You didn't know." She sat up straight. "Daddy made me go back to school. At the time, I fought him on it because I didn't want him to be alone. I thought he would need me. But now," she forced a small smile. "I'm glad he was insistent about it."

"So am I. Because if he wasn't, we probably never would have met."

She stood up to get a tissue. Randy's longing eyes followed her. "Some of my sorority sisters and I are going to The Club tomorrow night. You want to meet me there?"

It sounded like she was asking him out this time, which was a pleasant change. "Sure. What time?"

"Between 8:00 and 9:00 most likely. I'll call you if that changes."

"Alright. I can see if Jim and Trina want to go," he suggested. "We can double up."

"That sounds good."

Randy caught himself looking into her eyes, which had that gleaming glow back in them again. She seemed to be more at peace now than she was a few moments ago. Her smile returned and resumed its enticing effect on him. "I'll see you tomorrow night then." He rose to his feet and headed toward the door. With a kind smile, he said, "Goodnight, Jane."

"Goodnight, Randy."

He winked at her as he left.

Jim and Trina were already at The Club when Randy arrived. This nightclub had an open space with a cool vibe and lots of nooks, giving it a mellow feel. The dancefloor of this place was a large twenty-by-forty foot hardwood that could hold many gyrating bodies. Two full bars bordered the dance area lending easy access to cocktail needs. Booths and tables were available around the dancefloor to provide a more private place to chat with friends. It had the best sound system and put on the best live shows in the East Bay. Randy had been here several times before.

When Jim saw Randy walk in, he approached him with a huge grin. "Hey, Loverboy."

"Shut up, Jackass." The men pulled two tables together. Before they sat down, Randy took off his jacket and draped it over the back of a chair. He positioned himself so he could see the front entrance of the club. "Do you think you could possibly find the self-control to not make me the object of your mockery tonight, please?"

Jim had to laugh. "I don't know, man. Might take a tremendous amount of restraint."

"I'm sure you can handle it."

The music played loudly and the place quickly filled. Several friends joined them at the table, but not one of them was the familiar face Randy had come here to see. He didn't think Jane was ever going to show up. Feeling restless, he checked his watch for the thirteenth time and stared toward the front door. He became impatiently bored with the conversation and went over to the bar to get a drink.

Jim sensed Randy's anxiety and joined him. "I have never seen you so uptight. You alright, man?"

Randy took a deep breath and shook his head. "I feel like an idiot. I can't believe I've been sitting here for almost an hour waiting for this girl. She's not gonna show. I'm going to get stood up. That's never happened to me before."

Jim put his hand on Randy's shoulder. "Don't worry. She'll be here."

Randy took a sip from the drink he had in his hand then turned around to face the door. A huge grin instantly lit up his face. The beautiful Psychology major he had come there to see finally walked through the entrance. Her mesmerizing smile and beautiful, succulent lips caught his attention immediately.

As she approached him, Randy looked her over thoroughly. She was dressed in a pair of navy blue Capri's that hugged every curve of her body. Her low cut white blouse exposed some skin and revealed a bit of cleavage. She had on delicate pearl earrings and a simple gold necklace with a small pearl pendant. Her hair was pulled back into a hair clip. On her feet, she wore white sandals, revealing her brightly painted red toenails. Every detail was taken into consideration. She was flawless.

Men's heads turned when she walked by; their gawking eyes stared lustfully with every step she took. Knowing that the beautiful woman who turned all the men's heads was here to share the evening with him boosted Randy's confidence. "You're late," he said.

She greeted him with a hug. "I'm sorry I kept you waiting."

"Some friends and I grabbed a few tables if you want to join us," he suggested.

"Thank you. That would be great."

Randy gently placed his hand on her back and led her over to the tables. "Can I get you a drink?" he offered.

"No thanks. I'm fine." She set her purse under Randy's chair then took a seat next to him.

Throughout the night, Randy's eyes remained fixated on Jane. When she spoke, he watched her lips move. He carefully observed her body language, and every time she glanced his way, he gazed into her eyes. The way they sparkled in the neon lights of the club was so alluring.

After sipping at his drink for an hour but not really drinking it, he could stand it no longer. He had to be alone with her. He set his drink down, held out his hand to her, and asked, "Dance with me?"

"I would love to." She took his hand, and he led her onto the dancefloor.

All night he'd been dying to hold her in his arms. Now that he finally had the opportunity to do so, his heart raced. Normally, Randy wasn't the type of guy to let a girl get to him. He was cool, collected. It wasn't his style to overheat, much less fall for a girl. Yet tonight, he was quickly losing control.

Randy had been with many women in the past, dated casually, and even had a girlfriend back in high school, but he never felt the way he was feeling now. The effect she had on him was unlike anything he had ever experienced. Something about Jane drove him wild.

However, this emotional reaction posed a serious problem. He was in medical school. He had commitments and obligations and couldn't let this happen. He didn't have time for a woman in his life and really didn't want to become seriously involved with Jane. With his schooling schedule, he couldn't do that. It wouldn't be fair to her and would be too distracting for him.

But her lips stared at him, glossy and moist. He desperately wanted to kiss her. Trying to maintain a level head, he decided he needed to get out of this environment before he did something he was going to regret.

"You like ice cream?" he whispered into her ear. "I know a good place to get some."

This sparked her interest. "Sounds yummy, but let me use the ladies' room first. I'll be right back."

While she was gone, Randy grabbed his jacket.

Apparently, Randy was preparing to leave. Jim questioned this sudden decision. "Where you goin'?"

"Away from here."

The way Randy held Jane against his body and stared and ogled over her all night gave away his intentions. "Uh huh. Goin' somewhere so you can be alone?"

"Why do you have to be so meddlesome?" Randy asked.

"Everyone in this place saw the way you two were dancin' together. You were practically glued to her."

As much as Randy tried to hide the intense feelings he had for Jane, he now realized he hadn't done a very good job of it. As soon as Jane returned, she grabbed her purse and the two of them left the building.

After ice cream, they walked along Albany Waterfront Trail. The air was slightly chilly, and Jane's arms were folded across her chest. "Are you cold?" he asked.

She nodded. "A little."

He took off his jacket and draped it over her shoulders then rubbed her arms to warm her up. "That better?"

"Yes. Thank you."

She looked up at him with those tantalizing, hypnotic eyes of hers. Every time she looked at him, he was spellbound. He pulled her close and held her in his arms. The heat from her body generated onto his, warming him. He was dying to kiss her, and as much as he wanted to, he didn't dare. He knew he'd lose control if he did.

Jane tilted her head and stared at him inquisitively. "Do you think I'm pretty?"

What kind of a question was that? Shocked by this bold statement, he replied, "Of course I do." As he held her under the streetlight and the stars, he found her more and more irresistible. His heart pounded out of control, and that tingly feeling he had when they danced together once again filled his entire body. He swallowed hard, hoping to get rid of it. "Why would you ask me that?"

"Because I don't get it."

"Don't get what?"

Jane moved her mouth a bit closer to his. "How come you have never tried to kiss me?"

Randy raised an eyebrow at her question, a question he really did not wish to answer. "You don't really want me to answer that."

"Yes, I do." Then a discouraging thought popped into her head that made her pull away slightly. "Oh, god. You're not gay are you?"

This response made Randy laugh. "No. I'm straight as an arrow."

"Then why?"

He decided the best recourse was to tell her the truth. "Because I'm afraid that if I kiss you, I won't be able to stop."

She didn't fully understand his logic. "And that's a bad thing?"

He moistened his lips and caught himself drifting into her eyes. He desperately longed to kiss her, but knew he couldn't go there, shouldn't go there. It would lead to nothing but trouble. "It could be."

She drew herself closer to him, so close that their lips were almost touching. "Kiss me," she insisted.

He didn't do it. He didn't dare. If he did, there would be no turning back.

She closed her eyes, begging him to make physical contact. "Kiss me."

His heart raced. The last thing he wanted was to be emotionally attached to a woman, yet he was dangling on the thread of the very emotion he was trying to avoid. Kissing Jane would seal his doom. He couldn't give in to his urge. *Come on, Randy*, he thought. *Pull it together*. No matter how hard he tried, he found himself unable to resist her. Before he realized what was happening, their lips touched. The intense feeling left him weak in the knees. He interlocked his mouth to hers and their kiss became more succulent. The sensation was the most stimulating feeling he had ever felt. It sent chills down his spine.

Several minutes later, he broke away and came up for air.

She smiled. "See, that wasn't so bad."

Wasn't so bad? It was incredible, the best kiss he'd ever experienced. Randy was always physically attracted to Jane and found her personality alluring, but now he had completely fallen for her. Confused, he drew Jane in as close as he could and turned his eyes toward the starlit sky. He reflected on the events of the evening and couldn't believe he had allowed his emotions to get the best of him. He knew if he kissed her this would happen. Why did he have to kiss her?

When Randy walked Jane up to her door that night, she held his hand and said, "Thank you for meeting me tonight, Randy."

"Thank you for inviting me." He took a deep breath and moistened his lips. He wanted to kiss her again but was afraid to. In an attempt to shake it off, he exhaled deeply and closed his eyes. When he did, Jane took him by surprise and interlocked her lips to his. He made no attempt to resist her. He absorbed every taste, every touch, every delicious sensation she offered him. Yearning within him grew and he deepened the kiss, giving it more passion. Feelings of intense desire began to brew. Attempting to maintain his composure, he slowly pulled away from her before things got out of control. "I should go. I have my study session in the morning."

"Will you call me?"

"Of course."

She bit her lip seductively and slowly released him. "Goodnight, Randy Hanson."

"Goodnight, Jane. Bonne nuit."

Once she was safely inside, he returned to his car and drove home.

Randy didn't sleep well that night. His head spun a hundred miles an hour and the emotions he felt tormented him. He couldn't get Jane out of his head.

He awoke in the morning hoping the feeling would subside. It didn't. Still groggy, he rolled out of bed and trudged into the bathroom. He combed his fingers through his hair and looked in the mirror, reflecting on the events of the previous night. "Dammit. What the hell is wrong with me?" Hoping to clear the jumbled up mess inside his head, Randy called his father.

His father answered cheerfully. "Good morning, Randal. How are you this morning?"

Randy and his father talked for several minutes, discussing school and work and the recent research he had done for his thesis, before he finally got to his reason for calling. "I've met someone. Her name is Jane Davine. She's 21, Psychology major. She has amazing green eyes, a gorgeous smile, beautiful girl."

Randy hadn't talked about a woman in a long time. In fact, Dr. Hanson couldn't remember the last time Randy talked about a girl. "Is that right?"

"Her sorority supports Women's Cardiac Care, so she's an advocate for women's health. She does a lot of volunteer work at the children's hospital too. And get this, she loves basketball."

This woman definitely seemed to strike his son's interest. "Really?"

"I met her in Santa Cruz, at the beach, before school started. We played a game of volleyball together. After the game, we talked for a while. I ran into her again during lunch the next day. We really hit it off so I asked her out. We've been dating for several weeks now. Anyway, last night I met her at this club and this song came on. We danced together and the feeling of holding her in my arms, combined with that incredible perfume she was wearing, drove me crazy. At first, I thought maybe it was just the atmosphere we were in, so I suggested we leave. We went for ice cream then took a walk. The next thing I knew she was in my arms again. I didn't want to kiss her, but I couldn't help myself. She leaned into me and it just happened. It was the most intense kiss I've ever experienced."

Randy's dreamy state of mind made Dr. Hanson laugh. "So you like this girl?"

"I can't get her out of my head." He paused briefly to gather his thoughts. "Which freaks me out."

"Why?"

"Because I think I'm in love with her." Randy had never allowed himself to become emotionally attached to a woman before. He couldn't believe those words just came out of his mouth.

"Well now. That's something I've never heard you say."

"Yeah, I know," Randy confirmed. "And it scares the hell out of me."

"Have you told her how you feel?"

That was the most ridiculous suggestion Randy had ever heard. "I can't tell her that."

"Why not?"

Randy didn't have a reason, other than sheer fear. "Because I can't."

"I haven't heard you talk about a girl in a long time, Son. I think a girlfriend will be good for you."

"She's not my girlfriend."

Dr. Hanson knew his son well and knew exactly what Randy was thinking. "But you want her to be, don't you?"

With a sigh of admittance, Randy said, "Yes. I do."

"Then you're going to have to tell her."

His dad was right, but Randy was terrified to do it. "What am supposed to say? I can't just blurt out that I'm in love with her. Isn't that coming on a little strong?"

"You need to say something or she's going think you don't care about her."

"But I do care about her. I'm so confused."

Trying to get Randy to think rationally, Dr. Hanson offered some advice. "Sounds to me like you two have a lot in common. A strong foundation is forming and you have a good line of communication open. Tell her how you feel. For all you know she might feel the same way. But you won't know if you don't say something."

"I don't know what to say," Randy admitted.

His father reassured him. "Just be honest with her."

Randy contemplated this advice, but he wasn't sure he agreed with it.

"I do hope you are staying focused on school, Randal," Dr. Hanson insisted firmly.

"Don't worry. I am."

During his group study session that morning, Randy's head was full of turmoil. He had difficulty concentrating and seemed to be zoning in and out of the discussion.

Jim noticed this driftiness right away. "Randy," he called out, trying to get Randy's attention. No response. He tried again, a bit louder this time. "Hanson!"

Randy snapped out of his trance and returned to reality. "What?"

"You are in your own little world today. You okay?"

With a blank expression, Randy flipped the page in his book. "I'm fine."

Jim knew better. The muddled expression on Randy's face told him his best friend was not fine. "You wanna shoot some hoops later?"

"Sure."

When they met at the basketball court that afternoon, Jim had every intention of getting Randy to talk. They played for a while, but no words were spoken. Randy dribbled down the court taking all of his frustrations out on the ball. After his shot cleared the net, he plodded to the side of the court and picked up his water bottle. He carefully unscrewed the lid, slammed down a huge gulp, then sat on the floor with his knees bent. He leaned against the wall, wiping sweat off his brow with a towel. When he was finished, he aggressively tossed the towel to the side and raised his hand to his forehead as if his head hurt.

Jim watched him the entire time. Obviously his best friend was upset about something. He joined Randy on the side of the court and took a seat right next to him. "You alright?"

"My head is a mess."

"Care to elaborate?"

Randy took another drink and exhaled heavily. "I've been running this through my head over and over again and telling myself I'm crazy. I must be fucking crazy. There is no way this will ever work. I have enough upheaval and bullshit in my life. I definitely don't need this."

Unclear what Randy was referring to, Jim asked, "What are you talkin' about?"

"Everything was cool until last night."

"What happened last night?"

Randy explained, "I don't know what it is. She is so fun to hang out with and so damn easy to talk to. I can't get enough."

Now Randy's rant made perfect sense. The way he felt about Jane was getting the best of him. Jim sat back and let him continue his rant.

"As I held her in my arms last night, I knew. That's why I had to get out of there. The mood was…" His thoughts were all jumbled together and he couldn't think straight. "Dammit, I knew if I kissed her this would happen. Why did I kiss her?"

Jim raised his eyebrows teasingly. "You kissed her?"

Randy drifted into another world. "She is the most incredible kisser. I'm talking melt in your mouth, heart-stopping kisses."

With a smirk on his face, Jim said, "That good, huh?"

"Oh god, yes. She stood there staring at me with those hypnotic eyes of hers tempting me, teasing me. I couldn't help it. It just happened. What was I thinking?" Feeling flustered, he combed his fingers though his hair. "I can't stop thinking about her. I can't sleep, can't stay focused on anything, I can't concentrate at all."

Jim nodded in agreement. "Yeah. I noticed."

"This is driving me insane."

"Because you like her."

"I wish it were that simple." Randy nervously fidgeted with his fingers. "I can't shake this feeling. I've tried, but I can't. Every time I'm with her it grows bigger and stronger."

"What feeling?"

Randy turned his head, staring at Jim with a muffled expression on his face. "I'm in love with her."

Well, this was not what Jim expected. In fact, he was shocked to hear Randy say that. In the five years Jim had known Randy Hanson, he had never heard the word love come out of his mouth, at least not in reference to a woman. "Seriously?"

"Yes. And I don't want to be, dammit. I can't. I don't have time for a woman in my life. I have too much at stake. I can't afford to get distracted by her." Randy paced around the gym floor. "Why do these things have to be so goddamn complicated? The more I fight this, the harder it hits me."

Jim tried to be understanding, although deep down he was laughing his ass off. "Then stop fighting it."

"I can't. It doesn't make any sense, Jim. I shouldn't have kissed her. I knew if I did this would happen."

Before Randy could utter another word, Jim interjected, "You know what your problem is? You think too much."

Randy quit pacing and looked Jim directly in the eye. His sarcastic, backwards words of wisdom were not at all helpful in this situation. "What the hell do you know?"

"You're the kind of guy who always tries to rationalize things and come up with plausible explanations for every aspect of life. Well, I hate to be the one to break this to you, Bro, but not everything in life makes sense. Some things just happen, without explanation, and you have no control over them."

"I know, but this is different."

"Like hell it is. Listen to you," Jim lectured. "You need to quit thinkin' with your head and think with your heart for a change." Jim rose to his feet. "You know, some people spend their whole life searchin' for love and never find it. You're one of the lucky ones. Love flew off the beach and landed right in your lap. Don't try to rationalize this and don't try to make sense out of it. Just flow with it and let it happen."

Jim wasn't making Randy's situation into a joke. He was downright serious, a side of Jim that Randy rarely saw outside of medicine. "But Jim…"

"You can't just sit in the lineup like a buoy bobbin' in the waves. You have to push your limits and take the opportunity to ride some epic waves."

Although Randy was impressed by the length of the speech Jim had just given him, he wasn't exactly sure what Jim's surfing analogy meant. "What?"

"If you love her, like you just told me you did, you need to do somethin' about it. Because if don't, and you let that girl slip through your fingers, you are a damn fool."

Jim was right. Why did Jim have to be right? Randy hated it when Jim was right. Didn't his father say something like that to him too? Damn, his head hurt.

The emotional rollercoaster Randy had been riding on lately was messing with his head. Jim tried to ease his mind. "Love is the most powerful feeling in the world. Don't fight it so much."

For the reminder of the day, Randy couldn't focus on school or work or anything else no matter how hard he tried. All he could think about was Jane. Words of advice from both Jim and his father echoed through his head over and over again like an ominous voice plaguing him. Maybe they were right. Maybe he did need to tell her how he felt.

He contemplated calling her. He even picked up his phone a few times and almost dialed her number. Since he didn't know what he would say to her if she answered, he immediately set the phone back down. "What the hell is wrong with me? Why is this so hard?"

Chapter Six

The following afternoon, when Jane walked into the Alpha house, Lisa stared at her as if she was sprouting horns and green wings. Alarmed by this reaction, Jane looked down at her clothes thinking maybe she was mismatched. "What's wrong?"

Lisa reached for a large bouquet of roses and handed them to Jane. "These came for you earlier this afternoon."

"Really? From who?" With the vase in her hands, Jane sat on couch and read the attached card. *Meet me at the gym. We need to talk.* It was signed with Randy's name. She was excited that he sent her roses, but concerned about the meaning of the note. Since the day Randy got her number, he had called her every night, except for last night. Jane figured it was because he was busy studying for exams, but now she began to think otherwise. *We need to talk.* What did he mean by that? Was he about to tell her he only wanted to be friends? Or maybe he didn't want to see her at all. That was usually what a guy implied when he used those words with her. She feared her persistence the other night scared him away. Her eyes became cloudy with tears.

Lisa saw the look in Jane's eyes and came over to see what was wrong. "What is it?"

Jane showed Lisa the card.

Since the day they met, Jane had done nothing but talk about Randy. She stayed up every night anxiously awaiting his phone call. When he didn't call her last night, she was crushed. Offering comfort, Lisa said, "I'm sure it's nothing. He wouldn't have gone through the trouble of sending you flowers if he didn't want to see you anymore."

"Unless he wants to let me down gently." Jane was used to being let down. Every man she had ever been with treated her like a trophy or his prized possession. Men weren't interested in what she had to say; they only wanted to get her in bed. Sometimes she gave in, only to be let down the next day when she overheard the guy make degrading comments about her to his friends. But most of the time she kept her personal body parts to herself, which usually led to the *'we need to talk'* speech, at which time the guy would ditch her for someone more willing to put out.

But Randy was different. He was actually interested in what she had to say. He made it a point to take time out of his busy schedule so they could be together. He was the nicest person she had ever known, and the most romantic man she had ever dated.

Lisa gave Jane a hug, trying to offer encouragement. "Everything will be fine. Go talk to him."

Jane hoped she was right.

She arrived at the gym, not knowing what to expect. When she walked inside, Randy was dribbling a basketball across the court, working up a sweat. He ran to the hoop and easily made a layup. He let the ball bounce away and headed to the side of the court. Winded, with the slightest drop of sweat on his brow, he grabbed a towel and wiped his forehead. Then he reached for a bottle of water, unscrewed the cap, and chugged down half the contents.

That's when he spotted Jane. "Hey," he said, panting. "I didn't see you standing there. You been here long?"

"Not really." Jane walked onto the court, stopping right in front of him. "Thank you for the flowers. They're beautiful."

"You're welcome." He drank down one more swallow then screwed the lid back on.

"You didn't call me last night."

Admitting this fault, he replied, "I know. I'm sorry. I had a lot on my mind." Not exactly sure what he was going to say or how he was going to say it, he took a moment to pull his thoughts together. "You know, Jane, becoming a doctor is my dream. I've never let anyone or anything stand in the way of accomplishing that goal. Med school is my life. It's something I've worked hard to achieve and the only thing I've ever cared about...until I met you." He stepped closer and gazed into her eyes. "Since I met you, you're all I think about. Every time I hear your voice, see your beautiful smile, or look into your eyes, I get this feeling. And every time I'm around you, the feeling grows stronger. I can't fight it anymore."

She heard the words that came out of his mouth, but didn't fully comprehend what they meant. "Why are you saying?"

Butterflies fluttered in his stomach and his heart raced as he thought about what he was about to say to her. Baring his soul, he professed, "I'm in love with you."

She stared at him, unsure what to say. For several seconds, neither one of them spoke. Randy wished she would say something, anything to ease this pit in the middle of his stomach.

Breaking the silence, Jane finally said, "What did you say?"

He licked his lips and spoke from his heart. "I love you."

A smile filled her pretty face. "Really?"

He simply nodded.

She breathed a sigh of relief. Immediately her hands clasped around his neck.

He drew her closer and closed his eyes, groping for her mouth with his. Her lips—those soft, tender lips drove him mad with want. Her kiss was so satisfying, so pleasing; it made him tingle in agonizing pleasure. Feeling every moist curve and soft crevice of her lips, he opened his mouth a bit wider. Pleasure, nothing but pure pleasure. He let go of the world and completely absorbed himself in her and this incredible kiss.

At the end of their embrace, she nuzzled into his shoulder.

He held her in his arms and touched her forehead with the tips of his lips. "This could get really complicated."

She lifted her chin and said, "Randy, you need to promise me something."

"Anything."

"I know how important medical school is to you, and I know how dedicated you are. What you do isn't easy." She cradled his face with both hands. "I do not want to take medical school away from you or keep you away from it. You need to promise me that if you need space, if you need time to study or need to be left alone so you can concentrate, let me know, immediately."

"I will," he agreed.

"I mean it," she insisted. "We are in this together. And I'll support you any way I can, but you have to tell me."

Sensing her uncertainty, he kissed her to free her from worry. "I promise I will."

They stood forehead to forehead, nuzzled in each other's arms. "So, now what?"

"Well, for starters, I need a shower."

She laughed in agreement.

Randy picked up his basketball then he and Jane held hands and strolled toward Alpha together. When they got to the front porch, Randy said, "Would you like to join me for dinner?"

"I would love to."

"Can you be ready in an hour?" he asked.

"I can try."

"Good." He leaned over and kissed her. "I'm gonna hop in the shower." Reluctantly, he released her and turned to leave.

"Randy?" she called out to him.

"Yes?"

"I love you too."

Happy to hear those words from her, he smiled in contentment.

Randy slept better that night than he had in days. A burden had been lifted from his shoulders and he discovered a new sense of freedom. He had unlimited access to Jane's luscious lips, was able to hold her whenever he wanted to, and proudly called her his girlfriend. He felt so alive and so full of energy.

During lunch, Randy shimmied over to the table with a blissful smile on his face.

Jim recognized his friend's cheerful disposition right away. "You're in a good mood today. What are you so stoked about?"

Randy set his bag on the floor and pulled up a chair. "I took your advice and told Jane how I felt."

"I can assume by your mood that it went well?"

"Let's put it this way, Jane's officially my girlfriend."

Jim had never heard Randy refer to a woman as his girlfriend before. This was a very welcome change. "Grats, man. I'm happy for you."

As per their dinner conversation the night before, Randy planned to meet Jane for lunch and use the opportunity to introduce her to his circle of friends. When she walked in the building, he bounded to his feet to greet her. "Hey, Babe."

"I am starving. I haven't eaten anything all day."

"Didn't you eat breakfast?"

"I woke up late and didn't have time."

"Then let's get you some food." He carried her backpack over his shoulder and escorted her to the counter to grab lunch.

Randy piled a cup of coffee, a package of M&M's, and a bag of chips onto his tray. This food combination made Jane cringe. "I hope you're eating something healthier than that."

He inched a bit closer to her. "Oh yeah? Like what?"

She picked up a salad and handed it to him. "Here. Try this."

He stared at her with a crooked grin.

While Randy and Jane were choosing lunch pickings, the rest of Randy's friends arrived at the lunch table. "Yo, Peeps," Steve said as he approached the group. "What's up?" He set his bag down then glanced over at the food court. When he saw Jane standing right next to Randy, his eyes got huge. She was the sexiest woman he had ever seen. "Holy crap! Who is that hottie with Randy?"

Jim turned his head to see Randy and Jane side by side with his arm around her. Witnessing this made him smile. "You guys are not gonna believe this, but that is Randy's new girlfriend."

Bruce's jaw hit the floor. "A girlfriend? You're kidding?"

"Nope. No joke, man."

Bruce looked over at Randy right as he and Jane embraced in a kiss. He could not believe what he saw. Inquiring further, he asked, "When did this happen?"

"Been happenin' for several weeks now."

"Is this a steady thing or just another one of his run of the mill booty calls?"

"Oh, no," Jim replied. "This is the real deal. He is completely hooked on this chick."

"I can see why," Steve cut in. "Look at her. She is hot."

"Who is she?" Bruce wanted to know, curious about the woman who had whipped Randy into submission.

"Her name is Jane," Jim answered as he grabbed a handful of straws. "He met her right before school started when he and I were chillin' in Santa Cruz."

As Randy and Jane headed toward the table, he gave a basic overview of his friends' personalities. "I should probably warn you, some of my friends are a little…off. All of us are medical students, which explains the partial insanity we all seem to possess."

"I see."

"Now Jim you've met," he said. "He's my best friend, and the world's biggest smartass. He thinks he's a surfer, but he's never stepped foot on a surfboard in his life."

"Good to know."

He continued to say, "Mandy is slightly hyperactive. She's a sweet woman, but has a tendency to freak out over minor things. Sarah is really shy. She doesn't say much, but watch out for her Chinese insults. She can whip out some sort of vulgarity, although I have no idea what she's saying."

"Have you been on the receiving end of those insults?" Jane teased him.

"Occasionally, but I probably deserved it."

This comment made her laugh.

"Bruce is a great guy. Smart, serious, kind of your silent brainiac type. He's pretty private, but he's fun to hang out with. He's a good friend and would come to my assistance at the drop of a hat. Steve on the other hand..." Randy shook his head and sneered in disgust. "Steve is an ignorant ass. Every word that comes out of his mouth is either a lie or an exaggeration. He's arrogant and lazy. I don't like him much, but I'm forced to put up with him. I ignore most of what he says, which keeps me from beating his ass. He annoys the hell out of me."

Jane found his overview amusing. "Hmm, sounds like a stable group, these friends of yours. They would be good people to observe for my Psychology case studies."

After introductions were made, Jane sat in the chair beside Randy and chomped on an apple. He sipped from a cup of coffee and nibbled on a bag of chips. Jane had a class to get to, so she didn't stay long. As she picked up her backpack and prepared to leave, she said to the group, "It was nice meeting all of you."

Randy stood up with her and escorted her to the door. "I'll call you later."

"You better."

"I will." He leaned in closer and gave her an enduring kiss, trying to make it last as long as possible. As soon as they parted ways, Randy returned to the table and rejoined his friends.

"Hey, Jim, hand me a straw," Bruce demanded.

Jim corrected his friend, "Don't think of it as a mere straw, Buckman. Think of it as your tubular pipeline to instant, ice-cold refreshment."

Bruce peered at Jim sternly. "Just hand me the damn thing."

Jim reached across the table and gave Bruce a straw.

"She's a nice girl," Mandy remarked. Then she directed her attention to Bruce. "You need to wise up and get a girlfriend, Buckman." She playfully elbowed him in the ribs.

"Ow!" He rubbed his chest where Mandy jabbed him.

"There are women out there interested in you if you'd open your eyes and look."

"You had to jab my in the ribcage to tell me that? You could have been a little nicer about it." Bruce peeled the paper off his straw and stuffed it into the lid of his cup. "She is a sweet girl, Randy. Pretty too."

Steve could stand it no longer. He had to express his opinion. "Pretty? She is drop dead gorgeous, man. Sexy curves, firm ass. Bet she's tight as hell."

Randy did not appreciate Steve's lewd tone. "She is also unavailable, Fuckwad, so keep your damn hands off of her."

Mandy stepped in, in Randy's defense. "Yeah, Steven. Find your own woman."

Steve retorted, "Hey. I can get any woman I want at any time."

"Is that right?" Jim teased.

"Yes it is."

Jim could not resist the temptation. "Alright, Mr. Hall. What about Mandy?" he said, eyeing Amanda with a mischievous grin. "She's single, and she's a bodacious babe."

"James! You bastard!" Mandy yelled, appalled that he had suggested such a thing.

Mandy's reaction made him laugh. "I meant that as a compliment."

"There is no way in hell," she bellowed. "Not if he was the last man alive."

Steve snidely replied, "Your loss."

Then Jim offered Steve a challenge. "Care to put your money where your mouth is?"

"What do you mean?"

Jim scanned the room and pointed to a pretty redhead. "That one. I bet you twenty bucks that you can't dick that chick by this time tomorrow."

Steve didn't think that was a challenge at all. "You're on."

"I want proof. You have to show me her panties," Jim insisted.

Randy couldn't believe Jim was engaging in this infantile crap. "What, are you guys twelve?" He grabbed his bag and stood up to leave. "As much as I would love to partake in this intellectual debate, I have an appointment with Dr. Drenner. I'll see you guys later."

After class that evening, Randy stopped by his apartment to change into basketball shorts and a Lakers tee-shirt then headed over to Alpha to see Jane. When he got there, he stood on the porch with a basketball in his hand and knocked on the door.

Jane answered dressed in shorts and a tight tank top. Her hair was pulled back into a ponytail. "Hey, you. What are you doing over here?"

"Nice greeting. I thought you'd be happy to see me."

"I am."

"Then come here."

She stepped out to the porch and gave him a kiss. "What's with the basketball?"

He dribbled the ball, hoping to entice her. "I thought you might want to shoot some hoops with me."

She placed her hands on her hips and shifted from one foot to the other. "Are you sure you want to do that?"

"I don't know. Should I be worried?"

She snatched the ball from his hand. "Let's go."

While Randy laid his keys and phone on the bleachers, Jane dribbled in the middle of the court. "I'm not sure this is entirely fair," she said.

"Why is that?"

"Because I already know I'm going to beat you."

Wow! She was cocky and overconfident. Randy found this amusing. "Oh, you think so?"

"Uh huh." She passed him the ball. "You take out."

"As you wish."

Randy had a difficult time keeping up with her on the court. Not only was she quick on her feet, she also excelled at blocking. She handled the ball well and rarely missed a shot. When Randy dribbled down the court, Jane bumped into him and knocked him backwards onto the floor. She stole the ball and took off the opposite direction, firing a jumpshot straight into the basket. Once the shot cleared the net, she retrieved the ball and swaggered to the center of the court. "I win."

Randy looked up, astonished by what he just saw her do. Jane was confident when it came to basketball, and she had every right to be. Her skills were exceptional, and that was one of the best damn defensive moves he had ever seen. "Holy shit." He stood up, panting. "Where did you learn to do that?"

"I've had a lot of practice."

"I can see that." His chest heaved as he tried to catch his breath. She was tough competition. He couldn't remember the last time playing a game of one-on-one wore him out this much. "I'm pretty sure that last move was a foul, though."

"You gonna challenge me?" she asked haughtily.

Not wanting to debate with her, he conceded, "Nope. You win. You wanna grab some dinner?"

She nodded. "I could go for some food."

"Thought so." Jane was always hungry, and for a thin girl, she could eat a lot. "Mind if we stop by my place so I can change first?"

"That's fine."

They grabbed their belongings, exited the building, and walked toward the northern side of campus to Randy's apartment.

When they got to the front porch, Randy unlocked the door and gently put his hand on Jane's back, leading her inside. He tossed his keys on the table, set his phone alongside them, and placed the ball on a chair. "I'll only be a minute."

He disappeared into the bedroom, and Jane used the opportunity to look around. The place was roomy and comfortable. And for a bachelor's apartment, it was immaculately clean. From the look of the furnishings and stylish decor, the man had class. Nothing in here was cheap. His furniture was in impeccable condition. Tables were polished, and everything in this place was well taken care of.

He had a laptop, stethoscope, and open medical textbook spread out across the table. Next to the textbook, stacked neatly in a pile, was a *Sports Illustrated* magazine and two medical journals, one from the American Medical Association and another from the American College of Obstetrics and Gynecology.

In the living room was a large flat screen TV, an entertainment system with a surround sound stereo, and a combination DVD/ Blu-ray player. While browsing through the titles in Randy's DVD collection, a loud squawk startled her. She looked up to find a grey bird waving its claw at her from inside a large birdcage.

"Hello," the bird said.

"You didn't tell me you had a parrot," she called to Randy.

His voice trailed from the other room. "Yes, I do. His name is Mr. Fingers."

That was a strange name. She figured a name like that had some kind of significance. "Why did you name him that?"

"Because he'll bite your finger if he doesn't know you." Randy emerged from the bedroom right as Jane was about to put her finger in the bird's cage. "I wouldn't do that if I were you. He does bite." He came up behind her and gave her a kiss.

The bird wolf whistled and said, "Pretty girl."

Jane thought this was hilarious. "Did you teach him that?"

"Yup. He says all kinds of things. Sometimes he won't shut up."

The parrot started to sing, "You are my sunshine..."

"He's cute." She turned around to see Randy dressed in jeans and pearly white socks with a clean tee-shirt in his hand. He was bare-chested with his muscular chest, defined arms, and tight abdomen exposed in front of her. He had a well-toned physique. Obviously he took care of his body.

Jane crept closer and gently touched his skin with the soft tips of her fingers. Her touch gave him goose bumps. He felt a chill in his spine, as if someone had rubbed an ice cube down his back. A weak feeling overtook him, and his knees felt like Jell-O. Trying to ignore it, he slipped his UC Berkeley shirt over his head and headed into the kitchen.

Jane continued to browse his apartment at the various pictures and books he had on display. He had a collection of Michael Crichton novels, as well as a few by Stephen King. Randy's shelves were filled with all sorts of medical books, including a copy of Gray's Anatomy Coloring Book. Although he probably used it for medical school purposes, seeing a coloring book on a grown man's shelf made her giggle. Besides medical reference material, he also had several books about muscle cars, a few sports car models, and a framed, autographed picture of Dale Earnhardt positioned neatly on a shelf next to a mini replica of a vintage Aston Martin.

Randy opened the refrigerator and rummaged through the scarcity of their choices, searching for something edible to feed them. "You want a Pepsi?"

"Only if it's Diet," she called back.

He didn't like Diet Pepsi and didn't keep any in his apartment. He could see now, with a girlfriend that preferred Diet Pepsi, that he was going to have to keep a supply on hand.

Jane followed Randy's voice into the kitchen. He was staring at an open pantry with his back to her. Admiring his firm shoulders, she grazed her hand across his back as she passed by him.

Her gentle, arousing touch gave him tingles. It was amazing how Jane managed to get him excited simply by touching him. His heart thumped like crazy, and he developed a deep longing for her. He took her by the arm and pulled her close to him. Her lips called his name, teasing him with their sensuousness. He couldn't resist. He leaned in to kiss her, a deep, heartfelt kiss that left him breathless.

Jane was an incredible kisser. Tender and loving, yet passionate and intense. Kisses trailed down her neck and collar bone to the little crevice between her breasts. He caressed the small of her back and slowly worked his way down to her butt. He wanted her so badly it hurt. But he didn't want to rush things. He wanted to do this right and wait until she was ready. Swallowing hard, trying to hold back his fierce desire, he caught himself groping and withdrew his hands before things moved too far.

"So," Jane said as she brought her mouth close to his again. "What are we going to do about finding a suitable meal?"

"I don't know. What do you feel like?"

"Chinese takeout maybe?"

That sounded good. He hadn't had that in a while. Wanting to satiate her craving, he released his grip on her and picked up his phone.

Chapter Seven

Randy had been in an exceptional mood all week. He was full of energy, motivated, and life just seemed to be going his way.

Thrilled to see his friend in such high spirits, Jim couldn't let Randy's happy disposition go unnoticed. "You know, I gotta say, this mood you've been in lately looks really good on you."

Randy smiled, which he seemed to do constantly lately. "I feel pretty good. Thank you for knocking some sense into my stubborn head, Jim. Being in love is incredible. Since I've been with Jane, I've never been so happy."

"Told ya," Jim replied.

"Yes you did, and things are going great."

"Wish I could say the same," Jim complained.

"Why? What's going on?"

"Trina." Jim wadded up a piece of paper and tossed it in the wastebasket. "She was in a good mood last night, all snuggly and lovey, and then this morning when I got up, she went all agro on my ass and was totally buggin'."

Hearing this kind of complaint from Jim was not uncommon. However, recently it seemed to be a daily occurrence. "About what?"

"Some shit about how she works all the time and never gets to do anything. She says I'm never around and told me I don't hold my own weight as far as household chores go.

Then she had the nerve to accuse me of drainin' all her money. She called me a sponger."

That was extremely harsh. "Ouch!"

"Yeah. Bleak. She's constantly naggin' because I'm studyin' and can't spend every waking minute with her."

"But she knew all along that you wanted to go to medical school," Randy reminded him. "What does she want you to do?"

"Hell if I know," Jim said, shrugging his shoulders. "She pisses me off sometimes. She is so damn moody. One second she'll be all over me and the next she's findin' ten thousand reasons to bitch at me and doesn't want me to touch her. Fuckin' weak, man."

Jim and Trina had one of those on again, off again relationships. They had been together for eight years, when they could stand each other, and Randy didn't understand why Jim stayed in a relationship with a person he didn't seem to like very much.

"I can't figure her out," Jim continued. "I wish she'd make up her mind and decide what the hell she wants. I can't give her what she wants if I don't know what she wants."

"True."

"Maybe she's got cabin fever and needs to get out of the house. You wanna double up this weekend?"

"We can."

"Why don't we take the honeys to some fancy ass restaurant then go to The Club and chillax for a while. Trina says I never take her out."

Randy nodded. "Alright. I'll talk to Jane. I'm sure she'd love to go."

"Sweet."

As planned, Jim, Trina, Randy, and Jane had dinner together Friday night then went to The Club to go dancing. Trina had been drinking heavily throughout the night and was seriously intoxicated. Randy could sense Jim's aggravation with this situation. With every hour that passed, he became more and more annoyed by Trina's behavior. The smile left his face and his tone became increasingly rash. His cheerful disposition disappeared hours ago.

"Would you take it easy," Jim demanded.

Trina snapped right back. "Don't tell me what to do."

"You have had enough." He tried to take the glass from her hand, but she yanked it away, spilling it all over herself.

"I don't tell you what to do so leave me the fuck alone!" Her belligerence attracted the attention of everyone in the club.

"Lower your damn voice," he insisted.

"You are not the boss of me, James Ryan! I can do whatever I want!" Trina slammed down the rest of her drink and knocked the glass over as she pounded it on the table.

People gawked at them, disgusted by her conduct. Avoiding more confrontation, Jim backed off and left her alone.

While the four of them sat and talked, Trina scowled and climbed over the table, knocking all the cocktail glasses onto the floor. She quickly scurried into the bathroom. Concerned about Trina, Jane followed her.

Randy looked at Jim, not only disturbed by Trina's outburst, but also by Jim's reaction to it. "Are you alright?"

Jim pressed his lips tightly and rubbed the bridge of his nose. "Dammit, she never listens to me. She drinks too much, gets herself hammered, and makes a huge scene. Then she hurls all night, and I get stuck cleanin' up the mess."

Randy laughed over Jim's obvious aggravation of the situation.

"It's not fuckin' funny, man. She does this all the damn time. I have to live with her narf fest all night and deal with her feelin' like shit in the morning and blamin' it all on me. She gets fuckin' mean when she's drunk."

"I've seen her bitch at you before, but this time she was yelling at you in public and causing a huge scene. That's new."

"Yeah. I know," Jim admitted, perturbed about the entire situation. "Dammit. I really don't wanna deal with this tonight."

"You're the one who brought her here," Randy reminded him.

"I just wanted to get her out of the house, hopin' it would brighten her mood. You know, help her chill out. Guess I was wrong."

"Guess so."

A few minutes later, Jane approached the table alone. "Hey, you guys, Trina's sick."

"Shit!" Jim fumed. "She threw up didn't she?"

Jane nodded. "Yeah."

"Son-of-a-bitch. I knew it. Dammit, Katrina." He sighed. "I'll get my car. I need to get her out of here." He pulled his keys out of his pocket and headed out to the parking lot.

Randy turned to Jane and said, "Get Trina. I'll meet you out front."

"Ok."

Jane and Randy walked Trina out to Jim's car, trying to keep her from falling over. Once she was situated, Randy went over to the driver's side. Jim rolled down his window so they could talk.

"Is she going to be alright?" Randy asked.

"She'll be fine. She'll feel it in the morning though, when her head's throbbin' and she's nauseous all day. Then, undoubtedly, I'll get the third degree and she'll be bitchy as hell because her head hurts and she doesn't feel well. This is totally a no win situation for me."

Randy shook his head, not understanding his friend's devotion to that woman. Regardless, he tried to make light of the situation. "Fun times."

"Yeah, right."

"See ya later, Jim."

Jim rolled up his window and drove home.

Randy looked over at Jane, who was standing on the curb across the street. He slipped his hands in his pockets and walked over to her.

"Now what?" Jane asked.

"We can go over to my place and watch a movie if you want. I have a big selection."

"Sounds good."

When they arrived at Randy's apartment, he tossed his keys on the table and stepped into the kitchen. "You want something to drink?"

"Sure."

Randy had restocked his refrigerator and bought some Diet Pepsi for Jane. He reached into the refrigerator and pulled one out. She stood behind him, wrapped her arms around his waist, and started to nibble and kiss his ear, which sent chills down his spine. He set the soda can on the counter and turned around. With lips parted, he held her in his arms and kissed her intensely. Jane moved her hands up his chest and began unbuttoning his shirt. Her fingertips rubbed across his bare skin then worked their way over to his shoulders and down his arms. Her lips moved down to his chest, where she gave several soft kisses.

Randy closed his eyes. Her soft touches drove him wild, rousing his senses and making his whole body tingle. His heart raged in desire. Placing his hand behind her head, he clasped her long hair with his fingers. "Please don't tease me," he begged.

She moved her mouth to his ear and whispered, "Who said anything about teasing?" She reached around him to grab the can of Pepsi and retreated into the living room.

Breathing heavily, Randy's eyes followed her. He watched as she placed the can on the coffee table. When she bent over to thumb through his DVD collection, he stared lustfully at her backside. Her hips and buttocks enticed him, teasing him with fevered want. His heartrate elevated and he swallowed hard from the depths of his throat, fighting to keep his arousal under control.

Randy followed Jane into the living room, eyeing her with passion and longing. He slinked up behind her, moved the hair off her neck, then nibbled and kissed her soft skin.

Jane tilted her head slightly, giving him more access to her. "Randy," she said softly.

"Hmm?" he replied, sending kisses down the nape of her neck.

"I know why you brought me here tonight."

He knew why he brought her here too, but he wasn't about to admit it. "I don't know what you're talking about."

"Yes you do. I can see right through you."

He wanted her more than he could recall ever wanting any woman. He longed to feel his hands all over her naked body and kiss her for the rest of the night, but he couldn't tell her that. That would be entirely too forward, and he wasn't sure if she was ready or willing to go that far.

"If there's something you want, just say it."

This close contact, along with the erotic mood created from the neck nibbling, was pushing him over the edge. Sensing that she wanted it too, he moved his lips to ear and whispered, "I want you."

"Then what's stopping you?" She spun around and pulled his shirt over his head, exposing his bare chest and toned arms and shoulders.

His heart raced out of control, and his breathing became more erratic. Gently, he touched her cheek with the back of his hand. "You're so beautiful," he said. He grabbed the zipper on the back of her dress and slowly pulled it down. As the fabric slid off her shoulder and fell to the floor, he softly kissed her shoulder. She wore nothing but a lacy bra and skimpy black panties that were held onto her hips by two thin, lace-covered pieces of fabric. He put his arm around her, gently rubbing the soft skin of her tummy. Jane's eyes closed, tingling with every touch. His strong, yet gentle hands moved down her hips and buttocks, squeezing his fingertips into the flesh. With fingers spread, his hands found hers. They clasped them together and slowly made their way to the sofa.

Jane leaned back and rested her head on a pillow. Randy scooted in next to her, caressing her inner thigh. Her lips parted slightly, begging to be kissed, so he complied with her request. Any resistance he had was gone. His body throbbed, hunger burned inside him. Reaching his arms around her, he fumbled for the latch of her bra. He unfastened it then slipped it off her shoulders. Her beasts were round and firm, just the way he liked them. He cupped his hand over one of them and caressed her soft skin. Her nipple hardened between his fingers. He touched her breast with his lips, tempting her with the tip of his tongue.

Desire grew within him. Based on her reaction, she wanted him too. He squatted down by her feet and kissed her tummy, making her giggle. "You sure you want to do this?" he asked as he reached up and tugged at her panties. "Once it's done, we can't undo it."

She closed her eyes, dying to feel his touch again. "I want to."

Gently, yet with deep purpose, he kissed her. "Hold that thought. I'll be right back."

He didn't want to break the fervent mood that had developed between them, but he wanted to protect them both. So he got up and made his way to the bedroom. As much as he hated wearing them, condoms were a necessary evil in Randy's life. He grabbed one from the supply in his bedside table drawer then headed back out to the living room.

Jane's enticing, magnificently curved body was lying nearly-naked on his couch. He removed the rest of his clothes then returned to her side. His fingers roamed up her tummy and gripped the lacy fabric of her panties. Slowly, he slid them over her feet. With his hand, he spread her legs apart slightly and caressed the inside of her thigh. Then he crawled onto the couch and moved closer.

Jane's chest heaved as she watched him slip on a condom. Wanting him as much as he wanted her, she made no attempt to resist him. He kissed her on the lips as a token of the tenderness he felt for her then clasped both of her hands in his and held them above her head. Their bodies conformed into one figure, one motion.

Randy's whole body tingled. This intimacy they shared was the most bonding experience of his life. And the sounds coming from her mouth made it that much more intense. She gave herself to him completely, allowing him to touch her and kiss her as he pleased. Wrapped in skin, they clung together, memorizing each other inside and out. He felt every curve, bump, and crevice she had to offer him and explored every inch. Never before had he felt this feeling of complete ecstasy in a woman. His mind drifted into a world of pure pleasure, experiencing intensity and intimacy he had never experienced before. He was totally lost in the moment.

Even though he tried to hold back as long as possible, the sensation was too powerful to control. He succumbed to her easily, ending a long and very satisfying session. He leaned forward and kissed her then closed his eyes to fully take in the feeling. Satisfied, he reclined on the pillow and covered them with a blanket.

Jane rolled over and rested her head on his shoulder, her arm relaxed between his pecs. She closed her eyes and listened to his heartbeat as his chest rose and fell, taking in air.

Randy wrapped his arm around her, squeezing her closer to him. He kissed her forehead and lovingly stroked her hair. Jane was the best lover he had ever known, not because of the physical aspects, but because of the way he felt as he held her now. Being with her, sharing this moment, was the most bonding experience of his life. A serene feeling of contentment swept over him. "I love you," he said to her.

She smiled against his chest. "I love you too."

To hear the words, I love you, come from her lips made him feel more alive than ever before. He wanted nothing more than to make her happy. Now, more than ever, he was determined and more than willing to do whatever was necessary to make this relationship work.

Randy reached over and turned off the table lamp. Jane snuggled in closer. Entering into a world of peaceful dreams, he held her in his arms and drifted off to sleep.

When Randy got off work the next day, Jane was standing outside the student clinic waiting for him. She had her hands on her hips and carried a cross demeanor. Obviously not one of her better days. Hoping to cheer her up, he approached her with a smile. "Hey, Baby."

With a feisty tone, she fumed, "How many people did you brag to?"

Wow, she was a firecracker. Apparently she was mad at him, but he was completely clueless as to why. "What are you talking about?"

"I ran into your little friend, Steve, today."

Oh, great. That was the last person she needed to bump into. What the hell did Steve say to get her all riled up? "Baby, I told you about Steve. You can't believe anything he says."

"When were you planning on dropping me now that you got what you wanted out of me?" she cried. "Is that why you said those things you said? Is that why you told me you loved me, to get me to go to bed with you?"

That was a crazy accusation and not at all true. "Where is this coming from?"

"He told me that you say things like that to get girls into bed then once you get sex out of them, you dump them. He said…"

He pulled her into his arms and kissed her to get her to stop talking. Randy always knew Steve was a jerk, but had no idea he would stoop this low. "Baby, Steve is an asshole. He's a liar and you can't believe a word that comes out of his mouth."

"But he said…"

He didn't let her finish. "Janey, look at me."

She didn't want to look at him, but she forced herself to do it anyway.

"Have I ever given you a reason not to trust me?"

She shook her head. It was quite the opposite, in fact. "No."

"Then I need you to trust me now." The look on her face told him she was still upset. "I've been at work all day and haven't said a word to anyone, least of all him. I've told you the kind of person Steve is. He tries to stir up trouble and does everything he can to create friction. You cannot trust him, and you certainly can't believe anything he says."

Jane managed to smile, wishing now that she hadn't snapped at him like that.

"I'm not going anywhere, Babe. I very much want to be with you." Once she was calmed down a bit, he lifted her chin with his finger. Their eyes met and he smiled at her. "I had the most incredible night of my life last night."

"Really?" she asked, surprised he said that.

"Yes. You are absolutely amazing in every way."

She nuzzled into Randy's shoulder and felt his arms enclose around her. "I love you."

The sound of those words coming from her lips made him feel warm inside. "I love you too, and I don't say those words unless I mean them."

Randy met his study group at the SUB the next morning ready to beat the crap out of Steve. The minute Steve stepped into the room with his snotty little gait, Randy confronted him. It took every ounce of restraint he had not to punch him. "You son-of-a-bitch! What right do you have to say that to her?"

Jim saw the lividness in Randy's eyes and knew right away that this encounter was going to turn ugly quickly.

"I don't have to listen to you," Steve retorted.

"The hell you don't. You willingly and purposefully made derogatory, hurtful remarks to my girlfriend."

Steve sneered at Randy with an arrogant smirk on his face.

"Fess up, Asshole! You have something to say to me?"

Randy grew more irate by the second. Jim moved closer, prepared to break up anything that might occur.

Steve finally admitted his fault. "You know it's true as well as I do. I was just helping her see the light."

Seething through clenched teeth, Randy commanded, "Keep your big mouth shut and stay the hell away from my girlfriend, do you hear me?"

"It's a free country. I can talk to whoever I want." Steve folded his arms across his chest and pretentiously chomped on a piece of gum.

Randy had heard enough. He got right in Steve's face. "You pompous prick. I swear, if you go near her again…"

"What?" Steve taunted him. "What are you gonna do?"

Randy make a fist with his hand and lunged toward Steve.

Jim immediately stepped between them. "Come on, Dude. Let's get some coffee." He put his hand on Randy's shoulder and encouraged him to walk away. Jim had never seen his friend so angry, and had never known him to get violent. But right now, Randy wanted to punch Steve. "For fuck sake, calm down," Jim advised.

"I am calm!"

"Like hell you are. You're wound up tighter than a top."

Randy took a few deep breaths trying to compose himself. "I hate that son-of-a-bitch."

"What did he do?"

Randy glared at Steve while the jackass sat there with his feet on the table. "That asshole told Jane I was only with her for sex. Then he had the audacity to say I was planning to ditch her once I got my fill."

Jim glanced towards the table. He couldn't believe Steve would say such a thing. "He said that to her?"

"Yes. Jane came to the clinic yesterday all upset because of his lies. What right does he have to say shit like that to her? I swear I'm going to beat the crap out of that fuckup one of these days."

"He's just tryin' to rile you up."

"By harassing my girlfriend?" Randy wanted to know. "What did she ever do to him?"

"He's not doin' it to harass her. He's doin' it because he knows she is your weakness. He can get you worked up by gettin' to her."

This made perfect sense. But now Randy was even more infuriated because Steve chose to use Jane as bait. "What, he doesn't have the balls to approach me himself? He has to go through her because he is too chicken shit to deal with me?"

Jim recognized the fury in Randy's eyes—he was beyond livid. "Calm down, Dude," he told his best friend. "You are way wiggin'."

"I hate that mother-fucker!" Randy desperately needed caffeine. He stormed toward the cafeteria searching for a cup of coffee.

Jim followed him. "You seriously need to chill."

Sometimes Jim's 'peace, dude' attitude was exceedingly inappropriate. This was one of those times. "No, I do not need to chill. Why do we keep Steve around? He's a stuck-up little prick and the most indolent, self-centered person I have ever known. He never carries his own weight and does nothing except aggravate the hell out of everyone."

"He needs our help."

Jim had a bad habit of trying to help people who weren't worthy of help. Randy always felt that Jim should exert more of his energy helping people who really needed it rather than pitiful people who didn't deserve it or appreciate it. "Screw that."

"Randy, listen," Jim tried to get him to understand. "Steve's on academic probation. He's wipin' out and sinkin' in the swells out there."

After seeing some of the test scores Steve had gotten and the mediocre lab reports he always wrote, this news was not surprising. "Good. Maybe he'll get sucked up by the undertow and drown. Then he'll flunk out and leave me the fuck alone."

"We can't let him flunk out."

Randy gave Jim a displeased glare. "Why not? Why is it our responsibility to put a half-assed, lazy doctor into the care of patients when you and I both know he doesn't give a rat's ass about any of them? I wouldn't want my family anywhere near him. Would you?"

Jim didn't answer. Randy had a valid point.

"You want my opinion?" Randy continued, "Let the bastard flunk out and do the world a favor. I want nothing to do with it."

"Dude, come on." Jim followed him to the espresso bar. "He's part of our group. We have to work with him."

"Work with him?" Randy questioned. "There's nothing in any of our class syllabuses that require us to work with him. We haven't been required to even be in the same group with him since Anatomy class, Jim. We should not all have to suffer so Steve Hall can freeload his way through med school. Hell no. I have worked too hard for this. And unlike him, I actually want to be here. I am not willing to risk my education and my career to help that incompetent ass."

"We can't just kick him out."

"Why not?" Randy wanted to know.

Jim didn't know why.

"You want him to stay in the group? Fine. But keep him the hell away from me." Randy grabbed his coffee and stormed back to the study table, but sat as far away from Steve as he could. He couldn't wait to get out of there.

After the session, Bruce, Sarah, and Mandy stayed behind to talk to Jim. Bruce was disturbed by the friction that was so apparent between Randy and Steve, so he was the first to bring up his concerns. "Jim, there is some serious tension going on between Randy and Steve."

Mandy added her opinion. "It's not healthy, and it's really getting out of hand. What's going on with them?"

Jim tried to explain, "You know how Steve is. He tries to egg Randy on all the time, and, as you well know, Randy doesn't like him."

"Well duh," Mandy declared. "That's obvious."

Jim continued, "Steve was harassin' Jane yesterday, which created a ripple effect. She got upset, which of course trickled down to Randy, who went off on Steve."

"He was harassing Randy's girlfriend?" Bruce asked, appalled by this news. "That's extremely inconsiderate. Why would he do that?"

"I have no idea."

"Well, I don't blame Randy for being pissed," Mandy justified. "He's a good man to stand up for her."

"Regardless of that, we can't work like this," Bruce argued. "The tension is counterproductive. Randy is a key member of this group, and we can't do this without him. You all know that. If it's going to cause friction for him and Steve to be in the same room together then we need to loosen the tension somehow."

Mandy agreed. "He's right, Jim. We can't let this go on."

"What are we going to do?" Sarah asked, hoping they could find a solution.

Jim came up with a plan. "Let me talk to both of them. See if we can come up with some kind of compromise."

Randy walked into his apartment to find Jane diligently typing away on his laptop. He placed his bag on the table and sat in a chair watching her, enthralled by what she was doing. "Hey, Baby. Can you come over here for a sec?"

She looked up long enough to acknowledge him. "Sure. Give me a minute." She saved her work then joined him at the table. With a playful smile, she straddling his lap and clasped her hands behind his neck. "What's up?"

He put his hands on her hips. "I need to ask you something."

She scooted her body closer. "What do you want to know?"

"This weekend kind of added a new dimension to our relationship," he said with a smile.

Thinking about the last two nights of intimate passion and the most mind-blowing sex ever, she seductively bit her lower lip. "Yes it did."

"Well, I was wondering, are you on the pill by any chance?"

She shook her head. "No."

Pursing his lips together, he said, "Janey, I care about you. And if we are going to have an intimate relationship, I think it would be a really good idea if you were. I don't want to get you pregnant. Better to be safe than sorry, don't you think?"

"You're a sweetie."

This comment seemed a bit out of place. "Why do you say that?"

"Because you're so concerned about me." She leaned forward and kissed him gently in the lips. "I'll take care of it."

"Thank you. That would make me feel much better." He tried to kiss her back, but before he could, she hopped off his lap.

One of his medical textbooks was lying on the table. She reached over and picked it up. "What's this?" she asked.

"It's Immunopathology. Why?"

She flipped through the pages.

"What are you doing?" he asked, wondering why she was suddenly so interested in his textbook.

"Quizzing you."

"Quizzing me?"

"Yup."

Randy found this amusing. "Alright. Fire away."

She proceeded to ask him several questions from the first few chapters. Despite her efforts to trip him up, he knew every answer.

"How do you know all of this?" she asked. "I can't even pronounce most of these words."

"I noticed that," he replied with a laugh. "I'm retentive. I catch onto things quickly."

"Retentive, huh?"

"Yes, Ma'am."

She placed the book back on the table and took a seat on the couch. On the coffee table sat a newly developed pack of photographs. Jane picked it up and thumbed through the pictures while Randy grabbed a drink from the refrigerator. She examined a picture of a young woman with bleached blonde hair who was wearing a red bikini. This woman's arm was around Randy and both appeared to be laughing and having a good time. "Who's the blonde girl standing next to you in this picture?"

Randy sat beside her with a cup of coffee in his hand. When he saw the photograph she had, he grinned. "That's my sister. Those pictures were taken during our summer trip to Hawaii."

Jane picked up another photo. "You went to Hawaii this summer?"

"Yes I did. Every summer we travel somewhere exotic to experience culture. It's our annual family vacation. My family's done it every year since I was a kid."

"That's cool." The photo in her hand showed an image of attractive older couple holding a pineapple. The man in the picture had an obvious resemblance to Randy. "Are these your parents?"

"Yup."

"You look so much like your dad," she stated.

"That's what people tell me." Randy scanned through the pictures until he found the one he was looking for. It was a photograph of a teenage boy with attitude written all over his face. "And this is Robby," Randy said.

"He doesn't look very happy."

"He didn't want to go on this vacation and was mad that Dad forced him to go. He tried to make everyone miserable while we were there, but ended up having a good time and was smiling by the time we left." Randy glanced at the picture again. "I'm worried about him."

"Why?"

"Because he's always in trouble. He skips school and doesn't take anything seriously. He lacks ambition and has no idea what he wants to do with his life. All he ever does is work on his car and play video games."

"Maybe he just hasn't found his niche yet," Jane suggested.

"I hope he finds it soon." Randy showed Jane a picture of the whole family at the airport. They were dressed in shorts and sun dresses wearing flowery leis around their necks. "That was a fun vacation."

"Sounds like it." Randy's white tee-shirt was imprinted with the word Seattle. One of the T's was in the shape of the Space Needle. Knowing how much he loved talking about his family, Jane asked him about his hometown. "What's Seattle like?"

Randy leaned back and put his arm around Jane. He loved talking about his favorite city and often wished he could return home to get away from the stress and strain of school. "I love Seattle. But I actually grew up in a smaller city across the lake called Kirkland. There are tons of things to do there. Shops, nightclubs, water sports, fishing. It has some tourist attractions too, unique shops, world-class art galleries, parks and waterfronts. It's a marina city, pretty upscale."

"Sounds nice," she said, considering his description of it.

"Has some of the prettiest sunsets I've ever seen."

"Do you miss it?" she asked.

"I do, but I go home a lot. Every break I get, I fly home to see my family for a few days."

"Have you always wanted to be a doctor?"

"For as long as I can remember. When I was young, I totally idolized my dad. I always thought that what he did was the coolest job in the world, and I wanted to be just like him. When I finally hit high school, I took the necessary steps to pursue that career path. I buckled down on my grades, joined a local HOSA group, and focused on school. Medical school has always been my life's ambition." He ran his fingers through her hair. "What about you? What are you going to do with this psychology degree of yours?"

"I'm not sure. Clinical Psychology maybe. I really haven't thought about it much."

Randy leaned toward Jane and was about to give her a kiss when…

"SQUAWK! Pretty girl, pretty girl."

Jane started laughing.

Randy glared at Mr. Fingers. "Do you mind?"

The bird covered his eyes with his claw. "Naughty boy." It mocked him by making a smooching sound.

This was the funniest thing Jane had ever seen. "That bird of yours is a riot."

"He's a pest," Randy complained. Attempting to calm the savage beast, he plodded over to the cage and opened the enclosure. He put his hand inside and the bird perched on his arm. He brought him over to Jane. "Don't stick your hand anywhere near his head. I don't want him to bite you."

"Can I touch him?"

"Yes, but do it gently, and only on his tail. Don't do this unless I'm around though. Give him a while to get used to you first."

Jane pet the bird's tail.

"You can talk to him if you want."

Jane bowed her eyebrows. "What do you talk to a bird about?"

"I don't know. Ask him something."

Jane thought about this for a minute. "Hi, Mr. Fingers."

"Hello." The bird held one foot out and squawked. "Cracker."

This made her smile. "I think he's hungry."

"I'm hungry too."

"Are you?" Jane asked him.

"A little." Randy placed the bird on top of his cage and headed for the kitchen. First he pulled out a box of crackers and gave one to his parrot, then he searched the refrigerator for some edible human food.

Peering over his shoulder, Jane eyed a head of romaine lettuce. "I can toss some salads together," she suggested.

"Alright." He handed her the lettuce, spinach leaves, tomatoes, and a cucumber then pointed to a nearby cupboard. "Bowls are up there."

She pulled out two bowls and went over to the sink to rinse the vegetables.

In the middle of dinner prep, Randy developed an ornery look in his eye. He grabbed the sprayer from the sink and squirted Jane with it, dampening her shirt.

"Hey!" She splashed him with some of the water droplets on her hands.

"You sure you want to start that?" he challenged her.

"You started it, not me," she countered.

He filled a cup with water and held it over her head.

Backing away from him, she pleaded, "Oh, no. Don't you dare."

Now trapped in a corner, she had no place to run. "What's the matter? It's just water."

She pressed her lips against his long enough to distract him. Then she squirmed her way out of the corner and tok the glass of water out of his hand.

With his hands now free, Randy squeezed her tightly and embraced her with a kiss.

Shortly after dinner clean up, Randy received a phone call from Jim. They conversed for a few minutes before Jim said, "Bruce and the girls are concerned about you wiggin' on Steve today."

"He was being an ass, Jim. What did you expect me to do?"

"I know he was, and I know he's annoying, but try to let it go."

"You want me to let it go?" Randy declared.

"We need to keep the peace so we can get some studyin' done."

"You think I don't know that? If anyone in our group is concerned about getting studying done it's me. And why are you saying this to me? I'm not the one who started it."

"I know you're not," Jim explained. "And I've already talked to Steve. He said he's willing to lay off Jane if you're willing to lay off him."

"Lay off what?" Randy asked, wondering why Jim was posting blame on him. "He's the one who was talking a bunch of crap to my girlfriend. I didn't do a goddamn thing to him."

"All I'm sayin' is try to keep the peace. Lots of negative vibes goin' on."

"Oh, you think?" Randy quipped. "Fuck him."

"Tone it down, man. Be mellow."

Mellow. What the hell did Jim know about being mellow? Trying to get Jim to shut up and leave him alone, Randy said, "Fine, but he better back the hell off and quit talking shit to my woman. If he starts in on me, he's gonna get a fistful, and I will knock him down a notch or two."

"Understandable. So, peace?"

"Yeah," Randy agreed.

"Sweet."

Chapter Eight

The pressure of medical school started to build. Over the course of the next few weeks, Randy had multiple exams, several patient write-ups due, was submerged in research for his thesis, and he seemed to have his nose buried in a medical textbook 24/7. Throughout the week, he and his study group met multiple times and pulled an all-nighter. Likewise, Randy hadn't gotten much sleep. Aside from group study, he also studied on his own to prepare for next week's midterms. He was stressed, he was tired, and he was running low on fuel, functioning off several cups of coffee.

It had been a long week, and Jane knew Randy was feeling stressed. To offer her support, she decided to meet him after class so they could walk home together. She found a chair in the lobby of the Medical Sciences building and waited for Randy to get out of class.

As she sat with a book in her hand, Steve came out of the restroom. When he spotted her, he snuck up behind her and said, "Hey, Sexy."

She tried to ignore him.

Yet he remained persistent. "You need a real man. I have the biggest cock in the Western Hemisphere. I could give you the best time of your life. You want a taste?"

Disgusted by his crudeness and uncomfortable with his close proximity to her, she sneered at him and moved to another chair.

Steve refused to leave her alone. Inappropriately and rudely, he continued to harass her. "We should hook up. Let's meet at my place tonight around ten. I'll show you the best time of your life."

Once again she moved away.

Randy came out of his seminar joking with some of his friends. When he spotted Steve bothering Jane, the smile instantly left his face.

Jim quickly intervened. "Hanson, come on. Be mellow, Dude."

Randy promised he would maintain peace and try to be civil, but when he saw Steve persistently pestering Jane, and her trying hard to avoid him, he confronted him anyway. Glowering at the prick, he demanded an explanation. "What's going on?"

Trying to act innocent, Steve replied, "We're having a little chat."

By the look on Jane's face, Randy could tell she was annoyed. "It doesn't look like she wants to talk to you."

Tension was rampant. Jane had to intervene quickly before things got out of hand. "Randy," she stood up between them. "It's ok."

But Randy didn't listen. He glared at Steve fiercely. "Stay away from her."

"She likes it." Steve winked at her, making obscene gestures with his tongue.

Randy's blood boiled. "I mean it, man. Back the hell off."

Steve shuddered in fear, mocking Randy as he walked away.

Jane immediately took Randy's hand and led him out of the building.

They walked for a while, hand in hand, with no words spoken. The silence drove Randy nuts. "What did he say to you?"

She shook her head. "Nothing. It's ok."

Randy stopped, insistent on knowing what happened before he arrived on the scene. "What did he say?"

"It's no big deal. I can handle it."

"Come on Jane, talk to me. Tell me what he said."

She breathed deeply, knowing Randy was going to lose it when she told him what Steve had done. "He tried to hit on me."

Randy definitely did not like this. "He what?"

"Randy, let it go." He was already stressed from school. He didn't need this aggravation added to it.

"No. I'm not going to let it go. I want to know what he said."

She didn't want to tell him, but knew he wouldn't back down until she did. "He made inappropriate sexual remarks and tried to coax me to go to bed with him."

"Who the fuck does that bastard think he is?" he bellowed. "He can sit on his worthless ass and get carried through med school by the rest of us, and he can talk all the shit to me he wants, but when that son-of-a-bitch makes advances at my girlfriend and speaks to her inappropriately, that is where I draw the line. I have put up with a lot of bullshit from that cock sucker, but this time he has gone too fucking far."

Jane had never heard so many obscenities come out of his mouth at once. "Randy, please calm down."

"He has no right to do that, Jane."

"Don't worry about him so much." She leaned forward and kissed him, trying to get him to think about something else. "Are we still on for tonight?"

"Yes, Ma'am," he said with a smile, putting the annoyances of his day behind him. "I figured I'd cook dinner for you, if that's ok."

"You can cook?"

"I dabble a little."

She was anxious to see this.

After they ate and washed the dishes together, Randy grabbed a movie and moved over to the couch. He reached for the back of his neck with one hand and rubbed away the tension. "My head feels like mush today. I can't think clearly."

"You okay?" she asked, concerned about his wellbeing.

"I think I'm just tired. Too many late nights of studying this week and the all-nighter we pulled last night gave me brain fry."

Jane positioned herself behind him and began to massage his neck and shoulders. "You work too hard."

"I have to, Baby."

"And you have how many more years of this?"

With a slight scoff, he replied, "Three, after this year. It's a five year Master of Science/M.D. program. The curriculum is designed so I work on my M.S. and my M.D. simultaneously. This is what makes Cal and UCSF's Joint Medical Program different from other med schools. I'll walk out of here with a Master's Degree and my M.D."

"What happens after that?"

He explained, "Residency."

"And what does that entail?"

"That's where I get specialized OB/GYN training. It's different from med school though because I actually receive a paycheck and benefits. I have to complete four years of residency before I can practice on my own."

She calculated the time frame involved. "So you have seven more years of this?"

"Yup." He realized he had barely made a dent in his medical education.

"That's crazy."

"Perhaps." He sat up and pulled her onto his lap with one leg on each side of him. He reached into his pocket and handed her a key. "I wanted to give this to you."

Puzzled, she held the key between her thumb and forefinger. "What is it?"

"It's a key to my apartment. I know you're always looking for a quiet place to get some studying done and this way you can come over here any time you want. Feel free to come and go as you please."

"You're giving me a key to your apartment?"

"Yeah, I trust you."

She slid the key in her pocket. "By the way, Daddy invited you over next weekend."

Her father? Why would her father invite him over? "Really? Why?"

"He wants to meet you. I thought we could go next Saturday when you get off work. Midterms will be over by then."

Oh great. The classic meet the parents routine. Randy wasn't necessarily looking forward to this part. "That's fine." Getting more comfortable, he kicked off his shoes and grabbed the remote control. He lounged back on the couch and gestured with his index finger for Jane to come lie next to him.

With a smile that illuminated the room, she joined him on the sofa.

Randy turned off the table lamp, darkening the room. He put his arm around her and started the movie.

Around 12:30 A.M., he briefly recalled hearing someone call his name. He opened his eyes to see Jane's face looking down at him.

"Hello, Sleepyhead," she said in a sweet voice.

With a big yawn, he stretched his arms. "Oh, man. When did I go out?"

"About halfway through the second movie."

He rubbed his weary eyes. "I'm sorry, Baby."

"It's ok. It's been a rough week. You obviously needed to sleep."

"But I wanted to spend time with you."

"We'll spend more time together tomorrow." She gently kissed him. "Right now, it's late. I'm going to go so you can get some rest."

"No." He abruptly sat up. "There is no way I'm letting you walk alone in the middle of the night. I'll take you home," he insisted.

She placed her hands in his and pulled him off the couch. He draped her jacket over her shoulders then grabbed his coat and keys so he could drive her home.

When Randy got off work the next day, Jane was at his apartment curled up in a chair reading, as she often spent her free time doing. When she heard him come in, she set her book down and looked him over. He was wearing scrubs and had a stethoscope draped around his neck.

"Nice outfit," she remarked.

"Sexy, huh?" From the sour expression on her face, Randy could tell something was bothering her. "What's wrong?"

"I saw Daddy today."

Apparently that was a bad thing. "And?"

"I confirmed Saturday. He said that would be fine."

He removed his stethoscope and set it on the dining table. "Why the sour face then?" He came into the living room sat on the couch to talk to her.

"Remember how I said I would take care of getting on the pill?"

Based on her tone, this didn't sound good. "Yeah."

"Well, I went to the doctor and got the prescription, but I wasn't thinking and I used Daddy's insurance card. He received the claim from the insurance company, showed it to me today, and asked why I went to the doctor and what I got a prescription for."

Randy didn't see why this was a problem, but to her, apparently it was. "Did you tell him?"

"Yes. That's when he got upset."

Randy wondered why using a medical card would bother her father. Isn't that why she had medical insurance in the first place? "He's upset because you went to the doctor?"

"No," she clarified. "He's upset because he now knows you and I are sleeping together."

This didn't make a whole lot of sense either. "Why would he care about that?"

"Because he's always assumed I was a virgin."

"You never told him otherwise?" Randy asked, wondering why Jane would try to hide that from her father.

"No." Just suggesting that she openly admit that to her father was ludicrous. "That's not something I can easily explain to Daddy."

Obviously Jane being sexually active was a huge issue for this man, which to Randy seemed odd considering she was twenty-one. Thinking this was ridiculous, he had to make sure he clearly understood what she was saying. "So let me get this straight. You used your dad's medical card to get on the pill. He finds out we're having sex and gets angry because he assumes I'm the reason his daughter isn't a virgin?"

"Basically, yes," she clarified.

"Did you correct this misunderstanding?"

"Oh my god, Randy. He's already freaking out."

"Am I to assume then that you not being a virgin is a bad thing in your father's eyes?"

She seemed a bit worried. "You don't understand my father. Sex is unmentionable, disgraceful, sinful. God forbid his daughter have anything to do with it."

Randy combed his bangs off his forehead with his fingers. "Oh, shit. I'm so screwed."

"This has nothing to do with you."

He begged to differ. "That is where you are wrong, my dear. This has everything to do with me."

"How? Daddy doesn't even know you."

"Think about it, Baby," he explained. "Your dad has it set in his mind that you've never been intimate with a man before. He recently found out that we share a bed and now thinks I'm the one who caused his daughter to lose her virginity. I'm supposed to go over there next weekend and meet this man face to face. If he is as taboo about sex as you say he is, then he is going to have some serious issues with me. That is not going to be a good situation."

This made sense, now that he pointed it out. "I didn't even think about that."

He laughed inwardly then shook his head in disbelief. "Well, next Saturday should be interesting, and probably slightly awkward. But we'll figure it out. Your dad just needs some clarification, that's all." Getting to the heart of the matter, he asked, "You are on the pill now, right?"

She smiled. "Yes."

"Good."

On the last study session before the start of midterms, Randy dreaded going. He knew Steve was once again going to be his perverted and raunchy self, and Randy really wasn't in the mood to deal with it. He was forced to put up with Steve during multiple study sessions this week, and his obnoxious mouth was grating on his nerves. Randy had done his best to keep his promise to Jim about maintaining the peace, even though Steve had taunted him several times. Randy wasn't sure how much longer he would be able to remain peaceful before he killed the son-of-a-bitch.

When Randy walked into the room, he heard the shrill tone of Steve's voice and tried not to cringe. Throughout the session, Randy didn't say much, other than answering questions when it was his turn. Mostly he sat, giving Steve an angry stare.

Halfway through the session, Steve became bored with studying and tried to change the subject. "Did you guys see that voluptuous redhead at lunch on Friday? I could so do her right now."

Randy found him crude and immature. "When are you going to grow up?" he asked. "Stop thinking with your dick so we can get something done."

Steve scoffed at Randy. "Look who's talking."

"What's that supposed to mean?"

"Oh, come on, Randy," he snarled. "You're fucking the hottest chick to ever walk the halls of Berkeley."

His attitude was aggravating. Randy wished he could tell him to go screw himself. "What's your point?"

"My point is there's not a man in this room who wouldn't love to have your dick right now. Any guy would die to get into her pants. She is a hot chick with a tight ass."

Being around Steve annoyed Randy to no end, but this blatant rudeness was multiplying it tenfold. "You better keep your gawking eyes and perverted hands away from her."

Jim saw the ire fuming in Randy's eyes and knew his friend was going to lose it if Steve didn't shut up. "Lay off, man," he warned.

Randy tried hard to avoid confrontation with Steve. But the more the man opened his mouth, the more Randy despised the bastard. His patience was quickly wearing thin. "If you have something to say to me, why don't you grow some balls and say it instead of taking pot shots at my girlfriend."

Provoking him further, Steve said, "Oh, I guess she failed to mention that I was with her last night. She has some perky little nipples. Mmm, mmm, mmm."

"Shut up." Randy's rage escalated. He wasn't going to take this much longer before he exploded on his ass.

Irritated that Steve was goading Randy like this, Jim intervened. "Come on, Steve. Knock it off."

With an obnoxious grin, Steve prodded on. "By the sounds she was making, I'd say she liked it." He thrust his pelvis several times, and, in a high-pitched voice, taunted, "Ooh, Stevie, do me harder."

Randy had heard enough. He burst out of his seat and lunged toward Steve with his hand clenched in a fist, ready to beat the shit out of him. He would have hit him too, if Bruce and Jim hadn't held him back. "You son-of- a-bitch!"

Steve held up his hands, prompting Randy to take a swing at him. "Come on. Do it."

Randy lunged at him again.

Bruce grabbed Randy by the shoulders and yanked him back. He didn't want his friend to risk getting written up or kicked out of med school over this asshole's taunting. "He's not worth it, man!" Bruce said, leading Randy away from the table. "He's not worth it."

Jim glared at Steve fiercely. "What the hell is your problem?"

Steve pointed Randy's direction. "That spoiled, rich brat with his high and mighty attitude thinks he's smarter that all of us. He struts around here like some candy-ass flaunting his sorority slut girlfriend. I bet she's put out for every guy on this campus."

"Fuck you!" Randy bellowed. This flagrant disrespect for Jane was more than he was willing to tolerate. He stepped forward, clenching his fist until his knuckles turned white. Bruce continued to hold him back, which was becoming increasingly more difficult because Randy was stronger than he was.

Steve provoked him even more. "I could have given her a better fuck than you ever will."

"Stay away from her, Asshole!"

Bruce glowered at Steve in disgust. "Enough of this. Get out," he ordered, getting in the last word.

Steve grabbed his books and tore out of the room.

Sarah and Mandy stared at Randy, aghast over the openly violent outburst they had witnessed. He was usually so together. They had no idea he was capable of such fury. "Well," Mandy snorted. "Thank you very much for that lovely display. I couldn't have gone all day without seeing that."

"Let go of me," Randy demanded of Bruce, who still had him restrained.

"Not until you calm down."

"I'm fine. Let go."

Bruce granted his wishes and released him.

Randy jerked his arms out of Bruce's grasp then took a deep breath, trying to lower his blood pressure. His hands trembled. He flexed and relaxed his fists a few times to relieve the built-up tension.

The girls sat in disbelief. "Good god, Randy. What the hell was that all about?"

"I'm sorry," he said, feeling like an ass for wigging out like that.

"You ok, man?" Bruce asked.

Addressing the entire group, Randy declared, "I won't work with that asshole. He is deliberately tormenting me, and I don't have to put up with this crap. He said he would lay off if I did. Well, I kept my end of the bargain, yet he still provokes me and talks shit about my girlfriend."

"Come on, Randy, calm down." Jim tried to get him to relax. "He's just bein' a douche. Ignore him."

"Fuck that," Randy fumed. "I will not sit here and listen to him say shit like that about her, Jim. I can't do that. Jane doesn't deserve that and neither do I."

"You know how he is," Jim pleaded. "Let it go."

Randy shook his head. "I've let it go for far too long. This isn't about him and me anymore. It's more personal than that now. He pushed it too far when he got Jane involved. I refuse to work with that son-of-a-bitch. It's him or me, Jim. If he's not out of this group then I am. I can't do this anymore." Randy picked up his belongings and left the room.

The group needed Randy. They couldn't just let him leave. Since Jim was Randy's best friend, Sarah, Mandy, and Bruce turned to him for answers.

"Goddamn, Jim," Bruce said. "I know you feel obligated to help Steve, but not at this expense. We can't lose Randy and you know that."

Mandy chimed in, "With the two of them constantly at each other's throats, we aren't accomplishing anything. Steve does mess with him pretty harshly."

"He does," Sarah agreed. "What a jerk."

"This has gotten way out of hand," Bruce added. "Randy's a good guy. He's always trying to help all of us and he's a hard worker. He contributes so much to this group. But Steve? Steve is not only a slacker, he's an ass, and he shouldn't be saying those things about Randy's girlfriend. I gotta say, I agree with Randy on this one."

"I do too," Mandy said.

"Do something. Talk to him," Sarah begged. "Please, Jim."

Jim took a deep breath, taking in every argument they had. "Alright, I'll talk to him."

He went outside to find Randy sitting on the ground against the building. His knees were bent and his head was buried in his hands. Jim tread cautiously. "You ok?"

Feeling tense, Randy looked up. "Am I ok? That is the dumbest question you have ever asked me. No, I'm not ok." Antagonism was in his voice, and he still had an angry scowl on his face. "What did I ever do to that asshole?"

Jim tried to lighten the mood. "You have a mommy and daddy who love you and a pretty girlfriend. How dare you?"

Randy didn't find Jim's retort amusing. "Is that supposed to be funny?"

"Sorry. I'm just tryin' to get you to relax."

"I am relaxed," Randy argued.

"Like hell you are. If this is relaxed, remind me not to be around when you're uptight."

This comment made Randy smile.

Jim sat on the stairs across from him. "Don't worry about Steve. He's a fuck up."

"Fuck up? That is the biggest understatement of the year."

"Don't let him get to you. That's why he does it."

"I will not listen to him offensively talk smack about the woman I love." Randy stood up and grabbed his bag. "I'm sorry, Jim, but I can't do that. It's him or me."

"Randy, come on," Jim begged. "Don't be like that."

Randy looked him straight in the eye. "I refuse to endure this crap. It's him or me. Make a choice."

Jim watched his best friend walk away. He had always been able to reason with Randy, but this time the man wasn't budging, not one inch. Jim couldn't say that he blamed him. Steve had pushed it way too far.

As soon as Randy was out of sight, Jim went back inside to give the group Randy's ultimatum. He already knew what the outcome was going to be.

Randy was extremely uptight and irritated. Feeling overly stressed, he dropped his book bag off at his apartment and changed into shorts and a tee-shirt. He grabbed his basketball and headed up to Alpha to see Jane.

When she greeted him at the door, he wasn't very cheerful or talkative. All he said was, "Shoot hoops with me."

Concerned about his disposition, she slipped on her shoes and walked with him to the recreation center.

Randy didn't say a word, and Jane grew increasingly worried about him. Even after they played for a while, he still wasn't talking. This was very odd. Usually he was excited to tell her about his day. "Randy, are you ok?"

"Not really." His head was about to explode. He withdrew to the side of the court, where he sat on the floor and leaned against the wall.

Jane strode his direction and sat on the floor next to him. "What's wrong?"

He hands began to shake, finally realizing the seriousness of what happened. "I almost beat the crap out of Steve today. Thankfully, Jim and Bruce were there to hold me back or I would have hit him. I could have gotten myself into serious trouble. Might have been written up, red flagged, or even expelled from med school."

She tried to understand. "Things are that bad?"

"I completely lost my cool in front of my friends today, and I think I scared the girls half to death. I about ripped Bruce's arm off, then I placed an ultimatum on my best friend." Randy shook his head, feeling like a jerk. "I can't believe I did that to Jim."

She reached her hands up and massaged his shoulders. "You are way too tense, Mister. You need a break."

"I need Steve to stay the hell out of my face is what I need."

"You know what we should do?"

"What?"

Knowing how much he loved the water, she suggested, "Let's go for a walk by the pier. It will get you away from school for a while and help you relax." She held her hands out to help him get up. "Come on."

Being around water always helped Randy put the troubles of world behind him, and the pier was the perfect place to do that. "I'm sorry I've been crabby and uptight lately."

"It's ok."

"It's not ok," he argued. "I don't mean to take my stress out on you."

"Randy, I understand," Jane assured him. "You've had your nose constantly buried in a medical book and medical charts for the last two weeks."

He took her in his arms. "I told you this could get complicated. Thank you for being so supportive."

She gently kissed him on the lips. "And I told you we were in this together. Did you think I was kidding?"

With a grin, he admitted, "Actually, I kinda did."

"Well, I wasn't."

They drove back to campus, and Randy walked her up to the porch. Something was still bothering him. He wanted to discuss it with her, but wasn't sure how to bring it up. Rather than keeping it inside and letting it fester, he decided to speak his mind. "When are you going to tell your dad the truth?"

"About what?"

"About me. Remember, he has the misconception that I'm the reason you aren't a virgin anymore."

She had forgotten about this and hoped Randy would forget about it too. "But it's not true, so why does it matter?"

"Because your dad thinks it is the truth." The fact that Jane's father thought this about him tormented him more than he originally thought. He couldn't seem to get it off of his mind. "He's forming opinions about me based on false information. And I'm pretty sure the things he's thinking aren't positive. That's not right and it's not fair, Jane."

"Randy, I can't tell him I've had sex before you. He'll freak."

"I can't go over there next weekend and talk to this man when, in his mind, he sees me as something I'm not and is accusing me of something I didn't do."

"I can't control what Daddy thinks," she tried to justify.

"No you can't," he said. "But you can change his attitude by alleviating this misconception he has about me." Randy stood up, somewhat frustrated with her lack of seeing this from his viewpoint. "The way I see this, Janey, you have two choices. One, you tell your dad the truth. He might get upset and reproach you, but I'll have a clean slate. Or two, you do nothing and let your dad continue to form false opinions about me. This leaves you with a clean slate, but puts me in an uncomfortable situation. So you have a decision to make."

"Don't do this to me."

"I'm not the one who did this, you are. And you are the one who has to fix it. It's going to come down to what your priorities are."

She knew she had to set things right, but did not want to confront her father to do it.

Randy didn't like putting her in this position, but felt he had no choice. Deep down he didn't think Jane would tell her dad the truth and risk violating his trust. Now that he considered this, if she didn't tell her father, then she obviously didn't care enough about him to merit clearing his name of false information. He realized that the decision she made could potentially affect their relationship, and this made him uneasy. He wished he hadn't laid this burden on her. "I'm sorry, Baby. But you need to see this from my point of view."

And she did see it from his point of view. She just hated that it came down to her having to reveal hidden truths about herself to her father. She had kept things from him for years to leave him with the sense that she could do no wrong. His reaction would be unpleasant, and she really didn't want to go there with him. Since her mother died, her father had the mistaken idea that his daughter was an innocent bystander in the world, incapable of lust, sin, or any kind of wrongdoings. How was she going to break it to her dad that she wasn't the blameless child he had always pictured her to be? Admitting that to him was going to be the hardest news to break.

"I'll call you tonight, ok?" Randy said.

She nodded.

"I love you." He hugged her and gave her a kiss goodbye before he headed home to try to get some rest. Damn he was tired.

Randy managed to get in a few hours of sleep, but as he reflected back on his weekend, he realized how crappy it was. Bad situations seemed to creep up on him without warning all weekend long.

"Hey, buddy," Jim said as he sat down in a seat next to Randy, both prepared to undertake a week of assessment. "How you doin'?"

"I'm okay." Randy's tone was far from enthusiastic. "Had kind of a shitty weekend."

"Why?"

"Besides the crap with Steve, Jane and I planned to hang out Friday night. But after studying all night Thursday, as soon as we got some alone time, I was so tired that I fell asleep."

"That sucks."

"Yup, so much for that plan. Then Saturday," Randy explained, "Jane tells me that when she went to get a prescription for the pill, she used her dad's insurance card. Through this incident, he found out Jane and I are sharing a bed."

"So?" Jim shrugged, not seeing the significance of that.

"Under any other circumstances it wouldn't be a big deal. But in her father's eyes, this is a crime, mainly because he has the idea that I'm the one who stole his daughter's virginity. Jane was too scared to tell him otherwise, so her father now thinks this about me. To make matters worse,

I'm supposed to go over there next weekend and meet this man."

Jim could see why this was a problem. "Ouch!"

"I asked Jane about this yesterday and told her she needed to tell her dad the truth, but I'm not sure she will. She's afraid to upset her father, which scares me a little. If she isn't willing to tell him the truth and lets me take the rap for this, then I would have to seriously question how she really feels about me."

"What are you gonna do if she doesn't tell him?"

"I don't know," he admitted, trying not to think about that scenario. "Hopefully it won't come down to that. I hope she'll be the woman I think she is and make this right."

Jim didn't know how to respond to Randy's dilemma. "Damn, Dude."

"My weekend pretty much sucked. How was yours?"

"Well," Jim began, "the others and I were talking."

"And?" Randy waited he hear the verdict.

"You're my best friend, Randy. You don't deserve and the rest of us don't need the aggravation Steve causes. He's out, and we are set to meet at my place next Sunday, if that's ok."

This made Randy feel much better. "Good. Maybe we can make some progress and have a peaceful study session for a change."

"That's the plan."

The professor began his explanation, so Randy and Jim quit their conversation to listen.

Following a morning of exams, Randy was about to meet the others for lunch when he saw Jane standing outside the Medical Sciences building. "I'm going to talk to Jane for a minute. I'll meet you over there," he said to Jim.

"I'll save you a seat."

Randy exited the building and stepped outside to meet Jane. "Hey, Baby. What's up?"

"Do you have a minute?" she asked with a bit of earnestness. "I need to talk to you."

"Sure." He took her hand and led her to an empty bench under a tree.

When they sat down, she turned and faced him. "I saw Daddy this morning. I told him."

This surprised him. "You did?"

"Yes."

Her shattered expression was unnerving. "What did he say?"

"He's so angry, Randy. You should have seen the look on his face. He lectured me for twenty minutes about 'those kind of girls' then called me a cheap hussy."

That was a mean thing to say. Randy didn't understand why her own father would disdain her like that. "What?"

"I've never seen Daddy so mad. He thinks I'm a slut."

Randy felt awful. He didn't realize that asking Jane to do this would cause her so much pain. Feeling like a complete jerk, he held her in comfort. "I'm sorry, Honey. I shouldn't have put that burden on you."

"I couldn't let Daddy go on thinking that you were responsible for something you didn't do. I had to tell him the truth."

He softly kissed the top of her head. "It took a lot of courage for you to do what you did. And it means a lot to me. It tells me that you are willing to make sacrifices and take risks for us. I love you so much for that."

"I did it because I love you."

"I know. And knowing that means more to me than you realize." He gently wiped her tears away and kissed her on the lips. "You want to join us for lunch?"

With a bob of her head, her mouth curved into a smile.

"Good." He clasped her hand and walked with her to meet his friends for lunch.

Chapter Nine

A new weekend rolled around, much to Randy's relief. He was beginning to think the week was never going to end. With summative assessments, essays, practicals, and OSCE's behind him, he could finally relax.

Following the Friday night football game, he and Jane returned to his apartment. When Jane dug through her wallet to put her student I.D. away, Randy saw a photograph that caught his eye. It was a picture of a man and a woman—a beautiful woman with a tantalizing smile and beautiful green eyes, similar to Jane's. "Who's that?" he asked, eyeing the photograph carefully.

"My parents."

He reached into her wallet and pulled the picture out. "This is your mom?"

"Uh huh."

"She was beautiful."

Jane's cheerful glow suddenly disappeared. She took the picture from him and sat on the couch staring at it.

Randy sat next to her, curving his arm around her shoulder. "You ok?"

"Just thinking."

He listened attentively to everything she had to say.

"When Mom got sick, it was hard on all of us. But Daddy," she sniffled. "Daddy couldn't handle it. Seeing the pain in his eyes every time he looked at her. That was the first time I ever saw my dad cry. Losing Mom was bad enough, but seeing that look, that horrible, heartbreaking look on his face." She started to cry.

Randy cradled her head onto his shoulder, kissing her forehead as he did.

"I miss her," she said sadly.

"I can imagine. That must be really hard."

"Little things remind me sometimes. Images pop into my head."

Jane's hair had a sweet scent, and the soft, smooth skin on the nape of her neck was calling his name. He had to kiss it. Slowly, he worked his way up to her chin and finally to her succulent lips. They tasted fruity. "Mmm, what is that?"

"Watermelon lip gloss. You like it?" She smiled seductively.

"I love it."

"It comes in strawberry, bubblegum, cherry, and coconut flavor too."

Randy turned his nose up. "Don't get coconut. I don't like coconut."

She giggled and bit her lower lip. "Ok."

He wanted more of those sweet watermelon kisses. So he interlocked his mouth with hers, trying to get every last taste. All of this kissing was getting him excited. Still embraced, they stumbled toward the bedroom. Trying not to trip, he lifted her off the ground and carried her instead.

Once inside the room, Randy set her on the bed. She lay back onto the pillow and he crawled over top of her. Clothing began to come off one piece at time. He caressed her entire body from her hair down all the way down to her naked buttocks and hips. Feeling each other's breath and elevated heartbeat, their bodies intertwined, forming a silhouette of longing and intimacy.

Randy completely submerged himself into her, loving her, pleasuring her, getting pleasure from her. He drifted into a world where only the two of them existed. And for a moment, nothing else mattered.

He held her for a while afterwards, stroking his fingers through her hair. Jane snuggled in closer, and Randy gently grazed his lips across her forehead.

"Randy?" she asked in a sweet voice. "What are you thinking about?"

"Fishing, believe it or not."

"We make love and you think about smelly old fish?"

Her reaction made him laugh. "No, not fish, Baby. Fishing. Every weekend, my dad and I used to get up early, load the boat, and spend the day on the lake, talking and fishing for hours. I really miss that. When I was a kid, I used to swim off the dock and hunt for crawdads. Stephanie was so afraid of those things. I'd chase her around the yard with them, making her cry and scream. I used to get in so much trouble for teasing her like that."

"That's mean. You're a mean big brother."

"It was funny," he said. "And I'm not a mean big brother. I love my sister dearly. But back when we were kids, she was such an easy target. Everything made her scream—bugs, fish heads, worms, dead birds…you know all those cool things little boys like."

"My brother was ornery too. He used to take my bears out in the backyard and play football with them."

This sounded like something Randy would have done. "Know what my brother did once? I was probably sixteen, Robby had to have been eight or nine. I came in about two hours past my curfew, trying to be quiet so my parents wouldn't catch me. But Robby saw me and started screaming out my name. I did my best to shush him, but he kept yelling. Dad heard him screaming and came out to see what wrong. That's when he saw me sneaking in late. I was grounded for two weeks over that."

"You were a rebellious one."

"Not really," Randy said in his defense. "Just trying to find my place in the world. About midway through my sophomore year of high school, my dad and I were on our way home from a basketball game when a woman in the back of a cab was screaming in pain on the side of the road.

Dad noticed all the commotion and pulled over to see if he could help. Good thing we got there when we did because she was in labor and ready to push. Dad called me over to help. That was the first time I saw my dad in action, and the first time I witnessed a baby being born. It was the coolest thing that ever happened to me, and such an adrenaline rush. That night changed my life. I always knew I wanted to be a doctor but never really knew what specialty I wanted to get into until then." He lifted her mouth to his and kissed her. "You want to stay here tonight?"

She snuggled in closer and rested her hand on his chest. Randy took that as a yes. Getting more comfortable, he shifted his position slightly then clicked off the lamp.

The blinding light from the morning sun beamed through the window, waking Jane. She rolled over, still half asleep, and saw Randy on the bedroom floor pumping out sit-ups. His well-developed muscles were covered with sweat. Supporting herself with her elbow, she sat up and watched him.

"Good morning, Baby," he puffed, lifting his trunk to his knees again.

"You're up early," she declared.

He jumped off the floor and swung his arms around to loosen up. "Gotta work this morning."

"You remembered about going to Daddy's today, right?" she reminded him.

"Yup." Jane's naked body was wrapped up in a sheet. The smooth skin of her breast peeked out from under the covers. Randy cupped his hand around the soft curve of her skin while he leaned over the bed to kiss her.

He was full of an excessive amount of energy this morning. Jane wondered what pill he took that make him so spunky. "Are you always this cheerful in the morning?"

"When I wake up next to you I am." He took a few sips of water then pulled a fresh towel from the laundry basket. "I'm gonna hop in the shower. There's coffee brewing in the kitchen if you want some."

"I don't drink coffee."

"More for me then." Randy winked at her and headed into the bathroom.

Jane leaned back on the pillow and stretched. One of Randy's dark green tee-shirts was folded neatly on the bedside table. She reached over to grab it. *UCB-UCSF Joint Medical Program* was written on the front in white letters. She slipped the shirt over her head, stepped out of bed in search of her underwear, then walked into the kitchen to get a drink. With a book and a glass of milk in her hand, she curled up in a chair to read.

While Randy was in the bedroom dressing for work, his cellphone rang. "Can you get that, Babe?" he called out to Jane from the other room.

She set her book on the table and got up to answer his phone. "Hello?"

A male voice on the other end said, "I think I have the wrong number. I'm looking for my son."

Jane assumed it was his father. "Is this Dr. Hanson?"

"Yes."

"This is the right number. Hold on. I'll get him." She went into the bedroom and handed the phone to Randy, who was only half-dressed in slacks and socks. "It's your dad."

"Cool." He put the phone up to his ear and talked while he finished getting ready for work. "Hey, Dad."

"Good morning. Who answered the phone?" his father asked, unfamiliar with the female voice he heard.

"That was Jane. I told you about her."

"Oh, yes," his father said. "That girlfriend you keep talking about. What is she doing over there this early on a Saturday morning?"

Randy thought it was obvious. "Dad."

Teasing his son, Randy's father replied, "I see. You're using protection I hope."

"Of course we are," Randy reassured.

Dr. Hanson changed the subject. "How did exams go?"

"I think I did well. I should find out next week."

"And your grades?" his father probed.

"Grades are good. I started a new patient profile in clinicals class last week."

"You getting your thesis done?"

"Yes, Sir. Planning to do more research on it this weekend." It was unusual for Randy's dad to hound him about school. Randy wondered what the deal was. "Why are you asking me so many questions?"

"I know how you are with women, Randy. Are you able to study and stay focused with a girlfriend distracting you?"

Randy retorted, "She doesn't distract me. In fact, she is very supportive."

"Supportive, huh?"

"Yes," Randy affirmed.

"You need to remember why you're there," his father reminded him.

"I know why I'm here. Can you trust me on this please? School comes first, and Jane knows that."

"I hope so."

"Hey, can I call you later?" Randy asked politely. "I need to get ready for work."

"We won't be home 'til late tonight."

"I'll call you then," Randy promised.

"Be careful, Son. Don't do anything you'll regret later, and don't let her get pregnant," Dr. Hanson boldly warned.

"I won't, Dad. Don't worry."

"Have a good day, Son."

"You too, Sir." He set his phone on the dresser and went back to getting dressed. "That was interesting."

"What was?"

"My dad was grilling me about school."

"Does he usually do that?"

"No. He only did it because of you."

She didn't get it. Why would Randy's father give him the third degree because of her? "Me? Why me?"

Randy pulled a polo shirt off the hanger and slipped it over his head, tucking while he talked to her. "He's worried that I won't focus on school with you around."

"In other words, he thinks I'm keeping you from studying."

"Pretty much."

Randy didn't seem to think this was a big deal, yet Jane found it bothersome. "So what does that mean?"

"It doesn't mean anything. My father is not judgmental. He doesn't know you and hasn't met you, so he has no basis to form an opinion. He's a little concerned that I'll let you distract me, but I told him that's not how it is. Don't read anything into it." He grabbed his keys, his phone, and his stethoscope then gave her a kiss. "I have to go, but I'll see you when I get home."

"Alright."

"Have a good day, Babe." He patted her on the butt as he walked out the door.

Randy got off work early, which was ideal because he needed time to change and prepare himself to meet Jane's dad. Wanting to make a good impression, he stared at the clothes hanging in his closet debating over what to wear. After much pondering, he decided to go casual. He put on a nice pair of jeans, a grey button up shirt with the sleeves rolled up, and a pair of black loafers. He slipped his black leather jacket over top then hopped in the car to pick up Jane.

The outfit she was wearing looked nothing like her usual skin-revealing, tight-fitting, carefully accented attire. She had on a long denim skirt and a short sleeved solid white blouse, which she had buttoned all the way up to her neck. Her open-toed navy blue and white sandals exposed her toes, but she wasn't wearing nail polish like she usually did. In fact, she didn't have on any jewelry, makeup, or even lip gloss. Randy wondered why she was dressed so conservatively.

"Hi, Sweetie. How was work?" Jane asked.

"It was a little slow today. You ready?"

"Uh huh."

"Good." Meeting a girl's parents was not something Randy was particularly comfortable with. There was only one other time he had met the parents of a girl he was involved with and that was back in high school. Needless to say, this made him nervous.

When they got to the door of the Davine house, Randy took a deep breath to release some tension.

"You look great," Jane assured him.

"I don't want to screw this up." He feared that the anxiety he felt would turn him into an inarticulate buffoon, forcing him to say something stupid.

Jane gave him a kiss of reassurance. "Don't worry. Just be yourself."

"I'll try."

Jane knocked on the door, and Randy was immediately overwhelmed by a massive young man in a football jersey. He was about six foot three, probably weighed around two-hundred fifty pounds, and had muscles of steel—a giant compared to him.

"Hey! It's good to see you, Sis."

This mammoth boy gave Jane a hug. Randy was worried he was going to crush her to death.

"This is my brother Brian," she introduced them.

This young man might have been Jane's little brother, but he was anything but little; this kid was enormous. "Pleasure to meet you, Brian."

Brian shook Randy's hand, almost breaking it. "Come on in. Dad's waiting for you out back."

Randy rubbed his hand as Jane led him inside.

"Have a seat," Brian said. "I'll let him know you're here."

As soon as they sat down, Randy began tapping his fingers on the arm of the couch.

"Stop fidgeting," Jane told him.

"I can't help it. I'm nervous."

"You'll be fine. Just talk to him."

"Talk about what? What if we have nothing in common?"

At that moment, Jane's father walked into the room.

Randy stood up respectfully and offered a friendly handshake. "Mr. Davine, Sir."

Dale Davine stared at Randy's hand before he accepted the gesture. "You must be Randy."

"Yes, Sir." Randy returned to his seat.

Mr. Davine sat in a chair across from them, staring Randy down. "Jane tells me you're a medical student."

"Yes, Sir. That's correct."

"Any branch in particular you're planning on specializing in?"

"Obstetrics and Gynecology, actually."

"So you enjoy giving breast exams and examining the genitalia of women?"

That's not how Randy saw Obstetrics and Gynecology. This man was harsh and obviously trying to trip him up. In an attempt to clarify his beliefs, Randy defended, "That's not exactly what it entails, Sir."

"What made you chose that as a profession?"

The gruffness of this man intimidated him, but he held a strong composure. "My respect for women. Without them, none of us would be here. I want to keep women healthy so they can bring healthy babies into the world," Randy explained. "My father is an obstetrician. I'm planning on joining his practice when I graduate."

"You're a doctor's son?"

"Yes, Sir."

Mr. Davine stared at Randy with a snarl on his face, yet said nothing.

The silence made Randy increasingly more edgy. Seeking reassurance, he reached for Jane's hand, but her father gave him a vicious scowl. Being on the receiving end of this harsh glare made Randy draw his hand back, not touching her at all.

Brian joined the conversation to try to lighten the mood. "I heard Cal is really picky about who they let into their medical program. Is that true?"

"They only accept twenty-five medical students each year," Randy replied. "Hundreds apply, but only a small fraction get in."

"Yet you got accepted," Mr. Davine questioned.

"Yes, Sir."

"I see. And what are the grade requirements to stay in medical school?"

"Passing grade in every class is an eighty-five."

Mr. Davine expressed a bit of dismay over Randy's response. "An eighty-five seems unacceptable for someone who is supposed to save lives. To me, that's a low expectation. I would hope medical schools would demand more from our future physicians."

Randy's stomach felt queasy. His original observation about this man being harsh was a serious understatement. This guy was flat out scornful. He tried to say all the right things and respond respectfully, but the condescending tone this man used made remaining respectful difficult. Normally Randy was quite articulate. Being put on the spot like this made him tongue-tied. He felt like a faltering buffoon.

"What kind of grades do you have?"

That was really the question he wanted answered, wasn't it? "Currently, Sir, I'm carrying all A's."

Jane's father actually seemed impressed with that. "You mentioned you were going to join your father's practice. Where exactly is that? Is it here in San Francisco?"

"No, Sir. My family lives in Seattle."

Dale Davine sneered, not liking the prospect of his daughter being whisked away to another state.

Sensing the tension this conversation caused, Jane chimed in, trying to find commonality. "Randy is a Lakers fan like Uncle Ron."

"Is that so?" Dale replied, piquing his curiosity.

"Yes, Sir," Randy replied. "Big basketball fan."

Brian joined the conversation, now that the talk of sports was involved. "Basketball, bah. Football is my game."

Randy turned his attention to Brian, hoping it would ease the knot in his stomach. "Who's your favorite team?"

"San Francisco 49ers. Yours?"

"Seahawks."

Dale glared at Randy torturously, piercing daggers through his skull.

Randy had never felt so insignificant in his life. This man, the father of the woman he loved, stared him down painfully, dissatisfied with every word that came out of his mouth. Randy feared the impression he was making was not the one he intended. He was uncomfortable with the entire situation and didn't like the way the conversation was going.

While Jane's father stoked up the grill, Jane took Randy on a tour of the house.

In desperate need of an explanation, Randy said, "It's as cold as ice out there. I thought you told him."

"I did," she interrupted.

"Do you see the way he looks at me? What did I say to earn that eye-piercing glare?"

"Nothing, you're doing fine."

How the hell did she figure that? "Fine? Were you and I in the same room?"

"He does this to everyone, Randy. You are doing great." She wrapped her arms around his neck and tried to kiss him.

Randy resisted and pulled away. "Oh god, Jane, don't do that in your father's house."

"Why not?"

"Because he might kill me."

"No, he won't. Randy, stop it."

But Randy wasn't joking. He actually thought the man might kill him if he dared to kiss or even touch Jane. "That man hates me."

"No he doesn't."

She couldn't be serious. Was she talking about the same man? "Yes he does."

"Daddy's a little gruff around the edges. He comes across kind of brusque."

Brusque. Interesting choice of words there. Not the term he would have chosen. "He scares me. I keep expecting him to go out back and grab a shot gun yelling, stay away from my daughter."

Jane burst out laughing. "That is silly. Daddy doesn't even own a shotgun."

"He makes me nervous."

"You're doing fine. Just be yourself."

"I'm trying, but he's making it difficult." Randy scanned the room they were in. A bunch of trophies sat on shelves and framed newspaper clippings hung on the walls. He walked closer to get a better look at them. Most had Brian's name on them for football, but a lot of them were pictures and articles about Jane. One of the trophies had her name on it for Most Valuable Player. "You didn't tell me about any of this."

"They're just pictures."

"Just pictures? Damn, girl. You were a regular basketball megastar."

"That was a long time ago. I don't play anymore."

Randy began to wonder if there was more to her basketball story than what she had originally told him. Why would someone so good and so dedicated to the game suddenly quit playing and never look back? This seemed suspicious to him. But he decided that now was not the time or the place to bring it up. He would save that conversation for later.

Trying to shatter the ice that had built between them, Randy stepped into the backyard to see if he could offer Jane's dad some assistance. They ended up talking about fishing and sports cars, both of which Randy dearly loved. He had owned a sports car from the time he was old enough to drive and knew everything about them. It turned out this was something Jane's dad had an interest in as well, which eventually led to Mr. Davine wanting to take a look at Randy's car.

When Dale saw the shiny red Camaro sitting in his driveway, he inquired further. "What kind of specs does this things have?"

"Six speed, sports tuned suspension, 580 horsepower, V8 supercharged engine. Great muscle car."

"Does it get decent gas mileage?"

"Between nineteen and twenty-eight," Randy replied.

"Not bad."

As this conversation developed, Randy realized that he and Mr. Dale Davine had many common interests. They both liked sports cars, were both avid basketball fans, and both enjoyed fishing. Both men also loved and cared about Jane. The main difference was Dale Davine was extremely overprotective of her, to an almost irrational degree.

When the evening came to a close, Mr. Davine invited Randy back to watch a game. The air was chilly, so Randy left the top up as they drove home.

Jane unbuttoned the three top buttons of her shirt, exposing some skin. "Do you still think Daddy doesn't like you?"

"I don't know," he shrugged indifferently. "That look he kept giving me was merciless. I'm pretty sure he wouldn't have glared at me like that if he thought I was a decent guy."

"He does think you're a decent guy. You made an impression on him tonight. Daddy doesn't hand out return invitations to everyone." She grabbed a tube of lip gloss, flipped the visor down, and peered into the mirror to gloss her lips. When she was done, she pulled two rings out of her purse and slipped them on her hand.

Randy contemplated this situation. Her father's authoritarianism, Jane's conservativeness around him, and the fact that she was once exceptionally good at basketball and suddenly dropped it made him think there was more going on here than what she had led him to believe. He was convinced all of these were connected somehow. Hoping to gain more information, he asked, "How come you never told me about all of those trophies you had? Those are big accomplishments, Babe. You should be proud of those."

"It's just a game."

Just a game? How could she say that? She had more love for basketball than anyone he had ever met. He didn't understand why she was so nonchalant about the achievements she had made. "I see that spark in your eye every time you and I are on the court. I've never seen you play competitively, but I think all of those news clippings and trophies speak for themselves. Someone must have thought they were pretty important to keep them framed and displayed like that. You were a good player. I'm sure with your talent you must have played for a college team. Did you ever play for Cal?"

Knowing he wasn't going to drop this until she told him, Jane answered, "I earned a basketball scholarship as an incoming freshman and played for Cal for two years. I told you I don't play anymore, and I told you why."

"I know you did. But a PAC-12 NCAA team? Not everyone has the opportunity to do that. I can't believe you gave that up."

"It's not important to me anymore," she said brashly.

"How can you say it's not important? I saw your stats on that wall. You averaged eighteen points and five assists per game. That's good."

"It's ok."

"It's good and you know it," he corrected. "Would you ever consider playing again?"

"No."

He tried to convince her, "But you still have eligibility."

"So?" She quickly became frustrated with his insistence. "Why do you care so much?"

"Because I hate to see you throw that opportunity away. I wish you'd reconsider."

"I really do not wish to discuss this with you. Can you drop it please?"

She was getting upset with him, so he dropped the subject. Yet in the back of his mind, he wondered how much of that decision had to do with her dominating father.

Jane removed the clip from her hair and let it fall. Changing to a more positive subject, she said, "My sorority is planning a Halloween party."

"Why does that not surprise me?"

"I'd like you to come."

Randy didn't like that plan. "A sorority party, Jane? Do you have any idea how long it's been since I've been to one of those?"

"Oh, come on. It will be fun."

He looked at her skeptically. "I don't know."

"Please?" she begged.

"And what am I supposed to do there?"

"Hang out with me, mingle, meet people—it's called socializing. You can relax and have fun for a change."

"Is it on a weekend?" he asked.

"Yes, and I really want you to be there."

He didn't want to socialize with a bunch of frat boys and sorority girls, but for her he would suffer through it. "Alright."

She clapped quietly then carried on with the conversation. "You have to wear a costume."

"Seriously?" he said, not liking that idea.

"It's a costume party. And you need to invite your friends."

"Why would any of my friends want to go to a sorority party?"

"Because you medical students never take time to relax. This will be fun, and it will help them unwind."

He found her cute and convincing. "I'll tell them, but I make no promises."

Satisfied, she said, "Good enough."

Chapter Ten

As planned, Randy's study group met at Jim's house Sunday morning. Since Randy spent a great deal of time over there, he knew where everything was. Making himself at home, he sauntered into the kitchen and helped himself to a cup of coffee.

"Hey, where were you all day yesterday?" Jim asked. "I tried to call and kept gettin' voicemail."

"I had to work in the morning and was over at Jane's dad's house last night."

"Oh that's right. How did that go?"

Randy let out a discerning sigh. "You mean after he interrogated me for an hour?"

"Goddamn, Dude. You serious?"

"Yup." He stirred sugar into his cup and took a sip. "After spending an hour or so fearing for my life, he and I actually had a nice conversation."

"That's good."

"He tries to control Jane though," Randy stated, "Which bothers me."

"Controls her how?"

"He's overbearing—tells her what to do and tries to speak for her. Throughout the night, she expressed her opinion several times, and he completely blew her off. He's dominating, and I get the feeling he tries to hold a pretty short leash on her. I honestly think he forgot how old she is. He offered me a beer but wouldn't let her drink one. Every time I tried to touch her, he glared at me like I was some kind of leech."

Jim gave his analysis. "Sounds like an ass to me."

"Jane was acting really weird yesterday. You've seen the way she dresses."

"Oh, yes," Jim replied flirtingly. "She can be pretty risqué sometimes."

"Well, yesterday she had her shirt buttoned all the way up and her skirt was longer than usual. She had no skin exposed at all, no makeup, no jewelry. But the minute we left and drove back to Berkeley, she unbuttoned her shirt, took her hair down, and put on lip gloss."

"That's strange. I wonder why she did that?"

Randy wondered the same thing. "I don't know, but that's not like her."

"Did you ask her about it?"

"No. It seemed like a touchy subject at the time and I didn't want to push it." Randy took another sip of his coffee. "Jane's father doesn't know anything about her. She and I talked about things we like to do together and he responded with, 'Jane doesn't like that' or 'Jane would never do that.' He had no idea her favorite color was blue, didn't realize she liked cats, and was clueless about her love of dark chocolate. He also didn't know that she loves to read romance novels. I know all those things about her. How could her own father not know that?"

Jim agreed with Randy's assessment. "That's odd."

"That's exactly what I thought. He's completely oblivious to the person she is. And despite the fact that he negated everything she said and tried to order her around, she stood there and let him. She didn't even try to speak up for herself. I don't understand why she didn't say something to him. If I do things she doesn't like, she has no qualms at all about telling me."

"Is she afraid to stand up to him?"

"I don't know, but the entire situation was pretty uncomfortable."

"Sounds like it," Jim concurred.

As Randy got his notes and study materials out, the others began to show up. Since they didn't have to deal with Steve, their session was quite productive, and all of them really felt stress free for a change. They laughed together and had fun while they were studying, which was something they hadn't been able to do in a long time. Seeing how happy everyone was, Randy sat back in his chair and smiled in satisfaction.

After reviewing notes and discussing required readings and clinical work from the week, the five of them decided to play a game. They took turns going around the table quizzing each other. Their goal was to circulate four times with no one making a mistake. If someone did, they had to start all over again.

They went around three times already and were on the last person for round four. It was Sarah's turn. Randy did his best to encourage her. "Ok, if you get this one, we are twenty for twenty, Sarah. You ready?"

She took a deep breath, knowing she had been struggling with this class. "Yes."

Randy skimmed through his notes and asked a question he knew she would know the answer to. "This type of cancer is known to be a malignant neoplasm of the internal and external lining of the body that accounts for eighty to ninety percent of all cases. It's divided into two major subtypes: adeno and squamous cell. It spreads easily through soft tissue and affects organs or glands capable of secretion, such as the breasts, lungs, colon, prostate, or bladder. What is it?"

Sarah put her hand on her forehead.

Randy could see the gears turning in her head. "Come on, Sarah, I know you know this," he encouraged.

Everyone crossed their fingers, hoping she knew the answer.

Unsure of herself, she said, "Carcinoma of the epithelial tissues?"

Randy grinned. "You got it."

Everyone cheered. This was the first time that they had made it all the way around the table not only once, but four times. They celebrated with a group hug.

"Ugh, I hate this," Sarah said. "Remind me not to go into Oncology."

"Will do." Randy closed his book. "I say we end on a positive note. Besides, I'm hungry."

Their session ended and everyone shuffled home, except for Randy, who stuck around at Jim's for a while. They ordered pizza and watched the end of a football game together.

"Where's Trina?" Randy asked, not seeing her all day.

Jim shrugged. "I don't know."

"What do you mean you don't know?"

"She took off this morning pissed off. I haven't heard from her since."

Randy shook his head. "Man, how do you live in a relationship like that?"

"She gets moody sometimes."

"That sounds like more than just being moody to me. Does she disappear like this a lot?"

"Only when I tell her I need time to study. That usually leads to an argument."

Randy knew they argued over more than that. They seemed to disagree about almost everything. "What were you two fighting about this time?"

"I told her we were havin' our study session over here and we would need space to spread out. She went all postal on me and babbled on for about twenty minutes about how she's tired of putting her life on hold for my selfish needs."

"Your selfish needs," Randy scoffed. "She said that to you?"

"Yup. Then she said that I make her life more difficult than it should be, and she didn't see why she had to bend over backwards to conform to my schooling schedule."

"She does realize that you're going to school to make both of your lives better, doesn't she? That when you're done you'll be earning a doctor's salary? Does she think about that?"

"I don't think she's thinkin' that far ahead. All she seems to care about is the here and now."

"When was the last time you two had a conversation where you weren't yelling at each other about something?" Randy asked.

"We didn't yell at each other yesterday. Then again, we didn't really see each other yesterday."

"Don't take this the wrong way, Jim, but your girlfriend is a nag."

"I know," Jim admitted.

"So, I will ask again, why do you put up with that?"

"It's all good, man," Jim said with a grin. "I love her."

Randy didn't see it. How could Jim be committed to a woman who treated him like crap?

Randy returned to his apartment around 2:00 P.M. Jane was in the bedroom digging through his laundry looking for something. With an inquisitive stare and a silent laugh, he snuck up behind her and asked, "What are you doing?"

She flinched and pivoted toward him. "Stop sneaking up on me like that."

He sniggered. "Sorry."

"I think I left my white sweater over here the other day. Have you seen it?"

He opened a dresser drawer and pulled out a neatly folded white cardigan sweater. He hooked it on his finger. "You mean this one?"

"Thank you." She stood up to get it. "How was studying?"

"Productive." He kicked off his shoes and reclined on the bed with his hands clasped behind his head. "But I'm worried about Jim."

"Why?"

"He and Trina got into a fight again. That seems to be a daily occurrence lately."

She crawled onto the bed with him. "What's their story?"

Randy chuckled at her inquisitiveness. "It's complicated. They met in high school and have been together for eight years. Their relationship is rocky. They don't see eye to eye most of the time, and they argue over petty things. They've broken up at least six times that I'm aware of, yet somehow they end up back together. Trina has a tendency to blow things out of proportion, and she's nitpicky, in my opinion. Jim tries to study and focus on school, but she gets angry when he chooses school over her."

"Why are they still together if they don't get along?"

Randy didn't know why. "I've been asking myself that same question."

"What does she do? I don't see her around campus."

"She works over at First Bank. She's a computer specialist or something like that."

"And they live together?" Jane asked.

"They do. Jim and I were roommates up until last year. Trina got an apartment closer to the bank where she works and invited him to move in with her. She has a decent job and thought she could support them while he went to school."

"Jim used to live here with you?"

"Yup." He pointed to the room across the hall. "That spare bedroom over there used to be his room."

"And how long have you lived here?"

"Four years. Jim and I were roommates in the dorm my freshman year. After suffering through two semesters of that torturous hell, we decided to get an apartment together. I've lived here ever since." He put his arm around her and glanced as his watch. "When did you get here?"

"Right before you did. The girls and I have been out getting supplies for Halloween."

Curiously, he asked, "Does your dad know about all these parties and social events you do with this sorority of yours?"

"No, and he doesn't need to know. There are a lot of things I do that he doesn't know about."

"What would he say if he saw what you were wearing right now?" She had on a pair of white shorts, a curve-hugging electric green tank top that showed off her bust line, and electric green sling back sandals.

"I don't wear stuff like this around Daddy."

"I noticed that yesterday. You hide a lot of things from him, don't you?"

"What he doesn't know won't hurt him and can't upset him."

"So instead you play the role of the naïve little girl."

"Exactly."

Randy didn't agree with her doing this and didn't understand how she could be comfortable with this situation. "You're ok with lying to your father?"

"I don't lie to him," she denied. "If he asks me upfront, I tell him the truth. But I don't give him any reasons to ask. As far as he knows, I always dress conservatively, never drink, and wouldn't dare initiate physical contact with a man."

Randy busted out laughing at that blatant lie. "But that isn't true."

"I know, but he doesn't know that."

"Janey, you don't have to justify what you do," Randy explained. "You are twenty-one years old. You are old enough to vote, old enough to drink, old enough to get married or have sex if you want to, and there's nothing he can say or do about it."

"It's not that simple."

"Yes it is. You are far beyond your father controlling your life."

"He doesn't control my life. He just lives in the clouds. I do whatever I want."

"Not around him you don't," Randy added.

"No, not around him, but he's happy with that."

"Are you happy with that? Are you really happy knowing your father doesn't know who you are?"

"Not really, but it's easier this way."

Randy shook his head, baffled by this type of thinking. In his family, everyone talked and tried to work out differences and problems. They didn't hide things from each other or try to make people think they were something they weren't. He and his parents had a very open relationship. They didn't always agree, but they definitely knew who he was and what his convictions were, and at no time did they try to dominate him or make him feel inferior. "Easier isn't always better."

During class the next day, Jim seemed distant. Not at all himself. Normally he had a pretty cheerful disposition, but today not one grin, not one snicker, not one smartass comment. Instead, Jim Ryan looked dazed and almost fell asleep in class. Randy was worried about him.

As he was about to head home for the day, he caught up with Jim in the hallway. "Hey."

"Hey."

They walked together for a while, but the silence was awkward and uncomfortable. Randy broke it by asking, "What's up?"

"Nothin'."

Randy knew he was lying. He could tell by the distressed tone in his voice. "Did Trina ever come home yesterday?"

"She showed up a little after 8:00."

Jim wasn't in the mood to talk. Randy pushed the issue anyway. "Come on, man, talk to me. What's going on?"

"I told you, I'm fine."

"Liar. Either tell me what's going on or I'll sic the Anatomy students on you."

Jim stopped walking and turned around. He didn't say a word. Instead, his eyes grew misty, and he looked like he was about to cry.

Something was very wrong. "Jim?"

Jim stood on the stairs and stared at Randy with a desperate expression on his face. He struggled to find his thoughts. "Trina's pregnant."

"What do you mean, Trina's pregnant?"

Jim felt lightheaded and his knees suddenly gave out on him. He had to sit down. He hung his head to the ground, picking at bits of rocks and dirt in the cracks. "She found out Friday while I was takin' exams. She's been avoiding me because she didn't know how to tell me."

No wonder why Jim was so distant and dejected. Randy set his book bag down and sat on the stairs next to him. His heart ached for his best friend. However, he wasn't sure what to say or how to comfort Jim in a situation like this. Taking a deep breath to gather his thoughts, he replied, "Are you sure?"

Frustrated, Jim flung one of the rocks. "She took the test and went to the doctor Friday to confirm it. Yes, Randy, I'm sure. She's pregnant."

"Shit."

"Yeah." Jim's voice sounded bleak. This was not something he was prepared to deal with. Med school and a baby—not a good combination.

"What are you going to do?"

"I don't know." He couldn't think clearly, and honestly didn't know what he was going to do.

Randy tried to offer advice. "Are you sure it's yours?"

Jim glowered at him. "What the hell? Of course it's mine."

"Just exploring all the options."

"Well, that's not one of 'em," Jim snapped, appalled that Randy even suggested such a thing.

Randy didn't know what to say. With heartfelt empathy, he replied, "I'm sorry, man."

"I really don't need this in my life right now."

Trying to lighten the mood, Randy said, "You know, there is a little thing called birth control."

Jim didn't find Randy's statement funny. Defensively, he retorted, "Are you done lecturing me now? You're not helping me very much."

"Sorry." Randy thought for a minute before he asked, "Are you guys keeping the baby?"

"We've already decided that. We were up all night talkin' about it. But I'm in med school. How am I supposed to study and sleep with a baby in the house? We don't have enough money to support a kid. Trina and I barely bring in enough cash flow as it is. Trina's already uptight about our money situation, but I can't expect her to keep workin' with a new baby." Feeling defeated, Jim said, "I'm considering nixin' med school."

Randy's eyes widened at this statement. He didn't like that idea one bit. "Oh, hell, no. I will not let you do that. You have come too far to quit now. No way. That is not an option."

Desperate for answers, Jim pleaded, "You got a better idea?"

Anything had to be better than that. "We'll think of something, but quitting is not going to happen. Maybe your parents can help."

Jim had completely forgotten about his parents. His father was not a particularly understanding person either. Jim's father expected perfection from his only child, and Jim was never able to measure up to his father's expectations. His parents were going to be exceedingly pissed about this news. "Oh, Jesus, my parents," Jim panicked. "How the hell am I gonna tell my parents? My dad is gonna wig. I am gonna get the 'I told you so' lecture so badly. They didn't want me to move in with Trina in the first place. My dad told me this was gonna happen if I did. He will never let me live this down."

Randy exhaled deeply, feeling for his friend. "Ooh, yeah, I guess asking them is a bad idea."

"No shit. Do you know what my father is gonna do when he hears about this? I am so screwed." Jim had a horrible look on his face. He was screaming inside. "I am not ready for this. This is by far the worst thing that has ever happened to me."

Randy put his hand on Jim's shoulder, offering his support. "It's ok, man. We'll think of something. Try not to worry about it right now."

"That's easy for you to say. You're not the one with a pregnant girlfriend."

Randy walked Jim to his car then headed to the library to do some research.

After several hours at the library conducting research for his thesis, Randy stopped studying when he caught sight of a face he wished he hadn't seen. Steve Hall walked in the door and stared right at him. "Oh, shit," Randy said in a low voice, hoping no one else could hear him. He was not in the mood to deal with this asshole and didn't want to have a confrontation, but knew it was bound to happen.

"Well, well. If it isn't Randy Hanson." Steve deliberately sat in the chair across from him. "You always get your way, don't you? Who gives a shit what anyone else wants as long as Randy is happy."

"This is in no way my fault. You had to open your big mouth and talk a bunch of shit. Maybe you should learn to shut the hell up." He gathered his things to relocate when Steve grabbed his wrist. Randy jerked his hand away. "Don't ever touch me again."

"Can I touch your pretty little girlfriend, or is that a crime too?"

Randy shot him an evil glare "Stay away from Jane and stay away from me." He picked up his belongings and moved to another table.

But Steve remained persistent at trying to get a rise out of him. He followed him to his new location.

Irritated that Steve wouldn't leave him alone, Randy complained, "Dammit, Steve, don't you have something better to do?"

"That girlfriend of yours is a fine piece of pie. I might have to get myself a slice."

Randy raised his voice. "If you touch her, I swear to god…"

Steve grinned audaciously then sang the words to 'She's My Cherry Pie' as he walked away.

Randy hated that man. He had to be the most repugnant creature on earth. Thankful the confrontation was over, he tried to carry on with studying.

It was close to 9:30 P.M. by the time he was finished. As he walked back home to his apartment, he checked his phone messages. He had one from Jane. *I love you. Call me.* He immediately called her back.

When Jane saw Randy's name flash on her screen, she quickly answered her phone. "Hey, Stranger. Where have you been hiding all day?" she asked, wondering why she hadn't heard much from him today.

"Been at the library. Had some research I needed to do," he explained.

"Did you get it all done?"

"Yup."

Randy sounded tired. Concerned about him, she asked, "You ok?"

"I'm fine. It's just been a long day."

"You need to go home and rest."

"Heading that way right now." Feeling troubled, he said, "Guess what I found out today?"

"What?"

"Jim told me Trina's pregnant."

She thought he was joking. "She is not."

"I'm serious, Baby. She is."

By the tone of his voice, Jane knew he wasn't kidding.

"He's not taking it too well. Hardly said a word all day. He's thinking about dropping out of school."

"You can't let him do that," Jane insisted.

"Believe me, I'm trying. I told him not to do anything rash, but he's a little freaked out right now." He shifted his phone to the other ear and adjusted his backpack. "I also ran into Steve tonight."

Randy and Steve was a dangerous combination. The last encounter they had almost led to a fight. Jane hoped Randy was able to restrain himself. "You didn't have a confrontation with him, did you?"

"No, everything's alright," he reassured her. "What are you doing after class tomorrow?"

"Nothing that I know of. Why?"

"The Lakers are playing tomorrow night. You wanna come over and watch the game with me?"

"Sounds fun," she said. "I'll meet you over there."

Chapter Eleven

Randy agreed to meet Jane at her sorority house for the Halloween party Saturday night. He didn't want to go but promised he would be there. As Jane suggested, he invited his friends. Jim wasn't in the mood to celebrate, and Sarah said she had to study. Bruce and Mandy didn't normally socialize with party people, but they didn't want Randy to be stuck there by himself. They all arrived at the Alpha house around the same time.

When Randy saw them, he shook Bruce's hand. "Thank you for coming."

"Didn't have anything better to do tonight." The party had obviously been going on for a while because music blared from the house and some kind of chanting could be heard. "Sounds like a happening place."

"I'm only here because Jane invited me. And if I wouldn't have promised her I'd be here, I wouldn't have come. These Greek parties aren't really my thing."

Mandy chimed in, "Come on, Randy. Live a little."

Together, the three of them walked toward the sorority house. The door was open, so they stepped inside.

Randy quickly cast an eye over the area only to witness a rambunctious bunch of men wearing matching fraternity tee-shirts playing with beer bongs while they hollered, "Chug! Chug! Chug!" at one of their fellow frat brothers, trying to encourage him to drink himself to oblivion. A group of ditzy girls, obviously on the verge of being drunk, stood around in a circle urging them on. Randy wished he hadn't come.

Bruce, on the other hand, made the most of this situation. "I'm going to get a drink," he said to Mandy. "You want one?"

"Absolutely." She and Bruce headed to a cooler to grab a beer.

Randy felt uncomfortable being here. A sorority house full of drunk frat boys and dingbat tipsy chicks was not his idea of a fun time. "Well," he said cynically. "This should be enjoyable." He scanned the area hoping to find Jane. After a minute or two, he spotted her standing by a doorway in the kitchen. She was surrounded by a swarm of people, mostly men. But with the skintight, skimpy nurse's costume she had on, Randy wasn't surprised she was attracting so much attention.

When Jane saw him, a smile instantly filled her face. She came over and put her arms around him, greeting him with a kiss. She stared at his costume for a minute. He was wearing scrubs and a stethoscope. "A doctor, Randy? That's not very creative."

He didn't care. At least he showed up, which to him was good enough. "No, but dressed like that, you could be my nurse." He raised his eyebrows seductively.

Jane led him around the room from person to person, introducing him to her friends. He remained cordial, making small talk, while he nursed a bottle of Corona. Jane, on the other hand, had been drinking steadily throughout the night and appeared to be tipsy. Randy had never seen her drink like that before, so he was a little shocked.

After an hour, she began to stumble around and her speech became slurred. She tried to gulp down another beer, but as soon as Randy saw this, he took the bottle out of her hand.

"Whoa, Honey. Slow down."

Suddenly Jane felt lightheaded and almost fell over.

Luckily, Randy was right there to catch her. "You ok?"

"I don't feel well," she muttered.

Carefully, he escorted her over to the sofa and sat her down. "Honey, look at me."

She didn't hear what he said. She was in a daze and the room was spinning. Feeling dizzy, she closed her eyes.

"Open your eyes, Honey."

She did, but the room swirled around her.

Randy tried to get her to focus on him. "Baby, can you hear me?"

Feeling weak and unable to stop the room from twirling, Jane laid her head on the pillow and groaned.

Randy was worried about her. Her face was flushed and she was really out of it. He felt the temperature of her head, checked her pulse, and got a good look at her pupils.

Lisa saw Jane lying on the couch with Randy tending to her. Concerned about her friend, she came over to them and asked, "Is she alright?"

Randy's voice became taut. "How much did she drink before I got here?"

Lisa shrugged, "I don't know. A lot."

Randy grew increasingly worried. With the confusion, disorientation, lethargy, slurred speech, and dizziness Jane had, obviously her blood alcohol concentration was well beyond legal limits. "You don't know how much?"

"I lost count after about three."

"Wonderful," he mocked. "Where is her room?"

Lisa gave Randy the most dreadful scowl he had ever seen. In a harsh, accusatory tone, she said, "There is no way I am letting you take her upstairs. Not going to happen, Mister."

What kind of accusation was that? Was she insinuating that he was planning on having his way with his drunken girlfriend? He found this extremely insulting. "For Christ sake, Lisa, she's my girlfriend. She is drunk, and she needs to go to bed and sleep this off. Now, I am taking her upstairs and putting her to bed. If you are her friend, you will help me. Where the hell is her room?"

Lisa realized she had offended him. With Randy's insistence, she had no choice but to help him. "I'll show you."

Randy gently picked Jane up and carried her in his arms.

Lisa led him up the stairs and took him to a room on the second floor. "This is her room." She opened the door and showed him inside.

"Thank you." Randy carried Jane into the room and gently laid her on the bed, placing her on her side.

Jane moaned and softly called out his name.

"It's alright, Baby. Lie down." He slipped a pillow under her head and took off her shoes. "Get some sleep, Honey." He kissed her cheek then covered her with a blanket and tucked her in. Once Jane was snuggled in, Randy eyed Lisa. "Do not let her drink anymore."

"I won't."

Jane was passed out on the bed. Randy couldn't leave her alone in that condition. "Someone needs to stay here with her and make sure she's ok."

He was totally willing to take on this role, but before he could, Lisa offered, "I'll stay with her."

"Are you sure?"

Lisa sat on the floor and held Jane's hand. "Yes. I'll be right here."

Randy nodded, grateful to Lisa for doing this. Before he left, he wrote his cellphone number on a piece of paper and handed it to Lisa. "Keep an eye on her, please. If she gets worse, call me immediately. I don't care what time it is, just keep me updated."

"I will."

Randy headed toward the door. "I'll stop by after my study session tomorrow to see how she's doing."

Lisa could see that he was genuinely concerned about Jane and was not trying to take advantage of her in any way. The loving way he handled her and the gentle way he spoke to her convinced Lisa that Randy did indeed care about her.

She wished now that she hadn't so harshly accused him of such a heinous act. "Randy?" she called out to him.

"What?"

"I'm sorry about what I said. It's just that so many guys want to get a girl drunk and…"

Defensively, he retorted, "I'm not one of them."

Feeling apologetic, she said, "Thank you for caring about Jane."

"Of course I care about her. I love her." He pulled his keys out of his pocket. "I'll stop by tomorrow. Keep an eye on her, please."

Lisa promised she would.

The study group met at Randy's apartment that week. Right as Randy put on a pot of coffee, he heard a knock on his door. Bruce was the first to arrive. He stood on the porch with a backpack over his shoulder. "I smell coffee."

"Brewing now." Randy invited him inside. "Did you have a good time last night?"

Chuckling under his breath, he replied, "Those sorority girls know how to throw a party, don't they?"

"That they do."

"I think Mandy had too much fun last night. She was really ditzy when I dropped her off."

This made Randy laugh. "She'll probably be hungover this morning."

"Most likely." Bruce set his backpack on the table and shook his head. "How do you do it?"

"Do what?"

"I was at that party last night," he explained. "I saw what was going on."

Randy didn't know what Bruce was babbling about. "What did I miss?"

"Every guy in that room was staring at Jane's ass, and you know damn well each one of them wanted to get her upstairs. Doesn't that bother you?"

"No."

Bruce couldn't fathom how this didn't faze Randy. "If all those guys were gawking at my girlfriend with lustful eyes, that would make me uncomfortable."

"They can look all they want," Randy declared. "But the bottom line is I'm the one who holds her, I'm the one she's kissing, and I'm the one she sleeps with every night. So despite the fact that all of those guys lust after her, she always comes running to me. So no, Bruce, it doesn't bother me."

"You are a better man than I am then. I couldn't do it." Bruce pulled out his notes and placed them on the table. "I saw her passed out last night. Is she okay?"

"I called three times last night and again this morning. Lisa said she was still out. I'm gonna run over there when we're done and see how she's doing."

"Man, that girlfriend of yours was putting it away last night," Bruce remarked. "She was drunk off her ass."

"Yeah, I know. She'll regret it later when she wakes up."

"No kidding."

Randy headed up to the Alpha house immediately following his study session. When he arrived, he got a laugh out of Lisa and two of Jane's other sorority sisters standing on ladders trying to take toilet paper out of a tree. "Good afternoon, ladies," he said as he walked by them. "What happened here?"

"Apparently," Lisa said, stepping off the ladder, "someone found a roll of toilet paper and decided to decorate our tree last night."

"I can see that." Randy spotted a garden hose in the yard. With a playful grin, he picked it up and sprayed the tree with it, soaking the girls as well. When he was finished, he shut the hose off and set it back down in the grass. "Tree is clean."

Despite getting all wet, the water did remove all of the toilet paper. They looked at him, looked at the tree, then stared at each other and laughed. "Why didn't we think of that?"

Lisa walked toward Randy, dripping wet.

"How is she?" he asked, hoping Jane was feeling better.

"She's awake, she's been moving around a little."

"That's good. May I go in?"

"The back door's unlocked."

"Thanks." He let himself in and headed up the stairs to Jane's room. The bedroom door was partially ajar. He tapped on it lightly and poked his head inside. Jane was sitting on her bed dressed in sweats and a tee-shirt. Seeing her made Randy smile. "Hey, Baby."

With an apologetic slump, she replied, "I'm really sorry."

"Don't apologize." He sat down next to her and held her hand. "How you feeling?"

"My head is killing me."

He tried not to laugh. "I bet. You been drinking water?"

"Some, but it makes me nauseous."

"You need fluids, Babe." He kissed her softly on the lips. "I'll get you some more water and find you some Tylenol. Be right back."

As Randy walked out, Lisa walked in, drying her hair with a towel.

Jane giggled when she saw her. "What happened to you?"

"Your boyfriend sprayed all that toilet paper out of the tree. He got us soaked in the process though."

Jane thought that was funny.

"That man was worried about you last night."

"He was?" Jane asked.

"He's the one who brought you up here and put you to bed. It was adorable. He took off your shoes, covered you with a blanket, and kissed you on the cheek. He called over here three times last night and twice this morning to see how you were doing."

That was the sweetest thing Jane had ever heard. "He did?"

"Yup. And every time he called, he insisted that you drink water."

"That's why you've been shoving water down me all morning."

"Yes," Lisa explained.

Now Jane felt really foolish. "Oh, god. How embarrassing. I can't believe he saw me like that."

Randy walked back into the room carrying a glass of water and a bottle of Tylenol. He set the water on the desk next to Jane's bed and opened the bottle. "Take two of these and drink lots of fluids," he instructed her.

She covered her mouth with her hand to muffle a giggle.

Randy wondered what was so funny. "What?"

"You sounded like a doctor when you said that."

"I can't imagine why." He poured two Tylenol capsules in Jane's hand then he handed her a glass of water. "Drink all of this."

She stared at the glass and cringed. "Do I have to?"

"Yes," he insisted. "Doctor's orders."

She swallowed the pills and gulped down the water. When she was finished, she stared at Randy. "I am so sorry. I can't believe you saw me like that."

He took the empty glass from her. "Don't worry about it, Babe. Just feel better." He kissed her tenderly and set the glass down on the desk. "I'm gonna head over to the library for a bit, but I'll call you later. You have your phone?"

"Yes."

"Ok. Get some rest." He gave her another kiss then stood up to leave.

"Randy?" she called to him.

"Yes?"

"Thank you."

He winked at her as he left the room.

Chapter Twelve

Jim came over to Randy's apartment with a basketball in his hand. "Wanna shoot some hoops?" he asked.

"Sure. Let me change first."

Jim sauntered inside and followed Randy into the bedroom. He sat down on the bed while Randy put on shorts, a tee-shirt, and basketball shoes. "Trina and I have been talkin', and I want to kick some ideas at you."

"Alright."

"I'm not gonna quit school," Jim declared.

"That's good," Randy said. "I wouldn't have let you anyway."

"The baby's not due 'til June. School will be out by then and I'll only have my thesis to work on. I can get a job over the summer while Trina is home with the baby. She says she wants to keep workin', so when school starts up again, we'll have to find childcare."

"Doesn't sound too complicated," Randy said, offering support.

"And we've decided to get married," Jim added.

Randy stopped dead in his tracks. "Wait a minute. What did you say?"

"We're gettin' married."

Randy did not agree with this decision. "Marriage, Jim?"

"Yes. We've been livin' together for over a year, what's the difference?"

"Living with someone is not the same as marriage," Randy argued.

"I don't see the difference. Married people live in the same house, share bills, share income, sleep in the same bed. How is it any different than the arrangement I have now?"

"It's not the same. With marriage, you're committing your life to one woman forever. It's in writing, signed in front of witnesses and filed downtown. Marriage is a lifetime commitment, a legal bond, not something to be taken lightly. You should really think about this."

"I have thought about this."

"You are only marrying her because she's pregnant, Jim. Is that really a reason to get married?" Randy questioned, trying to talk his friend out of this rash and impulsive decision.

"Is it a reason not to?"

"Yes, it is. Don't get married for the wrong reasons, man. That leads to nothing but trouble."

Jim contemplated this for a moment, until he became distracted by an open condom wrapper on Randy's bedside table. With a smartass grin, he picked up. "Someone's been busy," Jim teased, completely changing the subject.

Randy took it away from him. "Give me that."

"How often does she stay over here?"

Randy snatched the basketball from Jim, completely ignoring his comment. "Come on. Let's play."

Jim openly laughed then the two of them went to the gym together.

Jane's sorority house was not far from the basketball court. After his game of one-on-one with Jim, Randy decided to pay her a visit.

Jane answered the door, surprised to see him at 4:30 in the afternoon. "What are you doing up here?" she asked.

Grinning ear to ear, he said, "Oh, I don't even get a 'Hi, Randy' or a hello kiss or anything? Is that any way to greet your boyfriend?"

She puckered her lips and gave him a kiss.

"That's better. You wanna go for walk?" he offered.

"Sure." She took his hand and went with him.

They ambled through the esplanade and playfully pranced to Sather Tower, enjoying the warm weather. "My parents called and asked about you today," Randy said. "They want to meet you and have invited you up to Seattle for Christmas break."

Jane had never spent a holiday away from home before. Although she loved the fact that Randy's parents had invited her to be a guest in their home, she was unsure about this proposal. "But what about Daddy? I can't leave him alone during the holidays."

Randy figured she would say that. "What about New Years?"

"What do you mean?" she asked.

"You spend Christmas with your family then fly up to Seattle and spend New Year's Eve with me."

That wasn't a bad idea.

"I'll even pay for your plane ticket," Randy added, trying to entice her further.

"Do your parents have room?"

"They have lots of room, and they want you to come. What do you think? Will you join me for New Years?"

She replied with a bob of her head.

"Awesome. I'll make airline reservations for you and call my parents to let them know."

Over the next few weeks, due to schedule conflicts and studying commitments, Jane and Randy only saw each other on weekends and occasional weeknights. Randy's class, work, and study schedule, as well as the clinical work he was doing, required many hours of his time and kept him exceedingly busy. He also spent a good amount of time doing fieldwork and research for the thesis he was working on. It seemed that the further into the semester he got, the busier he became. Despite this, he talked to Jane every day, and they exchanged text messages regularly, but it just wasn't the same as having her physical presence around him. Missing her company, he decided to send her flowers.

He came home Thursday from a long day of classes and a few hours of work to find his front door unlocked. Hoping he hadn't been so delirious that he forgot to lock it that day, he stepped inside his apartment. To his surprise, Jane was sitting at the table with books and papers scattered all around her.

When she heard Randy come in, she looked up. "Hey, Handsome."

He tossed his keys on the table and carefully set his stethoscope beside them. "Hi, Baby."

"Thank you for the flowers," she said with a smile. "They're beautiful."

"You're welcome." He drew her nearer and gave her a kiss.

"We haven't spent much time together lately so I thought I'd come over."

"I'm glad you're here." He draped his white lab coat over the back of a chair and went into the kitchen to grab a glass of water.

"Know what I discovered today?"

"What's that?" he asked, wondering what great world discovery she unveiled.

"Having a boyfriend who's in medical school is hard work. You are a busy guy."

"I tried to tell you that before you got yourself into this."

"I know you did," Jane confirmed. "And I'll take you anyway I can get you."

"You're not tired of all this yet?"

"Are you kidding?" she said with a giggle. "I wouldn't trade this for anything."

That response made him feel more secure. "I'm glad. Any other woman would have been long gone by now."

Jane turned around and bit her lip seductively. "Well, I'm not any other woman, am I?"

"That's for sure." He glanced at the mess she made on the table. "What are you doing?"

"Studying for a test I have on Friday. Do you have to study tonight?"

When did he not have studying to do? "Yeah. Mostly reading though."

"Tell you what," she proposed. "Why don't you get started while I make dinner."

Her devotion and dedication to him and the relationship they had established awed him. Jane was always doing small things for him, like massaging his shoulders when he was feeling stressed or fixing dinner on nights when he was swamped with homework. When she knew he was having a rough day, she would send him words of encouragement. It was truly inspiring

"Why are you looking at me like that?" she said, wondering why he was staring at her with a creepy grin on his face.

"You are amazing."

"Why?" she asked.

"You have more conviction than anyone I have ever met." He took her hand and pulled her over to him. "I'm sorry we haven't spent as much time together as we should. You deserve more than what I've been giving you. I don't mean to neglect you."

"It's ok," she reassured him, "I understand."

"Don't think I don't want to be with you."

"I don't think that at all. Now sit down and get your reading done. I'll make us something to eat." She kissed him softly and retreated into the kitchen.

Randy pulled his textbook out and began to read his required chapters. About twenty-five minutes later, a heavenly smell emanated from the kitchen. He sniffed the air taking in the delicious aroma of whatever concoction she was brewing in there. Following the scent, Randy picked up his stethoscope and tiptoed into the kitchen, hoping to sneak in undetected.

Despite his stealthiness, Jane saw him. "What are you doing?"

"Giving you a physical." With his stethoscope on his ears, he proceeded to examine her heart, lungs, and tummy.

"Are you getting kinky with me?"

He offered a suggestive glance. "Is that what you want?"

"Maybe, but not right now or dinner will burn."

He removed the stethoscope and set it on the counter then snuck up behind her and tried to grab a taste from the pot. "That smells incredible."

She gently smacked his hand, "Hey! Get your fingers out of there. You have to wait."

He retracted his hand and nibbled on her neck.

She giggled, "Randy, stop that."

But he didn't stop. He nibbled some more, trying to arouse her.

"Can we eat first?"

"What are you talking about? I am eating." He slowly worked his way up to her ear while he moved his hand inside her shirt, hoping to catch a feel of her breast.

Jane pushed his hand away. "Would you stop that? I'm busy."

"I'm busy too," he said playfully.

She turned around and locked her arms around his neck. "How 'bout setting the table? Dinner's almost ready."

Randy complied with her wishes.

Randy and his study group met at the SUB Sunday morning to go over information they all received from classes and seminars that week. In the middle of a discussion about epidemiology, Trina stormed in, steaming, and interrupted their session.

"Any particular reason, Jim Ryan, why you failed to tell me you were taking the car today?"

Jim looked at Trina as if she had lost her mind. "What are you doin' here?"

She continued her degrading, harsh-toned lecture. "You didn't stop to think that I might have needed it today?"

"Trina, I'm busy. Not now," Jim demanded.

"And when would you like to discuss this, James?"

Jim tried to remain calm. "You need to quit buggin'."

"I needed the car today!"

Her pushiness and refusal to diplomatically discuss this issue made Jim quickly lose his patience. "I have my study session today. I always have my study session on Sunday. What makes you think that this Sunday would be different from any other Sunday?"

"You could have asked me."

Annoyed by her attitude, he countered, "Excuse me? I was not aware that I had to ask permission to use a set of wheels I paid for."

"I need it!" she demanded obnoxiously.

"What for?"

"What difference does that make? Why do your needs always come first?"

"My needs? Dammit, Trina, don't start that shit again." He was about to blow up at her. Trying to keep his cool, he pursed his lips together and took a few deep breaths. "You want the car, fine." He pulled the keys out of his pocket and handed them to her. "Take the damn thing."

She snatched the keys out of his and left indignantly, without even saying thank you.

Randy watched this entire scene, appalled by the way Katrina treated Jim. Breaking up the session, he suggested, "Ok, guys, let's take a break. Get some coffee, grab some food, and meet back here at 10:15."

The others readily agreed.

As Mandy, Sarah, and Bruce dispersed to grab refreshments, Randy sat in the chair next to Jim, who was fuming. Randy stared at his best friend wondering what he was thinking.

Jim finally spoke up. "I swear that woman is gonna be the death of me. These damn pregnancy hormones are drivin' me insane. Nothin' ever satisfies her."

Randy felt sorry for him. Offering sympathy, he asked, "Why the hell did you do that?"

"Do what?"

"Let her come in here and throw a temper tantrum in front of your friends then give in to her like that."

"What choice do I have?"

"You could have told her no," Randy said.

"Then I would never hear the end of it, Randy. You don't understand."

"You're right. I don't," Randy agreed. "I don't understand why you are with a woman you don't get along with, who bitches at you constantly, and treats you like shit. That isn't love, Jim."

"What do you know?" Jim asked defensively.

"I know what a healthy relationship looks like, and I've never seen it look like that. You are miserable, and you can't blame it on pregnancy hormones either. I'm not buying it."

Jim had to get some things off his chest. Randy sat and listened, letting him vent. "She has done nothin' but complain about every aspect of our lives since school started. Nothin' I do pleases her." He paused briefly to collect his thoughts. "I don't know how much more of this I can swallow. I cannot stand livin' in the same house with her. I am so paranoid that I will do somethin' wrong which will undoubtedly lead to her biting my head off. Not only do I have to deal with my girlfriend bein' pregnant, I also never hear the end of how selfish I am because supposedly I neglect her needs and only think about myself. That is the biggest crock of crap I have ever heard. I have done nothin' but look out for her needs since the day we met."

Randy understood how Jim felt, which led to further confusion. "And you want to marry this woman? Is that really how you want to spend the rest of your life?"

Feeling trapped, Jim replied, "I honestly don't know what I want anymore. I wish I could nix this whole damn thing, but now I'm stuck in this situation and forced to marry her."

"Wait a minute. Forced into marriage? How do you figure that?"

Jim explained, "My mother says I need to be responsible and marry her since I'm the one who got her pregnant."

Randy stopped him before he said another word. "You're letting your parents decide that for you? Jim, come on. Don't do that. You're the one who has to live your life, not them."

"If I don't marry her, I'll end up spendin' my life's savings payin' child support."

Trying to get Jim to see this from another point of view, Randy said, "And how is that any worse than living the rest of your life with a woman you constantly argue with? Or worse yet, marrying her, getting a divorce, and ending up paying child support and alimony then having to give her half of everything you've worked so hard for. To me, that would be worse."

Jim felt like he was stuck between a rock and hard place and had no way of escaping from any of it. "Either way, I'm still forced to deal with the hell of it all. She is carrying my child."

"You and Trina had problems well before this baby came into the picture. This pregnancy is not the root of your problems with Trina and you know it. You're using that as an easy way out."

"You think this is easy?" Jim was getting angry with Randy now. "You have no fuckin' way of knowin' the hell I've been goin' through. Do you have any idea how pissed off my parents are right now? My dad has threatened to stop payin' for medical school because of this shit. My girlfriend is hormonally and chronically pissed at me, my parents don't even want to talk to me right now, and I'm not gettin' any sleep. Trina has taken my ride, and I now have no way of gettin' home. My life is goddamn nightmare. You honestly think I'm usin' this as an easy way out? Believe me, if I could find a way to get myself out of this fuckin' situation I would gladly do it, but it doesn't work that way, Randy. I'm not the kind of guy to get my girlfriend pregnant then abandon her to deal with it alone. I'm not an asshole."

Trying to convince Jim that he understood how he felt, Randy replied, "I didn't say you were. And I never said this was easy. I can't imagine the hell you must be going through. I just wish I knew what to do and say to help you, but I don't. Instead, I sit here and watch my best friend in pain, going through the worst time in his life, and there's not a damn thing I can do about it."

The two men stared at each other for a minute. Pain and extreme heartache was written all over Jim's face. Exhausted from the stress, he plopped his head on the table. "Fuck."

Randy hated to see his friend like this. He put his hand on Jim's shoulder, offering comfort. "I'm sorry, man. I know this is hard."

"Holy shit. That is an understatement. This fuckin' sucks."

His best friend was on the threshold of hell, and Randy didn't know what to say. "You want some coffee?"

Jim looked up. "Yeah."

"I'll get you a cup. And you can bum a ride with me later."

Jim managed to crack a smile. "Thank you. Make it black."

"You got it."

Chapter Thirteen

The Thanksgiving holiday approached and Randy couldn't wait to take a vacation and get away from the demands of school for a while. Jane came over to his apartment to help him pack last minute items and bid him farewell. She picked up one of his shirts, but before she folded it, she held it against her chest and stared down at his suitcase.

"What's the matter, Baby?"

She wrapped her arms around him and hugged him tightly, not wanting to let him go. "I'm gonna miss you."

He held her close and kissed the top of her head. "I'll miss you too, but it's only for a few days. We both need to spend time with our families. That's important."

"I know, but that doesn't mean I won't miss you."

He lifted her chin and examined her pretty features. "And I'll miss you, but it'll be ok. I'll be back before you know it." He folded the shirt and placed it in his bag. "You'll take care of Mr. Fingers for me while I'm gone?"

She bobbed her head.

"Be careful. I don't want him to bite you."

"I will."

He zipped up his bag, grabbed his airline reservations, his phone, and his keys then slipped on his jacket. "You ready?"

"Yeah."

"Let's go." He took her hand, locked up his apartment, and put his duffle bag and laptop in the trunk of his car.

As they sat at the coffee shop waiting for his flight, he reached into his pocket and handed her the key to his car. "I want you to take my car to your dad's house for Thanksgiving."

"You're leaving me your car?"

"Yes." Randy glanced at his watch. "I need to get through security or I'll miss my flight." With ticket and laptop bag in hand, he rose to his feet. "I'll see you on Friday. And I'll call you when I get there, so leave your phone on." They embraced in an enduring, heart-felt kiss.

"I love you, Randy."

He rubbed the back of his hand down her cheek. "I love you too. Drive carefully."

Hesitantly, she released him and let him go. With her arms hugged around herself, she watched him walk through security and toward the gates.

As Randy descended over Puget Sound into the SEA-TAC airport, he remembered how much he missed home. The beautiful Seattle skyline lit up the nighttime sky, and the glow of the lights reflecting off the lake brought back memories of fishing with his dad. Several sailboats floated on Lake Washington, and the lights from the Space Needle were breathtaking. He wished Jane could be here to share this sight with him.

Randy's parents met him at the terminal. His mother immediately swarmed him with hugs. "It's good to see you, Sweetheart."

"Hi, Mom."

"How was your flight?" she asked.

"Relaxing, actually."

She stood back and looked him over. He appeared to be well fed, well rested, and had a cheerful disposition. "You look healthy and happy. Been taking care of yourself?"

"I'm twenty-three years old. When are you going to stop worrying about me?"

"When you cease to be my son, I will stop being a concerned mom."

Randy gave his father a hug. "How's work? Keeping you busy?"

Dr. Hanson answered, "Yes, in fact I was up late last night. Had three of my patients check in around the same time, and all three delivered within an hour of each other."

"Wow. You have been busy."

"Did you eat on the plane?" his dad asked.

"You know I hate airline food. Is Stephanie here yet?"

"No, she's not coming in until tomorrow."

"Is she driving?"

"Yes. She said she'd call before she left."

"Where's Robby?" Randy wondered.

"At a football game. He'll be home later tonight."

Randy and his parents walked over to the baggage claim carousel and waited for his luggage to appear. "Where are we going to eat? I'm starving."

Mark laughed at his son's insatiable appetite. "I'll feed you. You need not worry."

Later that night, Randy called Jane to wish her goodnight. His mother overheard the conversation and saw the gleam in her son's eye when he spoke with his girlfriend. Obviously he was happy in this relationship.

When he hung up his phone, she asked, "How's Jane?"

"She's doing well." He sat on the sofa next to her.

She wanted to learn more about this woman her son was involved with so she pried for more information. "How serious are you about this girl?"

"What do you mean?"

"I know how you are with women, Randy. What's up? Are you steady? Are you casual? Are you committed? Are you only with her for sex?"

Randy blushed at her forthright comment. "Mom."

"You talk about her all the time. What's going on?"

"I'm faithful, if that's what you mean. And I'm not seeing anyone else, just her. I respect her, I trust her. What more do you want me to say?"

"Do you love her?"

162

Randy didn't falter one bit. "Yes I do. Very much."

"Do you want to marry her?"

For years Randy's mother had hoped he'd get seriously involved with a woman. She was always bugging him about 'settling down.' Although he was caught off guard by this question, he wasn't surprised that she asked. "What kind of a question is that?"

"So you don't want to marry her?" his mother assumed.

"I did not say that. We've only been together for three months. I'm sure as hell not going to rush into anything. Right now we want to enjoy our time together and get to know each other better. We're gonna take it slow and see how things develop. Why are you so eager to get me married?"

"I want my Randy to be happy."

"I am happy." He kissed her on the cheek. "Where'd Dad go?"

"I think he's out back."

Randy stepped outside to find his father standing on the dock gazing across the lake at the lights of Seattle. "Hey, Dad. Whatcha doing?"

Dr. Hanson turned around. "Just getting some air. Did your mother give you the marriage line yet?"

Randy chuckled. "Yeah, but that's alright. I was expecting it." He peered across the lake enjoying the view with his dad. "You wanna take the boat out tomorrow and throw in a few lines?"

"I was thinking that exact same thing," his father agreed. "But I have to run rounds in the morning first."

"I can get the boat ready. We'll head out as soon as you get back."

"Good plan. Think you can out fish me yet?"

"Possibly," Randy replied.

Dr. Hanson eyed his son with a content smile on his face. "It's good to have you home, Son."

"It's good to be home."

Randy always enjoyed fishing with his dad and was very much looking forward to doing it again. The morning air was crisp and the fog was beginning to lift when Randy and his father floated out on Lake Washington.

As Dr. Hanson threw in a line, he asked, "Everything going ok?"

"Everything's fine. Why?"

"Oh, I don't know," he said wondering why his son was unusually quiet this morning. "Normally you talk my ear off, yet this morning you've hardly spoken a word."

Randy lifted a shoulder. "Don't have much to say I guess."

"How's your thesis coming along?"

"It's going well. Brought my laptop with me so I could work on it a bit."

"That's good." A crooked smile quirked up one side of his mouth. "Every time your mother and I call you, you talk about this girlfriend of yours, but you haven't said much about her since you got here."

"I wondered how long it was going to be before you asked about her."

"Well?"

"Well what?" Randy replied. "What would you like to know that I haven't already told you?"

"It's been a long time since you referred to a girl as your girlfriend."

"I know," Randy concurred.

"You say you love her. There must be something about her you like."

"There are lots of things about her that I like."

"Such as?"

Randy found his father's persistence funny. "Well, I like how she curls up in a chair wearing one of my shirts and watches cartoons over a pint of ice cream. I like the way she gets frantic when she's running late or can't find something she's looking for. I like it when she gets so absorbed in the book she's reading that she completely tunes everything out around her. I like how she dabs grease off her pizza and gives me a hard time about the food I eat. I like that spunky, feisty attitude she gets sometimes. I like the way she seems to know what I'm thinking and I don't have to say a thing. I love the conversations we have and I like the way I feel when I'm around her."

His father interrupted, "And sex?"

"What?" This comment seemed abrupt and out of place.

"I know you have a physical relationship with her."

"Haven't we discussed this already? Yes, she's on the pill, and yes, we're being careful. I told you that."

"That's not what I'm asking," Dr. Hanson interjected. "I know you well, Randal, and with the other relationships you've had in the past, sex seemed to be the driving factor. Is your relationship with Jane purely physical or is there more to it than that?"

"It's not about sex, Dad. Although I'm not gonna lie. The sex is amazing. But with Jane and me it's deeper than that. She supports everything I do and she's right by my side to give me encouragement. She understands the importance of medicine in my life, and I've never known a woman who lets me take the time I need to study. Every other woman was always demanding of me and my time, but not Jane. She takes what I can give, and because of that I find myself wanting to give her more. Sometimes I feel like I don't spend as much time with her as I should."

"It all depends on how you use that time. Quality over quantity."

"I know. I love being with her. I can be myself and have fun, no pressure. It's incredible."

"You sound happy."

"I am very happy," Randy grinned.

Spending time with his family was exactly what Randy needed. He had fun fishing with his dad and enjoyed hanging out with his mother. But he wished Jane could be here with him.

He had a hard time sleeping that night. Images of Jane's beautiful smile and tantalizing green eyes ran through his head. He desperately wanted to be close to her. Tired of tossing and turning, he got up, slipped on a pair of sweats and a sweatshirt, and gave her a call. Afterwards, about 2:00 A.M., he sat out on the grass by the edge of the lake and chucked rocks into the water. The distant lights of Seattle reflected off the water and the faint sound of a train whistle carried in the cool breeze.

His mother woke up to get a glass of water and peered out the kitchen window. Randy was outside sitting in the sand. Considering it was thirty-eight degrees outside, she couldn't figure out why he was out there. She put on her robe and went out to see what he was doing.

Randy smiled when he saw her. "Hey, Mom."

"Why are you sitting out here in the freezing cold in the middle of the night?"

"Can't sleep." He threw another rock into the lake.

Mrs. Hanson sat beside him and put her hand on his back. "You only come out here and throw rocks in the lake when you have something on your mind. What's wrong, Honey?"

He threw another rock. "I just got off the phone with Jane."

His mother knew him well. She knew exactly what was on his mind. "You miss her, don't you?"

Randy nodded. "Yeah."

Trying to cheer him up, she said, "You've never shown us a picture of this girl. Do you have one?"

He pulled out his phone and searched for a picture of Jane. When he found one, he showed it to his mom. "This is Janey."

Jane was a beautiful woman. She had soft facial feature, long flowing hair, and gorgeous green eyes. "She's pretty."

"I think so," Randy concurred.

"Your whole face lights up when you talk about her," his mother remarked.

"Does it?"

"Yes, it does. This glow about you, this exceedingly pleasant smile you've had all day, I'm glad to see that. I love how happy she makes you," his mother remarked. "You look like a man in love."

"I am in love."

She gave his phone back to him. "You want some hot chocolate?"

"Mom, I'm not twelve."

"Oh come now. You mean to tell me that you don't like hot chocolate anymore?" his mother declared.

"I do."

"Then come inside. You're going to freeze out here."

They stood up and walked inside together, enjoying a bonding moment while they sipped on hot cocoa.

Thanksgiving morning, the house was quiet. Randy's dad was sitting at the kitchen table reading the morning paper, but no one else appeared to be home. Randy wondered where everyone went. "It's quiet in here this morning. Where is everybody?"

Dr. Hanson explained, "Went to pick up last minute items before Grandma and Grandpa get here."

"Robby and Stephanie went too?" He gripped a mug and poured himself some coffee.

"Yup."

Randy stirred sugar and creamer into his coffee then joined his father at the table. "Dad, can I talk to you about something?"

"Sure." He put the newspaper down and gave Randy his undivided attention. "What's on your mind?"

"It's Jane's dad. I've gone with her to her father's house a couple times now. At first, the man was really harsh towards me. Since that time, he and I have had more opportunities to talk, and I think we've established a decent rapport. But it makes me uncomfortable to see the interaction he has with Jane. I really don't like the way he treats her."

"Why is that?" Mark wondered.

"He's condescending towards her. He tries to control her life and denies the fact that she is a grown woman capable of making her own decisions. He talks down to her, doesn't really know her, and treats her like she is some kind of ignorant, naïve girl he can command. It really bothers me. But she won't stick up for herself and is afraid to say anything to him. She puts on a false front every time we go over there, leading her father to believe that she is someone she's not. It's not right, and I feel like I should say something to him about it."

Although Dr. Hanson valued the sentiment of his son's words, he had to speak his mind. "That is a very bad idea."

"But you always told me I should stand up for the woman I love, look after her, do whatever I could to protect her."

"Yes, I did say that, but this is not the appropriate time."

Randy didn't understand. "Why isn't it?"

"Because it involves her and her father. You have no right to stick your nose into it, Son."

"But you confront Grandpa when he gets overbearing and says things to Mom you don't like."

"That's different," Dr. Hanson claimed.

"How?"

"Because she's my wife."

"But Dad…"

Insistent and firm, Mark Hanson said, "You are not married to this woman, Randy."

His father had a valid point.

"Trying to get involved in a situation between Jane and her father will lead to problems. If you confront him, several things could happen. First, you will seriously jeopardize the rapport you have established with him. More importantly, you could potentially harm the relationship Jane has with her father. What do you think her reaction will be when she knows you confronted her father about this?"

After careful consideration, he said, "She'll probably get upset with me."

"Which could seriously harm your relationship with her. Do you really want to take that risk?"

"So I just sit here and do nothing?" Randy griped, not so sure he liked that idea.

"If Jane has a problem with her father, she is the one who has to deal with it. Not you," his father advised.

"But I can't stand to watch that."

"You don't have a choice, Son. You and Jane are in the very early stages of your relationship. It is not your right at this point to get involved in personal family conflicts."

Although he didn't like it, Randy knew his dad was right.

"I'm sorry, Randy. I know that's not the answer you were hoping for." He folded up his newspaper and neatly placed on the corner of the table. "You feel like grabbing some lattes and doughnuts before the family shows up?"

"Sure." Randy grinned. "Let me shower first."

"Take your time."

The day after Thanksgiving, Randy had to catch a 2:00 P.M. flight back to San Francisco. He traipsed into the living room with his luggage when he heard some commotion coming from the kitchen. He wandered that direction to see what was going on. Robby was throwing a fit about something while his dad fought to maintain a normal tone without losing his temper.

"That is not fair!" Robby hollered across the room.

"When you learn to care more about your grades, I'll care more about your social life," Dr. Hanson scolded. "These grades are unacceptable."

"I'm doing the best I can."

"I highly doubt that. If you would spend more time doing homework and less time working on your car or playing video games then your grades would be better. You will never get into college with grades like this."

"You can't control my life!"

"You're grounded until the grades improve."

"You're grounding me until report cards come out?"

"Yes," Dr. Hanson stated firmly. "This is not a debate, Son. Do something about these grades."

"That is not fair! You can't ground me for a whole month."

"You heard me, Robert. Give me your car keys." Dr. Hanson held out his hand expecting his son to hand over the keys.

"Fuck!"

"Do not use that language in this house, young man! I will not have it!" Dr. Hanson demanded, angry at his youngest son's belligerent disrespect. "Keys, now!"

Robby threw his keys at his father and stormed into his bedroom, slamming the door.

Shocked by this outburst, Randy stared at his dad in disbelief.

The man didn't make a sound. He simply picked up his cellphone, pager, and stethoscope and left the house.

The silence in the room was deafening. They could have heard a pin drop. Wanting an explanation, Randy turned to his mother. "What was that all about?"

"Robert and your father butting heads again."

"Again?" he questioned. "Does this happen a lot?"

"Unfortunately with your brother, yes, more often than it should. This year has been hard on Robby. He's neglecting school and has been belligerent, especially toward your father. And you know how your dad is; he has little tolerance for irresponsibility and disrespect, and your brother seems to be full of both lately."

Randy looked over at his brother's door, concerned about the outburst he had witnessed. "What's going on with him?"

"I wish I knew."

"Let me try talking to him." He roamed down the hall to his brother's room and knocked on the door.

"Go away!" Robby yelled through the door.

"Rob, it's me," Randy said. "Can I come in?"

"I don't give a shit what you do."

Randy opened the door and sat on the bed with his brother, who was lying on his back hugging his pillow. "What's going on, Rob?"

"I hate him," Robby blurted out harshly.

"You don't mean that."

Robby rolled over. He didn't feel like talking. "Don't tell me what I do and don't mean."

"You're just angry."

"What the fuck do you know?"

"I know Dad cares about you," Randy declared.

"Bullshit."

Randy tried to reason with his brother. "I know what it's like to have teenage hopes and dreams. I was there once, remember? I got in trouble sometimes and got caught doing things I wasn't supposed to do; it's part of growing up. But you need to step back and try to see this from Dad's point of view."

"His point of view sucks."

"No it doesn't," Randy countered. "It's just different from yours. He only wants what's best for you."

"He wants to tell me how to live my life and never lets me do anything," Robby complained.

"I find that hard to believe."

"He doesn't listen to anything I say. I don't want to go to college. I want to get a job and save some money so I can open up my own mechanics shop."

"That's a cool ambition. Did you ever tell Dad?"

"Fuck no. He wouldn't go for that. I told you he doesn't listen," Robby grumbled.

"Actually, Rob, Dad is a very good listener. I'm sure he would understand why you don't want to go to college if you gave him a reason and told him what you wanted to do."

"He won't listen."

"Have you tried?"

"No."

Robby was being stubborn. Randy pushed right back. "You need to sit down and carry on a conversation with him

171

without getting angry or defensive. Try to see things from his point of view."

"There's no point. He won't listen."

Randy remained persisted, "In my experience with Dad, I learned that if you give him legitimate reasons and act civilized, he's very understanding and supportive. But he can't read your mind, and he's not going to respond well if you're constantly combating him."

"He doesn't care about me."

"He does to," Randy said. "He might not always agree with you, but he does care about you. And I care about you. You're a good kid, Robby, and you can accomplish great things. But fighting Dad is not the way to go about it. Talk to him and let him help you. He wants to help you."

Robby just sat there staring at the wall.

Randy checked the time on his watch. It was almost 11:30. "You want to grab some burgers before I go to the airport?"

Robby lifted a shoulder. "I don't know."

"It's not every day I get to hang out with my brother. Come have lunch with me." He borrowed the keys to his dad's truck and drove to the nearest burger joint to get lunch.

Chapter Fourteen

Randy landed in San Francisco around 4:20 that afternoon. Although he loved going home to see his family, he was glad to be back. He anxiously stepped off the plane, knowing Jane's pretty face and loving arms would be at the terminal waiting for him. He beamed when he saw her.

She threw her arms around him and hugged him tightly, squeezing the air right out of him. "I missed you," she said.

"I missed you too." He held her close, giving her the deepest, most yearning kiss. Releasing his grasp on her, he eyed her from head to toe. "You look fantastic."

Once they arrived at his apartment, they barely made it through the front door before fervent desire took over. Randy immediately took Jane into his arms and interlocked his mouth to hers. A trail of clothing followed them from the front door, through the living room, and to the bed. Randy didn't even take the time to put on a condom. He knew Jane was diligently taking her pills and was confident that neither one of them had been sleeping around, so he didn't think twice about it. Bare skin on skin contact was something he never experienced before. As he penetrated her, every sensation was multiplied. It was much better than having a latex barrier between them. He had a feeling that his condom supply wasn't going to be used much after this. But that was fine with him. He hated wearing them anyway.

173

They rolled all over the bed, knocking the clock off the bedside table as they tumbled onto the floor. "Ssh," Randy said, placing his index finger over her lips. "I have neighbors you know."

They laughed together and continued their lovemaking down on the floor, which was now turning into more play than passion. Jane crawled toward the door, playfully trying to escape. She didn't get far before Randy grabbed her by the ankle and pulled her back. "Where do you think you're going?" he asked. "Get back here."

The moment their playful exploit was over, they both sprawled out on the floor, naked and completely out of breath.

"I'm hungry," Jane stated between breaths.

Her sudden random comment made Randy chuckle. "I'm not surprised." He rolled over and gave her a kiss. "Let's shower then go snag some food."

Radio on, they drove around San Francisco with the top down on the Camaro in search of a good Chinese restaurant. Afterwards, they stopped at Ghirardelli Square to pick up some chocolate for Jane then cruised around the city for a while enjoying the mild evening air. Close to sunset, they crossed the bay bridge back into Berkeley. Randy pulled over to the shoulder along Grizzly Peak Boulevard in the Berkeley Hills, where he and Jane perched on the hood waiting for the show to begin. Slowly the sun descended beyond the San Francisco skyline. It was a spectacular sight, surpassed only by the gradual glow as the city lights came up.

When the sight reached its magnificent zenith, Jane said, "That is beautiful."

"Isn't it?" He held her in his arms and kissed her. "I have another place I want to show you." Taking her hand, he escorted her back to the car and drove down to Lake Anza. They held hands as they walked along the water's edge.

"I can't believe I've lived here my whole life and never noticed how beautiful this city is," Jane admitted.

"It's one of the prettier cities I've been to."

"You've traveled a lot?" she asked.

"Not a lot. I've been places though. When we were growing up, Dad made sure that every summer we saw new things—new cities, new cultures, new scenery. He believed in expanding our horizons."

She tucked her hair behind her ear. "Not Daddy. Rarely did we leave San Francisco or go outside Silicon Valley. I saw more of the country playing basketball than I ever did growing up."

"Well," he gave her a kiss. "We will have to get you out to see some culture then. There's a lot of life out there beyond San Francisco." While Randy was in Seattle for Thanksgiving, he purchased something for Jane based solely on some information she had inadvertently given him. He reached into his jacket pocket and pulled out a red velvet jewelry case. "I got something for you."

She took the box from him. "What is it?"

"Why don't you open it and find out?" he teased.

She opened the box to reveal a blue sapphire pendant on a solid gold chain. Gasping, she said, "Oh my god, Randy, this is beautiful."

"You mentioned to me once that you have never owned any real gems or diamonds. Since your favorite color is blue, I though a sapphire was appropriate."

"This is real?" she responded in awe.

"Of course it's real. It doesn't seem right that a beautiful woman has never possessed precious gemstones." He took the necklace out of the box and clasped it around her neck, moving her hair back to reveal the pendant. "Stunning."

She bit her bottom lip. "I can't believe you did this. You are full of surprises, aren't you?"

"I told you, I aim to please."

"Well, Mr. Hanson, you certainly do."

Looking into her tantalizing eyes left him breathless. Never in his life had he found himself lost in a woman's eyes or found total contentment in her arms or complete joy in her smile. Every time she smiled at him, he felt like a king. "How did I get lucky enough to find you?"

"Randy," she blushed.

"I mean it. You are the most incredible woman I have ever met. You have done something to my heart that no other woman has ever been capable of doing. And believe me, they've tried. You have a way of making me laugh when I am in the worst mood, and you cheer me on when I feel discouraged. You're not demanding of my time, and even though I'm constantly studying or doing something for school, here you are, standing right by my side offering support, love, and a friendship that I've never experienced before. I'm so thankful for you."

She leaned forward and rested her head on his shoulder. "Randy, no one has ever treated me the way you do. You consider my feelings, always respect me, and put my needs first. You're such a caring, loving man."

Seeing her happy meant more to him than anything else in the world, and he would do whatever it took to keep her happy. "I love you, Jane."

She peered up at him. "I love you too."

They found themselves lost in each other's arms as they meshed together in a passionate kiss. He felt so lucky to have found this amazing woman and was determined to hang onto her. He held her tighter in his arms, never wanting to let her go.

The following evening, Randy wanted Jane to choose were they had dinner. She directed him to a bright and airy spot in the fashionable part of Berkeley. This was a place Randy had never been to before. Lots of impeccably fresh seafood was served in a surrounding of cathedral ceilings, sharp lines of brick and tile, and shades of scrubbed seawater blue. The ambience was cozy, the seafood selection and quality wine list were superb, and the restaurant had very attentive service. Randy was impressed.

"This place is nice, Baby," he said as he looked around. "There are some incredible seafood places in Seattle you would enjoy. I'll have to take you to one when you come up during Christmas break."

"I told Daddy about that."

"And what did he say?" Randy figured this was going to bad, considering Dale Davine tried to control Jane's life and was probably not happy with the idea of his daughter flying out of the state to meet her boyfriend's family, especially without him around to chaperone.

"He doesn't understand why I can't stay in San Francisco for New Year's."

Randy wondered how Jane responded to her overprotective, domineering father. "What did you tell him?"

"I explained to him how it wasn't fair that he had the opportunity to meet you, but your family had yet to meet me. Then I told him I was going, and it didn't matter if he didn't like it."

She actually stood up to him? That was a first. "You said that to him?"

"Yes I did."

"Really? That surprises me."

"Why?" she asked.

"Because I never expected you to stand up to your father. He wasn't mad?"

"Yes," Jane admitted. "But he doesn't have a choice. He assumed I was going to ask him for money to get an airline ticket, but I told him you already got one for me."

Still in shock over the fact that Jane stood up to her father, Randy questioned, "You really said that to him?"

"Yes. Do you know what else Daddy said to me while you were gone?"

Randy was afraid to ask. "What?"

"He wanted to know why I was driving around in your sports car, and told me it wasn't safe to do that."

"Why would he think that? He likes sports cars."

"I know, but he told me he didn't want me driving one."

"That doesn't make any sense."

"He also said that the sorority isn't good for me, and he wants me to move back in with him."

Randy laughed out loud at that preposterous request. "You didn't agree to that I hope."

"Are you crazy? No way."

He breathed a sigh of relief. "Good."

"He thinks you're a bad influence on me."

"What did I do that makes me a bad influence?" Randy thought he was a pretty good guy, although he could think of many reasons why Dale Davine would not want Jane around him. His sarcastic attitude, his smartass remarks, the fact that they were sharing a bed...

"That's what I asked him," she explained. "He seems to think that since I've been with you, I've had a bad attitude."

He couldn't wait to hear what Dale Davine had to say about this. "How does he figure that?"

"His argument was that I have never talked to him in such an argumentative tone, nor have I ever told him no or openly disagreed with him before I met you. He thinks I've become some kind of wild, radical, rebellious hippie or something. "

Randy almost rolled out of his chair. "Are you serious?"

"That's what he said."

"I have never seen you conform to conservatisms. The only time I ever see you do that is when you're around your dad."

"Yes, but Daddy doesn't know that."

"So he's blaming your independence on me?" he assumed.

"He thinks you've influenced my decisions somehow."

"That's ludicrous. Your father doesn't know anything about you. If he knew about half the things you did, he would flip his lid. What you choose to do has nothing to do with me."

"I know that, and you know that. But Daddy doesn't see it that way."

"I'm sorry, Jane, but your dad needs to get his head out of the clouds and come back to Earth. I still can't believe you said that to him."

"Are you proud of me?" she grinned smugly.

"Yes, actually, I am," he said. "Now when are you going to show him how you really dress and quit wearing conservative attire every time you're around him?"

"Oh god, Randy. My dad would have a heart attack if he saw me dressed like this."

"I bet he's never seen you in a bikini either, has he?" Randy asked.

"Hell no."

Randy snickered at her father's naivety. "I still can't believe that he really thought you were a twenty-one-year-old virgin. He can't really be that oblivious to reality can he?"

"He's only oblivious to me," Jane clarified.

"And that's my point, Babe," Randy said. "You can't go around deceiving him forever."

"He's pissed off enough right now. I think I went too far when I told him that I was going to Seattle whether he liked it or not."

"That might have been a bit harsh, but I'm glad you're taking the initiative to speak up for yourself and not letting him push you around."

She smiled proudly. "Thank you."

"You wear a size six, right?"

Questioning the randomness of this statement, she asked, "Why do you want to know?"

"It's a little too close to Christmas for you to be asking snoopy questions, Missy. Do you wear a size six?"

"Yes."

"Ok. That's all I wanted to know."

She wondered what he was up to. And Christmas? She almost forgot about that. What in the world was she going to get Randy for Christmas? She would seriously have to think about that for a while.

Chapter Fifteen

On Sunday morning, Randy didn't feel like getting up and going to his study session. He wished he could stay in bed with Jane all day, but knew he had to get motivated. He had enjoyed his relaxing time off and hadn't opened a medical book in the last four days. But alas, he had to get into the swing of school again and get his mind back on track.

Before joining the others at the table, he stopped and got a cup of coffee. Fifteen minutes passed and their scheduled meeting time had long since gone by. However, Jim hadn't shown up yet. Randy was getting worried, wondering where he was. He set his coffee down and addressed the group. "Have any of you heard from Jim at all?"

"No," Bruce said. "I figured he would have called you."

"Well, he didn't. Did he say he'd be here?"

"He didn't say he wouldn't," Bruce replied.

Randy picked up his phone and dialed Jim's number. When Jim answered, Randy asked, "Hey, man. Where are you?"

"Dude, I'm sorry. I'm on my way," Jim stated. "Give me ten minutes."

"Hurry up. We're all waiting for you." Jim seemed frazzled and stressed out. Randy hoped everything was alright.

After the session, Randy pulled Jim aside to see how he was doing. "How come you were late this morning?"

"Fuckin' Trina," Jim growled. "She went out last night with my car and didn't get in until 8:30 this morning."

"What the hell was she doing all night?"

"I don't know. But this isn't the first time she's done this."

"How long has this been going on?"

"About a month now. She takes off and disappears for several hours."

This was cause for concern. "Where does she go?"

"She doesn't tell me, and she gets pissy if I ask."

"Why would she go out all night and not come home until 8:30 in the morning?"

Jim gave his explanation, "Just to prove a point. I told you, she gets snarky with me because I'm studyin' all night and not payin' attention to her. She goes out just to spite me. It's aggravating as hell."

Randy thought there was more to it than that. "Don't get pissed at me, but when's the last time you two had sex?"

"What the fuck difference does that make?"

"I'm serious, man. How long has it been?"

Jim was getting defensive. "Randy, she's pregnant."

"So? Is there some rule that says you can't have sex with her because she's pregnant?" Randy argued. "How long has it been?"

"Why the hell do you care?"

"Because your girlfriend goes out all night but won't tell you where she is. It's been awhile, hasn't it?"

"Yeah, so?"

"How long?" Randy insisted.

"I don't know, over a month. She never wants to. She says she doesn't feel well."

Randy pondered this for a moment. "That's what I was afraid of."

"What the hell are you talkin' about?"

Dreading where this conversation was going, Randy hesitated. "Look, I'm not trying to stir up trouble, but I'm concerned about you. You said she's been acting like this for about a month now, the same amount of time you two have gone without sex. She takes off without notice, doesn't tell you where she's going, and disappears all night. Have you ever seen her sneak off to another room when her cellphone goes off?"

Jim didn't see the significance of that. "Sometimes. Why?"

"Does she tell you who she's talking to?"

"No. She tells me it's none of my business."

Randy suspected Trina was cheating. That's the only thing that seemed to fit into this picture. "This sounds suspicious to me, Jim. Something is going on."

Jim thought about what Randy was saying, and it made sense. Trina's behavior was indeed unusual. Aside from the sneaking away at night and not telling him where she was going, or running into another room to talk every time her cellphone rang, Trina had also been distant with him recently. This behavior was typical of a woman who was having an affair. Crushed and in total shock, he collapsed in the chair. He couldn't breathe. "That little bitch. She is fuckin' cheatin' on me."

"Calm down. We don't know that," Randy offered, trying to get Jim to think rationally.

The more Jim thought about this, the angrier he became. "If this was happening before…" He was about to have a nervous breakdown. "You know, this kid might not be mine. She fuckin' cheats on me, gets pregnant, then tries to make me responsible. This is so fucked up," he bellowed.

"Jim, calm down. We don't know anything for sure. You have no proof."

"I don't need fuckin' proof. It makes perfect sense— the late nights, the secretiveness, the mysterious phone calls she keeps gettin'."

Wishing now that he hadn't said anything, Randy declared, "You should at least ask her about it before you jump to conclusions."

"Oh, I can't wait to hear the explanation she'll give for this crap."

Randy took a deep breath, feeling for his friend and wishing there was something he could say. "I'm sorry, man."

"You're sorry? All hell is about to break loose at my house because of that cheating bitch. Things are gonna get hellaciously bleak." He stared at Randy, saddened and shaken.

Placing his hand on Jim's shoulder, Randy said, "I'll be here if you need me."

Jim left the study session angry and headed home to face Trina. When he walked into his apartment, she was sitting on the couch talking on her cellphone. He dropped his bag on the floor and pierced through her with his eyes. "Where were you last night?"

"I'll call you back," she said to the person on the other line. Then she hung up her phone and glared at Jim with a snobbish sneer. "I told you I went out."

Trying to remain calm, he tried again. "I will ask you this one more time. Where were you last night?"

"Why do you care?" she snorted callously.

His patience was gone. "Goddammit, Trina, stop fuckin' around and playin' this stupid game. I'm sick of it. Who the hell is he?"

She gasped, shocked that he would accuse her of such a thing. "What are you talking about?"

"Don't fuck with me. I know you've been sneakin' off to see someone." He glanced over at her cellphone. "Is that who you were talkin' to when I walked in?"

"That's ridiculous," she denied.

"Then tell me where you were last night."

She ignored him.

"Dammit, after eight years you owe me an explanation."

"I don't owe you shit," she snapped. "If anyone owes anybody anything you owe me for putting up with your medical school horseshit and for giving up my life so you could chase after your stupid dream of becoming a doctor."

Jim took a step back and almost sank to the floor. She squashed him down to a miniscule dust particle with that

183

lowly comment. "Stupid dream? That's what you think this is? A stupid dream? That's harsh, Trina."

"You don't really think you'll make it through this, do you?" she asked, breaking him down even more.

"What the hell is that supposed to mean?"

"Come on, Jimmy, you and I both know that you don't have what it takes to finish medical school and become a doctor. You're a California boy. People like you aren't cut out to be doctors. People like you own surf shops and wear shark tooth necklaces, not scrubs and stethoscopes."

How dare she say that to him? Glaring at the cruelty she possessed, he snarled, "What a fucked up thing to say to me. I have sacrificed everything to pursue this dream. Medicine is my life and the only thing I ever gave a damn about. You've known all along this is what I wanted."

"What about what I wanted? Did you ever stop to think that you pursuing this ridiculous dream of yours was fucking up my life?"

"Well, I'm so sorry to have cramped your style." He looked her dead in the eye. "Where the hell were you last night?"

"It's none of your business."

"The hell it's not. Goddammit!" He wanted to back slap the bitch, but somehow managed to restrain himself. Gritting his teeth, he asked again, "Tell me where you were last night."

She refused to answer.

Jim reached for her cellphone, hoping to find out who she had been talking to. But before he was able to grab it, she snatched the phone away from him. In retaliation, he snapped, "What are you hiding, Trina? Who the hell is he? And where the fuck were you last night?"

"You want to know where I was? Fine." She stood up, slipped her phone into her pocket, and walked toward the kitchen, turning her back to him. "If it will shut you up and get you off my back, I'll tell you." Knowing she had been caught, she no longer tried to hide it. "I went to San Jose and met a man named Aaron Starletto."

Breathing a bit heavier, his heart plummet into his stomach. "Who is he?"

She didn't answer.

"Dammit Trina, tell me the truth for once in your life."

She began to panic. "Jim."

"Answer the damn question!" He raised his voice at her, something he rarely did. "Is this the same man you've been sneakin' out of the room to talk to on the phone? The one you text all the time? The same one you've been supposedly havin' lunch with every goddamn day?"

Ashamed and embarrassed, she simply nodded. "He and I have been talking, but it wasn't…"

He didn't let her finish. "Son-of-a-bitch. How the hell long has this been goin' on?"

Trina stared at him with tears in her eyes.

Jim could not remember a time in his life when he felt as betrayed as he did at this moment. He was absolutely seething. "Have you shared a bed with this man?"

She refused to respond.

He remained persistent, "Is that what you were doing last night? Tell me the truth, Trina."

"I met him at a hotel," she finally admitted. "I wasn't planning on spending the whole night with him."

Holy shit! Randy was right. Jim glared at her and tightened his lips, trying not to lose control. "You knew damn well what was going to happen when you got there, you little bitch. Don't put on this bullshit innocent act with me."

Desperately trying to justify her actions, she said, "Things got out of hand. I never intended for it to go that far."

"And you think that justifies it and makes it ok? You've been fucking another man, Katrina!"

"Jim, please." She walked toward him.

He backed away from her. "Get away from me."

"Jimmy."

With his hand clenched in a fist, trying to suppress his anger, he said, "Don't call me that. You have lost your right to call me that." He flopped onto the couch and held his head in his hands. "Eight fuckin' years, Trina. How could you do this?"

"I'm sorry."

The look he shot her was chilling. "Oh really? Were you sorry when he had his hands all over you? Were you sorry when you let him stick his dick inside you? I bet you weren't sorry then." Jim fought hard to hold back his emotions. He felt like someone had ripped his heart out of his chest, stomped on it for a while, then buried it in a deep, dark hole in the middle of the frozen Siberian wasteland.

Trina tried to put her hand on him.

He jerked away from her. "Don't touch me. Stay away from me."

Tears flowed from her eyes. "I was lonely."

"Bullshit."

"I needed someone."

"Shut up!" Enraged by her actions, he covered his ears with his hands so he didn't have to listen to her. "I refuse to sit here and take this abuse from you." He glanced up at her with pain in his eyes, desperate and pleading. "Just tell me one thing, and tell me the fuckin' truth. Is that my child you're carrying?"

"How can you ask me that? Of course it is."

He didn't believe a damn word she said. "What were you plannin' on doin'? Lead me to believe I fathered a child so you could collect child support off my doctor's income for the rest of your life? Was that your plan? Because that is cold, Trina."

"The baby is yours. I swear."

"How do I know you didn't fuck some other guy to get yourself pregnant? You let this Aaron guy stick it in you. How many other guys have you been puttin' out for?"

She sobbed uncontrollably.

Jim held his head in his hands. He had never felt this much pain in his life. Wanting to get as far away from her as possible, he stood up and tore a suitcase from the hall closet.

"What are you doing?" she asked teary-eyed.

"What I do and where I go is no longer your concern." He pulled clothes off hangers and began packing his belongings.

"Jimmy," she pleaded.

"Don't fuckin' call me that ever again. And don't talk to me. I have nothin' more to say to you. When this baby is born, I want a DNA test. I want proof that this child is indeed mine. Until that happens, don't call me, don't talk to me, don't come near me. Stay the hell away."

"Where are you going?"

Giving her a taste of her own medicine, he coldly replied, "What do you care?"

After his bags were packed, he looked at her, heartbroken. "I cannot believe you did this. I will never trust you. I will never believe a word you say ever again. If this child, by some miracle, does happen to be mine, you can be damn sure that I will have my rights. If you ever try to keep me from that, fire and brimstone will rain down on you, Katrina Rogers. Attorneys will pound down your door night and day and your life will become a living hell." He exited the apartment and walked away.

She tried to stop him, but he refused look back. He drove away, taking with him two suitcases, a box of medical books, a bag of medical supplies, a shoebox full of his favorite CD's, and his book bag for school.

When Randy answered his door and saw Jim standing on his porch with a suitcase in his hand, he knew right away what that meant. "Oh Jesus, Jim. I'm sorry."

"Can I crash here tonight?" he asked his best friend.

"Of course." Randy opened the door, inviting him inside.

Jim stepped into the living room and set his bag on the floor. "You were right. That pretentious little bitch has been fucking another man. Maybe more than one. I don't know." He plopped onto the couch and buried his face in his hands, shaking his head in disbelief. And for the first time ever, Randy witnessed his best friend break down and cry.

Randy had no idea what to say. He felt the horrendous sadness Jim possessed but couldn't even begin to comprehend the heartache he must have felt.

"I cannot believe this is happening," Jim wailed. "I wasted eight years of my life with that woman. Eight years, Randy."

The pain Jim felt was tearing at Randy's heart. His best friend was miserable, and there was nothing he could do about it.

"This is a nightmare. She cheated on me, she's pregnant, and this baby might not be mine. She led me to believe it was and I fell for it. Son-of-a-bitch. Who knows how many men have had their hands all over her. And she let them dick her, Randy. That cheating little…" He stopped to catch his breath. "There's like this gash in my heart, man." He sat in silent, sad contemplation as tears streamed down his face.

"You know you're welcome to stay here as long as you need to."

"Thank you, Randy. You're a good friend."

Randy helped Jim unload the rest of his things then he grabbed his cellphone and stepped onto the porch to call Jane and tell her what was going on. When he came back inside, Jim was moving his belongings into the spare bedroom. Randy helped him.

While Jim unpacked, he tried to vent some anger and dejection. "You know, if she would've told me she needed space, I would've been cool with that, but this is unforgivable." Jim sat on the edge of the bed reflecting on this situation, trying to make sense of it all. "I should've ended it when we graduated from high school. Then I could've been rid of her and moved on with my life. But no, I had to be stupid and fall for her shit. I should've…" He couldn't continue. The pain and defeat he felt was breaking him apart. As hard as he tried to fight them, the tears returned.

Randy hugged his friend, trying to get him to calm down. "You can't change the past, Jim."

"I know that. But I wasted eight years of my life tryin' to make her happy, and look how far it got me. I have absolutely nothing to show for it."

Randy didn't like the way Jim was tearing himself down over Katrina. "Don't dwell on it. You did what you felt you had to do. It's her loss, not yours."

Once Jim was unpacked, he and Randy watched a basketball game together, which uplifted Jim's spirits quite a bit. He finally composed himself and was able to relax. As he readjusted pillows on the couch and fluffed a few of them to get more comfortable, he developed a strange look on his face. On the end of his finger, he held up a black lacy bra. He cleared his throat and passed it Randy's direction.

Randy reached over and took it from him. "Sorry. Wonder how that got there?"

Jim knew damn well how it got there. "Uh huh. And what else will I find around here?"

"Oh, I probably should have told you that."

"Told me what?"

"Jane has a key."

Randy never mentioned this before. "Are you two livin' together?"

"No. But she does come and go."

"I'm not imposing on you, am I? Because I don't wanna get in the way of whatever arrangement you and Jane have."

"Don't worry about it," Randy said. "Just don't be surprised if you wake up in the morning and she's in the shower."

"So she does stay here a lot," Jim deduced.

"A few nights a week." Randy stood up and took the bra into the bedroom.

Chapter Sixteen

Tuesday, after a two hour lecture about diseases of the red blood cells, the medical students were told they would be working in assigned small groups using data from blood smears, iron tests, hemoglobin electrophoresis, bone marrow biopsies, and reticulocyte counts to determine different types of red blood cell diseases. Randy thought this experience sounded intriguing and eagerly arrived to his small group session feeling confident.

The coordinator, who was also one of Randy's medical professors, read off names for pre-assigned groups. Randy stood at the back of the room with Jim and the others anxiously awaiting his assignment.

"Gonzales, Hall, Hanson, Jefferies."

Randy hoped he heard wrong. "Jim, did Dr. Drenner say Hanson and Hall in the same group?"

Confirming Randy's concern, Jim replied, "It sounded that way."

That's what he was afraid of. "Shit."

Randy did not like this group assignment at all. He had managed to avoid Steve for the most part, since his study group gave him the boot, and he was not looking forward to another encounter with him. After all assignments were handed out and groups were assembled, Randy reluctantly walked over to his lab table. Steve stared at him indignantly. Randy tried to ignore him.

Dr. Drenner gave the groups time to look over information and discuss results before she circulated around the room asking individual groups questions about their analysis of the data. When she came to Randy's group, he felt confident and was ready for any challenge she would throw their way. She examined the data his group had and asked, "Based on this information, what is this group's diagnosis?" With a clipboard in her hand, she directed the question at Steve. "Mr. Hall?"

Of everyone in this group, Steve was the worst possible person she could have asked. Randy knew he didn't know the answer. He hoped this was not a group grade or they would all be screwed.

"Mr. Hall? Do you have a diagnosis for your group?" the professor repeated.

When Steve didn't answer, Randy tried to respond to save him and his group from utter humiliation. "Dr. Drenner, with the destruction of the RBC's…"

The doctor glared at Randy angrily. "Mr. Hanson. I was not asking you this question. I was asking Mr. Hall. One day he will be examining a real live patient and will be expected to produce a diagnosis, and you won't be there to give him the answers, will you?"

Randy clenched his jaw. "No, Doctor."

"Your colleague is trying to think," she insisted. "Let Mr. Hall give his analysis."

"Yes, Ma'am." He decided it was best to shut up.

Dr. Drenner questioned Steve again. "Mr. Hall? Diagnosis."

The expression on Steve's face was mortifying. It was obvious that he didn't know the answer. And to make matters worse, every second year medical student at UC Berkeley was watching this scene. This was horribly embarrassing. As much as Randy hated Steve, he felt for him in this situation.

"I don't have a diagnosis," Steve responded.

"And why is that?" Dr. Drenner insisted.

In a quiet whisper, hoping no one would hear him, Steve admitted, "I did not read that chapter last night."

She found this completely unacceptable. "Mr. Hall. If this were a real patient in a real life and death situation do you really think the family of this person would accept that answer?"

"No, Doctor, they would not."

"The life of this patient is in your hands. The patient and family members are relying on you to give a diagnosis and find a treatment. And that is the best answer you can give them?"

Steve froze, unable to speak.

"I am very disappointed, Mr. Hall." Dr. Drenner addressed the entire group. "Is there anyone in this group who does have a diagnosis?"

To put an end to this horrific experience, Randy spoke up. "By the destruction of the RBC's, this is hemolytic in nature. Based on the data from the ferritin test, iron is deposited in the skin and vital organs resulting in hemochromatosis. DNA analysis indicates a mutation in the HBB gene, and since hemoglobin levels are low, splenomegaly has occurred. Symptoms of fatigue, weakness, and mild jaundice are present, thus we can conclusively say that this patient has Thalassemia."

Dr. Drenner lowered her clipboard. "That's correct. Very good, Mr. Hanson." Her attention returned to Steve, putting him on the spot. "Mr. Hall, patients and families do not accept excuses and neither do I. Do I make myself clear?"

"Yes, Doctor." Steve dropped his shoulders and slumped down in his chair.

"Groups are dismissed," Dr. Drenner announced. "Mr. Hall, come see me in my office, please."

When the session released, Randy rushed out the door. He couldn't wait to get out of that room. He stood outside the lab with his hand on his head as Jim, Bruce, Sarah, and Mandy gathered around him. "Did you guys see that?" he said. "Holy shit."

"Poor Steve," Sarah added.

"Is she allowed to do that?" Bruce asked. "There has to be some sort of professional or ethical breech involved here."

"I don't know," Randy answered. "But that was the worst experience of my life."

About ten minutes later, Steve walked right past them. The conversation instantly ceased and all eyes followed him. He drug himself to the opposite end of the hallway, dropped his bag on the floor, and sat on the stairs hanging his head.

"Is he alright?" Mandy asked, concerned about him.

"I don't know, but I'm gonna go find out." Jim started to walk down the hall.

Randy gripped Jim's arm and pulled him back. "No, Jim. I'll do it."

"Are you sure? I thought you hated him?"

"I'll go." Randy knew he needed to say something since he was the one who was directly involved with the incident in the lab, but he really didn't know what he was going to say. Hesitantly, he headed Steve's direction. When he got to the stairs, he said, "Hey."

Steve continued to stare at the floor. "If you came over here to rub this in my face or give me some kind of fucking lecture then get the hell away from me."

Randy sat next to him. "That's not why I came over here."

"Then why did you?"

"Look, Steve," he said in a thick voice. "What happened in there…no one deserves that. That was not fair."

"Like you care."

"I do care," Randy remarked. "That wasn't right."

"That's easy for you to say. You're the one who saved the group's ass."

Randy wasn't sure how to respond to that.

After a long, awkward silence, Steve ranted, "People like you have all the answers, don't you?"

"People like me?"

"Yes. People like you. Medicine is in your blood, it's imbedded in you. People like you make the rest of us look bad. You know all the answers, make all the right connections, grasp the concepts so quickly. You're the ideal medical student. I wish I had the capability of doing this as easily as you do, but I don't." Steve gathered his thoughts for a minute before he continued. "There are good, dedicated people out there who would give anything to be where I am. People who try to get into med school but can't. People who really want to be doctors more than anything else in the world. People with more heart for this than I have. People who care."

"If you didn't care you wouldn't be here," Randy replied, trying to console him.

Steve looked Randy dead in the eye. "You're right. I shouldn't be here."

Defending his words that Steve somehow twisted, Randy replied, "I did not say that."

"You don't have to." Feeling defeated, Steve stated, "I know that your opinion of me is one of incompetence. But you won't have to worry about me anymore. I'm done."

"What do you mean you're done?" Randy asked.

"Dr. Drenner is right. I don't belong here. I'm not dedicated, don't care about it enough. My heart," he swallowed hard, "is not in this." Steve stood up and grabbed his bag. "I'm out."

"You can't quit," Randy begged.

"I wasn't meant for this." He trudged down the hall, impassive and despondent.

Knowing that no words would be the right words at this moment, Randy called out, "For whatever it's worth, I'm sorry."

Steve didn't say another word. He simply walked out of the Medical Sciences building without looking back.

Steve didn't show up for any lectures, labs, review sessions, or classes for the remainder of the week. Friday,

Jim found out from several sources that Steve's name had been removed from the medical school roster. On the way home from class, he told Randy. His reaction was not what Jim expected.

"What?" Randy asked in shock. "He said he was done, but I didn't think he was serious."

"People are sayin' it's all because of what happened in lab the other day."

"He quit over that?"

"Rumor has it he didn't quit voluntarily. He was invited to leave."

"They kicked him out?"

Jim explained the situation. "After his meeting with Dr. Drenner, Steve met with Dr. Boyce and the whole panel of muck-e-mucks. Shortly afterwards, he went down to the registrar's office and withdrew."

"That's bullshit."

Jim thought Randy would be happy to have Steve Hall out of his hair, but instead, his friend seemed more upset about this incident. "I'm surprised you are so concerned about this."

"It sucks that someone put a year and a half into med school and they throw him out like that."

"It wasn't a sudden thing," Jim reminded him. "He's been on the verge of expulsion for a while. Once you've been red flagged and placed on probation, they don't fuck around. You know that."

"What happened to him? When we started this, he had his shit together. He really wanted to be a doctor."

"Maybe the pressure got to be too much."

Randy felt a sudden surge of guilt. "Damn, this is all my fault."

Jim didn't see how he reasoned to that conclusion. "How the hell do you figure that?"

"Because I knew he was a pain in the ass, and I threw a fit about it, forcing him out of the group. He wasn't able to get the help he needed, which caused his grades to drop to the point where he failed. They kicked him out of med school because of me."

Jim scoffed at Randy's irrational reasoning. "That's far fetchin'. Honestly, I don't think anything we could have done would have helped him much. He would have wiped out regardless, and all of us would have gone postal in the process. Don't even think you had anything to do with this, Dude. Steve brought this on himself."

Randy pulled his keys out of his pocket to unlock his apartment. "I guess you're right. It still doesn't seem fair." He dropped his book bag on the floor and placed his keys on the table. "By the way, Jane and I are going out tonight. You'll have the apartment to yourself for a while."

"Like I ever do anything. It'll be chill time for me." In a teasing tone, Jim remarked, "You are aware that there's a box of tampons in your bathroom, aren't you?"

With a sheepish grin, Randy replied, "Yeah."

"And there's Diet Pepsi and yogurt in your fridge. You detest yogurt. And since when do you drink Diet Pepsi?"

Randy sniggered, "It's not for me. It's Jane's."

Jim wrinkled his forehead. "This relationship of yours is pretty serious, isn't it?"

"Semi-serious."

"Bullshit. She has a key to your apartment and stays over here almost every night. You have food for her in your refrigerator, extra clothes, female products, makeup, a toothbrush…semi-serious my ass."

"Ok," Randy admitted with a smile. "You're right. We are getting pretty serious."

"I am totally infringing on your love shack stayin' here. Over Christmas break, while you're in Seattle, I'm gonna look for my own pad and leave you two alone."

"It's ok, Jim, really."

"Nah, I need to get my own place anyway. I'm gonna look for a job this weekend too. Try to get my life back together."

"Oh, that reminds me," Randy stated. "Carlos Gonzales told me that UCSF Medical Center is looking for medical students to do some part time work."

This was intriguing. "Really?"

"I hear they pay pretty well. You should check it out."

"I will do that." Jim set his things down and kicked off his shoes. "Where are you guys goin' tonight?"

"Dinner, then to see some local band at the Greek Theatre," Randy replied. "Jane snagged a few tickets from some friends of hers so we're meeting them over there."

"Sounds fun. Have a good time."

"We always do."

After Randy left for work the next day, Jane woke up and showered. While she was drying off, Jim barged through the bathroom door. The second he saw her standing there naked, he immediately drew back, red in the face.

As soon as Jane was dressed, she came out searching for Jim. "Jim, are you out here?"

Mortified that he had walked in on her, he said, "I am really sorry. I didn't know you were in there."

"It's ok. I should have locked the door."

Jim chuckled under his breath. "Man, I have got to get my own place. This whole girlfriend thing he's got goin' on…"

"Are you hungry?" Jane offered. "I'll make breakfast."

"You don't have to do that."

"It's ok. I don't mind. You need a good breakfast. Randy told me you were going to the hospital to look for a job today."

"Yes I am."

Jim was going through a tough time in his life. Jane was genuinely concerned about his wellbeing. "How are you doing?"

"I'm doin' alright. Better than last week. When you've loved someone and dedicated your life to them for eight years, it's hard, you know."

Offering support, she said, "If you need anything, let us know."

"Thank you. I will."

Jim didn't really know Jane that well, other than what Randy had told him about her and the few brief times they had all hung out together. But after staying with Randy during the week, observing the two of them together, and having conversations with Jane, he came to realize that she was a kind and compassionate person. She wasn't demanding, was very affectionate and forgiving toward Randy, and did whatever she could to support him. Randy and Jane had a solid relationship. Jim approved of his best friend's choice.

By the time Randy got home from work, Jim had returned from the hospital. "Hey," Randy said to him as he tossed his keys on the table. "What's going on?"

Jim was surrounded by paperwork. "Filling out W-4's and readin' through all these orientation papers."

"You get the job?" Randy presumed.

"Yup."

"Congrats."

"Thanks." Jim stacked the papers into a neat pile while Randy went to the refrigerator and grabbed a Pepsi. "Jane and I had a nice conversation this morning while you were at work," Jim said.

Randy sat in a chair across from him and popped the top on his soda can. "What did you guys talk about?"

"Nothin' in particular." Jim paused to roll up his sleeves. "You know, that girlfriend of yours is really sweet, and she genuinely cares about people. I can definitely see why you like her."

"Well gee, Dad, I'm so glad you approve."

Jim laughed. "I'm serious."

Thinking about Jane made him smile. "She's an incredible woman. I can't wait for my parents to meet her."

"She's goin' up to Seattle with you for Christmas break?"

"Only for New Year's," Randy clarified. "She wants to spend Christmas with her family."

"Makes sense. When's the last time you introduced a babe to your parents?"

"High school," Randy replied. "Never had a woman worthy enough to meet them."

Unexpectedly, there was a knock on Randy's door. Jim hopped up to answer it. When he saw who was standing on the porch, his heart plunged to the floor. "Trina."

"Hi, Jim."

Considering Jim never told Trina where he was staying, he was surprised to see her. "How'd you know where I was?"

"Randy's your best friend. I figured you would come here. Can I come in?"

"No." Resentment and distrust flooded his voice. "What do you want?"

"I want you to come home." Trina reached for his hand.

He pulled away. "Get away from me."

"But I miss you."

"Good." The fire in his eyes burned right through her.

"Jim, I'm sorry."

"I've heard that line from you before, too damn many times. It's too late for that."

"But it only happened once," she tried to substantiate.

"You can't justify it because it only happened once. Fuck that! I don't give a shit if it happened once or ten thousand times. Cheating is cheating. I don't trust you. I will never trust you again. And why should I? How do I know that you won't do this again?"

"Please come home."

"Hell no!"

"But, Jimmy…"

"I told you not to call me that." Filled with fury, he laid it on the line. "If you came over here to try to get me to change my mind, if you think for one second that I'm gonna come runnin' back to you, you are wastin' your breath. We are done, nixed. You are a cheating, lying deceiver, and I want nothin' to do with you."

"But what about your baby?" she pleaded.

"How the hell do I know it's my baby?" he argued. "The way you sleep around, it could be anybody's baby. So until the day I get proof of that, stay the hell away from me, and stay away from Randy's apartment. You are not welcome here."

Jim was about to shut the door in her face when Trina called out, "I love you."

He closed his eyes, trying to suppress his pain. "This is your idea of love? If anyone loved anyone in this relationship it sure as hell wasn't you. My commitment level to you was totally unrequited. I dedicated eight years of my life tryin' to make you happy. I gave you everything you wanted, yet I got nothing in return. You have managed to take everything you and I ever had and turned it into crap. So don't stand here and tell me that you love me, Trina. You don't have any idea what love is. You never knew what it was. Any small iota of love that I had for you is now gone. You flushed it down the toilet when you chose to be with another man. Take your bogus idea of love and tell someone who cares, because I no longer do." He closed the door and leaned against it, slowly sinking his body to the floor. He hung his head in his hands and let the tears flow freely.

Randy rushed to Jim's side to console him.

"God this hurts," Jim cried. "I can't believe she thinks I'm gonna crawl back to her after the shit she pulled. I am not a glutton for her punishment."

"Good," Randy said. "Stand your ground."

"This wouldn't hurt so much if I didn't still love her. That's what's killin' me."

"I know it is."

"I hate this." Jim wiped his eyes. "What the hell am I gonna do if this kid is mine?"

Randy toiled with that question, but had no answers. "I don't know. We'll cross that bridge if we come to it."

Jim walked into UCSF Medical Center excited to start his new job. He felt kind of foolish wandering around with a piece of paper in his hand that was supposed to be giving him directions, yet he couldn't make heads or tails out of it. He looked at room numbers on the wall trying to locate the area he was supposed to report to when a pretty blonde nurse dressed in scrubs bumped into him.

"I am so sorry," she said.

"No, I'm sorry," he apologized. "I should have been watching where I was going."

"You must be the new orderly from Berkeley."

"What brought you to that conclusion?" Jim asked.

"Because you look lost."

He grinned and extended an open palm. "James Ryan."

She shook his hand. "Jill Darcy. You'll learn your way around. It won't take long." She gave him a tour of the hospital. "There are twelve main examination rooms in the ER." She pointed to each one. "Triage is over here. ICU and radiology are right down this hall, and for surgery, go up the elevator to the second floor."

"Surgery. Second floor. Got it," Jim replied.

"Are you familiar with triage colors and what they mean?" she asked him.

"Yes I am."

"Good." She led him to a storage closet. "All equipment and supplies are in this cabinet. Chest tubes, breathing tubes, latex gloves, gauze, IV bags—everything you'll need to restock the carts."

"Alright."

"Dr. Gentry is the chief resident in charge during this shift. Have you met Dr. Lyons?"

"The head ER physician?" Jim asked, clarifying who he was. "Yes, I've met him."

"Good. Listen to that man," Jill advised. "He is one of the best. Dr. Lyons is right this way. Follow me."

She directed Jim to a man in blue scrubs. He had a stethoscope draped around his neck and a telephone receiver in his hand. Jim recognized him right away.

Dr. Lyons looked up and gave Jim the 'hold on a second' signal with his index finger while he continued his phone conversation. "Alright. I'll have CT on standby. Thank you for your help." He hung up the receiver and shook Jim's hand. "James Ryan. Good to see you again."

"You too, Sir."

"Welcome to the jungle. For the next six hours, do not leave my side, and don't do anything unless I tell you to do it."

"Yes, Sir," Jim replied, anxious to get into the action of the ER.

Jim had on a fresh pair of scrubs, ready to enter the exciting realm of the Emergency Room. "I see you are dressed for the occasion," Dr. Lyons remarked. "Scrub up. We have a code blue coming in, and I'm going to need your help."

"Absolutely, Doctor."

Jill smiled at Jim and left him in the guiding hands of this physician.

Chapter Seventeen

Randy finished his final exam early Friday, which meant he wouldn't have to rush to get to the airport on time. He fed and said goodbye to his parrot, loaded his luggage in the car, then drove up to Alpha to get Jane. She didn't have any finals that day, so they grabbed a quick bite to eat before heading to the airport.

After he checked in, they went to get coffee at Starbucks. Randy sipped from his cup while Jane stared at hers, not drinking any of it. She was unusually quiet.

"Honey," he said to her. "You okay?"

She shrugged and continued to stare at her cocoa.

He lifted her chin with his finger to get her to look at him. "What's the matter, Babe?"

Her eyes welled with tears. "I hate this."

"Hate what?"

"When you fly hundreds of miles away. I wish you didn't have to go."

He drew her closer. "I will call you every day and every night. I promise. We'll be together before you know it."

"I know. But I'll miss you."

"I'll miss you too." Her cup was still full. "You aren't going to drink that, are you?"

She shook her head. She wasn't in a cocoa mood.

He picked up her full cup and his empty one and threw them in the trash. They exited the coffee shop then Randy held her hand and walked toward the security checkpoint. "I'll give you a call as soon as I land."

She held him tightly, not wanting to let him go. "I love you," she said.

"I love you too. I'll see you on the 26th." He kissed her goodbye and made his way through the security line.

Randy was on the phone when he walked out of the gate area to meet his parents. They could tell by the smile on his face that he was talking to Jane. After he said goodbye to her, he greeted his mother, father, and brother with a hug. When he saw his sister, a huge grin filled his face. "Hey, Steph."

She gave him a huge squeeze. "Hey, Brat."

"When did you get here?" he asked.

"Flew in last night."

"Lucky you," he mocked. "I was taking an exam six hours ago."

"Ew. That sucks."

"Yes it does."

His father interjected into the conversation, "How did exams go?"

"Went well," Randy replied.

As soon as Randy claimed his bag, Mark Hanson said, "Dinner's on me tonight. Decide amongst yourself where you would like to go, just keep in mind that traffic is not the greatest this time of day."

They stopped for Italian food before returning to the Hanson home.

Randy spent the majority of the evening teasing his sister, when he wasn't beating her in a game of Operation.

"I hate this game," she complained. "You always kick my butt. I think you have an unfair advantage."

"This is nothing like the real thing, Steph. Real patients don't buzz and their noses don't light up if you do it wrong. In real life, you would kill someone." He poked her in the side.

She threw a piece of popcorn at him. "You are a pest."

"Didn't your mother teach you not to throw things?" He laughed and threw it back at her.

"When is Jane coming up?" Stephanie asked, completely changing the subject.

"The day after Christmas."

"I can't wait to meet her."

"You two will get along well I bet." Randy's cellphone rang. He reached into his pocket and saw that it was Jane. "Well, speak of the devil." He stepped into another room to talk to her more privately. They spoke for about an hour before Jane's dying battery forced them to end the conversation, at which time Randy rejoined his family upstairs.

"It immerges from the dungeon and blesses us with its presence," Robby remarked.

"I was talking to Jane."

"For an hour? What could you two possibly talk about for an hour?"

"We talk about all kinds of things."

"Like what?" Robby scorned.

"School, how our day was, family, friends. We talk about food sometimes."

"Why? Is she fat?"

"What?"

"If she thinks about food all the time, she must be fat."

Stephanie sneered at her younger brother. "Robby, that's rude."

"No, she's not fat," Randy declared. "How can you be so damn judgmental?" He whipped out his cellphone and scrolled for a picture of Jane. "She's a very attractive woman. See?" He shoved the picture in Robby's face.

Robby ogled over Jane's image. Indeed she was beautiful. "Damn, she's hot. What is she doing with you?"

"Shut up," Randy argued, snagging his phone back.

Jane went down to Randy's apartment the morning of Christmas Eve to feed and check on his parrot before she drove to her father's house for holiday festivities. When she pulled into the driveway, Dale Davine greeted her at the door.

"Hi, Daddy."

He stared at the red convertible. "This is the second time I've seen you behind the wheel of that thing. It's not safe for you to drive a sports car, Jane. I told you I didn't want you driving that."

"Since I don't have a car, I had to get here somehow. And someone has to feed Randy's bird while he's gone."

"You have a key to his apartment too?"

"Yes."

Dale's face formed a frown. "I don't like that, Jane. Not one bit."

"Daddy. He's my boyfriend. It's not a big deal." She walked past him and entered the house.

"I also don't like this attitude you've developed lately," he snarled.

"What attitude?"

"Speaking to me like that. I am your father."

"Yes, you are, and I respect that. But I have my own life," she argued.

"Randy puts you up to this."

"Please don't start that again."

"I don't want you flying up there."

She boldly replied, "I already have my ticket. I'm going."

"He's trying to keep you from your family."

"Why do you say things like that about him?" she countered. "Randy's a nice man, and he's good to me."

"Good to you?" her father mocked. "By giving you keys to his apartment and taking you into his bed he's good to you?"

Her father was being unreasonable, and it raked on her nerves. "Daddy."

"I don't like the influence he has on you, Jane."

"I am old enough to make my own decisions. I'm sorry you don't like some of them, but you can't blame Randy for what I do."

"That man is corrupting your mind and polluting your body with an insatiable appetite for sex. I don't like him having that kind of influence on my daughter."

She rolled her eyes at his stupid reasoning. "Sex is not a sin, Daddy."

"You are not married to him."

"So? You and Mom were having sex when you weren't married. It seemed to be just fine for you two, but you're telling me it's wrong. That is hypocritical."

Her lack of respect infuriated him. He raised his hand and slapped her hard across the face.

She held her cheek where he had hit her. Tears filled her eyes, not from the pain, but from the sheer shock of the fact that her father had done that. Crushed by his reaction, she ran out the door and drove over to Randy's apartment to get as far away from her father as she could.

Randy was sitting on the sofa drinking a cup of coffee and watching National Lampoon's Christmas Vacation with his brother and sister when his cellphone rang. Seeing Jane's name flash on the screen brought a smile to his face. "Hi, Baby."

She cried hysterically.

"Honey, what's wrong?" He got up and stepped into another room.

She sniffled and tried to get ahold of herself. "I hate him. He is the most stubborn, inconsiderate, narrow-minded, two-faced jerk."

"Whoa, Honey, slow down. Who are you talking about?"

"Daddy."

"Your dad?" What had her father said or done that brought about this abrasive reaction? "What happened?"

She told him what happened.

Randy could not believe this. "He slapped you for saying that?"

"Yes," she sniveled.

Outraged by her father's outburst and hurt by Jane's pain, Randy said, "That is a bit extreme."

"It's true. He is a hypocrite. I hate him, I swear I hate him." Tears flowed steadily.

"Honey, please calm down. Are you sure that's all you said?"

"You don't believe me?" she whimpered.

"I do believe you," he assured her. "But I don't understand why your father reacted that way simply because you said that. That doesn't make any sense."

"I think he's an idiot who has no idea what he's talking about," she cried. "He's a dominating ass and he's mean to me."

"You didn't say that to him, did you?" Randy feared.

"No. But it's true."

It took a while, but Randy was able to get her to calm down and think rationally, yet somehow he felt guilty for not being there to defend her. "Honey, I'm so sorry this happened."

"I'm not going back over there."

"It's Christmas Eve, Baby, you have to."

Jane didn't acknowledge him.

Randy thought he was pigheaded, but damn, she was far more stubborn than he was. "Janey, did you hear me?"

After an extended silence, she finally said, "I am not going over there."

"And what are you hoping to prove by doing that?" he argued.

"That I don't have to listen to him."

"No, what you're going to do is show him that you're acting like a child. I thought you were trying to demonstrate that you are an independent woman who has a mind of her own?"

"I am."

"Then you need to let him see that you are above this," he advised. "Show him that you will not let his reactionary outburst keep you from your convictions. You have to be bigger than that. Now get in the car and go back over there."

"I don't want to."

"I know you don't, but that is your family, Jane. Despite everything that may have happened between you and your dad, your family will always be there for you even if no one else will. You may not always like what they do, but you do love them for who they are. I know you do."

She contemplated what he said. "Yes, I do, but…" She didn't want to look at her father right now, let alone be around him, but she knew Randy was right. "I hate this."

"I know, Baby," he sympathized. "But you have to do it."

She let out a long drawn out sigh.

"Call me if you need me, ok? I'll be here. I love you, Honey."

"I love you, too." She hung up.

Randy stared at the phone in his hand. "Damn."

His father overheard him. "Everything alright?"

"No, not really. I hate the way Jane's father treats her."

"What did he do?"

"She expressed her opinion and called him out on something, and he slapped her."

"Why would he do that?"

"I told you he treats her this way. He belittles her and doesn't want her to live her own life. He's dominating and demoralizing and I…" Randy clenched his fist. "I can't watch this."

"Son, I know it's hard."

"Dad, he hit her," Randy complained. "And I'm not there for her right now when she needs me."

"There's nothing you could have done," Dr. Hanson told him.

"I would have stood between them so he couldn't have laid a hand on her." Randy leaned forward in his chair. "It kills me to watch her endure this crap."

"I know. But it's something she has to work out."

Randy didn't agree. "I'm sorry, Dad, I know you think that, but it's ridiculous for me to sit here and let him do that to her. What kind of a man am I if I let him bully her around and do nothing about it? I can't do that."

"You'll take a huge risk standing up to him. You'll jeopardize the relationship you've built. Do you really want to do that?"

"If it will get him to leave her the hell alone, it's worth it, dammit. There is no way Jane is okay with this. She was crying, Dad. She swore at him, saying she hated him, and Janey doesn't get like that. This really isn't right."

Knowing Randy was stubborn about these kinds of things, Dr. Hanson said, "So what are you going to do?"

"I don't know, but I'm not going to sit here idly and let the woman I love take this abuse from him or anyone else. She doesn't deserve that."

"Don't do anything you'll regret," his father warned.

"I won't. But I have to do something, because I am not going to let her suffer like this."

Randy had a hard time enjoying the holiday festivities that night. He was worried about Jane. Around 11:45 P.M., in the middle of family chitchat, eggnog, and Christmas music, he put on his jacket and went out on the deck to call and make sure she was ok. "Hi, Baby. How you doing?"

"I'm alright," she assured him. "I don't have a red mark on my face anymore."

"That's good." He thought about how he was going to express what he was feeling without upsetting her. "Honey, I think I should say something to your dad. I really don't like this."

"Randy, don't." She did not want him to get involved in her problem. "You'll only make it worse."

"He shouldn't treat you that way."

"He just gets frustrated."

"Stop making excuses for him," Randy stated.

"Please, let me handle this."

He did not agree with her, but he did let it go. "Fine, but I'm letting you know that I'm not comfortable about this at all." There was a moment of silence between them before Randy looked up at the sky and saw a very bright full moon. "Are you outside?" he asked her.

"I'm sitting on the patio."

"Look up. Do you see the moon?"

"Yes. I see it."

"I see it too. Our worlds aren't so far apart after all." As midnight rolled around, the air became crisper and a calm stillness filled the area. "It's midnight, Baby. Merry Christmas."

"Merry Christmas."

"Hey, since today is Christmas, you'll be flying up here tomorrow," he reminded her.

"I know. I can't wait. I miss you."

"I miss you too, terribly," he proclaimed. "Make sure you pack warm clothes and bring a jacket. It's cold up here."

December 26th, Randy awoke in an impeccable mood, whistling and bouncing all over the house.

His brother saw the way he was gallivanting about and had to comment. "Someone is way too cheerful this morning."

Randy simply grinned.

"Today's the big day, huh?" his dad asked.

"Yup," Randy replied.

Robby didn't know what they were talking about. "Big day for what?"

"I'm picking up Jane from the airport this morning," Randy reminded him.

"Oh, that's right," Robby remembered. "What time?"

"11:30."

"Can I come?" Robby asked.

"I haven't seen her in a week. I would really like to spend some alone time with my girlfriend before you guys steal her."

His mom set a plateful of food in front of him.

"Oh, no thanks, Mom," Randy said. "I'm gonna wait and have lunch with Jane. I'll take some coffee though." He got up and made himself a cup.

"Don't keep her away too long. We want to meet her." His took the plate away.

"I know. We'll go to lunch, I'll show her around a bit, and then we'll come home."

"We're giving you guys the family room downstairs," his father stated. "You'll have more privacy down there."

The family room of the Hanson house was roomy. It had a large sectional sofa that unfolded into a bed, two floor lamps for lighting, two end tables, a large screen TV, surround sound stereo system and DVD player, a bar with a mini fridge, and a bathroom complete with shower. And it was located downstairs by itself so there would be plenty of privacy. "Cool, thanks."

Robby complained, "How come Randy can bring a girl home and you let him share a bed with her downstairs, but when I want to bring a girl over you won't let us leave the living room?"

"Because Randy is twenty-three and in graduate school. You are sixteen and barely passing eleventh grade," Dr. Hanson answered.

Finding this unjust, Robby stormed out of the room.

"Cranky ass," Randy noted.

"He isn't much of a morning person," his mother added.

"I can see that."

Chapter Eighteen

Randy drove his father's pickup to the airport. Jane's flight was delayed thirty minutes, so he was forced to wait, impatiently. When passengers finally exited, Randy stood up and anxiously looked for her. He spotted her beautiful smile and green eyes and it instantly brought a grin to his face.

When Jane saw him, she threw herself in his arms. "I missed you."

He hugged her tightly and lifted her off the ground. "I missed you too." He groped her mouth with his, soaking in the moment. "Mmm, I missed that too."

She drew her lip between her teeth then looked into his deep, brown eyes.

He stared at her adoringly. "You did something different to your hair."

"I had it highlighted. Daddy hates it."

Randy didn't give a shit what her father thought. He thought it looked fantastic. "Well, I love it." He combed his fingers through it. "It's very beautiful."

"Thank you."

Jane had on a pair of skinny jeans, a short-sleeved black tee-shirt, and a pair of black sandals. "I hope you brought warmer clothes than that. We have snow forecasted for this week."

"Snow?" Her eyes lit up at the prediction.

Randy flashed her a crooked smile. "I bet you, in your secluded little California world, have never seen snow before, have you?"

"I've seen snow, on a mountain."

"I hope it snows while you're up here." He took her hand, snagged her suitcase, and ploughed toward the airport exit.

They went out for lunch then piddled around the emerald city, checking out Puget Sound, Seattle Center, and the Space Needle. Then he drove over the Evergreen Floating Bridge and gave her a tour of his hometown of Kirkland.

Kirkland was beautiful. The panoramic views of the lake, Seattle skyline, and Olympic Mountains were breathtaking. Waterfront parks, tree-lined boulevards, lanes of boutique shops and restaurants, intriguing outdoor sculptures, and all kinds of recreational activities invited and welcomed people from all walks of life. Jane thoroughly enjoyed the new scenery.

"So what do you think?" Randy asked.

"It's beautiful here. That Space Needle is neat."

"There's a restaurant on the top. Great view of the city. It revolves while you eat so you can get the full panoramic feel of Seattle. I'll take you up there before we leave."

Her nerves got shaky and she stated to panic.

"What's the matter?" he asked, seeing her sudden anxiety.

"I'm about to meet your parents."

"You don't need to be nervous about that," he reassured her.

"What if they don't like me?"

"They are going to love you." He reached over and put his hand on her thigh. "Don't worry."

When they pulled into the driveway of the Hanson home, Jane almost fell out of her seat. Their house sat on a ten-thousand square foot lot of intricately landscaped lakefront property. A huge double-paned glass window welcomed them, along with a three-car garage. It had to be the most elaborate home she had ever seen. "Oh my god, Randy, I can't go in there."

"Why not?"

"Look at this place." She felt even more nervous now than she was before. "This is your parents' house?"

"Yeah, what's the problem?"

"You didn't tell me about all of this. Your parents are obviously wealthy. How do I act around them? What do I say?"

Randy tried to ease her apprehension. "They aren't any different than I am. They just happen to live in a big house."

"This is really intimidating. Big house, lake property, doctor."

He thought her anxiety was unfounded. "Yes, my dad is a doctor. So what? My parents are wonderful people, and they are going to love you." He gave her a reassuring kiss. "Come on. It'll be ok."

As soon as Randy's mom heard them come in, she ran to greet them at the door. "Where is she?"

Randy put his arm around Jane. "Jane, this is my mom."

Jane nervously held out her hand. "Very nice to meet you, Mrs. Hanson."

"Oh no, Dear. That won't do." Instead of shaking Jane's hand, Randy's mother gave her a hug. "Welcome to our home. We have heard so much about you. It is good to finally put a pretty face with the name."

"Thank you."

Randy said, "I'm going to show her around."

"Make sure you introduce her to your dad," his mother reminded him.

"Where is he?"

"Around back."

Jane appeared less nervous as Randy gave her a tour of the house. The four bedroom, three bath home had a color palette of latte and cream, travertine, and slate. The gourmet kitchen with marble countertops and a suite of Viking appliances was a cook's dream. Ceramic tile and terrazzo flooring with fancy area rugs covered the entire kitchen and living area. Formal living and dining areas, with skylights and vaulted ceilings, were elaborately decorated with fine furnishings, glass tabletops, and exquisite fabric-covered throw pillows. The balcony, which overlooked the lake outside the master suite, had the most breathtaking view Jane had ever seen.

"I can't believe you grew up here," she said in awe. "This is beautiful."

"Mom will be happy to hear you say that. She's put a lot of work into this house."

Randy took her hand and led her out a pair of French doors, over a huge deck, and down to the backyard. Several large evergreen and bare deciduous trees shaded the area. A small sandy beach covered a portion of the backyard and a private boat dock looked out over the lake.

Randy spotted his dad walking toward the water's edge. "There's my dad," he said to Jane. "Come on."

"Randy." She gripped his hand tighter and began to breathe nervously.

With a reassuring smile, he said, "It'll be ok. My dad is the most understanding, nonjudgmental man you will ever know. You have no reason to be nervous." Leading her by the hand, he escorted her down to the lakeside. "Dad?" Randy tried to get his father's attention.

When Mark Hanson saw Randy holding hands with a beautiful brunette woman, a warm smile filled his face. "Well, there she is." He kindly held out his hand to welcome her. "Hello, Jane. We have heard many good things about you."

"Your home is beautiful," she commented.

"Thank you. Make sure you tell Ellen that. The house is her work of art, not mine."

Jane was more relaxed now, realizing that she was not being looked upon as an inferior being in this world of wealth. Randy was right. His parents were incredibly kind, very hospitable, and opened up their home to her unreservedly. After the initial shock, she soon made herself at home.

Following dinner with the family, Randy took Jane downstairs. He pulled the bed out of the sofa and folded back the sheets and comforter. "My parents absolutely adore you. I knew they would." He gave her a tender kiss on the lips. "By the way, we've been invited to attend a party with my parents."

"What kind of party?"

"One of my dad's colleagues is throwing a big New Year's Eve bash. A bunch of his doctor friends will be there."

"What I am supposed to talk to a bunch of doctors about?"

"The same things you talk to me about," he explained. "Think of it as a fancy sorority party. They'll be dancing, an open bar, socializing. You're good at that kind of stuff."

"Your parents dance?" she questioned.

"Actually, they are quite good. Do you want to go?"

She nodded. "Sure."

"Thank you. I'll be working with some of these people later on down the road. This will give me a chance to talk to them and introduce myself." He squatted down on the pullout bed, sitting on his knees.

"Is this formal?" she asked, wondering what kind of dress code a shindig like this had.

"Yes it is."

"I didn't bring anything to wear."

"Then you will have to go shopping with Stephanie and get something, won't you?" With his index finger, Randy signaled for Jane to join him. When she did, he pulled her closer and found the soft curves of her lips. "I need you." His kisses became more intense, and his breathing intensified. "I want you."

"Randy, we can't do this."

"Why not?"

"Because we're in your parents' house. They'll hear us."

"No they won't. And they don't care anyway. My dad gave us this room so we could have some privacy." Jane was apprehensive and overly cautious, not herself at all. Obviously something was bothering her. "Honey, what's wrong?"

Through bleary eyes, she said, "Daddy is so mad at me. He won't even talk to me."

Every time Jane was with her father, she felt overly emotional and sensitive afterwards. "I hate the way he treats you."

"He's my father. He has every right."

Randy disagreed. "No, Jane, that is where you are wrong. He does not have the right to slap you because you disagree with him, and he does not have the right to make you feel like crap. Just because he's your father does not mean he can push you around."

She hung her head.

"Baby, look at me." He gently lifted her chin with his finger. "He can't do this to you. I cannot stand to see this. Every time you're around him, you're miserable. It's not right. I don't know exactly what's going on with you and your dad, but this needs to stop."

She wiped her tears with her hand.

"Don't let him get to you. You're here with me now, and I will not hurt you or disrespect you or ridicule you in any way. Neither will anyone in my family."

She knew Randy would do everything he could to make her happy and would never try to hurt her. She felt safe with him.

"You ok?" he asked.

Her lovely, tantalizing smile brightened her face. "Yeah."

"Good. Now, where were we?"

Randy stepped out of the shower to a very strong scent of nail polish. He slipped on a pair of jeans and a tee-shirt then headed up to the living room where Jane and his sister were on the floor painting their toenails. They had out several different colors, including bright red, neon pink, and sparkly silver glitter, as well as various sticker adornments. "Good morning, ladies. What are we getting all decorated for?"

"I'm stealing your girlfriend today, Randy," Stephanie said.

"Oh, you are, huh?"

"Yes. I am taking her shopping, and we are going to have a girls' day out."

"Sounds fun." He leaned over and gave Jane a kiss. "Can I talk to you for a minute?"

She rose to her feet and joined him on the opposite side of the room, trying not to ruin the polish on her toes. "What's up?" she asked.

He reached into his wallet and handed her his debit card. "Here. When you are out and about today, get yourself a nice dress, shoes, whatever you need for that New Year's party we're going to tomorrow night."

"I can't take your bank card."

"I insist. Pull out some money and get what you need. The pin number is JAVA."

His coffee addiction was shining through. "Thank you."

"I love you, Babe. Have fun today."

She slipped his card in her pocket and went back to painting her toenails.

Before the New Year's Eve party, Stephanie worked diligently to help Jane get ready. Jane had picked out an elegant mid-length royal blue evening gown to wear that evening. A spaghetti string tied behind her neck, and a small brooch at the base of her bust bunched up the fabric from her waist. It hugged every curve of her body. Her opened-toed sandals with a two-inch heel were also royal blue. The shoe fabric compliment the waistline on the dress.

Stephanie French braided Jane's hair then Jane put on a touch of pink lipstick, just enough to add the slightest hue to her lips. To top off the look, she put in dangly crystal earrings.

Stephanie gave her one last inspection. "Wow! If my brother doesn't think you are a knockout, there is something seriously wrong with him."

Jane eyed her reflection in the full-length mirror. She looked like a movie star ready to walk the red carpet at the Oscars. Her transformation was a stunning success.

"You are going to knock his socks off, girl," Stephanie proclaimed.

"You think so?"

"Oh, yes. Most definitely."

Stephanie went into the living room where Randy and her parents were dressed and ready to go. She walked up to Randy, who looked incredibly handsome in the tux he was wearing. "She looks gorgeous, Randy."

Randy grinned anxiously. "Really?"

"You are going to die when you see her."

He couldn't wait to see for himself.

When Jane stepped into the living room, Randy's eyes lit up in amazement. He circled around to get the full effect. "You are the most beautiful woman I have ever seen in my life."

Jane fixed his collar. "You wear a tux well."

His hand found its way to the exposed skin on her back. Taking in the sweet perfume she was wearing, he moved his lips to her ear and whispered, "You smell incredible." With her lips that close to his, he couldn't resist any longer. He had to kiss her.

Dr. Hanson cleared his throat. "We have to go, Son."

Reluctantly, he broke away from Jane. He gently grazed his hand across her back and led her out to the car.

Jane was without a doubt the most beautiful woman at the New Year's Eve party. Men's heads turned when she walked in the room and women admired her lovely gown.

While Jane and Ellen mingled with a group of women, Mark introduced Randy to his colleagues. In the midst of a conversation, Randy caught himself staring at Jane.

"She truly is lovely, Randal," his father remarked.

Randy agreed. "She's gorgeous."

"Your mother and I would like to invite her to come on vacation with us this summer."

Randy pulled his eyes away. "Seriously?"

"Yes. Do you think she would like to join us?"

"I can almost guarantee it, and I appreciate you inviting her."

"She is always welcome. Does she have a passport?"

"I don't know, but I can find out."

"Yes, please do."

Randy's eyes drifted Jane's direction. Any resistance he had managed to maintain throughout the evening was now gone. He set his wine glass on a nearby table and gazed at her with loving eyes. "But right now I'm going to go dance with her. Excuse me."

Dr. Hanson and his wife watched Randy and Jane on the dancefloor. The tenderness Randy possessed and the loving and gentle way he touched her warmed their hearts. There was no denying that their son was in love.

"Oh, I hope she's the one," Ellen Hanson proclaimed.

Mark knew what his wife was thinking. "Now, Ellie, I know you want to see him get married, but you need to let Randy do this his way."

She pretended not to hear him. "She is such a sweet girl. She has to be the one."

He remained persistent. "Do not ask him about marriage and do not pressure him in any way. Let our son take his time, let him decide."

While Randy's parents watched him and Jane on the dancefloor, Randy saw something that put a smile on his face. "Janey, look." He pointed her toward the window. "It's snowing."

Her face beamed with excitement. She grabbed Randy's hand and ran over to get a better look.

Randy's parents joined them. "Well, it looks like you got your snow," Mark said.

Overjoyed, Jane gave him a hug.

Randy couldn't contain his joy. Family was important to him. Knowing they liked her and she liked them meant the world to him.

After everyone else had gone to bed, Randy and Jane snuggled in front of a warmly lit fire in the living room. All lights were off in the house, making the romantic glow from the fire project shadows onto the walls.

"I can't believe we're leaving tomorrow," Randy said. "Back to the 'ole college grind."

"But at least you are another semester closer," Jane reminded him.

"Good point."

Jane sank into his arms and sighed contently. "I don't want to go back. I had such a good time up here. Your family is fun."

"I tried to tell you that," he declared. "Speaking of which, I had a conversation with my dad earlier tonight. We're going to Puerto Vallarta this summer, and my parents invited you to come."

She's mouth gaped open. "Are you serious?"

"Yes, Ma'am. Do you want to come on the Hanson family vacation to Mexico this summer?"

She bounced up and down in excitement. "Oh my god, yes!"

Her reaction made him laugh. "Alright then. I'll let my dad know."

Jane got more comfortable, and Randy slowly moved his hand to her tummy, softly caressing the skin under her shirt. "Being alone with you here in the firelight is turning me on." He kissed her neck and raised his hand up to her breast.

Surprised by his forthright statement, she whispered, "Your parents will hear."

"Then we'll have to be quiet, won't we."

His mouth conformed to hers while he fumbled for the latch of her bra, slowly unfastening it. Clothes scattered throughout the living room. The image of her naked body shadowed by the firelight roused the senses. He put his hand behind her head and eased her down to the floor. He leaned against the couch and she straddled his lap. An uncontrollable moan left her lips as she slowly sank onto him.

He placed his finger over her lips. "Ssh."

She tried to control her impulse, but the intenseness was too powerful. Her heart jolted and her pulse pounded. She wrapped her legs around him and their bodies conformed into one.

Chapter Nineteen

Monday afternoon, Randy met his study group for lunch. He set his bag on the floor and was establishing his seat when he saw Mandy struggling with a man in a black hoody. Mandy tried to walk away, but the man violently grabbed her arm and screamed obscenities in her face. After a noticeably negative confrontation, he finally let go of her. Trying to hide the fact that this encounter occurred, Mandy moseyed over to the table as if nothing happened.

Being a concerned friend, Randy asked, "Who was that?"

She rubbed her arm. "Don't worry about it. It's nothing."

He gawped at her, knowing it would drive her nuts and eventually make her talk.

"Stop doing that," she said.

"Then tell me who that was," he insisted. "Is he that guy you've been dating?"

"*Was* dating." She shook her head. "But not anymore."

Randy was happy to hear that, especially after what he just witnessed. He visually examined her arm. It had a decent-sized red mark on it. "He has no right to grab you like that. What's going on?"

"Last week I told him I didn't want to see him anymore. Ever since then he's been texting me constantly and refuses to leave me alone. I've asked him several times to stop bothering me, but he won't. He spotted me outside and followed me in here. He got in my face, asking me why I was ignoring him and insisted that I give him another chance. I refused, which he didn't take too kindly to."

"That's harassment, Mandy. You need to report this."

After lunch, Randy and Jim walked across the courtyard together. "Have you met that guy Mandy was dating?" Randy asked.

"I've seen him around. Never talked to him though. Why?"

"Is he violent? Does he have a history of stalking or assault?"

"I don't know, Dude. Why would you assume that?"

"Because I witnessed something today that has bothered me. Mandy told the guy she didn't want to see him anymore, yet he still texts her all the time. And today he followed her to lunch and grabbed her arm pretty hard. Obviously he hurt her because she was rubbing it afterwards."

Jim shrugged it off. "Maybe he was pissed because she dumped his ass."

"That's my point. I saw how he treated her, Jim. He was mean and hurtful. The dude has some anger issues. If he reacts that way simply because she broke up with him, he has the potential to do something far worse. People do crazy shit over relationships."

"Did she report it?" Jim asked him.

"I told her to, but that doesn't mean she will."

"There's nothin' we can do if Mandy doesn't report it, Bro."

"Maybe we should say something to someone."

"I'm sure she'll handle it." Jim seemed so absolute.

But Randy was genuinely concerned and couldn't figure out why Jim blew it off as unimportant.

Following class that afternoon, Randy stopped by to see Jim's new place. The small studio apartment was surprisingly comfortable. Jim had moved in furniture and other belongings and personalized it with some beach and surfing décor.

"Man, you should have seen Trina's reaction when I went over there to get my stuff," Jim said.

"What did she do?" Randy asked.

"She got pissy with me and swore up and down that some of it was hers, then she begged me not to go. She should've thought about that before she decided to be a cheatin' little bitch."

"I'm sensing some bitterness there."

"Hell yeah, I'm bitter. Wouldn't you be? She got herself pregnant and cheated on me."

"Got herself pregnant?" Randy said. "I love how you put that. Last time I checked it took two to accomplish that task."

"You know what I mean." Jim put his feet on the table and relaxed. "My door is no longer open to her, that's for sure. I'm glad to be rid of her."

"When are you gonna start dating again?"

Jim shook his head. "Do you know how long it's been since I've been on the dating scene? In case you forgot, Trina was my girlfriend since high school. She's the only woman I've ever been with."

"I know that, which is why you need to get out and meet some women, expand your horizons. There are a lot of fish in the sea, Jim. You need to get back in the boat." Trying to help him out, Randy reached into his jacket pocket and pulled out his book of girls' names and phone numbers. He handed it to Jim.

Jim recognized this book. "Why are you handin' that to me?"

"I'm giving it to you."

Jim could not believe Randy was giving up his treasured book. "I can't take this."

"Why not?"

"Because it's yours."

Randy insisted. "I don't want it anymore."

"Every girl you've ever known is in here."

"I know."

Jim thumbed through the pages to take a peek at some of the names. There had to have been over two-hundred phone numbers in this book. "Damn, Randy. Who are all these chicks?"

"One night stands mostly. Ancient history I do not care to repeat."

Jim tried to give it back to him, but Randy refused to take it. "I told you I don't want it. If you have no use for it then burn it or shred it, I don't care. I haven't opened the damn thing in five months."

"Didn't you meet Jane about five months ago?"

"Yes."

"What the hell did she do to you?" Jim teased.

Randy smiled widely. "She's completely stolen my heart is what she's done."

Jim set the book on the table by his phone. "I never thought I would see this day. Randy Hanson, the most eligible playboy I've ever known, has actually committed to one woman."

"Yeah, yeah," he blew off Jim's gibberish. "I gotta get to work."

"Alright, Bro." They knuckle bumped. "See ya later."

Saturday night, Randy and Jane made plans to share dinner together then see the stage production of *Cabaret* at the local theatre. Anticipating a romantic evening with the love of his life, Randy whistled a happy tune while he finished getting dressed. As soon as he slipped on his pants, he heard a knock on his door. Thinking it was Jane showing up early, he left his shirt on the bed and hurried to answer the door. Standing in front of him was a young woman with bruises and lacerations all over her pretty face. She looked like she had gotten into a fight.

"Jesus, Mandy. What the hell?"

"Can I come in?"

"Of course." He showed her inside and helped her to the couch. "What happened?"

She proceeded to explain. "Ever since lunch the other day, Jack's been following me around and making constant threats. I reported it and even got a restraining order against him. Obviously he didn't take it seriously."

Randy's hunch had been right. He wished it hadn't been. "You broke up with him so he beat the crap out of you?"

She nodded to confirm.

"Bastard." He grabbed a wet washrag, some antiseptic ointment, and a Ziplock bag full of ice and doctored up her wounds. "Did you call the police?"

"Yes, but I can't go back to my apartment. He knows where I live, and that's the first place he'll go to find me."

"Good call," Randy concurred, thinking that was wise on her part. "It's not safe for you to be there by yourself right now."

She started to breathe heavily, fighting off tears. "I'm sorry, Randy, but I didn't know where else to go." She fell into his consoling arms and cried.

Right at that moment, Jane walked in the door. She dropped her keys on the floor and covered her mouth with her hand. "How could you?"

Randy turned his head. "It's not what you think."

Not believing a word he said, she stormed out the door, leaving her keys behind.

"Janey, wait." He hopped over the back of the couch and ran after her. Trying to prevent her from leaving, he grabbed her hand. "Can we please talk about this?"

"Let go of me."

"Give me a chance to explain."

She stared at his hand, insistent that he let her go. He honored her wishes. "How could you do this, after everything we've been through?"

"I didn't do anything. Please let me explain," he begged.

Heartbroken, she turned her back and ran away crying.

He called to her in desperation. "Jane!" When he realized she wasn't going to turn around, his knees weakened and he fell to the porch.

Mandy heard the hollering and came out to see what was going on. Holding a bag of ice on her cheek, she saw Randy sitting on the porch with his face buried in his hands. She put her hand on his shoulder and felt him shaking. She could only imagine what that must have looked like from Jane's perspective, and knowing this made her feel awful. "Randy, I am so sorry."

He lifted his head and clasped his hands together, touching his knuckles to his lips. "It's not your fault." He sat on the porch trying to figure out what to do. When he finally pulled himself together, he hopped to his feet and grabbed the keys Jane dropped on the floor. "Stay here," he told Mandy. "I'll be back."

He went out searching for Jane. When she wasn't at Alpha, he considered other options, trying to figure out where she might have gone. He checked in several places, all to no avail. Then he remembered a gazebo across campus where Jane sometimes went to study or be alone. He headed that direction, relieved to find her. She sat curled up in a ball hugging her knees. "I've been looking everywhere for you."

She turned her eyes to him, sobbing. "I can't believe you're having an affair with Mandy."

That was an extremely unsound conclusion she jumped to. "Jesus, Jane. Is that what you think? I would never do that. Never."

"I'm not stupid. I saw the way you were holding her."

"Nothing happened, I swear to you. Please listen to me."

"Why should I?" she wailed.

"Because I'm telling the truth. Nothing is going on with me and Mandy. She came to me because she needed help. That's all it was."

"Do you think I'm that naïve?" she cried. "I saw her in your arms, Randy. She was all over you, and you were half naked."

"No I wasn't. That's not at all what it was. If you'd let me explain." He desperately tried to explain himself and she was totally unwilling to hear anything he had to say. "Come on. Let's talk about this."

Her tears flowed steadily; she couldn't stop crying.

Distressed by her unwillingness to hear him out, he painfully laid it on the line. "I am one-hundred percent dedicated to you and our relationship. I've been loyal, faithful, and committed from day one, and I've always been truthful. I love you, Jane, and I would never cheat on you." He hesitated for a minute, trying to contain his emotions. "But it hurts, it really hurts knowing that you think I would." He laid her keys on the seat next to her and sulked all the way home.

He walked in the door and tossed his jacket on the floor, not caring where it landed. Feeling completely numb, he trudged into the living room and plopped onto the couch. Mandy was still at his apartment. She sat down next to him and gently placed her hand on his arm. "Randy?"

He didn't feel like company right now and wanted to be left alone. Wallowing in his own misery, he offered no reply.

The painful look on his face was more than Mandy could bear. "I am so sorry. If there is anything I can do." He didn't want to engage in conversation and almost seemed annoyed by her presence, so Mandy packed up her belongings and left.

Finally alone, he buried his face in his hands and cried.

Randy didn't show up for their study session Sunday morning and didn't answer his cellphone when Jim called. It wasn't like Randy to ignore phone calls or neglect school. Concerned that something had happened, Jim questioned Bruce and Sarah. "Have either of you heard from Randy this morning?"

They both denied having any contact with him at all.

"Hmm," Jim pondered. "He hasn't called me either."

Moments later, Mandy walked in and told everyone what happened. "Jane ran off crying and Randy lost it," she added. "He was pretty shaken up, Jim."

"Did you stay and talk to him?"

"He didn't seem like he wanted to talk."

"So he's been suffering through this alone?" Jim asked, annoyed by her lack of sympathy. "You should have stayed with him or called me or something."

Mandy's voice became brittle. "I was dealing with another issue and was flustered at the time. I'm sorry."

Somehow, Mandy felt like she was to blame for all of this, and Jim was adding insult to injury, making her feel even worse. In her defense, Bruce spoke up. "Give her a break, Jim. She's been through enough."

Jim took a few breaths to calm down. "I'm going over there." He grabbed his keys and immediately left for Randy's apartment.

The Camaro was parked out front, which meant Randy was probably home. But when he knocked on the door, no one answered. He tried again. Still no response. He pulled out his key, let himself in, and searched the apartment. "Hey, man, are you in here?"

Randy was sprawled out on the living room floor as if lying on a crucifix awaiting his death. Motionless, he didn't say a word, except for the pathetic groan he was making.

Jim sat on the floor beside him. "I hear you and Jane had a little mishap."

With sad eyes, Randy stared at the ceiling. "She hates me."

"No she doesn't."

"She accused me of cheating on her."

"That's ridiculous."

Randy slowly sat up. "I tried to tell her that, but she doesn't believe me."

"Did you try calling her?"

"She won't answer her phone and won't return any of my calls. She refuses to talk to me." Fearing their

231

relationship was on the verge of destruction, Randy hung his head. "I can't lose her, Jim. What the hell am I gonna do?"

Jim had never seen his best friend this miserable. He put his hand on Randy's shoulder and offered the only advice he had. "Maybe she needs some time to think. Give her some breathing room then try talkin' to her again. You two have always worked things out. It'll be okay." After some coaxing, Jim was able to talk Randy into coming to the study session with him.

The entire time they were studying, Randy stared at his cellphone. Jane wasn't calling and wasn't answering his texts. He was convinced their relationship was over. This thought remained in his head, haunting him, plaguing him with pain.

He had a hard time sleeping that night. Still, he did manage to drag himself to class in the morning. He spotted Jane walking across the courtyard, but when he tried to approach her, she turned away as if she didn't see him. Heartbroken, he came to the conclusion that the only way to repair this situation was to confront her face to face.

After class, he boldly walked up to the Alpha Phi house, prepared to get the break up speech. He didn't want to face that scenario, but tried to brace himself for it. He knocked on the door insistent on seeing Jane.

"She doesn't want to talk to you," one of her sorority sisters said.

"Tell her I'm not leaving until she comes out here." Randy folded his arms across his chest and refused to move. He waited on the porch for five minutes before Jane peeked her head out. Relieved to see her face, he stared at her for a minute. "We need to talk."

She considered what he said, but didn't respond.

"Please," he begged. "If our relationship means anything to you at all, you will come out here and talk to me."

Reluctantly, she stepped out to the porch and closed the door.

He tried to look her in the eye, but she turned her head away. "Please look at me."

She refused.

"Jane, I love you very much, but I am not going to stand here and waste my time trying to make this right if you are not willing to listen."

She finally broke the barrier and their eyes met.

"Are you ready to listen?" he asked, praying she would hear what he had to say.

She responded with a simple nod.

He slid his hands in his pockets and leaned against the porch pillar. "I was in the middle of getting dressed for our dinner date, which I was very much looking forward to by the way, when there was a knock on my door. I thought it was you, so I didn't think twice about putting on a shirt before I opened the door. But when I got there, it wasn't you. It was Mandy. She was bruised up, she was battered, and she was crying."

Horrified by what he told her, Jane cried, "Oh my god, is she okay?"

He sat on the stairs. "She broke up with this guy she'd been seeing and his reaction was to beat the crap out of her. She was hurt and she was scared. She didn't know where else to go, so she came to me. She's my friend, Jane, and I couldn't stand to see Mandy hurting like that. I tried to make her feel better by giving her a hug. That's all it was. A hug for my scared friend who needed my help. That's when you walked in. You freaked out and stormed off and never gave me a chance to explain. I did nothing wrong. I was simply comforting a friend in need."

She sat next to him, feeling unbearably guilty for falsely accusing him. "I am so sorry I didn't believe you."

Relieved, he held her tightly in his arms. "You scared the hell out of me. I thought I lost you." Trying to be open and honest with her, he lifted her chin. "Relationships involve trust. You have to learn to trust me."

"I do trust you."

He doubted the sincerity of that statement. "If you trusted me then you'd know I would never do anything to hurt you. I would never lie to you, and I would never, ever cheat on you."

"I know you wouldn't," she sniffled and held him close.

"If things like this happen, we need to talk about it. We can't work through misunderstandings if we don't communicate."

"I agree."

"Alright then, new rule. Neither one of us will go to bed angry. We will talk things out and find a solution. We will not make assumptions or jump to conclusions." With that, he gently touched the tip of her nose with his finger. "And no more silent treatment, ok?"

"Ok." She released her grip on him and crinkled her forehead, brooding. "Is Mandy alright?"

"She's a little shaken up, but she's gonna be okay."

"We missed our dinner date," she stewed, obviously disappointed.

"I know. But that's alright. We'll do it next weekend." He leaned in to kiss her. "I love you, Honey."

"I love you too."

Chapter Twenty

The next week, Randy and Jane met Bruce and Jim at the Cal State Golden Bears men's basketball game against UCLA. During the half time show, admission ticket stubs were drawn and the person who possessed the winning ticket would get a chance to walk away with $150. All they had to do was make three free throws within thirty seconds.

As numbers were read over the P.A. system, they all checked their tickets. Jane gasped when her number was announced. "Oh my god, that's me!"

Randy checked her ticket to confirm. "Get down there, Baby. Show them what you're made of."

She confidently stepped onto the basketball court.

Randy leaned toward Bruce with a haughty grin on his face. "She's about to come home with a hundred and fifty bucks."

"She won't make three of those, will she?" Bruce asked skeptically.

"Just watch." Randy clasped his hands behind his head and leaned back. He knew how accurate she was from the free throw line, and tonight was no exception. She was dead on, easily firing three shots into the hoop, one right after the other.

"Damn, Randy. Remind me to have her on my team next time we play."

"Hell no, she's all mine."

Jane pranced back up the bleachers waving several twenty dollar bills at Randy. "Looks like I'm paying for dinner tonight," she said.

Everyone sat slack-jawed over what they witnessed Jane do. Randy simply put his arm around her, grinning proudly.

After the game, Jane and Randy headed to his apartment. Randy kicked off his shoes and pulled out his textbooks to get some studying done.

"Daddy invited us over for dinner Sunday night," Jane said.

Randy groaned. "I hate going over there."

"Why?"

"Because I don't like the way he treats you. One of these days he's going to push it too far and I'm going to say something to him."

Jane thought he was overreacting. "Randy."

"Apparently you forgot what happened over Christmas break when you tried to speak your mind around your father. If he does that around me, I *will* step between the two of you and I *will* say something, Jane. I won't allow him to treat you that way."

"Will you meet me after your study session so we can go?" She gave him begging puppy dog eyes. "Please?"

He couldn't tell her no. "Alright."

"Thank you."

Randy used the remainder of the evening to get homework done, dreading the upcoming visit with Jane's father.

Randy woke in the morning with Jane in his arms. He leaned over to kiss her forehead, which felt hot to the touch. "Good morning, Baby."

"I feel horrible."

She sounded horrible too. Her voice was hoarse, and by the glossiness of her eyes and the grimace on her face, it was obvious she didn't feel well. He put on a pair of shorts and stepped out of the room. He returned with a thermometer in his hand. "Here. Put this under your tongue."

She stuck it in her mouth.

A few minutes later, he checked her temperature— 101.8. He slipped the thermometer back in its protective case and left the room again. He came back with a glass of water, a bottle of Tylenol, and a pen light. "Sit up, Honey."

She slowly sat up.

"Open your mouth." He shined the pen light in her mouth and examined her throat. She had white spots on her tonsils, her throat was bright red and swollen, and dark red blotches covered the roof of her mouth. "Looks like you might have strep." He handed her two Tylenol tablets. "Take these. It will help with your fever."

She swallowed the pills, and Randy grabbed his phone. "What are you doing?" she asked.

"Getting you into the clinic. You're gonna need antibiotics to get rid of this. You're not allergic to Penicillin are you?"

"No."

"Good." He called his boss and scheduled an appointment for Jane that afternoon. "Get some rest, Babe. I'll pick you up around lunchtime." He kissed her forehead and got ready for class.

In the lecture hall, Randy sat between Jim and Bruce, who already had their notes out. "Hey," he said to his friends. "I'm not gonna make it to lunch today."

"Why not?"

He pulled out his spiral notebook and prepared to take notes. "Jane's not feeling well. Looks like she's got strep. I'm gonna take her over to the clinic after class."

Bruce added, "If you've been kissing her, you're probably going to get that. Streptococcus is highly infectious you know."

Randy furrowed his brow. "I know that. But thank you, Dr. Buckman."

"No problem."

At the clinic that afternoon, Randy's boss, Dr. Stephens, immediately took Jane into an exam room. Randy went in with her.

"Randy tells me you're not feeling well," Dr. Stephens said to her.

Jane confirmed this statement. "My throat hurts."

Dr. Stephens turned his attention to Randy. "You want to do this?"

"Yes, Sir. I'd love to do this." He was thrilled to have this opportunity, but wanted Jane's permission first. "If that's ok with you, Babe."

"That's fine. I can be your guinea pig."

"Cool." He washed his hands thoroughly then swiped a digital thermometer across her forehead, noting the temperature on her chart.

"Talk it out," Dr. Stephens instructed.

"Fever of 100.3." He grabbed a tongue depressor and a throat culture stick then carefully inspected her throat. "Swollen anterior cervical lymph nodes. Marked tonsillar exudates. Petechiae on the soft palate." He took a throat culture sample and handed it to the nurse.

"What's your diagnosis?" the doctor asked.

"Streptococcal pharyngitis. Rapid strep test should confirm."

Jane had never seen Randy play this role before. She was impressed, not only with his level of knowledge, but also with how quickly he determined a diagnosis.

The test came back positive, confirming Randy's analysis. "Good," Dr. Stephens said, proud of his protégé. "Treatment plan?"

"She's not allergic to Penicillin, so either a ten day oral suspension or a single intramuscular injection of Penicillin G." He looked away from paperwork for a minute and asked, "You want ten days of meds or a one-time injection, Babe? Up to you."

She didn't know the difference. "Which one works faster?"

"Injection."

"I'll take that then."

Dr. Stephens instructed, "Four CC's of benzathine."

"Yes, Sir." He put her chart down and exited the room.

While Randy went to get a syringe of Penicillin, Dr. Stephens checked his work. "You'll start to feel better in a few hours," he said to Jane. "Tylenol will keep that fever down. Drink plenty of water, but stay away from citrus for a few days."

Randy reentered the room with a syringe, rubbing alcohol, and a cotton ball in his hand.

Jane's eyes widened when she saw the size of the needle. "You're not going to stick me with that, are you?"

"Sorry, Babe. It's either this or Dr. Stephens can write you a prescription."

"Just get it over with," she insisted.

Dr. Stephens washed his hands, slipped on a pair of latex gloves and injected her with Penicillin. "Ok, Ms. Davine, you are good to go." He washed his hands again then wrote her a doctor's excuse. "It was very nice to meet you, Jane. Now go home and get some rest."

"Thank you, Dr. Stephens."

The doctor left the room and Jane hopped off the examination table. "He seems like a nice man."

"He's a cool guy. I've learned a lot from him. He's really easy to work for, and he's super supportive."

Randy took Jane back to his apartment and made her go back to bed. He brought her some water and handed her the remote to the T.V. "You need anything before I go?"

"No, I'm fine." She gave him a thoughtful stare. "I'm impressed with what you did at the clinic today, Dr. Hanson."

"I'm not a doctor yet, but thank you." He leaned over and kissed her cheek. "I have to go. Get some rest please."

The day seemed to drag on endlessly. It might have been because Randy skipped lunch, which made his stomach growl all afternoon. He needed food. Before he headed to work, he stopped at the café and grabbed a quick bite to eat.

Bruce sat at a table scrolling through his cellphone. Randy pulled up a chair and joined him. "Hey, Buckman."

Bruce looked up. "Hey, man. How's Jane feeling?"

"Her throat still hurts, but she had a Penicillin injection. She should start feeling better soon."

"That's good." Bruce set his phone down. "She's a good woman, Randy."

Randy smiled self-assuredly. "Yes she is."

"I had a woman like that once. Her name was Heather Lucas—beautiful girl, funny, brilliantly creative, sharp as a tack. Our relationship was pretty serious. After dating for three years, we got engaged."

This was shocking information. "You were engaged?"

"Yes I was. We planned to get married when I graduated from college, and she had every intention of coming to Berkeley with me, but it didn't work out that way."

"What happened?"

He gathered his thoughts and tried not to get emotional. "On the day of our wedding, she left me standing on the altar. She never called, never left a note, never told me why, she just didn't show up. I never saw her or heard from her again."

What a cold and heartless thing to do. "Damn, Dude, that sucks."

He inhaled slowly and released a long drawn-out breath. "Her sister later told me that she couldn't go through with it, but she was afraid to confront me about it. Took me a while to get over that one," Bruce claimed. "It still gets to me sometimes. Every time I hear the name Heather, I turn my head."

Randy completely understood. "I bet."

Bruce checked his phone to see what time it was. "I better take off. Have some research to do."

"Alright. I'll see you tomorrow."

When Randy walked into his apartment that evening, Jane was up and about, getting a glass of tap water from the kitchen sink. He sneaked up behind her and kissed her neck.

She flinched and playfully smacked him on the arm. "Why do you always sneak up on me like that? Stop that."

Randy laughed at her. "You look like you're feeling better."

"Much better."

"Good." He put his book bag down, took her in his arms, and kissed her. They made their way to the bed and rolled around on top of the blanket for a while. Deeply engrossed in a kiss, Randy's phone rang.

"Let it ring," Jane insisted.

Randy's foot knocked the phone on the floor, inadvertently answering the call. "Hello?" the voice on the line said.

Jane kissed his neck and unbuttoned his pants, completely distracting him. She stripped off his pants and kissed the entire length of his naked body. When she began fondling, a pleasurable groan slipped from his lips. "Oh god, that feels good." He now had a full erection. He swallowed hard trying to curb his desire.

"Randy, are you there?" the voice called out.

Randy reached for his phone. "Dad."

Jane pulled her shirt over her head and sexily unlatched her bra, slowly sliding it off her shoulders. Randy stared in lustful delight, not listening to a word his father said.

"Everything alright, Son?"

"Everything's fine."

This was impossible. There was no way he could maintain a conversation with his father under these conditions. "You really caught me at a bad time. Can I call you back in about thirty minutes?"

"I guess so. Are you sure you're alright?"

"I'm fine. I'll call you right back." He hung up and pulled Jane on top of him. "What are you doing?"

"What's it feel like I'm doing?" She straddled his lap and forced his erectness inside her.

He let out a groan and reclined back on the pillow, letting her take complete control.

When she was finished, he grinned at her seductively. "I just hung up on my dad. How the hell am I supposed to justify that?"

"Tell him the truth."

Randy laughed. "Gee, Dad, I'm sorry I hung up on you, but Jane was taking off all my clothes, doing a little strip tease for me, and she and I were having sex. I can't tell him that." He gently lifted her off his lap.

She stretched onto her side with her head propped in her hand. "Why not? You told me your dad is open about sex. I'm sure he'll understand."

He dangled his feet over the edge of the bed and held out his hand. "Hand me my phone."

"What are you gonna say?"

"Just give it to me."

She handed it to him and he dialed his father's number. While it rang, he slipped on a pair of athletic shorts and moseyed into the living room.

Jane got up and got dressed. It couldn't have been more than five minutes before Randy returned to the room.

"So, what's the verdict?" she asked.

With a smartass smirk, Randy replied, "He was upset that I hung up on him, but he knew what we were doing."

This didn't seem to bother him at all. "You're not embarrassed?"

"Why would I be? I'm a big boy, I can have sex with my girlfriend if I want. I have no problem talking about it with my father either. You're the one who doesn't like to talk about it."

"That's not true."

"Yes it is," he teased. "You let me stick my dick inside you, but you never talk to me about it."

She cringed at his upfront statement. "That's perverted."

"It's not perverted. It's the truth."

"Ok. What do you want to talk about?"

He knew she wouldn't answer the question, but he asked it anyway. "How do you like it, fast and hard or more of a slow, deep ease in?"

Her jaw dropped. "Oh my god, Randy. I can't believe you said that."

"See, there you go again. Why won't you talk about it?"

"Sex might have been an open topic in your family, but in mine it was always taboo."

"Yeah, I know, and I don't get that," he said. "Sex is natural. What's the big deal?"

"It wasn't something we openly discussed. It's shocking to me how open you are about it with your parents."

"I'm trying to be open about it with you. I don't see why you won't talk to me about it. We do it all the time."

"Randy, please." She walked out of the room.

He followed her, not understanding her point of view. "Are you mad at me?"

"No, but you don't get it, do you?"

"No, I don't," he admitted. "I'm trying to understand. I'm not used to sex being such a closed subject."

"Daddy freaks out when the topic even comes up."

"But your dad isn't here, is he?" Randy reminded her.

"No."

"You're a grown woman with a libido. It's ok to talk about sex, especially with me." He sat on the couch and propped his elbow on the armrest. "So, tell me. What is your most erotic sexual fantasy?"

She wasn't sure she was comfortable talking about this. "Randy."

"Open up to me, Babe. I can't satisfy a fantasy if I don't know what it is."

"I'll tell you, but you have to go first."

"Alright." He cogitated over this for a minute. "Ok, I've got it. Sex on the beach, right where the waves hit the shoreline. The water showering our bodies while I'm hot and heavy with the woman I love. Moonlight glistening off the ocean, wet skin, soft kisses, extreme passion." Picturing this made him wish he could be there with her right now. "That would be heaven."

"Add a few palm trees, a couple tropical flowers, and the faint chirp of tree frogs, and I'm there."

"Nice touch," he agreed. "Your turn."

She bit her lip and revealed her deepest secrets to him. "Skinny dipping, but not just anywhere. One of those tropical lagoons surrounded by sweet smelling flowers and big palm leaves, making love under the waterfall."

This fantasy of hers intrigued him. "Sounds luscious to me. Any island in particular?"

"Bermuda maybe. I've always wanted to go there."

"I've never been there," he told her. "My parents have. They showed me pictures from their trip. Turquoise waters, white sandy beaches, beautiful natural pools. Lush vegetation and colorful flowers everywhere. Totally picturesque."

She tried to picture it in her head. "Sounds beautiful."

"I promise I will find you that waterfall someday. I do have a shower, though. Will that suffice for now?"

His creativity made her laugh. "Yes."

"Good. Let's hop in the shower then.

Chapter Twenty-One

Saturday afternoon, Bruce, Randy, Jim, and Jane decided to meet at the gym to play a game of two on two.

"I get Jane on my team," Bruce said.

"Oh, no you don't," Randy corrected. "My girl, my team."

"You won't even share her for a game of basketball?"

"Nope."

"Greedy bastard," Bruce teased.

"Damn straight."

Throughout the progression of the game, Randy and Jane consistently remained in the lead. Jim wasn't about to allow that to happen. In a huddle with Bruce, he laid out a game plan. "Ok, Jane is a lot better than I thought. Her accuracy on the line is hella good. We can't foul her anymore."

"I agree," Bruce confirmed. "Stay on Hanson. See if you can wear him out so Jane has to run alone."

"Good idea." They broke their huddle and tried their new strategy. It seemed to work for a while. Randy was getting tired. He had to stop a few times to catch his breath, which enabled Bruce and Jim to tie up the game.

Jane had seen enough. In an attempt to steal the ball, she slammed into Bruce and knocked him onto the court. She hijacked the ball then dribbled to the other end to make a layup.

Bruce sat on the hardwood floor rubbing his elbow. "Holy shit. Remind me not to piss you off."

She offered a hand to help him up. "You okay?"

"Yes. I'm fine."

She pranced to the sidelines to get a drink of water while the men gathered in the middle of the court, panting. "Dude, did you see that?" Jim said, struggling to regain air. "How the hell do you keep up with her, Randy? You must have the stamina of a stallion."

Bruce's elbow was raw and sore. "She's an aggressive player," he said. "Why isn't she playing for Cal?"

"I'm working on that," Randy declared.

The men said their goodbyes and Randy walked Jane home. When they got to the Alpha house, Jane led him up the stairs to her room.

"Why'd you bring me up here?" he asked.

"I want to give you something." She closed the door then grabbed the bottom of Randy's shirt and pulled it over his head.

Misinterpreting her intentions, he said, "We can't do this here, Babe. Your sorority sisters are all over the place."

She laughed internally at his false interpretation. "I don't want to have sex with you."

"Gee, thanks."

Jane reached up to the top shelf of her closet and pulled out a gift bag. Inside was a white tee-shirt with the Lakers logo printed on the front. She unfolded it and slipped it over Randy's head.

Randy looked down at the imprint. "You bought me a new Lakers shirt. Thanks, Honey."

"You're welcome."

He sat on the bed and pulled her onto his lap. "That was a pretty impressive move you made on the court today. I really enjoyed watching your intensity. Basketball is in your blood, Babe. I'd love to see you play competitively."

She got off his lap and stepped away, avoiding the issue. "Why are you bringing that up again?"

"Because you still have eligibility left, and I hate to see you throw that away."

"I told you it's not important to me anymore."

"It is important to you. I saw it in your eyes today. Why are you fighting this?"

"I'm not fighting it."

"Yes you are. Something is holding you back, something more than what you're telling me. What are you so afraid of?"

"You wouldn't understand."

"Did you forget who you're talking to here? It's me, Baby. You've always been able to talk to me." He stood behind her and wrapped her in his arms. "Whatever it is, I'll understand."

She stared blankly out the window. "I'm afraid to get into the game again because I'm afraid I will get so wrapped up in it that I'll lose everything I love. I can't afford to take that risk."

"What could you possibly lose because of basketball?"

"For one thing, Daddy won't approve."

"He doesn't have to. It's not his decision."

"And what about my grades?" she countered. "With the time commitment involved, my grades might drop."

"Tutoring sessions and study halls can help you work around that. "

"Then there's you." She looked up at him. "I don't want to lose you."

"I'm not going anywhere, Baby."

Despite his encouragement, she was worried. "Basketball consumed my life. It was all I ever did. I spent so much time focusing on my game that I lost track of the things in my life that mattered to me the most. Now some of those things are gone, and I will never get them back."

Affectionately, he kissed the top of her head. "I would never let basketball come between us."

"It involves so much."

He cut in, "And you miss every minute of it, admit it. Basketball drives you, it gives you that spark. It makes you happy."

"I'm happy being with you."

"But you would be happier if you played, and you know it."

She was even more confused now than she was before.

Randy tried to clear the waters for her. "Lots of things in life are important to me: my family, my friends, you. I love them all and would not give up one for the other. Look at med school, for example. Medicine is my passion. It motivates me and is something I get excited about it, but that doesn't mean I can't enjoy other aspects of my life. It is possible to have friends, maintain a relationship, and spend time with your family while playing basketball, if you're willing to work at it. It's a matter of balancing your time commitments. You're the only one who knows what you want, Jane, and ultimately, the decision has to be yours. No matter what you decide, I will support you. I just want you to be happy." He checked his watch. It was almost 4:00. "I have to get going. Have some research to do before we go out tonight." He grabbed his basketball and turned to leave.

"Randy?" she called out to him.

"Yes?"

"I love you."

"I love you too." He kissed her before he left.

Jane lounged on her bed with her arm dangling over the side and thought about what Randy said. Despite the happiness and contentment she felt in her life, something was missing. Perhaps basketball would fill that void. As her hand reached down to the floor, she felt something touching the tips of her fingers. It was Randy's shirt. She picked it up and held it close to her. It needed to be washed. She had other laundry to do anyway, so she put his shirt, along with some of her laundry, in the washing machine downstairs.

Jane met Randy at his apartment that night. Purposefully positioned on the table was a vase of long-stemmed red roses with a card attached. She walked over to read the note. *Janey, I will support you in all that you do and love you for all that you are.* It was signed with the letter R and a drawing of a heart. Sentimental tears filled her eyes.

Randy stepped out of the bedroom, surprised to see Jane there so early. "Good evening."

"Thank you for the flowers. They're beautiful."

"You're very welcome." The outfit she had on was simply, but looked elegant on her—a black skirt, white button up blouse, and a black cardigan. Her sexy black sandals showed off her brightly painted toenails. "You look nice."

"So do you." Jane reached her hand up and touched his face. "You shaved for me."

"Of course. Can't kiss a scratchy face. And I'm hoping for a lot of kisses tonight." He leaned forward and kissed her. "There's one. I'm on a roll so far."

"Are you going to count all night?"

"I might." He offered his hand to her. "Shall we go?"

"Yes."

On the way out the door, he grabbed his black leather jacket.

When the waitress brought the dinner check to the table, Jane grabbed it out of Randy's hand.

He raised his eyebrows. "Give it back."

She held it behind her back so he couldn't reach it. "No."

"Come on, Jane, give it to me."

"We've been together for more than five months now and you have never let me pick up the tab."

"That's right," he declared. "And I'm not going to start tonight. Give it back."

Reluctantly, she handed it back to him. "How come you never let me pay?"

"It's just a thing with me. I'm not into having a woman pay. I never have been. I don't think it's right." He pulled out her chair and offered his hand to help her up.

"It bothers me that you never let me pay for anything."

"Why?" he asked.

"You shouldn't have to spend your paycheck on me every week."

"I don't spend it on you. I spend it on us, and I do it because I want to." Jane was not satisfied with this answer. Aiming to please, he offered, "Fine, if it bothers you that much, you can take care of the tip."

She was satisfied with that.

They met a bunch of their friends at The Club that night. When they arrived, Randy immediately went to the bar and ordered two drinks—a strawberry daiquiri for Jane and a Screwdriver for himself. He joined Jim at the table and chatted with him while Jane visited with her sorority sisters. It wasn't long before Randy was back at the bar getting another drink. When he returned to the table, he moved the hair off Jane's neck and nibbled on the sweet, smooth skin underneath. "Will you dance with me?"

She took his hand and joined him on the dancefloor.

Randy held her close, kissing her neck as they danced. The scent of her perfume drove him crazy. "What is that perfume you are wearing? It's turning me on."

"It's called Seduction," she said with a suggestive grin.

"I can see why."

When their dance was over, they rejoined their friends. Randy quickly grew tired of the conversation and slammed down another drink. He leaned closer to Jane and suggested, "Come with me."

"Where are we going?"

"I want to be alone with you." He grabbed her hand and led her to a secluded corner of the room. When they got to the booth, he backed her against the wall and forcibly kissed her.

Trying to get him to back off, she said, "Randy, not here. People are watching us."

"With that perfume you're wearing, the soft lights in here, and the sexy way you're looking at me, I am really turned on right now." He pressed his body against hers and moved in closer, rubbing his hands all over her.

Sexual aggressiveness was out of character for him. But then again, he had been drinking steadily all night. His breath smelled of alcohol and his speech was slightly slurred, which led Jane to believe he was intoxicated.

He rubbed his hand up her thigh and locked his lips to hers.

Annoyed by his behavior, she said, "Randy, stop."

He reached his finger into her panties and tried to take them off.

She immediately pushed his hand away. "Stop it."

He quickly became frustrated. "Come on, Baby. I want you."

She had never seen this side of him before. "How many drinks have you had tonight?"

"I don't know. Why does that matter?"

"You're drunk. I need to get you home. Give me the keys."

Her tone sounded hostile. Randy was a bit drawn back by this. "Are you mad at me?"

"No, but you are drunk, and you need to go to bed."

"Ooh," he moaned seductively. "I will definitely go to bed with you."

She held her hand open. "Keys, Mister."

He reached into his pocket and handed her his car keys. "Does that mean no?"

She escorted him to the table to get their coats.

Jim saw the dazed look in Randy's eyes and knew right away that he was drunk. "Is he causin' you trouble?"

Although annoyed, Jane thought this whole situation was amusing. "Nothing I can't handle."

Laughing, Jim warned, "Watch out for this guy, Jane. He gets horny and a little tenacious when he's been drinkin'."

Yeah. She had that figured out. "Thanks for the tip." She picked up her purse, grabbed both their jackets, then took Randy's hand and led him out to the car. "Come on, Mister. We're going home."

On the way out, Randy said, "You never answered my question."

"And which question would that be?"

"Will you have sex with me tonight?"

She unlocked the car and opened the passenger side door. "Get in the car."

"I was just asking."

While Jane drove home, Randy fondled her thigh and moved his hand up her skirt. She continued to push his hand away. When she finally got him inside his apartment, he forced her against the wall, kissing her while he groped for her breasts.

She resisted. "Randy, no. You have had too much to drink."

"But I perform better after a few drinks. It'll be the best sex we've ever had."

He could barely stand. How could he possibly 'perform' at all in his condition? "Are you always like this when you're drunk?"

"Like what?" He kissed her neck and tugged at her panties, hoping to strip them off of her. "All I want to do is have sex with you and you won't let me."

"Go lie down on the couch," she insisted.

"Ooh," he said, expressing his approval. "You wanna do it on the couch?"

"No. I want you to lie down." She pulled herself away from him and walked into the living room.

"Shit, Jane. You're really gonna leave me here all night with a hard on?"

"You need to sober up, then I'll think about letting you touch me."

The room started to spin. To keep himself upright, Randy leaned against the wall. He raised his hand to his forehead and closed his eyes. "Whoa."

Jane rushed to his side. "Please sit down before you fall over."

She helped him hobble over to the couch, where he collapsed on the pillow. He was out almost instantly.

Jane put his feet up on the couch, took off his shoes, and left him there to rest. She went into the kitchen, grabbed a Diet Pepsi and an apple to munch on then sat in the chair to keep an eye on him.

About 7:00 A.M. he began to stir. His head throbbed and his eyes burned. His tongue felt like it was coated with mold. With a grumpy look on his face, he sat up. "My head is fuckin' killing me."

"I'm not surprised." Jane joined him on the couch.

The licorice flavored vinyl taste in his mouth made him gag. "How much did I drink last night?"

"I'm not sure. I wasn't monitoring you, but maybe I should have," she teased.

He collapsed back on the pillow, feeling weak and tired.

"Let me get you some Tylenol." She stood up and headed toward the bathroom.

Randy held his head in his hands and groaned.

Minutes later, Jane returned with a glass of water and two pills in her hand. She handed them to Randy. "You acted like a jerk last night."

He gazed upon her, guilt-ridden. "I didn't come onto you did I?" Jim told him horrible stories about things he did when he was drunk. He hoped he hadn't been forceful towards her. "Did I?"

She curled her lip and nodded.

He rolled his eyes, ashamed of himself. "I'm so sorry, Honey." He took both tablets and chugged down the entire glass of water. "I haven't had a hangover in years. Now I remember why." He looked over at Jane. Her eyes were puffy with dark circles under them, and her complexion was pale. "You look tired, Babe."

"I am. I slept in the chair all night so I could watch over you."

He held out his arms to her. "Come here."

She moved over and sat on his lap.

"I'm really sorry I acted like an ass last night."

"It's ok."

He put his arms around her and gave her a hug. "What time is it?"

"A little after 7:00."

"I'm going to hop in the shower. Hopefully that will clear my head. Will you put a pot of coffee on for me?"

"Sure."

Lovingly, he kissed her forehead. "Thank you for looking after me last night."

"You're welcome."

Randy reported to his study session that morning feeling like shit. This was definitely not one of his better days.

When he strolled into the room, Jim laughed at him. "Well, good morning!" he shouted, knowing Randy's head was throbbing. "You look like hell."

"Shut up," Randy retorted.

Jim couldn't help but make fun of him "Did you enjoy your bottle of Vodka last night?"

"Don't remind me, ok? I feel like I've been run over by a truck."

"Yeah, a Smirnoff truck."

His head hurt, and Jim's smartass remarks made it worse. "Are you finished now?"

Randy probably felt queasy. Jim had to tease him about it. "You up for some donuts?"

"Ugh!" Randy suddenly felt nauseous.

"I'll take that as a no."

When the others joined them at the table, Bruce got a chuckle over Randy's sour expression. "Glad to see you out and about. You were wasted last night. I think Jane was getting annoyed with you."

Randy confirmed, "I know. I'm pretty sure she's mad at me."

Mandy added, "Can't say that I blame her. You acted like an asshole last night."

"That's what I've been told."

"She'll get over it," Jim so conclusively put it, downplaying the situation.

"I hope so."

When the session was over, Jim walked Randy to his car. "Did I tell you I saw Nicole Jacobs the other day?"

Randy hadn't heard that name in a long time, and it was a name that he would just as soon forget about. Leave it Jim to bring up haunting incidents from his past. "Does she still hate me?"

"Yup," Jim grinned. "In fact, she pretty much told me that you are the most insensitive asshole she ever met."

"I'm not surprised she feels that way."

"Is it true that she broke up with her boyfriend to be with you?"

"That's what I heard." Randy wished Jim would leave the past well enough alone. "Why are you bringing that up?"

"I'm tryin' to make a point."

"Then make it," Randy demanded.

"You went out with her, what, three times? When she finally agreed to go to bed with you, you dicked her and told her to take a hike, didn't you?" Jim stated.

"Those weren't my exact words, but yeah, basically that's what happened. What's your damn point, Jim?"

"Man, you are an asshole."

Randy was not amused. "Very funny."

"Does Jane know you used to be a playboy?" Jim inquired.

"I don't do that anymore. You know that."

"I wonder what she would say if she knew about the screw and scrap side of you."

Randy was mortified. "She will never know. She has no reason to know. That is something from my past that has no significance or relevance to anything. I would rather that you put all of that back in the past where it belongs and leave it there. That's not a stage in my life I'm particularly proud of."

Jim laughed. "So, how pissed is she?"

"She's not happy, but at least she's talking to me. I have some serious sucking up to do."

"So it seems, Bro. So it seems."

255

Chapter Twenty-Two

Randy strolled through the door of his apartment later than usual Monday night. It was after 10:30 P.M. Jane was curled up on the sofa dressed only in a pair of underwear and one of his oversized dress shirts. She was so engrossed in the book she was reading that she didn't hear him come in, which made it easy for him to sneak behind her. "Hi, Baby."

She smacked him in the arm with her book. "Jesus, Randy. Don't do that."

He loved sneaking up on her like that. It always made her flinch.

She put her book down and sat up. "You're home late."

"Had a lot of research I needed to do." He plopped down next to her and kicked off his shoes. Feeling tense, he rubbed the back of his neck.

Jane scooted closer and massaged his shoulders. His muscles felt unusually tight. "You are really tense."

"I have a lot going on right now. Have midterms coming up in about a month and progress on my thesis has been slow lately."

"Are you getting enough time to study?" she asked. "If you're not, you need to say something."

"It's not that. It's me. I can't seem to organize my thoughts. I'm trying to piece all of the research together and sharpen it up. The information is scientifically sound, but it's not flowing the way I'd like it to."

"How much do you have done?"

"About twenty-one pages so far, but I'm not finished. I still have revising and editing to do. Dr. Grayson is helping me fine tune it, but I feel like a piece of my research is missing. I can't figure out what it is though." He closed his eyes and released a relaxed sigh. He felt much looser now. "Maybe I should have my dad take a look at it. He might be able to help me come up with something."

"Isn't your thesis based on Obstetrics anyway?" she reminded him.

"Yes, that and Toxicology mainly."

"Then an obstetrician might be the answer."

Randy nodded. "Dad is good at stuff like that too. He's written many articles for medical journals." He moved his head from side to side to loosen his neck more. "Dr. Boyce asked me to stop by his office tomorrow."

"What for?"

"He didn't say. All he said was that it was imperative I stop in and see him. I'm not sure if that's good or bad."

"I'm sure it's nothing to worry about."

During his hour-long break between a lecture and a lab, Randy reported to Dr. Boyce's office as instructed. He was a little apprehensive, wondering why the Dean of UC Berkeley's Joint Medical Program wanted to see him. He stepped into the Dean's office and spoke to his secretary. "Excuse me, Ma'am."

She looked up from her paperwork. "May I help you?"

"Yes. I'm Randy Hanson. I have a twelve o'clock appointment with Dr. Boyce."

"Yes, Mr. Hanson. He's been expecting you. Have a seat, and I'll tell him you're here."

"Thank you." Randy sat in a nearby chair and anxiously waited.

Dr. Boyce came out of his office, graciously extending his hand. "Randy Hanson. Good to see you again."

Randy stood up respectfully. "Thank you, Sir. It's good to see you too."

"Please," the doctor led him to a chair in his office. "Have a seat."

Randy did as he was asked.

Dr. Boyce took a seat across from him. "I understand you work over at the student clinic with Dr. Stephens."

"Yes, Sir. That's correct," Randy confirmed.

"He has told me wonderful things about you and is quite impressed with the work you're doing over there."

Knowing Dr. Stephens acclaimed him highly boosted Randy's confidence. "That's good to know."

Dr. Boyce got out of his chair and towered over Randy, intimidating him a little. "Have you ever heard of the Herbert W. Nickens scholarship?"

"No, Sir. I'm not familiar with that one."

"It is specifically designed for medical students entering their third year. It's awarded based on grades, research efforts, clinical work, leadership, medical professionalism, and university recommendation. Only five medical students in the country are awarded this scholarship each year. I've received several letters from your professors and Dr. Stephens recommending you for this scholarship. I gave this information to the scholarship commission, and they have agreed to award it to you."

Randy was not expecting such a prestigious honor. Unsure how to react, he simply replied, "I'm honored, Sir."

"You should be receiving more information sometime next week. There is some paperwork involved. Congratulations, Randy. You've earned it."

Randy rose to his feet and shook Dr. Boyce's hand. "Thank you, Doctor."

"Let me know if you need anything."

"Yes, Sir. I will."

Dr. Boyce showed him out.

Randy couldn't hold his excitement in any longer. Immediately, he got on his cellphone and told Jane the good news.

Sarah, Bruce, Mandy, and Jim all knew Randy was meeting with Dr. Boyce during lunch, so they were surprised when he waltzed over to the table with a huge smile etched on his face.

"How'd it go?" Jim asked.

"You guys ever heard of the Herbert Nickens medical school scholarship?" Randy asked the group.

"I have," Bruce said. "It's virtually impossible to get. Only five med students in the entire country are awarded that scholarship each year. It's a pretty hefty award too. Five thousand dollars or something like that."

"That's the one," Randy confirmed.

"What about it?" Bruce asked.

"Guess who the latest recipient is?"

They all saw the grin on Randy's face and knew he was talking about himself. "You have got to be shittin' me?" Jim said, thinking Randy was flipping crap at them.

"No, I'm not. Dr. Boyce just told me. I didn't believe him at first."

"Holy shit," Bruce said. "That's incredible!"

Mandy gave him a huge hug. "Congratulations!"

Jim could not believe his best friend had earned a scholarship only five medical students in the entire country receive. He was completely dumbfounded. "Jesus, Hanson. How the hell did you manage that? Make us all look bad, why don't ya."

Randy knew Jim was messing with him because he had a cheesy grin on his face. "I do my best."

Randy and Jim left class together and planned to play basketball for a bit, but as they exited the Medical Sciences building, Randy spotted something that made the smile instantly leave his face. A familiar woman with a pregnant belly was standing outside. Jim hadn't noticed her yet. "Jim, don't look now, but Trina is standing outside."

Jim turned to look. "Dammit. What the hell does she want?"

Randy hated that Trina kept popping up like this all the time. Right as Jim was getting over her and feeling pretty good about his decision to leave, Trina would show up, which made Jim reconsider his choice. Randy didn't like the way Trina treated him, and he especially didn't like the way she toyed with Jim's heart all the time. "You don't have to talk to her, you know," Randy said.

"If I don't, she won't leave me alone."

Randy tried to warn him. "Don't fall for anything she says."

"I won't." Jim stepped outside to talk to her.

Even though Jim didn't want to admit it, Katrina had been on his mind. He was trying to get over her and move on with his life, but her name always seemed to pop up in conversations he and Randy had. Randy carefully watched their interaction. At first, their confrontation was bitter and argumentative. But as they continued their discussion, Jim placed his hand on Trina's pregnant belly. This was not a good sign. They had broken up several times before and blindly Jim always ran back to her. Randy hated to interfere with their relationship, but this time Trina had gone too far and had seriously wronged his friend, wounding him badly. Randy was not going to sit around and continue to watch her to do this to him, so he took matters into his own hands. He walked over to them and said, "Come on, Jim. We have to go."

Trina smiled at him. "Hi, Randy."

He glowered at her and simply said, "Trina." He put his hand on Jim's shoulder. "Let's go."

Jim went with Randy but didn't say anything for several minutes. Once they were in the parking lot, he finally spoke up. "Why'd you do that?"

"Because I know what you're thinking," Randy said. "Do not forget what that woman did to you."

"I know, but…"

"No," Randy interjected. "I have never butted into your relationship with Trina but dammit, Jim, she has hurt you too many times. When are you going to figure it out? She has done nothing but deceive you, lie to you, and steal your soul. That woman is a succubus. There are a hell of lot better women out there who won't treat you like crap.

Stop falling for her deceitful lies. You're going to get hurt again."

"But I…"

"Don't do it, Jim, please. You are finally getting your life together, and without her nagging at you all the time, I've never seen you so happy. You don't need her."

"I know. I just…" He stopped and reflected on his circumstances. "I really miss havin' a babe around. Do you know how long it's been since I've had sex?"

Usually Jim was the one offering advice, but this time, he was the one who needed it. "Trina is not the answer," Randy advised. "There are other women."

Jim knew Randy was right. He grabbed his workout clothes, changed at Randy's apartment, then the two of them went to the gym to play basketball.

Chapter Twenty-Three

Jane's birthday was right around the corner, and Randy wanted to do something to surprise her. He knew she loved tropical motifs and dreamed of going to a tropical island, so he made reservations at The Tonga Room in the Fairmont Hotel in San Francisco. The restaurant had tiki huts, palm trees, and a lagoon in the middle of the dining room. It offered exceptional Pacific Rim Asian cuisine in a tropical setting complete with thunder and rainstorms. The festive atmosphere, with live entertainment and dancing, served tantalizing cocktails and exquisite delicacies. Jane was absolutely going to love it.

Randy prearranged to have the wait staff serenade her with the birthday song as they presented her with a cake. He also bought a bottle of wine that was chilling in his refrigerator and arranged to have flowers delivered to her. Her birthday present was wrapped and hidden from her in the bedside table drawer for safe keeping. Now, all he had to do was wait.

Jane was surprised to come home the evening of her birthday to a huge bouquet of roses. A note was attached. *Happy birthday, Baby. We have a date tonight. Be ready by 6:30. I love you, R.* She was so charmed by his secretiveness. He had not said a word about her birthday all week, and she thought he had forgotten about it. Obviously he hadn't. Biting her lip, she ran upstairs to get ready for their date.

Randy arrived promptly at 6:30, and he was in an impeccable mood. He greeted Jane at the door with a long, deep kiss. Her lips tasted fruity. "Mmm, strawberry. My favorite." He put his arms around her waist. "You smell great too. I love that body spray you're wearing."

"Thank you."

Excited to begin their evening together, he asked, "You ready?"

"Uh huh."

"Then let's go." He took her hand and escorted her out to the car.

At the restaurant, the host greeted them. "Good evening, Sir. How may I help you?"

"Reservations for Hanson, please," Randy said.

The host checked the reservation book to confirm. "Right this way."

He led them to a cozy table in the corner. Randy, being the gentleman he was, pulled Jane's chair out for her. She sat down gracefully, and he took a seat across from her.

"Your waiter will be with you momentarily. Enjoy your evening, Sir."

"Thank you."

Jane surveyed the surroundings. Tiki torches flickered all around them. "This is fantastic. Where'd you find this place?"

"A little hideaway I happened to stumble upon." The Tonga Room was considered the high-style Tiki bar of San Francisco. Randy had never been here before. The fun environment reminded him of a bar he went to in Waikiki. "It is pretty cool."

They ordered their entrees and a couple of cocktails. Jane's was a Mai Tai which came served in a coconut shell glass, and Randy had a coral-colored drink Jane had never seen before. "What is that?" Jane asked, watching him take a sip of it.

Randy grinned sexily. "It's called Sex on the Beach. You want some?"

She giggled and reached to take a sip from his totem head-shaped glass. "This is so much more than I expected. Thank you, Sweetie."

"I am hoping to sweep you off your feet tonight."

She smiled, overjoyed by his intentions. "You already have."

When the waiter brought out their meals, he draped a single red rose across Jane's napkin, as Randy had instructed him to do. She picked it up and sniffed its sweet scent. "I can't believe you did all of this."

"I would do anything for you." Randy reached into his jacket pocket and pulled out a box wrapped in metallic purple paper. "Here you go, Honey. Happy birthday."

She carefully peeled off the paper. Inside was a gold ring with a heart on it. On each side of the heart was a small blue sapphire. A matching gold bracelet with an alternating heart, sapphire pattern accompanied it. She slipped the ring on her finger and held up her hand to admire it. "I love it."

Randy took the bracelet out of the box and latched it around her wrist. "There. Now you are complete."

"Thank you so much."

"My pleasure."

After their table was cleared, the entire wait staff brought out a cake brightly lit with candles. They presented it to Jane while they sang 'Happy Birthday.' She was horribly embarrassed by this, but loved the trouble Randy went through to make this night so special for her.

Randy gazed at her with a grin on his face. "Did it work?"

"Did what work?" she asked, not knowing what he was talking about.

"Did I sweep you off your feet tonight?"

"You did that a long time ago."

They walked out to the car with leftover birthday cake. "I have a bottle of wine at my place," Randy said. "Can I interest you in a glass?"

"Depends."

"On what?"

"Will you take me to bed when we get there?"

He was a bit surprised by the boldness of this question. "I'll take you anywhere you want to go."

"Good. Then take me to the moon." She grazed her hands across his chest as her mouth interlocked with his. Desire burned within him, and they hadn't even left the parking lot yet. As soon as Jane was in the car, Randy had to take a few breaths to lessen the lustful craving he felt, at least long enough to drive home.

The following afternoon, Jane was sitting on the sofa reading a magazine when Randy came home from work. "Oh good," she said when she heard him walk in. "I'm glad you're home. What is an intraparenchymal hematoma?"

He chuckled at her mispronunciation. "A hematoma is a hemorrhage caused by a blood vessel rupture. This particular hemorrhage includes white matter injuries. The tear in the axon connections results in the neurons no longer having the ability to communicate, which can lead to serious brain damage."

"That sounds bad. Is it fatal?" she asked, curious about it now.

"It's definitely life-threatening if not treated properly. Where did you hear about that?"

"I read about it in this magazine."

He removed his stethoscope and placed it on the table. "How was your day?" he asked, leaning over the back of the sofa to give her a kiss.

"It was alright. I worked on a paper." She sat on her knees and peered over the back of the couch. "And I made cookies."

His eyes lit up. "Cookies? What kind?"

"Chocolate chip. They're in the kitchen."

"Sweet!" Chocolate chip cookies were his favorite. He hurried off to grab a few.

While Randy was in the kitchen stealing cookies, someone knocked on the door. "I'll get it!" Jane hollered into the kitchen. When she opened the door, her jaw fell to the floor. "Daddy."

Dale Davine frowned at the skin-tight shorts and skimpy spaghetti-strapped tank top Jane had on. "Put some clothes on."

"These are my clothes."

"Where were you last night?" he bellowed. "I tried to call you three times, and each time your phone went straight to voicemail."

"I was charging my phone and didn't have it on me."

"I was worried something had happened to you. I went up to your sorority house this morning and they gave me this address. They told me you were over here all night." He peered in the door. "Is this Randy's apartment?"

"Yes."

The makeup she was wearing irked him even more. "What the hell is that crap on your face?"

"Baby, who is it?" Randy called out. He came to the door to see who she was talking to. "Mr. Davine."

Dale Davine shot Randy an ice-piercing glare. "What have you done to my daughter?"

"Excuse me?"

"Jane would never dress provocatively, nor would she plaster cosmetics all over her face if it wasn't for your influence."

Offended by this man's vile tone, he said, "I don't force her do anything. Jane has a mind of her own. She does whatever she wants."

"Is that right?" Dale griped, outraged that Randy dared to question him. "She's too young to know what she wants."

"She's a grown woman, Sir. Perfectly capable of making her own decisions."

Dale glowered at Jane. "You've become a bed-hopping hussy now, is that it? Dressing like a slut and freely allowing yourself to act as this man's sex toy?"

Jane started to cry.

This scornful statement, and the fact that it was so hurtful to Jane, made Randy angry. He could no longer stand back and allow this man to belittle her. Despite his father's warnings, Randy had to intervene. "Now hold on. That was not necessary. Don't speak to her that way."

"She is my daughter. I can speak to her any way I please."

Randy disagreed. "Not to sound disrespectful, Sir, but no you can't. Jane has every right to express her independence and voice her opinion. She doesn't have to answer to you."

Dale grabbed Jane's arm and tried to drag her away. "You are coming with me, young lady."

She jerked her arm back. "No I'm not."

"Do *not* undermine me. We are leaving now!"

She defiantly stood her ground. "No, Daddy. I'm staying here with Randy. You can't make me leave."

Her father was about to raise his hand to her. Randy stepped between them. "Don't touch her," he demanded. "She is not a subservient child you can dominate and control."

Dale Davine stared Randy down. "Who are you to tell me about my daughter?"

"Sir, I'm sorry, but I cannot stand here and let you treat the woman I love this way. She is not a baby. She is an intelligent, beautiful, talented woman who deserves your respect."

The piercing way Dale stared at Randy was a bit disturbing. He began to wonder if he had done the right thing.

With fury in his eyes, Dale redirected his anger toward Jane. "I did not raise you to be an insubordinate party girl who undermines authority."

Jane went off on him. "Mom always told me to be true to myself. She encouraged me to question things that didn't make sense and to stand up for what I believe in. You are the one who tried to keep me locked away from the world.

You treat me like I'm some kind of porcelain doll that can easily shatter." Tears flowed steadily.

"Your mother would be so disappointed in you," he reproached.

Trying to dart his words, Jane ran off sobbing.

Randy scoffed at her father, disgusted by his attitude. He took a deep breath to swallow his rage before he said something he was going to regret.

"And you," Dale said, pointing his finger in Randy's face. "Look what you've done to my daughter."

Randy did his best to stay calm. "Mr. Davine, I am aware that you are Jane's father and you only want what's best for her. But at what point are you going to realize that Jane is a grown woman? She stands up to her convictions and fights for what she believes in. In your eyes, I know I am the bad guy in all of this, and you seem to think that I have put her up to no good. But despite what you think, I would never humiliate her, never criticize her, and never put her down. I would never disrespect her in any way, and I would never, ever raise my hand to her the way you did. You have hurt the woman I love, and that I will not tolerate. I will protect her and keep her safe, and because I love her, I cannot and will not allow you treat her this way. Your conversation with her is over. She is not coming back out here just so you can cause her more pain. If you have something else to say, then you will have to say it to me."

Dale Davine peered over at Jane. "That is not my daughter."

"Yes, Sir, she is," Randy retorted. "And she is a beautiful, intelligent, caring woman who thinks for herself, has strong opinions, and is passionate about the things she loves."

"You know nothing about my daughter," Dale sneered.

"That, Sir, is where you are wrong."

Dale Davine didn't say anything else. He simply turned his back and stormed off. Randy swore he saw smoke bellowing out of his ears.

He closed the door and joined Jane on the sofa. He detested what being around her father did to her. He pulled her close and held her tightly in his arms.

"I hate him," she sniveled.

Expressing his love for her, he kissed the top of her head. "I am so sorry, Honey. You shouldn't have to endure this crap. That isn't right."

She sniffled and wiped her eyes. "Thank you for standing up for me."

"I had to. I couldn't let him hurt you. I told you if I saw him treat you that way I was going to say something. I hope you aren't upset with me."

"No."

"I'll support you any way I can, Honey. You know that." Hoping to get her mind off this incident, he offered, "You feel like catching a movie, maybe grabbing some dinner?"

She nodded.

"Ok." He gathered his keys, his sunglasses, and his phone and headed out the door with her.

Chapter Twenty-Four

To prepare for upcoming midterms, Randy's study group met at his apartment Sunday morning. Jim arrived first, and he was in an impeccable mood. "Good morning," he said as he moseyed inside.

"You're overly cheerful this morning," Randy remarked.

Jim pulled out a thick textbook and a few notes. "You will never guess what I did last night."

"Won the lottery."

"Nope. Guess again."

Randy thought for a minute. "Got laid?"

"Ha, I wish."

Jane stepped into the room, threw her arms around Randy, and they embraced in a long, passionate kiss. "I'll see you tonight," she said. "Call me when you guys are done."

"Love you, Babe," Randy replied. "Be careful."

"Love you too." She blew him a kiss on the way out.

Jim chuckled. "Apparently you got laid though."

With a crooked grin, Randy gathered his study materials. "So what happened last night?"

"I was on a shift in the ER, and Dr. Lyons called me in to help with a code blue. Dude…" Jim had to stop for a second to let his heartrate decelerate. "It was so intense. Nurses and doctors runnin' around everywhere, EKG's beepin' like crazy, blood gushin'. It was a total rush."

"You're crazy."

"No way, Bro. The ER is where the excitement's at."

"I think you have some sort of secret morbidity obsession," Randy teased him.

"The ER is better than tits and ass."

"That's debatable."

As soon as Bruce and Sarah arrived, everyone gathered around the table, sipping on coffee and munching on breakfast tacos while they waited for Mandy.

She was late and appeared frazzled, panicking about something as she set her bag on the table. "This is the worst morning ever."

Randy wondered what was wrong. "Why?"

"I went to grab a latte this morning and some asshole busted out a window and stole my laptop out of my car. I lost all of my research for my thesis."

Mandy tended to blow things out of proportion. Because of that, Randy wasn't sure if she was serious or freaking out over nothing. "You didn't save it on a USB?"

"I had the damn USB drive in the bag when it was stolen. The last two years of my life were on that drive, all of my research, my data, everything. It's gone. This is horrible!"

"What the hell?" Jim said, disturbed by this news. "What kind of jackass does shit like that?"

"Damn, Mandy," Bruce added. "That's a lot of information to lose."

"I know." Amanda plopped her down in a chair. "What am I going to do?"

Randy narrowed his eyes. "Why were you carrying your USB with your laptop? That wasn't very bright."

"Thank you very much," she scorned. "I hope you're not planning on going into Psychiatry, Randy, because you suck at it."

"Sorry," he said, somewhat offended by her comment. "Did you call the police?"

"The police won't do anything. I am so screwed."

Bruce chimed in, "Randy's right, though. You should at least call. You'd be surprised what they can recover."

"You guys don't get it," she complained. "My research, my whole thesis is gone. That is two years' worth of work."

Yup, she was pretty much screwed. Why in god's name did she leave something as important as a laptop containing her entire Master's research thesis openly visible in her car simply for a cup of coffee? His thesis was saved on two different USB drives located in different places, as well as on a web-based drop box and his laptop's hard drive. He also e-mailed it to himself. That research was entirely too important to randomly leave lying around. A bulk chunk of their schooling was research based, and writing that thesis was their way of showing the university that they were proficient researchers and worthy of a Master's degree. Their thesis was their Master's degree.

"You seriously had a blonde moment there, Mandy."

Bruce stood up for her. "Don't pick on her because she's blonde."

"I'm not picking on her for being blonde. I'm picking on her because that was a stupid thing to do," Randy said, defending his argument. "She shouldn't have left it lying out in the open like that for some Joe off the street to see. Laptop in car, car left unattended. Do you protect two years' worth of research or run in to grab a cup of coffee? Priorities, Mandy."

Mandy rolled her eyes. "Ugh. Men, I swear."

"There isn't much we can do about it now." Bruce looked at his watch. "We need to get started."

The others agreed, and they began their study session, which ended up lasting longer than they had anticipated. After five and a half hours, five pots of coffee, two large pizzas, and several cans of Pepsi, none of them wanted to look at another medical chart or attend another Immunopathology seminar as long as they lived.

Randy slouched in his chair and rubbed his forehead. "Ok, I can't think anymore."

Now having brain fry, everyone gathered their belongings and headed out the door, except for Mandy, who lingered.

Randy smirked at her. "You know I was kidding, right?"

"I know," she assured him.

"If you need help redoing your thesis, I'll help you."

"It's ok. I still have the notes I took and a rough draft saved. But don't expect me to have a cheery disposition while I retype this damn thing."

Mandy's lack of enthusiasm made Randy laugh. "Do yourself a favor. Save it on multiple drives this time, and don't leave your laptop lying around, ok?" he reminded her.

"Duh. I'm not stupid enough to do that again." She stuffed her textbook in her bag and zipped it. "Can I ask you something?"

"Sure."

"Do you think men are attracted to me?"

That was not what he expected her to say. "What?"

"Well, I guess what I mean is…how do I get a guy to notice me? You're a guy. What grabs your attention?"

He never really considered this before. "I don't know. A pretty smile, a certain look she might give me, something about her personality that stands out. Why are you asking me?" he wanted to know.

"I'm trying to get a guy's attention, and he doesn't seem to notice at all."

"Have you been sending him signals?" Randy asked.

"Yes. All the time. But he doesn't see them, I guess."

"Maybe he has a girlfriend."

"No. He doesn't."

"Does he want one?" Randy asked.

"I don't know, but I'm hoping to convince him."

Randy brood over this for a minute. Mandy constantly flirted with Bruce, and the two of them always hung out together after hours. Putting the pieces together, he said, "Wait a minute. You're talking about Buckman, aren't you?"

Mandy hid behind her backpack. "You can't tell him. Please."

He openly laughed.

"Hush!" She rubbed her hand across her backside. "It's my butt, isn't it?"

"There is nothing wrong with your butt. Actually, you have a nice ass."

"Then what it is?"

"Some guys need you to spell it out for them. You know how Bruce is. He gets absorbed in his own world sometimes. Maybe he figures you're off limits because you two are friends. Or maybe he's not seeking a relationship." Trying to help Mandy out, Randy asked, "Did you ever tell him that you like him?"

"Not outright, but I've given him every hint imaginable."

"Try something different. Try asking him out," Randy suggested.

"I have. We have, but he takes it as a casual get together between friends, not as a date."

"Did you tell him it was a date?"

"No. I've invited him to dinner, and sometimes we hang out at his place watching movies or go to a club together, but he doesn't think anything of it."

"Bruce isn't the most open person in the world when it comes to his feelings," Randy said. "He might need that extra push from you. You're going to have to be more direct. Tell him how you feel. Don't expect him to figure it out on his own."

"How do I do that?" she asked, desperate for answers.

"Tell him you'd like to be more than friends. Suggest to him that you two have a romantic date together. See how he reacts."

"I don't know. That seems too forward to me."

"Subtlety isn't working with him. You may have to bite the bullet and say it." The perplexed look on Mandy's face made him laugh. "I don't know what you want me to say. Sorry if I wasn't much help."

"It helped a little."

"Good. See you tomorrow, Mandy."

Randy came home from a long day of lectures, and one of the more difficult exams he could ever remember taking, with a sore back and a slight headache. He dropped his book bag on the floor, tossed his keys on the table, and skimmed through his mail, too tired to open any of it. He stretched out on the sofa and laid his head on a pillow to relax for a bit. Getting more comfortable, he kicked off his shoes and clasped his hands behind his head.

Around 7:00 P.M., Jane came over hoping Randy hadn't eaten yet so they could grab a meal together. When she stepped into the apartment, it was quiet and appeared to be empty, yet she knew he had to be home because his keys were on the table. She found him sound asleep on the couch. Leaving him to rest, she went into the kitchen to prepare dinner.

Forty minutes later, Randy was awakened by a magnificent aroma permeating from the kitchen. He stretched glamorously then sat up and rubbed his eyes. Jane was at the counter slicing French bread. He rose to his feet, snuck up behind her, and kissed the nape of her neck, causing her to flinch.

"Oh god, don't do that," she said, startled. "Especially when I have a knife in my hand."

"Sorry." He gave her a soft kiss on the lips. "What's all this?"

"Dinner. You were asleep when I got here and I didn't want to wake you, so I made dinner for us."

He took in the heavenly aroma, drooling over the elaborate meal she was preparing. "That smells incredible. What is it?"

"Eggplant Parmigiana."

Jane was an exceptional cook, far better than he was, although he wasn't terrible. Her specialties included chicken dishes, cookies, pastas, and a variety of vegetable recipes. Randy always looked forward to eating a meal prepared by her. "Sounds amazing. Do I have time to hop in the shower before we eat?"

"If you hurry. You have about ten minutes."

He kissed her again before he plodded to the bathroom.

Over dinner, they had a pleasant conversation. However, the mood quickly turned when Randy asked, "Have you talked to your dad since Saturday?"

"Nope," she said stubbornly.

"Does he know you're coming to Seattle for spring break?"

"No, and he doesn't need to know."

"Are you at least planning on calling him before we leave?"

Her headstrong attitude was certainly shining through. "Wasn't planning on it."

"So, you're avoiding him now?"

"You see a reason why I shouldn't?"

"Yeah," he said. "He's your father."

"He's a mean, narrow-minded jerk is what he is."

"You're not going to accomplish anything by acting this way you know," Randy reminded her.

"Do I look like I care?"

Jane didn't seem to care at all, which was what bothered Randy. She blew off her father as if he didn't exist and refused to deal with the problem at hand. Her strong will was getting the best of her, and her obstinacy was counterproductive. "No, but maybe you should. You can't blow him off forever."

"Just watch me."

"You're avoiding the issue."

"Yes, and I'm doing it on purpose." Irritated that he continued to probe her about this, she said, "Are you finished now? Because I do not want to talk about this."

He didn't want to make her mad, so he changed the subject. "Make sure you get everything down here by 5:30 Saturday morning. We have to leave early if we're going get to the airport on time."

"I know.

"Pack your swimsuit," Randy advised. "Should be warmer this time. Probably a little rainy though, but nice enough to take the boat out and go waterskiing."

"Is Stephanie coming home for spring break?" Jane wondered.

"I don't know. I haven't talked to her in a few days. She usually does though."

"Your family's so nice, unlike mine," she grumbled.

Randy laughed at her indignant attitude. "You're just mad at your dad right now."

Circumventing the situation, she shifted the conversation again. "How did your exams go today?"

"See, there you go again," Randy stated. "Avoiding the issue."

"What's your point?"

"Ignoring this isn't going to make it go away. You're going to have to talk to him sooner or later."

"I don't want to talk to him, and I do not want to discuss this anymore. Why do you insist on bringing it up?"

"Me?" He denied having anything to do with it. "You're the one who brought it up this time."

"Will you drop this please?" she insisted.

He understood why this was such a touchy subject for her. He wasn't too fond of her father either, but avoidance wasn't going to solve the problem. He didn't want to upset her, which he could see now he was doing, so he let it go. "Alright. I won't bring it up again. I'm sorry."

Jane realized that she had unintentionally snapped at Randy and made him feel bad when he was only trying to help. She straddled his lap and clasped her hands around his neck, gazing into his eyes. "I'm sorry. I didn't mean to sound bitchy."

"It's ok. I understand." His lips found hers, taking in a brief bonding moment. "I'll take care of the dishes," he offered.

"Thank you."

Chapter Twenty-Five

Jane and Randy landed at SEA-TAC airport midmorning on Saturday. Randy's mother was there to greet them. "It's good to have you home, Honey," she said, embracing each of them with a hug. "Welcome back, Jane. I'm glad you were able to come see us again."

"Thank you, Mrs. Hanson."

Randy looked around for his father. "Where's Dad?"

"At the hospital. He received a page right as we left, but he wanted me to tell you he'd meet you at the house when he was finished."

Jane asked, "Is Stephanie coming?"

"Yes. She said she'd be here in time for the barbecue."

"What barbecue?" Randy wondered.

"Uncle Tom and Aunt Camille are coming over this afternoon for a cookout."

"Is Dad running the grill?"

"If he's back by then," Mrs. Hanson confirmed. "If not, we'll put you to work doing it."

"That's fine. I love to grill." They grabbed their bags from the baggage claim then Randy drove them all home.

Later that evening, after enjoying tasty barbecue with the family, Jane sat on the porch chatting with Stephanie. Randy walked over to them and said, "Hey, Beautiful. Wanna go for a walk?"

Stephanie shuddered at her brother's statement. "Ew, gross. Don't say things like that to me."

Randy sneered at her. "I wasn't talking to you. I was taking to Jane."

Jane stood up to join him.

Holding hands, they strolled down to the lake to take in the view. Randy hoped they could catch a sunset together. "Let's take the boat out tomorrow and do some skiing."

She thought that was a good idea. "Sounds fun."

"Steph and Robby will probably want to go with us. Stephanie wants to show us a dance club in Seattle where a bunch of local bands play. I've never been there, but she says it's cool."

"I could go dancing," she replied with a smile.

"Thought so." They got comfortable in the sand with Jane cradled between his legs. Randy held her in his arms as they watched the sailboats float across the lake. He clutched her hand in his then tilted his head slightly, kissing her as the sun set on Lake Washington.

The following afternoon, Randy and Robby loaded the boat with a cooler of Pepsis and water bottles. They snagged a stack of CD's, four towels, and a bottle of sunscreen then placed binoculars in the storage console to get close up views of the surroundings. Randy hooked the ski rope to the back while Robby pulled the water skis and ski vests out of the shed. When all ski equipment was gathered, Randy drove over to the marina to fill the boat with gas.

They took turns waterskiing, with Randy and Stephanie sharing driver duties and Robby and Jane sharing spotter duties. Three hours into skiing, Randy dropped Stephanie and Robby off at the shore.

While Stephanie and Robby put ski equipment away, Randy turned the boat around to dock it. Instead of pulling up to the dock, he parked the boat in the middle of the lake. Thinking something was wrong, Stephanie shaded her eyes from the sun and peered out to the water. "What is he doing?" she asked.

Robby turned to look. The boat was bobbing on the lake with the orange warning flag raised. He grabbed the binoculars to get a closer look. What he saw made his jaw drop. "Whoa!"

Robby was awfully interested in whatever was going on out there. Stephanie took the binoculars from him to find out what it was. "What are you looking at?" she demanded to know.

"Hey!" he yelled, trying to snatch them back.

Stephanie held them up to take a peek. When she saw Randy slip his hands down Jane's bikini bottom, she immediately lowered the binoculars, aghast that Robby was spying on them. "Robby!"

Robby reached for the binoculars, hoping to catch more of the show. "Gimme those."

Stephanie held them away from him. "No. You are not going to watch them," she scolded. "That is sick, Robby. He's your brother, don't invade his privacy."

"But it was getting good," he told her. "Come on, gimme the binoculars."

"No, no, and hell no." She put the binoculars back in the case and refused to let Robby have them. "I can't believe you were watching them."

Robby stared at the water, but without magnification, he couldn't see a single kinky detail.

At the dance club that night, Randy, Jane, and Stephanie found a table and ordered drinks. Stephanie stood up and scoped the scene. She saw a few people she knew. "Well, I'm here, and there are lots of single guys here. I'm gonna go find one." She hopped over the railing onto the dancefloor.

With Stephanie gone, Randy offered his hand to Jane. "Will you dance with me?"

She gladly accepted. "I would love to."

In the middle of a slow dance, Randy felt someone tapping his shoulder.

"Randy!"

He looked to his right to see Stephanie poking at him with a panic-stricken look on her face.

"Randy, come quick. We need your help." She grabbed him by the hand and ran with him to the other side of the room.

"What is it, Steph?" Randy asked, wondering what was going on.

She directed him to a corner where a large crowd had gathered around a young man holding a lifeless woman in his arms. He called out her name, shaking her and trying to get her to wake up.

Randy knelt down beside them. "I'm here to help."

This man shook in fear, not knowing what to do.

Stephanie reassured him, "It's ok, Lance. He's my brother. He's a medical student."

Reluctantly, the man laid the woman on the floor and allowed Randy to tend to her.

Randy quickly checked for breathing and a pulse, finding neither. He positioned himself on his knees beside the unconscious girl, clasped his hands over her sternum, and began chest compressions. While he was doing this, he looked up at Stephanie. "Call an ambulance. Inform them that she's unconscious, not breathing, and has no pulse. Tell them CPR is being initiated. Hurry!"

She immediately grabbed her cellphone.

He looked directly at a nearby bystander and declared, "See if there's an AED in this building. If there is, bring it to me quickly." The person ran off in search of an Automated External Defibrillator while Randy continued CPR—chest compression after chest compression over and over again. By now, everyone in this club had gathered around to watch. Determined to help this girl, Randy's energy and adrenaline skyrocketed. Compressions continued for several minutes while they waited for the ambulance to arrive. Although only a minute or two had passed, to Randy it seemed like an eternity. He continued to work to sustain the victim, hoping she would open her eyes and gasp for air. "Come on, dammit. Breathe!"

Jane sensed his frustration as he fought to keep this woman alive. She had never been as proud of him as she was at this moment.

Finally, the sweet sound of sirens. Randy continued CPR until the paramedics set up their equipment and took over.

Concerned about this woman, he watched the Emergency Medical Technicians place an oxygen mask over her face, check her pulse rate, and hook her up to a defibrillator. They injected her with a hypodermic syringe and shocked her with the paddles of the defibrillator twice before a pulse was detected. Relieved that they found a heartbeat, Randy moved his hair off his forehead and stepped outside. Without saying a word, he sat on the stairs with his elbows on his knees. He clasped his hands together and rested his forehead on the fist he made. His heart pounded, and as the adrenaline slowly left his body, he suddenly felt ill.

Jane followed him outside. She gently placed her hand on his back and could feel him breathing, slightly winded from this ordeal. "Randy, are you ok?"

He took a couple breaths. "Just getting some air."

"That was the most incredible thing I've ever seen."

Not feeling the heroism Jane saw, Randy stated, "That woman could have died tonight, Jane."

"But she didn't because of you. You were really a hero tonight."

He stood up and walked over to the side of the building, where he leaned against the wall with his forearms. He stared at the ground and continued to catch his breath.

Jane wondered what she said that upset him. She stood behind him and put her hands on his shoulders, hoping he would say something. "Sweetie, what's wrong?"

"All I've ever wanted is to be a doctor. I want to help people. But being out there tonight, trying to help that woman, I was terrified that we were going to lose her. I'm not a hero, Jane. I'm not a miracle worker. I'm a man, a man with limitations. I won't be able to save everybody no matter how hard I try. In medical school they teach us to stay as emotionally unattached to our patients as possible. But these are people, Jane. People with families. How can I be unattached and pretend not to care?" With defeat in his voice, he swallowed hard trying to get rid of the sick feeling in his stomach. "Doctors are not superhuman. We're people, ordinary human beings. We have feelings and doubts and make mistakes like everyone else. Medicine has limits. I have limits."

She held his hands, trying to reassure him. "You're wrong, Randy. These hands can work miracles. Doctors perform miracles every day. They save people's lives. Look at your dad. What about him? He brings life into the world, new life every day. What greater miracle is there than bringing new life into the world? And what about tonight? What do you call that? I witnessed a side of you tonight that I've never seen before—these caring, compassionate, loving hands—hands that refused to give up. I've never seen anyone with as much love and conviction as you have. You have a genuine concern for people, all people. I saw the determination on your face and the anguish in your eyes when she wouldn't breathe. Through it all, you took control and stayed calm. You were amazing, Sweetie. You should have seen yourself. You saved her life. Is that not a miracle?"

At a loss for words, he stumbled for the right thing to say. "It's like you search deep within my soul and find all the misgivings and reservations I have, then you rip them out and throw them in the burner like they never existed. How do you do that? Is that a psychology thing?"

"I know you better than you think I do."

"Thank you, Baby. I needed to hear those words from you tonight." He drew her closer and kissed her tenderly. "I'm going back inside to see how she's doing."

"I'll go with you."

The paramedics wheeled the woman out to the ambulance on a gurney. They pulled away with sirens blaring.

Stephanie ran up to Randy and gave him a huge bear hug, excited about what she witnessed her big brother do. "That was incredible. I can't believe I witnessed that tonight."

Randy rubbed the back of his neck. "Look, I'm sorry to be a party pooper, but can we leave now? All of this adrenaline careening through my body has kinda put a damper on my mood."

Stephanie smiled proudly. "Of course. Let me get my purse."

The pitter-patter of the rain and the heavenly aroma of coffee pulled Randy out of bed. Even though it was raining, he awoke in a good mood. He slipped on a pair of basketball shorts and a tee-shirt and headed upstairs to the kitchen. His dad sat at the table reading the paper and drinking a steaming cup of coffee. Still half asleep, Randy sat in a chair opposite him. "Good morning," he said groggily.

His father's eyes shifted his direction. "Well, good morning. Heard you had quite an eventful night last night."

"Don't believe everything you hear," Randy replied modestly.

"Stephanie said you saved some woman's life. How'd it feel?" Mark asked his son.

"How'd what feel?"

"Helping that woman, trying to save her life. How'd it make you feel?"

Randy grinned. "Miraculous."

"Yup, you've got doctor's blood. No doubt."

Randy rubbed his eyes. "Got any more of that coffee?"

His dad pointed to the coffee pot. "Help yourself."

Randy grabbed a cup and poured. "I'm making breakfast. You hungry?"

"Sure." Mark Hanson watched as Randy reached into the refrigerator and pulled out a dozen eggs. He couldn't believe how much Randy had matured over the years. He was a responsible, empathetic, motivated, and benevolent human being, one of the finest men Mark had ever known.

"I'm proud of you, Son," he said, pleased with the man his son had become.

Randy peeked around the refrigerator door. "Thank you."

After breakfast, Randy cleared and washed the dishes. While drying his hands, he glanced out the window and spotted his dad out by the boat. He wondered why he wasn't tending to patients at the clinic or conducting hospital rounds. He went out to the dock to find out. "Hey, Dad. Whatcha doing?"

Mark turned around. "You and I are going fishing today."

"You're not working?"

"No. I took the day off to spend time with my son. The boat's ready to go. Meet me out here in fifteen minutes."

"Alright!" Ecstatic to spend the day with his dad, but surprised by the spontaneity of it all, Randy quickly showered, dressed in appropriate fishing attire, and met his dad out by the boat.

Randy was extremely talkative, and Mark found it refreshing. "Where'd Jane run off to this morning?"

"She and Steph went shopping," Randy explained. "Give Stephanie a wad of cash and a shopping mall and she's gone. Jane's certainly not going to pass up the opportunity to shop."

"How's the thesis coming along?"

"I'm glad you asked me that," Randy replied. "Do you think you can read it for me this afternoon and tell me what you think?"

"Sure. I can do that for you."

"Thanks."

"Everything going ok with you? Do you need anything?"

"Everything's fine." His father continued to play twenty questions, which made Randy wonder what was going on. "What's with all the questions?"

"Just want to talk to you," Mark said. "I miss having you around."

"I miss you too, Dad." He reeled in, changed his lure, and cast back out.

Jane and Stephanie were back by four o'clock. They walked in the house to find Mark at the table scanning Randy's laptop while Randy stood at the sink scaling and cleaning fish. He sliced the fish's belly open and ripped out the insides. Grey and red fish organs fell into the sink with a wet sloshy splat.

Jane recoiled in disgust. "That is so gross."

"Why?" Randy chuckled. "It's only a fish."

"I hope you are gentler on your patients than you are with that poor fish."

He picked up the fish, turned its fishy face toward Jane, and moved its mouth as if it were talking to her. "I'm just a fish," he made the fish say in a deep playful voice.

The fish he butchered was actually decently sized. "That's a big one. Did you catch that one?"

"Yup. I outfished my dad today." Randy took the knife in his hand and cut the fish's head off.

"Ew," Jane grimaced, totally sickened by this.

Randy laughed at her. "Did you and Stephanie have fun today?"

"Yes we did. I got a new outfit I thought I'd wear to dinner tonight."

"Cool. Can't wait to see it."

She gave him a kiss and headed into the living room with Stephanie.

As soon as Randy was done cleaning fish, he and his dad sat and discussed his thesis. "This is excellent, Randy," his father commented. "The section on pre-eclampsia and PIH is very thorough."

Randy was surprised to hear his father say that. He worried his thesis wasn't quite adequate. "You think? I feel like it's missing something."

"I wrote down a few things you might want to look into." He handed Randy the notes he had jotted down.

"Look up endothelial dysfunction. That might help clarify some things."

"Thanks." His dad offered some excellent suggestions. Randy revised his paper and did internet research until dinner.

Around 9:00 P.M., Jane and Randy retreated downstairs to be alone for a while. Randy grabbed a couple of Pepsi's from the mini fridge then pulled the bed out from the couch and arranged the pillows. He sat on the mattress and leaned back, crossing his legs comfortably. "I've been thinking."

"Uh oh," she teased, sitting next to him.

"What I'm about to say might make you mad, but I'm going to say it anyway."

"Ooh, you're getting brave, aren't you?" Her curiosity was piqued now. "What is it?"

"I think you should play basketball again." Expanding his thinking, he stated, "I know we've talked about this a dozen times, and I've always listened and tried to be supportive. But now I'm expressing my opinion. You rock on the basketball court, Babe, and you need to play again."

She shook her head. "I told you, I don't need basketball."

"Yes, I know. I've heard that before. But I think you're wrong, Jane. You do need basketball, and you need to get back on the court."

"Randy, do you have any idea what it will take for me to get back to where I was three years ago? And even if I do get back on my game, who's to say I'll be good enough to make the team as a walk-on. The competition is tougher now, and I haven't played competitively in three years. It's not that simple."

"I'll help you."

"How can you help?"

"I'll shoot hoops with you, lift with you, spot you, whatever you need me to do. I just want to see you on the court."

"Basketball season is over."

"I know, but what about next year?"

She tried to explain, "I really don't think you realize what playing basketball entails. Sessions at the gym at six o'clock in the morning, class all day, practice all afternoon, out of town for away games, at the gym all day for home games. I was busy constantly from five thirty in the morning 'til nine o'clock at night, sometimes later."

"And you loved every minute of it," he added.

"Yes, I did, but the rules have changed."

"If you're talking about me, we've already discussed this."

"When would we have time to be together?"

"We'll make time," he said. "That won't be an issue. You love to play. If you let your last few years of eligibility slip away, you'll regret it. I already told you I'd help you. You'll have my full support."

She took a deep breath and sighed. "I'll consider it."

"Seriously consider it, please." He decided to lighten things up a bit. "There are some grapes in the fridge. You want some?"

"Did you know that grapes are considered a seductive fruit?" she remarked, giving her psychological insights.

This topic fascinated him. "Is that right?"

"Uh huh. Want me to show you?"

"Yes. Please do. I would love to see that." He rose to his feet.

"Where you going?"

"Bathroom. Maybe stop and grab some grapes on the way back. You have me curious now."

Randy returned with a bowl of grapes. He created a more romantic mood by turning off the lights, leaving only the soft glow from a small lamp. He hopped back onto the mattress and set the bowl between them. "Alright, Missy. Show me the seductive power of these little green things."

She picked one off the stem. "It's not the fruit itself that's sexy, it's the way you eat it."

"Show me," he insisted.

She slowly brought it to her lips, licking it with the tip of her tongue as she put it in her mouth.

Randy watched in fascination.

"The key is that we feed each other, that way the sensual feeling of the tongue on the fingertips is more arousing."

"Lemme try." Randy picked up a grape and proceeded to feed it her. His skin tingled when he felt her tongue on the tip of his finger. "I like that."

They continued to feed one other as they gradually removed clothing. It wasn't long before they succumbed to the passion of the moment and melted together.

In the morning, as the sun was just starting to come up, they made love again. Because it was so early, they assumed everyone was still asleep. But in the middle of the act, Randy heard what sounded like something falling off the shelf by the doorway. He stopped, panting from the heat of passion. "What was that?"

"I don't know," Jane replied.

They both looked toward the noise to find Robby hunched behind the shelf watching them. "You little shit!" Randy hopped off the bed and slipped on a pair of shorts, ready to pummel the nosey bastard.

Robby took off, running up the stairs.

Randy chased after him. "I am going to kill you, Robby!"

Mark and Ellen Hanson heard this commotion and barreled out of their room to see what was happening. Their two sons raced around the house, one acting as predator, the other as prey. "What in god's name is going on out here?"

Randy cornered Robby in the living room. "This fucking little pervert needs to mind his own damn business!"

"Do not use that language in this house," his mother scolded, shocked to hear such a foul word come out of his mouth.

Randy charged toward Robby with his hand clenched in a fist. Robby tried to dodge him.

"Randal!" his father demanded. "Sit down!"

"Dad, that little creep was watching us." Randy's blood boiled. He wanted to knock his brat brother down a notch or two.

"You need to calm down." Mark stood between his sons and held Randy back.

"You're damn lucky Dad is here to save you!" Randy told his brother. "If I get ahold of you, I'm going to kick your ass."

"You will do no such thing," his father commanded.

"Dad, that fucking prick was watching us."

"Jonathan Randal Hanson," his mother warned. "If you use that word again…"

Mark put his hands on Randy's shoulder and forced him to sit in a chair. "Randy, sit down right now. I will handle this."

Now that Randy was restrained, Robby ran to his room and slammed the door.

Seething, Randy hollered after him, "Yeah, you better run!"

Dr. Hanson desperately tried to get his son to cool off. "Will you calm down?"

"Dad, he…"

"Dammit, Randal. Sit in that chair and shut up."

Randy sat back and impatiently tapped his foot. He heard some arguing going on in Robby's room but couldn't hear what was being said.

Five minutes later, Dr. Hanson emerged and sat in the chair across from his oldest son. After a long awkward silence, he said, "Robby will have consequences, and I told him he owes you and Jane an apology."

"Thank you," Randy replied, grateful that his father handled the situation.

Mark gave his son some very serious advice. "You need to be more careful. There are certain people in this house who can hear and see things they shouldn't."

"How is this my fault?" Randy replied defensively.

"I didn't say it was your fault. But you need to be more careful."

"He knew Jane and I were down there. He had no business snooping into our private matters."

"You know how your brother is. If the opportunity presents itself, he's going to be in your business."

Yes, he did know his brother. He was a perverted, hormonal punk. "Jane and I are getting our own room when we go to Mexico this summer."

"That can easily be arranged."

Ellen Hanson put her hand on Randy's shoulder.

He reached up and touched her. "I'm sorry I was cursing, Mom."

"Is Jane alright?"

Oh, shit. Jane. In the heat of anger, Randy had forgotten about her. She was probably mortified by this. Calmer now, he rose to his feet and plodded back downstairs.

Jane was wrapped in a sheet hugging her knees. "That was the most embarrassing thing that has ever happened to me."

"Honey, I am so sorry." Randy said, with a pitiful, apologetic tone.

"Your brother is a brat."

"I told you he was a pest. Are you ok?"

After the fit of rage she just witnessed, Jane was more concerned about him than herself. "Are you?"

"Yes. I'm fine."

Thinking back on the incident, they both stared at each other and laughed.

Chapter Twenty-Six

Randy was anxious to finish his second year of medical school. He started the last leg enthusiastically, but as the week progressed, he became increasingly more stressed. Many of his professors seemed to think that the second year medical students had thirty hours in their day and nothing else to do, ever. Case studies piled up, lecture notes accumulated at an alarmingly high rate, and the required readings he had every night tripled from what they had been. Randy was in class, had a lab, or was practicing clinical skills from eight o'clock in the morning until 6:00 P.M. daily. He was also working twenty hours a week at the student clinic and wasn't getting home until close to 9:00 almost every night. When he finally did get home, he had hours of studying, research, and writing to do on his thesis, and all of it was making him lose his mind.

Over spring break, he discovered that two more of the second year students had either quit or failed, leaving only twenty-one of the original twenty-five that were admitted with him left in the program. He was beginning to feel that the university gained great joy in watching hardworking medical students fail or drop out from the pressure.

Hell week, as the second year medical students later nicknamed it, finally ended. Randy and his friends gathered at his apartment Sunday to review the week's excessive influx of information. The study session seemed to drag endlessly. No one was concentrating and Randy became frustrated with their lack of reasoning. Everyone seemed incapable of knowing the answers to anything. "Sarah," he snapped, "Did you even read what that said?"

"Yes, I read it."

"The answer is right there," he argued, rather harshly.

"This chart is confusing," Sarah complained.

"Look at it."

"I did. Excuse me for not getting it."

"Maybe if you would actually pay attention when Dr. Drenner is going over the information in class, you wouldn't be so confused."

Ok. Randy was incredibly grouchy and argumentative today. Jim didn't like his snippy attitude. He had to say something. "Jesus, Randy, chill."

"Yeah, man," Bruce added. "Leave her alone. She's doing her best. You seriously need to relax."

Randy was so frustrated that he tossed his notes on the table. "Ugh. We have been at this for three hours and haven't accomplished a damn thing. Can we all try to focus and at least attempt to think about the answers?"

Randy's attitude bothered Mandy. "Oh my god. On what the hell side of the bed did you wake up?"

Jane overheard how frustrated Randy's friends were getting with his foul disposition. She came out of the kitchen and sought his attention. "Randy?"

"What?" he barked.

"Can I talk to you for a minute?"

"We're studying. I'm busy."

"Just one second," she asked.

He put his book down and joined her in the kitchen. "What is it?"

"You are acting like a jerk. What is wrong with you today?"

"What are you talking about?"

"You are biting everyone's head off. Sarah didn't deserve that."

He leaned against the counter and folded his arms across his chest. "I am so sick of this crap," he complained.

"These damn professors must think we have nothing better to do with our time than sit around and read medical reference books all day. Two more of us dropped out over spring break, and I swear Dr. Drenner loves to confuse people with her toxicology ramblings." He rubbed his thumb and finger across his sinuses.

Jane put her arms around his neck. "Sweetie, your friends are going through this too. They are just as stressed as you are, and you are snapping at them for no reason."

Jane was right. They were all facing the same hell he was. He felt bad for snapping at them and giving them a hard time. "I know."

"Why don't you guys take a break for a while. I'll pick up some burgers for you."

He nodded. "That's a good idea."

"Find out what everyone wants."

"Thank you, Baby. I'm sorry."

"You're under a lot of stress. I understand. But they are too, just remember that."

He grabbed a piece of paper to collect orders from everyone. "Alright," Randy said as he approached the table. "We are taking a break for a bit. Jane is going to get burgers for us, so write down what you want. Speak now or forever hold your peace."

Sarah said, "Thank god. I am starving."

When Jane walked into the room, Jim remarked, "You are hellatiously awesome, Jane. Thank you so much."

Jane giggled at his flattery. "You're welcome. If you need a special order, make sure you write it down. And please write legibly so I can read it."

Randy collected money from everyone and handed the wad of cash and the list to Jane. "Thank you, Baby. You have no idea how grateful we are."

"No problem. You guys sounded like you needed nourishment." She grabbed her purse and Randy's car keys and headed out the door.

When she returned, five sets of hands frantically dug through the bags of burgers and fries she placed on the table. Randy sorted out drinks and milkshakes then they all leaned back in their chairs relaxing for a while before they continued their session, feeling much less cranky and more focused now that they had some brain food. After another three hours, productive ones this time, they wrapped up their session and dispersed.

As soon as everyone left, Randy came over to Jane and wrapped his arms around her. "That was the coolest thing anyone has ever done for me."

"All I did was pick up burgers for you guys."

"I know," he said. "But your timing was impeccable. We desperately needed a break, and you read that so well."

"You were about to lose it."

"I know. And I'm glad you saw that and called me on it. Thank you."

"You're welcome."

He smiled at her, and they embraced in a long heartfelt kiss.

Tuesday afternoon, Jane came over to the Medical Sciences building hoping to catch Randy between classes. There was something she desperately wanted to tell him and knew he wouldn't answer his phone when he was in class, yet a text message wouldn't suffice in this situation. She wanted to tell him face to face. When she walked into the lobby, a few people were moving from one room to another. A man she didn't recognize stood in the hallway scanning his phone. She walked up to him. "Excuse me. I'm sorry to bother you, but would you happen you know where Randy Hanson might be?"

"I might." He grinned enticingly, flirting with her. "Who wants to know?"

"I'm his girlfriend," she replied. "Can you tell me where he is?"

This man called out to a group of people exiting a room behind him. "Hey, Ryan! Is Hanson over there with you?"

Jim squeezed out of the huddle and moved toward this man. "Yeah. Why?" That's when he saw Jane. "Hey, Jane. What brings you over here?"

Jane was happy to see a familiar face. "Have you seen Randy?"

"He was right behind me." Jim glanced behind him but didn't see Randy anywhere. "Hang on. Lemme see if he's still in there." He poked his head inside the room to find Randy chatting with the professor. He waved to grab his attention.

Randy acknowledged his best friend with a head nod. As soon as his conversation concluded, he went to see what Jim wanted. "What's up?"

"Jane's out here lookin' for you."

With a smile on his face, Randy walked into the lobby. He greeted her with a hug. "Hi, Baby. What are you doing up here?"

"I need to talk to you."

"I'm kinda between classes right now. You'll have to make it quick." A throng of people moved about the halls. He took her hand and led her to the corner of the lobby where they could have more privacy. "What's going on?"

"I've been thinking, and I'm ready."

Randy didn't know what she was talking about. His face twisted quizzically. "Ready for what?"

"I want to play basketball again."

He stared at her for a second or two to make sure he heard her correctly. Slowly, his lips curved upward. "Well, this is good."

"I'm going to go talk to the coach this afternoon and let him know my intentions."

"Alright!" he proclaimed excitedly. "That is awesome, Baby. What can I do to help you?"

"I'll need to get back in shape, and I will need your help with that."

"I can handle that." He clasped both of her hands in his and looked into her beautiful green eyes. "I am overjoyed that you have decided to play again, and I will help you in any way I can, but right now I have to get to my next class. Why don't you meet me at my place tonight and we'll talk about it then."

With a nod, she agreed.

Their lips met in a soft, tender kiss before Randy released her. He watched as she left the building.

Jim sauntered into the hall. "What was that all about?"

"She's decided to play basketball again."

"That's cool. You've been tryin' to talk her into that for a while."

"I didn't talk her into it," Randy corrected. "I just got her to think about it. It was her decision."

"But you're glad she made it. I can tell by that shit-eatin' grin on your face."

Randy's grin became a bit wider. "Yes, I am. This is very good news."

"You've gone soft, man. Definitely suckered in by the love bug that's bitten your ass."

"A huge love bug, Jim. A mighty huge one."

When Randy came home that evening, it was nearly 8:00 P.M. Jane wasn't there, and he wondered what was keeping her. Right as he was about to pick up his phone and give her a call, she walked in the door. "There you are, Babe. I was starting to worry about you."

"Sorry. I lost track of time."

He pranced over and greeted her a kiss. "Did you talk to the coach today?"

"Yes, and he's looking forward to adding my name to the roster."

"Well, that's good news," Randy declared.

"Uh huh. Anyway, Coach Kline gave me a bunch of paperwork to fill out, and I have to get a physical."

"Ooh." Randy grabbed her buttocks and sank his fingers in. "A physical. Can I give you one?"

"Randy, I'm serious."

He moved his hands. "I'm serious too. Come down to the clinic. Dr. Stephens is letting me give athletic physicals now, supervised of course. But I'll do it for you. In fact, I have to work tomorrow afternoon. Why don't you stop by then?"

"I'll do that."

"What else did you find out today?"

"Practice starts the beginning of September, and he makes final starting position decisions by November, before regular season. I can start practicing with the team right away. I'll have between now and September to get back into shape. That's where you come in."

"Doing what?" he asked.

"I'm gonna have to start lifting again to get my muscle tone and strength up to par. I'll need you to spot me."

This sounded like a fun assignment. "Not a problem."

"I need more shooting practice. Playing with you will help, but see if can get Jim and Bruce to come along so it will be more challenging," she suggested.

"I can do that. However, getting Bruce to play after you knocked him on his butt might be difficult, but I'll certainly try."

"Tell him he can be on my team."

"That'll do it I bet. Want me to set up a game this weekend?"

"Yes, if you would. That would be great."

"No problem. Certain GPA requirements?" Randy asked.

"3.0. I need to keep my grades up, and I'll need a quiet place to study. Alpha's not the best studying environment. I'll probably come over here while you're at work, if that's ok."

"Of course it is," he declared. "You can come over here any time you want." He put his hands in her back pockets and squeezed.

"And I am going to have to study, Mister."

"I know. I need to study too, but that doesn't mean we can't mess around a little when we're finished." He winked at her suggestively.

"Randy." Her face flushed at his sexual suggestiveness.

"You know you like it." He pulled his hands away and said, "Can I ask you something?"

"What?"

"What made you decide to play again?"

She explained, "I was thinking about my mom. It's what she would have wanted. She used to love watching me play. She was my biggest supporter, and she came to every game. My dad hated it. According to him, the basketball court was no place for a girl. Daddy's never seen me play."

"What do you mean your dad has never seen you play?"

"He's never set foot anywhere near a basketball court I was playing on."

"You're kidding?"

"No, I'm not."

That wasn't right. If Randy had children who played basketball, he would be all over the court cheering them on. This made no sense to him at all. "Damn."

"I wish Mom could be there to watch me when I step onto that court again."

"She'll still be watching, Baby, just not from the stands."

This made her feel better. Randy always had a way of doing that.

"I'll be in the stands though, and go to every game I can."

She looked up at him. "This isn't going to be easy, you know. I'm gonna be on the road a lot. We won't see each other as much."

"We'll be alright," he reassured her. "It's not quantity that counts, it's quality. It doesn't matter how often we see each other. What matters is how good it is when we are together." He kissed her to confirm his dedication and devotion to her. "We'll be fine. We have a strong relationship. I'm not worried. You've supported me over the last year of med school. Now it's my turn to return the favor. We'll help each other."

She squeezed into him. "Thank you."

"Any time, Babe."

"I love you, Randy."

"And I love you."

They walked out to the porch to look at the stars on this clear night. He sat on the top step with her below him. She leaned back between his legs and he put his arms around her shoulders. Staring up at the nighttime sky, he exhaled heavily.

"That's a big sigh," she said. "What's on your mind?"

Concerned about the latest developments in medical school, Randy expressed his feelings. "Our class keeps dwindling. I can't believe Connie is out. That really bothers me."

"Some people aren't cut out to be doctors. There's nothing you could have done."

Showing empathy, he stated, "I feel bad for her, after all the time and effort she put into it. If I would have known she was having problems…"

She didn't let him finish his thought. "You're not responsible for everyone, Randy."

"I know, but she worked so hard and now she's out, just like that. It's not fair, and it makes me mad."

"That's because you care about people. Anyone who knows you can see that," Jane told him. "And it doesn't take genius or a psychologist to figure it out either. It shines through you. Look at the relationships you have. People like you, they trust you, and they listen to you. You have a certain rapport with people that draws them to you. That's a good trait for a doctor to have. And that night in Seattle, I saw firsthand the kind of dedication and genuine concern you have. You are an amazing man. I've never known anyone with a more caring heart than you have. That's one of the things I love about you."

"Thanks. That means a lot to me."

Sitting under the stars, they shared their thoughts and feelings about various topics. They had done this many times before, but tonight their conversation took a different angle than it ever had before. The information they divulged was beyond surface knowledge; they delved deep, discussing things that no one else knew and no one else had ever dug deep enough to find.

Chapter Twenty-Seven

The following day, Randy met with Dr. Thomas Boyce for his annual progress meeting. It was standard procedure for Dr. Boyce to meet with all the second year medical students in the spring to determine if they were ready to move on to the next phase of their training. Randy walked in that afternoon feeling confident, especially after the last meeting he had with the dean.

While Randy sat and waited, Dr. Boyce's secretary called out to him, "Dr. Boyce will see you now, Mr. Hanson."

"Thank you." Randy stood up and headed into the dean's office.

Dr. Boyce was at his desk flipping through a file when Randy walked in. "Ah, Randy Hanson." He directed him to an empty chair. "Please, sit down."

"Thank you, Doctor." Randy took a seat.

"I was looking over your file. Your midterm scores were outstanding."

"Thank you, Sir."

Dr. Boyce closed Randy's file and tossed in on his desk. "But I've seen your file before. I'm interested in more than what I see in there."

This statement confused him. "Sir?"

"Randy," he leaned back in his chair. "Your grades, academic standing, and entrance exam scores are exceptional, the best I've ever seen. But I want to know about you. Who is Randal Hanson?" The doctor folded his arms across his chest waiting for a response.

Randy wasn't sure how to respond. This was not the type of meeting he was expecting. "What would you like to know, Sir?"

"What do you do when you're not in class? Hobbies, interests, women?" Dr. Boyce glanced down at Randy's hand. "I don't see a ring on your finger, so you must not be married."

"No, Sir. I'm not married. I do have a girlfriend though."

"Ok, good. Now we're getting somewhere." He sat forward in his chair and proceeded with casual conversation. "Tell me about her."

Randy thought this was an odd conversation for an annual review. What did any of this have to do with his progress in medical school? Assuming Dr. Boyce had a purpose in mind, he played along. "Her name is Jane Davine. She's a Psychology major and an exceptional athlete."

"How long have you been dating this young lady?"

"Eight months now," Randy explained.

"Davine. Where have I heard that name before? You said she's an athlete?"

"Yes, Sir," Randy confirmed.

"Does she play basketball?"

Randy grinned. "Yes, Sir, she does."

"My daughter used to play basketball for Cal. Does this girlfriend of yours play on the team by any chance?"

What a small world. Randy didn't know Dr. Boyce even had a daughter, let alone one who played basketball. "She played a few years ago."

"That's where I've heard that name. I'm pretty sure she was on the team with my daughter," Dr. Boyce assumed. "She played point guard, if I'm not mistaken. But after only playing for two years, she left the team for personal reasons. Something about her mother being ill, if I remember correctly."

"That's correct, Sir,"

"The team was sad to see her go. She was one of their best players."

"She is planning on playing again next season," Randy declared.

"That's great! It will be good to have her back," Dr. Boyce said. "Are you a basketball fan?"

"Oh, yes. Big Lakers fan."

"But you're from Seattle, aren't you?"

"Yes, Sir."

"And you're a Lakers fan?"

"Always have been," Randy said. "A good friend of mine, Jim Ryan, is a Lakers fan too. He and I watch games together all the time."

"James Ryan is a friend of yours?" Dr. Boyce had known both Randal Hanson and James Ryan for two years, and all that time he never knew they were friends.

"Yes, Sir," Randy confirmed. "My best friend."

"I was not aware that you two were friends."

Randy explained, "Have been for many years."

"Well, I've learned a few things about you today. I know you have a girlfriend who plays basketball and is a Psychology major, you're a Lakers fan, and James Ryan is your best friend. We're making progress." Dr. Boyce seemed satisfied with the information Randy had given him so far. "I also understand your father is a doctor."

"Yes, Sir. He's an obstetrician in Seattle."

"And that is what you are planning for your specialty as well, is that correct?"

Randy still wasn't sure what any of this had to do with his end of second year progress check, but regardless, he enjoyed this conversation with Dr. Boyce. "Yes, Sir."

"How's the job with Dr. Stephens going?"

"I love it. I'm hoping to get more hours in next year. My schedule this year just wouldn't allow it."

"You sound like a well-rounded, very busy young man."

"I try to stay that way. Keeps my mind occupied," Randy replied. "And it keeps me out of trouble."

Dr. Boyce got a kick out of that comment. "Good. How's the thesis coming?"

Ah, discussing the thesis. Now that was more like the conversation he was expecting. "It's coming along nicely," Randy said. "Doing some research in toxicology at the moment."

"Very good. I look forward to reading it and hearing your presentation. I expect good things from you. I'll be anxious to see your final exam scores as well. They are always exceptional," Dr. Boyce praised.

"Thank you, Sir."

"You seem motivated."

"I am, Sir," Randy replied.

Then Dr. Boyce did something Randy did not expect. He stood up directly in front of Randy's chair and leaned on the desk. This was extremely intimidating, and it made Randy nervous.

"Randy, let's cut to the chase here and get to the bottom line," the doctor began. "You are the only medical student in Cal history who has received the Herbert W. Nickens scholarship. You are actively involved in the medical community on many levels. We've heard about your volunteer work at the Suitcase Clinic as well as the work you do with Dr. Stephens. I've been watching you very closely. Your professors have been watching you. You are making quite a name for yourself."

The doctor's flattering remarks were a bit overwhelming. "Thank you, Sir."

"I didn't call you in here this afternoon to review your file. I have already done that. I called you in here because I want to recommend you to the Awards and Honors Committee. I would like to have them interview you and review your file. Your academic standing and personal commitment are superior to anyone else in your class. Depending on your final grades and your performance next year, we'd like to give you Alpha Omega Alpha Medical

305

Honors. The well-roundedness I witnessed from you today confirmed that even more. Are you familiar with that honor?"

"Vaguely, Sir."

Dr. Boyce explained it to him, "Alpha Omega Alpha is a national honor given to only the top ten percent of medical students in the country. It's based on academics, personal commitment, involvement in the medical community, and other personal activities. I've had several local physicians, medical professionals, and professors write me letters personally recommending you for this award. Would you object to having the committee look into your file and interview you?"

Randy was shocked. Alpha Omega Alpha was a huge honor that very few people received. It was the Summa Cum Laude of medical school. "No, not at all, Sir. I'd be honored."

"There are people here at the university, as well as physicians and other committee members from various parts of the country, who would like to speak with you. I will call and arrange for them to meet with us during our next appointment. In the meantime, you keep up the good work." Dr. Boyce held out his hand to Randy, who in turn respectfully stood up and shook it. "It was a pleasure getting to know more about you. I would like to sit and chat with you again very soon."

"It was a pleasure visiting with you too, Sir."

Dr. Boyce escorted Randy to the door. "My secretary will be contacting you about that meeting."

"Thank you, Doctor." Randy slowly walked down the stairs and headed toward the student clinic for work. The corners of his lips gradually formed a smile. He pulled out his phone and called Jane to tell her the good news.

During the week, Sarah hadn't shown up for lunch and dispersed from class too quickly for anyone to talk to her, almost as if she was avoiding contact with anyone. Randy tried to text her several times during the week, but she did not reply. This raised red flags, as Sarah normally didn't act that way.

Randy and the other second year medical students were working in small groups Thursday afternoon doing some data analysis. In the middle of the session, Randy glanced over at the group Sarah was working with and saw the professor questioning her about something. He couldn't make out what they were saying, but when the conversation was over, Sarah had tears in her eyes, obviously distraught over what had occurred. He tried to talk to Sarah about it after class, but she left before he had a chance to. Then Friday morning, at the conclusion of their seminar, the professor handed back some graded lab reports. When Sarah checked her grades, she developed a disheartened look on her face and walked out of class without saying a word.

Randy got up and followed her, shoving his papers in his backpack without even looking at his scores. "Sarah," he said, trying to get her attention.

She kept walking as if she didn't hear him.

He continued to follow her out the door, walking faster this time. He finally caught up to her in the middle of the courtyard and gently touched her arm. "Sarah."

She turned around, her eyes welled with tears.

"What is it?"

She sniffled and wiped her eyes then handed him the paper she was holding.

The score at the top was a sixty-two. Offering support, he said, "It's only one paper."

She unzipped her backpack and pulled out a stack of papers, handing them all to Randy.

He stared at her, not understanding. "What are these?"

"Every lab report, quiz, and written assignment from this semester."

He skimmed through them. The highest score on any of them was a seventy-four, below the passing grade of eighty-five needed to demonstrate mastery of the content in medical school. According to these papers, Sarah wasn't making the cut. "Oh man," he said.

"And my midterm scores were terrible."

"Why didn't you say anything?"

"What was I supposed to say?"

"If you need help, I can tutor you, or we can have more study sessions."

She shook her head. "Randy, it's not your responsibility to help me."

"You're our friend, Sarah, and all of us are in this together." He looked her in the eye and declared, "We can help you."

"It's too late for that," she sniveled. "I have my meeting with Dr. Boyce this afternoon, and I know what he's going to say to me."

Randy remembered what he said to her at their last study session and the flack he had given her. He now realized why it upset her so much—she was failing and tried to hide it from her friends. He felt terrible for being so hard on her, in fact he felt like a complete ass, now that he thought about it. Of course at the time had no idea she was having these problems. She had hidden it well and never said a word to anyone about it. "But there's still time."

"They're going to put me on probation," she cried. "Every semester gets more and more difficult for me. If I can't make it through this one, how am I supposed to bring my grades up next year?"

"We'll help you."

"That would burden all of you, and I won't do that to you guys."

"Sarah, please," Randy pleaded. "You've only got one year left. We can help you get through this."

"And what about after that? How am I supposed to survive clinical rotations when I don't understand half of the things we're supposed to already know?"

"Let us help you. You're not in this alone."

She looked at him, teary-eyed.

He gave her a hug, feeling awful.

After shedding a few tears, she released him without saying another word.

"Sarah," he called out as she turned the opposite direction.

But she did not look back.

Randy wasn't sure what to do or how to react. When Sarah was no longer in sight, he joined the others for lunch. "Have any of you talked to Sarah lately?"

"Sunday was the last time I talked to her," Bruce said.

"I saw her this morning, but she didn't say much," Mandy declared.

Jim added, "She hasn't been around for lunch this week, and now that you mention it, I haven't talked to her in class either. Why?"

"Did she say anything to any of you about having problems with school?" Randy wanted to know.

Mandy asked, "What makes you think she's having problems?"

"Because I just talked to her, and she showed me her scores from the semester."

"So?" Bruce shrugged not seeing the connection.

"So…she's failing," Randy informed them.

Jim was shaken by this news. "What do mean she's failing?"

"Are you sure?" Mandy questioned.

"Yes, I'm sure," Randy clarified. "She showed me all of her graded assignments. I saw it with my own eyes."

Bruce dropped his menacing eyebrows, wondering how this was possible. "How can that be? We all study together. We cover the notes and textbook information pretty thoroughly."

"You mean to tell me that none of us knew about this?" Randy was appalled. How was it that no one took notice of this?

"She never said anything to me," Mandy claimed. Then she turned to Bruce, wanting to know if he heard anything. "Did she say anything to you?"

"No," Bruce replied matter-of-factly.

"How the hell did this happen?" Jim asked.

"I don't know, but this is not good," Randy said. "She has her progress check with Dr. Boyce this afternoon and is freaking out about it. When I talked to her after class, she was crying."

"Sarah was crying?" Bruce felt his heart break a little.

"Yes."

They all sat staring at each other, shocked over this news. "Well, what are we going to do?" Mandy finally asked.

"We are going to help her," Randy insisted. "We can't let Sarah fail."

Mandy hoped Randy was conjuring up another one of his brilliant ideas. "Do you have a plan?"

Randy suggested, "We tutor her and have extra sessions or something. Anything."

Bruce, Jim, and Mandy all discussed how they were going to help Sarah, and together they came up with an ingenious plan.

They met at Randy's apartment Sunday morning hoping Sarah would show up for their study session. Randy put on a pot of coffee and Mandy brought doughnuts for everyone. They waited impatiently, constantly checking the time on the clock. About twenty minutes after their scheduled meeting time, there was a knock on the apartment door. All eyes turned to Randy.

He took a deep breath. "There she is," he said as he got up to answer the door. "Here we go."

When Randy opened the door, Sarah stood on the porch with her book bag over her shoulder. He showed her inside.

All four of them stared at her. Sarah wondered why. "What did I miss?"

Randy responded, "We are going to get you through this."

"You told them?"

"I had to. We're all in this together, and we will not let you fail."

"We're here to help you, Sarah," Bruce added.

Sarah started to cry. Amanda immediately stood up and gave her a hug, allowing the tears to flow.

Randy was crushed. Seeing his friend hurting this much almost made him cry. Sarah was the sweetest, nicest person he knew, and she did not deserve this. "We will work together and do whatever it takes to help you get through this."

She wiped her eyes with the back of her hand. "I appreciate that, but…" She eyed Randy, heartbroken. "I can't do this anymore. That's why I came over here. To tell you all that I'm leaving."

Randy shook his head in disbelief. "No, don't say that. The semester is almost over. There are only six weeks left."

"There's nothing I can do in six weeks. Even if I ace my final exams, I'm still not going to pass. And I'm not going to put myself through the torture of taking these classes over again," she sniveled. "I can't."

"We'll help you," Randy offered.

"It's too late. There's no point." She didn't want to face them anymore so she turned her back, preparing to leave.

Frantically trying to get her to stay, Randy took her by the hand. "I won't let you do this. Sarah, please. Let us help you."

She whimpered, "I can't."

Bruce offered his support as well. "Come on, Sarah. Don't give up. We'll pull through this together."

"Yeah," Jim said. "We'll do whatever it takes. Just don't leave."

"No." She shook her head. "I will not burden you guys with this. It's not your load to bear."

"But you've worked so hard," Randy said, trying to get her to change her mind. "The semester is almost over. You can't give up."

"It's too hard and too stressful, and the pressure is making me physically ill." She placed her hand on her forehead and the tears surged. Obviously she felt like she had no other options.

As a gesture of support, Randy hugged her.

After a minute or two, Sarah regained her composure. "Dr. Boyce is right. He told me I need to seriously consider my purpose. And I have." She hung her head and wrung her hands together. "This is not my purpose."

Randy said, "You can't leave."

"Randy, it's over," she asserted. "I can't do this anymore."

He could tell by the look on Sarah's face that there was no convincing her. She had already given up. He gave her another hug. "I am so sorry."

The others gathered around her too.

"Sarah," Mandy said. "Please don't go."

Sarah halfheartedly smiled at all of them, trying to hide behind the pain. "Thank you. I know you would have tried, but there's nothing you can do now."

They all stared at her, feeling miserable.

Concerned about her wellbeing, Randy asked, "What are you going to do?"

"I don't know." Sarah turned her back to them and started to walk toward the door. "I'll really miss you guys."

Randy found all of this hard to swallow. How could they be losing Sarah? He knew medical school was going to be rough, but really didn't fathom how many of his friends, who were so excited and dedicated on their first day of Anatomy class together, could buckle under the pressure. What happened that caused them to not make it through this? And why Sarah? She was about to walk out of his apartment and out of medical school for good. He couldn't let this happen. "Sarah wait," he pleaded, stopping her from leaving.

Sarah glanced at him one more time, then without saying a word, he watched her walk out of their study session and close the door behind her.

"What the hell? This totally blows," Jim griped.

Mandy was about to have a panic attack. She paced back and forth holding her hand up to her forehead.

"I can't believe this," Bruce complained. "How did we let this happen?"

"No!" Randy protested. "We can't let her do this. This isn't right."

"How do you propose we stop her?"

"I don't know." He looked at the door sadly. But instead of chasing after her, he leaned against the doorframe and closed his eyes. "I don't know."

"She's already made up her mind," Jim said. "There's nothing we can do."

"It's not like she ever said anything to anyone," Bruce reminded them. "She was quiet, she didn't talk much."

Randy replied, "We cannot let this happen again. If anyone ever has problems, we need to speak up. We can't help each other if we don't talk to each other. We have been in this together from the start and, dammit, we will finish this together come hell or high water. We are not going to lose another one of us, so if you are struggling with a concept or don't understand something or need clarification then for god's sake speak up!"

They all agreed to be more open with each other and promised to share results of tests and written assignments if necessary to maintain the unity of the group. They continued with their session, trying to put the incident with Sarah behind them.

Four hours later, their study session ended with Randy still upset about it all. Wanting to get some things off his chest, he got out his cellphone and called Jane. It went to voicemail for some reason so he left her a message. "Honey, please call me when you get this. I really need to talk to you." He let his bird out of the cage for a while then sorted laundry and cleaned up his apartment. About a half hour later, his cellphone chimed. He rushed to answer it, hoping it was Jane. It was.

"Hi, Sweetie. You guys done?"

"Yeah. You busy right now?"

"No. Why?"

"I need you," he declared.

She sensed something was wrong. "You ok?"

"Can I come get you?"

"Yes."

"Be over in a sec." He hung up and drove over to the Alpha house.

Jane stood on the porch waiting for him. He pulled up with the top down on the Camaro and the CD player blaring. He had on his designer sunglasses, wearing a frown and nervously tapping the steering wheel of his car. Worried about him, she got in the passenger seat and asked, "What's the matter?"

He didn't answer her at first. He simply pulled away from the curb, squealing the tires.

"Randy? What's wrong?" Jane asked, hoping he would talk to her.

It took him a while before he said anything. Finally, thick with sadness, he told her, "We lost Sarah. She quit."

"Sarah?" Jane was surprised to hear this news. "What was her reason?"

"Apparently she was failing, and not one of us knew about it."

"Why didn't she say anything?"

Randy struggled for words. "I don't know. But I'm an idiot for not seeing it, and I feel like a jackass for giving her such a hard time last Sunday."

"You didn't know."

"That's not the point," he snapped. "I was being an insensitive prick, totally disregarding that other people might not see things the way I do. I should have considered her feelings, and I realize now that what I said to her was hurtful, rude, and totally thoughtless."

Jane reached over and held his hand. "Randy, you do not have to bear the weight of the world on your shoulders. Why do you do that to yourself?"

"Because I feel responsible. I should have seen it. I should have done whatever I could to prevent this from happening. I should have helped her," he said, outraged that he didn't try to do more for Sarah.

"And what would you have done?" Jane asked.

"I certainly wouldn't have harassed her about it."

She didn't recognize the route he was taking. "Where are we going?"

"The hell out of Berkeley. I am so pissed off right now."

He drove around San Francisco, down highway 101, and across the Golden Gate Bridge trying to calm down. Jane's conversation soothed him, and he finally came to a stop at the Cliff House Bistro, San Francisco's only oceanfront restaurant. The water always calmed him, so he figured this would be a good place to eat. They were lucky enough to see a few sea lions hanging out by the rocks and a California Pelican landed by their window, which made Randy smile. The ocean view and frolicking wildlife lightened his mood. He became more talkative and was smiling by the time they left.

Before he started the car, Randy turned to Jane and said, "Thank you."

"For what?"

"Listening to me vent. Being here when I needed you." He hugged her tightly, almost squashing her. "I love you, Honey."

"I love you."

He started the engine and turned on the radio. Jane caught him singing the lyrics to a few songs as they drove across the city with the top down, enjoying the evening air and the starlit sky. She found his boyish charm incredibly cute.

Chapter Twenty-Eight

Finals were approaching, and all week long Randy had spent long hours studying and staying up late with his study group. He also spent an hour every night at the gym helping Jane get back into shape. His mind was still plagued with the thought of Sarah, as well as a million other extraneous things, and he felt seriously overloaded. By the time he came home Friday evening, he was exhausted.

He and Jane planned to meet Mandy, Bruce, and Jim for pizza and bowling to have fun and get away from the stress of school for a while. But when Jane showed up at Randy's apartment at 7:00 P.M., he was sound asleep on the couch with his stethoscope and cellphone on the coffee table next to him. She knelt on the floor and kissed him softly on the lips. He didn't wake up. In fact, he didn't move at all. She tried again, this time forcing his mouth open with her tongue. That woke him up. He wrapped his arms around her and pulled her onto the couch with him.

"Hey, Sleepyhead," she said.

"Hi, Baby,"

"What would you have done if you opened your eyes and it wasn't me?"

"I knew it was you," he replied, still feeling sleepy. "I'd recognize your kiss anywhere. No one's ever kissed me the way you do."

Randy appeared run down. He was physically drained and did not have his usual energy level. "You okay?" she asked him.

"I'm tired," he said with a yawn. "This week kicked my butt."

"We're supposed to meet everyone for pizza in thirty minutes. Did you still want to go?"

He sat up, stretched, and rubbed the kink out of his neck. "Yeah, we can go."

"You sure? We don't have to if you don't want to."

"It's alright," he said. "We'll go."

Randy's eyes sagged and the muscles of his face hung loosely under his skin. "You sure you're okay?"

"I'm fine. But let me change before we leave." He crept into the bedroom and changed into a pair of jeans, his Periodic Table of Elements tee-shirt, and a pair of sneakers. He grabbed his wallet, his keys, and his phone then took Jane's hand and headed to the pizza parlor.

The group ordered two large pizzas and a pitcher of Pepsi then sat around the table and chatted over dinner. Jim laughed as Jane peeled the pepperoni off her slice and blotted the grease with her napkin.

"You can't be serious," Jim teased.

"What?" she asked him.

"Oh my god. Just eat it."

"I'm not putting that grease in my body. Gross."

Randy didn't say much during dinner. He was distant and quiet. Normally hanging out with his friends cheered him up if he was cross or down, but tonight it seemed to darken his mood.

When they finished eating, they all met at the bowling alley and took ownership of their lane. Randy's foul disposition was bringing everybody down. Jane sat on the bench next to him and put her hand on his shoulder. "You okay?"

"Janey, I'm fine." He leaned over to tie his shoes. "Why do you keep asking me that?"

"Because you're not talking to your friends or to me. What's going on?"

"Don't have anything to say I guess. I'm gonna grab a beer. Do you want one?" he offered.

"No, thanks."

He put his hand on her thigh, stood up, and headed to the café.

Something was bothering Randy. His unpleasant mood made it pretty obvious. Hoping Jane knew what was going on, Jim scooted next to her. "What's wrong with Randy? Mega negative vibes emittin' off of him tonight."

"You noticed it too?" Jane glanced over her shoulder, worried about his negative disposition.

"Yeah. What's up?" Jim asked.

"I don't know. He won't tell me."

Everyone at the bowling alley was having a good time. Jane felt out of place being with someone so joyless. Randy was really being a bump on a log. He returned with a beer in his hand and sat at the table behind everyone else, a distance away from the lane. He had a scowl on his face and didn't seem interested in what was going on. Throughout the game, he came up to the lane long enough to take his turn then returned to his position at the table.

"Hmm," Jim said, staring at Randy. "What gives?"

"Let me talk to him." Jane got up and joined Randy at the table, pulling up a chair beside him. "How come you're sitting back here all by yourself?" She reached out and grabbed his hand.

Feeling her touch, he looked up. "Did you say something?"

"What's wrong?"

"I don't feel like sitting down there."

Jane knew there was more to it than that. "What's bothering you?"

"Nothing. I'm fine." She didn't believe him, and he knew it. But he wasn't in the mood to discuss it with her.

She moved her chair closer. "Why won't you talk to me?"

"What would you like me to say, Jane?"

"What's on your mind?" she asked him again.

"Nothing," he insisted.

"I don't believe you."

"Sorry." He took another drink of his beer then got out of his chair to take his turn. He returned to the table without saying a word to anyone. This continued throughout several frames. He spoke to no one, simply sat blank-faced nursing his beer.

Jim turned around and saw the sullen look in Randy's eyes. "Does anyone else feel a chill in here or is it just me?"

"I feel it too," Bruce said. "What's with Randy tonight?"

"I don't know, but somethin's not right."

Jane moved behind Randy and put her arms around his shoulders trying to get him to relax. "Randy, Honey, your friends think you're snubbing them."

He didn't care. "So?"

"So, why don't you tell me what's bothering you?"

"I told you, I'm fine. Would you quit bugging me about it, please?" he demanded.

"No, I will not," she pushed right back. "I will keep bugging you until you talk to me."

"Ok, fine. You really want to know? I have a file cabinet in my head full of mumble jumble crap. Open a drawer and take your pick, Babe."

"Pick one and tell me."

"I've been thinking about what Dr. Boyce told me, and I don't think I like that kind of pressure."

"I don't think he said that to pressure you. You should feel honored that he thinks so highly of you. You usually perform well under pressure," she reminded him. "I don't know what you're worried about."

"I've never felt pressure like this before. If someone like Sarah buckles under the pressure, who's to say that I won't or Jim won't or any of us for that matter. I've got enough bullshit in my life with exams and clinicals and working on my thesis. Plus, I'm trying to set up a full time job for this summer, helping you train for basketball, and trying to prepare for exams. Yet I feel completely unprepared, like I'm regurgitating information pointlessly. And I haven't been spending as much time with you as I should. I'm about to lose my mind." He voice became a bit louder.

"Sweetie, calm down."

He glanced up at the scoreboard. "It's your turn."

She softly kissed his neck. "I'll be right back."

While Jane went down to take her turn, Randy took another sip of his beer. His head hurt. He rubbed his forehead trying calm down before he ruptured a vein.

When Jane stepped onto the bowling lane, everyone stared at her. Slightly concerned about the upheaval that came from their table, Jim asked, "Is everything alright?"

"Everything's fine," Jane replied.

"No offense," Mandy added, "But your boyfriend has a major bug up his butt tonight. Seriously."

"Yeah he does. Grumpy ass. What's the matter with him?" Bruce asked.

Jane acknowledged their concerns. "After this game we need to go outside and let him breathe. He is suffocating in here."

Jim agreed. "Good idea."

"Sorry Randy's so uptight tonight, guys. He's feeling a bit stressed. Once he gets some fresh air, I think he'll feel better." She bowled her turn then returned to their conversation, sitting in the chair next to Randy.

He looked over at her, wishing he hadn't snapped at her. "I'm sorry, Baby. I didn't mean to take this out on you. I feel like a walking zombie lately."

She held his hand. "I think you're worried about things you don't need to be worrying about. The weight of the world does not have to rest on your shoulders. You need to stop doing that or you're going to drag yourself down. It isn't your responsibility to hold everyone up."

Her comment annoyed him. "Don't psychoanalyze me."

"I'm not. I just know how you get right before finals."
She moved to his lap and put her arms around his neck.
"You need to relax before you wig out on me."

"I'm not wigging out," he denied.

"Yes you are." She kissed him softly on the lips.
"You're grumpy tonight, and I'm not the only one who's
noticed."

He gently placed his hands on her hips. "You know me
too well."

"I also know that your friends down there are worried
about you," she told him.

He peered down at them. They were laughing and
having a good time together, yet he had been a total buzzkill
all night. "I have been kinda hiding under a rock tonight,
haven't I?"

Jane nodded. "Some fresh air will be good for you."

He managed to muster up a smile. "I think you're
right."

They nuzzled forehead to forehead. "And an ice cream
cone would be nice."

"Definitely." He closed his eyes, parted his lips, and
moved his mouth to hers.

Mandy saw Jane and Randy embraced in a kiss. "Hey
guys. Look."

Bruce and Jim turned their heads. "That's awesome,"
Bruce said. "Looks like he's feeling better."

Jim developed a mischievous grin. "Wanna see me ruin
a romantic moment?"

"Jim." Mandy whacked him on the arm. "Leave them
alone."

But Jim, being the ornery person he was when it came
to Randy, could not resist. "Hanson!"

Randy broke his kiss with Jane and lovingly gazed into
her eyes. "Never a private moment."

"Of course not," she giggled.

Jim called out, "Are you two gonna sit up there makin'
out all night or are you gonna come down here and finish
this game?"

"Yeah, yeah. We're coming." Randy kissed Jane one more time before she hopped off his lap and the two of them joined the others. Randy felt better now, still muffle-headed but at least more sociable.

They left the bowling alley and headed to the shoreline for ice cream. The five friends strolled around the path discussing summer plans. Jane and Randy held hands, straggling behind the others. When Randy realized where they were, he stopped and grinned. "Well, well. This looks familiar."

Jane recognized this location. "I know where we are."

"I would hope so. This is where we shared our first kiss."

"Yes it is."

Randy pulled her closer to him. Their eyes met briefly before he found himself lost in her kiss.

Jim looked around. Randy and Jane were nowhere to be found. "Where did Randy and Jane go?"

Bruce turned around and saw a couple kissing under a streetlamp. He pointed that direction. "They're over there kissing…again. Good lord. Don't they ever quit?"

"I should have guessed," Jim said. "And no, I don't think they do. Perma glued."

"Those two are perpetually lip locked," Bruce protested. "Every time I see them together they're kissing."

"They're in love," Mandy remarked. "Maybe you should take a few lessons from him."

"What are you implying?" Bruce asked. "Are you saying I don't know how to attract a woman?"

"There's a reason why women swoon to him."

Bruce burst out laughing. "Swoon. That's a good one, Amanda. He just knows how to sweet talk them and use romance to his advantage. If every guy did that, there would be mushy, sappy, romantic crap all over the place."

"So? What's wrong with a little romance?" she argued.

"Nothing, unless it's in excess." He peered over at Randy and Jane again, who were still kissing. "And those two are extreme."

"I don't think so," Mandy debated. "I think it's sweet."

"If they stay like that much longer, we might have to surgically remove them."

"Good," Mandy snapped. "It will be good practice for you."

"Ooh," Jim commented, laughing at Bruce. "She burned you, Dude."

"Shut up," Bruce complained.

Changing the subject, and trying to get a rise out of Mandy, Jim blurted out, "Dude, did you see that chick at the seminar this morning?"

Bruce played along. "The one with the incredible ass?"

"Ass? Fuck yeah. But did you see her face up close?"

"No," Bruce replied.

"Totally hideous nose job. Man, that hag was a full-on Monet."

Mandy did not find their shallowness amusing. Apparently Bruce was attracted to whoever it was they were talking about or else he wouldn't have made that comment about the woman's ass. Mandy wondered what was wrong with her butt that caused Bruce to never notice.

Reluctantly, Randy came back to the world and removed his lips from Jane's. His heart beat out of control and his body still quivered from the moment.

Playfully, Jane hopped on Randy's back, and he gave her a piggyback ride over to where the others were debating. When they got there, Amanda seemed upset about something. "What's going on?" he asked, gently setting Jane on the ground.

"These guys are a bunch of male chauvinist pigs," Mandy grumbled.

Randy retorted, "Is there a man alive who doesn't suffer that fate? We're all pigs, according to women. Insensitive, unemotional, only interested in the carnal pleasures of sex—it's what makes a man a man."

"Ugh," Mandy rolled her eyes, not impressed with his witticism. "You're as bad as they are."

Jim and Bruce both laughed.

"You guys are assholes!"

Randy leaned toward Jane and whispered, "Want to go home with me so we can be alone?"

"Sounds like an intriguing proposition, Sir."

"You interested?" He nibbled on her ear.

"Very."

He leaned over and kissed her again.

Jim teased, "Get a room for god's sake."

"I heard that, Ryan. And I don't need a room. My bed will work just fine."

Jane's jaw dropped. "Don't tell him that."

"Why not?" Randy innocently stated. "It's true."

"You're obnoxious."

"And you love it." He gave her a quick peck on the lips then told the others, "Jane and I are gonna take off. See you guys on Sunday." Randy turned his eyes to Jane. "You ready, Baby?"

"Yes."

They walked over to his car and drove home.

When they arrived at Randy's place, Jane kicked off her shoes. Randy collapsed on the sofa. "I'm sorry I was such a killjoy tonight. I know it's not an excuse, but I have so much crap buzzing through my head right now, I feel like I'm about to lose control."

"You're not losing control," she assured him. "You just need a break. School will be over in a couple weeks then you'll be able to relax for a while. We could have stayed home tonight, you know."

"No, I needed to get out of here." Randy raised his hand to his forehead.

"Headache?" she asked.

"Yeah."

"I'll get you some Tylenol." She headed toward the bathroom.

Randy opened the birdcage, releasing his parrot to fly free. Then he sat on the couch and took off his shoes. Slowly, he laid his pounding head on a pillow.

Jane walked in with two Tylenol capsules and a glass of water in her hand. "Here you go, Sweetie."

"Thanks." He swallowed the pills and chugged down the entire glass.

Jane sat next to him. "You feeling ok?"

He rested his head on her lap. "Tired. I've been living off about four hours of sleep every night for the past week because I've been getting up early to get some studying in before class."

"Why didn't you tell me?" she asked, feeling guilty for adding to his stress. "And I've made it worse by dragging you into the gym every night."

"I'll be alright. I need a good night's sleep. I always sleep better with you by my side, so I hope you're planning on staying here tonight," he suggested.

"I was."

"Good." He placed her hand in his. "I'm sorry I've been so stressed lately. I can't seem to get all this crap out of my head. It's like someone took all of the organized files in my brain and threw them around randomly, making a jumbled mess. My thoughts are going in a thousand different directions at once and it's making my head spin."

"You need a day to relax."

He brought her hand up to his lips. "I love hanging out with you," he added. "I can let go of all the confusion in my life and be myself. No pressure, no stress, I love it."

She ran her fingers through his hair.

He closed his eyes and took in the relaxing sensation.

"I talked to Brian yesterday," she said. "He invited us to his graduation on the eighth of June."

"That's fine with me, Babe, but what about you?" He opened his eyes and looked up at her. "Won't your dad be there?"

She nodded. "I know. I thought about that."

"You know, Janey, it kills me to see the relationship you had with your dad unravel like this. I know you're angry, but you're going to have to talk to him sooner or later."

"Talking to him is like talking to a mule," she griped.

Randy laughed at her scrutiny. "I know. But you need to stick to your guns and let him know that you won't back down. Do it in a respectful way, of course. At that point he'll either accept it or he'll stay mad, but at least then the ball will be in his court. He needs to know how you feel, even if he doesn't agree with you."

"Dad's gonna flip when he finds out I'm playing basketball again."

"But it's not his decision," Randy reminded her. "It's better to be upfront and honest with him about it. You need to stop hiding things from him."

"He's gonna blame you for that, you know."

"Yes, I'm sure he will accuse me, but let him."

"But that's not fair," Jane declared. "I'm not going to let him fault you for every decision I make that he doesn't like."

"That's probably the way it's going to have to be. It's easy to post blame on me. After all, I stole his daughter away from him," Randy stated.

"You didn't steal me away."

"We'll go to Brian's graduation, but you're gonna run into your dad, and you're going to have to talk to him."

"I know."

"I'll be there with you if you need me." He kissed her hand. "By the way, I have something for you." He rolled off the couch and walked into the bedroom, returning with an envelope that had her name on it.

She took the envelope from him and opened it. Inside was a card with a rose on the front. She turned it over to read the words on the back. *My darling Jane, I'm sorry I've been oversensitive and crabby lately. You've been patient and very understanding with me. You are an amazing woman. Thank you for being who you are. I love you. XOXO Randy.* She bit her lip and smiled. "Aww, thank you, Sweetie." Also inside the envelope where two tickets to a Maroon 5 concert Jane had been dying to see. Her mouth gaped open. "You told me these were sold out."

Grinning slyly, he replied, "I lied. We have front row seats for tomorrow night."

"No way."

"Yup. You didn't already have a date for tomorrow did you?"

She threw her arms around him, almost knocking him over. "Oh my god, Randy, I can't believe you did this!"

"Whoa, Baby. Take it easy," he said, stumbling backwards.

"I've been wanting to see this concert ever since I heard they were coming to San Francisco!"

"I know. That's why I got tickets."

"Thank you so much." She held the tickets in her hand, super excited that he had done this for her.

"You're welcome."

She hugged him tightly. "I love you so much."

His heart beat wildly at the sound of those words. "I love you too." He held her firmly, never wanting to let her go.

Chapter Twenty-Nine

Randy felt a tremendous weight lifted off his shoulders and an incredible feeling of liberation when he turned in his last exam. He stepped outside the Medical Sciences building and took in the fresh air. Two years down. What a phenomenal feeling to complete another year of medical school. He glanced at his watch and realized he had finished his exam earlier than he thought, so he went up to Alpha to see Jane.

Outside the sorority house, several of the girls were lying out in the sun listening to music. Randy loomed toward them. "I am one lucky guy," he remarked. "Surrounded by all these beautiful women. Lookin' good, ladies."

One of the girls shaded her eyes with her hand and looked up to see Randy towering over her. "Hey, Doc, you're blocking my sun. Move."

"Sorry." He moved out of the way. "Is Jane inside?"

"I think so. The door's open."

"Thanks." He snuck through the back door and walked inside. "Hello?" he called out. No one answered. He went upstairs and found Jane in the bathroom wearing a very short pair of shorts and a bikini top. She had earbuds in her ears and was dancing in front of the mirror while putting her hair up in a ponytail. He crept behind her and said, "Hello, Gorgeous."

She smiled at his reflection in the mirror. "Hey! What are you doing up here? I thought you were taking a final?"

"I finished it," he boasted.

"Already?"

"Yup."

Once her hair was in place, she set her brush on the counter. "How do you feel?"

"About?"

"You just finished your second year of med school."

He took her in his arms and spun her around. "I feel fabulous. In fact, I feel like celebrating. Let's go down to L.A. for a few days, just you and me."

"Are you serious?"

"Yeah, it'll be fun. We'll grab a hotel down there and spend a few days chilling out. We'll check out Malibu and go to Disneyland. Neither one of us has any commitments right now, so let's get out of here for a while and take a mini vacation."

She liked this plan. "That sounds fun."

"Cool. Let's make reservations."

They strolled down to his apartment where he did some internet searching, got out his phone and his credit card, and made hotel reservations for Friday and Saturday night. When he was finished, he drew her nearer. "Ok, we're all set, Babe. We'll drive down in the morning, stay in Anaheim tomorrow and Saturday night, then drive home Sunday."

"Randy, this is crazy," Jane declared.

"Oh, but it will be fun. It's the spontaneity that makes it fun." He kissed her softly on the lips. "I will give you the best time of your life this summer, my dear. I promise you that."

"I can't wait."

As soon as Jane and Randy returned from Southern California, Randy logged onto his student account to see if final grades had been posted. He earned a ninety-five on his final written exam and a ninety-eight on his practical. Respectable scores. He called Jim to let him know grades had been posted.

"I know," Jim replied. "I already checked mine."

"What did you get?"

"Ninety-three and ninety-one."

"Good job." Despite all the personal hell he'd been through this year, Jim pulled it off. "Are you home?"

"Yup."

"I'm on my way over."

Jim answered the door holding an unopened envelope in his hand. "Hey, man. How was your lovers' outing this weekend?"

"We had a blast." Jim stared at the envelope with a fearful look in his eyes. Randy questioned this reaction. "What's that?"

"It's from the hospital. Trina had the baby while you were gone."

"A boy or girl?" Randy asked curiously.

"A boy. Had a paternity test done immediately afterwards. This is from the lab. It has the results in it."

Randy and Jim stared at each other. Jim was nervous, and Randy knew it. A simple nod indicated that Randy was behind him one-hundred percent.

With bated breath, Jim slowly pulled the letter out. As his eyes scanned the contents of the letter, a grave expression filled his face.

"What does it say?" Randy asked.

The letter fell out of his hands, and he started to breathe heavier. The weakness in his knees forced him to sit down.

Randy rushed to his side, hoping Jim didn't hyperventilate. "Jim?"

"It's conclusive." He held his head in his hands; he couldn't breathe.

"Calm down, man. Breathe."

"Goddamn. I'm a father. I can't believe this." He combed his fingers through his spiky hair.

Randy felt Jim's emotional turmoil right along with him. "So now what?"

Swallowing hard to clear the lump in his throat, a feeling of certainty suddenly overtook him. "I'm gonna go see my son." He snagged his keys.

"I'm coming with you."

When they arrived, Jim started to panic. "I can't do this. What the hell am I supposed to say to her?"

"Show her the letter and tell her you want to see your son."

Terrified that he would do or say something he was going to regret, and knowing Randy would be there to watch over him, Jim said, "Don't let me do anything dumb."

"I've got your back." And on that note, they stepped out of the car.

Jim closed his eyes and took a cleansing breath, trying to calm his nerves before he knocked on the door.

Trina answered, surprised to see Jim and Randy standing on her doorstep. "Jim."

Jim hesitated before he spoke to her. "Hi."

"What are you doing here?"

He handed her the paper confirming his biological connection to this baby.

She read the letter, unsure what to say.

"I'm here to see my son," he declared.

She opened the door and let them in.

A tiny infant slept in a bassinet. Jim and Randy crept closer and peeked inside. Jim stared at the baby for a minute. It seemed unreal to him that this tiny being was his flesh and blood. The reality of it all was frightening. "What's his name?" he asked Trina.

"Christopher. Christopher James Ryan."

Jim jolted his head to the right. "You named him after me? Why?"

"Because he's your son. I told you that."

Jim reached into the bassinet and gently supported the baby's head, lifting him out.

Randy looked on. Even from first glance, there was absolutely no doubt that Jim was the father of this baby. The infant had his eyes, his facial features, his blonde hair—he was a carbon copy of James Ryan. "Damn, Jim," Randy said. "He looks just like you."

Jim sat on the couch and gently touched the infant's tiny fingers and toes. The baby opened his eyes, which made Jim smile. "Hey, little one."

Trina sat next to him and gave him an envelope.

"What's this?" Jim asked, not sure he wanted to take it from her.

"You can have those," Trina replied. "They're pictures of Christopher my dad took at the hospital."

"Thank you."

"He has your eyes," Trina noted.

Jim stared at his son. "Yes. I see that." He watched the baby squirm. Now realizing that this child was indeed his son, he felt a sudden urge to protect him, provide for him, ensure that this baby had everything he needed. "Are you nursing?" he asked Trina.

"No. Bottle feeding."

Jim was quick to question this decision. "Why? It's better for him if you're nursing. It gives him the antibodies he needs until he gets vaccinated."

"It will be too hard to nurse when I go back to work," she declared.

Jim looked over at her, not liking what he heard. "When are you planning on doing that?"

"Six weeks, hopefully."

A six-week-old baby was far too young for daycare. "What are you gonna do with him?"

"My mom."

"I wanna be able to see my son."

"You can come over here and see him anytime you want," Trina told him.

"I want parental rights."

"James, I will never keep you from him."

Jim caught himself gazing at her, which he didn't want to do. He had to force himself to look away. "Do you need anything? Diapers? Formula?"

Trina touched his arm, trying to get him to look at her again. "Jimmy."

He pulled away and laid the baby back in the bassinet.

"I want us to be together again, for Christopher's sake."

Still angry and hurt by her previous acts of infidelity, Jim laid it on the line. "There is no us. You threw us away."

"But we can fix that."

"Look," he stated, feeling betrayed and used. "I will get you whatever you need, and I will be responsible for my son, but don't," he shook his head. "Don't pretend like everything is ok between us."

She eyed him sadly, feeling dejected because he was being so cold and distant with her. "James, please."

His jaw tightened and his lips drew a hard line. "You betrayed me, Trina. You lied to me and you broke my trust. I can't live with that." Jim kissed the baby on the cheek then headed toward the door.

Randy stood up, ready to walk out with him.

"Jim," Trina implored. "I'm sorry."

He gave Randy 'the look' indicating that he was ready to leave, so Randy escorted him out.

With an abundance of thoughts and emotions running through his head, Jim didn't say much during the car ride back to his apartment. Wishing Jim would talk to him, Randy broke the silence. "You ok?"

"Yeah."

"I can't believe how much he looks like you. Even without a paternity test, there's no denying he's your son, Jim."

Jim nodded. "I know. I'm gonna have to tell my parents."

"How do you think they'll react?" Jim's parents, especially his father, overreacted to situations and weren't always the most supportive people in the world when it came to complicated issues like this.

"They already knew there was the possibility that the baby could be mine and they're prepared for it. But I'm not sure I am. I don't know the first damn thing about bein' a dad or caring for an infant," Jim said, fearing this new responsibility in his life.

"Looked to me like you were handling yourself pretty well back there."

"Christopher James, huh?" Jim said with an agreeable smile.

"I like it."

"I like it too."

Although Randy was enjoying his summer vacation, he was not looking forward to having another confrontation with Jane's dad at Brian's graduation. Jane hadn't spoken to her father in months, and the last time they did speak, the conversation was argumentative.

Randy and Jane sat on the bleachers in the high school gymnasium watching the graduates parade in to 'Pomp and Circumstance.' The valedictorian gave a speech and the graduates walked across the stage one at a time to receive their diplomas.

When the ceremony was over, Jane suggested, "Let's go down and talk to Brian. But I need to use the ladies' room first. I'll meet you down there."

"Alright." Randy barreled through the hordes of people to get to Brian. When he found him, he shook his hand. "Congratulations."

"Thanks. Glad you guys could make it." Brian scanned the area for his sister. "Where's Jane?"

"She went to use the little girls' room. She should be here in a minute." That's when Randy spotted Jane's father. He dreaded this moment. And where the hell was Jane?

Dale Davine shot Randy a wicked glare. "What are *you* doing here?"

Apparently he was on his own until Jane got back. "I'm here with Janey."

Dale sneered at Randy maliciously. "Janey? Is that what you call her? That is not her name."

Randy tried to remain respectful, but that comment irritated him. Every time Jane's dad was around, he felt like a bug about to be squashed. He'd had enough of it. He wanted answers for the way Dale Davine treated him. "Excuse me, Sir, but have I done something to offend you?"

"Knowing you have your hands all over my daughter offends me."

"I'm sorry you feel that way."

"She never would have done any of the inappropriate things she's been doing if you wouldn't have told her to do them."

What a ludicrous accusation. "Meaning no disrespect, Sir, but I don't tell Jane what to do. And even if I did, she probably wouldn't listen to me anyway."

Dale's glower grew colder. "For some reason beyond my understanding my daughter seems to think she's in love with you. I don't see how that is possible unless you put the idea into her head somehow. I'm not as blind as she is. I can see you for what you really are, Mr. Hanson."

Remaining polite became increasingly more difficult the more Mr. Davine opened his mouth. He seemed to have a way of pushing Randy's buttons with his constant degrading insults. "Sir, if you have a problem with me, that's fine. I can deal with that. But Jane is not this immature girl you keep saying she is. You speak of her as if she's a vulnerable child, and she most definitely is not. She's a beautiful, intelligent, strong-willed, independent woman. Pardon me for being abrupt here, Sir, but I have never known Jane to be the kind of person you make her out to be. And you continuing to say those things about the woman I love is beginning to upset me."

"The woman you love? Do even know what love is?" Dale asked, displeased with Randy's bold statement.

"Yes, Sir, I do. And I know how I feel about Jane. There is nothing I wouldn't do for her."

"Jane seems to think she has some kind of future with you. But if you think for one second that you can whisk her away from us, you have another thing coming, because I will *never* allow that to happen." Dale glared at Randy; his voice was abrasive and cold.

Not only did Randy not like the tone Dale Davine used, he also did not like those hostile and intimidating words.

Jane walked up behind them and overheard the harsh tone her father directed towards Randy. She stopped him before he said another word. "Daddy."

Dale Davine snarled at his daughter. "Why did you bring him here?"

"He's my boyfriend, and he was invited." She stood proudly by Randy's side with her arm around him.

"I will not talk to you with him here. What I have to say to you is none of his business," Dale Davine insisted.

Jane was insistent right back. "Then I guess you won't talk to me. Anything you have to say to me, you can say in front of him."

Wow, she was being tough and standing her ground in a way Randy had never seen before. She was downright persistent.

Dale refused to speak.

Jane continued, "I hate the way you are acting. What did Randy ever do to you?"

Randy was curious to hear the answer to this question.

"Any man who has the gall to take my daughter into his bed without having the decency to marry her first is not trustworthy. That tells me that's all he wants from you. That's not love, Jane."

"When are you going to stop treating me like a child?" she demanded to know. "Yes, Daddy, I know what sex is. I've heard the word. I've used the word. I've seen it, and I've done it. So what?"

Fury brewed in Dale's eyes. Trying to alleviate this bad situation before it escalated into something worse, Randy grabbed Jane's hand. "Come on, let's go."

She pulled away from him. "No, I'm not finished."

"Jane." Randy leaned toward her and whispered in her ear, "Let's go before this gets out of hand."

But instead of walking away, she moved closer to her father. "What would Mom say if she knew the way you were treating Randy? Treating me? She would be disgusted!"

"I've heard just about enough of this, young lady," Dale warned.

"Oh yeah? You wanna know what else? I'm going to play basketball again because I love that game, and I know that's what Mom would have wanted me to do. At least she supported me in that, which is more than I can say about you. You never cared about anything I love."

Her father's eyes penetrated Randy like daggers. "Is this the kind of influence you have on my daughter?"

Randy fought to remain civil and courteous. "She makes her own choices and lives her own life, and whether you like it or not, Sir, she has chosen me to be a part of it. I'm not a father, and I have no desire to be one anytime soon, but I would think that if your daughter is happy, you would be happy for her."

In a threatening tone, Dale Davine seethed, "If you ever do anything to hurt her..." He stormed out of the gym.

Although this distressing scene upset Jane, Randy was glad she finally stood up for herself, and for him.

"That went well," Brian stated, his sarcasm intentional. "But at least you let him know where you stand. And he needed to hear that. Ever since Mom died, he's been acting like a dick. It took a lot of guts to call him out on it."

"I'm sorry, Brian," Jane said. "I didn't mean to ruin your graduation."

"No worries, Sis." He shook Randy's hand and gave Jane a hug. "Thanks for coming."

As Brian walked away, Randy lifted Jane's chin. "Are you ok?"

"I'm fine."

"That was ugly. But I have to say, you were very strong today. You stood up to him, and I'm proud of you. I do think you got a little carried away though. You could have handled that with more tact."

"I don't care," she said, being pig-headed.

"Your daddy is very angry with you," he stated. "Being a bit less callous when you told him the news about basketball might have made him react more positively. You were kinda harsh there, Babe."

"I told you I don't care. I am not going to stand here and let him say things like that. I can't believe he spoke to you that way."

"Well, this was eye-opening, to say the least. I can certainly see where you get your temper and willfulness," he teased. "I've had the lovely privilege of being on the receiving end of two Davine tempers now."

She had lost her temper and been stubborn with him a few times in the past. She felt horrible about it now. "I'm sorry."

The pathetic look on her face made him laugh. "It's alright, Babe. It happens. I can be tenacious and obstinate and let my arrogance get the best of me sometimes. Don't worry about it."

"I wanna go home," she said. "This has turned out to be a really crappy day."

"Alright." He took her hand. "Come on."

Jane desperately needed a pepper-upper. To lighten the mood, Randy suggested, "Jim has the baby this weekend. You want to stop by and see him?"

She gasped in excitement. "Ooh, can we?"

"Sure. But I want to get him a gift first." They stopped at Target and bought a newborn outfit, a tiny squeaky basketball, a package of diapers, and a rattle with little basketballs on it. They placed it all in a decorative baby print bag and both signed the card before they headed over to Jim's apartment.

When Jim answered the door, Jane handed him the bag.

"Thanks." Jim had purchased an infant car seat and a baby cradle for Christopher to sleep in. Between that and all the baby clothes, bottles, and toys lying around, his tiny studio apartment was starting to look like a baby lived there. "Nice timing. He just woke up."

"Where is he?" Jane asked, anxious to see the baby.

Jim showed them in. Right away, Jane headed for the cradle. "Aww, he's so cute. Can I hold him?"

"Sure," Jim replied.

Jane carefully, and quite naturally, held the baby while Randy talked to Jim. "How you doing?"

"I'm doin' alright. Christopher's a good baby. As scared as I was about this whole daddy business, I have to admit, I love my son very much. I'm still not sure I know what I'm doin', but I'm gonna try my best." Jim watched Jane interact with Christopher and a smile brightened his face.

Jane was a natural at handling the infant. She tenderly stroked his arms and held his little hands and talked to him with the most loving and caring voice. She definitely had that maternal instinct. When the baby started to fuss a bit, Jim handed her a bottle.

"I wish his mother wasn't so selfish," Jim said. "But at least she's willing to cooperate, so I guess things could be worse."

"True." Randy sat next to Jane and the baby.

"She had my name added to his birth certificate," Jim declared.

"So it's official now?"

"Yup."

Jane held the baby out to Randy. "You want to hold him?"

Although he was in no hurry to have one of his own, Randy loved babies and had handled several over the years. Babies would one day be his livelihood. He held his arms out and took the infant from her. "Hello there, Christopher Ryan." The infant reached for Randy's finger and squeezed. "Whoa. He's got a good grip," Randy said as he glanced over at Jim. "He's really alert for a newborn."

"I know," Jim concurred. "He's a pretty good snoozer too. Only woke up once last night."

Randy repositioned the baby on his shoulder. "Did you get your work schedule changed?"

"I have weekends off, at least until school starts again."

"That's good. That will give you some bonding time with him."

"My parents came over last night to see him."

"How did that go?" Randy asked, hoping everything went well.

"They brought over a bunch of crap. Bottles and diapers and baby blankets. My parents are actually bein' pretty supportive. Although my dad was buggin' me to find a way to patch things up with Trina."

"You told him what she did to you, right?"

"Yeah."

"And he's ok with that?" Randy questioned.

"No. In fact, both my parents are pissed at her and are gonna go postal on her ass if they see her."

"Then why would your dad want you to get back together with her? That doesn't make sense."

"Sayin' some shit about how it's all for Chris's benefit and that the baby needs stability, yadda, yadda, yadda…"

"Don't know how stable being with Trina would be."

"Exactly," Jim affirmed. "I can't trust the bitch. I pretty much told my dad that was never gonna happen."

Randy smiled, proud of his friend for standing his ground. "Good for you."

"I'm gonna move into a bigger apartment in a few weeks. There's a two bedroom available downstairs. That way Christopher can have his own room."

"Cool." Randy gave the baby back to Jane. "Do you need anything?"

"I'm cool right now, but thanks."

"Let us know if you think of anything," Randy offered.

"Will do, Bro. You guys all packed for Mexico?" Jim asked.

"Yup. We leave on Tuesday."

"I'll watch your bird for you," Jim offered. "But the featherhead better not bite me again."

Randy had to laugh. He remembered the story Jim told him about how Mr. Fingers latched onto his thumb and Jim had to pry him off, leaving broken skin and beak marks on his knuckle. "Don't fuck with him and he won't."

"I don't fuck with him," Jim defended. "All I do is feed that damn thing and he bites me. Didn't you teach him not to bite the hand that feeds him?"

Randy got a chuckle out of this.

"I swear that bird hates me."

"Thanks for looking after him for me," Randy stated, grateful that his friend was willing to endure getting bit to help him out.

"No problem," Jim replied.

"Check the mail for me too, and call if anything weird happens."

"Like what?"

"I don't know," Randy said. "Weird shit has been known to happen in that apartment complex. You know that. You used to live there."

Jim recalled a few incidents.

Randy then glanced at Jane, who was still ogling over the baby. "You gonna be able to give him up so we can eat?" he asked her, hoping they could get some food soon.

Jane smiled at baby Christopher. "He's so sweet."

"Yeah, he's a cutie, but we have to go."

She gently handed Christopher to Jim, who handled him like a pro now. "Thanks for stoppin' by, guys," Jim said. "You'll call when you get to Mexico?"

"Yes we will."

"Take lots of pictures."

"I always do." Randy and Jane walked toward the door.

"Have fun."

"See ya later, Jim." Randy waved at the infant. "Bye, baby."

Jim moved the infant's hand up and down and said, "Bye, bye," as Randy and Jane left.

Randy thought about Jim's interaction with the baby and was impressed with what he saw. Jim was responsible, caring, and gentle, and really seemed to have a handle on this parenting thing. For being a brand new dad, Jim didn't flinch and was surprisingly relaxed. As Randy walked out to the car with Jane, he said, "He's going to be a good dad."

"So will you," Jane added.

He stopped abruptly and swung his head to one side. "What?"

"I saw how you handled that baby in there."

He shrugged, "I have nothing against babies. I like babies, as long as they're someone else's. I don't want one right now."

"Will you ever want one?" she questioned.

Why was Jane bringing up children all of a sudden? This was a topic that had never come up in their conversations before, and he wasn't sure what to make of it. "Someday I want to have kids, but I have to get through medical school before I even think about having a family."

"You do want a family then?"

Although she was probing him, it was actually refreshing to hear her talk about future plans. "Eventually. I'm not in a hurry though." He decided to turn the conversation to her to see how she felt about all this. "What about you?"

She nodded. "I want a family."

That's all she had to say about that? Simple yet decisive answer. She certainly knew what she wanted. Maybe someday, when he was ready, he could give her that.

After working another shift in the Emergency Room, Jim walked out to his car. The ER nurse, Jill Darcy, was standing outside the hospital waiting for a bus. He walked over to her. "Hello, Jill Darcy."

She turned to his voice. "Oh, hello, Mr. Ryan."

"Why are you waitin' for a bus? Where's your car?"

"It's in the shop. The brakes needed to be fixed."

"I can give you a ride."

"I don't want you to go out of your way."

"It's no trouble at all."

"Thank you." She picked up her bag and followed him.

He unlocked the car and opened the passenger side door for her. An infant car seat was strapped to the back seat.

"You have a little one?" she asked.

Jim stared at the car seat. He thought he took that out of the car. Guess not. "Yes. My son."

"How old is he?"

"Was born two weeks ago."

"Congratulations to you and his mother."

"I'm not with his mother anymore," Jim instantly corrected.

"I'm sorry to hear that," she replied, trying to show a little sympathy.

Jim gave a crooked smile. "Don't be. I'm not."

There was a bit of an awkward silence. Jill wondered what the story was behind that. "What's his name?"

"My little boy?" Jim wanted clarification.

"Uh huh."

"Christopher."

"I have a daughter," she stated.

Curious now, Jim wanted to know more. "Do you?"

"She's three. Her name's Sabrina."

"That's a pretty name."

"I raise her alone."

How she managed to do that and work the inconsistent hours she carried in the ER was beyond his understanding. "You get child support and help from her father I presume?"

"No," she replied. "He's out of my life and hers, and I'd like to keep it that way. Sabrina doesn't know him, I don't talk about him, and she doesn't ask."

"How do you raise a child by yourself? That must be hard." He was kind of hoping to get some constructive insights from her experience with this.

"It's challenging. Babysitters are expensive and my ER shifts can have some terrible hours."

"How do you handle that?" he asked.

"She stays with my parents. They are really good with her, and I know they'll keep her safe."

"It's good that you have their support."

"They've been helpful," she agreed.

Jim drove across town talking with Jill about parenting and taking in the advice she offered. When they pulled up to her apartment, he kindly asked, "You need a ride to work tomorrow afternoon?"

"No. I'm supposed to pick up my car in the morning, but thanks anyway. And thanks for the ride."

"Anytime," he replied. "It was great talking to you. You really gave me some good advice."

"I'm glad I was able to help." She got out and headed inside her apartment complex.

Jim ran into Jill again the next day when he went to the coffee shop across the street from the hospital before his shift started. He grinned when he saw her. "Hello, Jill."

"Hello, Mr. Ryan."

"No need to be so formal. Call me Jim, please," he insisted.

"Getting coffee, Jim?"

"Oh yeah. The largest caffeinated latte I can get my hands on. Coffee any good here?"

"The best in the city," she claimed. "They make an almond vanilla latte that's to die for."

"That sounds good." He ordered one then sat with her in a booth.

"Are you thinking about pursuing Emergency Medicine?" she asked him.

"I am."

"Really? What draws you to it?"

Interesting question. He gladly told her. "This may sound kind of morbid and messed up, but I love the thrill of havin' someone's life in my hands. Trauma patients need more help than any others—blood and broken bones and life threatening injuries—and I get to save them. I get a rush from that."

"I like that too. Not so much the blood and all, but knowing I'm helping to save the lives of the most critical patients. Kind of my way of giving back to the community."

"Yeah," he took a sip of his coffee. "Definitely with ya on that."

"You're working my shift tonight," she stated.

"Awesome. I've seen you in action, and you are one helluva good ER nurse. Very caring and compassionate."

"Thank you."

"Hopefully, when I start clinicals, I'll get the opportunity to work with you more directly."

"Hopefully."

He smiled pleasantly and finished his cup of coffee before he had to report to the hospital for his shift.

Chapter Thirty

Randy and Jane flew out of San Francisco Tuesday morning and headed to Mexico. When they landed in Puerto Vallarta, a shuttle bus picked them up and drove them to their hotel, the Grand Velas. This elaborate resort, located on the Mexican Riviera, offered twenty-four-hour concierge services, a unique world-class spa and fitness center, and a wide beach right behind the hotel. It had three on site restaurants, and sponsored various activities including snorkeling, kayaking, boogie boarding, and introductory scuba diving classes.

"Wow, look at this place," Jane said, reading over the offerings of the beachfront hotel. "This is going to be awesome."

Randy checked them in, and since he hadn't heard from his father since they left the airport, he asked the hotel desk clerk if the rest of his family had arrived.

The man checked the hotel register. "Yes, Sir. They checked in about an hour ago."

"What room are they in?" Randy wanted to know.

"608, Sir. Right across from yours."

"Great. Thank you."

They wheeled their bags into the elevator and headed up to the sixth floor. Their room was an Ambassador Suite with a king-sized bed, private Jacuzzi, and a balcony with an ocean view. Jane stood wide-eyed. "This view is amazing."

Randy closed the door. "I'm gonna run across the hall and let my parents know we're here."

Jane followed him. "I'm coming too."

Randy handed her a room key then they went across the hall and knocked on the door of room 608.

Stephanie answered, screaming in excitement. "Dad, Randy's here."

Randy's dad came out of hiding and greeted them. "Is your room ok?"

"The room is fantastic. Thank you."

Ellen Hanson hugged her son. "Did you guys just get here?"

"Yup," Randy answered. "That was a long flight. I'm starving."

Mark Hanson checked the time on his watch. "Anyone else hungry?"

Robby overheard the food conversation and rushed out to see what was going on.

Agreeing on a dinner choice, they all went down to the hotel's casual oceanfront restaurant, Azul.

Before everyone returned to their rooms for the night, Mark pulled his oldest son aside. "Randy, can I talk to you for a minute?"

"Sure." He gave Jane a kiss and said, "I'll be there in a minute." Jane headed inside the room and Randy went with his dad. "Yes, Sir?"

Mark reached into his wallet and handed Randy a wad of cash. "Take this."

Randy refused to take it. "You don't have to do that. We have funds that we specifically saved up for this."

"I want you two to enjoy yourselves. I know you're on a budget, Son."

"Dad, we're fine."

"Randal, don't argue with me," his father insisted. "Keep it in a safe place. The hotel has lockboxes in all the rooms."

Randy reluctantly took the money. "Thank you."

"Everything in the hotel is paid for, and if you need a car, Mom and I rented one."

Although Randy appreciated his father's generosity, he found it a bit extreme. "You don't have to do all this."

"I want to. Consider it my gift to you for completing your second year. Congratulations, by the way."

"Thank you."

"How'd you do?" Mark asked, hoping his son fared well.

"I have my grades in my carryon."

"You can show me later. We'll meet for breakfast tomorrow and discuss plans from there. Enjoy yourselves tonight. See you in the morning."

"Good night, Dad." He returned to his room. "Wow," he said, closing the door behind him.

Jane was unpacking her suitcase, but stopped what she was doing to see what he was so excited about. "What?"

"My dad just gave me a thousand bucks to spend while we're here."

"Are you serious?"

He flashed the money at her. "Yes."

"Oh my god, Randy. This is going to be the best vacation ever. Can you believe this room?" She walked out to the balcony and looked over the edge then shuffled back inside. "And did you see the Jacuzzi we have?" She moved over to the bed and picked up a mint from the pillow. "There are mints on the pillows. Mints."

Her child-like excitement made him laugh. "You've never been in a luxury hotel before, have you?"

"No."

"Well, then," he moved closer and wrapped his arms around her. "You are in for a treat, my dear. Everything you need or could possibly want is right here in the hotel. However, the best part is out there." He pointed toward the window. "The beaches, the culture, the tropical paradise of Mexico. I can't wait to introduce you to it. We'll need to figure out what we want to do while we're here. There are a lot of choices."

He gave her a kiss then pulled out brochures, travel guides, and a hotel registry of activities that he picked up from the lobby. They sat together and discussed a tentative itinerary for their ten day stay, leaving some days open for family activities.

Jane lounged in the sand in her bikini with her hands clasped behind her head. Randy was in his swim trunks, lying on his side propped up on his elbow beside her. The waves lapped at their feet; the white sand filtered through their toes. Palm trees extended their leaves out to the sun and the faint aroma of tropical flowers perfumed the air. Even though it was evening and the sun was low in the sky, the air was still warm and the water was pleasant. It was truly paradise.

Jane let out a relaxed sigh. "I could get used to this. I'm not going to want to go back."

A content smile decorated Randy's face as he gazed down at her. "Not bad for a family vacation, is it?"

"I can't believe your dad did all this. I'm having so much fun."

"This is what it was like for me growing up," he explained. "Except when I was younger, we went to places like Disney World, wild animal parks, the Ben and Jerry's ice cream factory, and Legoland."

Jane was a little jealous of the escapades Randy experienced as a child. She never had the opportunity to do any of those things.

"I thought all families went on vacations like that, until I was older and realized how privileged I was. Being a doctor's kid had its advantages. It had its disadvantages too."

"Like what?" Jane asked.

"Like having my dad's work hours so unpredictable that we would be in the middle of opening presents Christmas morning and he would get a page to go to the hospital. He would sometimes miss birthday parties or other family functions because of his schedule. Obstetricians are always on-call. Can't predict deliveries. Babies come when they are ready."

"That must have been tough."

Randy brushed it aside as unimportant. "Mom was a trooper about it, and we kids were used to it. That's why I'll be glad to join his practice. It will make the job easier for both of us because we can share on-call duties. And with two physicians in the clinic, we'll be able to double appointments and patients we have. Everyone wins."

It seemed like Randy had planned this all out very well and knew exactly where he wanted to be in five or ten years. "You two have this all worked out, don't you?"

"Not all the details, but Dad and I do have a plan. I have a long way to go before that happens though."

"One year less now," she reminded him.

He grinned at this actuality then stood up and grabbed Jane's hands. "Come on. Let's go for a swim."

After the sun set, they came back up to the sixth floor in wet swimsuits and sand-covered flip flops.

Randy's dad ran into them in the hallway. "Good evening."

"Hey, Dad."

"You guys about ready to eat?" he asked his son.

"We'll need to get dressed first, but give us twenty minutes?"

"Alright. Come get us when you're ready."

"Will do."

Jane and Randy frolicked into their room, laughing and kissing. Mark Hanson enjoyed watching his oldest son's giddy schoolboy playfulness every time he was around Jane. It was refreshing to see.

Randy's father had made reservations at Frida, located on the second floor above the lobby. Frida offered traditional Mexican cuisine with a delicious mix of aromas and flavors. Every dish was a work of art, presented in native colors reflective of Mexico's culinary history. They indulged in mouthwatering local cuisine in a lovely dining room with stunning ocean views while serenaded by a mariachi band.

After dinner, Jane and Randy snuck off to their room. Randy hung the DO NOT DISTURB sign on the door and warmed up the Jacuzzi. He called room service for a bottle of champagne, pulled two wine glasses out of the minibar, and filled a bucket of ice to keep the champagne cold. Then he and Jane relaxed in the Jacuzzi bubbles while they sipped on champagne.

"You know, Baby, I've been thinking," Randy said.

"You're on vacation. You're not supposed to think."

With a grin, he said, "You're not going to like this, but hear me out."

She snuggled in closer and took a sip from her glass. "Not going to like what?"

"I think I know a way to fix this problem with your dad."

Champagne dribbled down her chin and she almost choked from his outrageous suggestion. "Uh uh. We are not discussing this."

"Hear me out."

"No." She set her glass down and covered her ears. "I'm not listening."

He removed her hands from her ears and turned so they were facing each other. "I think this might actually work."

"Why are you bringing this up now?" she demanded to know.

"Because I really think I have a good plan. At least listen to my idea."

She sighed. "Ok, what is it?"

"When we get back, you are going to get on the phone and invite your dad over to my place for dinner."

That was the most outlandish thing she had ever heard him say. "This is a bad idea." She picked up her glass and took a huge drink, gulping down every drop.

"I'm not done." He took the glass out of her hand and set it on the edge of the Jacuzzi. "Janey, listen to me. We have to do something calm and peaceful to let him know we are making an effort to fix this. He is convinced that our entire relationship is based on infatuation and physical lust and doesn't think we love each other. The reason he thinks that is because he doesn't know us, as a couple. I think that if he sees us as we are, no holds barred, he'll see that we…"

"I cannot believe you are actually suggesting this," she interjected.

"Why?"

She stumbled over her words. "Because…it's…we just can't."

"I really think this will work. We'll be on our territory for one thing, not his. And maybe if he sees how serious we are about each other then perhaps all of this petty stuff that seems to bother him won't be such a nuisance. If nothing else, he'll see that we are making an effort. It will fall on him after that."

"I don't know." She tightened her lips, not sure she agreed with him.

"It's worth a try, don't you think? Can't be any worse than what it is now. This way we can all sit down and have a polite conversation over a pleasant dinner on our territory."

Jane had doubts. "You don't really think he'll come over to your apartment, do you?"

"I don't see why he wouldn't. Especially if we are sincere. And even if he doesn't, at least we did our part to try to make amends." He set his glass down and took her hands in his. "Honey, I'm not saying this is the miracle cure-all or that everything will be peachy after this, but maybe things will at least be civilized. As it stands now, you two can't even be in the same room together."

"I hate it when Daddy gets like that."

"Will you call him when we get back?" he beseeched as he looked into her eyes.

"I don't know about this."

"Come on, Baby. What harm can it do?"

"This is crazy."

"Maybe. But will you promise me you'll think about it?"

"I'll think about it."

As she reached for another glass of champagne, he snuck in close, stealing a kiss before she could get a sip in. She almost spilled her champagne as he intensified the kiss and pulled her even closer. Before she dropped the glass, Randy took it out of her hand and set it on the edge of the tub. Then he reached his hand behind her head forcing her mouth to his again. She didn't resist him. In fact, she gave into him completely.

A knock on their hotel room door came entirely too early for Randy's liking. Who was awake before the crack of dawn, and why in god's name did they feel it necessary to knock on his door at this ungodly hour? Groggy and a bit cranky, he slipped on a pair of shorts and answered the door.

Stephanie's overly cheerful face shrieked, "Good morning!"

He sneered at her. "Good god, Steph."

She removed the DO NOT DISTURB sign from the door and handed it to him. "You left this on your door."

He snatched the sign from her hand. "Yet you still knock on my door. Apparently you can't read."

"Dad told me to make sure you were awake. We're all going on that ecotour this morning, remember?" She peeked in the door to see Jane partially covered with the sheet, naked underneath. An almost empty bottle of champagne and two glasses sat on the bedside table. "Rough night?"

"We were up late. What time is it?" Randy searched the room for a clock.

"6:30. Dad wants us out the door by 7:45. That gives you forty-five minutes, if you want breakfast before we leave."

"I need some coffee."

"What do you want me to tell Dad?"

"Tell him we'll be ready." He brushed the hair off his forehead and held the DO NOT DISTURB sign in her face. "And learn how to read."

Randy closed the door then woke Jane up. They showered together, got dressed, and he and Jane were ready in time for breakfast.

They chose to spend the afternoon lounging on the beach. Randy leaned back on a towel soaking up some rays while Jane was on her tummy next to him, propped up on her elbows with a book in her hand. Over by a nearby palm tree, Robby sat in the sand by himself watching some young people frolicking on the beach. Randy watched him for a while. He could tell his brother wanted to go over and mingle with the group, but for some reason he wouldn't join them. "I'll be right back." He leaned over and gave Jane a kiss then hopped to his feet and sauntered across the sand to his brother. "Hey, Rob. Whatcha doin'?"

Robby ogled over a young girl wearing a white flowered bikini.

"You like the redhead, don't you?"

Robby continued to stare at her. "She's totally hot, and look at her smile."

"Why don't you go over there and talk to her?"

Robby pulled his eyes away from the girl. "I can't."

"Why not?"

"I don't know her."

"You don't have to know a girl to talk to her, Robby," Randy advised.

"I…uh," he stumbled over his words. "I'm not good at talking to girls. I get all panicky and my palms get clammy. I never know what to say."

"Talking to girls isn't so tough."

"That's easy for you to say. You seem to be a natural at it."

"Strike up a conversation with her."

Robby stared at the girl, dreamy-eyed. "What do I say?"

"Say hello, introduce yourself. Ask her if she's on vacation, ask her if she's enjoying her stay, ask her where she's from. Asking questions tells her you're interested in what she has to say."

Robby's whole body tensed up.

"What's the worst that could happen?"

"She can totally reject me and humiliate me in front of all those people."

"Worst case, yeah, but so what. You don't know any of them, and it's not like you'll ever see any of them again. But she could respond to you, and you two could hit it off. You won't know if you don't try," Randy instructed.

Robby was reluctant to take his brother's advice.

To encourage him, Randy put his hand on his brother's shoulder. "Go on. Talk to her. Just be yourself. You'll be fine."

Robby stood up, dusted the sand off his shorts, and put his hands in his pockets.

"Lose the pockets, Robert. Be confident."

Robby pulled his hands out of his pockets and strode across the beach to join the group.

Randy sat and watched, hoping his brother wouldn't crash and burn. Robby approached the red-haired girl and said something that struck her attention. This was a good sign. As Robby spoke, the girl sat down in the sand. Robby sat next to her. Things seemed to be going well, so Randy left them alone and returned to Jane's side.

"Where'd you go?" Jane asked him, now that he had reclaimed his spot on the towel.

"Helping Robby get hooked up with that girl over there." Randy's eyes drifted that direction. "He was sitting there staring at the girl, afraid to talk to her, so I gave him a few pointers."

"Oh you did, did you?" she teased.

"Yup."

"And what did you tell him?"

"I told him to ask her questions. That way she'll think he's interested in what she has to say."

She sat up and cocked her head. "Oh, is that how it works?"

"I'm not into pick-up lines. They're lame and they don't work. But if a girl really thinks you're interested in what she's saying, you're in. Girls like to talk, and if she has a chance to do that, and a guy appears to care about what she's saying, he's good as gold."

"Oh really?" she mocked. "You mean you don't actually have to be interested in what she says, you just have to pretend to be?"

"Basically, yeah."

"Randal! That is a terrible thing to tell him."

"What? It's true. It always worked for me."

She couldn't believe he said that. "You mean to tell me that you just pretend to listen to what I'm saying?"

"No," he defended himself, realizing he probably dug himself into a hole. "That's not what I meant. You're reading things into this. I never told him not to listen to her, I simply advised him to ask questions to get her to talk. For pick-ups it never fails. And I was trying to help my brother." He leaned forward and kissed her. "You know I love you, and I am very interested in what you have to say."

She leered at him.

"Baby…" He slid his hands onto her hips and pulled her over to him. "I thoroughly enjoy our discussions. The conversation you and I shared when we first met was one of the things that attracted me to you."

"Really?"

"Yes, really. I thought you were the most interesting person I had ever met. I love talking to you. It's one of my favorite things to do." Randy quickly found himself drifting into her eyes. "And your eyes, god I love your eyes. I always have." He rubbed his fingertip across her lips. "And you have the prettiest, most enticing lips that I love to kiss. They drive me wild."

She seductively bit her lip and grinned at him.

"I love it when you do that."

"Do what?"

"Bite your lip like that. It is so sexy." He caressed her bare back and moved in to kiss her. He explored her mouth with his tongue and leaned back on the towel, taking Jane with him. Jane's knee bent slightly, and she rubbed her foot on his leg as they kissed under the warm tropical sun.

Someone stood over them, clearing their throat. Hearing this caused Randy to break away from Jane long enough to look up.

His dad stared down at them. "Are you two planning on coming up for air to eat something tonight?"

"Depends what's on the menu."

Mark plopped down in the sand next to them. "Feel like French cuisine?" he asked his son, knowing French food was his favorite.

Randy asked for Jane's opinion. "What do you think?"

"Sounds good to me."

Randy turned his attention back to his dad. "Guess that's a yes."

"Good. Where's your brother?"

Randy pointed to where Robby and the pretty redhead were sitting. "Over there."

Mark's youngest son was laughing with an attractive young red-haired girl. "Oh, I see. Did you have anything to do with this?"

Randy grinned cunningly. "Maybe."

Mark chuckled at his oldest son's playful tendencies. "The French express leaves for dinner in forty-five minutes."

"Alright." Since they needed time to shower and change into appropriate dining attire, Randy stood up and took Jane's hands, lifting her off the sand. "Rob!" he hollered at his brother. "Dinner in forty-five!"

They made a slight detour toward Robby. Randy leaned closer and whispered, "Establish a meeting place for later."

Robby beamed confidently as Randy and Jane headed back to the hotel holding hands.

Moments later, Robby ran after them. They stopped walking and waited for him to catch up. "So? How'd it go?"

The excitement on Robby's face was priceless. "She's going to meet me out by the pool tonight."

"See, I told you. Never fails," Randy confirmed.

Jane rolled her eyes.

Randy touched the tip of Jane's nose with his finger then kissed her tenderly. He slipped his arm around her and the three of them headed back to the hotel together.

Midway through dinner, Jane's cellphone vibrated. She glanced down at the incoming number and crinkled her brow with a scowl on her face, but didn't answer the call. Randy wondered why she reacted that way. Instead of discussing it in front of his family, he decided to wait until they had the opportunity to be alone.

After dinner, Randy and Jane walked barefoot along the beach. Now that they were alone, Randy used this opportunity to question her about the earlier phone call. "Who called you at dinner?" he asked her.

"Daddy."

"Why didn't you answer it?"

"I didn't feel like it," she boldly stated. "Besides, we were all having dinner together, and I didn't want to be rude."

"Are you going to call him back?"

"No."

"Why not?" he asked.

"Because I don't want to listen to his lecture."

"Lecture? About what?"

"About being down here."

"Your dad doesn't know you're in Mexico with me and my family?"

"No," she plainly stated.

"Why didn't you tell him?"

"My father doesn't run my life. He doesn't need to know where I am or what I do all the time."

Randy explained, "Baby, you went out of the country. You really don't think that was important for him to know?"

"No," she insisted.

Her indifferent attitude concerned him. "You should have told him. You can't go on keeping secrets from your father."

"I can if I want. What Daddy doesn't know won't hurt him."

He tried to get her to understand. "You told me once that you wished you could have a relationship with your father like I have with my parents."

"Yes, but Daddy is too close-minded for that to happen."

"Would you like to know why I have such a good relationship with my parents?" He stopped walking and looked at her. "I have never lied to my parents or kept secrets from them or tried to lead them to believe that I was someone I wasn't. My parents and I have always had an open line of communication. We talk to each other."

"Daddy is too stubborn to listen."

"Seems to me like the stubborn one here is you, Babe," he countered. "He tried to call you and you ignored him. I thought you wanted to end the discord between you and your father?"

"I do."

"And you think that lying to him about your whereabouts and refusing to take his call is going to accomplish that?"

She considered the implications of her actions and realized he was right. "No."

"Then get on the phone and call him back."

"He's going to be mad that I'm down here," she fretted.

"He's going to be even angrier that you didn't tell him you were coming in the first place." Randy's eyes met hers as he took both of her hands in his. "Baby, if you want your dad to trust you and support the decisions you make then you have to give him a reason to trust you. If you keep secrets from him all the time and don't tell him what's going on in your life, that is never going to happen. You lie to your father constantly. How do you expect to build any kind of relationship with him that way?"

"I don't lie to him. I just don't tell him everything. Every time I tell him something, he gets angry."

Seeing the way she handled her relationship with her father forced Randy to say something he didn't want to say because he wasn't sure how she would react. "Hiding things from someone is considered lying. And you do it to your dad all the time. He gets angry because he's finding out that you've been deceiving him. Think about it, Honey. Do you really blame him? How would you feel if I did that to you?"

"I'd be hurt and feel betrayed and have a hard time trusting you."

After months of trying to get this point across to her, she finally figured it out. "My point exactly." He reached his hand into her pocket and pulled out her cellphone. "Call him. You need to tell him you are down here, and you need to tell him you're with me. And while you're on the phone, invite him over for dinner next weekend so we can fix this."

She looked down at her cellphone, scared and hesitant.

"There is no other way," he definitively stated.

Reluctantly, she dialed her father's number and sat by a palm tree. Randy watched and listened. He only heard one side of the conversation, which appeared to be a little confrontational from what he could tell, but as it developed, it seemed to lighten up somewhat. A few tears were shed, and the conversation came to a close with Jane trying to convince her father to join them for dinner when they got back to San Francisco. The answer her father gave was unclear as Jane hung up the phone.

Wanting to get a response from Jane, Randy asked, "Well?"

She slipped her phone in her pocket. "He agreed to come for dinner."

"That's good."

"He was angry that I was down here, just like I told you he would be."

"Angry that you were in Mexico with me or angry that you didn't tell him you were coming?"

"Angry that I didn't tell him," she admitted. "But he was glad I called and told him the truth."

"See. Honesty is the answer, Jane, I'm telling you. On a different note, I got a text from Jim today," Randy said. "There's a nurse at the hospital he's gaining an interest in."

This grabbed Jane's attention. "Really?"

"Yes. Her name is Jill. He seems to really like her."

"A girlfriend?" Jane said, hoping for the best.

"Nothing's developed into that quite yet, but maybe. Apparently she's divorced and has a three-year-old daughter. Jim hasn't been on the dating scene in a long time. Trina is the only girl he's ever been with, so the fact that he's even interested in another woman is a huge deal."

"Does this nurse know he has a baby?"

"Yes. And if she will get his mind off Trina, I'm all for it," Randy claimed, happy that Jim was getting his life back on target.

On their last night in Mexico, Randy reached for Jane to get her to sit closer to him. She scooted over and sat between his legs. The waves lapped on the shore and the light from the moon reflected off the water. He wrapped his arms around her and said, "Now you can say you've been to Mexico."

With a content sigh, she said, "Yes."

"Did you have fun?"

"So much fun. I love it here."

"I love Mexico, too," he said. "Definitely one of my favorite vacation spots."

"This was the most memorable vacation I've ever had."

"That's good. We got a ton of pictures too, so we have lots of memories to take back with us. I want the memories we make together to be extraordinary. I want to be the most unforgettable experience of your life."

"You already are."

Randy's heartrate elevated and his breathing deepened a bit. He touched Jane's face with his hand, which made her close her eyes. "You are so beautiful," he said to her. The tip of his thumb moved across her lip, stroking it lovingly. While her eyes were still closed, he leaned forward and gently kissed he lips.

When she opened her eyes, he was staring at her. "What?" she asked.

"I'm just thinking."

She sat on her knees facing him with her arms around his neck. "Thinking about what?"

The smile on his face looked more like a devilish smirk of mischief. "You don't want to know."

"Yes I do. I always want to know what you're thinking."

"I was thinking about a conversation we had a long time ago about sexual fantasies. And now here we are, alone on a beach in Mexico in the moonlight with the waves and the warm tropical breeze. Ironic."

She gave him a seductive stare. "So what are you thinking?"

"I told you, you don't want to know."

She moved closer. "I bet I know what you're thinking." Jane saw the hunger in his eyes. She moved her mouth up to his ear and whispered, "You want to make love on the beach, don't you?"

He felt her breath in his ear and closed his eyes. She knew him well, too well.

"Randy?" she whispered, trying to get him to respond. "That's what you're thinking, isn't it?"

It was a crazy idea. They were out in the open, exposed for the world to see them. They couldn't have sex here. What if someone walked by and saw them? He looked into her eyes again and his heart thumped out of control. Longing increased by the second.

"Isn't it?" she asked.

"We can't."

"Why not?"

"Because this is a vacation resort, and we are out on a public beach. Someone will see us."

Jane looked around. The beach was completely empty. "Who? There's no one out here." She pressed her body against his as she rubbed his chest with her hands.

He closed his eyes and enjoyed her loving caresses. Her touch was alluring, her kiss intoxicating. "Baby, don't do this to me."

"But this is your fantasy." She teased him by gently licking his lips with the tip of her tongue. "We can fulfill it right here, right now." She reached down and felt that he was hardened. "I know you want to."

Her loving touch made him long for her even more. They sat on their knees facing each other. Waves hit their feet and legs as they intertwined together, kissing under the moonlight. "I want you," he finally admitted.

She moved her mouth to his ear and nibbled on it a bit before she whispered, "I want you too."

Randy loved Jane's spontaneity and the way she was always willing to play along with his crazy whims. This was a fantasy he had been longing to fulfill, and she was completely encouraging it. Yet this was the craziest thing he had ever considered. How could they even think about doing this here?

"Take me," she whispered.

Passion grew by the second. He unbuttoned his shorts while Jane repositioned herself in front of him with her back against his chest. Once she was in position, he slid his shorts down to his knees. His finger slowly crept up her thigh, fondling in sensitive places. Then, sliding her shorts and panties off, she leaned forward onto her hands and knees. He wrapped her up in his arms and slid inside. Sex under the moonlight and the stars of the Mexican Riviera was the most erotic, yet romantic experience of his life. The cool water splashed them and the breeze hugged their bodies as they made love on the beach, fulfilling a long awaited fantasy.

Chapter Thirty-One

Returning to California was not particularly welcomed, but Jane and Randy needed to return to reality sooner or later. They spent the weekend unpacking, doing laundry from the trip, cleaning out the birdcage, and giving the apartment a thorough cleaning to prepare for Dale Davine's scheduled arrival.

While the main dinner dish was in the oven, Jane took some down time to gather her thoughts.

Randy could sense her apprehension and tried to mollify the anxiety she felt. He put his arms around her and pulled her close. "Take a deep breath."

She obliged.

"We are here to make amends with your dad. You being on edge like this isn't going to help. You need to calm down."

"I can't."

"You need to try," he advised. "Think before you say anything. Do not be reactionary. You tend to be too forthright in expressing how you feel when you're angry. Think tactfully, clearly, and control your actions. Remember to communicate peacefully, not argue."

"Ok."

With his finger, he lifted her chin so they were eye to eye. "Put your angry feelings aside and think. Be patient and understanding. Listen to him. Don't just hear him, really listen. Communicate here, Baby."

"I'll try."

"That's my girl." He kissed her to show his support. "Now I'll be here, but I can't speak for you. You're on your own there, Babe."

"I hope this works."

"He agreed to come, didn't he?" Randy reminded her. "That's a good start. The goal is to get you two talking again. The rest will come later. We'll have to take it one step at a time."

"I'll do what I can, but what if Daddy isn't willing to make peace?"

"Oh, I think he is," Randy said, "or he wouldn't have agreed to come. Now you sit down, unwind, and collect yourself. I'll finish up here."

Right as Randy finished setting the table, there was a knock on the apartment door. Jane jumped up nervously.

"Calm down. It'll be ok." He opened the door and welcomed Jane's father, who was standing on the porch with a teddy bear in his hand. "Good evening, Sir. Please, come in."

Dale Davine didn't say a word. He simply walked inside.

Jane greeted her father cordially. "Hi, Daddy."

He handed her the teddy bear. "I brought this for you."

"Thank you." She led him to a chair in the living room. "Can I get you a drink?"

"Yes, thank you."

Jane brought a Pepsi to her father and sat on the sofa across from him. She tried to make peaceful conversation, avoiding the topic of basketball, while Randy brought food out to the table.

The conversation over dinner went well, except for the fact that her father completely ignored Randy. Randy didn't mind though. He was just happy that Jane and her father were communicating.

After they ate, Jane helped Randy clear the dinner dishes. When they were alone together in the kitchen, she had to speak her mind. "Daddy is being so cold toward you. He won't even acknowledge that you're in the room."

"I don't care," Randy declared. "At least you two are communicating. That's what matters right now."

"I hate this," she complained.

"I know you do, but you're doing great, Honey," Randy assured her. "I'll finish cleaning up. You go out and talk to your dad. I'll be out in a minute." His lips brushed against hers. "Go on."

Reluctantly, she returned to the living room.

When Randy emerged a few minutes later, he sat on the couch next to Jane and put his arm around her. Doing this caused Jane's father to sneer at him, but he didn't care.

"They want to recommend Randy for Alpha Omega Alpha Medical Honors," Jane remarked, hoping to bring Randy into the conversation.

For the first time all evening, Dale acknowledged Randy's existence. "What's that?"

Randy gladly answered, "It's a national honor that only the top ten percent of medical students in the country are eligible to receive. It's based on strong academic standing, professional commitment, and diverse background experience in the medical field. I'm up for nomination, but the process of actually getting the award is tedious and time consuming."

Mr. Davine actually seemed impressed by this news. "You are in the top ten percent of medical students in the country?"

"At the moment, yes, Sir. And I'm currently ranked top of my class here at Berkeley."

"That's impressive," Mr. Davine acknowledged.

"Thank you, Sir."

For the first time in a long time, Jane's father said something nice to Randy. But this kindness was short-lived. With a sudden change in tone, her father stated, "I would like to know what gives you the right to convince my daughter to play basketball again when she knows it's against my will to do so?"

Randy calmly answered, "It was her decision."

"I don't believe that. Jane would not do anything against my wishes unless someone convinced her to do it."

"Daddy," she interrupted. "The decision to play was strictly mine. I've done a lot of things you didn't approve of. I just didn't tell you about them."

Jane's father held his hand up to his head, trying not to get angry. "Jane, I do not approve of you playing and you know that."

"But I love to play. Why are you so against it?"

"What I'm against is you sneaking around and doing things behind my back. You say one thing then do another without even bothering to check with me or discuss it with me first."

Jane responded with, "Daddy, I love you, but I am an adult and I can make my own decisions."

Dale's face developed an angry frown. "And I suppose the decision to have sexual relations with this man was strictly yours as well?"

"Yes," she said. "Randy makes me happy. Why can't you accept that?"

"Because I know you are over here every night sharing his bed. Your relationship is purely physical, and I will not support that."

"Sir, if I may," Randy interjected. "That statement is not true. I love your daughter. Jane and I have a special relationship. We discuss things, we laugh together, we cry together, we support each other, and we lift each other up. We understand one another, and we have a connection."

Dale responded defensively. "What I see is two young kids mistaking lust for love. Love is a commitment, a promise you make to someone. Physical pleasure and true emotional commitment are not the same thing."

"No, Daddy, they are not," Jane admitted. "But Randy and I are committed to each other. We're in love."

Not convinced, Dale stood up and headed toward the door. He feared Randy would break his daughter's heart, and he couldn't live with that. "I truly hope you are right, Jane."

Randy and Jane stood up with him. "Thank you for coming, Sir," Randy offered.

"Thank you for dinner," Dale returned, almost politely.

"You're welcome." Randy graciously offered a handshake.

Dale stared at Randy's hand but refused to accept the gesture.

"Thank you for the teddy bear," Jane added.

Her father gave a quick nod then turned and walked away.

Jane closed the door. "Thank God that is over with."

"I thought that went well," Randy said.

"He's still upset."

"But you two are talking. That's good. And he brought you a bear," Randy grinned.

"I have never felt so much tension in my life."

"You handled it well, Honey." He drew his lips to hers and kissed her. Then the two of them returned to the couch to watch a movie together.

While Randy and Jane were relaxing on the sofa, Jim finished another shift at the hospital. Jill was heading out to her car. He walked a bit faster to catch up with her. "Hey, Jill," he called, trying to get her attention.

She turned around. "Hi, Jim. I'm glad I ran into you because I wanted to give you something." Jill reached into her purse and handed him a piece of paper with a phone number on it. "She's a really good babysitter, if you ever need one."

"Thanks." Jim took the paper from her and put it in his wallet. Jill Darcy was a kind-hearted person. He enjoyed her company and looked forward to the conversations they had.

"Looks like you're fitting in well with the ER crew," Jill remarked. "Dr. Lyons likes you. He's impressed with how quickly you've stepped up to the plate."

"That's good, I guess."

"If he didn't like you he would have fired you by now. He's fired more orderlies than I care to tell you."

"Really?" Jim asked, a bit concerned about his job security.

"The fact that he's still allowing you to stick around says a lot about you."

Jim found this funny.

"Hopefully you'll be able to get a good night's sleep tonight after the busy day we had," Jill said.

"I hope so."

"This must be hard for you with an infant in the house."

"Sometimes. But I'm doin' alright." He caught himself gazing into Jill's eyes. The cloud cover blocked the moon's reflective light and the sound of traffic, distant horns, and sirens filled the nighttime air. Far from a romantic setting, but to Jim it didn't matter. His eyes kept shifting from Jill's lips back to her eyes. Finding himself unable to resist the urge, he leaned forward and kissed her. When he realized what he had done, he backed away and apologized for his lack of self-restraint. "I'm sorry. I shouldn't have…"

Before he could continue, her mouth covered his.

He closed his eyes and wrapped her in his arms.

After several minutes, they stood staring at each other. Jim stumbled for words, feeling awkward about what had happened. "Well, I guess I'll see you tomorrow."

"Goodnight, James." She got in her car and drove away.

When Jim saw Jill at work the next day, he wasn't sure what to say to her. He approached her during a break, hoping things wouldn't be uncomfortable between them. "Hey, Jill."

She turned her head and smiled. "Hi, Jim."

"You got a minute? I need to talk to you."

"Yeah, sure." They stepped into the resident break room. "What's on your mind?"

He gazed at her lips. They were more persuasive than he cared to admit. "Please tell me not to feel weird around you."

"Ok. Don't feel weird around me."

He laughed. "Thanks." Searching for the right words, he said, "Look, Jill, about last night. I was wonderin' if by that kiss you meant…"

She pressed her lips on his.

Her kiss was slow and thoughtful, and it was the most invigorating feeling he had ever known. He closed his eyes, butterflies flittered around in his stomach. When she broke their embrace, Jim was left weak and confused.

"Does that answer your question?" she asked.

He grinned bashfully, embarrassed that they had done that at work. "Yeah, actually, it kinda does." He swallowed to loosen the knot in his throat. "I saw on the schedule that you're off tomorrow night."

"Yes I am."

"I was hopin' you might like to have dinner with me."

The corners of her mouth curved in approval. "I'd love to."

Thrilled that she accepted his offer, he said, "Great! How's six o'clock sound?"

"Sounds wonderful."

He straightened his shoulders and stood a bit taller. It had been a long time since he'd been on a date. Although he was excited about this, it also made his nerves jumpy.

"I wanted to give you my phone number, in case we don't see each other at work and you might want to talk or something." She reached into her pocket and handed him a piece of paper with her cellphone number on it.

He glanced down at it. "Thanks."

"Oh, and Mr. Ryan?" She tapped her watch. "Your break is over. You might want to get back to work before Dr. Lyons gets upset with you."

"Yes, Ma'am. I am on my way." And on that note, he returned to the ER, feeling on top of the world.

Chapter Thirty-Two

Jim sat in the living room of his newly acquired bigger and better apartment doing some research and working on his thesis with Christopher sleeping soundly in the other room. The apartment was quiet, until someone tapped on his door. He set his textbook on the coffee table and got up to answer it. Trina was on his doorstep. He stared at her, eyes full of contempt. "My weekend isn't over yet. What are you doin' here?"

"I need to talk to you."

He didn't want to talk to her. He would have much preferred to slam the door in her face. "About what? What is so important that it couldn't have waited until I dropped him off?"

"It's about Christopher."

"What about him?"

"Can I come in?" she asked.

He glared at her, reluctant to let her in. "Make it quick. I have things to do."

She sat in a chair by the kitchen table. "Jimmy."

Immediately he snapped back, "Don't fuckin' call me that. I told you never to call me that."

She cast her eyes downward. "Why are you so cold toward me?"

"Are you serious?" He refused to answer that question. She already knew why. "I know you're not that fuckin' stupid, Trina. Figure it out."

"I'm sorry our relationship has come to this."

"You did this, not me," he reminded her.

"I never meant to hurt you."

"That is the biggest load of crap I have ever heard. You knew exactly what you were doin'." Annoyed by her obvious attempt to drag out this conversation, he demanded, "What do you want?"

"Please don't be angry."

"Don't be angry?" he mocked. "You have got to be fuckin' kidding me. I gave you everything, Trina, my heart, my soul, my life. Yet despite everything I did, you lied to me, deceived me, stabbed me in the back, and took every part of my soul and sucked me dry. If you think for one second that I am gonna stand here and let you screw me over without bein' angry about it, you have got another thing comin'. As it stands now, I don't give a fuck about you. In fact, I have absolutely no feelings for you whatsoever. My priorities have changed. Now I do everything for our son so he can get what he needs, live the life he deserves, and have a good future."

"Jim," she pleaded. "I'm so sorry things turned out this way."

"I don't give a shit if you're sorry. I will not be your crutch, and I refuse to be your doormat."

"Don't be like that."

"No? And how should I be, Trina, when I gave you everything and didn't get a damn thing in return. All you did was shit all over me."

With a forlorn frown on her face, she hung her head.

But he felt no sympathy for her at all. "What the fuck do you want?" he asked again, annoyed by her hanging about.

"I don't know how to tell you this," she began with a brittle quality in her voice. "I'm moving to Denver with Aaron."

"Denver?" he sneered. "You mean to tell me that you stood here wastin' your breath tryin' to apologize to me only to announce that you're moving to Colorado with the man you fuckin' cheated on me with? That's convenient, isn't it?"

"James, please try to understand."

Feeling even more betrayed, he bellowed, "You are not takin' my son to Colorado. Hell no! I will fight you tooth and nail on that."

She tried to justify her decision. "I need some time to think and figure out what I want. I need to get away from here, away from you, away from the baby."

"What do you mean, away from the baby?" Jim didn't like where this conversation was going. "You're gonna leave and abandon your son?" he questioned, hoping to God that wasn't what she was implying.

"I'm not abandoning him. I'll come back and get him."

"The hell you will," Jim corrected. "If you leave here and turn your back on Christopher, I guarantee you will never have any kind of custodial rights, joint or otherwise, ever again."

"He's my son," Trina begged.

Her self-seeking motivations annoyed the crap out of him. "Yes he is, but obviously your egocentric needs are more important to you than your own flesh and blood."

She swiftly looked away.

"Jesus, Trina, are you really that selfish, that you can shove your son on the back burner for a cheap thrill? You gave birth to him for Christ sake."

"I'm sorry, but I can't handle this responsibility right now," she beseeched.

"And what am I supposed to tell him when he asks about his mommy?" Jim asked, getting angrier every time Trina opened her mouth. "That his own mother didn't want him?"

"That is not true." Tears flooded her eyes.

However, her tears meant nothing to him. Cold hatred created a stony mask on his face. "Goddammit, Trina! You gave up our relationship, my friendship and my trust, and now your son, for what? So you could have a selfish, lustful thrill ride with your man-whore? I gave you everything I had. I committed myself to you and dedicated eight years of my life to you. Eight years, Trina, and you just threw it all away."

"It's not that simple," she cried.

"Don't fuck with me!" he roared. "Why? Why did you throw away eight years for cheap, meaningless sex? I think I deserve an explanation."

"It was hard for me."

"That is bullshit. You had it easy. I busted my ass in school and gave every ounce of energy I had left to our relationship, and all I ever got was flack and criticism from you."

She was blatantly honest with him. "There was no excitement in our lives. I got bored."

"That is the lamest excuse I've ever heard. Bored with what?"

"It was always about medical school, Jimmy. You were always too busy. You didn't have the time or the energy for me. There was never any excitement and we never did anything fun. Being with you was boring."

Ouch. That was a low blow. Not only did she deceive and cheat on him, she now informed him that he was boring and no fun. This kept getting better and better. Agitated even more, he questioned this statement, "What?"

"There was no variety. I needed someone more exotic. Something more exciting. It was always the same thing— every night we were in our bed, and every day I woke up with you."

Oh, now he understood. Their sex life wasn't exciting enough for her. An even bigger blow to his ego. "Oh, so you would've liked a threesome or the ability to bring home a random man whenever you felt like it so you could have some variety? S and M maybe? Bondage? Would that have given you more excitement? Is sex all it was about for you?"

"How can you expect me to limit myself to one man, living the same ordinary life, and doing the same ordinary things day after day, year after year?"

"That's how relationships work, Trina," he spouted. "There are two words called faithfulness and commitment, neither of which you know the meaning of because they are not in your vocabulary. You have to have both to make a relationship work."

Ignoring his comment, she stated, "I have to go. My plane leaves in three hours." She stood up and walked toward the door.

"Oh, just like that, huh? It's that easy for you to leave? You don't even have the decency to say goodbye to your son?"

"I have a plane to catch."

Jim's eyes blackened with fury. "You little bitch. You really are selfish, aren't you?"

"Tell Christopher I love him."

"You don't know the meaning of love." She was about to walk out when Jim stopped her. "Trina, I implore you. Don't turn your back on Christopher. He didn't ask for any of this. You can shit on me all you want, but please, don't do this to him. He's just a baby; he needs his mother. If there is any love left at all inside that cold heart of yours, you won't do this."

Crying now, Trina stood frozen in the doorway.

"Dammit, Katrina, listen to me."

"I can't," she sniffled. "I just can't. Goodbye, Jim." She gave him one last glance then opened the door and walked out.

Jim froze in blankness. "Shit! What an insensitive, selfish bitch." Immediately, he got on the phone and called his lawyer.

Randy was offered a full time position in Dr. Stephens' office over the summer, which he thoroughly enjoyed. Following a full day at the clinic, he had to report to the airport to pick up his sister who was coming to visit for about a week. Jane was excited about Stephanie coming to San Francisco, and Randy was glad Jane was around to keep her entertained so he wouldn't have to do it. They stopped for dinner on the way home and returned to his apartment around 7:00 P.M. that night. Jane and Stephanie sat on the sofa and chatted while Randy checked his voicemail for anything he might have missed while driving. There was a message from Jim, so he called him back.

"Hey, buddy. What's up?" Randy asked when Jim answered.

"Guess what happened to me today?"

"You and Jill had sex," Randy teased.

"That would be totally stellar if we did, but no, it's not that," Jim declared. "Trina came over here."

"I thought you had Christopher until Sunday?" Randy asked, wanting clarification.

"Well, looks like I'm going to have him for a lot longer than that. Trina informed me this afternoon that she was movin' to Denver with that guy she's been bonin'. She took off and left Christopher without even sayin' goodbye to him."

Surprised by this news, Randy exclaimed, "What the hell?"

"Yup. Her flight left this afternoon. She just up and left her son. Now I get to be a single dad and raise my son by myself. Can you believe that shit?"

"Damn. What are you going to do?" Randy asked.

"I've already called my lawyer."

"What did he say?"

Jim explained, "I can get sole custody for abandonment if she doesn't come back by the time the papers go through, which she won't. The custody dispute that Trina and I had going on will now be uncontestable because she left him here and won't be around for the court date. When it's all over, they'll track her down and serve her the custody papers with my terms."

"And what are your terms?"

"I want sole custody, and I pay her nothing. By the time school starts again, I'll be legally free of her and have no obligations to her whatsoever."

"That fast?"

"Yup, pretty much," Jim said. "With the crap she pulled today, she has made a jivel mess of her life and totally screwed herself. She has turned all custodial care over to me, and since I am sole caregiver, I don't owe her a goddamn nickel. Nil. And it will be at my discretion whether or not I let her see Christopher. Legally I don't have to. She totally wiped out today by gettin' on that airplane. She left and didn't even stop to look at her son before she took off. Not a single glance. Can you believe this woman? What a selfish bitch."

Randy found this hard to swallow. "Man, how could she do that? What are you going to do while you're working? And when school starts and you're talking care of a baby full time, how the hell are you going to manage that?"

"I've already called my parents. They're gonna help," Jim declared.

Relieved that Jim had a solution to this predicament with a support system behind him, Randy replied, "That's good. You didn't think they would."

"Well, with all the crap Trina has pulled recently they've been very supportive."

"How are you feeling about all of this?" Randy asked, concerned about his best friend's state of mind. "You've had a lot of shit go down in your life lately."

"I'm feelin' good about the legal proceedings, but I'm nervous about tryin' to raise this kid by myself, especially when I'm tryin' to finish med school. And I'm pissed. I can't believe she left so easily. She never looked back. She simply walked away, just like that, and left everything behind." Jim's voice began to crack. "And the hardest thing, Randy…"

Jim was about to lose it. Offering support, Randy said, "It's alright, Jim."

"I'm hurt," Jim continued. "She left Christopher like it was no big deal, like he means nothing. It was bad enough that she threw away the eight years we had as if it was meaningless, but now she's thrown away her son too. It's killin' me."

"This is going to take time, Jim. Healing isn't going to happen overnight."

"I'm gonna totally start buggin'."

"You have to keep it together," Randy advised. "For Christopher. You have a little boy who needs you. Cry if you need to, punch something if you need to, but don't let yourself fall apart. Don't let this take control of you. You're stronger than that, and you're not alone. I'm here for you, Bruce and Mandy are here for you, your parents want to help you. Ask for help if you need it. Your friends and family will be here. And what about Jill?" Randy reminded him. "I'm sure you've told her about your situation, and I'm sure she understands. You have people who love you, Jim, and we will do what needs to be done to help you."

"That doesn't make this any easier, Dude."

"I know," Randy confirmed. "But you need to know that you're not alone. I will come to your aid at the drop of a hat and you know that. If you ever need anything, just tell me. That's what I'm here for."

"Thanks, Bro," Jim said, knowing Randy was right.

"Hang in there, man. I'll see you in the morning. Bring Christopher if you need to."

"Alright. Thanks for listenin'."

"Anytime, Jim. You know you can always vent to me."

"Yeah, I know. Talk to you later, Bro."

"Later."

Chapter Thirty-Three

Sunday morning, Jane took Stephanie over to the sorority house, allowing Randy and his friends time to study. By the time they came back, the study session had dispersed. The only one still lingering was Bruce.

"Did you girls have fun?" Randy asked them.

"Yes," Stephanie said. "Those sorority sisters of hers are great."

Randy had to laugh. "Yeah, if you're into party chicks."

Bruce eyed Stephanie from head to toe. She had long, bleach-blonde hair, a thin frame, and a curvy figure. Her smile was infectious, and her pretty hazel eyes shone like gleaming porcelain. A small butterfly tattoo peeked out from the back of her waistline, playing peek-a-boo with him. Her hip hugging jeans were low enough to expose her midriff and belly button, which was pierced with a glowing dangly diamond bead ring. He watched every move she made, wondering who this woman was.

"We're going to get sandwiches from Subway," Jane said. "You want one, Sweetie?"

"Yes I do," Randy replied. "Get me a BLT with avocado and a Dr. Pepper."

"Alright. Be back in a bit." She gave him a kiss then took off with Stephanie again.

When the door closed, Bruce asked, "Who's that girl with Jane?"

"My sister."

"*That* is your sister?" Bruce raised an eyebrow. "You failed to mention what a knockout she was."

"Guess I never noticed."

"Does she have a boyfriend?" Bruce asked.

"At the moment, no. But that probably won't last long," he teased with a smartass grin. "She switches boyfriends more often than I change my socks."

A strange, faintly eager glint flashed in Bruce's eyes.

The look on Bruce's face made Randy laugh. He had a feeling he knew what Bruce was thinking. He also knew Amanda liked Bruce. To help Mandy out, he tried to discourage his friend from pursuing his sister. "She's only going to be in town for two more days then she's going back to Pullman."

"Pullman?" Bruce had never heard of that town before. "Where the hell is that?"

"Eastern Washington. WSU."

This didn't deter him. In fact, it sparked his interest further. "How old is she?"

"Just turned twenty one. She's starting her junior year this year."

"What's her major?"

"I'm not sure what it is anymore. She changes it all the time. She's indecisive that way." Randy wasn't sure he liked all these questions Bruce was asking about his sister. "What's on your mind, Buckman?"

Bruce moistened his lips and inhaled, trying to find a way to say this. "Would you mind if I treated her to dinner tonight?"

Initial observation confirmed. "You want to ask Stephanie out?" That was the most outlandish idea he had ever heard. "Dude, are you high? I would strongly advise against that."

"Why?" Bruce set his bag on the table and sat back down.

"Because she's not your type. Trust me."

Bruce didn't necessarily agree. "How do you know?"

"She's a flirtatious party girl. She's high maintenance and can never make up her mind what she wants. She doesn't take anything seriously, and she's kind of a nymphomaniac." Knowing how low key Bruce was, Randy was convinced that would turn him off.

Bruce developed a crooked smile that Randy had never seen on him before. "She sounds fun."

Ok. He was wrong. Bruce wasn't turned off by that at all. In fact, he seemed even more intrigued by her now. So much for that plan. "Yeah, I gotta give her that. She definitely knows how to have fun."

"Do you mind if I ask her?"

Stephanie instead of Mandy? Randy didn't see it, but ok. Whatever turned him on. "Why would I mind?"

"Because she's your sister," Bruce reminded him.

"So? She's a grownup. She can go out with whoever she wants. She doesn't need my approval."

When the women came back from Subway, Bruce was still hanging around. Jane greeted him with a smile. "Hey, Bruce."

Before Bruce could respond, Randy took Jane's hand and led her into the kitchen.

Jane wanted to know what was going on. "Why did you drag me in here?"

"Because Bruce is going to ask Stephanie out."

"Really?" She peeked out the door, bug-eyed. "I wanna see."

"Jane, stop that." He pulled her back.

"He likes Stephanie?"

"Apparently. But I think he's crazy."

"Why?"

"Because Stephanie lives in Pullman. I'm telling you, this is a bad idea. He's not her type," Randy said. "She's more into frat boys, not a school-oriented guy like Bruce. Buckman is far too relaxed for her, too serious, and too dedicated to medicine. He won't spend every waking moment with her, and she's not going to like that. They are not right for each other."

"Opposites can attract."

"Opposites?" he questioned. "They have absolutely nothing in common."

Bruce gathered his belongings and left, so Jane and Randy came back into the living room.

Stephanie stared at Randy with an inquisitive grin on her face. "You knew he was going to do that, didn't you?"

"Yes," he replied. "What did you say?"

"I told him I'd let him take me out to dinner. He's cute."

Randy did not agree with this. "This should be interesting."

"Interesting how?" Stephanie wanted to know.

"You two are very...how should I put this? Different. Let's leave it at that," he said definitively.

The following afternoon, Randy ran into Bruce at the library. He joined him at the table. "Buckman."

Bruce looked up from his reading. "Hey, Randy."

"How'd it go last night? Did she drag you along on one of her stay-up-'til-dawn-wreaking-havoc-through-the-city escapades?"

"We had fun, but I think I may have crossed the line last night," Bruce admitted.

"What do you mean?"

"Well," he said. "Things kind of got out of control. I tried to resist her, but..."

Randy knew what that meant. "What the fuck, Buckman? You slept with my sister?"

"I'm sorry. I didn't plan it that way. She totally threw herself at me."

"You could have told her no."

"I tried to. But that girl is crazy." A thoughtful smile curved his mouth. "And I kinda like her."

How could this be possible? Stephanie, the rebellious nympho with a tattoo and body piercings? What did conservative, clean cut Bruce Buckman possibly see in her? "You have got to be kidding me?"

"Oh no. She is fun as hell."

They seemed to be complete opposites, from Randy's point of view. Stephanie was wild and reactionary, and about as free-willed as they came. She was more interested in guys than school and seemed to be seriously lacking in the morals and common sense department. Bruce. Buckman was a scholar, wasn't much of a paint the town red kind of guy, and was definitely not a big party person. Amanda was more his type, and Randy was still rooting for Mandy. "I don't see it. She doesn't seem like your type. And even more so, you're not her type, at all."

"Last night was the wildest night I've ever had."

"I bet. But Bruce, this is never going to work. She lives in Washington," he reminded.

"It could work."

Bruce was officially delusional. "She's not that kind of girl. You don't understand. All she cares about is sex."

Acknowledging Randy's assessment, yet not fully understanding what he meant, Bruce replied, "I can live with that."

In the evening, Stephanie was getting ready to go out with Bruce again. Worried that Bruce was going to end up hurt, Randy questioned her motivations behind this decision. "Steph, don't lead him on."

"Who says I'm leading him on?"

"What about tomorrow when you go back to Pullman?" Randy warned. "You live hundreds of miles away, and I know damn well you have no intention of making any kind of commitment to him."

"I don't want a commitment. I want sex."

"And that's the problem."

"He and I will have to make an arrangement," Stephanie rationalized in her own twisted way.

"What kind of arrangement?"

"We get together whenever we have a break like Thanksgiving or Christmas. In the meantime, we can see whoever we want."

She couldn't possibly be serious. "There is no way he's going to go for that. He's not going to want to share you."

"How will he know if he's hundreds of miles away?"

"Bruce is my friend, and I will not let you do this to him. You need to be upfront and honest with him. If you have no intentions of building a relationship with him then you need to tell him."

She ignored him.

Randy didn't like her attitude. "Dammit, Stephanie. What is wrong with you? Do you have a conscience at all?"

Stephanie continued to argue, "How is what I'm doing any different than what you did for years? You took a girl home, brought her into your bed for a one night stand, then never spoke to her again. You did it all the time, so don't lecture me, Randy!"

"This is not the same thing and you know it. I never lied to any of those women. I never once led any of them to believe that I wanted a relationship. I told every one of them straight up that I wasn't looking for anything serious. But you are leading Bruce to believe he may have a chance with you when you have absolutely no intention whatsoever of going beyond the bedroom with him. And what's worse is you don't even have the common decency to tell him."

"This really is none of your business," she said crossly.

"When my friend is concerned, damn straight it's my business." He stood in front of her, blocking the bathroom door so she couldn't get in.

Stephanie tried to push her way through, but Randy wouldn't let her. "Do you mind?"

"Don't do this, Stephanie. I'm warning you."

"Move out of my way!" She shoved her way past him and slammed the door.

Jane heard the commotion and came out to see what was going on. "What are you two arguing about?"

Randy retorted, "Stephanie is so shallow. How can she live with herself?"

"What did she do?"

"She has absolutely no intention of telling Bruce that she doesn't want a relationship with him. She wants to deceive him into thinking that she will be with him exclusively when she and I both know that there is no way in hell that she will."

"Why would she do that?"

"Because that's how she is, Jane." He raised his voice, hoping Stephanie would hear every word he said. "She doesn't seem to think people have feelings!"

"I heard that!" Stephanie yelled from the bathroom.

"Good!"

Stephanie stepped out of the bathroom right as Bruce pulled up.

"You better tell him, Steph," Randy demanded.

"Why don't you mind your own business?" She grabbed her purse and walked out the door.

Randy snorted under his breath. "Where the hell did she learn to be so egocentric and superficial? I know damn well my parents didn't raise her to be like that."

Jane gave him a hug. Her touch soothed him.

"My sister is cruel. What a conniving bitch."

Jane couldn't believe those words spilled out of his mouth. "Randal Hanson. That is your sister you're talking about."

"Yes, Jane, I am aware of that, but it's true."

In the morning, Randy awoke with a kink in his neck. He and Jane had fallen asleep on the couch, still in their clothes. The TV was on, so he reached for the remote and clicked it off. He stretched then stumbled into the kitchen to put on a pot a coffee. Stephanie stood at the counter drinking a glass of milk and fiddling with her phone. He walked past her and opened the cupboard to pull out a bag of coffee. "Morning."

She turned around and looked directly at him. "You look like hell."

"I feel like I slept in a sardine can all night."

"Why?"

Randy explained, "We fell asleep on the couch last night and now my arm is tingly because Jane was lying on it."

"Why didn't you move it?"

"Because I didn't want to wake her up," he stated. "Unlike you, I'm not selfish."

She sneered at him. "Very funny."

He started a pot of coffee then raised his eyes to watch her. "You told him I hope."

"More or less."

"What do you mean more or less?"

"He knows I don't want anything serious, but I do want to see him."

"As what? Your San Francisco booty call?" Randy questioned, not liking this arrangement.

"Pretty much."

"Stephanie." Randy's dark eyes widened, disgusted that his sister was purposefully treating Bruce this way.

"What? I told him I didn't want to make any commitments. He seemed cool with that."

"Oh really? He's cool with the fact that other guys will be in your bed and he gets leftovers? I'm sorry, but I don't picture that." This didn't seem like the kind of thing Bruce would do. As Randy considered this further, he realized Stephanie hadn't told Bruce her true intentions. "You didn't tell him you'd still be sleeping with other guys, did you?"

"No. He doesn't need to know that."

"So you lied to him," Randy concluded. "Telling him you want to see him is not that same as telling him that you want to have regular sex with him but screw other guys on the side. What you said is deceiving. You failed to tell him the other side of this."

"But I do want to see him," she added. "He's a nice guy. And he's good in bed."

Randy cringed at the thought. "Oh god, Steph. I don't want to hear that."

"Bruce and I are both wise enough to know that long distance relationships don't work. We'll get together whenever we can."

"And in the meantime?" Randy questioned.

"We see who we want."

Randy corrected her. "You mean you sleep with whoever you want."

"If you want to put it that way, yes."

"Dammit, Stephanie. What other lies did you tell him?"

"Nothing."

Randy doubted that. "Nothing at all?"

"No."

"Bullshit.

"I'm offended that my own brother thinks I would do something like that. Geez, what kind of person do you think I am?"

"You will do anything to get your way, even bend the truth," Randy shook his head, appalled by his sister's actions. "Dammit, Stephanie. I knew you would do something like this."

"What? We both win. I get sex; he gets sex."

"Except you get sex with other people too. You failed to mention that part to him," Randy scolded, upset that Stephanie was being deceitful and dishonest.

"I never told him he couldn't have sex with other people. I want him to."

"But he won't because you telling him you want to keep seeing him implies that you are exclusive, and he's not the kind of guy to disrespect you like that."

"It's not my fault if he misinterprets what I said," Stephanie declared.

Randy prepared a cup of coffee, scowling at his sister's insensitivity. "You should have told him the truth. I can't believe you've done this."

Jane awoke heavy-eyed and joined them in the kitchen.

Randy captured her eyes with his. "Hey, Baby. Good morning." He gave her a kiss then reached out and touched her arm.

She leaned into him and rested her head on his shoulder. Still sleepy, she rubbed her eyes and squinted at the clock. "You're up early."

"My arm was numb," he replied with a gentle voice. "You fell asleep on it last night."

"I'm sorry."

"Don't worry about it. I love it when you fall asleep in my arms." He gently kissed the top of her head. "But I couldn't lie on that couch anymore. There's really not enough room on it for both of us to be comfortable."

"I know. My muscles are all cramped." She turned to Stephanie and asked, "What time do you have to be at the airport?"

"Three," Stephanie replied.

Jane looked up at Randy. "I get off at one. I can take her, if you want."

"That would be great if you could."

"Don't you need to get ready for work?" Jane asked him.

"Yes I do."

"You want some breakfast before you leave?"

"You don't have to do that."

"For you, I will."

He gazed at her for a moment. "Thanks, Babe. You're awesome." He gave her a kiss then disappeared to take a shower.

Chapter Thirty-Four

The first week of school proved to be exceedingly busy for both Jane and Randy. He was swamped with classes, working, volunteering down at the homeless clinic, doing research for his thesis, and studying. She had pledge week, the busiest portion of Sororityhood. Thank goodness it was almost over. With their busy schedules, they hadn't seen each other much that week. When Randy got off from work Friday, he decided that he and Jane were going to have a romantic date night.

When he knocked on the front door of the Alpha House, Jane was surprised to see him dressed in khaki pants, a light blue long sleeved dress shirt, and a pair of brown loafers.

"Bonsoir, mademoiselle." He took her hand in his and drew it to his lips. "Je t'aime."

"Why are you dressed like that?"

"I thought you might like to have dinner with me tonight. A nice romantic candlelight dinner for two with some sweet red wine, perhaps?"

She wrapped her arms around his neck, intrigued by his proposal. "I'm interested.

"Good, because we have reservations in an hour."

"Can you give me fifteen minutes?" she asked.

"Sure. Just hurry."

She gave him a kiss then dashed upstairs to change her clothes.

About fifteen minutes later, she stumbled down the stairs, trying to put her shoes on her feet while she walked, which caused her to almost trip.

Randy laughed at her. "That was graceful. Are you okay?"

She finally regained her footing. "Yes, I'm fine. Just klutzy."

He looked her over from head to toe. She had on a black knee-length floral dress with feminine black sandals on her feet. Her toenails were painted pink, and she left her hair down, exposing the delicate flower earrings in her ears. To top off the look, she carried a black clutch bag. Randy couldn't take his eyes off her. "You like gorgeous."

She offered him a sweet smile. "Thank you."

He leaned in and kissed her. "You ready?"

"Yup. Where are we going?"

"I felt like French cuisine tonight, so we're going to Le Café de Louge," he said with a French accent. "We'll dine on ze French cuisine and drink Pinot Noir. Do you object?"

"No. Not at all."

"Très bon." He brought her hand up to his mouth and kissed it. "Je t'aime beaucoup, l'amour de ma vie."

His silly antics made her laugh. "Can we eat now?"

"Oui, mademoiselle."

They left holding hands.

As soon as they were seated at the restaurant, Randy ordered a bottle of wine. The waiter poured some into each glass then placed the bottle in a bucket of ice by the table.

Randy took a sip.

"I was hoping to get Daddy to a game or two this year, but I doubt that will ever happen. He's still mad that I decided to play again"

Randy found this unacceptable. "It shouldn't matter if he doesn't like you playing or not. You're his daughter, and he should support you by coming to a game or two."

"I know, but he won't."

Randy reached over and held Jane's hand. "Doesn't it bother you that he's never come to any of your games?"

"It does, but there's nothing I can do about it. I'm tired of trying to please him. I am who I am, and I'm going to do what I want. If he doesn't like it, that's just too bad for him."

What did she just say? Those words couldn't possibly have come out of her mouth. "Wow! There's a switch. What side of whose bed did you wake up on this morning?"

"I'm tired of trying to make Daddy happy all the time. It's not worth the time and energy I put into it."

"I agree." He took another sip of his wine. "My class lost another one over the summer."

"Oh, Sweetie, I'm sorry." She knew how much it got to him when that happened.

"I knew medical school was going to be rough, but damn. There is no way I could do this without you. You give me something to look forward to. When I'm with you, I can relax and unwind. No pressure, no stress. I can put the chaos behind me for a while." He set his wineglass down and took both of her hands in his. "I know this hasn't been easy for you. You've put up with a lot from me over the last year. You've seen me at my worst, when the stress gets the best of me, and I know I can be a real bear to be around when I get like that. Yet you're still here by my side. No one else would have stuck this out." He truly appreciated how supportive Jane was. No matter what was going on in his life, she was always right by his side. She was encouraging, uplifting, and supportive on every level. She inspired him in many ways. "Thank you for loving me and being here for me."

"You're welcome."

While the waiter brought their food out, Randy stared at Jane; his eyes brimmed with tenderness and passion.

"Enjoy your meal, Sir," the waiter said.

"Thank you." He unfolded his napkin and draped it over his lap. "Filet mignon and Pinot Noir are perfect together."

"Kinda like us," Jane added. "Can't have one without the other."

"Exactly like us." Randy raised his glass. "D'amour."

Jane had no clue what he was saying. "What's that mean?"

"To love," he clarified.

"To love." She raised her glass and gently clanged it to his.

After class the following Friday, Jim frantically tried to get Randy's attention. "Hanson!" he hollered in the hall of the Medical Sciences building.

Randy turned around. "Yes?"

"I need a mondo favor, Dude."

"What is it?"

"I need you and Jane to babysit for me tomorrow night."

He wondered what the big emergency was. "Why? What's up?"

"Jill invited me over to her place for dinner. Her daughter will be with her parents and we'll finally get a chance to be alone."

Of course Randy would do anything for Jim, but he wanted him to suffer a little. "I don't know, man."

Jim implored, "I'm beggin' you, Bro. This could be my chance with her."

Randy teased him. "Ooh, someone wants to get laid."

"Come on, Randy, please. I need this."

Randy couldn't hold it in any longer. He burst out laughing. "I'll babysit for you."

"Sweet. Thank you so much."

"What time?" Randy asked.

"Is six ok?"

"That shouldn't be a problem," Randy confirmed. "I'll call Jane and let her know."

"I owe you one, Dude," Jim replied thankfully.

Jim dropped Christopher off at 5:45 Saturday evening. He handed the baby to Randy then set a diaper bag and a port-a-crib on the porch. "There are tons of diapers and formula in there. He'll scarf it down pretty fast, so watch him or he'll make himself sick. If he does, he'll hurl all over you."

Randy scoffed, "Great."

"You have no idea how grateful I am," Jim declared.

"It's no problem," Randy assured him. "You go out and have a good time tonight."

Jim grinned, eternally grateful to his best friend. "Thanks, Bro. You're a life saver."

"Get the hell out of here."

Jim rushed to his car and drove off.

Randy grabbed the diaper bag and the port-a-crib and went inside. He stared at the infant for a minute. "Well, looks like it's just you and me. Auntie Jane should be home soon." Getting more comfortable, he reclined on the couch with Christopher on his chest. "You need to be good for your dad. He's working hard in medical school and he needs rest. You better start going to sleep at night, little guy."

The baby cooed and grabbed his finger, making Randy chuckle.

"Your daddy wants what's best for you, and he's trying to make that happen. He'll give you everything you need, but you have to be patient with him. He's doing his best to support you while he finishes med school. And you know what? When he's all done with this, you'll have it made, Kiddo. You're going to be a doctor's son. Uncle Randy knows a lot about this. My daddy is a doctor too."

The baby kicked his feet excitedly and chewed on Randy's finger.

At that moment, Jane walked into the room. She set her bag on the floor. "Hi, Sweetie."

"Hey. How was your meeting with your coach?"

"It was good. Practice starts next week."

"You ready?"

"I feel confident. I need to get a couple new pairs of basketball shoes though," she said.

"Really? More shoes?" he teased her. "You have four pairs of basketball shoes already."

"Basketball shoes wear out quickly when I use them all the time."

Jane had an obsession with shoes. She had a whole closet full of them. Yet every time she went shopping, she always returned with another pair. "Can you take him for a minute?"

Jane gently took the baby off Randy's chest, greeting him with a kiss while she did.

Randy sat up. "Do you want me to get dinner ready while you sit with the baby or do you want me to sit with him?"

"I'll keep him."

"I knew you were going to say that."

While Randy was in the kitchen, Jane changed the baby's diaper and fed him a bottle. When his tummy was full, she sat on the couch burping him then rocked him to sleep.

Randy came out and joined her. "Is he asleep?"

"Uh huh."

"Good." Randy set up the port-a-crib in the middle of the living room and spread a blanket across the bottom of it. He took the baby from Jane, handling him carefully, and laid him in the crib. "That wasn't so hard. He seems like a good sleeper."

"Let's hope it stays that way."

After dinner, Randy turned on the TV and flipped through the channel guide until he found something he liked. The baby was still sound asleep. "I can't believe he's still sleeping," Randy said, peering into the crib. "I don't know what Jim's talking about. He says Christopher keeps him up all night."

Jane joined Randy on the couch. He put his arm around her and kissed her. The baby disturbed them by making noises, which made Randy turn his head. "Cover your eyes, boy. This is X-rated stuff for you."

Jane giggled. "He doesn't understand you."

"Sure he does." Randy peeked into the crib. "Did you hear what she said about you?"

Christopher started to cry.

"See, look what you did," Randy declared. "You hurt his feelings."

"He's probably hungry." Jane reached into the crib and picked the baby up.

They fed him, burped him, and changed his diaper then played on the floor with him for a while.

Finally, around midnight, they were able to get him to go back to sleep. Randy set up the port-a-crib in the bedroom and laid the baby down. "It's about time," he said.

Jane started to get up, but Randy grabbed her waist and gently eased her onto the bed. He kissed her long and hard as his hand slowly slid across her belly.

"Randy, we can't. We'll wake the baby."

"We'll have to be quiet then, won't we?" Once again he moved his mouth over hers, devouring its softness. His hands explored the feminine lines of her waist and hips, searching for pleasure points. The shapely beauty of her naked body gradually curled into his.

In the height of pleasure, Christopher let out a blood-curdling scream. Randy broke position, very close to climaxing. Still aroused, he flopped backwards on the bed. "Dammit."

Jane got up and cuddled the baby, trying to console his crying.

Randy propped himself up on his elbow, panting to catch his breath. "What's wrong with him?"

"I don't know. Let's try making him a bottle."

Randy slipped on a pair of shorts and went into the kitchen to prepare a bottle. The apartment was dark and he couldn't see where he was going. As he made his way through the living room, he tripped over the diaper bag and bashed his shin on the table. "Ouch! Shit!"

Jane called to him from the bedroom, "Are you ok?"

"Yes, I'm fine." He grumbled then returned to his bottle making duties. He returned to the bedroom a few minutes later with a freshly made bottle of formula in his hand.

Jane tried feeding the baby, but Christopher didn't want to eat. Next, she checked his diaper, which was dry. The baby continued to cry. "What's the matter, little guy?"

"Let me try." Randy grabbed the infant's pacifier and carefully put it in his mouth. Then he took the baby from Jane and nuzzled him into his shoulder while he gently rubbed his back. He softly sang "Twinkle, Twinkle Little Star" until Christopher's crying ceased. Randy was so gentle and loving with this infant, soothing him and snuggling him. It wasn't long before his magic touch lulled the baby to sleep.

"Randy, he's sleeping," Jane whispered.

Randy gently laid the baby back in his crib.

Jane reclined on the bed with her legs dangling over the edge, thankful that he had stopped crying. "I told you that was going to happen."

"I'm still horny as hell." He traced his fingertips across her lips then brushed a gentle kiss across her forehead. "We didn't finish. We can't end it like that."

"He's going to wake him up again."

"Ssh." He put his index finger over her lips then rubbed his hand across her inner thigh while his tongue caressed her nipples. "Now, where were we?" He removed the shorts he had on and resumed the position, uninterrupted this time.

In the morning, Jim was the first to show up at Randy's apartment for their weekly study session.

Jane didn't want to disturb them, so she decided to spend the morning at Alpha. Before she left, Randy laid a big, wet kiss on her, tasting the lip gloss she was wearing and trying to kiss off every last bit of it. "I'll call you tonight," he said to her.

"You better." She sexily drew her lip between her teeth. "I love you."

"I love you." As soon as she departed, Randy pulled his notes and textbooks out of his book bag.

Jim had to laugh. "Damn, Dude. Did you get in deep enough?"

"She was wearing lip gloss. I had to get all of it."

"If you like it so much, why don't you put it on yourself?"

"Now what fun is that? I can taste it better when it's on her."

"Oh yeah? What flavor was it?" Jim asked curiously.

"It was strawberry." Randy set his notes on the table. "How was your date last night?"

With a Cheshire Cat grin, Jim said, "It was good."

"Just good? You have no details for me?"

"I have some. Where would you like me to start?" Jim asked.

"You did have sex with her, right?"

"Why am I not surprised that is the first question you would ask me?"

Randy laughed.

"Oh man, Randy. It was epic. We had a nice talk over dinner, deep conversation, Dude. Then we cuddled and kissed on the sofa for a while, and by the end of the evening we ended up in bed together, and we didn't have to worry about Christopher or her daughter disturbing us. It was incredible."

Randy hadn't seen Jim this happy in a long time. "That's awesome, man. I'm happy for you."

"Thanks again, Bro. Jill and I are really hittin' it off."

"When do I get to meet her?" he asked.

Jim shrugged. "I don't know. Gettin' childcare is sometimes an issue. But maybe we can share a sitter one night and the four of us can go out."

"Sounds great."

Bruce showed up about five minutes later. He tossed his bag on the table and plopped down in the closest chair. "This has been a busy ass weekend."

"Why?"

"Flew in from Pullman late last night and I'm exhausted."

Randy stared at Bruce, thinking he was nuts. "You are crazy trying to do this."

"Do what?" Jim asked.

Jim hadn't heard about what went on with Bruce and Randy's sister. Randy filled him in. "After my sister came down here this summer, Bruce seems to think that he and Stephanie have some sort of thing going on."

This sparked Jim's interest. "Your sister Stephanie?"

"Yes." Randy said, still not approving of this situation.

Jim couldn't stop laughing. "Oh my god. That is rich. What the hell are you doin' with a chick like that, Bruce?"

"What?" Bruce defended. "She's cool."

"She's a maneater," Jim said. "That girl would wear a man instead of pants if she could get away with it."

"Hey," Randy warned. "That's my sister you're talking about, Ryan. Watch it."

Bruce ignored their dispute and headed to the kitchen for a cup of coffee.

The second Mandy walked in the room, the men got quiet. She wondered why. "Ok, how come you guys are deep in conversation until I walk in the room? What were you saying about me?" she asked.

"Nothing, Mandy." She was going to be upset when she found out Bruce was involved with his sister. Randy tried to lead on that he knew nothing about it.

Chapter Thirty-Five

Over the next several weeks, Jane's game improved considerably. As her strength training progressed, she became stronger, faster, and more powerful. She was pumped up about the upcoming exhibition game and ready to compete.

On his way to work, Randy saw Jane walking down the sidewalk in front of him. "Jane!" he called out to her.

She turned to his familiar voice and flashed him a beautiful smile. "Hi, Sweetie."

He greeted her with a kiss. "Where are you going?"

"I have practice in an hour. I'm going home to change."

Randy checked the time on his watch. "I have about ten minutes. Stay and talk to me for a bit."

She held his hand and strolled toward the clinic with him. "Coach Kline said that after Sunday's game he was going to make final decisions about who was starting for the season."

"And how do you feel about that?" he asked.

"Really good. I'm playing well and feel confident."

"Good for you."

"You'll be at the game Sunday, right?"

"Of course," he declared. "I already told you I would. You don't really think I'd miss the opportunity to see you play, do you?"

"No, but I still wish Daddy would come. It would mean a lot to me if he would see me play in at least one game."

"I know, Baby, but try not to let it bother you. You need to stay focused. I wanna see you get that starting position."

"That would be nice."

"Wanna meet me at my place after practice?" he suggested. "We'll grab some dinner and, since I know how much you love to read, I thought we'd head over to Barnes and Noble to pick out some books you like."

"That sounds fun," she agreed.

"I figured you'd like that." When they reached the clinic, Randy stated, "I have to go to work, but I'll see you tonight." He kissed her tenderly and they parted ways.

Randy was disturbed by the fact that Jane's father wasn't making an effort to come to her game. He was more disturbed that it bothered Jane so much. He couldn't stand to see her disappointed, thus he decided to step in and take matters into his own hands. He picked up the phone and dialed her dad's number.

"Hello?" Dale Davine answered.

"Hello, Mr. Davine. This is Randy Hanson." Dead silence. "Sir, as you know, Jane started playing basketball again. Her first game is this Sunday at 2:00, and it would mean the world to her if her dad came to watch her from the stands."

"Who are you to tell me about my daughter?" he barked. "I have known Jane her whole life, and she has known all along that I don't approve of her running around and sweating all over a basketball court. Why would you have the gall to suggest that I watch her do that?"

"Because she's your daughter, Sir, and she loves to play. She would be thrilled to see you sitting in the stands cheering her on. She really wants her father's support."

"Nothing you say will get me to change my mind about this. Quit trying to offer me advice about my daughter, Mr. Hanson," Jane's father scolded.

"No, Sir, that's not…" Dale Davine hung up on him. That was not the reaction Randy hoped for. He stared at his phone, frustrated that Jane's father wouldn't even listen to what he had to say. "That's not what I meant."

Randy arrived at the pavilion just in time to watch the team warm up. He found a seat toward the middle of the stands and scanned the court looking for Jane. He spotted her practicing a layup, wearing a ponytail which swung back and forth along her back.

When Jane came over to the side of the court to rehydrate, she looked up and saw Randy, offering his support as promised. She smiled and waved at him.

He returned the gesture then sat back and watched the ladies warm-up before they pounded the hardwood in their first game of the season.

Randy made previous arrangements to meet Jane outside the locker room after the game. As soon as the crowd cleared, he moseyed that direction. He paced around impatiently, glancing at his cellphone a few times while he waited for Jane. When he stopped to read a poster on the wall, an ominous voice spoke out from behind him. "Hello, Randy."

He turned around, surprised to be face to face with Dale Davine. He wasn't expecting him to be here, and wasn't sure what to say. Being cautious, fully expecting a confrontation, he said, "Mr. Davine."

Dale's eyes narrowed. "I've been doing a lot thinking over the last few weeks, and I've come to the undeniable conclusion that basketball is a big part of Jane's life. My wife painted the word Davine on a poster and brought it to every one of Jane's game, holding it high to make sure Jane saw it. Barbara was Jane's biggest and loudest fan. I figured I owed it to her, and to Jane, to be here."

Well, this was a pleasant change. Dale Davine was actually making an effort to speak peacefully and be supportive of his daughter. "Jane will be excited to see you."

"Randy, I have something to tell you that I think you should know," Dale declared. "The transition we've had to go through since losing Barbara has been difficult for all of us. It's been especially hard on me, and I've been unfair to Jane because of it."

Randy wasn't sure what he meant. "Sir?"

"You see, Jane is a carbon copy of her mother. They think alike, they look alike, they have the same mannerisms, and they even laugh the same way. Now that she's grown up and Barbara's gone, it's very hard for me to look at Jane. I see Barbara every time. I lost my wife too soon. I don't want to lose Jane too."

This picture became clearer to Randy. No wonder why her father treated her the way he did—sheltering her, babying her. He was trying to keep her to himself and lock her in a bubble so she wouldn't leave. The fog was lifting, and the pieces of this odd situation were starting to come together.

Tears began to form in Dale's eyes. "My kids are all I have left."

Randy tried to offer his sympathy. "Sir, I do see where you're coming from, but you have to understand that Jane is longing for your acceptance. She needs to know you care about her and will be there when she needs you."

"I do care about her. She's my daughter, and I love her very much."

"I love her too," Randy continued. "And if you'll allow me to be honest here, Sir, Jane's confided in me. She told me you two were once close, and she's hurt over this lack of communication you now have."

After several minutes of silence, he admitted, "I want my daughter to be happy. I know I haven't been showing it, but that is what I want."

"She doesn't think so, Sir," Randy told him.

"I know she doesn't, and I'm sorry. I'm also sorry I said the things I said to you. I haven't been very kind to you, in fact I've been extremely callous towards you. What matters is Jane's happiness, and she's happy with you."

What brought about this drastic change in attitude? Dale Davine had done a complete three-sixty here and

Randy wasn't sure what to make of it. "Sir, may I say something?"

"Please do."

"I appreciate your honesty, but I really think you are saying all of this to the wrong person. Jane is the one who's been hurt through this. I've just been here to listen and offer support. You should be telling Jane…"

"Tell me what?" Jane said as she walked out of the locker room. That's when she saw her father. "Daddy. What are you doing here?"

"You played a sensational game, Sweetheart."

"You saw the game?"

"Yes, and you were wonderful. You really are a tremendous athlete."

She squeezed her father tightly. "Thank you, Daddy."

Jane and her father making amends was a sight long overdue. Jane's smile beamed. Randy couldn't recall a time when he'd seen her so happy.

Randy and Jane walked out of the arena holding hands. "I love to see you smiling after talking to your dad," Randy remarked.

"I can't believe he came to the game. I wonder how he found out about it?"

Randy was about to tell her something that was most likely going to make her angry, but he needed to say it. He gritted his teeth and prepared himself to face her wrath. "I called and invited him."

She released her grip on his hand and stopped in midstride. "You called my dad?"

Yup. She was angry, just as Randy feared she would be. "I'm sorry. I should have told you, but I thought you'd be upset if you knew."

"Randy."

"Well, you weren't sending him an invite, and I thought…" He tried to justify his actions, but feared he was digging himself into a deeper hole instead. "I thought you were just being stubborn. I figured maybe he might come if he actually received an invitation, and since you weren't calling him, I did." She wasn't as angry as he thought she was going to be, but she was still mad. "I'm sorry Baby. I had to."

"Why didn't you tell me?"

"It worked, didn't it? He came to your game." Randy was pretty proud of himself for pulling that off.

"What were you and Daddy talking about before I got there?" she demanded to know.

"Janey, please. Do we have to discuss this right now?"

"Yes we do. What did he tell you?"

Randy hesitated to answer. She was going to be upset if she knew what her father had said. But he sucked it up and told her anyway. Her reaction wasn't exactly what he expected.

Her face turned pale as if she'd seen a ghost. Her legs grew numb and she fell to the ground then she buried her face in her hands and cried.

This reaction confused him. "Honey?"

"I'm the reason he's so miserable. I make him feel this way. This is my fault."

Randy held her tightly in his arms. "No, Honey. That's not what he said. You remind him of your mom is all, and that's hard for him. Don't take it so hard. You always let your dad work you into a frenzy and then you fall apart. Don't let him get to you like that."

She wiped her eyes. "Well, thank you, Dr. Hanson, for that psychoanalytical glimpse into my life."

He wasn't sure if he should laugh or be offended by that remark. With a gentle hand, he wiped the rest of her tears. "You played well today, Babe. I was keeping track of your stats. You snagged four rebounds, scored thirteen points, and were four for four on the free throw line. You played strong defense too. I'm impressed."

"Coach made his decision today." She stared at the ground dolefully.

By the look on her face, Randy feared that she didn't get her position on the team. "What's the verdict?"

A cheerful grin lit up her whole face. "I made starting point guard."

He lifted her off the ground spun her around. "Alright! A starter! I knew you'd get it." He gave her a kiss and set her back down. "I'm proud of you. But you better watch it or you're going to find yourself getting into foul trouble."

"I get into my game."

"And that's good, just be careful and watch those fouls. I don't want to come to a game to watch you warm the bench the entire time."

"I'll be careful."

They headed toward town to get her some much needed nourishment. The air was a comfortable temperature so Randy put the top down on the Camaro. "I was reading through your schedule and noticed that you don't have any games until next Sunday, am I right?"

"Yes."

"So you're available next Saturday night?" he asked for clarification.

"Depends on what you need me to be available for."

"The College of Medicine is hosting a banquet for this year's M.S. candidates, and I need a date. Don't suppose you'd want to put on a pretty dress and accompany me to dinner with a bunch of doctors and medical students would you?"

"Of course I do," she said joyfully.

"Good. My advisor is dying to meet you."

She knew Randy was under a lot of stress and pressure with the Awards and Honors Committee breathing down his neck. He seemed to have a lot of homework lately too. He'd been up late studying most nights, and he was more tired than usual. She reached for his hand and squeezed. "How's school going? You haven't talked much about it lately."

"I feel like I've been in school forever, but the other day I came to the realization that I'll have my M.S. degree in only five months." He perked up at this prospect. "Five months, Jane, and I'm done with this bullshit. I am very much looking forward to my clerkship."

"When do you make arrangements for that?" she asked.

"My advisor and I will sit down together in January and plan it out. I'll have to take the first part of my Medical Licensing Exam before I start though. Can't participate in clinical training until I pass that exam."

"When are you taking that?"

"They offer an administration in February. I'll to try to take it then."

She wondered how he found the time to accomplish all of the things he needed to get done. "Have you been studying?"

"Oh yeah. I have an MLE study guide that has some practice tests in it. And I've been reviewing every note, chart, and diagram I've ever had over the last two and a half years."

"That's a lot of information."

"No, not really," he explained. "I already know that content, I'm just refreshing my memory. And it will give me something to do while you're off stomping the hardwood playing basketball. In a way, basketball has been a blessing in disguise. It will give me time to prepare for that exam."

"Well, that's good then."

"Yes it is."

Chapter Thirty-Six

The night of the banquet, Randy dressed in a pair of black slacks, a light gray long-sleeved silk dress shirt, a black and grey patterned tie, and a black sport coat. He slipped on a pair of black patent leather dress shoes then pierced a gold Caduceus pin through his lapel. He looked polished and professional when he picked Jane up at 6:30.

She came to the door wearing a very elegant emerald green, mid-calf length cocktail dress that had spaghetti straps and a sequin embellished pattern across the front. The sparkly silver heels she wore complimented the dangly diamond earrings that hung from her ears. Her hair was in a French braid and she had on a light touch of makeup. In her hand, she carried a simple emerald green rhinestone embossed handbag. She was an absolute vision.

"That dress is fabulous," Randy remarked. "It really brings out your eyes."

She looked him over. "Looking good yourself, Doctor."

"I'm not a doctor yet."

"To me, you are."

On their way to the Berkeley City Club Ballroom, where the banquet was being held, they had a pleasant conversation. "There are probably going to be over a hundred people at this banquet tonight, including some UCSF medical professors and clinical staff, local physicians, preceptors I've worked with. I was even told that some of

407

the Awards and Honors Committee members were invited to attend tonight."

"I bet that makes you nervous," Jane assumed.

"A little," he disclosed. "But I'll be ok. I feel confident."

They pulled up to the Berkeley City Club and Randy parked the car. He sat for a minute to loosen his nerves. "You ready for this?"

"Are you?" she returned.

"Yup." His eyes traveled from her emerald green dress to her lips and back again. "I'll make a good first impression, especially with a gorgeous woman like you by my side." He gently rubbed her cheek with the back of his hand as he looked into her eyes. "Thank you for coming with me tonight." He kissed her softly on the lips. "Let's do this."

When they got out of the car, Jane linked her hand onto Randy's arm and he proudly escorted her into the ballroom. Jane's radiance filled the room, and several heads turned when they made their entrance.

Randy scanned the area. He saw several faces he didn't recognize but others that were all too familiar—one of them was Jim's. He was standing in a corner of the room intermingled among a group of fellow medical students holding hands with a petite blonde woman Randy didn't recognize. He assumed it was Jill. He and Jane made their way toward them. "Hey, guys."

Jim broke into an open, friendly smile. "Hey, Hanson. You look great." Jim introduced the woman standing next to him, "This is Jill."

Randy shook her hand. "Well, well. Nice to finally meet you, Jill. Jim has told me a lot about you."

"Likewise," she replied.

Jill was only about five foot two, busty with a curvy figure, and she had the most beautiful blue eyes Randy had ever seen. Randy could easily see why Jim liked her.

"Is anyone else here yet?" Randy asked.

Jim replied, "Mandy's around here somewhere, but Bruce hasn't shown up yet. A bunch of muck-e-mucks from the Awards Committee have been scopin' the place lookin' for you."

"Really?" Randy said, feeling slightly overwhelmed by the attention he was receiving.

"Over there." Jim pointed to a group of men and women in business suits.

Randy eyes drifted that direction. "I should go introduce myself." He took Jane's hand and led her over to this group.

Over dinner, Randy and his interrogators engaged in pleasant conversation. He never once lost his composure. In fact, he openly appeared calm and collected, even though deep down, he was nervous.

When Jane left to use the restroom, Randy scanned the room. Mandy was sitting at a table by herself. Not wanting her to be alone, he decided to join her. "Hey, Mandy. You look lovely tonight. I've never seen you in a fancy dress before."

"Never have a reason to wear one."

"You should wear one more often. You really are a beautiful woman."

She offered him a shy smile. "I wonder why Bruce isn't here," she remarked, concerned that he hadn't arrived.

"I don't know. I was wondering the same thing."

The smile Mandy was wearing turned to a frown as a disturbing thought popped into her head. Bruce had been distant with her lately, and she had a hunch she knew why. "He's seeing someone, isn't he?"

Randy didn't want to talk about this topic. "Mandy."

"I know he is. I'm not ignorant." She remained persistent. "Do you know who it is?"

He didn't want to tell her, but he could see he was about to be forced to.

"I know he said something to you. Who is it?"

He hesitated for a moment before he said, "My sister."

"Your sister? Doesn't she live in Washington?"

"Yes, she does."

A glazed look of despair spread over her face. "She's pretty, isn't she? She must be if he'd go all the way to Washington to be with her."

Randy didn't like Mandy's despondency. "Stop it. You are a beautiful, intelligent woman and I think he's ignorant for not seeing it."

She couldn't bear the thought of Bruce being alone with another woman. She decided to change the subject. "I was watching you with those people from the Awards Committee. You were outstanding—poised as usual. And you look really handsome tonight."

Randy grinned at her flattery. "Thank you."

The fact that Bruce was a no show for the dinner banquet had Randy concerned. He didn't show up for their study session on Sunday either, and he didn't call—completely uncharacteristic of Bruce Buckman. Randy tried calling him several times, but his phone went straight to voicemail. Worried that something had happened, Randy and Jane went over to Bruce's apartment. No one answered. His truck wasn't parked in its usual slot either. Randy called Stephanie thinking maybe he went to Washington for the weekend, but Stephanie said she hadn't heard from him.

"Where the hell is he?" Randy asked.

"Did he have someplace he needed to be this weekend?" Jane suggested.

"If he did, he didn't say anything to me about it." He phoned Jim and Mandy that night to see if either of them had heard from him. They hadn't.

"Maybe he'll show up to class tomorrow," Jane said, trying to ease his mind.

"I hope so. This isn't like him."

Bruce eventually made his appearance, but not until Tuesday morning when Randy ran into him at a coffee shop.

"Buckman, where the hell have you been, man? We've been worried sick about you. You missed the banquet, our study session, and class yesterday. Why didn't you call?"

"Sorry." Bruce's voice was extremely brittle.

When Randy got a closer look at him, he noticed the saggy eyelids and disheartened frown on his face. "Hey," Randy probed, worried about his friend. "You ok?"

Bruce sat at the table with a cup of coffee in his hand. He frowned into his cup, trying to hide his inner misery.

Randy sat in a chair beside him. "Bruce, what's wrong?"

He looked at Randy, eyes darkened with pain. Grief and despair tore at his heart. "I received a rather disturbing phone call after class Friday. My brother was in a car accident."

"Is he alright?"

Bruce hung his head. "He had severe head trauma and suffered a basilar skull fracture. All of the internal damage caused an intracranial hematoma. They got to him too late, they tried to…" He swallowed hard and bit back tears. "There was nothing they could do."

Randy covered his mouth with his hand, dismayed by this news. "My god, Bruce. I am so sorry."

Sniffling through his tears, Bruce announced, "He was only eighteen. I told him not to buy that motorcycle. And dammit, why the hell wasn't he wearing a helmet? The shitty thing about this is I didn't get to say goodbye. He was gone by the time I got there." He wiped his eyes and cleared his throat, trying to shake it off. "I'm sorry. Here I am blubbering like a baby."

Sorry? Bruce had nothing to be sorry about. Randy couldn't believe he was apologizing. "It's alright. He was your brother."

He took a deep breath to calm himself. "Anyway, that's where I was this weekend."

"Damn, Bruce. You need to be with your family. What are you doing here?"

"I needed to come back to school," he declared. "I'd already missed a day of class. I couldn't afford to miss another. There's nothing for me to do at home anyway. We already had his body cremated. It's done." He shook his head and sighed, "I'm gonna have a shit ton of work to make up."

"We'll help you," Randy offered. "And I'm sure the professors will understand. Did you talk to them and tell them what happened?"

"I'm going to this morning. I have a written excuse from the hospital and the mortuary for missing class."

Randy offered a sympathetic smile. "I'll buy you lunch later."

"You don't have to do that."

"I want to. And don't worry, we'll get you caught up this week."

"Thank you."

Randy told Jim and Mandy what happened so Bruce wouldn't have to repeat it and get all emotional again. Bruce spoke to all his professors and was able to make up all the work he missed. They added another study session to their schedule that night to help him get caught up. By Thursday morning, he was doing better emotionally, even though it was going to take some time to fully recover from this ordeal.

Chapter Thirty-Seven

Early Friday morning, Jane's basketball team hopped on a bus to catch a flight to New Jersey for a game against Rutgers on Saturday. Randy escorted Jane to the gym parking lot to bid her farewell before he went to class.

During lunch that day, Randy had a bit of a somber air about him. Concerned, Jim questioned him about his mood. "Randy, you alright, Dude? You're kinda in your own little world today."

Randy settled back in his chair. "What the hell am I supposed to do all weekend without Jane?"

"Oh, that's right. She's out of town this weekend." Jim offered a suggestion, "You should go out."

"Go out?" Randy asked, thinking that was a ridiculous idea. "And do what?"

"I don't know. Somethin'. You and I could shoot some hoops after class."

Randy liked that plan. "Alright."

"And there's a Lakers game on tomorrow night. I'll come over and we'll watch it together."

"Sounds good."

"Then Sunday we have our study session, and doesn't she come home Sunday night?" Jim reminded him.

"Yeah."

"Well then, there you go. You'll be busy chillaxin' this weekend."

Jim and Randy enjoyed spending time together, something they hadn't done in a while with Jim playing daddy and both carrying part-time jobs and attending medical school full time. They munched on tortilla chips and salsa, ate Oreos, and drank Coronas while they watched the game.

"Man, this brings back memories," Randy said. "I remember when we used to do this every weekend."

"Before med school, girlfriends, and babies got in the way."

"I hear ya." Randy gulped down the rest of his beer. "How come you're not hanging out with Jill tonight?"

"She's on night shift at the hospital."

Curious about this woman Jim was involved with, Randy probed further. "What kind of nurse is she?"

"ER."

"Right up your alley."

"Yup," Jim replied with a smile.

"How old is her daughter?"

"Three. She is as cute as button too."

Randy popped the top on another Corona. "How serious are you about her?"

Jim was completely honest with him. "Takin' it one day at a time. Not pushin' anything. Her marriage ended badly and apparently her ex-husband was a real assmunch, so I don't wanna rush her. It's goin' well though."

"That's good. You seem a lot happier since you've been with her."

"Yeah," Jim said contently. "She has a way of makin' me smile even if I don't feel like it. She goes out of her way to make me happy. She calls just to say hello. She can tell when I'm havin' a bad day and knows exactly what to say to brighten my mood. I've never felt this way before."

"Uh oh," Randy teased. "Sounds like someone's in love."

"I think I might be."

"Does she feel the same way about you?"

Confidently, Jim replied, "You know, I think she does. When we were together last night, the way she looked at me…totally made my heart skip a beat, man." Jim nodded with a glowing smile. "There's definitely somethin' happenin' here."

"That's awesome, buddy. You deserve to be happy." Randy liked Jill. And more importantly, Jim liked her. He hoped this relationship would turn into something serious later on down the road. "She's really pretty, by the way," Randy commented. "She has gorgeous eyes."

"I know," Jim agreed. "Definitely a bodacious babe."

Randy was able to relax, refresh, and recharge over the weekend. For Jane, however, the weekend had been exhausting. She and her basketball team played in a tournament all weekend and didn't get back to Berkeley until late Sunday night. The women hadn't had a day off in weeks. The minute Jane got home, she collapsed. Since she didn't have practice Monday morning, Randy let her sleep in.

Jim stopped by Randy's apartment on his way to class. Jane's athletic bag was on the floor and the apartment was unnervingly silent and dark, except for the light that was on in the kitchen. "Why is it so quiet in here?"

With a steaming cup of coffee gripped in his hand, Randy said, "Jane's asleep. You want some coffee?"

"Sure."

Randy headed into the kitchen to get Jim a cup.

Jim set his book bag on the table and followed him. "I would've thought Jane would be headin' to the gym this mornin'. She doesn't have practice today?"

"No, this is the first day since the season started that she hasn't had practice. She's been working her tail off and she's exhausted."

"How has all of this basketball stuff affected your relationship? Dingin' it up, I bet."

"Why would it?" Randy asked.

"Because she goes out of town all the time. That's gotta be hard on you."

"I miss her, but it gives us something to look forward to when she comes back. It's actually strengthened our relationship."

"How the hell do you figure that?" Jim leaned against the counter.

Randy handed him a cup of coffee. "Because the time we spend together has become more valuable. We cherish every second we have together and make the most of it. I do admit, though, that it has been a little more challenging with both of us having insane schedules this year, but playing basketball is something she loves and something she's been wanting for a while. I believe this is an incredible opportunity for her, and I'm going to stand by her side and offer whatever support I can. I get more satisfaction from doing something that makes Jane happy than from anything else I have ever done."

"Jane has you wrapped around her finger, my friend."

With a good-humored grin, Randy said, "Fuck you, Jackass. I just want her to be happy, and I'll do whatever it takes to make that happen."

Jim finished his cup of coffee then glanced at his watch. "We better jet, Bro."

Randy gulped down the last of his coffee and set his mug in the sink. Jim placed his cup next to Randy's, then each of them grabbed their backpacks and headed out the door.

Chapter Thirty-Eight

With work, class, labs, clinicals, studying, and Jane's basketball games, Randy found it difficult to fit everything into his schedule. Since finals were coming up soon, his study group had pulled late-nighters over the last few weeks to prepare. He was functioning off very little sleep. Exhausted from the stress, he awoke in a foul mood.

He was irritable and overly cranky as he sat at the table eating his breakfast.

Jane came into the kitchen and greeted him with a kiss. "Hey, Sweetie. Good morning."

"That's debatable."

She detected a hint of cynicism in his voice. "You ok?"

"I hate finals," he complained.

"So do I."

He sneered at her with a distinct hardening of his eyes. "Yours are nothing like mine." He claimed his irritation as he jumped to his feet. He slammed his coffee cup and oatmeal bowl in the sink then fumbled around in his bag.

She watched him intently. He moved about the apartment harshly with cold derision in his eyes.

"Where the hell is my phone?" he asked, frantically searching for it.

She grabbed it off the coffee table and handed it to him.

He snagged it out of her hand and shoved it in his pocket.

Aware of his aggravation, she tried to coax him into a better mood. "Sweetie?"

He shot her a penetrating glare. "What?"

"What's wrong?"

"Why do you keep asking me that?"

"Because you are ratty and irritable this morning."

"Ratty?" Her words weren't soothing him at all, in fact, they seemed to increase his annoyance. "What the hell is that supposed to mean?"

"Nothing. I…"

"You know, Jane." His straight glance and mocking tone shot right through her. "If you don't have something constructive to say to me then be quiet." He picked up his bag and searched for his keys.

"I was only trying to help you."

As soon as he found his keys, he left for his study session, without even acknowledging what she said.

Throughout the morning, Randy had a guilt-ridden conscience. He realized the words he said and the tone he used with Jane made him sound like an asshole.

Jim watched Randy fidget with his pen, taking it apart a couple times before he scribbled all over his notes. After drinking three cups of coffee, Randy folded his empty sugar packets into triangles and sharpened his pencil at least ten times. And somehow he managed to poke several holes in his empty Styrofoam coffee cup. He drew a heart on the side of his cup, labeled it with the word *Jane*, then tore the eraser off the end of his pencil.

This peculiar, extremely distractible behavior made Jim wonder what was wrong with him. He was drifty and appeared to have something on his mind. When they stopped to take a break, Jim questioned Randy about the mess he made of his area. "You ok, man?"

Randy hung his head, ashamed of himself for the way he treated Jane. "I'm such an ass."

"I already knew that, but what finally made you realize it?" Jim attempted to bring humor and sarcasm into this to make Randy feel better. It didn't work.

Randy picked up his coffee cup and looked at the heart he drew. "I can't believe I said that to her."

"To who? And what did you say?"

"Jane and I got into an argument this morning. I said some shit I shouldn't have said and I feel like an insensitive prick." Even his normally cheerful voice was drab.

"You and Jane were arguing?" This was something they never did, so Jim was surprised to hear about this. "About what?"

"Basically I told her that my finals were more important than hers."

Those were mean and unnecessary words. Jim could see why Randy was upset. "Damn, Dude. That was harsh. You big meanie."

"I know. I told you I'm an asshole. With all this crap going on with school right now, the Awards and Honors Committee breathing down my neck, and her damn basketball schedule, I'm about to go nuts."

"So you bitch at Jane?" Jim questioned, agreeing that Randy had acted like an ass.

"I know, I know. I feel like crap."

"Couples break up over that kind of shit."

Randy's heart plummeted to the floor. "Oh, Jesus. Don't say that."

"Hey, I'm just sayin' I've seen people break up over lesser shit than that. You better do some serious ass kissin', Bro."

Randy poked more holes in his cup.

"Why don't you grab another cup of coffee and try not to worry about it," Jim suggested.

But Randy did worry about it. He tried to trudge through the rest of his study session, hoping Jane would forgive him.

On the way home, he stopped by the flower shop and picked up a dozen roses, a box of chocolate, and a huge teddy bear holding a big heart-shaped, helium-filled Mylar balloon that said *I Love You* on it. He walked into his apartment with his hands full. Jane wasn't there, and her purse was gone. He figured she had probably gone up to Alpha. Desperately trying to make amends, he made his way up there, hoping she would be home. He got lucky.

When Lisa saw Randy standing outside with suck-up supplies in his hands, she went to fetch Jane.

Jane came to the door puffy-eyed, making Randy feel worse. She had probably been crying all morning because of him. He set the roses, chocolates, and teddy bear on the stairs and pulled her into his arms. "I am so sorry."

She sniffled and wiped her eyes. "I didn't mean to make you mad."

"You didn't." He held her tightly in his arms, stroking her hair with his hands. "I get crotchety and stressed out this time of year, but that is not an excuse. I had no right to take any of this out on you. I shouldn't have yelled at you like that." He held her hand and knelt down on one knee. "I am begging for your forgiveness."

She laughed at his lame attempt to regain her favor. "Randy, get up."

"Do you forgive me?"

"Yes. Now get up." She eyed all the stuff he had on the stairs. "What is all this?"

"My way of saying I'm sorry." Randy picked up the bear and maneuvered its hands playfully. "See, he's sorry too."

She took the bear from him and squeezed it.

Randy did not understand Jane's dedication to him. He bogged her down with medical crap and let his grouchiness get the best of him. Yet somehow, despite all of this, she stood by his side, faithfully. "You have got to be the most patient woman in the world. I don't deserve you."

"I love you, Randy."

"I love you, too." He held her in his arms, floating on the clouds. He couldn't remember now why he had been so afraid of love and commitment. Jane was the best thing that had ever happened to him, and in his eyes, she was the most incredible woman in the world.

Randy breathed a sigh of relief when he turned in his last exam. His features became more animated; satisfaction pursed his mouth. While he made his way home from the Medical Sciences building, he called Jane.

"Hi, Sweetie. You finished?"

"Yes I am," his heart sang with delight. "How about you? You done with practice?"

"Yup. Heading home now."

"Where do you want to go for dinner tonight?" he asked her.

"I don't know. How about that place where we saw the seals," she suggested. "That was fun."

"The Cliff House?"

"Yes."

"Sweet," he approved. "I love that place."

Once again Randy and Jane would be apart on Christmas. As much as he looked forward to going home over the holidays, he didn't like the idea of leaving Jane to do it. She had practice and game commitments and needed to spend time with her family.

Being sneaky, Randy grabbed a long white box decorated with a little red bow and stuck it in his pocket before he left.

As soon as the waiter took their orders, Randy reached into his pocket and handed the box to Jane. "Merry Christmas."

"Randy," she replied. "Why didn't you tell me you were bringing this? I left yours at home."

"That's ok. You can give it me later."

She removed the lid and pulled out a ruby double heart pendant with diamond accents. There were matching earrings that went with it. "Oh my god. These are beautiful." She happened to be wearing a red sweater, and these matched perfectly. She removed the necklace and earrings she was currently wearing and put these on instead. "What do you think?"

Randy straightened the pendant and laid it back down on her chest. "You're beautiful." He reached across the table and held her hand. "Does your coach know that you'll be flying out to Seattle after the Pullman game?"

"Yes, I talked to him." The lady Golden Bears had a game against UW in Seattle, which Randy planned to attend. Immediately following that game, her team was flying to Pullman for a game against WSU. He planned to see that one as well. Before returning to San Francisco, he and Jane were going to spend a few days together in Seattle. It was going to be crazy and chaotic, but it was the only way they could spend the holiday break together.

"I hope one of these years we can spend Christmas together. Just once I want to hold you under the mistletoe on Christmas Eve," he said.

"I'd like that too."

Randy awoke Sunday morning snuggled under the blankets with Jane. He really didn't want to get up; he was far too comfortable. Trying not to wake her, he carefully lifted the blanket and snuck out of bed. He slipped on a pair of shorts and moseyed into the kitchen to make a pot of coffee. As soon as it began to brew, he came back into the bedroom and leaned against the doorframe, watching Jane sleep. A smile filled his face as she rolled over and hugged her pillow. "Good morning, Beautiful."

She stretched elegantly and opened her eyes. The sheet slid down, exposing the soft skin of her breast.

Randy sat next to her. He reached over to hold her hand and pulled the sheet back up to cover her.

"When do you have to be at the airport?" she asked.

"Couple hours. I thought we could share breakfast together before my flight, if you feel like it."

"That sounds good."

He leaned over and gave her a kiss. "Might want to get up then. Never know what traffic will be like."

By the time they arrived at the airport, Randy had about an hour and a half before his flight was scheduled to leave. He dropped his baggage off at the check in counter then headed to Starbucks. Jane ordered cocoa and Randy ordered a cup of coffee. In the middle of their conversation, Randy glanced at his watch. Flight time was quickly approaching, and he still had to get through the security line.

"I'll call you when I get there," he said.

She held him close. "I miss you already."

"I'll miss you too." Randy hated these departures. He wished he didn't have to say goodbye. "Play hard this week, and watch those fouls."

"You sound like my coach," he giggled.

"Maybe you should listen to him." He cradled her face with his hands and gazed into her eyes. Before he departed, he kissed her. "I love you. Honey. I'll see you in a few days."

"I love you too." She slowly released him and watched him walk away.

Chapter Thirty-Nine

That evening, Randy walked along Lake Washington to get some fresh air. Robby stood on the dock staring out at the water. Hoping to have a bonding moment with his youngest sibling, Randy went over to talk to him. As he got closer, he saw Robert puffing on a cigarette. "Rob?"

Startled, Robby flinched, hiding the cigarette behind his back. "Jesus, Randy. You scared the shit out of me."

"Sorry."

Robby pulled the cigarette out and took another puff.

"When did you start smoking?"

"That's none of your business."

"That shit is bad for you. Nicotine and tar…"

Robby glared at his brother, annoyed that he had brought that up. "You know what, I don't give a shit. I am tired of hearing about things that are bad for my body and things I shouldn't do."

"People die from that crap, Rob. How many of those things do you smoke every day?"

"Half a pack." Robby put the cigarette back in his mouth.

"Don't pollute your body with that shit."

"Don't tell me what to do. You are not my father."

"Alright, then I'll tell Dad," he threatened.

Robby snarled at him. "Fuck, Randy! You're as bad as he is."

"I've seen what that crap can do to your lungs, and it's not pretty. I had to analyze a lung fucked up by cigarettes. Trust me, you don't want to go there."

"You know," Robby said. "All of this doctor bullshit is getting old. Does anyone ever stop to think what I want?"

"Do you really want to end up with lung cancer? Have you ever watched a person suffer from that? You don't want to. Cancer is not something to fuck around with."

Robby finished his cigarette and flicked it into the lake.

"Oh, you're polluting the lake now?" Randy lectured. "Get that out of the water."

Robby put his hands in his pockets and walked off the dock.

This radical change in attitude and behavior had Randy worried. He fished the cigarette butt from the lake then ran after his brother. "What is going on with you?"

"What makes you think something is going on with me?" Robby grumbled.

"Well, for starters you're wearing nothing but black, and you have chains hanging all over you."

"It's Goth."

"Goth?" Randy questioned. "That's what you're into now? Dad told me you got arrested a couple weeks ago."

"He told you that?"

"Drinking and driving, Robby? You have a DUI and underage drinking on your record now. You're gonna lose your license and you're gonna kill someone if you get behind the wheel of a car in that condition."

"Dad took my keys. How the hell am I supposed to drive if I don't even have my fucking car?"

"I'm glad he took your keys, if you're going to be irresponsible."

Randy was beginning to sound like his parents, and Robby didn't like it. "I didn't ask for your opinion. Stay out of my business and leave me alone." Robby moped inside the house.

What the hell happened to the sweet little kid Randy once knew? He didn't want to get his brother in trouble, but he was concerned about his wellbeing. Randy stepped inside the house and searched for his mom, who would take the news of Robby smoking better than his dad would.

He found her in the kitchen baking cookies. Randy sat on a stool opposite her and grabbed a cookie off the cooling rack. "Did you know Robby was smoking?" He took a bite of the scrumptious treat and waited for his mother to respond.

She looked up from her baking with a horrified expression on her face. "What?"

"Robby. I was outside talking to him. He had a cigarette in his hand. He's smoking."

She dropped her measuring cup in the sink. "Oh crap. You father is going to flip."

Randy took another bite of his cookie. "What's going on with him?"

"I wish I knew. It started a few weeks ago. He began dressing in black, arguing with authority, and raising all kinds of hell. Robby hasn't talked to us much lately, and when he does, he's usually yelling at your father. He hasn't been out of the house since that DUI incident. Your father won't let him out of his sight."

"Understandable. But if that's the case, where did he get those cigarettes?" Randy asked, troubled by his brother's attitude.

"I don't know, but I will tell your father. Thank you for letting me know."

Randy hated to tattle on his brother and hated even more that his father was going to have to deal with it, but for Robby's safety, he felt he had no choice.

The aura around the house was a little tense, as Randy's dad had heard about Robby's smoking habit and was livid. Dr. Hanson tore Robby's room apart and took every pack of cigarettes he had hidden. And because Randy told his parents about it, Robby refused to speak to him. To make matters worse, Robby was suffering from nicotine withdrawal.

Christmas Eve, after the family festivities, Robby retreated to his room. Randy followed him. "Rob?"

"Get away from me, traitor!"

Even though he wasn't invited, Randy entered Robby's room. "I'm sorry. I care about you, Rob, and I'm worried about your recent behavior."

"If you cared about me, you'd leave me the fuck alone."

He sat on the edge of Robby's bed.

Robby threw a pillow at him. "Get out! You are a backstabber and a fuckin' stoolie!"

Trying to get Robby to understand his perspective, Randy explained, "I know you're having some problems right now, but we can't help you if you don't talk to us."

"Like any of you would care," Robby whined. "You'll just tell Mom and Dad and get me in trouble. I can't believe you narked on me."

"I'm concerned about you. That's why I told them. And if there's something I can help you with, I will, but you have to tell me, Rob. You can't hide in here."

Robby sat up, staring at his hands with vacant eyes.

Randy tried to persuade his little brother to open up. "Come on, Rob. You've always been able to talk to your big brother."

Robby's world was collapsing, and he wanted to cry. Feeling crushed, he confided in his brother. "My girlfriend dumped me, Mom and Dad don't understand me, and I feel like I want to die."

Oh, so this was about a breakup. Robby was taking it hard. "Did she give you a reason?"

"She told me she didn't want to be with a loser for the rest of her life."

Randy cringed at that demeaning statement. "Ouch. That hurts."

"I tried to talk to her, but she won't listen to me. She just hangs up on me and laughs when she sees me in the hallway at school."

"Breakups can be rough."

"You ever had a girl dump you?"

"Yes," Randy admitted. "My junior year in high school, a girl I was dating dumped me when I ditched her for my friends. Looking back on it now, it was definitely for the best. And after graduation, I broke up with Alison. You remember her?"

"She was cool. I liked her."

Randy explained, "You know, Rob, sometimes people need to go their separate ways. When you don't share common goals and don't see eye to eye or life pulls you in different directions then it's time to move on. The whole dating scene is to help you find that special someone. And you will go through many relationships and breakups in the process."

"Breaking up sucks."

"I know it does, but you can't let it consume your life, and you sure as hell can't self-destruct over a girl. You're only seventeen. You have your whole life ahead of you. And you know what?"

"What?"

"You will find another girl better than the one you were with," Randy reassured him. "One who will make you happier than you've ever been. It might take you a while to find her, and she'll probably come into your life when you least expect her to. But someday you'll fall in love with an incredible woman and your life will never be the same again."

"But what if she was the one?"

"I firmly believe that if she was the one then you wouldn't have broken up. Your soul mate is someone who forgives your misgivings, loves you unconditionally, always stands beside you, and digs deep, knowing you inside and out. Was she willing to dig that deep?"

"Well, no," Robby admitted.

"Then there you go. You weren't meant to be together."

Robby was perkier now. He sat up straight and actually had a smile on his face. "What about Jane?"

"What about her?"

"Does she dig that deep?"

This conversation made Randy uneasy. As he spoke to his brother about love and life partners and soul mates he was beginning to realize the person he described was Jane. The thought of lifelong commitment frightened him. But lately the prospect of Jane being 'the one' was an incredible vision. Coming to this realization made him queasy.

Robert probed further, demanding an answer from Randy. "Does she? Is she the one?"

Randy seriously pondered over what Robby asked him. Already he was starting to picture himself married with a family. And now that he thought about it, Jane did fit the qualifications in every way. Their relationship had stood the test of time, good times and horrible ones. Jane was the supportive woman Randy had always hoped for, and the thought of having her in his life indefinitely was a vision he welcomed wholeheartedly. His mouth slowly curved into a smile.

Seeing the grin on Randy's face made Robby tease, "Oh, so she is the one."

After careful consideration of this question, Randy replied, "You know, now that you ask me that, I think she might be."

"I'm starved," Robby said. "Let's eat some turkey sandwiches then I'll whoop your ass at basketball."

"I think not. You're going down, little bro."

Randy waited for a phone call from Jane telling him that she and her team were in town. When the call finally came, he rushed to answer his phone. "Hey, Baby."

"We just finished with practice. I'm free for a while."

He gathered his jacket and the keys to his dad's truck and dashed toward the door. "Where are you staying?"

"The Best Western at Seattle Center."

"I know where that is. What room are you in?"

"218."

"Alright. I love you, Honey. I'll get there as quickly as I can."

His reaction amused her. "Don't go too fast. I don't want you to get a speeding ticket."

"I won't. I'm just anxious to see you. I'll be there soon."

Without hesitation, Randy hopped in the truck and pulled out of the driveway. He swerved in and out of freeway lanes to dodge traffic, which wasn't moving fast enough for him. When he arrived at her hotel, he trekked upstairs to room 218 and knocked on the door.

The minute Jane saw him, she melted in his arms. "I missed you."

He smothered her with kisses. "I missed you too." Wanting to see her pretty face, he pulled away slightly. "Oh man, you are a sight for sore eyes. Can you leave the hotel or are you glued here?"

"No, I can leave. But I have to be back by eight for a team meeting."

Randy thought this was funny. "Ooh, a curfew. Well, in that case, we better get going."

Over the last few months, Jane had discussed with Randy the possibility of going to graduate school and getting her Master's Degree in Psychology. Randy fully supported this decision, and since he was familiar with grad school enrollment procedures, he helped her with the application process. She had already taken the GRE and filled out all necessary paperwork, and now awaited her acceptance letter from the department.

"Have you heard from the Psychology Department yet?" Randy asked her over dinner.

"No. Not yet."

"What specialty did you end up going with?"

"Sports Psychology."

"Sounds like a good match for you."

Before taking Jane back to the hotel, Randy drove them to a secluded spot under a bridge by the waterfront to admire the view of the skyline. They sat on the tailgate of the truck and watched the sun descend over the city. Randy scooted closer and put his arm around her; their feet dangled over the side of the bed. The evening air chilled their skin, but being close to each other made them feel warm.

The moment the sun set, Randy hopped off the tailgate and stood on the ground in front of Jane. He positioned himself between her legs and placed his hands on her hips. His gaze met hers, which drew a smile to his face. He was about to kiss her when he felt Jane's hands unbuttoning his pants.

He cocked his head slightly and shot her an inquisitive eye. "What are you doing?" He quickly checked their surroundings. They were in the middle of downtown, and even though it was dark outside, people and cars were all around them. "We cannot do this here."

She scooted to the edge of the tailgate and wrapped her legs around him. "Why not?"

"Because we're in public."

"So?"

"You do realize, don't you, that public sex is frowned upon. It's considered lewd and lascivious conduct in the eyes of the law."

"Only if we get caught," she encouraged. "You're always so worried about rules and regulations."

"Because I'd rather not get arrested." Although he was dying to take her in his arms and explore the luscious curves of her body, he did have a sense of morality and public decency. "I'm all for excitement in our love life, Jane, but let's find a more private location where we're not freezing our asses off." He kissed her then helped her off the tailgate. "Besides," he tapped his watch. "You have a curfew tonight. And if we don't get moving, you're going to be late." They went inside the truck cab and Randy cranked up the heat. They thawed out for a few minutes before he turned the truck around and headed back to the hotel.

Randy and his family arrived at Alaska Airlines Arena on the University of Washington campus around 1:00 P.M. the next day, right as Jane and her teammates stepped onto the court to warm up. As soon as they found their seats, Randy told his family, "I'll be right back. Gonna talk to Jane for a minute." He tromped down the stairs and made his way to the side of the court. Trying to get her attention, he hollered, "Jane!"

She turned to his voice. "Hi, Sweetie."

"How you feeling? You ready?"

"I'm ready." She looked up at the stands of the pavilion. "Where are you guys sitting?"

Randy pointed to a section in the middle where his parents and Robby sat waving at them. "We're up there."

"I see." She waved back.

"Where can I meet you after the game?" he asked.

"Why don't you wait in the stands. I'll meet you out here."

"Sounds good. Good luck today. Play hard," he encouraged her.

"I will." She went back to her warm-ups, and Randy returned to his family.

Jane played one of the best games of her life that afternoon. She scored the first six points for Cal, hauled in a career high ten assists, snagged two steals, nailed her two free throws, and hit a three-pointer with thirty-nine seconds on the clock at halftime. She scored eighteen points overall, a double-double game for her. It was an action-packed hardwood court battle that had some of the most precision perfect fundamentals Randy had ever seen.

When the game was over, Randy's dad remarked, "That is a talented athlete you've got there, Son."

Randy completely agreed. "Yes she is. She's an aggressive player too. I love watching her play."

"We're gonna take off and give you two some alone time for a while," Mark suggested, grinning at his son.

"Sounds great." Randy leaned back in is seat waiting for the arena to clear. Thirty minutes later, Jane walked across the court carrying an athletic bag. He bounded out of his seat to greet her. "Awesome game, Babe."

"Thanks."

Parting his lips, he kissed her, then he threw her athletic bag over his shoulder and escorted her out of the building. "What time do you have to be back?"

"Six thirty. Coach made dinner reservations at the hotel for all of us."

He checked to see what time it was. Four o'clock. "What should we do for a couple hours?"

"I don't know. This is your hometown, not mine."

"You know what? Winterfest is going on right now. Local art, ice sculpting, live music—I heard there's some kind of illumination and light show going on down there too. We should check it out."

"Sounds like fun."

When Jane's team dinner reservation time approached, Randy drove her back to the hotel. "My flight leaves at 12:20 tomorrow," he told her. "I'm gonna get a hotel for two days. I'll be there in plenty of time to see your game on Friday."

"What hotel did you make reservations in?"

"The Holiday Inn by the university."

"We're staying there too."

"Even better. You have your return ticket to Seattle, right?"

"Yes, Sweetie," she said with teasing laughter because she knew he was an incessant worrier.

"Ok, just making sure. I've been looking forward to having those four days with you in Seattle."

"I know. I have been too."

"I'll call you when I get to Pullman." Once again he had to bid her farewell. As happy as he was that she was playing basketball, he couldn't wait for the season to be over so he could have her to himself again. He swore they said goodbye more in the last two months than the entire first year of their relationship. "Have a safe trip, Baby. Call or message me tonight if you have time."

"I will."

He put his arms around her and held her close. Every time they said goodbye, he felt an agonizing pain in his heart. "I love you."

"I love you."

They parted with a kiss, and Randy slowly let go of her hand. She gave him once last glance before she joined her team for dinner.

Randy took a shuttle from the Pullman airport to his hotel. He was about to call Jane to tell her he was in town when a text message from her popped up on his phone. *At practice. Will call u when I'm done.* He messaged her back then searched the area for a cup of coffee.

With a Starbucks cup in his hand, he reported to his hotel room. Right as he was about to flip on the TV, his cellphone rang.

Jane's sweet voice resounded on the other end. "Hi, Sweetie."

"Well, hello," he said. "You at the hotel?"

"Yup. Meet me in the lobby."

Without hesitation, he dashed downstairs to meet Jane. The instant he saw her, his pulse quickened. He swept her into his arms. "How much time do you have?"

"A couple hours. Coach wants us to hang around the hotel 'cause he needs us to be available to go over plays before dinner."

Randy developed an ornery grin. "Two hours, and you have to stay in the hotel. Whatever shall we do?"

Jane knew what was on his mind because she was thinking the exact same thing. She gave him that 'come here baby' grin, that same look she gave him when she was in the mood. Catching her drift, they snuck away to his room.

Lying naked under the sheets, Randy rolled over and positioned himself on top of Jane. With one elbow on each side of her head, he grazed his thumb across her lips. "I haven't been sleeping very well."

"Why not?"

"Because I have a hard time sleeping when you're not lying next to me." His hand slowly worked its way down to her thigh.

His gentle massage sent rushing currents of desire throughout her entire body. "Hey, Mister. No cavorting."

"I don't see a sign anywhere saying it's illegal, do you?"

"No."

"Well then, seeing as I'm a law abiding citizen, and since we're alone in the privacy of this room, not out in public view," he teased, "I really don't see what we're waiting for." He explored the recesses of her mouth with his tongue while he stimulated her with his finger, making her well lubricated. She bent her knees and squirmed around on the bed. Obviously he was getting to her. Grinning devilishly, he moved in quickly, not wasting any time.

Trying to lower his heartrate after a long and breathtaking session in the sack, Randy swallowed hard from the depths of his throat. His chest heaved, and he desperately tried to regain air. With sweat beaded on his brow, he flopped on the mattress, weary and muscle fatigued.

Jane gave him a quick peck on the lips then crawled off the bed to freshen up. When she looked in the mirror, a shocked gasp escaped from her lips. "Jonathan Randal!"

What did she call him? No one, aside from his mother, ever called him that, and that was only when he was misbehaving. "What's the matter?"

"Look at this." She pointed to her neck. "You gave me a hickey."

He rolled with laughter.

She looked in the mirror again, trying to cover the mark with her hair. "I can't go to a team meeting with this hickey on my neck."

"Good. Skip it and stay here with me."

"I can't skip it." She shook her head in utter disbelief.

"Guess they'll know what you were doing for the last two hours, won't they?" He raised his eyebrows lustfully.

"Oh god, Randy," she said. "This is embarrassing."

"They all know you have a boyfriend. Do you really think they don't know what goes on behind closed doors?"

"Well no."

"How long is this meeting?"

"I don't know." She grabbed a washcloth and turned on the water.

"Are you tied up afterwards or will you be free to go?"

"Coach said something about wanting to get another round of shootarounds in tonight."

"Are you going to be able to break free and see me at all tonight?" he asked.

"Hopefully." She turned the water off then dried her hands. "I'll call you and let you know." She put her clothes back on and gave him a kiss. "I have to go."

He pouted his lip. "Boo hoo."

"I love you. I'll call you later."

"Love you, Babe." After she left, Randy stretched his muscles, which were now tight. He took a hot shower to help loosen them up.

Chapter Forty

Jane and Randy enjoyed their trip to Seattle together, but had to return to San Francisco for basketball practice, work, and a new semester of classes—the last of undergraduate school for her and the conclusion of stage one of medical training for him.

Randy's study group met at Amanda's apartment that week. Randy arrived earlier than the others and caught Mandy wrapped in a towel when she answered the door. "Damn, Mandy! Put some clothes on."

She showed him inside. "I'm sorry. My alarm didn't go off and I'm running way behind."

Randy stepped into the kitchen to pour himself a cup of coffee. Out of the corner of his eye, he saw Amanda knock a pile of magazines off a table and stub her toe on a chair. When she leaned over a laundry basket to get some clothes, her towel fell off.

Realizing Randy had seen her naked, she quickly covered up and ran into the bedroom.

When she came back out, fully dressed this time, Randy had a smirk on his face. "You are frazzled more than usual this morning."

"Shut up!" she demanded. "I do not wish to be the object of your amusement, Randy Hanson."

"You're the one who took off your towel and bared all in front of me."

"You're not going to tell anyone about that, are you?"

"You know I wouldn't embarrass you in front of Bruce like that," he tittered. "I gotta give you credit though, you have very nice breasts."

She smacked him on the arm. "Asshole!"

"Ow!" He drew back, rubbing his arm where she hit him. "I meant that as a compliment."

When Bruce and Jim arrived, Randy snorted under his breath, trying to contain his laughter.

"What's so funny?" Jim asked, noting the mischievous smirk on Randy's face.

Amanda glared at Randy, begging him not to say anything.

"A little inside joke between me and Mandy." He winked at her flirtingly.

The table quickly filled with chips, dip, and several opened cans of Pepsi. Debating over an answer, the group bickered back and forth.

"It is not," Mandy insisted.

"Mandy," Jim argued. "It's the zygotic membrane."

"You guys are wrong."

"Look it up, prove your answer," Randy said. "We're not accomplishing anything by arguing over this." He stood up and stretched. "Why don't we take a quick break. Get some air, use the restroom, eat something of substance."

"Excellent idea." Bruce traipsed into the kitchen to snag some food.

Jim trailed right behind him.

Mandy sat at the table, frantically flipping through her medical book trying to find evidence to support her answer.

Randy leaned over and said, "You're not going to find it in there."

That didn't stop her from looking. In fact, she rather violently turned the pages, almost ripping them. "This is driving me crazy."

Randy put his hand on hers to get her to calm down. "Mandy, relax. You're spazzing out."

"What does she have that I don't?"

He turned to the page she was searching for and pointed to the words in bold print. "The zygotic membrane. It's right there in big black letters."

She glared at him.

"I'm sorry this is bothering you, but try to stay focused." He joined the others in the kitchen.

Around 3:00 P.M., all the pages started to jumble together. Randy announced, "Alright, look. We're all tired and we're not thinking clearly. Why don't we call it a day? Where do we want to meet next week?"

"We can meet at my place," Jim suggested.

"Same time?" Bruce asked.

"I have to work next Sunday. We'll need to meet a little earlier."

"About eight?" Randy asked. They all agreed that eight would be fine.

Following their session, Bruce lingered behind. He couldn't help but notice that Mandy had been standoffish toward him lately, and he was hoping to get an explanation. "Why have you been avoiding me?"

She denied this accusation. "I'm not avoiding you."

"Yes you are. You and I used to hang out all the time. Now you hardly say two words to me."

"I heard you're seeing Randy's sister," Mandy finally said to him.

"Does that bother you?"

Mandy sat in the chair beside him. "I'd like to know what you're thinking, Buckman. From what I've heard, she doesn't appear to be the type of woman you'd be interested in. Seems she only wants you for one thing."

Mandy was one of his closest friends, and he valued her opinion. He took to heart every word she said. "Maybe. But maybe I want it that way."

She doubted his sincerity in that statement. "That doesn't sound like you at all."

Bruce tried to explain, "I'm not ready for any kind of serious commitment. With her in Washington, I still have my space. It remains casual, no pressure. I'm not giving up my freedom and we both have mutual benefits from this arrangement."

"Are you in love with her?"

"I never said I was." Wanting to reconnect with Mandy, Bruce suggested, "I'm gonna grab some tacos. You wanna come?"

"Sure."

He carried his bag over his shoulder. "I'll drive."

Chapter Forty-One

When Randy came over to Jim's apartment Sunday morning, Jim was out on the porch talking to Jill, who held Christopher in her arms. A blonde girl with pigtails stood next to them both. This made Randy's day. She was one of the cutest little girls he had ever seen. "Good morning," Randy said as he walked closer to them.

"Mornin', Randy," Jim answered.

This little girl handed Jim a picture. "It's for you."

Jim squatted down to her level. "This is a beautiful drawing."

She pointed to child-like sketches of people. "This is Mommy and this is me. And this is Chris and this is you," she said, showing him the characters she had drawn.

"What are we doing in this picture?"

"Going to the park."

Jim gave the girl a hug. "That's awesome, Sweetheart. Thank you very much." He stood up and grinned at Jill.

"I told you," Jill said to him. "She adores you."

This scene was absolutely precious. Apparently Jim had become quite popular with this little girl. He seemed to have a soft spot for her as well.

Jim leaned in to kiss Jill. "You sure it's not a problem to watch Chris for me?"

"No," Jill replied. "Not at all. Call me when you guys are done."

"I will."

She threw Christopher's diaper bag over her shoulder and headed toward the car. The little girl turned around and waved at Jim before they left.

"That is a cute little girl," Randy commented.

"Yeah she is," Jim replied.

"What's her name?"

"Sabrina."

"You have really gotten into this whole daddy thing, haven't you?"

Jim walked into his apartment with Randy trailing close behind. "Christopher and Sabrina make my day so much brighter. Yesterday Jill and I took the kids to the park. Sabrina was down on the grass playin' with Chris and she gave him a kiss on the cheek. It was classic, man." He picked up some baby toys and tossed them in a plastic bin.

"How old did you say she was?"

"She's four."

Randy placed his bag on the kitchen table and pulled out his notes. "You want me to put on some coffee?"

"Could you, please?" Toys were scattered everywhere. Jim grabbed a baby doll and a plastic toy baby bottle and put them in a neat pile on his couch then grabbed a few more toys and tossed them in the plastic bin with the others. "The kids kinda trashed my place last night."

"Last night? Did Jill stay here last night?"

"She came over to have dinner with me, but Sabrina fell asleep on the couch. Jill didn't want to wake her so she shacked here with me."

Randy grinned cunningly. "Hmm, nice excuse."

"Hey, whatever works."

"That little girl has really taken to you, hasn't she?" Randy remarked.

"She's a good girl."

"Where's her dad?"

"Jill doesn't know," Jim stated. "He walked out on Jill and Sabrina right after she was born. Jill hasn't heard from him since."

"Running away from responsibility?" Randy assumed.

"Maybe. The way she talks about him, sounds like he was a dick." Jim grabbed his notes and books out of his bag and joined Randy at the table. "Jill filed for divorce when he didn't come back. He didn't contest it and didn't fight her for custody. But now Sabrina has no father figure."

"And you are gladly taking on that role I see."

"Sure. And Jill is great with Christopher."

Randy saw where this was going. "Oh, I see."

"She's an incredible woman, Randy. She is accepting and understanding, and she's patient with me as far as school goes. She's the most empathetic person I've ever known."

"The complete opposite of Trina."

Jim considered this, not quite sure how to react. "Now that you mention it, yeah. She is."

"Don't take this the wrong way, Jim, but I never liked Trina."

Jim knew Randy wasn't a big fan of Katrina, but he never actually said anything about it to his face before. "I know."

"She treated you like crap, and I never did understand why the hell you were with her in the first place. Was she the only available girl when you guys were in high school?"

"No. She was the homecoming queen."

Randy laughed loudly. "You have got to be kidding me. And what were you, the chump boyfriend who worshipped the ground she walked on and followed her around like a lost puppy dog?"

"Not exactly. I was the starting quarterback on the football team."

Randy's mouth dropped open. "You were a jock?"

"Fuck you. You weren't on any sports teams in high school?"

"I screwed around on the basketball court, but I wasn't the damn team captain or the starting quarterback." Randy had a hard time containing a snicker. "How cliché is that, the quarterback and the homecoming queen."

"In hindsight I should've known it wouldn't last," Jim said. "But I felt damn proud walkin' down the hall holdin' the homecoming queen's hand. In high school, that was the bomb. She wore my letter jacket, we shared a locker, we went to the prom together. She was the most popular girl in school, and she put out. Damn, Randy, what teenage guy would pass up the opportunity to dick a goddess?"

"Fuck that. I would have passed her up if she was a bitch, no matter how popular or pretty she was. You know, I went out with the head cheerleader in high school, until she started talking a bunch of smack about me behind my back that I later found out about, then I dumped her ass."

"Why does it not surprise me that you dated a cheerleader in high school?" Jim teased. "Probably because your girlfriend now is a sorority chick."

"I like my girls a bit on the dirty side." Randy prepared a cup of coffee. "How come you never told me you played football?"

"High school was somethin' I wanted to put far behind me as quickly as possible. I'm not one of those guys who relished in reliving my juvenile hormonal stage. Those were not my glory years, as some people might like to think they were."

"Were you any good?" Randy asked.

"Never won any awards or scholarships for it. Wouldn't have played in college anyway even if they offered it to me. I had better things to do. Wanted to focus on medicine."

Randy could relate. "Makes sense."

Rethinking his relationship with Katrina, Jim said, "I think what finally made Trina wig was the fact that six years after we graduated from high school, she realized she wasn't the center of the universe. She was an average person with a normal job who lived an ordinary life like everyone else. She was no longer the popular high school princess."

"Maybe." Randy glanced at his watch. Bruce and Mandy would be showing up any minute. "So…Jill…you really like her, don't you?"

Jim smiled in delight at the mere mention of her name. "I've totally fallin' for her, Dude."

"That's great. As long as she's good to you, I'm all for it." A knock at the door ended their conversation. Jim got up and answered it.

Chapter Forty-Two

The next few weeks were busy for Randy. They were the last weeks of his Clinical Skills class before his final Objective Structured Clinical Examination, or OSCE, and the last weeks of his Contextually Integrated Case-Based Curriculum class before his last written final exam. The reality of being only weeks away from ending his medical classes and receiving his M.S. had finally begun to sink in. His workload seemed lighter this semester then it had been in the past and he wasn't as tired as he remembered feeling over the last three years during finals week. In fact, he felt a new burst of energy in anticipation of ending the first stage of his medical training and beginning his clinical rotations.

Randy awoke the day of his OSCE prepared and ready. After showering and shaving, he dressed in preceptorship professional attire then sipped a quick cup of coffee and ate a hearty breakfast. He grabbed his white lab coat with his nametag, *J. Randal Hanson, UCSF-UCB Joint Medical Program*, then slipped his stethoscope, reflex hammer, and eye chart into the pockets of his lab coat. He read through the checklist on his syllabus one last time to make sure he hadn't forgotten anything.

Jane woke up still sleepy-eyed from a busy weekend of games and practice. She emerged from the bedroom to see Randy carrying his lab coat in his hand. "Hey, Sweetie." She yawned. "You look great."

"Thanks."

She straightened his tie. "You ready for your exam?"

"Yup. Feeling confident."

"Good. What time are you guys meeting today?"

Randy scheduled his OSCE on a Sunday morning so he wouldn't miss work. His study group still planned to meet, but they adjusted their meeting time to accommodate Randy's exam. "1:30. We're gonna meet at the SUB and grab some lunch before we get started. Shouldn't be any later than 4:00."

"Can I meet you for lunch?" she asked, hoping it would be ok if she joined them.

"Sure, Babe. Don't know how exciting the conversation will be when we're preparing for finals, but you are always welcome to join us." He pressed his lips on hers. "I gotta get to my exam. Think about what you want to do this afternoon when I get home."

"Alright, I will."

"I love you, Baby. I'll see you later," he said.

"Love you too. Good luck."

"Thanks." He grabbed his backpack with study materials in it and walked out the door.

When Randy finished his exam, he texted Jane then moseyed over to the SUB to meet his friends for lunch. Jim, Mandy, and Bruce were already there. "Sorry I'm late, guys."

"No problem," Bruce said. "How'd your exam go?"

"I think I performed well." Randy draped his lab coat over the back of a chair and set his backpack on the floor.

"Two more weeks," Jim exclaimed, excited about being nearly finished with the classroom portion of their training.

"Yes, thank God," Randy said. "And the best part is we have that break during basketball playoffs. I'll be able see every one of Jane's games before we start rotations."

"Her team made the playoffs?" Bruce asked.

"Yup. They are ranked twelfth right now."

Bruce was impressed. "Nice."

Just as he said that, Jane walked through the door. "Well, there she is." Randy put his arms around her and gave her a kiss. "Hello."

"Hi, Sweetie."

She had a manila envelope in her hand. "What's that?"

"It came in the mail while you were at work yesterday, and in the chaos of my game last night, I forgot to give it to you."

The return address was from Alpha Omega Alpha. Randy took the envelope from her, and pulled out the letter. As he read to himself, his entire face lit up.

"What's it say?" Jim asked.

Randy read a portion of it out loud. "Dear Mr. Hanson, after thorough review of your file and careful consideration by the panel of the Awards and Honors Committee, you have been selected for induction into the Alpha Omega Alpha National Honor Medical Society."

"Congratulations, man!" Bruce said.

"Show off," Jim teased. "Grats, Dude."

"Thank you," Randy boasted.

Jane threw her arms around him. "I'm so proud of you."

Randy was in complete shock. "Wow. This is too much."

Following the study session, which was actually quite productive, Randy returned to his apartment. "Honey," he called out to Jane. When she didn't respond, he dropped his bag on the floor and searched from room to room. "Baby, are you here?" Still no response. Obviously she wasn't there. He took out his cellphone and dialed her number. "Hey, Baby. Where are you?"

"Up at Alpha. I'll be down in a bit. I want to make dinner tonight."

Yes! She was going to cook. This evening was going to be incredible. "Sweet. How long 'til you get here?" he asked, hoping she would hurry.

"Thirty minutes or so."

Thinking about eating a meal prepared by her made his mouth water. "Can't wait. I love you, Baby."

"Love you too. See you soon."

He hung up his phone and used this opportunity to straighten up the apartment before she came over.

While Jane started dinner prep, Randy stood in the kitchen leaning against the counter watching her. "Are you going to come up to Seattle with me over spring break?"

"Yes, if I'm invited."

"Of course you're invited." He pulled a glass out of the cupboard and poured milk into it. "This month-long break before clinical training is gonna be nice. I can chill out, put on my shades, cruise the city with the radio blasting…"

Jane laughed. "You think you're Mario Andretti, don't you?"

"You mean I'm not?" he asked teasingly.

"No, and I'm glad. Racecar driving is dangerous. If you had a dangerous job like that, I'd go crazy with worry."

"Instead you're with a guy with an insane schedule who'll be on-call all the time."

"But at least as a doctor you'll be safe. I'd go nuts if I had to spend each night hoping I was going to see you in the morning."

"Then I guess I shouldn't go bungee jumping or skydiving any time soon."

"Oh god no. That would scare the hell out of me."

Randy stood behind her and pulled her hair off her neck. He kissed the soft skin behind her ear. "We're having a big banquet the night before graduation. Dr. Boyce has asked me to give a speech."

"Really?"

"Yes. I need you there for support." He wrapped his arm around her and rubbed her tummy. "My parents are coming down for that too." He considered the significance of this. "Oh, great. I have to make a speech in front of my dad. I hope I don't make a fool of myself."

"You're always so hard on yourself, and you worry too much." She put some linguini noodles on to boil.

"I know. You tell me that all the time." He kissed her then let her finish making dinner.

When Randy walked into his apartment after work Saturday afternoon, Jane was sitting at the table reading something from one of her Psychology books.

She glanced up at the clock. It was two hours later than he said he would be home. "Where have you been? I texted you and you didn't answer me."

Randy took her by the hand and pulled her to her feet. "Come outside with me and I'll show you where I've been."

Parked out by the curb was a brand new metallic, crystal red convertible. The top was down, showing off the black leather interior. Her mouth gaped open. "What is this?"

"That, my dear, is a Corvette Stingray Convertible. Isn't it sweet?"

"Whose is it?" she asked.

"Mine."

"What?" she gasped. "What happened to the Camaro?"

"I traded it in."

She paraded around the car, checking out every detail. "When did you do this?"

"I went in a couple weeks ago and looked at Corvettes. I customized all the accessories on this one and picked it up this afternoon."

Worried about the financial aspects of this, she questioned, "How much did you pay for this?"

"About sixty-thousand."

"For a car?" she said, sticker shocked. "That's extreme, don't you think?"

"New stage in my life, new car. With the trade-in and the down payment I made, my payments will be within my budget."

"How are you going to make payments on this? In case you forgot, you won't be working with Dr. Stephens anymore."

He explained, "That's the other thing I wanted to tell you. I received a phone call from a local OB by the name of Susan Wells. She's been looking for a medical student who's interested in specializing in Obstetrics to help out in her office. Apparently Dr. Stephens knows her and recommended me, so I went in and spoke with her this afternoon. She offered me a part-time job in her clinic."

"That's wonderful, Sweetie."

"It's perfect timing too. She'll work around my clinical schedule, and the pay is decent. This is going to be an incredible experience." He broke into a wide open smile as he pulled a set of keys out of his pocket. "You wanna go for a ride?"

"Yes."

He opened the passenger side door and she stepped inside, admiring the leather interior. "This is nice."

Randy sat in the driver's seat. "Wait 'til you hear the engine purr. This beauty has some massive power." He started the engine and let it rev. "Can you hear that?" he asked, loving the sound it made. This car was a beast.

Jane knew how much Randy loved sports cars. He collected models of them, read magazines about them, and researched them on the internet constantly. She enjoyed watching him play with his new toy. However, she figured a car with this kind of power was bound to suck down gas. "What kind of gas mileage does this get?"

"Eighteen city, twenty-six highway."

Just as she thought. "A gas guzzler."

"Hey, but for the power and the look of this baby, it's worth it." He slipped on his sunglasses and pulled away from the curb. This car rode smoothly, was extremely comfortable, and wow, the power it possessed. Randy might not have been Mario Andretti, but he sure felt like him now. He was in sports car heaven. "This car is so sweet. Jim and Bruce are gonna have a fit when they see this."

The opportunity to show them presented itself the following week when Randy invited both of them over to his place to watch the Lakers game. When Randy answered his door, Jim peered over his shoulder, admiring the Corvette parked outside. "Whose car is that?"

"Mine," Randy bragged.

"Shut the fuck up, liar."

"I'm not lying. I picked it up on Saturday."

"Holy shit." Jim bounded over to get a closer look at it.

Randy unlocked the doors to show off the leather interior.

Jim peeked under the hood at the horsepower this car bore. "Damn, Dude. This is sweet. Bet this baby can haul ass."

"Oh yeah."

Bruce pulled up in his truck and stepped out to join them. "Whoa, nice car. Where'd this come from?"

"Randy bought it," Jim said.

Bruce didn't believe him. "Bullshit."

"No shit, man. Check it out."

So Bruce did. He looked at every detail, from the intricate instrument panel to the engine. "Nice, man. What did Jane say when she saw it?"

Randy closed the hood. "She was surprised, but she likes it."

"Of course she does," Jim declared. "What babe wouldn't want a guy with a fancy ass sports car? Very sweet ride, Bro."

After gawking and admiring the shiny red beauty, the men went inside and got comfortable on the sofa with beer, chips and queso, and Oreos as the pre-game show came on.

"Hey, Bruce," Randy asked. "When you going to Pullman again?"

"Leaving Thursday night, actually. Gonna stay 'til Sunday."

"Steph said she wasn't coming home for spring break this year. Something about you guys going to Florida."

"Fort Lauderdale," Bruce replied. "Figured we'd spend some time together while I have a break. She talked about transferring down here for her senior year, but I don't know how I feel about that. I'll be busy with clinical training, and I'm not so sure I want that kind of distraction."

Jim took a sip of his beer. "You're still seein' Randy's sister?"

"Yes, I am."

"That's trippin'," Jim huffed, objecting to this arrangement.

"Why?"

"Because you're dickin' Randy's sister, that's why."

Randy openly laughed. "Why the hell do you care, Jim?"

"I'm surprised you don't," Jim argued. "Man, if one of you guys was sleepin' with my sister, I'd beat your ass."

"You don't even have a sister," Randy said. "Stephanie is an adult. She does whatever she wants. I'm sure as hell not going to interfere. I'd rather she was with Bruce then some psychopath who might get her pregnant. At least with Buckman I know she's safe." Randy gave Bruce the evil eye. "You are being safe I hope. 'Cause if you get my sister pregnant or give her an STD, I will beat your ass."

Bruce's mouth twisted wryly. "Yes, Sir."

Jim chimed in, "Since we're talkin' about vacations, what are your plans this summer, Randy?"

"Paris. Jane's coming too."

"Damn. Paris with your girlfriend? Better watch it, man."

"Why?" Randy asked.

"The city of love, the romance capital of the world. Don't get the nads to do somethin' stupid."

Randy didn't know what Jim was talking about. "Like what?"

"Like gettin' yourself married or some shit."

"I don't want to get married right now." As he thought about this more intently, being married to Jane was actually an alluring prospect. "Although…"

Jim warned, "See, there ya go, thinkin' crazy ass shit, and you're not even in Paris yet, Bro."

"I'm not gonna do anything crazy, Jim. I'm just going to spend some time with my family and my girlfriend in gay Paris."

"Speaking of which, where is Jane?" Bruce asked. "Haven't seen her around tonight."

"Practice," Randy replied. "They have playoffs tomorrow, Thursday, Friday, and maybe Saturday, depending on how they do. But she's done after that."

"You seem happy about that."

"This NCAA PAC-12 basketball schedule sucks from my point of view," Randy complained.

"But it was cool to see her on the court."

"It was. I love watching her play. She has a strong competitive spirit, but I'll be glad to have my girlfriend back."

"Have her back," Jim scoffed. "Whatever, Dude. You make it sound like you haven't seen her in years. She's over at your place every damn night."

"But basketball wears her out," Randy declared.

Jim laughed. "Oh, so she's too tired to have sex, in other words."

Randy's tone became hostile. "My relationship with Jane is not about sex. I have told you that a hundred times, Jackass."

"Maybe not, but sex is certainly involved."

"Why are you so hung up on the fact that I share a bed with my girlfriend?" Randy demanded to know. "Are you not getting any? Is that why you feel the need to snoop into my sex life, to satisfy your unresolved itch?"

"Shut up," Jim retorted.

"You are a cranky ass today."

Jim denied this accusation. "I'm not cranky."

"The hell you're not. Are you teething like Christopher is? 'Cause I can get you a chew toy."

Jim gave him a brutal and unfriendly stare.

"Seriously though," Randy said, sensing Jim's aggravation. "You ok?"

"Fuckin' Trina called me this morning," he replied.

"That would put me in a foul mood too. What the hell did she want?"

"Money."

"Screw that. Don't give the lying bitch a damn dime," Randy ordered.

"I'm not going to. But the fact that she had the gall to ask me really pisses me off. Why doesn't she ask her lover for money and get schwag from him?"

"Did you tell her that?" Randy wondered.

"Hell yeah, I told her that. Then she got all pissy and started yellin' at me about how, since I'm gonna be a doctor and all, I can afford to spare some dinero for her. She seems to think I owe her that."

"You don't owe her shit."

"That's what I told her."

Randy was glad to hear that.

"You should change your cellphone number so she can't call you anymore," Bruce suggested. "Otherwise she's gonna hound you about money 'til your balls turn blue. And if you give her any, she'll just ask for more, and she'll never be satisfied until she's sucked you dry. She's a fuckin' gold digger. Don't give her shit, man. She doesn't deserve it."

"That's true," Randy added. "And the more you make, the more she'll ask for."

"I hate money grubbing bimbos," Bruce said. "Gold diggers like that won't say two words to you until they find out you're a doctor, then they go ape shit and hang all over you. Do they really think we can't see right through them?"

Randy laughed at his cynical attitude. "I don't know."

Chapter Forty-Three

Randy worked about thirty hours a week in Dr. Stephen's clinic training the new assistant and helping the doctor wrap things up before he left to start his new position with Dr. Wells. Since basketball season was over, Jane's schedule wasn't as full, which allowed them more time together in the evenings. It was a welcome change.

Wednesday was Jane's birthday, and since she didn't have to be in the gym at 7:00 A.M., Randy made her breakfast in bed. He put on a pot of coffee then sliced up a cantaloupe and put it in a bowl. While he waited for the coffee to brew, he poached an egg for Jane and toasted her a whole wheat English muffin. Then he placed it all on a silver serving tray with a glass of milk and a single red rose. He brought the tray into the bedroom and set it on the bedside table. "Janey," he said, leaning forward to kiss her cheek.

She stirred a little.

He called to her again, "Jane, Honey, wake up."

She opened her eyes. "Hey."

"Good morning, beautiful. Happy birthday."

She sat up and stretched. "Thank you."

"I made you breakfast."

She inspected the contents of the food tray. "Looks delicious."

"Wanna watch cartoons or something while you eat?" He handed her the remote to the TV in his bedroom.

"Thank you."

"I'm gonna grab a cup of coffee. Enjoy your breakfast." He kissed her softly on the lips then returned to the kitchen. When he came back, he had a steaming mug in his hand.

"Daddy wants us to come over for cake and ice cream this afternoon."

"Alright," he agreed. "As long as I get to take you out to dinner."

"Where are we going for dinner?" she asked curiously.

"I know how much you love Chinese food. A new Xian-style restaurant just opened up not far from here. I thought we'd check it out."

"Ooh," she said with a smile. "Yummy."

"Meet me after work. I get off at 3:00. We can go right after."

"Sounds good."

That evening, while Randy was getting dressed for dinner, he stopped and watched Jane for a moment. She stepped into a pair of black pants then pulled a short sleeved light blue sweater over her head. Her pretty black sandals showed off her toes, but she hadn't put on any makeup or jewelry, other than the diamond and sapphire ring he had given her. He snuck up behind her and brushed his lips across her neck. "Why do you always dress like that when we go to see your dad? He's not stupid, you know. He knows damn well this is not your normal attire."

"What's wrong with the way I'm dressed?"

"There's nothing wrong with it, it's just more conservative than what you usually wear. It's missing something though." He opened a dresser drawer and pulled out a small box wrapped in purple metallic paper. "Here."

She took the box from him and peeled off the paper. Inside was a teardrop-shaped black sapphire solitaire pendant on a long gold chain. A pair of matching gemstone earrings sparkled in the box with it. "These are beautiful."

"Put them on."

Jane shook her head. "Daddy doesn't like it when I wear jewelry."

457

Randy pulled the necklace from the box and latched it around her neck. "There is no way your father can object to the way you look. You're elegant, sophisticated. I love this look."

"You do?"

"Yes. I think you look much more beautiful when you dress less scantily."

Normally men loved the revealing clothing she wore. She found it hard to believe that Randy preferred she didn't dress like that. "I thought you liked the way I dress."

"I do like it. You have an amazing body and should feel free to show it off. But in all honesty, Honey, I much prefer the more delicate nuance over the sexy look. It really accentuates how beautiful you are."

She put her arms around him, thankful that he was always so honest with her. "Thank you, Sweetie."

He kissed her softly on the lips. "You should wear your hair up tonight."

She pulled the sides of her hair back and held it in place with a clip. Then she put the earrings in her ears and checked her reflection in the mirror.

Randy stood behind her, compelled by her beauty. "Perfect. You ready?"

With a bob of her head, she said, "Uh huh."

"Cake and ice cream on the way."

The visit with Jane's father was surprisingly civil. Randy, Jane, and Dale had a pleasant conversation, and Randy even held Jane's hand without ice-piercing daggers being thrown his direction. Her father admired the jewelry Jane wore. When Jane told him Randy gave it to her, he acknowledged Randy with a smile of acceptance. Most young men his daughter dated were never willing to give her gifts of that value, if they even took the time to give her anything at all.

Randy and Jane had been together for over a year and a half now, which showed Dale that Randy was committed to his daughter. Right from the start Randy professed his love for Jane. Perhaps he had been telling the truth all along. As Dale thought about this and other things Randy had said and done, he realized that the young man his daughter was involved with was not the selfish shirker he originally took him for.

"Are you parents coming down for graduation, Randy?" Dale asked him.

"Yes, Sir. My entire family is flying down."

"I would love to meet your parents."

"I can definitely arrange that."

When Jane and Randy were ready to leave, Dale walked them out. He stopped short when he saw Randy's car new parked in the driveway. "You bought a Corvette."

"Yes, Sir." Randy and Dale had a conversation about the car, and Randy let him take a peek under the hood. Then, much to Jane's surprise, Randy handed Dale the keys. "You wanna take it for a spin?"

A look of pure joy filled Dale Davine's face. "I would love to."

Randy sat in the passenger's seat and let Dale take over the wheel.

The men were gone for quite a while before they pulled back into the driveway. Dale positively beamed as he stepped out of the car and returned the keys to Randy. "That is a magnificent vehicle."

"Yes it is," Randy replied.

"I've always loved Corvettes."

"Me too. So I decided what the hell and bought one. I'm happy with it."

Jane stood by Randy's side and put her arm around him.

Randy curved his arm around her shoulders and kissed the top of her head. "We have to get going, Baby. Birthday dinner awaits."

Then, unexpectedly, Dale extended his arm to shake Randy's hand. This was something he had not done in a long time. "Thank you for coming, Randy. I enjoyed our conversation."

"Thank you for your hospitality, Sir."

Dale reverted his attention back to Jane. "Happy birthday, Sweetheart."

Jane hugged her father tightly and bid him farewell. "Thank you, Daddy. I'll call you this weekend."

Randy pulled out of the driveway with the top down. As they cruised through the city, Jane gazed at him with loving eyes.

The way she gawked at him brought a sense of uncertainty. "What did I do that's making you gawp at me like that?"

"You let Daddy drive your car."

"He likes cars. I thought it seemed appropriate."

She still found this hard to believe. He never let anyone drive his car except her. "But that's your new sports car and you let Daddy drive it." She reached over and held his hand. She loved how hard he tried to gain her father's acceptance. "You have no idea how much something like that means to Daddy."

"I'm trying, Baby."

"I know you are," she commended. "And I'm proud of you for that."

"He seems a bit more trusting of me, now that I'm starting my clinical training. Guess he figured I wasn't serious about med school."

"I don't know," Jane responded. "But whatever you did, it made him happy. He shook your hand, Randy."

Randy grinned. "I noticed that."

"Oh my god. This is so cool."

"And did you see his reaction when you told him about graduate school?"

"He was thrilled."

"Yes he was. We are definitely making progress." At a red light, he leaned over and kissed her. "I love you."

"I love you too."

He winked at her and fiddled with the radio dial before the light turned green.

Chapter Forty-Four

Randy and Jane's flight to Seattle was scheduled to leave at 5:20 P.M. They would land in the emerald city around seven o'clock that night. When they arrived at the airport, Randy parked in long term parking then he and Jane headed to the terminal to check in. They stopped at Starbucks to grab a cup of coffee before they made their way through security.

"It was nice to pack a suitcase and leave with you for a change," Randy said.

"Yes it was. I am so ready for a break. This year has been rough."

"You've been traveling all over the country and playing your heart out, Honey. You deserve some relaxing time off. I know I've enjoyed the last three weeks," he claimed, feeling refreshed after spending a huge chunk of time away from the stress of school.

"I bet you have."

"I'm looking forward to my clerkship though. And the cool thing is, since I opted for the fifth year, I automatically get twelve weeks off during my clinical training. The non-JMP people only get three. I'm taking one of those weeks to go to Paris."

"What rotation are you doing first?" Jane asked, trying to get a better handle on Randy's schedule.

"Next week is orientation, training seminars and such. But after that, my first core block is right up your alley."

"Why is that?"

"Four weeks of Neurology and four weeks of Psychiatry," he said. "Then I'm off for a week before I start the next rotation. Dr. Wells is gonna put me to work in her clinic full time during that week."

"Psychiatry I could do, but Neurology sounds complicated."

"Very intricate," Randy clarified. "Not really my thing, but Bruce is into Neurology. He's really leaning towards Neurosurgery as his specialty."

"Wow. That's complex."

"Yes it is," Randy replied. "He excels at it though. Bruce is the master of the human brain. He knows its anatomy and delicate workings inside and out."

"What about Mandy?"

"Pediatrics. And Jim loves the action in the ER, all that trauma shit." He gulped down the last of his coffee. "You know, considering all the crap he's been through over the last couple years, he's done an amazing job. His grades were better this term. He managed to make a 3.8 while being a single dad with a baby in the house. I'm impressed. I don't know if I could have done that with a pregnant girlfriend, a bad break up, and a custody and paternity suit. I'm proud of him."

"He's been through a lot."

"That he has. Jill's been good for him. I like her. She's supportive and goes out of her way to help him. But you know what I really like about her? She doesn't treat him like crap," Randy bluntly stated. "She understands the life of a physician in training because she's around them all day and knows what he's going through. And she helps him with Christopher. A lot of women would have been turned off by a twenty-five-year-old single medical student with a baby. That's not an easy undertaking."

"But she's single and has a child too, so she can relate to him," Jane reminded him.

"Which is good. Those two have some kind of family thing going on. Jim loves it. I've never seen him so happy."

When their boarding call sounded, they each grabbed their carry-on and headed to the gate. Once they claimed their seats, Randy leaned back in his chair, relaxing. "You know what just dawned on me?"

"What?"

"I'm celebrating my birthday with my parents this year. That hasn't happened in years."

"And it's your twenty-fifth one too," she reminded him.

"Yup. I can't wait to see them."

Both of Randy's parents met him and Jane at the airport baggage claim. The moment Randy spotted them, he took long, purposeful strides toward them. "There they are," he said to Jane. He greeted them both with a hug.

"Hello, Son. How was your flight?"

"Flight was good." Randy reached into his carry-on and pulled out the letter he received from Alpha Omega Alpha. He handed it to his dad. "Read this."

Mark put on his reading glasses and unfolded the letter while Jane and Randy stepped up to the baggage claim carousel to get their luggage. While he read, his eyebrows raised inquiringly. "Well, I'll be damned."

Ellen Hanson studied her husband's face. "What is it, Mark?"

"Alpha Omega Alpha, Ellie."

She stared at him, astonished. "Who? Randy?"

"Yes. Randy."

She snatched the letter from him and read it for herself. Her mouth gaped open and tears of joy filled her eyes. "My Randy is in Alpha Omega Alpha?"

"That's what this letter says." Mark's glance turned to Randy, who stood at the baggage carousel with his arm around Jane. "That kid. Where the hell did he get his dedication from?"

"From growing up watching the dedication his father has," Ellen declared, matter-of-factly.

Mark's face brightened at that suggestion.

"It's true. He's always admired you, Mark. When he was little, he ran around in your lab coat and played doctor. When he was ten, he found one of your medical books and became enthralled by it. He wouldn't put it down. He read what he could and was fascinated by the pictures. He watched those medical science programs on the Discovery Channel, he was a member of HOSA in high school. He's been following in your footsteps since he was a little boy."

"I can't wait to see what that kid can do." Words couldn't begin to describe how proud Mark was. He stood in the baggage claim holding the letter in his hand, staring at Randy.

Randy and Jane rejoined his parents, both wheeling a suitcase behind them. "Did you read that?" Randy asked his dad.

"Yes I did. You never cease to amaze me, Son. That is a remarkable accomplishment."

"Remember that pre-graduation banquet I told you about?"

"Yes."

"I've been asked to give a speech, so you get to listen to me babble over dinner that night."

"Oh good. I'll take pictures."

"Please don't," Randy begged. He took the letter back from his dad and returned it to his pocket.

"You should save that letter," his father advised.

"I have a certificate."

"Good. Frame it. Display it on the wall in your office along with your M.D. and Medical License. Let your patients see that."

Randy didn't see the point in this. "Why?"

"Because people like to know their doctor is the best."

Randy laughed. "I am far from being the best, Dad. You're the best."

"I just have more experience. I've been doing this for twenty-seven years. But I wasn't as good as you when I started my clinical training. You have the potential to be the best, Randy. Once you finish your training and establish yourself during your residency, I guarantee word will get out. Already there are people up here who have heard about you."

"Who?" Randy wondered.

"Ian Strombolt. He's a local surgeon and a colleague of mine. He's also Pete Stephens' friend."

Randy was unaware that his former boss had connections in Seattle. "Dr. Stephens?"

"Yes. He speaks very highly of you, and apparently he talks about you all the time."

This was interesting information. "He does?"

"That's what I hear. Your reputation precedes you, Son, and that reputation will spread quickly."

Randy had a hard time sleeping. A particular comment his father made at the airport really got to him. He couldn't get the thought out of his mind. In the morning, when he heard his parents upstairs, he crept out of bed and joined them at the kitchen table.

"Good morning, Randy," Mark Hanson said, gripping his coffee mug.

"Dad, I need to talk to you."

"About what?"

Randy spit it out. "I need to know that you haven't been using your medical connections to influence people on my behalf."

Ellen's jaw dropped at this insane accusation. "Jonathan Randal Hanson! How dare you accuse your father of that!"

"No, Ellen. It's alright," Mark interjected, understanding his son's concern. "Randy, I have never and would never do that. It is unprofessional and unethical. I don't know what kind of influence you seem to think I have, but I don't have that kind of power. The only person who has made any kind of influence on anyone is you."

"I don't want people to think that I'm making it through this because of my dad's connections in the medical community."

"No one thinks that, and you shouldn't either. You know damn well that medical school doesn't work that way. If you don't make the cut, you are out, and they don't care who you are or who you know."

Randy stepped over to the coffee pot and made himself a cup. "I don't deserve all this."

"You've worked hard for your achievements. Someone recognized your talent and told the right people. I don't see why you're upset about this. I would have given anything to be initiated into Alpha Omega Alpha at your age."

"I feel like all of these honors and awards I've received are unwarranted. Why was I chosen for Alpha Omega, and why do they want me to make this speech at the banquet?" Randy questioned.

Randy's nerves were getting the best of him, and Mark recognized it. "Is that what this is about? The speech you have to make?"

"I don't know." Randy sipped on his coffee. "What the hell am I supposed to say? I don't even know where to start, and I only have four weeks to figure it out."

"You did minor in Communications, didn't you?" Mark reminded his son.

"Yes."

"Then utilize those skills. You are bright, Randy. You'll think of something."

"Like what?"

"If someone else was standing up there giving you a speech the night before you received your Medical Science degree, what would you want to hear?"

Randy couldn't think of anything. "I have no idea. I am not good at this kind of thing."

"You are very good at this kind of thing," his father corrected. "Quit second guessing yourself. You'll be fine."

"I'm going to say something stupid and make a complete fool of myself in front of my friends, my professors, and other people's parents," Randy feared.

"No you won't," Mark encouraged. "You are way too hard on yourself."

"Jane tells me that all the time."

"My son, the perfectionist. Where did you get that from?" Mark looked at his wife with an accusing smile.

Ellen put her hands on her hips and dropped her jaw. "I am not."

"Oh yes you are," Mark reiterated. "And you've rubbed off on our son."

"I did not."

Randy agreed with his father. "It's ok, Mom. I love you for it. You always expect nothing but the best from me, and I appreciate that."

"Your father's right though," she said. "You need to relax and do your best. You did fine on your valedictorian speech in high school."

"That was high school, Mom. This is medical school. And in high school I didn't care if my speech was lame. I wasn't trying to impress anyone. But here it matters. These are my fellow medical colleagues."

"Quit worrying. You'll do fine. You always do."

Later that afternoon, following a tour of the Lake Washington's floating houses and lakeside mansions, Randy sat downstairs watching TV while Jane searched for a letter she received from the Psychology department. She paused briefly to see what he was watching, confused by the show's content. "What is this?"

"A medical show about abnormal serum sodium levels."

"I won't even ask what that is." Jane sat beside him with the letter in her hand.

"What's that?" he asked.

"Graduate school information. I need to sign up for fall classes when we get back." She flipped through the pages while Randy focused his attention back to the show he was watching. "Randy?"

"Hmm?"

"After graduation I won't be able to live at Alpha anymore. Only undergrads can live there."

He heard what she said, but wasn't really listening.

"I'm trying to figure out what to do. Daddy wants me to move back in with him."

She now had his full attention, and he didn't like what she said. "That is a very, very bad idea."

"My only other option is to get an apartment. Lisa and I looked at one together, but they want two months' advance rent. I wanted to get a part time job anyway, but working enough hours to pay rent and utilities while I'm trying to go to graduate school is going to be next to impossible. And since I don't have a car, I have no way of commuting unless I take the bus. It's hard to find apartments close enough to campus to walk. What should I do?"

"I don't think you should move back in with your dad."

"So you think I should get an apartment?"

"You don't have to spend money on an apartment either when you already have one at your disposal," he suggested.

She didn't catch his drift.

"Move in with me." He had never said this to a woman before, but the thought of sharing an apartment with Jane allured him.

"Randy."

He sensed her apprehension and tried to make his argument solid so there would be no way she could dispute it. "Look, Honey, you're at my place almost every night anyway. My apartment is close to campus, and you'll be able to walk to class. I'm ready to take this step in our relationship. I wanna be with you all the time, not just in the evenings for pizza and basketball or for nights of romance and passion. I wanna share my closet, my bathroom, and all my bad habits with you. I wanna fall asleep in your arms every night and wake up next to you every morning." Now that he'd stated his argument, he took her by the hand and said, "Move in with me."

This commitment scared her, but at the same time she was glad he felt so strongly about their relationship to open up his home to her. Obviously he was serious about her. She stared at him for a minute, unsure what to say.

With her silence, Randy feared he pushed their relationship too far forward. He hoped he hadn't screwed up by suggesting this. "Awfully quiet over there, Babe. What are you thinking?"

As much as she wanted to take that step with Randy, her father posed a problem. "What about Daddy?"

"What about him?" Randy refuted.

"He won't approve."

"So what? I thought he didn't control your life?" he countered.

"He doesn't but…" she stopped in mid-thought.

"But what?"

"What am I supposed to tell him?"

"Tell him the truth. Tell him I offered and you said yes. You are agreeing to this I hope."

"Yes."

Overjoyed with her response, Randy embraced her tightly, found her mouth, and kissed her.

They discussed this arrangement in detail and Jane decided she wouldn't even wait until after graduation. She would move in with him as soon as they returned to Berkeley.

The next morning, while Jane was in the shower, Randy shared a cup of coffee with his dad, discussing how abnormal serum sodium levels might affect prenatal health. In the middle of the conversation, he rather abruptly blurted out, "Jane's moving in with me."

Dr. Hanson almost choked on his coffee. "What?"

Randy figured his parents might not approve of this decision, but that was not quite the reaction he expected. "Jane's moving in with me."

"I heard you the first time." Mark set his coffee cup down and cleared his throat. "This is a little sudden, isn't it?"

"No, I don't think so. We've been together for almost two years. I'm ready to boost our relationship up a notch, and so is she."

"But moving in together, Randy? That's a huge step," his dad questioned.

"Yes. I am aware of that."

His mom overheard the conversation and offered her thoughts. "Are you sure about this?"

"Yes. I'm sure. What's the big deal?"

"The big deal is you'll be living together. That's a huge commitment, Randy. You'll be sharing living expenses, personal space…" his mother warned.

Randy tried to defend his argument. "She can't stay at her sorority house after graduation, and it's dumb for her to have to spend money on an apartment when living with me would be easier and more convenient for both of us. You always told me you wished I'd get involved in a serious, committed relationship, didn't you?"

"Yes, but this isn't what I had in mind."

"And what did you have in mind, a marriage proposal?"

Mark objected to his son's obstinacy. "Randy, that's not necessary. Watch your tone."

He upheld his argument. "Isn't marriage and even bigger commitment? I'm not legally tied to anything this way."

Though Ellen didn't respond, the expression on her face spoke volumes.

"Jane and I are serious, and we're committed."

"Randy," Mark cut in. "Don't jump into anything so deep that you drown in it. You are still in medical school."

"I know that. And Jane has been right by my side through it all. I'll be making good money with Dr. Wells, and Jane's going to get a part time job. We'll be fine. We'll support each other."

"It's not the financial aspects I'm concerned about," Mark confirmed. "It's the emotional ones. She can't just go home if you need space or if you disagree. She will be living there with you, whether times are good or bad. Things can get cramped quickly if you're not careful. Be certain that you know what you're getting yourself into."

"I know what I'm getting into," Randy maintained.

"Don't do it for the wrong reasons, and don't do anything you will later regret."

"It sounds like you don't trust me." Randy tightened his lips, a bit perturbed that his parents didn't support his decision.

"Neither one of us said that. We do trust you."

"You're not acting like it."

"Just be careful is all we're saying," Mark said.

"I know, Dad. We will."

While Jane and Mrs. Hanson went shopping to get a cake for Randy's birthday, Randy went fishing with his dad. Mark watched intently as his oldest son reeled in a catch and removed the hook from the fish's mouth. Randy's earlier behavior, along with his argumentative tone, baffled him. "Randal, what's going through your head?"

"What do you mean?"

"You know damn well what I mean. What's up with this sudden decision to have Jane move in with you?"

Randy baited his hook again and recast his line. No matter how ridiculous something sounded, Randy had always been able to talk to his dad. His father lent him an understanding ear and did his best to offer advice when he asked for it. But right now, Randy was tormented by mixed emotions. Some of the thoughts going through his head were muffled and didn't make any sense. He knew his dad would understand if he opened up and talked about it, but he wasn't really sure how to disentangle the mess in his head. "I know what you're thinking, Dad."

"You have no idea what I'm thinking. But I would like to know what you're thinking."

"I've been wanting to ask you something, but it's a stupid question."

"Doubtful. Fire away."

Randy opened up. "How did you know Mom was the one?"

Mark understood now why his son was troubled. Randy was a sworn bachelor, but since he'd been with Jane, thoughts of commitment, long-term commitment, weighed heavily on Randy's mind. "That's an interesting question, and I'm not sure how to answer it."

"I mean, was there a sign, or something she did or said? What was it?"

"It was a combination of things," Mark tried to explain. "The same things that attract me to her now, the same things that keep me here."

"Like what?" Randy wanted to know.

His father began, "Like the way she looks at me. The way I feel when I'm around her. The way your mother and I are able to talk and understand each other. The way she supports me and my career. It's the little things she does, like rub my feet when I've had a hard day or bring me a cup of coffee when I have a 2:00 A.M. page. The way she seems to know what I'm thinking and I don't have to say anything. Your mother is my best friend, Randy. She is a person I can always depend on and a person I know will always be there even when times are tough. We work as a team. It wasn't one particular thing that attracted me to her. I just knew she was the one."

A lump formed in his throat because he came to the realization that the way his father described his mother was the same way he felt about Jane. "How can I be sure I've found her?"

"Only your heart can tell you that. No one can spell it out for you. It's not like an illness. There are no signs or symptoms."

A war of emotions raged within him. He had to fight to control them. "I'm getting a little freaked out."

"About what?"

"The thoughts and feelings I have. I look at Jane now and honestly can't picture my life without her in it."

Mark understood. "And that scares you."

"It scares the hell out of me. I used to be gung ho about school and my career simply for the sake of my pride and proving to the world that I was the best. But it's different now. It's not just about me anymore. My motivation has changed. I want to be successful so Jane and I can have a good life together. It's gone beyond my pride. I've swallowed my pride. It's come down to wanting to provide a future for Jane."

Mark understood completely what his son was going through. "You're getting thoughts of marriage, aren't you?"

His mind reeled with confusion. "Yes. And it scares me."

"It happens to every man at some point."

"But I don't want to make a mistake and think I've found her when I haven't," Randy tried to rationalize.

"There you go, worrying again."

"I don't want to marry her then come to find out later that we're really not compatible. And what if we aren't following the same dream? What is she finds out she hates being a doctor's wife? Our perfect marriage turns sour and we end up getting mad at each other and fighting all the time then we both end up miserable and our life turns into a living hell."

"Randy," his father interjected. "Stop it. For one thing, you are getting worked up over circumstances that are unlikely to happen between you and Jane. Also, there's no such thing as a perfect marriage. There never has been and never will be. A relationship between a husband and wife encounters bumps in the road occasionally. Is Jane a woman who will make sacrifices for you and someone you are willing to make sacrifices for in order to reach a compromise and make your relationship work?"

"We already do that," Randy said. "But I want to be certain, and that's what I was trying to tell you and Mom this morning. Yes, I admit, I am getting thoughts of marriage. I've been thinking about it a lot lately. But I need to know that Jane and I can live together, and even when the apartment feels cramped, that we can talk and work things out. Because I agree with you, that is extremely important. Which is why I have asked Jane to move in with me."

473

"I understand."

"I'm sorry I snapped at Mom this morning, but I am really freaked out about the way I feel right now. I know Mom wants me to get married, but I don't want to be pressured by her or anyone else. I need to know it's real. For my own peace of mind, I need to know I'm making the right decision. You can't tell Mom we had this discussion, please. You know what she'll do if she knows I'm getting thoughts of marriage."

Mark chuckled. "Oh yes. She'll never leave you alone about it."

"Which is why I didn't bring it up at breakfast. I need some time to sort this out and make sure. But if Mom knows, she'll pressure me."

"I know. I won't say a word until you're ready," Dr. Hanson promised.

"Thank you."

Randy had a fabulous birthday with Jane and his parents. They spent the day at the aquarium then took him out to dinner. Upon returning home, they ate cake and watched him open his gifts. From his parents, he received a new stethoscope and a check for five-hundred dollars. Jane presented him with two boxes, one larger than the other. In the larger box was a Spalding basketball with Kobe Bryant's autograph on it, which was obviously rare. The smaller box contained a die-cast mini-replica of a Chevy Belair, decorated in the Los Angeles Lakers colors and designed with the team graphics. Jane knew him well and had managed to find a gift that consisted of two things he loved, cars and the Lakers.

That night, as they prepared for bed, Randy asked her about this rare gift. "Where the hell did you get that basketball?"

"When we went down to L.A. for our game against UCLA, we had a practice session at Staples Center. Kobe was there and he signed it for me."

"Are you shitting me?" Randy's jaw dropped. "You met Kobe Bryant?"

"Yup."

"And you never told me about this?"

"I couldn't very well tell you if I was planning on giving it to you for your birthday, now could I?" she declared.

"Holy shit. That is incredible. He signed this personally?"

"Yup," she said with a big grin.

"Well, thank you. That is the coolest gift anyone has ever given me."

She leaned over and gave him a kiss. "Happy birthday, Sweetie."

"Thanks."

Chapter Forty-Five

When Jane and Randy returned to San Francisco Saturday afternoon, Randy drove over the Bay Bridge to get to Berkeley. "Take me up to Alpha," Jane said. "I want to pack some boxes this afternoon and move everything down to your place tomorrow while you guys are studying."

"If that's what you want to do." The more they talked about the new adventure they were about to engage in, the more excited Randy became. "Are you going to need my car to haul things?"

"I might."

"I'll leave the keys on the table for you then."

Even though Randy and his friends didn't have any classes right now, they still met every week to go over information for the second part of their Medical Licensing Exam. They reviewed old notes, and Randy purchased several MLE study guides to help them prepare. He brought these, along with old First Aid books, to the UCB Student Union Building. He arrived Sunday morning, several minutes before their scheduled 9:00 A.M. meeting time, smiling widely and whistling a happy tune.

Jim looked up from tying his shoelaces. "You are far too cheerful this morning, Bro. What are you so stoked about?"

"First off, I'm in love with the most incredible woman in the entire world. Secondly, her dad has decided I'm not an asshole. And third, Jane is moving all of her stuff down to my apartment as we speak."

Jim had to make sure he heard him correctly. "She's movin' in with you? Are you serious?"

"Yup," Randy confirmed.

Bruce added his two cents worth. "That's a pretty serious step, Randy."

"I know that."

Jim chuckled with a dry, cynical laugh. "How the hell did you talk her into shackin' up with you?"

"What makes you think I had to talk her into it? I simply offered the invitation; she took me up on it."

"Oh," Jim teased. "That simple, huh?"

"Yup," Randy replied with a smug grin.

Mandy walked in with a bakery box in her hands. "Hey, guys. I brought doughnuts." She set it down on the table.

Randy reached in and grabbed a glazed one.

The table was far too quiet for Mandy's liking. "You guys were talking about me again, weren't you?"

"No, we weren't," Jim said. "We were talkin' about Randy."

"What about him?"

"His girlfriend is movin' in with him."

Mandy gasped. "Oh my god, Randy, that is so cool!"

He couldn't have agreed more.

When Randy returned home that afternoon, he walked in to find boxes spread out all over the floor. Treading through the obstacle course, he put his book bag down and made his way to the kitchen to grab something to eat.

About a half hour later, Jane arrived with clothes-filled hangers in her hand. She had to dodge cardboard barriers to get to the table to give Randy a kiss. "I got all of my stuff moved down here."

"Yes, I can see that. You've been busy, haven't you?" He peered at the cardboard boxes lying around, dying to know what mysteries hid deep within them. "What's in all these?"

"My teddy bear collection, my basketball equipment, shoes, books…all my stuff."

"I cleaned out three dresser drawers and made room in the closet for you," he said.

"I know. I filled them already, and already used all the closet space."

He wrinkled his forehead, amazed that she had managed to occupy so much space in such a short amount of time. "You used all that closet space?"

"Uh huh. And I still have more clothes I need to hang up."

He laughed at the overwhelming size of her wardrobe. "There's a closet in the other bedroom you can use if you need more room. All that's in there are suitcases and my old high school letter jacket, but I can move them."

"You lettered in high school?"

"Yup."

He had never mentioned this to her before. "In what?"

"Basketball. Lake Washington High School. Home of the Kangaroos. Played on the varsity team my Junior and Senior year."

"What position?" she asked, curious now about his basketball playing history.

"Shooting guard."

"You didn't tell me you played basketball in high school."

"You never asked." The multitude of boxes in his apartment was a bit overwhelming. He hoped he had room for all her belongings. "What are we going to do with all these boxes?"

"I have more at Daddy's."

More? How could she possibly have more? "Ok, and when were you planning on getting those?"

"Tomorrow night maybe," she suggested.

"I have orientation tomorrow," he reminded her. "I probably won't be home 'til five or six."

"And I have class 'til three. But maybe we can stop by when you get home and get something to eat after." Talking about food made her want some. "Speaking of which. I'm hungry."

There she goes. Her stomach was taking control again. "Are you sure you don't have some sort of alien parasite hosting off of you?"

"I'm an athlete, Randy. I have a high metabolism."

"I know, Baby. I'm messing with you."

While Jane grabbed herself a snack, Randy picked up the millions of clothes she had draped across the bed and carried them across the hall to the closet in the other room.

Randy, Bruce, Mandy, and Jim met at UCSF Medical Center and piled into a room with forty-two other Berkeley and UCSF medical students. They listened to a lecture about clerkship guidelines and requirements, reviewed schedules and grading procedures, then read through a medical ethics document.

Their duties included examining patients, writing admission orders, and performing procedures such as blood draws, IV's, and lumbar punctures. They also had to check vital signs, analyze laboratory results, and review nurses' notes. Throughout all of this, daily SOAP notes were required, which reported subjective and objective findings. Once these notes were collected, an assessment and plan for treatment was formulated. Each medical student would present these detailed notes to colleagues during pre-rounds.

Grades were given on a pass/fail basis. Occasionally, the honors grade was awarded to students who demonstrated outstanding performance on all aspects of their clerkship, including clinical knowledge, clinical skills, and professional and personal attributes. To earn honors, students needed to be judged as 'outstanding' or 'superior' by all of their supervising faculty and residents. Honors recognition was limited to twenty-five percent of students who took each core clerkship. Randy was determined to be one of them.

After the initial introduction and a talk about appropriate cellphone use, they all received a grand tour of the hospital. Since Jim worked there as an orderly and already knew his way around, he thought this was a waste of time. "And this is the medical supply room," he whispered to Randy in the middle of their tour. "And now we are approaching the Emergency Medical facilities of the hospital."

"Ssh, you're distracting me," Randy complained.

Jim rolled his eyes. "This is lame. I already know my way around this place."

"Well some of us don't, so hush."

They walked past the Emergency Room to the elevator. Jim had long ago lost interest in the tour guide and now scanned the entire ER, hoping to catch a glimpse of Jill. He frowned when he didn't see her.

After the tour, they all attended a seminar about infectious diseases, blood-borne pathogens, and the proper use of latex gloves. To Jim, this was pointless and ridiculously mind-numbing. He didn't see why the university was wasting its time telling post-Master's Degree medical students something they should have already known. He hoped the rest of the day would be better than the morning had been.

Jim, Mandy, Bruce, and Randy met downstairs at the hospital cafeteria to grab some lunch together. Randy expressed his opinion of their first few hours. "If this afternoon is anything like this morning was, it is going to be a very long day. They told us about all the requirements we have, but dammit, I want to see some action. And who the hell was that guy? He has got to be the most boring speaker I've ever heard. Talk about monotone. I think everyone in the room was falling asleep."

Jim agreed. "I hear ya, Bro."

"I'm gonna need a strong cup of coffee after that."

Bruce yawned as he made his way to the table. "Holy crap that guy was drab."

"Jim and I were just saying that."

Mandy walked over to the table, frazzled. "Oh my god. Think they have enough for us to do? There goes my social life."

"What social life?" Jim asked. "I wasn't aware that you had one."

"Shut up," she snapped. "And what was up with the latex glove demonstration? Do they think we are a bunch of morons or something?"

"Apparently." Randy looked at his watch. "I'm gonna step outside and give Jane a call. I'll be right back."

The afternoon session was much better than the morning. They read and signed the Computer Security and Use Statement, were trained on the use of the Clinical Display System/Patient Information Database, then they all received laminated CDS cards. They went over information about the Health Insurance Portability and Accountability Act, were given a link to the on-line required reading of *The Clinical Guide: A Guide to the Clinical Years*, and received a copy of *General Guide to Writing Prescriptions*.

By the time Randy arrived home that evening, he was drained. He draped his lab coat over the back of a chair and skimmed through the mail on the table. "Hey, Baby. I'm home."

Jane stepped out of the kitchen and greeted him with a kiss. "How was your first day?"

"We had a ton of information crammed into our heads today. I am going to be busier than hell."

"Isn't that what you wanted?" Jane reminded him.

"Yes, but I want to get my hands into the action."

His comment amused her. "They aren't going to let you jump right in without some kind of orientation."

"I know, but after hearing about everything we're going to do, this is gonna be blast. I can't wait to get started."

"Are you going with me to Daddy's to get the rest of my stuff?"

"Have you told him you've moved in with me?" He hoped she had at least mentioned it.

"I was going to tell him tonight."

"So you haven't told him yet?"

"No."

"Great," he scorned. "Is he expecting us?"

"No."

"Have you at least called to see if he's home?"

"He'll be home," Jane assumed.

Randy was uncomfortable with the idea of dropping this news on Dale Davine tonight. This information probably wasn't going to go over too well. "He's gonna be pissed, isn't he?"

"Probably."

That's what he feared. "Let's get it over with."

As Randy suspected, Jane's dad was furious when she told him she opted to move in with Randy instead of him. He became even more indignant when she told him that she had come home for the rest of her belongings.

She went into her former bedroom and grabbed a box of yearbooks and school pictures. She filled another with family memorabilia, photo albums, and her old basketball uniforms, then she packed up all of her basketball trophies, newspaper articles, and awards. She placed all of these items in the trunk of Randy's car.

"I don't approve of this, Jane," her father griped.

"I know, and I'm sorry you're upset. But I need to live my own life."

All Randy wanted to do was go home. He had some required reading to complete and wanted to relax for a few hours before returning to another busy day of training. Hoping for a quick retreat, he said, "We have to go, Honey."

Jane hugged her father, bidding him farewell. "I love you, Daddy. I hope you can support my decision."

Despite the fact that Dale was angry, he remained gracious. "I'll try."

Randy and Jane returned home around seven o'clock that evening. Jane prepared dinner, and Randy logged on to his required reading: *The Nerd's Guide to Pre-Rounding*. This title amused him, but as he began reading, he actually found the information helpful.

The months ahead were going to be stressful, and Jane's understanding and support would be especially important. After dinner, Randy sat down with her and talked about the things he would be doing and the hours and expectations required of him. He explained his work hours with Dr. Wells and the time he would need to set aside for research, hoping she would gain a full understanding of his upcoming schedule.

He was going to busy, but she was excited about the work he was doing. As always, she was supportive and promised she would do her best to help him adjust to his new schedule.

The next evening, following a day full of seminars, training sessions, and a brief orientation with Dr. Wells, Randy strode into his apartment with his white lab coat and stethoscope in his hand. Jane was sitting on the floor staring at piece of paper. Curious, he set his supplies on the table and sat on the floor with her. "Whatcha looking at?"

She handed him a crinkled up note. "Mom gave this to me."

He took the note from her and read it: *My darling Jane, As you enter into this adult world, remember that I'll always be here for you. If you get lonely, call me. If you need anything, don't hesitate to ask. The sky is the limit, Darling, and your dreams are right in front of you. Now spread your wings and fly. I love you. Mom*

A photograph of Jane and her mother was taped to back of this note. Randy's heart broke a little. "When was that taken?"

"The day I came to Cal. I forgot I had this picture."

Randy snooped through the box and pulled out a necklace with a pearl pendant dangling from it.

"That was Mom's," she said. "Daddy gave it to me when we cleaned her things out of the house."

"I bet that was hard."

"It was, but Brian and I couldn't let Daddy do that by himself."

"You are such a strong woman, Jane," Randy said. "It amazes me how tough you can be, even through the hardest times. I don't know how you do it."

"What choice did I have?"

"But it's more than the strength you showed with your mom. All through medical school, when I know damn well there were times you wanted to wring my neck, you stuck it out with me. And now, when I'm going through some challenging and very stressful times in my training, you take it on, wholeheartedly. I love that about you."

Her mouth curved into a smile. "You've always been there for me when I've needed you, now it's my turn."

"Thank you, Honey. You don't know how much I need you." He leaned forward and kissed her, grateful to have such a supportive and understanding woman by his side.

Chapter Forty-Six

One of the many frustrating things about medical school was something the students termed as pimping. Pimping occurred when an attending physician or resident doctor tried to catch medical students ill-prepared. Randy got a taste of this one afternoon when the resident he worked under handed him a patient file and questioned him, hoping to trip him up. "What do you think of this patient's shortness of breath?"

Although Randy thought this was incredibly patronizing, he flowed with it as best he could. Luckily this chart belonged to one of the patients he was following, and he had read up on as many of this patient's problems as he could. "Well, I know this patient has CHF, which can cause shortness of breath. But in general, when I think of shortness of breath, I first consider lung-related problems. Problems in the lungs that could be infectious, such as pneumonia or empyema, or vascular, such as an embolism. Or it could be due to a cancer or other space-occupying lesion, or surgical trauma, causing a pneumothorax. There are also cardiac-related problems that could cause shortness of breath, such as congestive heart failure leading to pulmonary edema. There could be a hematological cause, like anemia as well."

The resident eyeballed him and simply said, "Hmm."

Medical school was nothing but a tortuous test of will and consisted of ruthless competitiveness which produced a great deal of disharmony among people. Because of this, Randy vowed to look for opportunities to extend assistance to his peers whenever appropriate. Instead of competing with them, he was going to compete with only himself. He swore that as he moved up the ranks in his medical training that he would not be the insensitive, arrogant ass many resident doctors above him appeared to be. Success through this was going to depend on his ability to survive and thrive. Every day he was inundated with the complexity of the tasks he engaged in, but at the same time he was amazed at the true privilege it was to take care of patients and felt blessed to be able to be a part of it.

Weekly study sessions became not only a time to prepare for their MLE, but also an enormous venting session for Jim, Bruce, Amanda, and Randy. They shared stories about experiences they were having in their individual rotations and tried to prepare each other for each placement. They updated one another on articles they had read and tried to relax and have fun together. Even though they rarely saw each other during the week, the support the four of them offered each other on Sunday mornings was invaluable.

Jim and Randy managed to get together most Saturday afternoons to shoot hoops or catch a game and talk. Jim spent a good amount of time complaining about his schedule and wished he could spend more time with his son. Randy felt horribly guilty for no longer being readily available by phone or otherwise for Jane if she needed him and really wished the resident he worked under would lighten up.

"Hey, Randy, did I tell you what happened last week?" Jim asked over a cup of coffee.

"No."

Jim started to laugh. "I was in surgery with my attending, and this medical student walked into the operating room havin' no idea what procedure we were doin'. That in itself is a bad idea. Anyway, when he caught a glimpse of a vessel, he blurted out, 'Is that the aorta?' This was funny because the procedure was a popliteal bypass. He was lookin' at the patient's knee."

Randy laughed with him. "Oh my god. What a moron."

"The resident doc I'm workin' with right now is awesome. I'm learning a lot from him. We exchange information all the time and he values my opinion. It's been a great experience."

Randy took a sip from his cup. "Wish I could say the same. The flow of knowledge between me and the resident I'm working under is more unilateral rather than collaborative, at least he seems to think it is. He's convinced he's right about everything. But I totally called him out yesterday."

"What'd you do?"

"He tried to tell me there was no abnormality in my patient's CT scan when my SOAP notes clearly stated that there was. We looked at the scan together, and I pointed out the abnormality to him. The attending was standing right behind me and he saw it too. When the attending questioned him about this, he glared at me and stormed out of the room."

"Seriously?"

"Yeah. He's either a spoiled baby or he's playing hardball to try to intimidate me. I don't think he likes me very much, and I wouldn't be surprised if he gave me a bad evaluation even though I've always been prepared and professional around him."

This concerned Jim. "He can't give you a bad evaluation just because you were right and he was wrong, can he?"

"I don't know. But he sure seems to think he's the center of the universe. He hates it when I know the answer to something. Thank God I'm finished working with him after next week. He is annoying as hell."

"Damn. I hope he doesn't hurt you because he's a whiner."

"Me too."

Their friendship grew stronger through these conversations, and the closeness Jim and Randy shared offered the most support because they each knew what the other was going through.

Over the last four weeks of his Neurology rotation, Jane had been exceptionally supportive. She helped him gather his gear in the morning and packed lunches for him, which really helped relieve some of the initial stress he felt. She usually had dinner prepared when he got home and allowed him time to research the latest treatment methods for his cases.

The last day of his first rotation, Randy's attending physician pulled him aside to go over his performance evaluation. The attending physician gave him an outstanding evaluation, and much to Randy's surprise, the resident doctor did too. Maybe he was just playing hardball. Either way, Randy was happy with his honors grade for that rotation.

Chapter Forty-Seven

The biggest event of the year was the graduation banquet for the UCB-UCSF JMP students receiving their Master's Degrees. The Dean of Berkeley's Joint Medical Program, as well as most of their professors and other local doctors and attending physicians, were expected to flood this event.

Randy dressed in professional attire then looked over his speech one last time. "Honey?" he called to Jane. "Should I say welcome ladies and gentlemen or welcome honored guests?"

"Honored guests makes the people sound more important."

"I'll use that then." He jotted that down on his notecard.

"How are you doing? Are you nervous?"

"A little. Not because I have to give a speech, but because my dad is going to be there to hear it."

"But your dad's not critical of you," she reminded him.

"Oh, he can be, if I screw things up, which is why I try not to."

She came out of the bathroom wearing an absolutely gorgeous black sequined gown. Her hair was up in a bun. The black sapphire necklace and earrings and elegant black strapped heels she had on accented her dress perfectly.

"Wow! You look amazing, Baby. So glamorous." He kissed her softly on the lips. "You ready?"

"Yup. Let's go, my handsome doctor." She proudly interlocked her arm in his.

He grabbed his keys as they headed out the door.

Jim, Jill, and Jim's parents were already there when Randy and Jane walked in. Jim's father stood up and shook Randy's hand. "Randy. It's good to see you again."

"Yes it is, Sir. It's been a long time." He introduced Jane to them then sat down and waited for his family.

It wasn't long before Stephanie, Bruce, and Dr. and Mrs. Hanson walked in.

Dr. Boyce stood at the podium and started the banquet. "Ladies and gentlemen, may I have your attention, please."

Everyone in the banquet hall took their seats and the festivities began.

Dr. Boyce made a few announcements, recognized some faculty members, and acknowledged the students' achievements. "Here at UC Berkeley-UCSF Joint Medical Program, we take pride in the clinical abilities, research efforts, and intellect of our medical students. We uphold high standards and expect nothing but the best from our future doctors. We've graduated many successful physicians from this university. This particular class was exceptional in many ways. They pulled together as a team on several occasions, they encouraged each other, and they worked diligently to meet the highest standards put before them. This class is graduating with the highest average GPA and MLE scores of any class to ever pass through the doors of our Health and Medical Science Program."

Applause resounded through the room.

When the noise subsided, he carried on. "This year we were blessed to receive national recognition. Every year, the National Medical Board gives the Alpha Omega Alpha honor to only the highest-performing medical students in the country. An honor very few students qualify for, let alone receive. The requirements for induction into this medical honor society are strict. Eligible candidates must perform academically within the top ten percent of all medical students in the nation. They must demonstrate outstanding character and possess exceptional dedication to the field of medicine. There was one student among this group who excelled in every aspect. He shows immense dedication to the medical profession and volunteers his time to the community. His exam scores are phenomenal, and his clinical work is always outstanding. Unquestioningly, he wrote and presented one of the best thesis papers I've ever read. He performs over and above what is expected of him and puts in extra hours, not only for his own benefit, but also to aid his classmates. He's an exceptional student and has a heart of gold. This young man has been evaluated by his peers, professors, and medical professionals who have worked with him directly, as well as outside physicians and parties from all over the nation who interviewed him and watched him perform. One student in this graduating class has exceeded all the requirements that the National Medical Board placed before him, and tomorrow, he will be graduating in the top of the class."

All of the medical students were now looking at Randy. Jim poked him with his elbow.

Dr. Boyce continued his introduction. "We are all very proud of him, his accomplishments, and his recent induction into Alpha Omega Alpha Medical Honor Society. It is my pleasure to introduce you to Mr. Randal Hanson."

The room echoed in applause. Randy was the kind of person who would go out of his way to help people. Because of that, everyone liked him. The medical students were thrilled that he was receiving this honor. Thus, they cheered the loudest when he approached the podium.

Overwhelmed by this introduction, Randy stood proud. "Thank you, Dr. Boyce." Randy viewed his audience, focusing his eyes specifically on Jane. She offered a smile of reassurance, which made him more confident. "Welcome honored guests."

He spoke for about ten minutes about the value of education and emphasized that no matter how tough things become, perseverance pays off in the end. He took a moment to moisten his dry throat before he continued. "Medical school takes dedication and hours of commitment. But choosing to pursue the path of a physician was not a mission I took on alone. Many people helped me along this road and gave me the support, motivation, and inspiration I needed to help me pursue my dream. First and foremost, I want to thank my parents, Dr. Mark and Mrs. Ellen Hanson, who not only supported me financially, but also offered constant encouragement. My father's love of medicine inspired me to follow a career in medicine, and my mother's high expectations pushed me to perform at my very best. Thank you, Mom and Dad. I love you. Next, I want to thank my friends, especially James Ryan, Bruce Buckman, and Amanda Stevens. Together we climbed mountains. We slipped and fell occasionally, but we picked each other up and carried on. We supported one another, cried on each other's shoulders, and offered a complaint box to file grievances in, and lord knows we had plenty of those."

The crowd laughed at this comment, particularly the other medical students because they knew how true it was.

"We never would have made it this far without each other's support. Your friendship is invaluable. And to Jim, who has been my best friend for seven years." He stared right at him. "From the very beginning, you and I were determined to make it through this together. We ran into roadblocks along the way, but we did it, and now here we are. Thank you for your support and your friendship."

Jim acknowledged with a shaka gesture.

With loving eyes, Randy turned his attention to Jane. "Last, but definitely not least, Jane, my love and inspiration in life. Jane has been my biggest supporter. She stood by my side through the stressful times and boosted my confidence when things didn't quite go the way I'd planned. Her constant encouragement motivated me and gave me a reason to work as hard as I did. She inspired me to push myself beyond any goals or expectations I ever set for myself. And she loved me, unconditionally, despite the hours of studying, my grouchiness when I was stressed, and all the pressures of everyday life in medical school. I wouldn't be standing here now if it weren't for her strength, devotion, patience, and advocacy. Janey," he looked directly into her eyes. "I never could have made it through this without you by my side. Thank you for your constant faith in me. I love you."

Her smile radiated through the room. She was truly honored to be a part of his life and his dream.

Randy faced his audience and made his closing remarks. "The Alpha Omega Alpha honor was a surprising, yet welcomed conclusion to my classroom training. Alpha Omega Alpha isn't just an honor I have achieved, it's for every professor, medical student, and physician in this room who had a dream. It's for every person who contributed even the slightest bit of encouragement to me and other medical students over the years. It's for you Mom, Dad, Jane. Thank you for your support and your love and for helping me make my dream come true. I love you and couldn't have done this without you." Randy stepped away from the microphone, took his plaque and an envelope from Dr. Boyce, and returned to his seat.

The medical students in the room gave him a standing ovation.

Over dinner, Randy reached across the table for Jane's hand. "I meant what I said, you know. I need you. I can't do this without you."

"Randy, it has been a pleasure walking down this road with you," she said. "I will support you in any way I can. You know that."

"I know, and I'm grateful for that."

When the banquet was over, Randy joined his friends in a corner of the room.

Jim said, "Some of us are gonna meet over at Elam's Tavern for some brewskies. You and Jane wanna come?"

"Not tonight," Randy answered. "I'm gonna hang with my parents for a while. I don't get to see them very often."

"A'ight. I'll see you tomorrow then, Bro." Jim left with Jill, Mandy, and a few other medical students.

Bruce stayed with the Hansons.

"Who's up for pie?" Mark suggested.

Agreeing to this suggestion, the family met at Marie Calendar's.

For the graduation ceremony, Jane and Randy lined up for the promenade in separate sections. Jane was close to the front with the B.A. recipients and Randy sat in the back with the other medical students receiving their Master's Degrees.

Departments were announced one by one and the graduates made their way across the stage. When the Psychology Department was beckoned, Randy anxiously awaited Jane's name to be called.

When she finally received her diploma and turned her tassel, she had to walk down the center aisle and around the back row to return to her seat, which meant she had to walk past Randy.

He held out his hand as she passed by. "Congratulations, Babe."

"You're next," she said. Then she gave him a high five and continued to her seat.

The medical students were the last to walk the stage. After painfully sitting through two and a half hours of watching the entire graduating class receive their diplomas, it was finally Randy's turn. This would be his final walk as a Berkeley student. The next time he made this walk, he would be receiving his M.D. degree from UCSF. This was the end of an era for him and the beginning of a new one.

Randy found Jane among the hordes of graduates. He squeezed her tightly in his arms and spun her around. "You did it, Babe. I'm proud of you."

"Thank you. I'm proud of you too."

He looked around California Memorial Stadium trying to locate his family. "Find your dad and Brian then meet me back here."

"Ok."

He slowly released Jane's hand and searched the stadium for his parents.

To celebrate their graduation, Mark Hanson offered to take Randy and Jane out for dinner. He invited Bruce to join them. Wanting to include Jane's father in the celebration, Mark offered, "We would love to treat you to dinner."

"I don't want to impose."

"I insist," Dr. Hanson said. "Please. Join us"

After some coaxing, Dale Davine agreed.

Following dinner, the Hanson family met at Randy and Jane's apartment. Randy waltzed into the kitchen to put on a pot of coffee with Stephanie close behind him.

"Hey, I'm mad at you," she said giving her brother a dirty look.

"Why?"

She poked him in the chest. "Why didn't you tell me Jane was sharing this apartment with you? When did this happen?"

"About a month ago."

"You brat. I can't believe you didn't tell me. Do Mom and Dad know?"

"They knew about it before it happened."

"You could have called and told me," Stephanie complained.

"I could have, but explain to me why it's your business?"

"Because you're my brother, and I care about your life."

Randy folded his arms across his chest. "Ok, so now you know."

"Your girlfriend had to tell me. How long were you planning on keeping this from me?"

"I didn't keep it from you on purpose, Steph," Randy claimed. "Don't get your panties in a wad."

She playfully smacked him on the arm.

Chapter Forty-Eight

Monday morning, Randy reported to his second rotation, Psychiatry, ready for a new challenge. He didn't know much about this particular area of medicine, but he walked in the door excited and eager to learn. Little did he know what he was about to walk into.

A young doctor snarled at him, seemingly irritated about something. "Who are you?"

This was not the kind of welcome he expected. "I'm Randy Hanson, the new medical student working in this rotation."

The doctor tossed a file at him. "I would like to know why this patient is getting dizzy spells and feeling faint. Can you answer that for me?"

Randy was taken by surprise at this rudely abrupt greeting. He had only been in the building for five minutes and hadn't opened this patient's file. "Sir?"

"You did go to medical school, didn't you?"

"Yes, Doctor."

"Then tell me what you've got." The doctor impatiently waited for an answer.

Tongue-tied, Randy replied, "I haven't seen this patient's file."

"And that's all you have for me? Dizzy spells, faint. Come on. Think. You say you went to medical school, act like it."

"Dizzy spells can be caused by many things, Sir."

496

"I'm listening." He leaned back in his chair giving Randy a brash stare.

"Postural hypotension or adrenal insufficiency can cause this patient to feel faint. Or it could be caused by hypoglycemia or ear disease. Any disturbance of balance in the inner ear may cause dizziness. Hyperventilation, chemical sensitivity, poisonings by pesticides, gas fumes, and carbon monoxide, or withdrawal symptoms from caffeine, alcohol, or prescription drugs can cause a patient to feel faint. Even allergies, not getting enough quality sleep or exercise, hypothyroidism and stress…the list goes on, Sir."

The doctor glared at him, unimpressed. "Is that your generic answer?"

Was this doctor really expecting him to know the answer when he had barely started this rotation and didn't even know where the restroom was in this building? This made Randy mad, and he felt like an idiot not knowing what answer this doctor wanted. "I don't have specifics, Doctor. I haven't done any tests on this patient."

"Well, I expect a full report by eight o'clock tomorrow morning, Mr. Hanson. No exceptions and no excuses."

"Yes, Sir." The doctor walked away leaving Randy dumbfounded as he held this file in his hand. This was, by far, the most humiliating experience of his medical school career.

Randy spent the morning running tests on this patient and interviewing her. His afternoon was dedicated to going over test results and writing down SOAP notes.

Upon arrival home that night, Randy was overly stressed and had no idea where to even start with the report he was supposed to have generated by eight o'clock the next morning. He threw the file on the table and collapsed in a chair. "Shit!"

Jane heard him come in. "Hi, Sweetie."

Randy pinched the bridge of his nose with his thumb and forefinger.

"Randy?" she asked again.

"What?"

His foul mood took her by surprise. "Geez, Grouch. What's wrong with you?"

He lifted his head. "I have a detailed report I have to write by eight o'clock tomorrow morning. I don't have complete information, don't have all my lab results back, and the patient is unclear about the symptoms."

"Then you'll need do some research," she suggested.

"How the hell do you know what I need to do? You have no idea what I need in order to generate this damn report!"

"Why are you yelling at me?"

"Why are you bothering me? I have a shit ton of work to do. Leave me alone."

"Fine." She stormed into the bedroom and slammed the door.

Randy felt like an ass. It wasn't her fault his attending physician threw this file in his face. He walked over to the bedroom door. Jane had locked it. "Janey."

"Go away. I wouldn't want to bother you," he heard her say.

He realized now that he had screwed up. "Come on, Baby. I'm sorry."

"You wanted to be alone. There you are. Enjoy yourself."

"That's not what I meant," he pleaded. "Please open the door."

Stubbornly, she replied, "No. Go away."

Getting nowhere, he went to work on his report, leaving her to cool off.

Around eleven o'clock, he wrapped up his research. He glanced over at the bedroom door, which was still closed. Jane hadn't emerged and hadn't spoken a word to him all night. Concerned about her silence, he closed his case file and crept over to the door. He stood and stared at it for a minute before he knocked. "Honey."

"What do you want?" she snapped.

"Please open the door and talk to me."

"I don't want to bother you."

498

Her voice was paved with attitude, and her tenacity grated on his nerves. "Dammit, Jane. Open this door!"

"No. And don't tell me what to do."

He growled in aggravation. Obviously this wasn't working. Hoping to get through to her, he tried a different angle. "I have to work tomorrow. All my clothes are in there, and I need to get some sleep." He stood outside the door waiting for her to give in.

About a minute later, she opened the door. But instead of letting him inside, she threw a blanket, pillow, and some clothes at him then slammed the door in his face.

With a stiffened posture, he held a pillow in his hands. "What the hell?"

"You wanted to be left alone. Fine. You can sleep alone then."

Was she implying that he sleep on the couch? "You have got to be shitting me."

"Good night." She ended the conversation.

Randy could not believe this was happening—exiled from his own bed to sleep on the couch. He picked up his clothes, made up the couch with the blanket and pillow, and attempted to get some shut eye. He hoped by morning her temper would pacify and the 'wrath of Jane' would be out of her system.

Randy woke with a horrible cramp in his neck. He hadn't slept well, and he felt unprepared for his report. "This is going to be a splendid day," he muttered sourly. Unable to sleep any longer, he decided to get up. He put on a pot of coffee and headed to the shower, noticing that the bedroom door was still closed. He stared at it with a heavy heart. Why did he have to be such a grouch last night and take his frustrations out on Jane? He couldn't say he blamed her for being mad at him. He acted like an asshole.

By the time he was dressed, the bedroom door was open. He peeked inside the room, but Jane wasn't in there. He heard her in the kitchen, so he took a deep breath and headed that direction. Standing in the doorway staring at her, he attempted to make conversation. "I put some coffee on if you want some."

"You know I don't drink coffee," she replied.

Yes, he did know that. He stood behind her and tried to touch her arm, but she moved away from him. "You still mad at me?" he assumed.

She swiveled around with her hands on her hips, glowering at him. "You know, Randy," she began.

Uh oh, here it comes. He was about to be lectured by her. As much as he dreaded this, he took it like a man and endured her wrath.

"If you needed time to get something done you should have said so. But no, you had to be a cranky ass and yell at me," she scolded.

"I'm sorry. I was stressed about this report."

"Was it my fault that you had a report to do?"

"No," he admitted, feeling horribly guilty.

"Then why the hell were you yelling at me?"

"I'm sorry. I didn't mean to take it out on you."

"I'm trying to help you," she said. "Don't yell at me because I offer a suggestion."

Obviously she was still angry. But after the way he treated her last night, he figured he deserved it. "This doctor I'm working with is pressuring me."

"Again, that is not my fault."

"I know. You've said that already."

"And I'm saying it again." She turned away and reached into the refrigerator for the carton of orange juice.

He reached out and touched her. "Honey, please. I made a mistake. Give me a chance at redemption here."

She didn't pull away, but wouldn't look at him either. Closing her eyes to hold back tears, she sat the carton of juice on the counter.

"Please look at me." Randy moved his hand down to hers, trying to get her to turn around. "Baby, I'm sorry."

A tear streamed down her face.

His heart was crushed. He shouldn't have gotten angry with her because she tried to offer assistance. What the hell was wrong with him last night? He wiped her tear and pulled her into his arms.

She laid her head on his shoulder. "I hate it when we fight."

"I know. I don't like it either. I didn't sleep worth a crap last night."

"I'm sorry. That's my fault."

"No it's not," he clarified. "I deserved what you dished out to me."

"But now you're going to be too tired to give your report."

"No I won't," he reassured. "But I gotta tell you, sleeping on the couch sucks. I missed you last night." He lifted her chin. "I thought we agreed to talk about things and not go to bed angry."

"We did."

Randy let out a sigh. "Then what happened last night?"

"Your attitude made me mad."

"I'm sorry. I shouldn't have said what I said to you."

She smiled in reassurance.

"Do I get bedroom privileges again tonight?"

"Maybe. I might even give you a chance to redeem yourself."

He raised his eyebrows at this prospect. "Really?"

She bit her lip seductively and pulled away from him.

Relieved that she wasn't angry anymore, he grabbed her hand and pulled her back into his arms. He was dying to kiss her. He moved his mouth to hers and indulged in her luscious lips.

Several minutes passed before Jane broke away. "You better get going or you're going to be late."

He already was. "I love you, Babe. We'll talk tonight."

She poured herself a glass of orange juice, returned the carton to the fridge, then left him to finish getting ready for work.

When Randy walked into the clinic that morning, the doctor greeted him at the door. "You're late."

"I know, Dr. Nichols. I'm sorry. I was held up in traffic." Randy wasn't sure how he felt about this particular doctor. The man seemed to be on a mission to make his life as miserable as possible.

"Do you have that report for me?" the doctor asked.

"Yes, Doctor, I do."

"Let's hear it then."

Randy pulled out all of his notes, research, and test results. He presented his report to the doctor expecting this man to find some sort of flaw in his analysis. He nervously stood before him and waited for the worst.

The doctor leaned back in his chair and folded his arms across his chest. "I gave that same file to another med student three weeks ago. He had the same information you started with, but even after three weeks he couldn't come up with as detailed a report as you did."

Randy wasn't sure how to respond. "Sir?"

"When did you do all this?"

"I ran all the tests yesterday and spent four hours last night analyzing the results and coming up with an assessment."

"That is impressive." The doctor relaxed his arms and leaned forward in his chair. "It's Randy, right?"

"Yes, Sir."

"Randy, I would love to buy you lunch today. We'll talk and get to know each other."

"Yes, Doctor."

Over lunch that afternoon, Dr. Nichols took ownership of his unprofessionalism. "I'm sorry I came across as coarse and uninviting."

At least the doctor recognized the harshness he bestowed and had the decency to apologize. "Thank you."

"You interested in Psychiatry?" the doctor inquired.

"Actually, I'm heading towards OB/GYN."

They talked about medicine, family, and what they did for fun. Throughout the conversation, Randy learned that Dr. Nichols wasn't the mean, undermining hardass he originally took him for. He was actually a pretty nice guy who had recently completed his residency, became board certified, and had only been practicing Psychiatry for a little over two years. Dr. Nichols gave Randy another file to take a look at, but this time he gave him plenty of time to analyze it and really soak it in.

Randy was anxious to get home and see Jane that night. He walked in the door with a smile on his face.

Jane was in the living room reading a magazine. "Hey," she said in a cheerful tone, turning her head toward him. "Better day?"

He set his case file on the table and leaned over the sofa to give her a kiss. "Yes. Much better." Getting more comfortable, he untucked his shirt and kicked off his shoes. "Dr. Nichols is cool. He bought me lunch today."

"Is this the same man who threw a file in your face yesterday?" she asked. "I thought you hated him?"

"He apologized."

"He did?" Jane asked.

"Yup." Randy lifted her out of the chair and moved his hands down to her hips, pulling her closer to him. "I'm hoping to redeem myself for treating you like crap last night. I'm sorry, Baby."

"It's ok. I forgive you."

He completely sized her up while his hands explored the hollows of her back. "So," he said as he gazed into her eyes. "What are you thinking?"

"What are you thinking?" she directed back at him.

"I asked you first."

She drew her lip between her teeth and gave him a seductive stare.

"I know that look." He squeezed her bottom with the flesh of his fingers.

"I have been thinking about it all day." In an attempt to seduce him, she traced his lips with the tip of her tongue.

He lifted her of the floor and sat her on the table. "I say we do it right here."

"Here?"

"Oh yeah," he said firmly. "Right here, right now." Wasting little time, he pulled her shorts and panties off and tossed them over his shoulder. Then he reached his hand up her blouse and unlatched her bra. His lips quickly found hers, exploring every inch of her mouth as he unfastened his pants. They fell down to his ankles and he stepped out of them. One hand clasped hers while the other one found its way to the curve of her hip.

Jane wrapped her legs around him, which allowed him to penetrate her from a standing position while she sat on the edge of the table. This deep, rapid rhythm quickly built up pressure. At this rate, the intenseness was going to cause him to release too soon, so Randy slowed the rhythm to make it last longer.

Jane's breath quickened and her eyes closed. She felt frisky tonight and wanted more, which was always good. Randy had a feeling it was going to be one of those nights when an encore performance awaited him.

Randy met Jim for lunch the next day, which was something they hadn't done in a while. As they sat down to eat, Randy said, "Jane and I want to get Christopher something for his birthday. Any suggestions?"

"He likes noisy shit. If it rattles, sings, beeps, or bangs, he loves it."

Randy laughed. "Alright, I will keep that in mind."

"Man, this daddy business is hard work. Do yourself a favor, Bro, and don't rush into it."

"I don't intend to. We actually use birth control," Randy teased him.

"Yeah, yeah. Rub it in my face." He sipped his soda from a straw. "How's Jane?"

"Doing well. She was offered a part time job at the library and is excited about grad school. We got into a fight the other night."

Jim didn't believe him. "You and Jane?"

"Yup. Huge."

"Over what?"

"This doctor I'm working with threw a case file in my face and insisted that I give him a full report by eight o'clock the following morning. That night I came home cranky and took it out on Jane. Well, it pissed her off, so she locked herself in the bedroom and made me sleep on the couch."

Jim laughed out loud. "You got couch treatment? That is fuckin' funny."

"It wasn't funny at the time. It made me mad."

"Is she still speakin' to you?"

"Oh yeah. We talked about it in the morning, and last night when I got home from work, we had makeup sex," Randy said with a snide grin. "Jane and I rarely argue. But on the rare occasion that we do, we always work things out. We are both strong-willed, which can cause problems sometimes, but even if she's angry, she doesn't stay mad very long." Randy gulped down his coffee. "I can't say that I blame her for getting angry. I acted like an ass. That woman's put up with a lot of shit from me."

"That she has. Any girl who is dumb enough to hang out with you all this time must be a glutton for punishment," Jim teased.

"Shut up, Jackass," Randy said with a crooked smile.

"Why did you ask her to move in with you? I've been curious about this because I know how much you value your personal space."

Randy knew Jim would hound him about this sooner or later. "If you must know, Jane and I have a connection—a bond I've never experienced before. I love her with all my heart, but I want to make sure she's a woman I can live with and that we can handle everyday situations that may come up in our lives."

Jim cogitated over this for a moment. When he finally realized what Randy was implying, his eyes widened and a smirk crept upon his face. "Holy shit! You're thinkin' about proposing to her."

Randy looked at Jim with a very solemn expression on his face. "Thinking about it."

"Damn, Dude. Marriage is like the biggest thing in your book. It's the mother of all commitments. Jesus, Randy, this is huge."

"Look, don't make a big issue out of it. I don't want to jump into anything unless I know for sure that Jane and I can live together. Dating someone is different than making a home with them. Just because you love someone doesn't mean you can handle sharing living arrangements and all the habits that go with them. I don't want her to feel obligated to stick around if she can't handle me being on-call or working a hospital shift all night or stressed over patient files. I have to be sure, so I'm gonna try this on for size and see how it fits me."

"I never in a million years expected this from you, man. Mr. I'm-Afraid-of-Commitment. The man who swore he would forever be a bachelor. Berkeley's local wave horny playboy."

"Give me the benefit of the doubt that Janey has given me a change of heart."

"Bet that scares the hell out of you, doesn't it?"

Randy explained his thinking. "I've gotten to the point in my relationship with her where I can't picture my life without her in it. Everything I do and all my plans for my future seem to revolve around her now. And yes, I admit, it scares the hell out of me. Which is why I need to do this."

"Why didn't you tell me?" Jim asked, somewhat bothered over the fact that Randy hadn't said anything to him about this.

"Because I know how you joke around about stuff like this."

"My best friend is gettin' marriage vibes. There is no way I would joke around about that. This is way too serious a thing."

Deep down Randy knew that. He had always been able to confide in Jim.

"So…Jane's the one, huh?"

"Yup. I believe she is. We've been sharing an apartment for a few months now."

"And?" Jim questioned, wondering what was going on in Randy's head.

Randy smiled contently. "I like this. I like it a lot. It fits me very well."

"That's awesome, man."

Chapter Forty-Nine

Randy arrived home from work excited about his and Jane's trip to Paris with his family. They loaded their luggage in the trunk of the car, grabbed some dinner together, then headed to the airport to catch their flight.

From previous experience, Randy knew that the problem with flying internationally was that they would be leaving San Francisco that night, sleep on the plane, cross a bunch of time zones, and arrive at their destination when it was night the next day, but physically it wouldn't seem like it to them. It tended to mess up sleep schedules. Their flight into Paris Charles de Gaulle airport was not direct. They had a ten and a half hour flight into Dublin, where they had a three hour layover before making their connecting flight.

Randy was dying for some coffee, so he grabbed a cup while he had time. Stephanie joined him and used the opportunity to call Bruce. Randy overheard part of the conversation, which appeared to be lighthearted and friendly. When she got off the phone, Randy asked, "What's going on?"

She shrugged, not knowing what he was talking about. "With what?"

"Bruce tells me you want to come to San Francisco and move in with him."

She was surprised Randy knew about this. "He told you?"

"He is my friend, Steph. He does talk to me."

"I'd like to stay with him, but he pretty much told me he doesn't want me to."

Well, at least she was accurate in her analysis. "You know why, don't you?"

"No. He didn't really give me a reason."

"He's worried that you'll keep him from studying."

"I would never…"

"Yes you will," Randy cut in. "You can get pretty demanding, Steph. Admit it."

She tightened her lips.

"He's scared that you'll distract him and keep him from doing the research he needs to do on his patient files, which could be detrimental to his grades."

"I grew up around doctors," she said. "I know what doctors do."

"This is not the same. Medical school is demanding, and if we trip up on our clinical placements our grade suffers, and we might have to repeat a rotation."

"I know that."

"Do you?" He didn't think she did. "Do you know how important this is to him? Do you know how hard he works?"

"Doesn't look to me like he's working that hard. When I'm around him, he never studies," Stephanie observed.

"And that's exactly what he's worried about. He's a good student, Steph, dedicated, hardworking, always puts school first. Bruce hits the books pretty intensely. All of us in med school do. We have to. I'm always doing research on something and constantly have my nose buried in a book. Ask Jane," Randy said. "My point is you need to understand what he goes through. Medical school isn't easy. He takes it seriously and he's always done well."

Curiosity brewed now. "How well?"

"He scored in the ninety-ninth percentile on his MLE exam and graduated second in my M.S. class."

Stephanie had no idea Bruce was so scholarly. "He did?"

"Yes. They rank us as we proceed through med school. He's always been right behind me." Randy couldn't believe Stephanie didn't know any of this. Medicine was Bruce's life, yet Stephanie seemed to know nothing about it. "Has he told you what line of medicine he's interested in?"

"No."

Randy told her. "Neurosurgery. Do you know how complex and complicated that specialty is? The intricacy of the brain is far more complicated than I care to get involved in. But Bruce is damn good at it."

"I had no idea," Stephanie declared.

"He is a bright man. Knows the inner workings of the brain like the back of his hand. Neurology is definitely his forte and his obsession. You should listen to him talk about it sometime." Randy found it strange that Stephanie didn't seem to know very much about Bruce Buckman. How was this possible when they'd been dating for so long?

"He doesn't talk about school or medicine. He thinks that since I grew up in a doctor's house, I wouldn't be interested."

"Medicine is his life, Steph. And he knows more about it than almost anyone I know."

"So you're telling me my boyfriend is smart?" Stephanie asked.

"Super smart. He pretends not to be because he doesn't like to draw attention to himself. He's kind of reclusive that way." He looked at Stephanie with some concern for his friend. "I know this whole transferring thing that you've been talking about has been bothering him, and I wanted you to understand why. He does want you closer to him, but he's scared, Steph. He's afraid that having you around will keep him from doing his job."

"But Jane does it, and it doesn't seem to bother you."

Randy burst out laughing. "I love you, Steph, but you are not Jane."

"What are you implying?" she retorted.

"You know damn well how high maintenance you are. You demand attention constantly. Bruce won't be able to pay attention to you all the time. He's busy."

"Jane doesn't want you to pay attention to her?"

Randy explained the situation. "She knows I have a job to do, and she makes sure I do it. She doesn't demand anything from me; she takes whatever I can give her. Are you willing to allow Bruce to do his job and not expect him to be joined at your hip all the time? Are you willing to let him put school first?"

"I can do that."

He shook his head, knowing she was incapable of putting other people first. "Let me ask you something. Do you love him, or are you merely thinking about the pocketbook?"

She glared at him, offended that he said that. "You're an asshole. I'm not a gold digger."

"I know you well, Stephanie. Bruce will be raking in the bucks when he is done, especially with the specialty he's going into. A doctor, Steph, and a neurosurgeon at that. Money, lots of money," he tempted her. "With your high maintenance lifestyle, and the fact that you were raised off a doctor's salary, I know damn well the money has come into play and influenced you somehow. Don't tell me it hasn't."

She admitted he was right. "Ok, maybe it has."

"I know it has." He hesitated for a minute before he offered her some serious advice. "Make sure you are in this relationship and coming to San Francisco for the right reasons. Don't let money or sex be your driving force. I'm your brother, and I don't want to see you jump into something you're not ready for, or even worse, something you'll regret. Because I guarantee you won't want to be involved in dealing with med school if you don't love him." Randy looked his sister in the eye and very seriously asked her, "Do you love him?"

With a bit of resentment in her voice, Stephanie said, "What kind of a question is that?"

"I don't want you or Bruce to get hurt."

"I know."

Randy threw his empty coffee cup in the trash. "Come on. We have a flight to catch."

The sky was dark when they arrived in Paris. But all the glimmering lights made Paris at night brilliant and vivacious. The Eiffel Tower illuminated over the city. Nothing could compare to its unbridled grandeur; it was an absolutely spectacular sight.

When they stepped out of the cab, Jane looked up at the glorious structure. "Randy, look at that."

"Merci beaucoup, Monsieur," he said as he tipped the cab driver. Then he observed the sight himself. "Oh wow. That is beautiful."

"This is going to be so cool."

"Yes it is. I've always wanted to visit Paris."

After a good night's sleep, they stepped outside the hotel into the morning sun. Randy took in a huge breath of fresh air. "Ah, Paris."

Jane's gaze quickly swept over the area. All of the street signs, billboards, and building banners were written in French. "Oh my god. I can't read any of this." She was about to have a panic attack. "We are never going to find our way around here."

"Calm down. We'll be fine." Easing her worry, he approached a gentleman standing outside the hotel. "Excusez-moi, Monsieur."

The man kindly acknowledged him, "Oui?"

Randy chattered with this man for a moment, exchanging French dialogue and shifting his eyes in the direction the man pointed. When Randy was satisfied, he shook the man's hand. "Merci beaucoup."

The man concluded with a few selected words then walked away.

Randy returned to Jane. "See, no problem."

"What did you say to him?"

"Asked him which way the Louvre was and how far it was from here. He says it's about ten blocks that way."

Randy pivoted that direction. "We can walk from here if you want."

"Ok. It will be fun to walk around Paris and check it out."

"Alrighty." He offered her his arm. "Voulez-vous marcher avec moi, mon chéri?"

She cocked her head. "What?"

"Walk with me," he said. "You're going to have to learn some French, Missy."

She giggled then interlocked her arm with his. They leisurely strolled down the street checking out the sights on their way to the Louvre.

After a day of touring the art museum, they decided to try their hand at genuine French cuisine, which Randy was very much looking forward to.

"This menu is written in French." Jane turned the menu upside down, trying to figure out what it said. "I can't read this."

He turned it right side up. "Helps if you turn it the right way, Babe." He scanned the menu for something she might like. "Try crudités with lemon oil or coq au vin. That's a chicken dish."

She trusted his judgment and decided to let him order for her.

Randy placed their order, along with a plate of escargot, hoping Jane would be adventurous and try it.

When the escargot came out, Randy poked one with a fork, dipped it in garlic butter sauce, and ate it. "Honey, you have to try this."

"Escargot? Isn't that snails?"

"Yes."

Just the thought of this turned her stomach. "Gross."

"Oh no. It's a delectable dish." He put one on a fork and coated it in garlic butter, moving it toward her mouth. "Come on. Try it."

"Yuk."

"We're in Paris, Baby. Try some of the local cuisine. I promise you it's good."

"It's a snail," she said, sickened.

"Yes it is, but a mighty tasty one." He moved it closer to her mouth. "Open up," he teased her with the fork.

She turned her head away. "I'm not eating that."

He tried to entice her. "Come on. One little bite."

With a grimace on her face, she held her breath and opened her mouth. He fed her one and let her savor it.

"Well?" he asked, curious as to what she thought.

The nasty expression left her face. "It's good."

"Told you. See, you have to trust me." He poked his fork into another one, dipped it, and popped it in his mouth. When the waiter walked by, Randy ordered two glasses of wine to drink with their meal. For dessert, he ordered Chocolate Mousse.

Enjoying the nighttime air on their walk back to the hotel, they stopped to get a good look at the illuminated Eiffel Tower. Randy put his arm around Jane as they stood staring at its glory and splendor. "That is spectacular," he said.

Jane snapped a few shots of it with the digital camera. "I wanna go up to the top."

"Oh, we will. Don't worry."

"I bet there's an amazing view from up there."

"I bet there is." He pulled her closer and gently rubbed his hand across her cheek. "Je t'aime."

"I love you too."

"No, you're in France," he corrected her. "It's je t'aime aussi."

She attempted to say it in French, although her pronunciation was bad.

Under the lights of Paris, the city of love, Randy held Jane in his arms and kissed her with all his heart and soul. "This is incredible," he said.

"What is?"

"Standing under the stars of Paris kissing the woman I love with the Eiffel Tower glowing in the background."

"It's romantic," she added.

"Yes it is." He smiled and kissed her again. "I am a happy man."

Throughout the week, Randy had several opportunities to practice his French and indulge in genuine French cuisine, which he thoroughly enjoyed. They toured the Musee d'Orsay, visited the Notre-Dame Cathedral, and posed for a picture by the Arc de Triomphe. They witnessed the view from the top of the Eiffel Tower, explored the shops and local culture, and drank coffee in a French café. They explored a masterpiece of Renaissance architecture—the Château de Chambord—then admired the ornate architecture of the Opera De Paris, where they saw statues of regal winged horses, splendid columns, and elegantly sculpted friezes.

The family booked reservations on a scenic nighttime dinner cruise down the Seine River. They enjoyed a relaxing, enchanted evening of live music and a three-course meal amid the soft glow of light reflecting off the water.

When they returned to the hotel, Jane leaned back on the bed with her hands behind her head. She sighed contently.

"What's up, Babe?" Randy asked her.

"This vacation has been so fun. I can't believe it's almost over."

He moved a stray hair off her face. "Gotta return to reality sooner or later." He scooted closed and propped himself up on his elbow. "Graduate school awaits you."

"I know. I'm excited about it."

"You ready?" he asked, hoping she felt confident.

"I am. I got my new work schedule for the library."

"Hopefully they're working around your class schedule."

"They are. In fact, a lot of my work hours coincide with yours."

"That's convenient." He meandered his finger across the exposed skin between her breasts as he looked at her face, deep in thought. "I know living with the demands that are placed on me and the crotchety moods I get into can be frustrating for you."

She reassured him, "Randy, I love you. I love everything about you, including your moods. Everybody has bad days once in a while."

"My schedule is about to get nuts. I'm going to start my ER rotation when we get back. That will most likely keep me at the hospital all night."

"That's ok."

"But you'll be alone."

She giggled at his unnecessary worrying. "I'm a big girl. I can take care of myself."

"I know you can, but I won't be there to hold you at night."

"It's ok. You were left alone sometimes when I was on the road playing basketball."

"That's true."

"Stop worrying. I'll be fine." She wrapped her arms around him. "Now stop talking and kiss me."

"Yes, Ma'am." He kissed her with so much passion, it left him breathless. The passion he felt quickly turned to sexual arousal. His clothes came off one piece at a time then he stripped Jane naked, leaving her in only her panties. Between kisses and lustful caresses, he yanked on her delicate lacy undergarment. "These need to come off or I'm going to rip them off."

"Those are Victoria Secret, Randy. Don't you dare rip them."

"Then take them off," he demanded playfully.

"You take them off."

He squeezed her buttocks and slipped them over her hips.

She kicked them onto the floor.

He leaned forward, grazed his lips across her shoulder, and covered her neck with tender kisses. "God, I love you." He wrapped her in his arms and indulged in the pleasure of a slow, sensuous rhythm.

While they waited at the Dublin airport for their connecting flights, Randy went on a quest for a cup of coffee. His dad went with him. "Thank you for this trip, Dad," Randy said. "We really had a good time, and I had the opportunity to use my French on several occasions."

"Good. I'm glad you enjoyed yourself."

"I start my ER rotation on Monday." Randy had been told that this particular rotation was extremely demanding. He would work long shifts off minimal sleep and wouldn't have time for much of anything else.

"Do you?" his father replied. "That's a busy one."

"I'm a little worried about leaving Janey alone in that apartment at night by herself."

"She'll adjust. And isn't that what you wanted to find out? To see how she would handle the demands of living with a doctor's schedule?" Mark reminded his son.

"Yes."

"Looks like you're going to get your chance then, Son. That ER rotation is one of the toughest ones, at least I thought it was. You're going to have a lot of responsibilities placed upon you for the next eight weeks, and you'll be working long and late shifts. It's going to be stressful and it's going to be physically and emotionally draining."

"I know. I'm nervous about it."

"Best piece of advice I can give you is sleep when you can so you're fresh and alert. Don't let the emotional aspects get to you, and try to relax. Learn from people who have experience. Listen to your superiors and do what they say. Don't try to be a hero."

Listening intently to his father's advice, Randy replied, "I won't."

"When you have a break, grab a cot and sleep. That's the biggest thing. Make sure you are eating well also, so you can keep up your energy. Pack yourself lunches or have Jane bring you some healthy food. That would be much better than trying to live off coffee, Randal," Mark suggested, knowing his son was addicted to coffee and would probably drink entirely too much of it during this rotation.

"I'll talk to Jane about that."

"I'm not going to lie to you or make this rosy for you. It's going to be eight weeks of hell. This will be a good opportunity for Jane to really support you. And if that is what you wanted to find out, this will be the rotation to see it."

"I hope I do."

"I hope you do too."

Chapter Fifty

Despite his father's advice and warnings, Randy wasn't sure what to expect during this rotation. When he walked into the Emergency Room, a physician dressed in green scrubs hurried to greet him. "Please tell me you are Randal Hanson."

"Yes, Sir, I am."

"Good. We are seriously understaffed and super hectic today. We need you now. Put on some scrubs, lock your stuff in a locker, and get out here."

Shocked by this abrupt greeting, the only words that came out of Randy's mouth were, "Yes, Sir." He found the physicians' locker room, slipped on some clean scrubs, and put on his *MEDICAL STUDENT* name badge. Then he locked his belongings in a locker and headed out to the ER with his stethoscope draped around his neck.

"Hanson, get over here!" the doctor called out to him.

Randy hustled down the hall to see what he could do to help.

By 3:00 P.M., the ER slowed. Randy had been running around like a mad man and hadn't had a break all day. Throughout the day, adrenaline careened through his body that his heartrate was in constant acceleration mode. He was physically and emotionally drained. He sat on a bench in the locker room, leaned forward, and rested his head in his hands.

Jill was about to go on shift when she saw Randy sitting there. She knew how tough ER rotations could be, so she came over to see if he was alright. "Hey, Randy."

When he heard her voice, he looked up. "Jill. Man, it's good to see a familiar face."

"How you doing?"

"I'm starving, and I am dying for a cup of coffee."

"Have you eaten anything?"

"No. I haven't had time."

"Eat something and relax for a bit," she suggested. "I'll run down and grab you some coffee."

"I would love it if you would do that."

"I'll be back in a jiff."

After Jill left, Randy grabbed a quick bite from the lunch Jane packed for him, enjoying a brief but much needed break.

Jill came back several minutes later with a large cup of coffee in her hand. "I didn't know what you wanted in it so I brought some sugar and creamer."

"Thank you so much. You are a life saver." He dumped three packs of sugar and two creamers in his cup then stirred and took a sip. It was terrible coffee, but it was better than no coffee at all.

The caffeine gave him a boost of energy before he rejoined the ER in time for the next big rush. They had an asthma attack, four women in labor who needed to be wheeled upstairs, a broken arm, several car accident victims, a man complaining of chest pains which required them to call in a cardiologist, and a man who severed his finger.

At 6:30 P.M. they received a gunshot wound. The ambulance drivers quickly wheeled in a teenage boy who was bleeding profusely. He had an IV sticking out of his arm, an oxygen mask slapped on his face, and several EKG leads attached to his body. The patient wasn't breathing, the heartrate was in arrhythmia, and the pulse was virtually nonexistent.

"Hanson!" the doctor yelled, running with the gurney.

Randy slipped on a pair of latex examination gloves and rushed over to assist.

"Chest compressions," the doctor ordered.

"Yes, Sir." Randy immediately began CPR while the ER staff worked to stop bleeding and supply oxygen.

"Clear!" the doctor yelled.

Randy moved out of the way so they could try to jumpstart the patient's heart. No response. He resumed chest compression.

When the defibrillator was recharged, they tried again. "Clear!"

Still nothing.

Suddenly the heart went asystole. The doctor injected the boy with a shot of vasopressin, hoping the medication would kick in. If a regular sinus rhythm was not restored within ninety seconds, it was unlikely that the patient would be revived.

The electrocardiograph was flatline.

They continued desperate life-saving efforts, all to no avail. Roughly seven minutes went by before the attending physician removed his gloves, threw them in the hazardous waste can, and glanced up at the clock. "Call it," he declared, then he walked out of the room.

Randy stared at his blood-covered hands, as if they had betrayed him.

"Time of death, 6:52 P.M." The resident doctor noted the time on the chart. "Clean up and call downstairs."

"Yes, Doctor," Randy replied.

After changing into clean scrubs, Randy saw the attending physician speaking to the family in a private room. Since the door was closed, he couldn't hear what the doctor was telling them, but through the glass window he could see the family members crying. One woman was on the floor gripping the leg of a man sitting in the chair beside her. Through it all, the doctor showed no emotion, no feeling whatsoever. Informing a family of a patient's death was something Randy had never done and hoped he never had to do. This was not something they had rehearsed in medical school, although now that the situation came up, he wished they had. He did not feel prepared for anything like this.

Randy combed the hair off his forehead with his fingers then took in a cleansing breath. He couldn't wait to get home. It had been a very long day.

The minute Randy walked in the door, he collapsed on the couch. He had never been so exhausted in his life.

Jane heard him come in. "Hey, Sweetie."

"I am drained. I was in the ER for eleven hours today and didn't get much of a break. I have to be back for another eight-hour shift tomorrow morning."

She could tell he was tired. His eyes were droopy and his voice lacked its usual energy.

"We lost a patient tonight," he said with a disheartened frown.

Disturbed by this news, and worried about how he was handling it, she sat next to him and gently rubbed his shoulder. "Oh, Randy. I'm sorry."

"It's ok. There was nothing else we could have done." He put his hand on his growling stomach. "I'm starving."

"I'll make you something to eat." She bounded to her feet, gave him a kiss, and plodded into the kitchen.

Jane was so supportive and always willing to offer a listening ear in any situation. He loved her for that. But right now, the only thing he cared about was sitting on this couch. Randy couldn't figure out how Jim found any joy in this kind of work. Yes, the action got his blood pumping and the adrenaline rush was unlike anything he'd ever experienced, but damn he was tired.

Jill was on shift with Randy the next day, which made life in the ER a little more bearable. Randy was in the supply cabinet retrieving bandages when Jill came up to him and said, "Jane is up front looking for you."

"Thank you." He closed the cabinet and stepped out to the waiting room where only three patients were waiting, along with Jane.

Jane stood up when she saw him. "Hi, Sweetie."

"Hey, Babe. What are you doing over here?"

"Stopped by to see how you were doing."

"I'm running on fumes," he admitted. "This has been a busy day."

She handed him a cup of coffee. "See if this helps."

He took a sip from the steaming cup. Caffeine instantly flowed through his system. "Thanks, Babe. This really hits the spot."

He stood in the waiting room and talked to her for a few minutes before he was beckoned by his attending physician. "Hanson, I need you."

"Yes, Doctor. I'm on my way." He returned his attention to Jane. "I have to go."

"I heard."

"I'll see you in a few hours." He gave her a quick peck on the lips and resumed his duties in the ER.

Randy ended up working two extra hours that day to cover an influx of patients that came in. When he walked into the apartment, Jane threw her arms around him. He was so worn-out he could barely stand, but somehow he managed to muster up the strength to hold her.

"You look exhausted."

"I am. Every joint in my body aches. I feel like I'm going to collapse." He sat down on the sofa and kicked off his shoes. "I've been working ten to twelve hours every day with straight adrenaline running through my body. I've depleted every ounce of energy I have."

She leaned over and gave him a kiss. "Do you have to go in tomorrow?"

"Yes, but not until 3:00. I'm working the night shift tomorrow."

She offered her support. "I bet you're hungry."

"I'm starving. And I am dying for a decent cup of coffee. I cannot survive off the hospital's liquid sludge. That stuff is terrible. Starbucks needs to open a shop at UCSF Medical Center. They'd certainly get my business."

"I'll start dinner."

"Thanks."

Not only was Jane supportive and understanding, she actually seemed to enjoy looking after him during his extended shifts and pampering him on his off times. Once again, she had amazed him with her diligence, dedication, and devotion. His dad had told him that when he found 'the one' he would know. He knew, without a doubt. Jane was indeed doctor's wife material.

Later that week in the ER, while Randy was standing at the sink washing his hands, Jill placed both hands on his shoulders and directed him into the physicians' break room.

"What are you doing?" Randy asked, wondering why they were in here.

"I brought something for you."

"Something for me?"

"Yup."

In the corner was a freshly brewed pot of coffee, a bag of his favorite Starbucks coffee beans, and a station where Jill had set up some Styrofoam coffee cups, sugar, and creamer. This made his day. "Oh man, this is awesome." He walked over to the pot and fixed himself a cup. As he stirred, he asked, "Why did you do this?"

"Because ER rotations are tough," she explained. "Especially if you're not used to it. You're Jim's best friend, and I know you love coffee. The coffee the cafeteria brews up isn't good. Even though you didn't say anything, I could tell by the look on your face that you didn't like it."

Jill had to be one of the most sympathetic and caring people Randy had ever had the privilege to know. She completely went out of her way to make his life in the ER more tolerable. "Thank you."

"You're welcome. I'll try to keep it brewed for you." She smiled at him and left the room.

Jill was a good nurse. She was fast, she was thorough, and she was always willing to help the doctors in any way she could. Her rapport with patients was extraordinary. Everyone loved her, especially the kids, and she looked cute in nurse's scrubs. Jim deserved a nice woman. Jill definitely had Randy's vote.

Randy met Jim at the rec center Saturday afternoon to shoot some hoops. When the two men took a break, Randy wiped his brow with a towel and chugged down an entire bottle of Gatorade. "Jill is incredible," he stated.

"You don't have to convince me of that, but what made you come to that epic conclusion?" Jim asked.

"She set up a coffee station in the ER break room last week, just so I could have a fresh cup. It was the sweetest thing."

"Yeah, that sounds like somethin' she would do."

"She's cool," Randy stated with a nod of approval. "I like her. And she makes a mean cup of coffee."

"I'm glad you approve. How's the ER treatin' ya?"

"I've never worked so hard in my life."

"Exciting though, isn't it?"

"I gotta give it that. And you want to do that every day?"

"Hell yeah. The ER is where it's at, man."

Randy laughed at Jim's overenthusiasm. "I don't mind the ER. It does have its downfalls though."

"Like what?"

"The adrenaline is..."

"Dude, I love the adrenalin rush," Jim interjected. "It's massive."

"It's not the adrenaline I have a problem with, it's the tired feeling after the adrenalin goes away that wears me out. And I really don't like being away from home and leaving Janey alone at night. Those over night shifts are killer."

"OB's are gone at night too, you know," Jim reminded his best friend.

"But not all night. Long enough to make a delivery then I get to go back home. It's an on-call status, not an all-nighter. There's a difference."

"That's true I guess," Jim concurred.

"Stephanie has decided to move down here for the fall semester. Evidently she's coming next week to look for an apartment while Bruce is off."

"An apartment?" Jim mused. "How come she's not movin' in with Bruce?"

"He doesn't want her to."

"Why not?"

"He's not stupid, Jim. He knows damn well Stephanie will distract him. And he sure as hell isn't going to want her to invade his privacy by sharing living quarters with her. That would most definitely cramp his style."

"No kidding," Jim agreed.

"But Jane has a couple of sorority sisters looking for another roommate. Steph might end up with them."

"Your sister is a trip, man."

"Tell me about it."

"What the hell is Bruce doin' with her? They don't seem compatible at all."

"I know," Randy agreed. "From what I can tell, they don't know each other that well. I get the impression it's a relationship of convenience, but it's not really my business."

"Isn't that awkward for you?" Jim wondered. "I mean, she is your sister, Dude."

"Not really. I try to stay out of it. Regardless of what happens between them, she'll always be my sister and he'll always be my friend. Stephanie knows that."

Jim changed the subject. "Jill and I have been talkin' about gettin' an apartment together."

"Really?"

"Yup. She thinks havin' my male influence around is good for Sabrina. And it's kinda bogus for both of us to pay rent and cough up dough for two babysitters all the time. We're lookin' at a three-bedroom. It's a little pricier, but overall it will be cheaper than payin' for two apartments."

"That's true," Randy said. "You heard from Trina?"

"Not recently. As you know, I changed my cellphone number. She has no way of contacting me. Doesn't mean she won't try though."

"What are you going to do if she does?"

"I don't need her and Jill to have a confrontation, that's for sure. Jill would be fine, but I don't know how Trina would handle that. She'd probably go off on one of her rampages. I have contact with her parents on a regular basis, and they told me she moves around a lot. Apparently she can't hold down a job. They don't even know where she's livin' right now. The last time they saw her, she became violent with them and was beggin' for money. They think she might be a Loadie."

Although hearing that Trina was involved in drugs was sad, Randy wasn't surprised. "She really lost touch with reality, didn't she?"

"Yup, which is why I don't want Chris around her. If she's really bent out on drugs and livin' that kind of lifestyle, I sure as hell don't want my son exposed to that shit."

"No doubt."

Chapter Fifty-One

The next three months flew by quickly for Randy. He was so busy with clinical rotations and work that he barely had time to breathe. It was now mid-October, and Randy and his study group were scheduled to meet at his apartment to review information for their upcoming MLE practice run. About twenty minutes before the group was supposed to meet, Jane grabbed a sweater and her purse and headed toward the door.

Randy gently took her arm and pulled her close to him. "Wait a minute. Not so fast. Where are you running off to?"

"I'm hanging out at the mall with Stephanie and the girls."

"Any idea what time you'll be back?"

"I'm not sure. I'll call you later, though, and let you know."

"I'll have my phone right beside me." He kissed her.

"I love you, Randy."

"I love you, Babe," he replied. "Have fun today."

"I will."

As soon as Jane left, Randy slipped into the kitchen to put on a pot of coffee and make himself a bowl of microwave oatmeal.

During a break in their study session, Bruce came out of the restroom with a smirk on his face. "Your bath towels have flowers on them."

"Yes, Bruce," Randy replied, "I am aware of that."

"You used to have the sweetest bachelor's pad. Now it's filled with feminine, frilly fluff."

"Jane lives here too. I want her to be comfortable."

Disgusted by this turn of events, Bruce picked up a copy of Cosmopolitan Magazine off the coffee table. "Cosmo, Randy?" He snooped around and pulled a book off the bookshelf. "Is this a romance novel?"

"Most likely," Randy replied. "There are some dresses, ten thousand pairs of shoes, satin sheets, and lingerie in my bedroom too, if you really want to investigate."

"Damn, Randy. This girl has really gotten to you." Bruce picked up a framed picture of Randy and Jane standing in front of the Eiffel Tower. "What the hell happened?"

"Love bit me in the butt."

"Looks like it's infected your brain." Bruce set the picture back on the entertainment system shelf. "Don't start painting your walls pink."

Mandy snarled at Bruce, unimpressed with the comments he was making. "You're just insensitive, Buckman. I think it's sweet that Randy's made her such a big part of his life."

"Big part of his life?" Bruce retorted. "She's taking over his apartment."

"No she's not," Randy argued. "Besides, it's not my apartment anymore. It's our apartment. She has every right to express herself here."

Jim was shocked that Bruce was being so insensitive. "It's a damn good thing you didn't have Stephanie move in with you. What do you think she has all over her place?"

"Frilly, fruity pink shit. Which is one of many reasons why she's *not* living with me."

Following their study session, Bruce and Mandy met at Starbucks. Over the last few weeks, Bruce had been overly sensitive and particularly short-fused. Mandy was worried about him. She sat down at a table with him and got a good look at his face. He had dark circles under his eyes and appeared run down. "Are you ok?" she asked him.

"Why do you ask?"

"You seem easily irritated lately, and you look exhausted."

"I've had a lot of things on my mind."

"Care to share?"

"Where would you like me to start?"

Bruce didn't always express his emotions well, but Mandy knew something was bothering him. "You and I have been friends for a long time. You've always been able to talk to me."

With a sigh, Bruce said, "My schedule is kicking my butt. We have clinical training ten hours a day then I'm off to work for another six hours. I'm functioning off five hours of sleep every night, if I'm lucky." He leaned back in his chair and took a sip of his coffee. "I'm normally not a big coffee drinker, but lately I've been living off this stuff. And to make matters worse, Stephanie has been giving me a hard time. She demands that we go out every night. Not only do I not have time, but I'm too damn tired and don't have the energy to keep up with her spontaneous whims. I tried to explain to her the demands of my schedule and told her I needed some space, but she got all huffy about it." He raised his hand to his head, which felt like it was about to explode.

Seeing the added strain Stephanie was putting on him, Mandy reached out and gently touched Bruce's arm. "If you were having problems, why didn't you come talk to me?"

"I really didn't think you'd want to hear about my problems with Stephanie. I know it bothers you that she and I are dating, and you always seem irritated when I talk about her."

"You know I'll always be here to listen. Don't try to take on so much by yourself. I want to help you."

"I know, and I appreciate that."

Trying to help him clear his head, she offered, "Come on. I'll buy you a cookie."

"No," he countered. "I'll buy *you* one."

Agreeing to his proposal, they each ordered an oatmeal cookie. Bruce picked up the tab then they sat and talked until Bruce had to report to work.

Bruce, Jim, and Randy all had placements in the same hospital that week, so they made plans to meet for lunch. After making his food selections, Bruce sat down at the table. "Both of you are crazy," he said, pointing first to Jim then to Randy.

"Why?" Randy asked.

"The single life is the way to go. No demands, no stress, no female moodiness to deal with. Just peace and quiet and all the time in the world to myself."

Jim and Randy looked at each other, somewhat surprised that Bruce had made such a bold statement. Yet Randy had a hunch he knew what caused Bruce to feel that way. "You and Steph broke up, didn't you?"

"Yes, but I'm glad."

"You're glad?" Jim questioned.

"I am," Bruce reiterated. "Being in a relationship consumed way too much of my time. Now I'm free to do what I want, when I want."

"Wow," Randy said. "You are taking this amazingly well."

"Women are not worth the trouble. They only complicate things." He focused on his lunch and didn't say another word about it.

Later that evening, Randy was able to catch Bruce alone. After the way he acted earlier, Randy questioned his state of mind. "Are you ok?"

"I'm fine." He pretended like nothing was wrong. "Why wouldn't I be?"

"You and Steph just split up. I can't believe you're not the least bit affected by this. I'd be going out of my mind if it were me."

"Well, it wasn't you, was it?" Bruce slipped his stethoscope into his lab coat pocket.

"What happened?"

Bruce explained, "Despite the fact that I made it very clear to her that I didn't want her moving in with me, she continued to push the issue, saying some shit about how she can't afford an apartment down here. I reemphasized to her multiple times that she couldn't live with me, yet somehow, more and more of her stuff ended up at my place. She totally blew me off and moved her crap into my apartment anyway. That's kinda what set off the whole thing. She was smothering me, and I couldn't breathe."

"I wondered if that's what it was."

"I was perfectly happy sitting on cruise control and coasting along, but she had to try to push this into overdrive. I'm not ready for that level of commitment, and she knew that. I had every right to let her know I wasn't comfortable with how fast she was trying to move this."

Randy agreed, "Yes you did."

"She and I don't see things the same way. I hope there's no hard feelings," Bruce said.

"No, not at all."

Stephanie was quick to put Bruce behind her, which was painfully obvious when Randy saw her kissing a man dressed in black leather out by the curb in front of his apartment. "Great," he said out loud. When she came inside to visit for a while, Randy probed her about what he witnessed. "Who was that?"

"Butch Vargas."

Randy raised an eyebrow. "His name is Butch?"

"Yes."

"Where'd you meet him?"

"At a club last night."

Randy rolled his eyes. "Stephanie, you need to be careful who you go home with."

"Why do you care?" She plopped down on the sofa, completely disregarding his advice. "Is Jane here?"

"No, she's not." Annoyed that his sister ignored him, he asked, "Did you hear what I said?"

"Yes I did, and you are not my father, so don't try to be." She tried to dodge the subject again. "Where did she go?"

Randy wouldn't let Stephanie off the hook that easily. "I'm not trying to be Dad. But I am your older brother, Steph, and I'm telling you that you can't go home with strange men you meet at clubs. That's dangerous."

"I'm an adult. I can do what I want."

"I know that, but you are also a young, pretty female, and you are far too trusting. There are some sick people out there, and I don't want to see my sister in a rape center, on the headlines of the missing person's page, or lying in a body bag, dammit. This is San Francisco."

"You worry too much."

"You're my sister, Steph. So yes, I worry about you."

"Well, stop. Where did Jane go?"

"She's at work. She'll be home in about twenty minutes."

Stephanie opened the refrigerator and pulled out a Diet Pepsi, patiently waiting for Jane.

Snuggled in bed under the covers that night, Jane laid her head on Randy's chest. He hadn't said much that night. She knew something was on his mind. "You're awfully quiet tonight."

He softly rubbed her arm. "I'm worried about Stephanie."

"Stephanie? Why?"

"Her promiscuous nature really scares me. She's always been kind of rebellious, but she's getting out of control. She goes home with complete strangers, taking no consideration of the risks involved. Something bad is going to happen to her one of these days."

Jane tried to get Randy to relax. "She's just impulsive."

"She's reckless, Jane. She's going to bring home an STD or get herself pregnant or something worse."

"You can't always be there to protect her, Sweetie. Stephanie is going to do what she wants. You know that," Jane reminded him.

"I wish she'd think a little more about consequences before she does shit like that. If something happens to her…"

At 2:00 A.M. Sunday morning, Randy received a phone call that woke him from a dead sleep. Wearily, he reached over to answer it. "Hello?" He listened intently for a minute before he asked, "Why are you crying?" The person on the other end of the line said something that made him burst out of bed. "Jesus, Steph." He began frantically pacing around the room, searching for a pen and a piece of paper so he could write something down. "Where are you?" He held the phone between his ear and shoulder while he wrote down the address. "Stay inside and do not leave. I'm on my way." When the conversation was over, he quickly slipped on a pair of jeans then grabbed a tee-shirt out of the closet. "Shit!"

The volume level of the conversation woke Jane up, who had overheard the entire thing. "What's going on?"

He pulled the shirt over his head and reached into a drawer for a pair of socks. "Stephanie got dumped on the street in front of a gas station."

Distressed by this news, she gasped, "Oh my god. Is she ok?"

"She says she is. I need to go pick her up."

"Do you know where she is?"

"Yes. She gave me the address." He sat on the edge of the bed and put on his shoes. "Dammit. I knew something like this was going to happen."

Jane sat behind him and wrapped her arms around his shoulders, kissing the back of his neck. "Be careful."

"I will." He grabbed the piece of paper he wrote the address on and slipped his phone into his pocket.

When Randy arrived at the convenience store, Stephanie was standing inside hugging herself. The moment she saw Randy step out of his car, she rushed out the door and threw herself into his arms, wetting his jacket with her tears.

He hugged her and let her cry.

"I'm sorry, Randy."

"It's ok." He leaned back a bit and carefully examined her. She had a laceration on her cheek, her hair was disheveled, and her face was flushed. She reeked of alcohol. Fearing the worst, he asked, "Did he…?"

Reassuring him, she shook her head. "No."

"Thank God." He helped her into the car and took off down the road. On the way home, he tried to gather more information from her. "What happened?"

"I was driving around with this guy I met at the bar…"

Randy gritted his teeth and scolded her. "Dammit, Stephanie. I told you not to do that."

"I'm sorry." She held her face in her hands and sobbed.

She was starting to become hysterical. Randy thought she was going to hyperventilate. "Calm down, Steph. Breathe."

Once she composed herself, she explained what happened. "He forced himself on me, but I told him no. Well, he tried anyway, so I kicked him. He started shouting obscenities at me then opened the door and shoved me out of the car."

At a red light, Randy stopped and quickly glanced her direction. "How did you get that cut on your face?"

"I banged it on the door when he pushed me."

He was glad she was ok, but angry at her for not taking his advice. "For god's sake, Stephanie. Will you listen to me now? I told you something like this was going to happen. You're lucky it wasn't worse. He could have raped you or beat the shit out of you or left you for dead somewhere." The light turned green; he continued to drive. "You can crash at my place tonight."

"Thank you."

When they returned to Randy's apartment he told her, "Clean up your face, and get some sleep." He put his keys and phone on the table then went into the bedroom, leaving

Stephanie alone in the living room to ponder her own stupidity.

In the morning, Randy grabbed the biggest cup of coffee he could find and loaded it up with caramel, chocolate, and whipped cream, hoping it would wake him up. He sat at the table and rubbed his eyes.

Jim couldn't help but notice Randy's feet dragging this morning. "Dude, you look like shit."

"Thanks," Randy grumbled. "My sister called me at two o'clock this morning. Some guy dumped her on a street corner downtown."

Bruce overheard this comment and lifted his head in disbelief. "Is she ok?"

Randy told him, "She's fine. She has got to outgrow this juvenile behavior. I swear."

"What happened to her?"

"This guy she met at a bar tried to come on to her. She denied him and he pushed her out of the car."

"She was drunk, wasn't she?" Bruce assumed.

"Yes."

Bruce looked at Randy with genuine concern in his eyes. "Where is she now?"

"She's at my place. Jane's going to take her home later."

Bruce drew his lips in thoughtfully. "That's good."

Following the study session, Bruce stopped by Stephanie's apartment to make sure she was alright.

When she opened the door and saw him standing on her front stoop, she didn't know what to say.

"Randy told me what happened," he said.

She leaned against the doorjamb and sulked.

He examined the laceration on her face. "You're hurt."

"It's nothing."

Bruce felt a bit guilty for not being there when she needed him. All he could think to say was, "I'm sorry."

"It was my own fault. You had nothing to do with it."

"I'm not talking about that. I never meant to hurt you, Steph. I…"

She put her finger on his lips. "Ssh." Then, to Bruce's surprise, she kissed him.

He stared at her, dazed. "Why did you do that?"

She kissed him again. It wasn't long before she drug him into her apartment.

Bruce and Jim came over to Randy's apartment that evening to watch the Lakers game with him. Bruce walked in and was immediately overwhelmed by the heavenly aroma that filled the air. "Oh man. It smells incredible in here. What is that?"

"Jane's chili," Randy said. "That stuff is awesome."

Randy offered Bruce a Corona, which he gladly took. He plopped down on the couch and put his feet up, getting more comfortable. "I went and saw Stephanie this afternoon."

Randy seriously questioned Bruce's rationale behind that decision. "Why?"

"I had to make sure she was ok."

"And were you satisfied?"

"Yes." Bruce grinned. "But things didn't quite go as I expected."

"What do you mean?" He took a drink of the Corona he had in his hand.

"We were able to patch things up. She agreed to give me the space I need and I agreed to dedicate one night a week just to her."

"And she was ok with that?"

"She was totally cool with it. She realized she was pressuring me, so she agreed to back off and just let things flow, which is what I wanted all along."

Hearing this actually made Randy happy. "Well, good. I'm glad you two were able to work things out." He still didn't think they were right for each other, but at least with Bruce, he knew his sister would be safe.

Chapter Fifty-Two

With his clerkship schedule the way it was, Randy only had one day off for Thanksgiving this year. Instead of flying home to Seattle, he decided to celebrate Thanksgiving with Jane and her family instead. Randy was apprehensive about being in a house with Jane's dad all afternoon, but was excited that he and Jane were finally going to spend a winter holiday together. It had been a while since Randy had been to her father's house, so he was due to make his appearance.

Jane and Randy walked up to the porch carrying a green bean casserole, Grilled Cinnamon Pears with yogurt dip, and a pumpkin pie Jane had made. "I hope we don't end up playing a game of twenty questions again," Randy scoffed.

"Stop that," Jane insisted. "It will be fine."

The evening was surprisingly enjoyable. Dale made a conscience effort to be friendly and cordial toward Randy. They talked about basketball and fishing, at which time Randy suggested they go fishing together sometime. Dale agreed that was a good idea so the two of them made plans to do it over Christmas break before Randy went to Seattle.

Before they left, Dale gave Jane some leftover turkey and the rest of the pumpkin pie to take home, which Randy was grateful for. He loved pumpkin pie.

On the drive home, Jane put her hand on Randy's thigh. "That was wonderful how you suggested that you and Daddy go fishing together."

"I figure if we're stuck together on a fishing boat, we have no choice but to talk to each other. You ever been fishing?"

Jane curled her lip. "Eww. Slimy worms and smelly fish?"

He laughed at her reaction. "You ever tried it?"

"No."

"You might like it," he suggested. "I could help you bait your hook and take the fish off the line for you. That way you won't have to touch it. I think it would be fun to go fishing with you."

"You'd laugh at me."

"I might. But it would all be in good fun. I'll take you out in Dad's boat when we go up for Christmas break. It's too cold to go skiing, but we can always go fishing." Driving over the Bay Bridge, Randy asked, "Have you told your dad yet that you're coming to Seattle for Christmas?"

She shook her head. "Not yet. I'm trying to figure out how to break it to him. I've always spent Christmas at home."

"You know, you don't have to come up for Christmas if you don't want to. I don't want you to feel like I'm dragging you away from your family."

"I don't feel that way at all. I want to go up there," she reassured him. "We've never spent Christmas together, and I get to see Daddy all the time. You don't see your parents that often. Besides, we spent Thanksgiving with Daddy."

"True. And we got pie out of it." Randy grinned.

Randy and Jim went Christmas shopping together to get gifts for family members and friends. They perused through several sporting goods stores before they headed to a toy store to purchase some gifts for Sabrina and Christopher. On the way, they passed by Bath and Body Works.

Randy declared, "I need to go in here for a sec."

Jim gave Randy a funny look. "What for?"

"Jane. She loves the lotions and body sprays from this place and I want to get her some." He walked in and picked out a few for her.

Jim couldn't believe the extravagant gifts Randy had purchased for Jane. Aside from the body sprays and scented lotions, he bought her a diamond accent heart pennant necklace, a bottle of French perfume, and a pretty cashmere cardigan sweater. "Jesus, Dude. Do you always get Jane gifts like that?"

"You have a problem with that?"

"It's your money. Spend it however the hell you want."

"She's worth it to me. I love spoiling her with gifts. It gets me laid a lot. You should try it sometime," Randy teased with an obnoxious grin.

Offended by that remark, Jim replied, "Shut up. I get laid."

Randy laughed. "I'm messing with you. Relax."

When the men had their fill of shopping, Randy dropped Jim off outside his apartment building. "Thanks for coming with me, Jim," Randy said, grateful that his best friend was willing to brave the holiday shopping hoards so he wouldn't have to go alone.

"No problem. I needed to get a few gifts for the kids anyway."

"I'll see you tomorrow."

"Yup. Nine o'clock." They knuckle bumped. "Later, Bro."

Jim took his bags upstairs to his apartment, but when he go there, Trina was sitting on his doorstep. His smile instantly turned to a frown. "What are you doin' here?"

Upon examining Trina further, Jim noticed she had lost a significant amount of weight, unhealthily so. And as the dark circles under her eyes and droopy eyelids indicated, she appeared to be wasted. She had a lot of nerve showing up in this condition.

"I want to see my son," she demanded in a hostile tone.

"He's not home." He walked past her and unlocked his door. She attempted to push her way in, but he blocked her at the door. "Where do you think you're goin'?"

"Coming inside."

"The hell you are. You're not comin' in here."

Inside Jim's shopping bags were some balls, a truck, and other toddler toys. Trina also spotted a few gifts for a little girl. "Why did you buy a doll?"

"That is none of your goddamn business. What do you want?"

"I've lost my job and my apartment, and I have no place to go. My parents told me I can't stay with them. I need your help." Her speech was garbled and incoherent and she seemed disoriented, as if she had forgotten where she was. Suddenly, she went pale-faced and passed out.

Jim tried to catch her before she hit the ground, but he was too late. She fell onto the concrete in front of his door. He picked her up, brought her inside, and laid her on his couch. "Trina," he said. "Can you hear me? Open your eyes." He shook her shoulders, trying to get her to respond. "Trina, wake up."

She recognized his voice. "Jim?"

"Open your eyes."

She groaned and lifted her eyelids, trying to figure out where she was.

When she moved her arm, her sleeve slid up slightly, exposing the skin on the crook of her elbow. Jim immediately noted the track marks on her skin. "You're shootin' up now?"

Weary-eyed, she wiped her runny nose.

He checked her pulse. It was slower than it should have been, and her breathing was short and shallow. She was extremely lethargic and weak. Concerned about her health, he reached for his penlight and quickly shined it in her eyes. Her pupils were constricted. "Fuckin' heroin?" He sat in the chair across the room, leaned his elbows on his knees, and stared at her pitifully. "Where did you get it?"

She didn't acknowledge the question. Instead, she threw up in the wastebasket next to the couch then began to nod off again.

Jim grabbed his phone. "I'm checkin' you into a detox clinic."

Following their study session Sunday, Jim pulled Randy aside. "Trina was at my doorstep when you dropped me off yesterday."

Randy's eyebrows shot down in surprise. "What the hell? What did she want?"

Jim explained what happened. "She said she wanted to see Chris then she passed out in front of my apartment. She was wasted, Randy. She had track marks on her arm and she looked like hell."

"Heroin?"

"Yup. A fuckin' junkie," Jim explained.

"How did she find you?"

"I talked to her parents last night and apparently she showed up on their doorstep Friday night totally wasted. She started tearin' their house apart lookin' for drug money so they threw her out. Somewhere along the way, she found my address and came scopin' me out."

"Damn."

"I checked her into a detox center yesterday," Jim said. "They put her on Methadone."

"Did Jill and the kids see this?"

"No. They weren't home at the time."

"Does Jill know about it?"

"I told her last night," he sighed.

Based on Jim's reaction, Randy feared this was not a good thing. "What did she say?"

"She wasn't happy about the situation, but she understands."

"What the hell happened to Trina?" Randy asked, somewhat concerned about the woman.

"The fuck if I know," Jim griped. "But that woman standin' outside my door yesterday was not Katrina Rogers. She probably only weighed ninety pounds and she looked like a fuckin' zombie. Then in the car when I was drivin' her to the treatment center, she started rubbin' her hand up my thigh and spattin' off a bunch of shit about how sorry she was and how she never meant to hurt me, beggin' me to take her back."

"What'd you say?" Randy asked.

"I told her she was wastin' her breath," Jim replied. "That I didn't love her and didn't want her around me or my son, especially when she was doped out. She went all agro on me and said I had no right to keep him from her. There is no way in hell I'm exposin' Christopher to that shit. No way!"

"She really thought you'd take her back after everything she did to you?"

"I don't know what the hell she's thinkin'. She isn't thinkin', that's the problem. She was so damn drugged out, I'm not even sure she knew where she was. That shit will fuck you up, man."

Randy completely agreed with him. "You had an interesting afternoon yesterday, didn't you?"

"Why the hell did she come back here? I really don't want to deal with her."

"Then don't. Make her parents do it," Randy advised. "Trina is not your responsibility, Jim. You did your ethical duty as a medical professional and got her medical treatment. Leave it at that. Let her parents deal with it now."

Randy had a good argument, and Jim felt better about the situation after talking to him. "You know, you're right. Screw her."

Randy was glad that was settled. "Wanna grab some burgers?"

"I would love to. Let's blow this Taco Stand."

Chapter Fifty-Three

Clasping Jane's hands in his, Randy leaned against the wall, lost in her kiss. "You know what I was thinking?" he asked, grazing his thumb across her lips.

"What?"

"I bet you have never been on a pair of snow skis before, have you?"

"No."

His mouth curved into a smile. "We might have to go up to Mt. Rainier and get you on a slope."

"But I don't know how to ski."

"I'll teach you." Wanting her close to him, he released his grasp on her hands and drew her nearer. "Two weeks with you in Seattle is going to be incredible." Finding her harder and harder to resist, his lips found hers again.

"Ok you two, break it up," Jim's voice rang out, disturbing the moment.

Randy raised his middle finger, ignoring Jim's request.

Jim laughed at him and joined their friends at the table.

"Hey, Jim, did you hear about the…" Bruce peeked over the brim of his beer and instantly went slack-jawed. "I'll be damned. Look what the cat dragged in."

All heads turned.

"Sarah!" Jim greeted her with outstretched arms. "It's good to see you."

Sarah quickly scanned the room. "Where's Randy?"

"Take one guess," Jim remarked, pointing to the wall where Randy and Jane stood together, engrossed in a kiss. He cupped his hands around his mouth and hollered, "Yo, Hanson! Get over here!"

Irritated by Jim's apparent lack of respect for his privacy, Randy broke his embrace with Jane and turned around. "What the hell do you want, Ryan?" That's when he saw Sarah. "Sarah!" Releasing his grip on Jane, he rushed to the table and gave Sarah a hug. He had kept in touch with her via text messages and e-mail, but hadn't seen her in ages. She looked better than ever—healthier, happier, and she had lost some weight, making her figure more defined. And with her pretty Asian features, she drew quite a bit of attention from the single men in the room. "Wow! Look at you. You look fantastic!"

"Thank you." She pulled up a chair and sat down.

Randy occupied the seat right beside her. "What are you doing in town?"

"My sister is in Cal's production of *The Nutcracker* this year. My whole family came down to see her perform."

"That's right," Bruce remembered. "Elaine is a dancer."

"Yup," Sarah said. "And since I was coming into town, I called Mandy. She told me you guys were all meeting over here tonight, so I thought I'd drop by."

Randy's eyes darted over to Amanda. "You knew she was coming into town?"

Mandy nodded.

"Gee," Jim complained, "Thanks for tellin' us."

Mandy told them, "Sarah wanted to surprise everyone."

It wasn't long before the five of them were completely lost in conversation, catching up, laughing together, and recalling old memories. It was a joy to see the group together again.

Mid-way through the conversation, Randy devoted his full attention to Jane. "You want a drink, Baby?"

"I could go for a…"

"Daiquiri?" he finished her thought.

She smiled and nodded. "Yes."

"Coming right up." He winked at her and headed to the bar.

Jane watched him for a second then excused herself. When she got to the bar, she stood next to him, leaning on the counter with her elbows. "How long did you want to stay here tonight?"

He swiveled the barstool, facing her. "Why?"

"Because I was hoping we could get home early." She bit her lip seductively and stood between his legs, clasping her hands behind his neck. "We'll turn down all the lights in the apartment, and I thought I might model my new lingerie for you." She teased him by nibbling on his ear then ambled back over to the table.

"Sir," the bartender said.

Randy didn't hear him. He was too busy staring at Jane.

"Your drink, Sir," the bartender repeated.

Randy spun around on his stool. "What?"

"Your drink."

"Oh." He paid the man, slipped off the barstool, and carried Jane's drink to the table.

Jane moved her lips up to his ear and whispered, "Thank you." Purposefully trying to entice him, she rubbed her fingertip across the edge of the glass then licked the condensation off. She unbuttoned the top two buttons on her blouse, exposing some of her breast to him then meandered her finger down her bustline, all while she sexily sipped her daiquiri from a straw.

Randy's heartrate went through the roof. He began to breathe heavier and had to swallow back pent up desire. After watching this display for several minutes, Randy retreated to the men's room. He leaned over the bathroom sink, resting his body weight on the edge.

Jim came in behind him, concerned that his friend might be ill. "You alright, Bro?"

Randy's face was flushed, and he was panting. He turned on the faucet and splashed water on his face. "Jane is totally coming onto me. I'm getting a fucking hard on out there. I had to get out of that room."

"Is she drunk?"

"No. That's the only drink she's had tonight, and she's not even drinking it. She's using it to seduce me." He dried his hands with a paper towel and tossed it in the trash. "Holy shit. She's never come on to me like this before. Not in public anyway."

Jim laughed. "You need to get her horny ass home."

"But we were all going to hang out tonight, and Sarah's here."

"Randy, go home," Jim teased.

Randy left the men's room and immediately advanced toward Jane. "Let's go," he said. He grabbed his jacket and headed for the car.

She set her drink down, grabbed her sweater, and chased after him.

In the morning, Randy was awakened by a knock on his door. He slipped out of bed, put on a pair of shorts, and trudged out to answer it.

Jim stood on the porch with a basketball under his arm. "Well, good morning, Casanova."

Randy scratched his head sleepily. "Hey."

Clothes and undergarments were spread out all over the floor, leaving a trail from the living room to the bedroom. Jim had to laugh. "Hmm, looks like you had a heavy night."

"Fuck you." He bent over and picked up the clothing, quietly tossing them into the bedroom, being careful not to wake Jane. "What are you doing here so early?"

"Early?" Jim shoved his watch in Randy's face. "It's ten thirty, Bro."

Feeling groggy, Randy stepped into the kitchen to put on a pot of coffee.

"You up for a game this mornin'?" Jim asked.

"Can I wake up first?"

"Sure." Jim hopped up on the counter, placing the ball beside him. "So, how was it?"

"How was what?"

"Last night? After all the come on she was givin' you, it must have been pretty hot."

"I'm not answering that."

Jim grabbed a cookie from a container, taking a bite. As he chewed, he examined it carefully. "Dude, these are kickass cookies. Did Jane make these?"

"Yes." Randy reached into the cupboard and pulled out his Lakers coffee mug. "Why aren't you home with your son today?"

"Jill's off for the next four days and agreed to watch the kids so I could spend some time with my best friend. You're not workin' today, are you?"

"No." Even though the pot was still brewing, Randy let it trickle from the spout directly into his cup.

"Jill wanted me to invite you guys over for dinner before you take off for Seattle."

"When?"

"You on-call Tuesday night?"

"No, Monday and Thursday."

"What about Jane? She doin' anything Tuesday night?"

"Not that I know of." Randy doctored up his coffee with creamer and two tablespoons of sugar. Gripping his mug, he took a sip.

"Tuesday then," Jim confirmed.

"You need us to bring anything?"

"Nope. Just yourselves." Jim checked the time on his watch. "How long 'til you're ready, Bro?"

"Give me ten minutes. I'm gonna get dressed." Randy slipped into the bedroom to put on some clothes.

As promised, Randy went lingcod and sturgeon fishing with Jane's dad. When he returned home that evening, he smelled like fish, but had a sixty-inch sturgeon that weighed about fifty pounds to showoff to Jane. It was neatly wrapped in ice.

When Jane saw the size of this fish, she was pleasantly surprised. "Oh my god, Randy. That is huge." She jumped off the couch and followed him into the kitchen.

"Yup," he replied, slapping it down on the counter. "Five footer." He took off his sweatshirt and searched for his fillet knife. "We can get several meals out of this bad boy."

"Did you catch that?" She lifted the butcher paper to get a better look at it.

"Yes I did." He set his knife on the counter and pulled out a large wooden cutting board.

"Did Daddy catch anything?"

"He hooked a pretty good-sized lingcod." Randy grinned pompously. "Mine was bigger." After sharpening his fillet knife, he washed his hands and took the fish out of the paper to reveal it in its entirety. "Look at this beauty." He had cleaned it on the boat but still needed to cut it into hefty steaks. "Can you get me some freezer bags, Babe?"

Jane pulled a box of gallon-sized heavy duty freezer bags out of a drawer. She labeled the bags with a black permanent marker then held each bag open so Randy could drop two fish steaks inside.

When they were finished, he thoroughly disinfected his knife and cutting board and dumped the smelly fishy paper and scraps in the trashcan outside. "This is good eats, Babe. Going to make a nice dinner." He set two good-sized fish steaks aside and put the rest in the freezer for future use.

While Randy was in the shower removing fish slime, Jane threw the sturgeon in the oven and put some rice in the rice steamer.

Randy could smell the fish cooking. "Mmm," he stated, emerging from the bedroom. "That smells incredible." He stood behind Jane, who was tossing a salad together, and kissed her.

"What did you and Daddy talk about today?"

He stole a carrot slice from the salad and ate it. "Basketball, sports cars, and we talked about you."

"What about me?"

Randy leaned against the counter facing her. "There's nothing that man wouldn't do for you, Jane. He talked about you a lot today."

"What did he say?"

"He told me stories from your childhood and bragged about your accomplishments. He's proud of you."

She seemed shocked by this. "Really?"

"Yup. How come you never told him you made the Dean's List?"

"Because I didn't think he'd be interested."

He grabbed another carrot slice and popped it in his mouth. "You don't tell your dad much, do you?"

"I tell him what he needs to know," she claimed.

"Your father doesn't know you. I think that's sad."

She slipped on some oven mitts and reached into the oven to pull the fish out. "It's not my fault Daddy never took the time to get to know me."

"Actually, it kind of is. How's he supposed to know you if you don't tell him anything?"

She put the pot holders on the counter and turned the oven off. "What are you getting at?"

"You need to talk to your dad. I think he knows more about me than he does about you."

"Daddy wouldn't be interested in what I do."

"You're wrong, Jane. I think he'd be very interested in what you do."

"Why would Daddy care about my basketball stats or be interested in the research I do for Psychology?" She dished the fish onto a serving plate.

"He would care because it's you." He reached into the fridge and pulled out two bottles of salad dressing, French for him and honey mustard for her, then helped her move the rice, fish and salad to the table. "Your dad said something to me today that made me feel sorry for him."

She turned her head and looked him in the eye. "What did he say?"

"He told me he misses you and wishes you would make more of an effort to talk to him about your life. He enjoyed fishing with me today, but said neither one of his kids ever took the time to do things like that with him. I didn't know how to respond to that, Jane."

She stared at Randy, not sure what to say.

"When's the last time your family went on a vacation together?"

"I don't remember," she admitted.

"When's the last time you called him?"

"I haven't talked to him since we went over there for Thanksgiving."

That's what he was afraid of. "Your dad lives alone in that house. His wife is gone and his kids don't visit him or even talk to him on the phone. He craves your attention."

She walked past him to get plates, napkins, and silverware, but didn't acknowledge what he said.

"Your dad and I had a good time today. We had a nice conversation. He talked about you and your brother with pride. He laughed and shared fond memories with me, and he got excited when the fish were biting. I would gladly go fishing with him again, but he wants to spend time with you." Randy took Jane's arm and turned her body, forcing her to look at him. "Honey, you need to take the time to call him or spend a couple hours over there on the weekend. Bake him some Christmas cookies and deliver them to him."

"When do I have time to do that?"

"How long does it take to pick up a phone and dial a number, Jane? It's not like it's a long drive to get to him. He's right across the Bay Bridge."

She hung her head shamefully.

Randy lifted her chin. "Try to put yourself in his shoes for a minute. You and your brother are all he has left. All afternoon, every conversation we had turned to you, and he's the one who brought it up, not me. He loves you. And I know you love him. He is your father and you are his daughter, but you are not a family, Jane. You know nothing about each other and rarely spend time together. Call him, talk to him, invite him over for dinner sometime, send him funny e-mails, but don't isolate him like this."

Her eyes began to mist.

"I love you. But you need to fix this." He kissed her softly on the lips. "Come on. Let's eat. We'll talk about this later."

Chapter Fifty-Four

This Christmas was going to be the best Randy had in a long time. This year he would have a full two weeks, not only with his family, but with his girlfriend and Bruce as well, who had been invited up to Seattle this year. Randy felt like a little boy anticipating the arrival of Santa Claus. He loved going home to be with his family.

As the plane approached Seattle, Randy pictured Jim in a fluffy red and white Santa suit. This image brought a smile to his face.

Randy's grin made Jane ask, "What's on your mind?"

"I was just thinking about Jim. He's been looking forward to Christmas for months. He even went out and bought a Santa suit for the occasion."

"Are you serious?"

"Yup. Bet his house is going to be a riot Christmas morning."

The ground was white when they landed at the airport. Jane excitedly looked out the window. "Ooh, look. There's snow on the ground."

Randy leaned over to look. Jane had on sandals, inappropriate attire for the current weather conditions. "Your feet are gonna freeze, Babe. Do you have another pair of shoes in your carryon?"

"No."

He shook his head and laughed. "You have got to learn to dress for Seattle."

When they pulled into the driveway of the Hanson home and stepped out of the truck, they had to cross the snow-covered driveway to get to the front door. Randy's dad took both bags while Randy lifted Jane onto his back giving her a piggyback ride so she wouldn't freeze her toes in the snow. When they made it safely to the porch, he set her back down then collected their luggage.

In the middle of unpacking their bags, Randy's mom came downstairs. "You guys doing ok? You need anything?"

"Nope. We're good. Thanks, Mom," Randy replied.

Ellen kissed her son's cheek. "Your dad has some appointments this week, but he didn't schedule anything Thursday or Friday. You'll get the whole weekend with your dad, Honey."

Excited about that, Randy said, "Good. We can go fishing."

"He's looking forward to it."

"So am I."

Monday morning, Randy and Jane picked Bruce and Stephanie up from the airport. Bruce was nervous about spending two weeks in Seattle with Stephanie and her family, but felt more comfortable about it knowing Randy was going to be there.

When they came through the gate, Randy gave his sister a hug then slapped Bruce's palm with his hand. "Hey, Buckman."

"Hey." Bruce quickly scanned the area. "Your parents aren't here?"

"Dad's working and Mom ran to the grocery store to restock before the whole clan showed up. She should be home by the time we get there. Have you guys eaten?"

"Not yet," Bruce replied.

"You hungry?"

"I am," he said. "I don't know about Stephanie."

Both men turned around to get the girls' opinions, but they were too busy chatting to even hear what the men were talking about. "Women," Randy chuckled. "I say we go eat."

Bruce nodded in agreement. "I'm right there with you."

The girls followed Randy and Bruce around, oblivious to where they were going and not really seeming to care one way or the other. Randy was excited that Bruce was in Seattle and hoped this would be a good opportunity to coax him to come out of his shell a little.

When they arrived at the Hanson home, Randy's mom was straightening pillows on the couch. She turned around and saw Randy and Bruce standing together. "I saw the girls go by and wondered where you guys were." Usually Ellen greeted guests with a hug. Uncertain about Bruce's comfort level and not sure how he would react, she offered him a friendly handshake instead. "Welcome to our home, Bruce. Make yourself comfortable."

"Thank you, Ma'am."

Randy asked, "Where are Bruce and Stephanie staying so we can set these suitcases down?"

"In her room."

Randy and Bruce headed that direction.

When they opened the door to Stephanie's room, Bruce drew back slightly. The room was good-sized and had a TV, but the bed was covered in pink fluffy pillows and the windows were adorned with flowered curtains. Stuffed animals lined shelves and a vase with bright pink flowers sat on the dresser. Bruce's eyes widened. "Oh my holy hell. This is a nightmare."

Randy set the suitcase on the floor. "I grew up with a girl in the house. I'm used to it." Trying to make Bruce feel less overwhelmed, he sat on the queen-sized bed and bounced. "Hey, at least the bed is comfortable."

Bruce began to have serious doubts about all of this. "I hope I didn't make a mistake coming here."

"It'll be fun. And if you need to escape for a while, I'll be here."

Randy showed him around the rest of the house. When they entered the living room, Stephanie and Jane were sitting on the couch. "Hey," Randy said. "There you are." He gave

Jane a kiss then looked over at his sister. "Why am I giving Bruce the grand tour? Isn't that supposed to be your job?"

She waved him off. "You guys are doing fine."

Randy sniggered at her and brought his friend into the kitchen where Randy's mom had just pulled freshly baked cookies out of the oven. Randy grabbed a few then offered some to Bruce. "Cookie?"

Bruce took one. "Thanks."

Randy sat on a stool by the kitchen island. "When is Dad supposed to get home?" he asked, taking a bite of his cookie.

"I think he said his last appointment was at three." Ellen turned her attention to Bruce. He was a quiet young man. She knew he was a good friend of Randy's and obviously saw something in her daughter, but other than that, she didn't know much about him. Needless to say, she was curious about him and the odd relationship he seemed to have with Stephanie. "Tell me about yourself, Bruce."

Bruce wasn't sure what to say. Sharing intimate details of his life with people he barely knew made him uncomfortable. He stumbled over his words. "Um…I'm originally from Thousand Oaks, California. Graduated from Cal State Northridge with a Biology Degree. Received a Master's Degree in Health and Medical Sciences from Berkeley. Currently doing my medical clerkship at UCSF. Pursuing a Neurosurgery Residency Program."

"Any preferences as to where?"

"Hoping for UCLA."

"And what do your parents do?"

Bruce hated talking about his family. Even the thought of it made him cringe. But he didn't want to be rude to Randy's mom so he suffered through the question. "My dad is a business executive at a large corporation in San Diego." That was a nice way of describing his father's position at work. The man was a slave to his job and was constantly bossed around by people higher up the ladder. He hadn't gotten a raise or a promotion in years and seemed content with being the office garbage boy. "My mom doesn't get out much." She didn't get out because she was passed out on the sofa, too drunk to go anywhere. His father worked his life away trying to avoid her, and he spent more time at the office than he did around his wife and kids. Bruce was forced to raise his younger brother, and his parents never seemed to care what either one of them did. When he was fifteen, his father had an affair with his secretary and his parents ended up divorcing over it. Bruce and his brother moved in with his dad, leaving his mother in peace to drink herself to death. Growing up, Bruce rarely saw his father, and even when he was home, he was too busy doing paperwork to even notice that his sons were around. But Bruce didn't want to say that. He was hoping Mrs. Hanson would accept the answer he gave and drop the subject.

Ellen sensed that talking about family was a sensitive topic for Bruce and seemed to upset him, so she didn't push the matter any further.

The Hansons spent the next few days doing last minute gift shopping. The girls baked Christmas cookies and made preparations for Christmas dinner while Bruce and Randy helped Mark shovel snow off the front sidewalk and driveway after a big snowstorm.

Bruce enjoyed being at the Hanson house, especially with Randy there to keep him occupied. He had never experienced family closeness and bonding like this. The family made him feel welcome.

Up on Crystal Mountain Ski Resort, Randy and the others geared up, ready to hit the slopes. Jane was having trouble trying to figure out how to attach her ski boot to the ski. Randy sent the others off without him so he could help her. "Honey, don't fight it so much. Relax."

She put her hand on his shoulder to keep from falling over and tried again. She still couldn't get it.

Randy buckled it for her. "There's one," he teased. "Now let's see if we can latch the other one without taking an hour this time."

"Hush. I told you I've never done this before." She attempted to put on the other one, balancing herself by holding his shoulder while he stood and watched her with a smirk on his face. "Will you help me please?"

He buckled the other ski onto her boot. "Ok. First step. Skis one, Jane zero."

"Be quiet."

He had to laugh. "I'm sorry. But those skis kicked your ass." He handed the poles to her. "Ok, take these. Let's move over here so we aren't standing right in front of the lodge entrance." He helped pull her over to a large flat section where new skiers were learning how to balance and control their skis. "Now, don't let the snow take control of you. You have to control the snow." He showed her how to keep her skis together, which was easy for her to comprehend because she knew the importance of that from water skiing. Then he showed her how to slow down, stop, and steer using the snowplow technique. He told her how to use her poles to help her balance then sent her over to the bunny hill to practice and learn to gain control of her skis. He squatted down and watched her technique. So far she was doing well.

"Good," he said with a smile. "You're getting it."

Right as he said that, she fell and couldn't get herself up. He held his hands out to her and tried to pull her off the snow, but she pulled him down with her instead. They sat in the snow laughing for a minute before Randy finally helped her up.

After about an hour of practicing and finally figuring out how to get herself off the ground if she fell, Randy wanted Jane to experience a green slope for beginners. He showed her how to negotiate a chairlift and together they rode to the top of the slope. Being an accomplished skier, Randy felt sort of silly going down a green slope, but he wanted Jane to feel comfortable and get a good handle on it before he left her alone. When they both made it down to the bottom, they hopped on the lift together and rode back up to the top.

"You're doing well," Randy said. "Skiing takes a lot of practice, and the more you practice, the better you'll get."

"You stop by skidding sideways. How do you do that?"

"You need to gain a little more control before you worry about more advanced techniques, Honey."

"You make it look easy," she declared, somewhat annoyed that she couldn't ski like he could.

"I've been skiing since I was seven. I've had a lot more practice. Let's try another run down the green slope. We'll see how you do this time."

He went down the run with her again, but this time he skied down a ways then stopped and watched her come down so he could observe her form. She was gaining good control and getting more confident on a pair of skis. She wasn't moving very fast yet, but he would rather she went slow and had control than try to speed down the beginner slope and fall, potentially hurting herself. After successfully navigating the green slope, they went back to the chairlift.

On the way up the mountain, Randy held her hand. "You ready to try it by yourself?"

Jane was slightly apprehensive about that.

But he encouraged her, "You can do it. You went down last time and didn't fall once. You're gaining good control. Up to you though."

She decided to try by herself.

"Be careful, Babe."

"I will."

"I'm going down a different run. You gonna be alright?"

"Yup. You'll probably beat me down," she said.

"Probably, but that's ok. I'll wait." He gave her a kiss and sent her on her way. "Good luck, Honey. See you at the bottom."

She smiled and took off down the slope by herself.

Randy went down a black diamond slope, finally able to get a good run in. When he got to the bottom, he slid over to the end of the green slope and took off his skis. He reached into his jacket pocket and pulled out his phone to call Stephanie and Robby to ask about grabbing lunch at the lodge. After about fifteen minutes, everyone made it to the lodge. One by one, they stuck their skis in a snowbank outside and walked inside to warm up.

Randy led the way to a table. He pulled off his gloves and hat and said, "Coffee time."

Unzipping his jacket, Bruce remarked, "Man, I've missed this. I haven't been skiing in a long time."

"You know, Lake Tahoe isn't that far from us. We could make a weekend run out of it," Randy suggested.

"That sounds fun. I'm in," Bruce agreed.

"Me too," said Stephanie.

They ate lunch together then made a few more runs down the mountain. Jane felt confident and was running down the green slope pretty well by herself now. She and Randy agreed to go their separate ways for a bit to allow him to run the more challenging slopes while she practiced on the beginner slopes.

New Year's Day, Randy slept in until almost ten. Some commotion upstairs woke him up. He opened his eyes to discover Jane's spot on the bed was empty. He sat up, stretched, and grabbed a pair of basketball shorts and his Alpha Omega Alpha tee-shirt. As soon as he was dressed, he headed upstairs to see what was going on. Bruce and Mark sat at the table discussing something about angina, and Stephanie and Jane were down on the kitchen floor cleaning up a raw egg they had dropped.

"Well, it lives," Bruce remarked.

Jane momentarily glanced up. "Good morning, Sweetie."

"Good morning." He joined Bruce and his father at the table. The chemical formula, $C_3H_5(NO_3)_3$, was written on a napkin. It immediately grabbed Randy's attention. "Glyceryl trinitrate?"

"Yup," Bruce replied.

"Glyceryl what?" Stephanie asked, confused about the foreign language all the men in her life seemed to use all time.

"Nitroglycerin," Bruce replied. "It's a vasodilator. It's used to treat angina."

"Actually, it's not a treatment for angina," Randy corrected. "It's more effective at preventing angina attacks rather than reversing them once they have commenced."

Irritated by Randy's self-righteous attitude, Bruce retorted, "It's an antihypertensive agent that provides therapeutic effects during episodes of angina pectoris. It works to subside chest pain, decrease blood pressure, and increase heartrate."

Jane was quick to notice Bruce's aggravation. Randy was so wrapped up in his own self-importance that he wasn't thinking about how his haughty attitude affected other people. With a stern glare, she said, "Uh, Randy, can I talk to you for a minute?" She headed toward the stairs expecting him to follow her.

But he didn't move. Instead, he simply turned his head and stared at her.

"Now!" she insisted.

Randy raised his eyebrows, shocked by her demanding tone. He rose to his feet and traipsed downstairs, wondering what Jane was all huffy about. "What was up with that?"

"Why are you arguing with Bruce?"

"I wasn't arguing with him."

"Yes, you were. Why do you do that? You really need to think about how you come across when you say things like that to your friends. It makes you sound like a pompous ass, and it's rude."

He stood there listening to her, but didn't know what to say.

"They know just as much about medicine as you do, yet sometimes you act like you're the only one who knows anything. That smug attitude is hurtful and mean."

"But I…"

She didn't let him continue. "Don't, Randy. You've said enough." She went back upstairs, upset with him.

Randy wasn't quite sure what just happened because he wasn't able to get a word in edgewise. But he did know Jane wasn't happy with him at the moment. Was he being disrespectful to Bruce? If he was, he didn't mean to be. Maybe she was right, maybe he did have a patronizing attitude. If that was the case, he owed Bruce an apology. He didn't want to be bigheaded and scornful like the doctors and residents he had contact with on a daily basis. That's not who he was. Wanting to make things right, he trekked back up the stairs.

Mark glowered at Randy from behind the newspaper. Bruce eyed him with a look of condemnation. Even Stephanie gave him a disapproving stare. All of these dirty looks made Randy feel like a jerk. "I'm sorry, man. I didn't mean to be condescending."

"It's cool," Bruce replied. "Don't worry about it."

Randy turned to Jane and their eyes met. She knew he had a hard time admitting when he was wrong. Taking the initiative to apologize was all she wanted to see him do in this situation. Satisfied that he displayed humility, she smiled in approval.

Mark went back to reading his paper. Stephanie and Jane returned to making breakfast.

Randy stepped into the kitchen and prepared a pot of coffee. "Where's Mom?"

His father looked up from the paper. "Your mother's not feeling well today."

"Is she alright?"

"Yes, she'll be fine. Just a little under the weather. We need to be quiet and let her rest."

After breakfast, they all gathered to watch the Rose Bowl. Brian Davine went in on several plays, and even though her brother was in the game, Jane didn't seem interested in it at all. She was standoffish, and Randy feared she was still mad at him about the incident this morning with Bruce. After the last play, giving a victory to USC, Jane grabbed a basketball, put on her jacket, and went out to the driveway without saying a word to anyone. Randy stared outside the window watching her. Something was bothering her. He wished she would talk to him and tell him what was wrong.

The tension between Randy and Jane was noticeable. To ease his son's mind, Mark stood up and placed his hand on Randy's shoulder. "Communication, Son."

Without further hesitation, Randy slipped on his jacket and stepped outside. "Hey, Babe."

Jane dribbled around as if she didn't hear him.

The silence drove him nuts. He couldn't stand it any longer. When she fired a jump shot, he stole the ball from her and held it under his arm. "You've hardly said two words to me all day. What's going on?"

She stared at him for a minute; her eyes were sad, cheerless.

"Did I say something, do something?"

"This has nothing to do with you."

Intently, his eyes followed her to the front step. She sat on the porch and hung her head. He sat next to her. "Talk to me."

She fidgeted with her fingers. "I've been thinking about what you said."

He said a lot of things. What exactly was she referring to? "About what?"

"About Daddy and my family. And you're right. I don't have a family." She looked up at him. "Stephanie and your mom have such a connection. They bake cookies together and talk about girl stuff and have manicures and go shopping." She started to cry. "Stephanie has her mom and I don't. It's not fair."

Randy set the ball down on the ground and put his arm around her, letting her cry. She hadn't talked about her mom in a long time. She hadn't broken down in tears like this in a long time either. Randy could see how watching the interaction between his mother and his sister over the last week would upset Jane, especially this time of year.

She wiped some of her tears and sniveled again. "Why didn't Daddy send her to the best doctors? Why didn't he get her the best treatment?"

Was Jane blaming her dad for her mother's death? That was harsh and unfair, and in no way did Dale Davine deserve that kind of accusation from his daughter. "Honey, you cannot blame your dad for this. He loved her as much as you did. I'm sure he did everything he could. Cancer doesn't always respond to treatment, and everyone reacts to treatment options differently."

"I can't bake cookies and go shopping with my mom because of that stupid disease." She sobbed inconsolably. "Why did this happen? Why did she have to leave us?"

Randy didn't know what to say or how to console her. He squeezed her closer and kissed the top of her head.

When the tears were out of her system, they went back inside. Jane went downstairs to take a refreshing shower. Randy joined his mom in the living room and helped her fold towels. "Hey, Mom. You feeling better?"

"Yes, much better. Thank you."

Randy folded a towel and set it on the couch. "I'm worried about Jane."

"Why? What's wrong?"

He told her, "You know how you and Stephanie do all that mother-daughter stuff? She's been witnessing all of that, and it made her cry."

His mother blinked with bafflement. "Why would that upset her so much?"

"Because she doesn't have her mom to do those things with. She's angry and hurt over it, and I don't know what to do to make her feel better. In fact, I feel like everything I say makes it worse. The woman I love is in pain, and I don't know how to fix it." Randy rubbed his fingers through his hair trying to figure out what to do. Desperate for advice, he asked, "What do I do? How do I help her?"

Ellen had an idea. "Tell you what. Why don't I take Stephanie and Jane out tomorrow and we'll have a girls' day.

We'll go shopping and see a movie and get our hair and nails done."

Randy liked that idea. "That would be great."

"Your dad has to work tomorrow, but I'm sure you and Bruce can manage on your own."

Grateful for her openness, he gave his mother a kiss on the cheek. "Thanks, Mom. You're awesome."

Randy lay in bed that night with his hands clasped behind his head. Jane was on her tummy propped up on her elbows with her knees bent, sticking her feet in the air.

He rubbed the back of his hand across her cheek. "I wanted to thank you."

"For what?"

"For intervening this morning with Bruce."

"You acted like a jerk," she boldly stated.

"I know, and you called me on it. Thank you." He lifted his head and kissed her. "I get on my pedestal sometimes and my arrogance breaks loose. I'm glad you're here to knock me down a notch and kick me off my high horse when I need it."

"I'm sorry I got all moody on you today, Randy."

"It's ok. I understand. The holidays must be tough." He clasped her hand and gently rubbed her fingers. "Did my mom talk to you about tomorrow?"

She smiled at him with eagerness in her eyes. "Yes, and it's going to be so much fun. I can't wait."

"I know it's not the same as being with your mom."

"No, but I appreciate the gesture," she said gratefully.

"I talked to my dad today. How would you feel about Acapulco this summer?"

"Really?" Jane said excitedly.

"Yup, you've been invited. You wanna go?"

The Hansons were always so kind and open to her. Jane felt comfortable around them and loved how they invited her on family vacations with them. "Yes. I would love to."

"Thought so. I'll let my dad know."

Chapter Fifty-Five

Over the last several months, Randy had been researching various Allopathic Residency Programs. There were certain criteria he was looking for. Among the non-negotiables on his list of strong OB/GYN programs were lots of hands-on experience with deliveries, gynecological surgery, and high risk obstetrics. He wanted state of the art care, supportive supervision, and fellowship among residents. Research and leadership opportunities were a must, including teaching other residents and contributing to the educational experiences of medical students. He also sought ultrasonography and mammography training as well as family planning educational opportunities and infertility. He had written to the residency directors of several programs to request additional information. Based on the information he received, he narrowed his choices down to four programs—University of Washington School of Medicine, Santa Clara Valley Medical Center in San Jose, Stanford University School of Medicine, and the University of California Davis Health Systems in Sacramento. University of Washington was his first choice, not only because it would bring him back home and allow him to establish a reputation in Seattle, but also because their program offered everything he was looking for. The problem was they only accepted six OB/GYN residents a year. The competition was going to be tough, but he was determined to attain one of those positions.

He registered his profile with the Electronic Residency Application Service and worked on his resume, listing all of his honors, research, clinical experiences, and test scores. He also gathered letters of recommendation and typed up personal statements so his applications would be ready to submit once he received his MLE scores in June.

He was in the middle of responding to a post on the medical school and residency forums when Jane walked in the door. He stopped typing and turned around in his chair. "Hey, Baby. Guess what happened to me today?"

"What?" She set her bag on the floor and dropped the mail on the table.

"I got to assist with a delivery."

"That's great!"

He told her all about it. "It was incredible. The adrenaline rush and the excitement of bringing a new life in the world and holding that brand new baby in my hands as it took its first breath, man, it was intense. The miracle of birth is amazing. It was the most exhilarating experience I've ever had."

The obstetrical training Randy received and the information he gained from his ACOG journals always excited him. Jane thought it was cute when he spoke of his experiences in the OB/GYN clinic or the maternity ward of the hospital. Truly he was meant to be an obstetrician.

Randy hopped out of his chair and kissed her. "I won't be home 'til late tonight."

"How late?"

"I don't know. Twelve maybe. Bruce and I are taking Jim out for hot wings and a few rounds of pool for his birthday. Did you invite your dad over for dinner next weekend?"

"Yes. Sunday night. Is that ok?"

"Perfect. I have my study session in the morning, but we're usually done by one. That will give us plenty of time to prepare." He perused through the stack of mail, but stopped when he came across a large manila envelope from the

University of Washington School of Medicine. He set the rest of the mail down and opened this envelope first.

Jane came over to see what sparked his interest. "What's that?"

"Hopefully the information I asked for about their residency program." Inside the envelope were several brochures and pamphlets, rotation schedules, payment stipends and benefits, hospital maps, elective alternatives, contact names, and a list of several websites and books of interest. There was even travel information about Seattle and a realtor's book listing local houses on the market. He opened the real estate booklet and skimmed through it. "This will give me a place to start."

Jane picked up a pamphlet and scanned through the benefits and pay scale of resident doctors. "Sixty thousand to start off?"

"That's pretty standard."

She pointed out some of the highlights. "Three weeks paid vacation, seventeen days of sick leave per year, one week of leave for attending educational events, and a two-hundred fifty dollar education allowance." They also offered a retirement plan, free health, dental and life insurance, disability coverage, hospital parking, free in-house and on-call meals from the hospital cafeteria, discounted home buying options, and a Tuition Exemption Program that allowed access to college courses. UW took care of their resident doctors. "Oh my god, Randy. These benefits are incredible."

"I know, but that's not even the good part. They also provide professional liability insurance coverage."

"What's that?"

"Malpractice insurance. They cover it in full while I'm a resident at UW."

"Really?"

"Yup, and that is a huge expense. And since I'll be affiliated with UW, I'll have access to all of the events and services offered at the university. Their OB/GYN training is superb with lots of research opportunities," Randy explained.

"Sounds like it's just what you're looking for."

"It is. The problem is they only offer six positions a year." He set the real estate book on the table to browse through later.

"When do you start the application process?" she asked.

"I already have. I'm taking the MLE in May, and I've already collected a few recommendation letters. Can't send anything off until September first; they won't accept applications before that. The deadline is October thirteenth, but they did say if I turn everything in prior to that date, I could get an earlier interview."

"When do they make their decision?" Jane asked curiously.

"Before December first usually."

"So you'll know before the end of the year."

"Hopefully. We'll have to wait and see."

At the bar, around ten o'clock that night, Randy hunched over the pool table to take his shot. A young woman in a black dress kept staring at him. She had been staring at him since they walked in the door, and her leering eyes made him uncomfortable.

"That chick over there has been givin' you the eye all night," Jim teased.

"Yeah," Randy said, chalking his cue stick. "I noticed." The ball he attempted to bank shot went in the corner pocket.

Jim peered over at the woman. She was licking the neck of her beer bottle, purposefully flirting with Randy. "Dude, she is totally comin' onto you."

Randy ignored them and took his next shot. He missed this time. "I'm going to grab a beer. Be right back." He leaned his cue against the wall and headed to the bar to order a beer.

As the bartender poured from the tap, this young woman approached him. "Hi," she said in a seductive voice. "You are the sexiest man I have ever laid eyes on."

Randy showed no signs of interest.

"There's a table in the corner where it's nice and dark. Care to join me?" She moved her lips up to his ear and tried to touch him.

Avoiding her, he pulled away. "Please don't do that. I have a girlfriend."

"She doesn't need to know." She walked toward the table, glancing over her shoulder, while she gestured with her index finger for him to follow her.

Randy ignored her. He paid the bartender, grabbed his beer, and returned to his game of pool. Since it was his turn again, he picked up his cue, set his beer on a nearby table, and took his shot.

Jim and Bruce gawked at him. "Holy shit," Bruce said. "She was all over you."

Randy didn't care. "So?"

Jim peered over at the girl who now sat at the table by herself wearing an angry scowl. "She looks pissed. What did you say to her?"

"I told her I wasn't interested." He casually drank from his beer stein.

"An incredibly sexy woman just came on to you and you didn't even flinch," Bruce observed.

"Why is that so surprising? I have a girlfriend. I don't give a shit if ten thousand girls come on to me. Not gonna happen. I'm not a cheating bastard."

Jim probed, "You've never even thought about it?"

"No, Jim, I haven't. Why? Do you think about it?"

"No, but I'm not you."

Jim's smartass mouth was starting to irritate Randy. He really wasn't in the mood for his bantering tonight. "What are you implying, Ryan? That because I used to easily be persuaded by a woman and was quick to bring her home for a one night stand that means I'm going to do it now? I am involved in a relationship, a very serious, very happy relationship with an incredible woman whom I love very much. What the hell kind of douchebag do you think I am?"

"Jesus, man. Chill."

"Do you cheat on your girlfriend?" Randy asked in his defense.

"No."

"Well, neither do I." His words were cold and exact.

After dropping Bruce off, Jim drove Randy home. Before Randy got out of the car, Jim said, "I'm sorry I was messin' with you earlier. I didn't mean to piss you off."

"It's ok," Randy assured him.

"Are you alright?"

Randy looked at Jim. A tumble of confused thoughts and feelings cluttered his mind. "You know what I caught myself doing yesterday?"

"What?"

"I walked into a jewelry store and was actually looking at engagement rings."

Jim knew Randy had been thinking about marriage, but now he was starting to act on it. This must have terrified him. "Engagement rings, huh?"

"I was just walking down the street, minding my own business, and the next thing I knew I was staring at a glass case full of diamond rings, like it was preprogrammed or some shit. It freaks me out."

In Randy's book, marriage was a sacred obligation, a lifelong responsibility, and a promise that he didn't take lightly. Jim never thought Randy would commit to marriage, but could see now that his best friend was indeed ready to pledge his allegiance to Jane. "Why does marriage scare you so much?"

Randy rambled, "Because when I'm only looking out for myself and I fuck things up it's my own fault, I have no one to blame but myself. I'm the one who has to suffer the consequences. But when another person's life is involved, a person I love, and things go awry then I fuck up her life too. Marriage is a huge commitment, a big responsibility. With marriage, we go from being two people with two different lives to becoming one entity, sharing the same goals and dreams, the same house, same bank account, same cars, same name, same everything. It's a legal bond saying that she is the only woman I will ever kiss or have sex with until the day I die. The only one." Randy stopped himself for a minute. "But suddenly the name Jane Hanson has a very pleasing appeal to it. And the thought of her being the mother of my children and spending the rest of my life with her, for some strange reason I'm drawn to that. I never thought I would welcome sharing my life so intimately with another person. But Jane knows shit about me that you don't even know. She reads me so well and knows what I'm thinking before I even say a damn word. This is the woman I have completely given my heart to and have shared every aspect of my life with. I have never done that with a woman before."

"Sounds like you've made up your mind. But you didn't really answer my question," Jim replied.

"It's not marriage that scares me. It's the fact that I'm picturing Jane as my wife not knowing if she feels that way about me. Does she want to be a doctor's wife? Does she want to have babies with me? Does she want to spend the rest of her life living with my arrogance and pigheadedness? Does she picture me the same way I picture her? Am I the man she wants to be married to? This feeling I have, this commitment I want to make, how do I know she wants that?"

"So you do want to marry her?" Jim knew Randy was trying to be serious but he found this whole situation funny.

"Yes, Jim, I want to marry her. But just because that's what I want doesn't mean that's what she wants. And that's what I'm afraid of."

"Look, Randy. I'm tryin' to understand, but I really don't know how you feel. I've never been in a relationship where I've cared so deeply for someone that I wanted to make that person a part of my life forever."

"Bullshit. You were going to marry Trina," Randy countered.

"That's different and you know it. I was only gonna marry her because she was pregnant, not because I loved her and wanted to grow old with her. Even you knew that." Jim tried to offer some advice. "I don't completely understand your relationship with Jane. You two have a dynamic I've never experienced and an understanding for each other I've never known. I'm really tryin' to understand, but what I don't get is, if you love the woman and want to marry her then why don't you buy a fuckin' ring and ask her?"

"Because it's not that simple, Jim," Randy tried to explain. "This is Jane's life we're talking about."

"It's your life too," Jim reminded him.

"But it's not about me anymore. It's about her. Her desires, her dreams, her happiness, and her life. That's what matters to me now. And if Jane's not happy then it's not worth it to me. I am not about to blindly propose marriage to my girlfriend if I don't feel she's ready to make that commitment. Jane is too important to me to take that risk. But along the same lines, I don't want her to think our relationship has no future either. I am madly in love with this woman and very much want to make her a permanent part of my life, but I don't know how to approach this."

"So what are you gonna do?"

"I don't know, and that's what I was trying to tell you." Randy sat on the stairs, feeling overwhelmed.

Jim could see his friend's predicament. Randy was scared to death that Jane was going turn down his marriage proposal if he offered it. Feeling the turmoil his best friend was going through, he sat on the stairs next to him. "Randy," he said trying to get Randy to look at him.

Randy turned his head, frustrated and scared.

"Buddy, I know this must be hard for you. I know what a commitment of this magnitude means to you. And I know how much you love Jane."

"She's my life, man."

"I know she is. But the only advice I can offer you is to take your time if that's what you need to do. Save some money for a ring if you have to. And when the time comes and you need someone to go ring shopping with, that's what I'm here for. I'll always be here for you, Bro. You know that."

Randy took a deep breath, trying to release the stress he felt. "I know."

Jim put his hand on Randy's shoulder. "But what I wouldn't do is worry about it. Let it flow and let it happen. You'll know when the time is right."

"How?"

Jim replied, "I don't know, but I'm sure you'll figure it out, and I'll be right by your side when you decide you're ready to do this."

Randy laughed. "Like hell you will. When I propose to my girlfriend, I will do it alone with her."

"You know what I mean."

Randy stood up. "I gotta go. Jane's been waiting up for me."

"Alright. I'll see you tomorrow."

"Happy birthday." He and Jim knuckle bumped.

"Thanks."

With the insane schedule of his surgery rotation, Randy wasn't home as much as he'd hoped. He had call nights quite often, but learned a lot from this experience. Throughout this rotation, Randy realized he didn't know as much about this particular specialty as he'd hoped. He felt ill-prepared and found that he needed more practice in this rotation than any of the others he'd had previously. In an attempt to provide himself with more training, he spent extra hours in the surgical lab and researched various surgery electives to better prepare for surgical issues that were bound to arise in his practice.

As usual, Jane was a real trooper, supporting him in any way she could. Even with her own work schedule and class load in graduate school, she made breakfast for him every morning and packed him a lunch before he left, unless he had prior lunch plans. She offered him a listening ear to vent to and gave him time to work on patient files or conduct research as needed. Even through the most stressful times, she stood right by his side.

Every year for Valentine's Day, it seemed like they did the same ordinary things. This year, Randy wanted to do something more personal and memorable to show Jane how much he appreciated everything she did for him. After much consideration, and some internet research, he decided to get them a room at the Ritz Carlton hotel for the night and made reservations for dinner at the hotel restaurant, Parallel 37. He reserved them a one bedroom suite and arranged to have a bouquet of roses waiting for her in the room.

Randy wanted this to be a surprise, so he packed an overnight bag and a duffle bag with a change of clothes for both of them and tossed it in the trunk of his car when she wasn't looking. After work, he stopped by the hotel and checked them in. He dropped off their bags and left the hotel with the key card to their room in his possession.

Randy had never been to Parallel 37 before. He never had a reason to go. It was a five star restaurant offering a superb showcase of globally-inspired, artistically creative California cuisine. Valentine's Day at Parallel 37 consisted of a special five-course delectable prix fixe meal. The menu included fresh linguini, Dungeness crab, and a selection of oysters. Their meal was perfectly paired with a bottle of Spanish wine and dessert. It was an incredibly romantic evening.

Randy paid the tab, which was rather pricey for dinner for two people, but tonight he didn't care. He was going to splurge. He corked up his bottle of wine and put it in a bag to take with them.

Being the gentleman he was, he came up behind Jane and slipped her sweater over her shoulders. With his hand placed gently on her back, he escorted her out of the dining room and toward the elevator.

She questioned his actions. "Why are we going this way? The car's that way." She pointed out the front door to the parking lot.

"We're not going home." He pushed the elevator button and waited.

"What do you mean, we're not going home?"

"I got us a suite here tonight."

"Why?"

"Because tonight I want you to have first class, five-star treatment." When the elevator door opened, he took her hand and stepped inside. He pushed the button to the fifth floor.

"You don't have to do things like this to impress me."

"I'm not doing it to impress you," he said. "I'm doing it because I love you and you deserve the best. We will relax here tonight in a romantic atmosphere and get away from the world. For the next twenty-four hours, it's just you and me, Babe." The elevator stopped on their floor and Randy escorted her out.

"But we don't have a change of clothes or toothbrushes or anything."

"Au contraire, mon chéri," he stated. "I packed us everything we would need and dropped it off after work. Don't you worry. I've got it taken care of." He unlocked their room and showed her inside. A dozen fresh roses sat on the table along with a box of her favorite Ghirardelli chocolates.

The room was gorgeous. Fancy furnishings with glass tabletops, incredible ambiance mood lighting, and a large glass plated window with an amazing view of the bay. She couldn't believe that Randy had gone through all the trouble to pull this off for her. "This place is spectacular."

"And in the morning, you are going down to the spa to soak in the hot tub and enjoy a full body massage. You can even get a pedicure and a manicure if you want."

Jane beamed with excitement. "Are you serious?"

"Yes." He closed the door behind them. "But tonight, it's just you and me alone together in this incredible room." He held up the bottle of wine. "We have the rest of this bottle, a box of chocolate, and a warm, comfortable bed."

"Randy, you really didn't have to…"

Before she could finish her thought, he pressed his mouth to hers and kissed her long and hard.

An empty wine bottle and several chocolates later, Randy propped himself up on his elbow with the bottom half of his naked body covered in a sheet. He held the stem of a rose in his hand, softly grazing the pedals down her cheek, neck, chest, between her breasts, and down to her tummy.

She closed her eyes and breathed in deeply, feeling the soft pedals sensuously caress her skin. Then Randy held the rose up to her nose so she could take in its sweet scent. She opened her eyes. "I don't deserve all the things you do for me."

He laid the rose on the bedside table and gazed into her eyes. "You deserve more than I can give you. I want to make all your dreams come true, Babe."

She reached her hand up to his face. "You already have."

More than anything, Randy wanted to make Jane a permanent part of his life. Just like the words in the song, the one they decided was their song, he wanted to be the wind that filled her sail and the hand that lifted her veil. That last line really got to him—the hand that lifted her veil. If he wasn't so scared and unsure, he would have proposed to her right then. He was ready. But he didn't have a ring yet. He made the decision to seriously pursue pricing engagement rings and save up the money to buy her one.

Chapter Fifty-Six

The next six weeks were hectic. Not only did Jane have exams to prepare for, but Randy struggled through a new rotation of Pediatrics while he studied for the second part of his Medical Licensing Exam he had to take in about a month.

When Jane met Randy at Mt. Zion Pediatric clinic, he was dressed in his white lab coat squatted next to a little girl in the waiting room. "There you go." He gave the girl a lollipop then handed her a big sticker that said, *I went to the doctor today!* "And you get a sticker for being so brave."

"Thank you," the child said. Her mother picked her up and carried her toward the door. The little girl waved at Randy on the way out.

As soon as Randy spotted Jane, he winked at her, opened the door that led to the examination rooms, and signaled with a wave of his hand for her to come back with him.

"Will you get in trouble for having me back here?" she asked.

"No," he replied. "But you'll need to wait a minute. I have one more patient to see before I can leave."

She found a chair by the scale and sat down to wait.

Jane watched intently as Randy grabbed a chart and quickly examined it before stepping into an examination room. Another doctor followed him. About ten minutes later, Randy came out writing something on this chart. He slipped the chart back in the slot by the door, put his pen in his lab coat pocket, and went into the back room. After a minute or two, he returned to the exam room with a syringe and a test tube. She hoped he wasn't going to poke the child with that thing. Seconds later she heard a child scream, which made her cringe. Randy emerged from the exam room holding a test tube in his hand, but this time it was full of blood. He put it in a sealed Ziplock bag and brought it back to the lab.

Before he returned to the exam room, he pulled a lollipop out of the jar and took a sticker off the front desk. A child exited with tears flowing down his cheeks, holding his mother's hand while the doctor discussed something with Randy. Then the doctor handed Randy a different chart and walked away. He held the chart in his hands and stared at it for a minute before he reported to Jane. "Now we can go. Let me get my stuff."

Right as Randy was about to leave, the doctor said to him, "Goodnight, Mr. Hanson. I'll see you in the morning."

"Goodnight, Dr. Kingsley."

"Let me know in the morning what you find out."

"Yes, Sir."

The doctor disappeared to his office.

Jane was curious what that meant. "Find out about what?"

"I have to do some research tonight." He slipped his stethoscope and this chart into his bag then took Jane's hand and walked out to his car. "A patient of ours is having a ton of problems. We got all the lab results back this afternoon and Dr. Kingsley wants me to look into the data and see if I can come up with a diagnosis and a plan of action."

"Tonight?" she questioned.

"Yes, and it's going to be part of my grade, so I might be up late. Sorry."

"No problem." Trying to make things easier for him, she suggested, "You want to stop and get takeout somewhere?"

"I think that's a good idea."

For two solid hours, Randy browsed through medical databases and flipped through several medical books, leaving pages open and marked. He read through some information in one of his medical reference books, checked something on the internet, then turned his eyes to the reference book again. A petrified expression consumed him. "Oh shit."

Jane turned her head to see him slumped down in the chair with and his head in his hand. "What is it?"

"This is bad, this is very bad."

"What?" she asked, wondering why he reacted that way.

"Leukemia." He closed his eyes and rubbed his forehead. "Dr. Kingsley is going to make me to talk to this patient's parents. How the hell am I going to tell these people that their child has leukemia?" Upset by this, he closed the patient's file. "This is the part of my job that I really hate. And why the hell did something like this have to happen during my Pediatrics block? Dammit."

She rubbed his shoulders, trying to get him to relax.

Randy touched her hand. "I need a vacation."

Instead of going to Seattle for spring break, Randy discussed with Jane the possibility of having her family get together for a vacation at Lake Tahoe to go skiing for a few days. She thought it was a great idea. She discussed it with her father and Brian, who also liked the plan. It was the end of ski season, but spring skiing was nice because the weather was warmer. Where else could Randy ski in jeans, sunglasses, and a tee-shirt, then go out for some fishing and all night fun afterwards? Randy booked reservations at the resort to ensure they had rooms available for this excursion. For him and Jane, he reserved a romantic townhouse with a jet tub and private balcony. It had a fabulous view of the lake. Dale and Brian booked a one bedroom suite right next to theirs. It was college week so they were able to get a good deal. This mini-vacation was going to be a fun weekend getaway that would give Jane and her family a chance to bond, which was well overdue.

On his way home from the clinic, Randy got walloped by the weather. Torrential rain and high winds whipped over the Bay Bridge. Huge swells and waves plummeted throughout the bay. The storm wreaked havoc across San Francisco. It was the worst weather he had seen in the bay area. Traffic was backed up, firefighters were trying to remove trees from the roads, and Randy had been trying to get home for over an hour.

He walked in the door around seven o'clock that night, tired and stressed from the traffic, the weather, and road-raged drivers. "I hope the weather isn't like this at Tahoe this weekend." He took off his jacket and draped it over the back of a chair. "It is pouring down rain and windier than hell out there."

Jane gave him a hug. "I'm glad you made it home safely. I was watching the news and saw the traffic and weather reports. Trees are falling down and there were a ton of accidents on the freeway."

"I'm gonna see how the roads and weather are over at Tahoe." Randy went on-line to check. Tahoe received two new feet of snow, but the roads were open and the resort was running in full force. "There's snow on the roads. It would probably be safer if we all crammed into your dad's SUV. It has better traction and four wheel drive. It will be a lot safer than my Corvette." Not only that, it would force them all to be together in one vehicle. "Call him and see if he can pick us up tomorrow. We'll all go together. And if he's not comfortable driving in the snow, tell him I'll do it." Also if Randy was concentrating on driving, Jane, Brian, and Dale could talk to each other.

"Alright." She called her dad and they arranged to go together in the SUV with Randy driving.

Lake Tahoe was beautiful in the spring with its Sierra peaks, endless views of snow-flocked pines, and one very blue lake. Throughout the weekend, they experienced outstanding fishing, which Randy convinced Jane to take part in. Even though she didn't want to touch the slimy fishes and would flinch and scream every time one came near her, which Randy found incredibly cute, she had a good time on the boat with them. They hiked on winding trails, went snowmobiling in the back country over miles of terrain, and spent time on the slopes.

Dale and Brian took ski lessons and tried the green slopes with Jane while Randy careened down black diamond slopes, leaving the three of them together to practice and refine their skills. Jane, Brian, and Dale laughed together on the snow as they fell down and tried to help each other up. Jane had more experience on the slopes from skiing with Randy, so she tried to help her brother and father as best she could. It was funny to watch them.

It became evident to Randy that since the death of Jane's mother, the Davine family had distanced themselves from one another. However, the reason for this was unclear. It was obvious that they were once close but had withdrawn into their own worlds for several years as a result of this tragedy. Throughout the week, the topic of Barbara Davine seldom came up, but when it did, the three of them spoke of her fondly. Randy couldn't even begin to imagine how rough that whole experience must have been for this family, but was glad to see them deal with it together rather than withdraw into their own worlds of grief and try to hide from it all. They were acting like a family—helping, supporting, and talking to each other. Randy wanted them to communicate. To accomplish this, he tried to keep the three of them together as often as possible and did his best not to step in too often. As the week progressed, laughs were shared, memories were reminisced, reconnections were made, and tears were shed. They were getting to know each other again.

On their last night at Lake Tahoe, Randy sat back and watched the Davine family interact during dinner. They were getting along quite well. Randy had never seen Jane this happy around her father. She even wore her normal clothing attire—jewelry, nail polish, makeup and all. It was a welcome sight.

Dale looked at Randy with a smile of gratitude as they walked back to their rooms for the night. "Randy," he said. "Thank you for suggesting this. This is the most fun I've had with my kids in years."

"You're welcome, Sir," Randy replied. "I had a good time, too."

"We should do this every year."

"Ooh, can we?" Brian asked. "That would be so cool."

Jane hugged her father. "Thank you, Daddy. I love you."

Dale stood between his children and the three of them walked arm in arm together.

That night, relaxing in the jet tub in their room, Randy couldn't stop smiling. "You know, Jane, I have to say this."

She rested her head on his shoulder. "What do you have to say?"

"Watching you with your dad and brother this week was incredible. I have never seen you smile so much."

Chapter Fifty-Seven

The scientist in Randy couldn't keep away from research-based projects. To appease this itch, he applied for a summer fellowship through the School of Medicine's Student Research Training Program. With the guidance of a faculty sponsor, Randy was approved to participate in a four week oncology-based research project before beginning his final year of rotations.

With Jane's mother as his inspiration, his project would concentrate on the behavioral, environmental, and genetic factors that affected the risk of developing certain cancers in women. During this period of research, he would spend the majority of his time at the University of California San Francisco Comprehensive Cancer Center, where he would gain valuable experience in Radiation Oncology, Gynecological Oncology, and breast care, including diagnostic mammography. He was excited about this research opportunity and hoped to learn something helpful from it.

Randy sat on the sofa intently reading an article about ovarian cancer when Jane snuck up behind him and put her arms around his shoulders. "Hi, Sweetie. How's it going?"

"Actually this is very interesting," he replied. "More than seventy-four thousand women in the United States were diagnosed with a cancer affecting the reproductive organs last year, and more than twenty-seven thousand women in the United States died from some form of gynecologic cancer, some of which could have been prevented." He looked up from his reading. "Have you had an HPV vaccine?"

"No. I don't think so."

"You need to get one. You know how to give yourself a breast exam, right?"

"Yes," she replied.

Randy was adamant about Jane keeping up on annual exams and procedures and insisted she go to the doctor regularly. "Make sure you do that at least once a month. When's the last time you had a pelvic exam and a pap smear?"

"I'm not due to go back until September."

"Good. Keep up on that." He closed his medical journal and set it on the table. "Your mom had uterine cancer, right?"

"Yes," Jane confirmed.

"The good thing about that is there are no demonstrable genetic markers or patterns for uterine cancer."

"What does that mean?" she asked, not understanding his medical language.

"In other words, it's not hereditary." He kissed her lightly on the lips. "At any rate, we need to get you an HPV vaccine. Get started on that as soon as possible."

"I will."

"You know, once I'm a licensed physician, I'll be able to do that for you, and I'll give you free medical care and write prescriptions for you whenever you need them."

"I never thought about that before," she said. "You're going to be handy to have around, aren't you?"

"Hopefully I'm handy for more than that."

"You're handy for a lot of things."

"Oh yeah? Like what?"

"Like eating the cookies I bake."

"I like that job." He probed for more. "What else?"

"Like fixing the laptop when I can't get it to work right and being a critic on my clothes before I go out. I love how you are always honest with me about that, by the way."

"I'm glad. Some women would get mad if I told them their blouse didn't look good with that skirt. I half expect you to backhand me when I say that to you," he admitted.

"No. I appreciate your honesty."

He drew his lips in thoughtfully. "I would never lie to you, Honey."

"I know, and that's one of the things I love about you. You've always been honest with me."

"And I always will be." Randy stared at her for a minute, thinking about honesty, which they definitely had in their relationship and something that was extremely important in a marriage.

"By the way," Jane said as she clasped her hands behind his neck. "I wanted to tell you that this cancer research you're doing, I think it is a remarkable thing."

He was glad she approved. "If any findings I have or conclusions I come up with could potentially help in the development of a cure or better preventative measures, I'm all for it. Someday, someone will develop a cure. I firmly believe that. It might not be until the next generation of doctors, but someone will. And any little thing I can do to help whomever that person is with that endeavor, it will benefit so many people and save so many lives. That's what medicine is all about, Baby. Helping people and saving lives. And that's where my passion for it comes from."

Randy and his study group met at Jim's place that Sunday. Randy arrived forty minutes early. When he got there, the kids were running around and toys were scattered everywhere. Both Jim and Jill struggled to get the kids ready. Finally, after about ten minutes of bedlam, the kids were dressed, all their toys were picked up, and Jill had everything ready to go.

"Are you sure it's not a problem?" Jim asked her.

"I'm fine," Jill replied. "Call me when you're finished."

"I will." He gave her a peck on the lips and she left the apartment with the kids.

"Wow," Randy commented. "Are your mornings always this chaotic?"

"Sometimes they get a little hectic." Jim put on a pot of coffee. "Jill and I tag team. I watch the kids while she's at work and she watches the kids while I'm at work. Sometimes we have to take the kids to my parents or her parents because we both have to be somewhere, but we've developed a system."

Randy set his bag down and pulled out a notebook and an MLE practice exam book. "What are you doing next Saturday?"

"Nothin' that I know of. Why?"

"I was wondering if you would come with me to look at rings."

Jim stopped what he was doing and turned around. By rings, Randy meant engagement rings. "Rings?"

"Yeah. You told me you'd come with me when I was ready. I want to look around and see what my options are. But I can't tell Jane I'm going shopping because she wouldn't buy it for one second. She knows I hate doing that. I'll have to tell her we're going out to lunch or something. Something that doesn't sound suspicious."

"I can't believe you're talkin' about this, man."

Randy wholeheartedly stated, "You know how I told you I was scared that she might not see me as someone she could spend her life with?"

"Yeah."

"Well, recently we've been having conversations about that. The other day I received a bunch of information from UW's Residency Program and included in that was a book of real estate listings. Out of the blue, Jane picks it up and starts scanning through it pointing out houses she liked."

"That's good, I guess." Jim wasn't sure how he felt about all of this. He was glad his friend was happy in a relationship and wanted to commit to this woman, but a part of him knew that once one of them committed to marriage, they wouldn't be together as often. That was the part he didn't like. "It's strange hearin' you talk about this. I never thought you'd be the first one to walk down that aisle and say those vows. I always thought I'd be the first one to tie that knot."

"You almost were."

"I know. And that would have been the worst mistake of my life," Jim admitted.

"You seem to be doing pretty well now."

"I can't complain. Jill and I are happy together, but marriage is not somethin' either one of us is in a hurry for. However, I see the tables have turned for you in regards to that matter. You're talkin' about commitment and lookin' at engagement rings. Never imagined it would be you, Dude."

Randy slipped into the kitchen and made himself a cup of coffee. "I'm not buying anything yet. I just want to do some pricing and comparing and see what's out there."

"But you *are* lookin'."

With a crooked grin, Randy said, "I want to get her something nice. And I want to do this right and plan it out. Everything has to be perfect."

"Oh yes," Jim laughed. "Mr. Perfect."

"I only have one chance to do this. I want to make it a memorable experience for her. Are you going to come with me or not?"

Jim tried not to laugh. "Yeah. I'll come with ya, but you better buy me some grub."

"I will."

Saturday morning, Randy woke in a cheerful mood. He had an excessive amount of energy that needed to be released. He slipped on a pair of athletic shorts and a tee-shirt and got down on the floor to begin his morning exercise ritual.

Jane sat up in bed and saw him on all fours pumping out a bunch of pushups. "What are you doing?"

He stopped, somewhat winded, and stood up. "Getting the blood pumping. Jim and I are gonna grab some lunch and hang out for a while today."

"Any idea when you'll be home?"

"One-ish maybe. I'll call you later." He leaned over the edge of the bed and kissed her. "Shower time for me." He winked at her and headed to the shower.

Jim grabbed his wallet and his cellphone, after dropping it for the third time. He was fidgety this morning and couldn't seem to hold a grip on anything.

Jill caught onto this right away. "Are you ok?"

He shoved his phone in his pocket. "Yeah. Why?"

"You've been acting strange all morning, frantically running around and dropping things left and right. What's going on?"

"Do you know what Randy and I are doin' today?"

"Yes, going to have lunch. At least that's what you told me."

"That's not entirely true," Jim clarified. "He is buying me lunch, but the whole purpose of today is because he wants me to go with him to look at engagement rings."

Jill's mouth opened wide. "Engagement rings? Oh my god, Jim. He's going to propose?"

"He's sure as hell been talkin' about it a lot lately."

"That is great news."

Jim didn't seem as convinced. "I guess."

"James." She walked closer to him, concerned about his downcast face. "I would think you'd be happy for Randy."

"Oh, I am. I'm stoked for him. But…" He looked Jill in the eye. "He's my best friend. I can't believe he's serious about this. He and I shared an apartment for years. I saw him bring home so many babes and engage in so many one night stands that I lost count. Hell, I didn't even know the names of half the woman he brought home. He was never interested in the responsibilities of a relationship or commitment of any kind, until Jane came along. I was there the day they met, you know."

"You were?" Jill said. "I didn't know that."

"Yes I was. He and I were playin' volleyball in Santa Cruz when Jane came over to us with one of her friends and challenged us to a game. He was oglin' the hell outta her and couldn't keep his eyes off of her. And he hasn't even looked at another woman since that day. He calls her every night, sneaks away in the middle of the day to meet with her, goes off on secluded romantic weekend getaways with her. He has spent a butt load of money showerin' her with gifts and I don't even know how many dozens of roses. He even developed some serious agro and almost beat the crap out of someone over her once."

She couldn't believe this. "Randy? I've never seen him get a violent outburst like that."

"That's my point. Not in his character at all. I remember well the day he told me he was in love with her. He was scared shitless and tryin' to talk his way out of it. He even gave up that book he had with the names and numbers of all the chicks he'd ever slept with. I couldn't believe he was givin' that up. He carried that book with him everywhere he went. He was the biggest playboy I'd ever met. But now, he has loyally and faithfully been with the same girl for almost three years. He gave her a key to his apartment, took her up to Seattle to meet his parents, invited her to move in with him, took her with him on family vacations, and now he's lookin' at engagement rings for Christ sake. He's actin' real rattly and it's freaky, Jill."

"You told me yourself how much he loves her," Jill reminded him.

"Oh, he does. There's no doubt in my mind that he loves her. I knew he liked her before he would even admit it. He's crazy about her, but that's what worries me. He loves her so deeply and so passionately that if this doesn't work out for him the way he's hopin', I'm the one who's gonna have to pick up the seriously shattered pieces of my best friend's heart and help him put his life back together, and I do not want to go there," Jim admitted.

Jill could see why Jim was upset about this, but she tried to comfort him. "It's not every day your best friend thinks about proposing to his girlfriend, Jim. The best thing you can do right now is be supportive."

"I know that, which is why I'm goin' with him today. I hope he doesn't get his heart broken over her."

Jill gave him a hug. "You are a good friend, James Ryan. I hope Randy knows how lucky he is to have you."

"I feel lucky to have him," Jim countered. "Randy is a mad cool dude that I have utmost respect for. He and I have been through everything together and he's always been there for me. I would do anything for him. I hope to god that when he finally does pop the big question, Jane says yes. If she doesn't, his world will come crashin' down." Jim glanced at the clock. "I'm gonna meet Randy out front. He should be here any minute."

"Ooh, you get to ride in the Corvette."

"Yup, and that son-of-a-bitch better buy me lunch like he said he would." Jim grabbed his sunglasses and a CD then gave Jill a kiss goodbye. "See ya later, Honey Bun. Love ya."

"Love you too, James. Have fun."

Randy pulled up with his sunglasses on, the top down, and the radio blasting.

Jim grinned devilishly. "Yo, Mario."

"Good morning."

Jim sat in the passenger's seat and closed the door. He handed Randy a CD with one of his favorite songs on it. "I brought this for you."

It was his favorite Nickelback album. "Oh sweet." He put the CD in the disc changer and pulled away from the curb. "Coffee. I gotta get some coffee before we do anything else."

Jim laughed. "Why does that not surprise me?"

Randy skidded away and headed towards Starbucks.

The following afternoon, Randy called his father. He hadn't talked to his dad in a while and was pleased to hear his voice. "It's good to hear from you, Randal. How have you been?"

"Busy as hell." Being fully open with his father, Randy stated, "I went and looked at engagement rings yesterday."

"You did?"

"Yup. I haven't picked one out yet, but I did see a few that I liked. I'm not really sure what I'm looking for. I want to get her something nice that isn't bulky or uncomfortable."

Mark knew it was a matter of time before Randy decided he was ready for marriage. "So, you're ready to take that step?"

"Yes, I am. I want to do this right though. I'm gonna plan it all out, find the perfect ring, find a place with just the right romantic flavor to it, and wait for that perfect moment. I want everything to be perfect."

"Of course you do," Mark said. "You're always a perfectionist."

"Well, yeah. This will only happen once, Dad, and I'm not about to sludge my way through it. I'm going to make this moment something she'll never forget. Flowers and wine and a romantic dinner together."

"Oh, my son's a romantic, is he?"

"I have my moments," Randy replied. "This is my marriage proposal to Jane, the only chance I'll have to make the woman I love a permanent part of my life. I want it to be perfect." Randy gulped down the rest of his coffee and swallowed hard. "I'm gonna be honest with you though. I'm scared."

"Scared about what?" Mark asked.

"Jane's never left San Francisco. She was born here, raised here, she's lived here her whole life. Everything she's ever known is in this city, her family, her friends, and she's in the middle of grad school. I won't just be asking her to marry me. I'll be asking her to drop everything for me, to leave everything she's ever known and spend the rest of her life with me. That's a lot to ask someone."

"Yes, it is," Mark agreed.

"And if she's not willing to do that, do I give up my dreams of practicing with you in Seattle because she doesn't want to leave San Francisco, or do I go to Seattle alone? I don't know if I could do that, Dad. I can't lose her. I can't live without her."

Trying to get his son to calm down, Mark said, "Randy, I've been there. I really do know how you feel. Proposing marriage can be stressful and very scary. And I know all the questions that are going through your mind. I wish I had answers for you, but I don't. The only thing I can tell you is to follow your heart. You're the only one who knows what you want, Son. Sometimes in life you have to make tough decisions. Marriage is not a decision to be taken lightly."

"I'm not taking it lightly," Randy said. "This is something I've been contemplating for a long time. Why do you think it's tormenting me so much? This is my life, Dad."

"I know it is."

"You can't tell Mom I'm planning this. Please. You know what she'll do if she knows."

Mark laughed. "Don't worry, Randy. I won't. When you decide you're ready, you can tell her yourself."

"Thank you."

Jane and Randy were invited to Chuck-E-Cheese for Sabrina's birthday party. After chomping on pizza and watching Sabrina open all of her gifts, Randy and Jim took off with the kids to play games, leaving Jane and Jill at the table to clean up wrapping paper and bag up all Sabrina's presents and leftover cake. "I hear Randy's all set to apply to UW for his residency," Jill said.

"He's been ready for a long time." Jane replied. "UW has always been where he's wanted to go. He's just waiting for the application window to open."

"Jim's applying to a few places here in San Francisco." Jill crumpled up some wrapping paper and threw it in the trash. "You know, Jane, when graduation comes and Randy gets a residency slot at UW, those two men are going to have a difficult time going their separate ways."

"I know," Jane concurred. "I was thinking about that too."

"Separating from Randy is going to be hard on Jim." Jill gazed across the room and spotted the two men laughing together, excited over a game of air hockey. "I don't think they've realized it yet."

Randy was always smiling when he was with Jim. The two of them were like brothers. Each would gladly lay down his own life for the other, and Jane knew it. And now that she thought about what Jill had said, her heart ached for Randy. Parting from Jim was going to be heartbreaking for him.

"They're going to need us more than ever when that happens," Jill remarked. "Because I'm pretty sure Jim will have many sleepless nights over it."

"It's going to be hard on Randy too." In fact, Jane was pretty sure Randy would break down and cry when it all went down.

Chapter Fifty-Eight

September first, Randy eagerly submitted his residency applications. He hoped his quality medical experiences, solid personal statement, excellent references and performance evaluations, honors grades, and high test scores would sell him over and above the other applicants. He wanted to leave an impression on the University of Washington so they would have no doubts about considering him for one of the six available positions.

He didn't expect to hear anything from them for a while because they were accepting applications until the middle of next month. But three weeks after submitting his application, he received a call from the director of University of Washington's Residency Program to schedule an interview.

As soon as he got off the phone, his entire face lit up. "Guess what?"

Jane immediately recognized his excitement. "What?"

"I just got off the phone with UW. I have an interview next Friday," he proclaimed.

Jane gasped and threw her arms around him. "Oh, Sweetie, that's great."

"The director invited me to dinner Thursday night to meet everyone prior to my interview. I'm gonna have to fly up to Seattle for a few days. I hope there are flights available." He went on-line to book an airline ticket. He was able to schedule a late Thursday morning flight. This would give him time to unpack and gather his thoughts before meeting his potentials.

When Randy arrived in Seattle, his mother picked him up from the airport. "What time is your dinner tonight?" she asked him.

"Six."

"How you doing? You nervous?" She was nervous enough for both of them.

"Actually, I'm doing fine. Looking forward to it."

She put her hands on his face and kissed his cheek. "I'm so proud of you, Honey."

"Thanks, Mom."

Members of UW's Residency Program hosted a casual dinner for Randy that evening. He enjoyed the conversation, even though he knew they were examining every move he made and evaluating every word that came out of his mouth.

The actual day of the interview, Randy listened to a presentation about the program, went to a morning conference, and then met individually with some of the members of the selection committee in the afternoon, which included a personal interview with the program director.

Overall, Randy was impressed with the program, and he felt they were impressed with him as well. After his interview, he headed back to his parents' house to have dinner with them.

While pouring himself a cup of coffee, Randy saw his dad out on the dock gazing across the lake. Wanting to discuss something with him, he went downstairs and grabbed a small box out of his carryon bag then stepped outside to join his father on the dock. "Hey, Dad."

With deliberate, casual movements, Mark turned to face him. "Hello, Randal. How did your interview go?"

"I think it went well. The director and I discussed my credentials, and he wanted to know about what kind of work I've done in Obstetrics and Gynecology."

"Any indications as to a decision?"

"Most of the people I talked to today seemed excited about my application," Randy declared. "The director said I should hear from him in a few weeks."

"That's a good sign," Mark said. "Good luck."

"Thank you." Randy checked the surrounding area to make sure his mom wasn't around. When the coast was clear, he reached into his pocket and pulled out a small velvet-covered box. "I bought a ring." He handed the box to his father. "Tell me what you think."

Mark carefully opened the box to reveal a diamond solitaire engagement ring with ten round cut diamonds encircling the band. "This is an elaborate ring. When are you planning on doing this?"

"After I hear back from UW. I want to confirm my residency match first."

"So this is it, huh?"

Randy took a deep breath. "This is it."

Mark started to get choked up as he closed the box and handed it back to Randy. "I know I don't say this to you enough, but I'm proud of you, Son."

"Thank you." He put the ring back in his pocket and enjoyed the view with his father.

"Beautiful night tonight."

"Yes, Sir, it is."

Three weeks later, the University of Washington Residency Director offered Randy a position in the OB/GYN department, and if he was interested, he would start June 23rd. Randy was ecstatic. After suffering through four and a half years of medical school hell, he finally saw light at the end of the tunnel. Since he had now received his acceptance call, the time had come for Randy to show Jane how much he needed her.

Randy made dinner reservations Saturday night for what he referred to as a romantic night out to get away from the world, but he wouldn't tell Jane where they were going. He wanted it to be a surprise. Jane adored his sneakiness and looked forward to whatever he had planned.

While Jane was out shopping with her friends, Randy paced around the apartment in nervous anticipating, which made him feel ill. He tried to shake it off by drinking a strong cup of coffee, but that only made it worse. He attempted to burn off some nervous energy by pumping out as many pushups and sit-ups as he possibly could. All that did was make him feel more anxious. He tried a shower hoping that would help. It didn't.

He sat on the edge of the bed and glanced over at the dresser where he had the ring hidden in the back of his sock drawer. Slowly, he opened the drawer and pulled out the velvet box. He stared at the ring inside. The butterflies in his stomach were having one hell of a party and the joints in his fingers hurt. "Why am I so nervous about this?" He combed his bangs with his fingers then leaned forward. He took a few deep breaths trying to calm his nerves. He checked his watch. It was only three o'clock. Had it really only been forty minutes since the last time he checked the time? Damn, this day was dragging. This had to be the longest day of his life.

Randy put the ring back in his sock drawer and stared at his cellphone while he nervously drummed his fingers on the bedside table. He stood up and paced around the room again. His nerves were getting the best of him. To combat this, he did the only thing he could think of—he picked up his cellphone and called his dad.

"Hello, Randy."

"Hey."

Mark immediately recognized the nervousness in his son's voice. "What's wrong?"

"I think I'm going to be sick. My palms are sweaty and I've got nervous twitches. I've paced around this apartment at least fifty times in the last hour."

This was odd behavior. "Are you alright?"

"Is Mom with you?"

"No."

"I'm proposing to Jane tonight," he said.

"Tonight?"

"Yes. I couldn't sleep last night, I can't stop shaking, and I feel like I'm going to throw up." Randy admitted his fears to his father. "I don't want to say something stupid and botch up this whole thing. And what if she says no?"

"Randy, calm down."

"But Dad, I only have one shot at this."

"You are getting yourself all worked up, and you're going to hyperventilate. Sit down," his father insisted.

Randy did what he was told.

"What you need to do is get out of that apartment and keep yourself busy. Do something fun or go somewhere to unwind. Sitting around waiting is going to drive you crazy. Get out of there."

That was a good idea. Some fresh air and a refreshing drive would be good for him. He left a text message for Jane telling her he was going over to Jim's, then opened his sock drawer and pulled out the box, putting it in his pocket. He grabbed his phone and his keys and drove over to Jim's apartment.

Jim was surprised to see Randy standing on his doorstep. "Yo, Bro."

"Hey. You busy?"

"Nah." Jim let Randy in. "I'm just tryin' to get some things done around here while Christopher is nappin'. What's up?"

Randy took a seat on the couch. "Where's Jill?"

"Sabrina had Gymnastics."

Randy tapped his fingers on the arm of the couch. "Jim, I need your opinion on something."

"Whatcha need?"

Randy pulled the box out of his pocket and opened it.

Jim grinned. He knew exactly what it was and what it meant for Randy. "It's an engagement ring."

Randy laughed. "Thank you, Captain Obvious. I know it's an engagement ring." His face suddenly fell. "And I have so many damn butterflies in my stomach; I feel sick."

Jim sat on the couch next to him. "Nervous?"

"Nervous," Randy admitted. "And scared. There is the possibility that she could say no."

Although Randy was worried about this, Jim knew it was an unsound fear. "That's crazy, Randy. That woman loves you."

"It's not just about love, Jim. There's more to it than that."

"What do you mean?"

"I've been offered a position in UW's Residency Program."

Jim's smile grew wider. "That's great. Grats, man. That's what you wanted."

"Yeah, that's what I wanted."

"Then what's the problem?"

Randy took in some air, trying to clear his head. "Janey's never left San Francisco. She was born here, she grew up here. All of her friends are here, her family. Everything she's ever known is in this city."

"What does that have to do with anything? She loves you, doesn't she?"

"But does she love me enough to give up everything she knows? Enough to leave her entire life behind?" Randy stared at the ring in the box. "The possibility that she might not is in the back of mind and it's driving me crazy."

"I think you're worryin' over nothin', Randy. She's not gonna turn you down."

"But what if she does?"

"She won't."

"What if she does?"

Obviously Randy wasn't going to drop this. The pain and turmoil was eating away at him. "Then you move on."

Tears began to form and a horrible pain penetrated his heart. "What if I can't?"

"That isn't gonna happen," Jim reassured him. "You have everything to offer her. You're good lookin', smart, have money, job security, you're a doctor for Christ sake."

"But it's not that simple. Jane and I have come to a point in our relationship where it's all or nothing."

"What the hell are you talkin' about?" Jim wanted to know, unclear what Randy meant by that remark.

"Her answer determines my life. It's gonna come down to two things. One, she says yes. She then comes to Seattle with me and we live happily ever after. Or two, she tells me she can't. Then that's it. It's over. There is no way I can maintain a long distance relationship while I'm doing my residency if she doesn't want to come to Seattle. If she says no, I've lost her. And I honestly don't know if I will be able to handle that." Randy's hands began to twitch and he felt nauseated again.

"Calm down, Dude. You are totally wiggin' over somethin' that is not gonna happen. Jane would climb mountains and swim oceans for you, and you know that. Think about it. Who has stuck with you through med school even when you were stressed out and grouchy, and who has been there to support you and give you unconditional love regardless of the crap goin' on and endless hours of studyin' and on-call hours? Who's been right by your side through thick and thin even through the worst of times when she could have easily walked away?"

Randy thought for a minute. "Jane."

"That's right. Jane. What the hell woman would put herself through that bogus bullshit if she didn't love you and didn't see herself as havin' a future with you? Not one would. I guarantee it. She has stood by your side through the stress, the chaos, the schedule conflicts, the pressure, and she has supported you wholeheartedly through it all. Do you really think, after goin' through that hell, she's gonna turn down a marriage proposal from you? No fuckin' way."

When Jim put it that way, it made sense—a lot of sense. Jane had been by his side through the good times and the bad times. The jumbled mess inside Randy's head became a little less cluttered with Jim's words of wisdom.

"Would you stop worryin'? You are gonna be fine. You're gonna ask her to marry you and she's gonna say yes. And you two are gonna spend the rest of your lives in joyful marital bliss, have a stellar life together, and make a ton of babies."

A smile slowly returned to Randy's face. "Yeah."

Jim put his hand on Randy's shoulder. "When were you plannin' on doing this?"

"Tonight."

"What?" Jim said, bowled over by this response. "Do you have a plan in place for this?"

Randy closed the lid to the box, putting it back in his pocket. "I'm taking her to the Fleur de Lys."

"The Fleur de…" Jim recognized that name. "Wait a minute. That's where you took her on your first date."

"Yup. And I've arranged to have us sit at the same table. I'm gonna order the same wine, same entrees, reproduce that night as best I can. And I bought her roses that night. I'm going to stop and pick some up on the way home."

"You did all that on a first date?" Jim teased.

"For her I did. I wanted to give her a night she'd never forget."

Jim smiled. "Even then you liked her."

"I liked her from the first moment I laid eyes on her on the beach in Santa Cruz. And if I wouldn't have seen her at the SUB that day, I would have tracked her down somehow."

"What are you gonna say tonight?"

Randy replied, "I have no idea. I'm hoping the words will come to me. But I'm a little worried that I'll be so nervous that it will all come out wrong and I'll say something stupid and make a complete fool out of myself."

"Nah. You've always been good with words, man," Jim assured him.

"This is more nerve-wracking than my interview to get into med school was." Randy felt ill again. "I've never been so nervous in my life."

"Everything's gonna be fine, Dude. You'll see."

Randy took a deep breath, trying to ease the tap dance in his stomach.

"I'll have my phone on waiting to hear the good news."

Randy grinned with anticipation. "I hope so."

"When are you supposed to go to dinner?"

"Six."

Jim checked the time. It was almost five o'clock. "You better get ready to go then."

Randy stepped toward the door, but before he left, he said, "Thank you for calming me down, for helping me see this differently."

"That's what friends are for. Good luck tonight."

"Thanks." Confidently, Randy walked out the door. He stopped at the nearby flower shop and bought a dozen roses before he headed home.

Jane was in the process of brushing her hair when she heard him come in. "There you are," she said, happy to see his face. "I was wondering where you ran off to."

He softly kissed her bare shoulder. "You didn't get my text?"

"Yes, but I figured you'd be here by the time I got home."

Randy presented her with the roses. "For you, my love."

She took the flowers from him and sniffed them. "I love roses. Thank you, Sweetie."

"You're welcome."

Randy was still in jeans and a tee-shirt. She wondered why he hadn't changed yet. "You told me to wear something nice. If you go out in that, you're going to make me feel overdressed."

He chuckled and said, "No. I need to change. But it won't take me long. I'll be done before you have your hair and makeup finished." He kissed her on the lips and went to put on more appropriate attire.

When Randy pulled into the parking lot of the Fleur de Lys, a huge smile brightened Jane's face. "You didn't tell me we were coming here."

"Nope. Wanted to surprise you." He parked the car, offered his arm to her, and escorted her inside.

Throughout dinner, Randy wasn't very talkative. He kept picking at his food, not eating much of it, and he had a troubled look on his face. "Sweetie, are you ok?"

He managed a smile. "Yeah, Baby. I'm fine."

She reached out and touched his hand. "You're shaking."

"Am I?"

"Yes." She hoped he wasn't getting ill. "Are you sure you're alright?"

It was stupid to prolong this any longer. He bit the bullet and began his speech. "UW offered me a position."

With a gasp she said, "That's fantastic! I'm so proud of you."

He poked around at the ice in his glass. "You know what that means, right?"

She nodded, trying not to think about the cold, hard truth that he was leaving at the end of the semester. "I know."

Randy reached for her hand. "Janey, we have come so far and…" He paused to gather his thoughts. "I need you. You have been my rock and my motivation through all of this. You've been by my side even in the toughest times. I never could have done this without you. I don't want to finish this without you. You are so much a part of my life now, I can't imagine not having you by my side." Rubbing the back of her hand with his thumb, he continued, "I know you have your family here, and you're in the middle of graduate school, and everything you've ever known is in this city, but…" Swallowing hard to moisten his throat, which suddenly felt extraordinarily dry, he stated, "I want you to come to Seattle with me."

"Randy, I…"

"No," he interjected. "Let me finish, please." He cleared his throat trying to get rid of the butterfly feeling in his tummy. "Jane, I know that expecting you to drop everything to follow me to Seattle is asking a lot, but I love you. I need you, and I want to spend the rest of my life with you." Randy got out of his seat and knelt down on one knee in front of Jane, looking her straight in the eye.

"What are you doing?" she asked, thinking this behavior was extremely odd. He reached into his pocket and pulled out a velvet-covered box. That's when it clicked—the restaurant they went to on their first date, roses, news of residency match, getting on one knee. She knew what he was about to do.

Randy's hands couldn't stop shaking. His heartrate accelerated, his breathing became heavier, and an intense feeling of nervousness consumed his entire body. The butterflies he had earlier flew back with a vengeance. They would not stop fluttering around, and they were about to make him ill. This was the moment of truth. He opened the box and presented the ring to Jane. "I want you to come to Seattle with me as my wife. Jane Elizabeth Davine, will you marry me?" His whole body went numb. Never had he felt as vulnerable as he did at this moment.

Jane's trembling hand went up to her mouth as a tear fell down her cheek. She couldn't breathe.

Her tears and the long, awkward silence made Randy anxious. By now, the entire restaurant, including customers and wait staff, had stopped to watch him make this proposal. His heart pounded a hundred miles a minute and he felt weak from almost hyperventilating. He wished she'd say something, anything to break this deafening silence.

She jumped out of her seat and threw her arms around him. "Yes!"

Applause resounded from the surrounding tables. Randy breathed a sigh of relief and squeezed her as tightly as he could. At that moment, he was the happiest man on Earth. He kissed Jane then pulled the ring out of the box. He took her left hand in his and carefully slipped the ring on her finger. When it was securely in place, he said, "There. Now it's official."

Still shaking from the shock, she held out her hand, admiring the welcome addition on her finger. "It's beautiful."

The glow on Randy's face resonated through the room. "I love you."

"I love you." She leaned forward and kissed him, overcome with joy. All existence faded, leaving the two of them to relish in the joy and excitement of the moment.

Jim paced the floor of his kitchen, checking his cellphone every thirty seconds.

Jill questioned this unusual behavior. "What is wrong with you?"

He looked at his phone again. "I'm waiting to hear from Randy."

"Randy? Why?"

"He's proposing to Jane tonight."

Jill's face beamed with excitement. "Are you serious?"

"Yeah. And the fact that I haven't heard from him yet is not a good sign. Please, Jane, for the love of God, say yes."

Jill laughed. "I'm sure everything is fine."

Right at that moment, Jim received a text message from Randy that simply read, *She said yes!!* Attached to the message was a picture of Jane's hand wearing the engagement ring. Jim plopped down in a chair, finally able to relax. "Thank God."

"Send them a congratulations or something," Jill insisted.

Jim typed, *Gratz, man! I'm happy for you.*

Randy's dad stood at the kitchen sink peeling potatoes when his phone beeped. He took it out of his pocket and saw he had a text message. He read it then called to his wife, "Ellie, can you come here for a minute."

She joined him in the kitchen. "Yes?"

Mark handed her his phone.

On the screen was a picture of a female's hand wearing a diamond engagement ring. Underneath were the words, *She said yes!!* She stared at it for a minute. "Mark? Is that Jane's hand?"

He grinned deceitfully. "Yes, it is."

"He proposed to her?"

"Yup. And evidently she said yes."

She jumped up and down and did a little happy dance right there in the kitchen. "Our son is getting married," she squealed, overcome with excitement.

Her response made him laugh. "Yes, he is."

"You knew he was going to do this, didn't you?"

"Yup."

"Why didn't you tell me?" she asked.

"Randy asked me not to."

"Why wouldn't he want me to know about this?"

Mark smirked at her. She knew exactly why Randy didn't want her to know. "Because he knew you'd make a big deal out of it if you found out he was thinking about marriage."

"How long has he been planning this?"

"Several months."

Ellen smiled proudly. "I told you she was the one. I knew it."

"Yes, you did. And you were right."

Snuggled in bed that night, Randy held Jane in his arms, playing with the ring on her finger.

"This was the last thing I expected from you tonight," Jane said.

"Then my plan worked." He kissed her softly on the lips. "This residency program starts in June. I'm going to have to give them an answer soon. I know you've never lived outside San Francisco. Are you going to be alright leaving and moving to Seattle?"

"Randy, I would follow you to the frozen wastelands of Siberia or the bug infested jungles of Africa if that's where medicine led you," she proclaimed.

"Really?"

"Yes. Honestly, I was afraid you were going to leave here without me."

"Not on your life. I would never leave you behind." He removed a stray hair from her face. "I have my study session tomorrow, but as soon as I get home, you and I are going to sit down and pick a date. I want to make this the wedding of your dreams."

"Let's get married on the beach," she suggested.

He loved that idea. After all, they did meet there. "That sounds great." He fused his lips with hers. Then a thought came to him that made him break away. "Jane Hanson," he said, loving the way the name sounded. "You are planning on using Hanson, aren't you?"

"Yes."

"Good. I can't wait 'til we start our lives together as husband and wife. This is the best day of my life." He drew his mouth to hers again, not stopping this time.

Randy elegantly pranced into his study session on Sunday with a huge grin on his face. Normally, he was the first one there, but today, he was the last to make an appearance.

"You're late," Jim said.

Randy didn't care. He set his bag down and addressed everyone. "Before we get started, I have something I need to tell you."

They all turned their attention to him, everyone except Jim, who already knew what Randy was going to say.

Randy stood tall and proudly announced, "Jane and I are getting married."

Mandy gasped and leaped out of her seat. "Oh my god, Randy! Oh my god!" She ran over and gave him a huge bear hug.

"Congratulations, man," Bruce said, slapping his palm. "When did this happen?"

"Last night," Randy replied.

Jim sat in his chair with a pompous grin. "Told you she was gonna say yes."

Mandy stared at Jim, her eyebrows raised inquiringly. "Wait a minute. You knew about this and didn't say anything?"

Jim clarified, "It's not my place to say anything. It's Randy's."

"Thank you, Jim," Randy confirmed.

Mandy could hardly contain her excitement. "So when? When's the big day?"

Randy sat down. "I don't know. We haven't talked about it yet. We're gonna look into that when I get home." With a heartfelt, yet serious expression, Randy eyed his best friend. "Jim, I want you to be my Best Man."

"Absolutely. I wouldn't miss this for the world."

"Bruce, I want you up there with me too."

"Of course," Bruce agreed. "I'd be honored."

"Thanks." Randy addressed Amanda. "You better be there, right in the front row where I can see your face."

"Are you kidding?" she said. "There is no way I'm missing the biggest event of the year."

"Thanks, guys. That means a lot to me."

The warmth of Randy's smile brightened the room when he walked into his apartment that afternoon. "Hey, Baby. I'm home." He set his bag on the table.

Jane came out of the kitchen and threw her arms around him. Parting her lips, she raised herself to meet his kiss. "I missed you."

"I missed you too." He unzipped his backpack and pulled a pocket-sized academic planner out of his bag. "Ok, come over here and sit down with me for a minute." Randy took her hand and led her to the couch. He opened the calendar and flipped through it. Almost every box was full with training seminars, Grand Rounds, presentations, schedule differentiations, rotation switches, or some sort of report that was due. "I don't want to get married until I'm finished with med school. Way too much going on." Jane agreed. He turned to May, which wasn't nearly as full. "My last day is the 18th. Graduation is Friday the 21st." As he skimmed over May's available dates, an idea came to him. "You know, my entire family is going to be down here for graduation anyway." He pointed to the empty box on May 22nd. "Why don't we get married that Saturday? Save everyone a trip." Wanting her input, he asked, "What do you think?"

"May 22nd?"

"Yeah. That will give us almost seven months. We can plan a wedding in seven months, can't we?" he inquired.

"I'm sure we can. May 22nd it is."

"Sweet!" In the May 22nd square of his pocket calendar, Randy wrote the word *wedding* in bold letters and drew two interconnected hearts around it. He closed his calendar and stared at the diamond on Jane's hand. "What's your dad gonna say when he sees that ring on your finger?"

She shrugged.

"When are you going to tell him?"

"I don't know."

"How about right now?" Randy suggested.

Jane's eyes got huge and her stomach lurched.

The expression on her face made him laugh. "What's that look for?"

"Right now?" she asked, making sure she heard him correctly.

"Yes. Now is as good a time as any."

She gave him a questionable stare, not sure she agreed with this plan.

"Baby, you have to tell him." He stood up and held out his hands to her. "Come on. Grab your purse, put on some shoes, and let's go over there and do this."

Hesitating, she said, "Ok."

While Jane was getting ready to go, Randy called his parents. He hadn't actually talked to them since his engagement and he wanted to know how his mother reacted. A crooked smiled filled his face when his mom answer the phone.

"Randy! Congratulations, Sweetheart. I am so happy for you."

"Thank you. Guess that means Dad told you the news last night?"

"Of course. Do you have a date set yet?" his mother insisted on knowing.

"We do. May 22nd, the day after graduation. Figured that'd be the easiest since many of our relatives will be in San Francisco that weekend anyway."

"Good plan. Let us know what we can do to help with wedding plans. We want to contribute," his mother said.

"We will," Randy promised. "We haven't even started that process yet."

Randy and Jane had not yet realized the complex tasks involved with wedding planning. Ellen didn't want to burst their bubble. She figured they'd find out soon enough.

When Randy hung up his phone, he winked at his future bride. "You ready?"

"Uh huh."

"Then let's go."

Driving over to Dale Davine's house, Jane stared out the window. When they came to a stoplight, Randy briefly turned his eyes to her. She had an intense look of concentration on her face. "Deep thoughts there, Babe?"

"Trying to figure out how I'm going to tell Daddy."

"Just be honest with him." He put his hand on her thigh. "We'll do it together. It'll be alright."

Before Jane got out of the car, she sat for a minute trying to collect her thoughts. Her lips drew a hard line and her facial muscles tightened up.

Randy could tell she was nervous. "We'll be fine, Baby. I'll be right there with you."

She stepped out of the car and walked up to the door. Randy stood right by her side.

Jane's father was not expecting them and was surprised when he opened the door to find Jane and Randy standing on his doorstep. "Jane. It's good to see you. Come in." Dale shook Randy's hand. "Randy."

"Sir." Randy followed Jane inside and they both took a seat at the kitchen table.

"Would you like some lemonade?" Dale asked.

"Yes, please. That sounds good," Randy replied.

Dale grabbed three glasses from the cupboard then pulled a pitcher out of the refrigerator. "How's school going?" he directed to his daughter.

"Good," Jane said. "I have midterms in a few weeks."

"You ready for them?"

"Yes."

Dale handed them each a glass of lemonade then redirected his attention to Randy. "How are you?"

"Been busy," Randy replied. "Working in the ICU right now. Recently found out I've been nominated for the Dean's Prize for some oncology research I did over the summer."

"That's good."

Deciding not to drag this out, Jane said, "Randy asked me to marry him."

Unresponsive at first, Dale turned his head to his daughter. "And what did you say?"

She held her hand out to show him the ring on her finger.

"Oh. I see." Dale stared at the ring on his daughter's hand. It looked expensive. "You're going to be a doctor's wife then?"

"Yes, Daddy."

Dale raised his head, showing almost no emotional response. "Congratulations."

Randy couldn't read Dale's face. He wasn't sure if he was angry, sad, or in shock over this news. "Thank you, Sir. We're very excited."

Dale took a drink of his lemonade. "Have you guys set a date yet?"

"Yes," Jane answered. "May 22nd, the day after Randy graduates from medical school."

Dale's expression hardened. "What happens after graduation?"

This was the part Jane was dreading—having to tell her father that she was going to be leaving San Francisco. "Randy's been offered a residency position at UW."

That was not what he wanted to hear. Even though he knew this inevitable moment would come, the idea of his daughter being whisked away to another state made him uneasy. His face instantly developed a frown.

Randy felt the need to intervene. "Mr. Davine, Sir, I'll be receiving the best training in the region. UW's Residency Program is superb. And since I'm planning on practicing in Seattle, it's important that I establish a reputation for myself up there."

But Dale was more concerned about Jane. "What about Jane's graduate studies?"

"She can transfer," Randy reassured him. "UW's Clinical Psychology Program is one of the best in the nation."

"Is that so?"

"Yes, Sir."

Although Dale wasn't necessarily thrilled about this situation, he had no choice but to accept it. "Well then. I guess that'll have to do."

They visited with Jane's father for about an hour. As Randy and Jane were about to leave, Dale escorted them both to the door. He shook Randy's hand and said, "You take care of yourself, and keep working hard."

"I will."

Dale gave Jane a hug and said his goodbyes. When she was strapped in the car and the passenger's side door was closed, Dale called out, "Randy?"

Randy turned around and faced his future father-in-law. "Yes, Sir?"

"I want you to know that I trust you to take care of my daughter."

In awe, Randy grinned. He had finally earned the trust of Jane's father. "Thank you. I'll do my best." He got in the car and put the keys in the ignition. But he didn't start the car right away. He sat in the driveway with his hands on the steering wheel staring out front windshield.

Jane couldn't figure out what he was waiting for. "Randy?"

"Do you know what your dad just said to me?"

She shook her head. "No. What?"

He looked over at Jane. "He told me he trusted me to take care of you."

Jane's lips parted and she sat breathless for a second. Her eyes began to water. She looked out the window to the front door of the house, but her father had already gone inside. "Daddy," she cried. She couldn't believe he had said that.

"Yeah," Randy said. "That's pretty cool." He started the car, backed out of the driveway, and headed back to Berkeley.

Chapter Fifty-Nine

Monday morning, Randy arrived at his clinical rotation feeling revitalized. The excitement he felt seemed to give him inexhaustible energy, then again it might have been the cappuccino he was drinking. He and Jim were at the same hospital that week, and they happened to run into each other in the parking lot. "Good morning, Mr. Ryan."

"Hey, Bro. How you doin' this mornin'?" Jim asked, acknowledging Randy's overly cheerful disposition.

"Never been better. Thanks for agreeing to be my Best Man."

"I'm gonna throw you the most hellacious bachelor party in history. It's gonna be kickass."

Randy rolled his eyes. "Jim, please."

"That's part of the fun of bein' Best Man." He patted Randy's shoulder. "Congratulations, man."

"Thank you."

"Have you told Jane's dad yet?" Jim asked.

"We told him yesterday. He was cool about it."

"That's good."

"Jane and I talked about wedding plans last night. Suppose we could borrow Sabrina and Christopher?" Randy asked.

"What for?"

"Sabrina as a flower girl, and Chris is old enough to handle being a ring bearer, isn't he?" Randy questioned, hoping Jim would agree to this.

"All he has to do is carry a pillow, right?"

"A pillow with expensive rings on it," Randy added.

"If we practice with him, I think he can handle that. You guys have a date now?"

"May 22nd," Randy confirmed.

Jim questioned the rationale behind that decision. "The day after graduation?"

"Yup."

"Damn, that's gonna be an exciting weekend for you, Bro. Your M.D. and a new wife all the same weekend."

"We planned it that way. It'll save a lot of my family members a second trip down here if we do it all at once."

"Good thinkin'."

They walked across the parking lot toward the hospital entrance. "We decided to get married by the beach, since that's where we met."

"No shit?" Jim said with a grin.

"Yup. Sunset maybe. Haven't decided for sure."

"Romantic as hell, Dude. Mushy ass shit."

Randy agreed, "Yeah, but it's our wedding, and if we're going to pay a fortune for this, we might as well give people a show."

"True enough. Hey, you wanna meet me for some grindage later?" Jim asked, hoping Randy wouldn't be too busy to join him for lunch.

"Sure."

"Sweet. I'll call you."

Randy refuted that plan. "ICU, won't have my phone on. Let's meet out front at one."

"Alright, but we're goin' somewhere off these premises. I am not eatin' cafeteria food. I can't stomach that today."

Randy laughed in total agreement.

About 6:00 that night, Randy came home from the hospital. He draped his lab coat over the back of a chair and gently set his stethoscope on the table. Jane was on the couch in one of his dress shirts with her hair wrapped up in a towel flipping through a copy of Brides magazine. Randy snuck up behind her and kissed her neck. "I love it when you wear my shirts. It's sexy as hell." He peeked over her shoulder. "Whatcha reading?"

"A catalog with wedding gowns and bridesmaids dresses in it."

"Find anything?" He eyed the page she was fixated on.

"I like these." She pointed to a picture of a red strapless satin side-ruched ball gown with a diagonal beaded waistband.

"Red? I thought you might have gone with blue since that's your favorite color."

"Yes, but red is more vibrant, and you like red," she justified. "And if we go with red, we can use red roses in the flowers."

He hadn't thought of that. "True. Did you find a dress for you in there?"

"I don't need one," she declared. "I'm going to wear Mom's dress."

That was the most remarkable gesture of love Randy had ever heard. Jane was going to become his wife wearing her mother's wedding dress. What an extraordinary way to include her in the ceremony. "That's great."

"It's been in a closet for twenty-six years. It'll need to be dry-cleaned. Daddy and I are going to pull it out this weekend."

While Randy kissed Jane's neck, he reached his hands down and unbuttoned the top two buttons of the shirt she was wearing, exposing the bare skin underneath.

"Behave," she declared.

"Was hoping we could have sex tonight," he said with a sexy grin.

She gave him an ostentatious stare while he brushed his hand over her breast. "Randy."

"What?" He sent more seductive kisses down her neck and shoulder, trying to stir up arousal. "I want to touch you, kiss you, and rub strawberry scented body oil all over your naked body." He could tell he was getting to her because she closed her eyes and moaned softly. Her chest heaved and her body squirmed beneath his hands. He unbuttoned two more buttons then roamed intimately over her breasts. Grazing his lips on her ear, he whispered, "Wanna go in the bedroom?"

She reached her hand behind his neck and instinctively drew her lips to his, kissing him intensely. Her luscious lips radiated through his entire body, leaving him unable to breathe.

Trying to regain air, he said, "Is that a yes?"

She drug him into the bedroom.

Following dinner that night, Randy took Jane's hand and pulled her into his arms to dance with her. While they danced across the living room floor, he sang the song lyrics to her.

She looked at him and smiled. "The first time we danced together they played this song."

"I know. I remember. This is our song." He lifted her chin and kissed her softly. "We need to dance to this song at our wedding."

Having wedding plans on her mind, she asked, "What kind of cake do you want for the wedding? Chocolate or white?"

He suggested, "Let's get an Oreo cake."

"An Oreo cake?"

"Oreos are good. And they're chocolate. Everybody likes chocolate. Besides, chocolate is considered an aphrodisiac."

She thought he was insane. "You want everyone at our wedding to be seduced by the cake?"

"Sure. Why not? It would certainly be memorable, wouldn't it?" he said, being obnoxious.

"Randal Hanson. Stop that."

"I'm just playin'."

Knowing his love for cheesecake, she suggested, "They make cheesecake wedding cakes."

This perked him up. "They do?"

"Yes."

He considered this suggestion. Cheesecake sounded good to him. "Ooh, get chocolate cheesecake. The best of both worlds." Jane always made Randy smile. She let him be silly and was a good sport at playing along with his insufferable teasing or ornery raillery. He loved her for that. "I wanted to show you something I found," he said to her.

"What is it?"

"It's this place overlooking Monterey Bay in Santa Cruz called Seascape Resort. They offer luxurious weddings by the beach. Their package deals include rehearsal, the wedding ceremony, and the reception. They'll include white garden chairs for our guests, our choice of wedding arches, and a reception room. They provide hors d'oeuvres, they'll serve dinner at the reception with a wait staff, and provide cake cutting service. They have a nice wine list too. We also have the option of having an open bar, and they have a dancefloor. It's all inclusive. And the ceremony will be right by the beach, like we wanted."

It sounded like everything they were looking for, but it also sounded pricey. "That sounds expensive."

"It's $1,200 for the ceremony for up to two-hundred guests. Plus a $2,000 deposit. It'll cost about eighty dollars per person for the reception."

She calculated the math in her head. "Twenty thousand dollars?"

"Give or take a few grand, depending on how many people we invite." He knew planning a wedding wasn't going to be cheap, but he didn't want to skimp on theirs. He wanted nothing less than what Jane deserved, and she deserved the best. "How much did you think this wedding was going to cost?"

The budget factor of this location posed a problem. "That's a lot of money."

"My parents want to help. We'll get the deposit back afterwards. Aside from a cake, flowers, a photographer, and a DJ, everything else will be taken care of. If the pictures I saw on the internet are any indication, the place is extraordinary. As an added bonus, all of our family members that come into town for the wedding can stay there at a discounted rate. It's certainly worth checking out."

"Ok," she agreed with a smile. "Sounds cool."

"Great! We'll drive over there tomorrow. We better plan on at least a hundred to a hundred and fifty people for this wedding, Babe. My family alone, including all my cousins and aunts and uncles, will be fifty or more. And all of our friends, medical colleagues, your sorority sisters. Damn, this is gonna be huge."

An excited grin lit up her face and brightened her eyes as they discussed plans for their wedding. She was thrilled Randy was getting so involved.

"I can't wait to marry you," Randy declared.

"I can't wait to be your wife."

He moved in for a kiss. "Are you sure you're ok leaving San Francisco, or are you just saying that because you know I want UW?"

"I want to go," she assured him. "I'm ready for a change in scenery."

He hoped she was being honest with him. "You sure?"

"Uh huh."

"Ok, because I gave UW my intent, and I've contacted the state medical board about licensure in Washington. I've gotten that process started. Going to start checking out real estate in the area too, Kirkland in particular. I need you to fly up there with me at some point so we can look at houses together."

Jane loved discussing their future plans. "You just tell me when."

"Washington takes at least sixty days to process medical license applications. And it will take about a month to close out escrow on a house. By the end of spring break, we'll need to make some decisions."

She agreed, "Alright."

Randy considered the hundreds of things they would need to get done within the next few months. It was going to be crazy. "Holy hell, we have a wedding to plan, a school transfer to take care of, a new job to prepare for, a house to buy, and a move to another state to organize. Glad my workload is light this year."

This comment made Jane giggle. "Good thing I'm not playing basketball anymore."

"Oh good god, imagine if we had to deal with that too. Finishing up my clerkship and you going to graduate school is enough."

"We're definitely going to be busy," she added.

That statement couldn't have been truer.

Over the next six weeks, Jane and Randy were busy taste testing wedding cakes, picking out invitations, getting bridesmaids sized for their gowns, and discussing details with the Seascape Resort. Wedding plans slowly began to fall into place.

On Sunday, while Randy met with his study group, Jane went over to her father's house. Her mother's wedding dress had been dry cleaned and pressed, but Jane had to see if it needed to be sized. She slipped it on and zipped it up then stared in the full-length mirror. This beautiful sleeveless wedding gown had a lace-covered bodice that seemed to drip down the front. Lace lined the bottom edge of the skirt, and the curve-hugging waistline supported a lace-trimmed train. Simple, yet elegant, and it fit perfectly. As she looked at her reflection, a soft knock rapped on the door.

"Jane," her father's voice called out.

"Come in, Daddy."

Dale Davine had to fight back tears when he saw his daughter wearing his wife's wedding dress. "You look lovely, Honey."

"Thank you."

"Turn around and let me see the back."

She posed to give him the full vision. She was the most beautiful bride he had ever seen. She looked so much like her mother, he had to swallow back the lump in his throat. "Your future husband is a lucky man." He handed her a small box. "These were your mother's. She wore them with that gown the day she and I stood on the altar. She wanted me to save them for your wedding day."

Jane opened the box to reveal a delicate and intricately detailed crystal and pearl drop necklace with matching earrings. "Daddy, these are beautiful."

Dale clipped the necklace around Jane's neck while Jane put the earrings in her ears. "You look just like your mother."

Those sentimental words brought tears to her eyes.

"When you were a little girl, I read you stories about princesses who were swept away by prince charming. Do you remember?"

"I remember."

"You used to wrap yourself up in a white sheet, put on your mother's heels, and parade around the house pretending you were a bride. You told me that someday you'd meet prince charming. Now, here you are. Five months away from your own happily ever after."

"I wish Mom was here."

"I wish she was too. She would have loved to see you walk down that aisle." A terrible ache filled his heart as he kissed Jane's cheek. "I hope Randy knows what a wonderful young woman he is getting."

"Daddy, of course he knows. He loves me."

"You're beautiful, Jane. I love you very much."

She put her arms around her father's neck and hugged him. "I love you too, Daddy."

When Jane got home that afternoon, Randy was surrounded by paperwork. He browsed the internet and read a pamphlet, all while filling out some kind of form. "Hi, Sweetie."

"Hello, Beautiful," he said, looking away from his reading. "What's the verdict on the dress?"

"It fits perfectly."

"Good. When do I get to see it?"

"You're not supposed to see it until the wedding."

"Says who?"

She had absolutely no idea. "I don't know, but you're not supposed to."

"Whoever made up these wedding rules did it to torture the groom I think." He laughed at his own ill humor then stood up and gave her a kiss. "I wanted ask you something."

"What?"

"How would you feel about writing our own wedding vows?" he suggested.

"What's wrong with the traditional ones?"

"They don't say what I want to say. I'd like the opportunity to express how I feel in my own words. But if I write my vows, you'll have to write yours too, that's why I wanted to talk to you about it. This would really mean a lot to me."

Personalizing wedding vows was a huge undertaking. Jane wasn't sure how she felt about this. "You're better at that kind of thing than I am."

"You're good with words too, Babe," he stated. "If we write our own vows, our true feelings will come out. The words won't be scripted. It will be more meaningful."

"But I'll have to say them in front of everyone."

"No, you'll say them to me while standing on that altar. No one else will exist at that point, at least for me they won't. So what do you think?"

"Sounds challenging, but more personal."

"Exactly. You in?"

She drew her lip between her teeth. "Yes. Let's do it."

"Awesome! Thank you." He kissed her once more then slid the paperwork in an envelope.

"What are you doing?" Jane asked him.

"Filling out paperwork to get my state of Washington medical license. They received my MLE scores and transcripts. They'll need an updated copy after I graduate, but this will get me a temporary license until my M.D. is confirmed through the university." He sealed the envelope and put a stamp on it. "Three-hundred, seventy-five bucks."

"Ouch!"

"Yeah. My thoughts exactly."

Randy and Jane visited several jewelry stores to look at wedding rings hoping to find something they both liked. They wanted matching rings, but they both had very different tastes, which made this task much more taxing than they originally thought it was going to be. The entire escapade was rather amusing. How could two people so in love with so much in common be so different when it came time to search for the perfect wedding ring?

"What's wrong with this one?" Jane asked, showing him an elaborate ring she found.

"I am not wearing that," Randy complained. "It's gaudy and too ornamental for my liking. I want something simpler than that."

She pointed out a plain gold band instead. "What about this one?"

Randy shook his head. "No. I need something with more style. I'll know it when I find it."

They walked into jewelry store number nine anticipating yet another debate of the rings. Before they approached the display counter, Randy looked at Jane and said, "Ok, we have been at this for almost six hours now. There's got to be something in this city we both like."

"You're the picky one, not me," she accused.

"Hell yeah, I'm picky," Randy declared. "If I'm gonna have a ring on my finger for the rest of my life, I want it to be a nice one. And I'm a doctor. I use my hands all the time. I have to have a ring that won't get in the way or distract me."

At the counter, Jane peered into the glass case. "Some of these are really expensive."

"So? How often will we buy wedding rings?"

"Once," she declared.

"Exactly. This is a ring that will be on your finger all the time. It should be comfortable and look good. Don't worry about the cost, Babe. Find something you like."

A salesman offered his assistance. "May I help you, Sir?"

"Yes," Randy replied. "My fiancé and I would like to look at wedding rings."

The salesman pulled out several styles. They looked at matching sets as well as individual rings. Jane found a round-cut channel set diamond band that really sparked her interest. She slipped it on her finger alongside her engagement ring to see how they looked together.

"That looks nice, Babe," Randy commented. He tried on the men's three stone diamond diagonal design ring that matched the one Jane had. "Hmm," he said, scrutinizing over the details of this ring.

Jane watched him intently, waiting for his opinion.

He held out his hand to see what it looked like. This ring was classy, comfortable, and masculine. Definitely his style.

"Well?" she asked, hoping he finally found something he liked.

"This is a nice ring." A huge smile lit up his face. "I could wear this."

"Finally," she replied.

Randy said to the salesman, "We'll take these."

"Very good." The salesman happened to have rings in stock in their sizes which allowed Randy and Jane to bring them home that day.

Now that the ring buying task was complete, Randy ran through their to-do list. Wedding gown, bridesmaids' gowns, flower girl dress done. Invitations ordered, reception and ceremony hall reserved. Entrees and hors d'oeuvres selected, cake ordered, and rings bought. They still needed to purchase flowers, hire a photographer, find entertainment, and get decorations for this event. And at some point, Randy needed to go with Jim to pick out tuxes.

Then a thought struck him that put him in a state of panic. The honeymoon. Oh shit! That was most important part, and he had completely forgotten about it. Where in god's name was he going to take Jane for their honeymoon? He reverted back to a conversation they had ages ago where Jane fantasized about going to a tropical island and making love under a waterfall in a lagoon. But where the hell did she say she wanted to go? For the life of him, he could not remember. Was it the Bahamas, Barbados, or Bali she had mentioned? He wished now he had paid more attention. It was definitely a B word. This toiled his mind for days while he fought to remember what she had said.

"Bermuda!" he exclaimed when it finally came to him.

"Bermuda?" Jim questioned, wondering why Randy randomly blurted out that word. "What the fuck are you talkin' about?"

"Jane mentioned to me once that she's always wanted to go to Bermuda. That's where I'll take her for our honeymoon." He considered this for a minute. "Wonder how much that will cost?"

"A pretty penny, I'm sure," Jim said.

"I just spent $2200 for wedding rings, I'm gonna end up spending a good chunk of my savings on a down payment for my new house, have to pay for a move, and now a honeymoon." Randy rubbed the back of his neck. "Damn. Getting married is expensive."

Jim laughed at Randy's ramblings. "Thought you said your parents were helpin' you."

"They are," Randy clarified. "They're paying for the wedding ceremony and reception, which is going to end up totaling about twenty-thousand dollars."

"Jesus, Dude. What the hell kind of wedding are you two plannin'?"

"A huge one."

"Sounds like it."

"Jane's dad is taking care of her dress and veil and hair and whatever the hell else she needs," Randy commented. "Pretty much all of Alpha Phi is providing decorations. Jane's bridesmaids all insisted on paying for their own dresses, so that'll help."

626

"I'll cover Sabrina and Chris, and I'll pay for my own tux," Jim offered. "I'm sure Bruce will too."

Grateful for Jim's offer, Randy replied, "Thanks, man. Know where we can get a good DJ?"

"How the hell would I know that? Jane's the party girl. After four years in a sorority, she's bound to have some connections."

"Oh yeah." Randy grinned. "Good point."

Randy seemed flustered and stressed. Jim hoped he didn't buckle under all the chaos. "You alright, man?"

"I'm fine. I just have a shit ton of stuff to do, and for a change it's not school related."

"Better you than me. Hey, I've been meaning to ask you something. Since our last day is the 18th, and graduation is the 21st, I thought we might have your bachelor's party on the 19th. That will give you a day to recover before graduation," Jim suggested.

Randy didn't like the way that sounded. "Recover from what? What the hell kind of bash are you planning?"

"The biggest damn party of the year, Dude."

Randy shook his head, knowing Jim was planning to go far beyond what was necessary to embarrass the hell out of him. "Is that really necessary?"

"Why yes. Yes it is."

Jim had something on his mind he wanted to discuss with Bruce and Mandy, but he didn't want Randy around to hear it. He called both of them, and they all agreed to meet discreetly the following afternoon. "Yo guys, I have an idea," Jim stated.

"What's up?" Bruce asked.

"You know how we were talkin' the other day about what to get Jane and Randy for their wedding? Well, I have the answer."

"And what's that?"

"I was hangin' with Randy yesterday and he mentioned that Jane has always wanted to go to Bermuda. He really wants to take her there for their honeymoon, but he was buggin' about how he was gonna pay for it with everything else he had goin' on—gettin' a new house and buyin' wedding rings and all that. So I was thinkin' we could all pitch in and get them some kind of honeymoon package in Bermuda. It wouldn't cost as much if all three of us split the expense, and that way Randy won't have to worry about it and can enjoy all of this excitement he's havin' right now. What do you think?"

Bruce and Mandy looked at each other and smiled. "You know, Jim," Bruce declared. "That is an excellent idea."

"It's the best idea you've had in years," Mandy agreed, teasing him.

"Oh, ha, ha. Very funny," Jim said, not amused by her comment.

"How much vacation time do they have available?" she asked.

"Two weeks I believe. But if we're gonna do this, we need to do it quick, before he makes his own reservations."

"I'll look up Bermuda honeymoon packages and see what's available."

It took them a few days, but they ended up with a nice package which included roundtrip airfare and a twelve night stay at Cambridge Beach Luxury Resort. They all paid Jim their share, and Jim booked the trip with his credit card. He bought a card, which all three of them signed, then Jim placed the airline reservations and resort information inside the envelope along with a note. *Our gift to you, Randy and Jane. May you live a long and happy life together. Enjoy your honeymoon! We love you. Jim, Mandy, and Bruce.* They planned to present this to Randy and Jane Sunday during their weekly study session.

They held their session at Randy's apartment that week. Halfway through studying, Jim announced, "Randy, can you have Jane come in here for a minute."

"What do you want her for?"

"Because what Mandy, Bruce, and I are about to say involves her."

"What are you talking about?"

"Will you tell her to come in here please?" Jim insisted. "Jesus, Hanson. Humor me."

"Alright. I'll get her." Randy got out of his chair and went into the bedroom where Jane was folding laundry. He came back out holding her hand. "Now tell me what's going on."

Jim announced, "The three of us wanted to get you guys a wedding gift. But under the circumstances, we felt this couldn't wait." Jim handed Randy an envelope.

"What did you guys do?" He let go of Jane's hand and tore the envelope open. Once he discovered what was inside, his jaw dropped. "Holy shit. I can't believe you guys did this. This is incredible." He looked up at Jim, Bruce, and Amanda, overcome with emotion.

"What is it?" Jane asked, wondering what Randy was getting worked up about.

He handed the reservation information to Jane. "Look."

When she realized what she was looking at, her mouth gaped open. "Oh my god."

Bruce declared, "You have a luxury suite at your disposal for twelve nights."

"And your airline tickets have already been reserved in your name and paid for, Randy," Mandy added. "You'll just need to pick them up."

"These rooms are stellar too," Jim said. "Ocean views, hot tubs, private terrace. All that mushy romantic shit you love."

Jane gazed at Randy with tears in her eyes. "I can't believe this." Then she turned her glance to Bruce, Mandy, and Jim. "This is too much. Thank you."

Randy was completely at a loss for words. "I honestly don't know what to say. I was not expecting anything like this."

"How about a thank you," Jim teased.

"Definitely. Thank you," Randy replied gratefully. "Thank you so much."

"Congratulations, Randy," Mandy said. "You two deserve it."

One by one, Jane hugged Mandy, Bruce, and Jim. She thanked them again before she returned to what she was doing.

After Mandy and Bruce left, Randy lounged casually in his chair and stretched out his legs. "Dammit, Jim. You didn't have to do that."

"Surprise," Jim said in return. "And it wasn't just me. Bruce and Mandy contributed."

"But obviously you put them up to it," Randy accused, knowing Jim was guilty as hell.

"Yes. But we've been toilin' with what to get you guys for a while. And when you said that whole honeymoon Bermuda thing, it finally came to me. Enjoy."

Randy and Jim knuckle bumped. "That is really cool. Thank you."

"You're very welcome."

Chapter Sixty

Winter break came around again, and this year Randy and Jane would be parted for Christmas. Understandably, Jane wanted to spend her last Christmas in San Francisco with her father and her brother. But Randy opted to fly home. He stared out the window of the 747. Snow-covered Mt. Rainier overlooked the city. Descending into Seattle, Jane was on his mind. Already he missed her beautiful smile and loving touch.

Randy's mother picked him up at the airport, greeting him with a hug and a kiss on the cheek. He looked a little gloomy. "You ok?"

"I'm alright." He let out a melancholy sigh. "Janey was crying when I left."

Ellen hoped this wasn't a major problem. "Is everything alright?"

"It's hard to say goodbye, and I hate to leave her like that."

"I understand." Trying to get his mind off of it, she said, "We'll keep you busy. You won't have time to think about her."

"I always think about her, Mom."

"I know. But you can call her any time you want," his mother suggested.

"I know, and I will." They headed to the baggage claim where Randy grabbed his luggage.

On the way out to the car, Ellen told her son, "Your father wants me to drop you off at the clinic."

"Why?" Randy asked.

"He wants to take you out to lunch."

"I need to talk to him anyway. I have a million things I need to do while I'm up here."

"Like what?" his mother asked him.

"Like go to UW and talk to the Residency Director and see if I can get a tentative schedule. Oh, by the way," he remembered, "UCSF is giving me the Deans' Prize for Medical School Research."

Ellen's mouth dropped. "Oh, Sweetheart, that's fantastic."

"I'm excited about it. I'm ranked first in the class right now too. There's a vote for the Gold-Headed Cane award coming up and I've been nominated. The bad thing is, Bruce is up for nomination too, but I kinda hope he gets it," Randy admitted. "I've gotten so many other awards, I'd really like to see him get this one. Bruce is a good student." Randy placed his bag in the trunk of the car then he and his mother drove to his father's clinic.

While she drove, his mom asked him, "How are you and Jane coming along with wedding plans?"

"We're getting stuff done," he replied. "I never knew how much crap was involved in planning a wedding."

"Dad wants to give you some money to help out."

"I think you guys have done enough with the ceremony and the reception, Mom. Twenty thousand is a hefty expense."

"Weddings are expensive, Randy, and you're gonna need money once you and Jane move up here. Please, let us help."

Randy grinned gratefully. "Thanks."

"Your dad and I are so proud of you, Honey. You are one semester away from graduating from medical school, you've already secured a residency slot for yourself, you're getting married to a wonderful woman, and now these two new honors you've achieved."

"Honestly, all I care about right now is getting my residency situated, getting Jane transferred over here, and trying to find a place for me and my future wife to live after we get married," Randy declared.

"Your dad can help with that," his mother suggested.

"I'm counting on it."

When they arrived at Dr. Hanson's clinic, Randy sauntered over to the receptionist. "Good afternoon, Sam."

She looked up at him and grinned. "Oh, what a treat. The other Dr. Hanson."

Randy chuckled. "Not quite. Five more months. But I do think I have an appointment with Dr. Hanson. Any idea where he might be?"

Mark Hanson peeked around the corner when he heard Randy's voice. "Hello, Randal."

"Hey, Dad." Randy stepped around to the back of the clinic and gave his dad a hug. "How's it going?"

"Going well. How's Jane?"

"Doing well," Randy replied. "Beautiful as usual."

Ellen prompted, "Tell your dad the news."

"What news?" Mark asked.

Randy told him, "I've been given the Dean's Prize for Medical School Research."

"Good job, Son. You're brilliant."

Dr. Hanson's nurse overheard this conversation and asked, "When are you coming to join us?"

Randy answered, "I wish I could, Mary. Still have four years of residency to complete before I can."

"We'll have a nametag and a door sign waiting for you when you get here."

"Thank you. It's nice to feel wanted."

Mark handed a patient file to his file clerk then curled his arm around his son's shoulders. "Let's get some lunch."

Later that afternoon, after dropping his father off at the clinic, Randy unloaded a few gifts from his bag and placed them under the tree. Then he kicked off his shoes and picked up the paper, skimming through the house listings in the Kirkland area.

His mother came in to see what he was doing. "You want some coffee, Honey?"

"Thanks, Mom. That would be great."

"What are you doing?" she asked curiously.

"Searching for houses that are on the market around here. You have a pen?"

She handed him a ballpoint pen.

"There's a house for sale right down the street from you guys. Have you seen it?" Randy asked.

"I wasn't aware there were any houses on the market in this neighborhood."

The description of it really intrigued Randy. He read it aloud to his mother.

"Sounds like a nice place," she commented, handing Randy his cup of coffee.

He took a sip. "I'll definitely have to check that one out."

Randy always enjoyed spending time with his family, but he hadn't seen Jane in four days and was looking forward to picking her up from the airport that afternoon. He hopped around the kitchen, singing along to the song that was on the radio.

Stephanie laughed at his fidgetiness. "Would you stop jumping all over the place?"

"No, I will not," Randy declared. "I'm in a good mood because I get to see my fiancé today." He took a sip from the steaming mug in his hand. "And I don't know what Mom does to this coffee, but this is really good."

"I think you've had too much caffeine. You're bouncing around like a jumping bean on crack."

"Can't help it," he said. "I love her. And I'm going to run to her and take her in my arms and kiss her like a mad man."

Stephanie cringed. "Eww. TMI."

Randy laughed at the look on his sister's face.

Thankfully, Jane's flight landed on time. Randy waited at the bottom of the ramp, anxious to see his fiancé's beautiful face. As soon as they spotted each other, they embraced in a hug and a long intimate kiss.

"I missed you," she said.

"I missed you too." They headed down to baggage claim, hands clenched tightly together. "We have a lot to discuss," Randy said. "I've found several houses I want us to take a look at and picked up a tentative residency schedule. My parents are going to pay for flowers and want me to tell them the final cost when we finally decide what we want."

The bulk of the wedding expenses were being covered by the Hansons. Dale Davine didn't have near the means to pay for as elaborate a wedding as Jane wanted, so they did their part to help out. Mr. Davine was, however, covering little things like the cake knife, the flower girl's basket, a pillow for the rings, as well as anything Jane needed, like shoes, and her updo and manicure for the event. Randy was grateful the families were working together to make this event possible for them. This was becoming a dual family and multiple friend group effort that everyone they knew seemed to have a major roll in.

After claiming Jane's bags, they walked across the sky bridge to the parking garage. Randy unlocked his dad's truck, put her suitcase in the bed, then pulled Jane into his arms. "Mom had mistletoe all over the place and I had no one to kiss," he said with a pout.

"You do now."

"I know. And I plan on taking full advantage of that."

When they pulled into the driveway, Ellen Hanson met them at the door, greeting them both with a hug.

"Hi, Mrs. Hanson," Jane said.

"Oh no, Dear. It's Mom to you now," Ellen corrected. "Let me see this ring my son gave you."

Jane proudly held out her hand.

"That is gorgeous," his mom said, approving of his choice.

The family shared a delicious homemade lasagna dinner together, which everyone helped to prepare. Randy cleared the dinner dishes and helped his sister load the dishwasher then he took Jane by the hand and disappeared downstairs to be alone with her. Together they looked at the real estate book he had picked up, reading through descriptions of some houses that interested him.

Jane and Randy spent the majority of their time in Seattle viewing houses for sale in the Kirkland area. Randy had never purchased a house before and he had a blast shopping around with Jane, viewing different layouts, waiting to see what caught her eye. He wanted her to have something cozy she would love, yet roomy enough to expand their family later on down the road. Unfortunately during this visit, they didn't find anything within their price range that they liked. They returned to San Francisco empty-handed, but planned to try again over spring break.

Chapter Sixty-One

Between January and March, Randy was so busy with rotations and finalizing residency paperwork, the wedding date crept up faster than he anticipated. Randy, Jim, and Bruce went to various formal wear shops to look at tuxes together, debating over many different styles. Randy finally decided on black slacks and black three-button coats with notch collars. The coat lapels were finished with matte satin, matching the satin covered buttons. White laydown collared shirts, black satin vests, and white satin ties accompanied the look. All they needed now were matching black dress shoes. He figured the three of them and his brother would take care of that when they all got fitted for their tuxes in May.

Following the tuxedo adventure, the three men drove to Randy's apartment to watch the NCAA basketball playoffs. They were lounging on the sofa drinking Coronas when Jane came in with a plate full of cookies. "You guys want a cookie?"

Jim grabbed the entire plate. "Ooh."

Randy tried to grab a cookie, but Jim pulled the plate away. "Hey, didn't your momma ever teach you to share?"

"Nope," Jim retorted. He handed one cookie to Randy and another one to Bruce then kept the rest of the plate for himself.

The men drank Coronas with their chocolate chip cookies. Jane thought that was the most revolting food combination she had ever seen. "Cookies and beer? That sounds totally gross."

"The three of us have discovered the secret of life," Randy said.

"Is that right?" This ought to be good. The secret of life discovered by three partially insane medical students.

"Yes. There are only three things a man needs to be happy."

Jim added, "Basketball, beer, and a babe that bakes. You have those three things, and life is complete. Total karma, man."

"Oh, it's that simple, huh?" Jane asked.

"Yup." Randy took a bite of his cookie.

"And I always thought you were a complex thinker, Randal Hanson. Boy, did you prove me wrong."

Randy, Bruce, and Jim all laughed.

For spring break, Randy and Jane returned to Seattle with the goal of choosing a house. After viewing several styles of homes priced within their budget, nothing seemed to catch Jane's eye. Randy was beginning to worry that they would never find anything they both liked. While driving through the neighborhood, they stumbled upon a home that had just been put on the market that day. It was one of twenty single family homes located within a two and a half acre gated community right across the street from Lake Washington. The contemporary style home with classic brick exterior finish was only about six years old. It had a strong and sturdy slate roof, was close to downtown, and not far from his parents' house. The house was only a short drive away from the 520 bridge, which Randy would be crossing every day to get into Seattle. They decided to check it out.

The interior was stunning with its European design and vaulted ceilings. It featured three bedrooms, three baths, a fireplace, and a two-car garage. The beautiful finishes of granite, marble, crown molding, ceramic tile and Brazilian Tigerwood flooring immediately caught Jane's eye. A spacious master suite with sitting area, walk in closet, and an elegant marble bath with jetted tub made her jaw drop. This house had multiple elements that she loved—upper level bed and bathrooms with a small sitting area, lower level office space and utility room, open daylight living room, gourmet kitchen with a pantry, and a wall of windows overlooking the yard from the living and dining area.

Randy was drawn to the roominess of it—all 3,230 square feet, a big and comfortable space with enough room to grow a family. The double paned storm windows would keep the cold out in winter, and forced air heating and cooling would create lower utility bills. The high tech cabling would support his HD surround sound entertainment system. The security system and gated entry would keep them safe. Randy loved the view—a deck extended into a garden-view courtyard. The yard was professionally landscaped and the lake was within view. The fact that he was only a hop skip and jump away from the park and close to the marina attracted his attention. It wasn't exactly lakefront property, but it was close enough.

Despite what he liked, the excitement on Jane's face as they toured the house was all he needed to see. She was in love, and to Randy that was all that mattered. He would have to negotiate the price to see if he could talk them down a bit, but for a first house for him and his fiancé it was elegant and roomy.

Since it was an estate house and the family wanted to sell it quickly, Randy's real estate agent was able to negotiate the purchase price, reducing it by quite a bit. Luckily Randy had impeccable credit, and because he had a resident doctor discount, he was able to get an exceptionally low interest rate on financing and lower their monthly payments.

Five weeks later, after another trip to Seattle to sign paperwork, escrow closed on his house. With one less thing on his plate, Randy could now focus his energy on preparing for graduation.

Lisa and Stephanie hosted Jane's bridal shower. While Jane was having fun with the girls, Randy tried to find ways to keep himself occupied. He decided to pack some boxes. As he was packing things up, he came across a box full of Jane's keepsakes. He sat on the floor and rummaged through the box. Inside, he discovered old family photos, some basketball pictures, Jane's high school athletic letter and class ring, concert and theatre ticket stubs, and even love notes he had written to her.

An opened envelope with Jane's name on it attracted his attention. He dumped out the contents—a locket on a gold chain. Randy opened the locket to reveal a picture of Jane's parents on one side and she and Brian on the other. There was also a note inside that was sealed with a basketball sticker. Curiosity got the best of him. He pulled it out and read it.

My darling Jane,

Having you as my daughter has been a treasure. You've been more than just my daughter; you've been my inspiration, my strength, my reason for living. I love you. Don't ever lose that joy and laughter you have for life. Pursue your dreams. Brighten the world with your beautiful smile and loving heart. Keep playing basketball and know I'll always be watching over you.

Find love and happiness, Sweetheart. Open your heart to a man and let him give you his. Make memories together. And someday, when you walk down that aisle, know that I will be there with you in spirit. In your heart is all the love in the world. Share it.

You can talk to me anytime you want, simply look up at the stars and you'll see me there; I'll always listen. Take care of Daddy and Brian for me.

I'll be with you always, Mom

Randy's heart grew heavy as he read this. Barbara Davine obviously wrote this when she knew her life was about to end. He slipped the note and the locket back inside the envelope and put it back in the box. Digging further, he discovered a long skinny box. Inside he found a dried, pressed rose wrapped up in a paper towel. Written in Jane's handwriting were the words *Jonathan Randal Hanson,*

September 23. He recognized that date, and the rose. That was the rose he left for her the morning after they made love for the first time. "I'll be damned. She kept it."

He packed a few boxes then headed toward the kitchen to get a drink. Sitting on the table was a spiral notebook with doodles all over the front of it. He flipped through the pages finding various song lyrics and poems. A small piece of light pink heart-shaped paper fell out onto the table. Randy set the notebook aside and picked it up. It said *Wedding Vows* on the top. Not wanting to spoil the day, he folded it back up and slipped it back in the notebook.

Also on the table was an envelope with metallic red foil lining. Inside was one of their wedding invitations. On the front, along with the words *Randy and Jane*, was a single red rose with a silver stem. He opened the card and read:

Dr. and Mrs. Mark Hanson
And
Mr. Dale Davine
Are pleased to announce the
Marriage uniting their children,
Jane Elizabeth Davine
And
Jonathan Randal Hanson,
And request the pleasure of your company
Saturday, May the 22nd,
At four o'clock in the afternoon.
The Seascape Resort
Monterey Bay, CA
Reception immediately following.

An RSVP card with the address and directions to the Seascape Resort was enclosed in the envelope. He had read the words on this invitation a hundred times yet it still moved him. He carefully returned the invitation to its envelope then decided to get something to eat.

Three hours later, Jane walked into the apartment with both hands full.

Randy hopped over the back of couch and greeted her with a kiss. "Hey, Babe. How was your bridal shower?"

"Fun. I have a surprise for you."

"Oh yeah? What is it?"

"New silk sheets for our bed."

Sexy and slippery—sounded fun to him. "I like it."

"I got some new lingerie, and Lisa bought me a bottle of edible strawberry flavored body oil."

Randy smiled seductively. "Ooh, we're gonna have fun tonight."

She shook her head, refuting his suggestion. "Uh uh. It's for our honeymoon. You have to wait."

"Ah, man." He snooped through the bags she had. "What else did you get?"

"Scented candles, a wedding keepsake book, a CD of love songs, and a garter to wear under my wedding dress."

He liked the sound of that. "Keep talkin'."

"I have a bottle of wine and two engraved wine glasses, his and hers bath towels, oh, and here's something you'll like." She reached into the bag and pulled out a book called *The Art of Sensual Massage.*

He turned the book over and read the description on the back. "Sensual massage? Can't wait to try this." He enjoyed Jane's gifts as much as she did. "We are going to have the time of our lives on our honeymoon."

During their final day of medical school, Randy sat at the table with Jim, Bruce, and Mandy to go over the graduation checklist. Bored with the discussion, Jim focused his eyes on the clock. He couldn't believe how slow the hands were moving. "Come on, dammit, ten minutes." As he watched, the minute hand on the clock moved backwards. "Shit!" he blurted out loud enough for everyone in the room to hear him.

Bruce, Randy, and Amanda stared at him. Unfortunately, so did the doctor conducting this seminar. "Mr. Ryan, is there a problem?" the doctor asked.

"No, Sir." Jim rejoined the conversation. "Damn clock. They really should fix that thing."

Randy laughed. "I don't think that clock has ever worked right."

"I have your bachelor's party planned for Wednesday night. The guest list is piling up."

"Please don't do anything to embarrass me, Jim."

Jim smirked. "Now why would I do that?"

Randy shook his head, not sure he was prepared for whatever veritable hell Jim was bound to put him through.

When Randy arrived home that evening, he was beaming with excitement. He dropped his bags, books, and all of his medical equipment on the table. "Jane!" he hollered as he walked in the kitchen looking for her. "Janey!"

She rushed out of the bedroom. "What? What is it?"

He took her in his arms and spun her around. "I survived medical school! I am finally finished!" He kissed her lovingly on the lips. "This is incredible."

Celebrating with him, she said, "Yay! Congratulations, Sweetie."

"God, this feels good. Dr. Hanson, here I come." He set her back down on the floor. "Let's celebrate."

"Ok. What do you want to do?"

"You know what?" He grinned at her. "Let's pig out on pie."

Jane giggled. "I have to be able to fit into my wedding dress, Randy."

"Oh, you will. But if for some reason you don't, we can always get married naked," he teased.

She gasped and smacked him with a pillow. "Randy! We're not having a nude wedding."

"I know," he tittered. "I'm teasing. But I do want pie." He took her hand and led her out the door.

Wednesday, Jane brought her wedding dress, the bridesmaids' dresses, and all of the accessories over to Lisa and Stephanie's apartment so they would be ready the day of the wedding.

"Put on your dress and let's make sure you're not missing anything," Lisa suggested.

Jane carefully stepped into the dress, and Lisa zipped it for her. To get the full effect, she put on the shoes and jewelry as well.

Lisa beheld Jane's beauty. "Perfect."

Jane viewed her image in the full length mirror. Tears began to fog her vision.

"What's wrong?" Lisa asked, touching Jane's shoulder in comfort.

"I can't believe I'm marrying my best friend in three days."

Lisa hugged her. "He's a wonderful man, Jane."

"He's the man I've waited my whole life for."

Lisa straightened out Jane's dress. "Randy is going to fall head over heels when he sees you. You look gorgeous."

Jane looked into the mirror again. "Jane Hanson," she said, trying out the sound of her new name. "Mrs. Jane Hanson. Mrs. Randal Hanson. Dr. and Mrs. Randal Hanson." She thought about the last thing she said—Dr. Hanson. "I'm so proud of him. He's worked so hard for this."

Wondering how Randy was feeling about all of this, Lisa asked, "Suppose he's nervous about the wedding?"

"He's too jacked about graduating from medical school to be nervous about the wedding yet. That part hasn't really hit him I don't think. It might tonight."

"What's going on tonight?" Lisa asked.

"His bachelor's party. Wanna come over to the apartment and hang out? We can watch a movie or something," Jane suggested so she wouldn't have to be alone.

"Sounds fun. I'll come over."

Around 5:30 that evening, Jim hammered on Randy's door.

Jane answered. "Hi, Jim."

"Hello, the future Mrs. Jane Hanson. Is your fiancé ready to go?"

"Almost. Come in."

Jim let himself in. "We're gonna keep him out pretty late tonight so don't wait up for him. And be prepared. Most likely he'll be drunk when I bring him home."

"Thank you so much," she scorned.

Randy walked out of the bedroom ready to go.

"Yo, Hanson, the groom." Jim flashed him a shaka sign. "Surf's up, Dude. You ready to have some wicked fun with the guys?"

"Yup." Randy grabbed his wallet and his phone. "Where we going anyway?"

"It's a surprise. You'll find out when we get there."

Randy kissed Jane quite intensely and grabbed his leather jacket. "I have no idea what time I'll be home, Babe."

Jane smiled at him. "Don't worry about it. Just have fun. And be safe please."

"I will." He kissed her again. "I love you."

"I love you too."

Randy winked at her then left with Jim. "Why won't you tell me where you're taking me?"

"You'll see," Jim grinned devilishly. "I will only tell you that you will have the time of your life tonight enjoying your last fling as a single man. Chill out, lay low, and have a kickass time, Bro."

Jim took Randy to a place called the Thirsty Bear Brewing Company, which was a beer pub and grill. Several of their medical school friends gathered around a table—seven men in all, including Randy. Behind the table was a huge banner that said, *Congratulations, Randy!* Several pitchers of beer were spread across the table and an oversized fishbowl full of flavored condoms, body oils, and a pocket sized book called *How to Give a Woman an Orgasm* served as a centerpiece.

"Jim, I am going to kill you," Randy said, trying not to laugh.

Jim showed Randy to the seat of honor and handed him a greeting card. "You have to read this before you open the box, otherwise it won't make sense." He handed Randy a box wrapped in paper with silhouettes of naked women all over it.

Randy took a deep breath and opened the card. Inside was a rather long epic soliloquy written in Jim's handwriting. "Goddamn, Jim. Were you bored or something?"

"You have to read that out loud." Jim poured Randy a beer.

Randy cleared his throat and began. "Here's a little something to brighten your day. James Ryan's list of worthless trivia. Number one: A pig's orgasm lasts for thirty minutes." Jim made several side notes beside each tidbit of information. Randy read these aloud as well. In this case, Jim's note said, "How'd they figure this out, and why? Do people really get paid to sit around and watch the coitus of pigs all day? In my next life, I want to be a pig." Randy and the others roared in laughter. He took a drink from his beer before he continued. "Two: Humans and dolphins are the only species to have sex for pleasure. Is that why dolphins are smiling all the time? And pigs get a thirty minute orgasm. Doesn't seem fair. Three: The strongest muscle in the body is the tongue. Did they teach us that in Anatomy class? Good to know next time you're French kissing. Hmm…I still can't get over that pig thing. Number four: A cockroach will live nine days without its head before it starves and dies. Can it have an orgasm without its head? Did taxpayers pay for this research?" By now, everyone at the table was rolling on the floor, and Randy couldn't maintain a straight face long enough to read the rest. "Oh my god, Jim. These are great."

"Keep readin'," he insisted.

So Randy did. "Five: The male praying mantis cannot copulate while its head is attached to its body. The female initiates sex by ripping the male's head off." The men cringed when Randy read this part. "Ouch. Sucks for him. Honey, I'm home. What the…? And, gentlemen, to top it all off, she eats it when they orgasm. At least pigs get a break there." The men all laughed. "Six: Some lions mate over fifty times in one day. I wonder how long their orgasms are? In my next life, I still want to be a pig. Quality over quantity. Number seven: An ostrich's eye is bigger than its brain. I know some people like that, don't you? Thirty minutes, can you imagine? And why pigs? All I can say is lucky pigs. Don't you wish you were a pig? Happy orgasm, Randy." Still laughing, Randy commented, "You and your worthless information, Jim."

"The question of the night is would you rather have a thirty minute orgasm like a pig or do it fifty times a day like a lion?" Jim asked.

"I don't know."

"You have to pick one. Pig or lion," Jim insisted.

Randy thought about his choices for a few seconds before he finally said, "Definitely a pig."

Jim grinned widely. He knew Randy would pick that. "Now open the box."

Randy ripped the paper off and removed the lid to discover a huge stuffed pig wearing a tee-shirt with the words *Thirty Minutes* printed on the front. Randy rolled his eyes. "Oh Jesus. What the fuck am I supposed to do with this?" He pulled the pink plush pig out of the box.

"Put it next to your bed as a constant reminder," Jim suggested.

Randy shook his head. "Just what I always wanted."

Steadily throughout the night, they drank several pitchers of beer, except for Jim because he was the designated driver. They ate steak fries and burgers while they joked around and told each other stories. Finally, it was time for Randy to open the goodies from the fishbowl.

He fished through the bowl and pulled out a plastic bag. With a twisted expression on his face, he read the label on the outside. "Edible panties, Jim? What the hell?"

"Hey, I didn't put those in there. Rick did," Jim replied.

"Gee, thanks."

Rick smiled and said, "You're welcome."

Randy dug further into the bowl. As he dug around, he thought this whole fishbowl thing was funny as hell, even though it was a little sick and perverted. He never realized how depraved some of his medical school classmates were. He never pictured them as men who would lick strawberry lotion off a woman then try to please her with cherry flavored condoms. He always saw them wearing lab coats and stethoscopes with scalpels and pens in their hands. He laughed as he pictured some of these twisted thoughts in his mind. "You guys are deranged." He picked up *How to Give a Woman an Orgasm* and laughed at the title. "They actually wrote a book on how to give a woman an orgasm? Like we can't figure it out for ourselves?"

"Actually," Bruce said, "There's some positions in there I've never seen before."

"Really?" Randy developed a mischievous smile and thumbed through it.

"Well," Jim said to the others. "Shall we take him to the next attraction?"

Randy cocked his head slightly. "What attraction?"

"We are takin' you to the Gold Club, gettin' you drunk, and partaking in luscious exotic dancer babes."

Randy hoped to god Jim wasn't serious. "Please tell me you're kidding."

"Nope."

"Great," Randy mocked.

They stayed at the club until the early hours of the morning, drinking and watching the strippers. By 2:00 A.M., Randy was seriously inebriated and could barely walk. Jim helped Randy to the door, attempting to hold him up so he wouldn't fall over. "Easy, buddy."

Randy stumbled around, which caused him to trip over the bottom step. "Ow!" he bellowed when his shin bashed into the concrete. "Jane is gonna kill me."

"No she's not," Jim assured him. "Now watch your step. Don't fall and hurt yourself." They finally made it to the porch where Jim unlocked the door and dragged Randy into the apartment.

Jane was on the couch reading a book when she heard them come in. When Randy stumbled inside, she knew right away that he was drunk. "Oh my god, Jim. What did you do to him?"

Supporting Randy's body weight, Jim led him into the bedroom. "He'll be fine. He's just a little drunk."

"A little?" she scoffed.

"He had fun tonight, but I'm not sure he'll remember any of it in the morning."

Jane helped to move Randy onto the bed, where he collapsed on the pillow. "How much did he drink tonight?"

Jim had to laugh. "A helluva lot. I'd keep an eye on him for a while."

Randy overheard what Jim said. "I'm fine," he claimed. He sat up and the room started spinning. His hand went up to his forehead. "Whoa. My head." He decided to lie back down.

With Randy in his drunken state, it was hard for Jim to maintain a straight face. "Yup, he's full-on drunk. Pretty fucked up."

Slightly upset with Jim for letting Randy drunk that much, Jane complained, "Jim."

"He'll be alright. Nothin' a good night's sleep won't cure," Jim explained. "There's a bag of his out in the car. I'll go get it. Be right back."

Jane took off Randy's shoes.

"Janey?" Randy said, barely conscious.

"Yes?"

"I saw strippers tonight. Naked women," he told her.

"It looks to me like you were drinking tonight too."

"I had a few beers."

"You had more than a few, Sweetie."

"You're not mad at me are you?"

"No. But you need to lie down." She kissed his cheek. "Get some rest."

"Baby?" he said.

"Yes?"

Wanting reassurance from her, he asked, "Do you still wanna marry me?"

He was barely coherent, but she tried not to laugh about it. "Of course I do."

"Good." He laid his head back down on the pillow and passed out.

Jane kissed him on the cheek, knowing he was going to regret this in the morning. "I love you, Randy Hanson." She closed the bedroom door and met Jim in the living room. "He's out."

"Is he?" Jim grinned. "Sorry."

"Don't worry about it. I'll look after him. What did you guys do tonight?"

"We took him to a beer pub then went to the Gold Club."

"You took him to the Gold Club?" Jane questioned.

"Yup." Jim handed her the bag. "These are his."

She peeked inside. "What is all this stuff?"

"Some gag gifts we were teasin' him with. He'll remember this night for a long time, maybe, once he sobers up."

"Thanks for bringing him home, Jim."

"No problem. I'll come by and check on him in the mornin'."

"Thank you," Jane replied.

"Later, Jane."

She closed the door and stood there laughing before she checked on Randy again.

Randy awoke in the morning with a hellacious headache, a dry throat, a repugnant taste in his mouth, and he needed to pee so badly he couldn't stand it. He was tired, beat down, and felt like shit. He looked over at Jane's pillow. It hadn't been slept on. And why was he lying on top of the comforter still in his clothes? "What the hell?" He attempted to sit up, but soon found out he was slightly lightheaded. Holding his throbbing head in his hand, he headed to the bathroom, where he relieved himself and brushed his teeth.

The taste of the toothpaste almost made him gag. He moseyed into the living room to find Jane sitting on the couch painting her toenails. He plopped on the sofa beside her.

"Welcome back to earth," she teased.

"Barely," he complained, feeling lethargic and a bit nauseous.

"Do you remember anything about last night?"

"Some of it." He hoped the alcohol hadn't turned him into Randy-the-aggressive-sex-monster last night. "I didn't maul you, did I?"

With a giggle, she said, "No."

"Good."

"You passed out right after Jim and I put you to bed."

"I did?" he asked, ashamed for letting himself get that drunk.

"Uh huh."

His head felt like it was going to explode. He curled his lip and suddenly felt ill. "My head is killing me. What is that smell?"

Jane screwed the lid back on her bottle of nail polish. "Let me get you some Tylenol."

"Thanks, Baby." Randy rested his head on the pillow. Then his cellphone rang, which made his head throb even more.

Jane ran to answer it, "Hello?" She paused to listen. "He's a little indisposed at the moment. Can he call you back?" She hesitated before she concluded with, "Ok, I'll let him know." She hung up the phone and brought Randy two Tylenol tablets and a glass of water.

"Who was that?" he asked.

"Your dad."

He swallowed the Tylenol and chugged down the entire glass of water. "What did he say?"

"They're in town."

"Oh, good." He set the glass on the table in front of him and leaned his head on the back of the couch. "Come here," he said, eyeing Jane.

She down sat next to him.

He took her hand and pulled her onto his lap. "Thank you for your patience and understanding with me. You're the best."

She leaned over and kissed him. "I'll make you some coffee. You lie here and rest."

"Thanks." While Jane was in the kitchen, someone knocked on the front door. Randy rubbed his eyes and wearily trudged over to answer it.

Jim stood on the front porch eyeballing Randy with a funny grin. "Yo, Bro. How you feelin'?"

Sneering, Randy invited Jim inside.

"You look like shit," Jim said, making his way to the couch.

Randy sat down with a groan. "I feel worse than that."

"I'm not surprised. You drank a *lot* last night, Dude. How much do you remember?"

"I remember the pub and that damn pig." Jim's loud guffaw made Randy cringe and rub his throbbing forehead. "Dude, not so fuckin' loud. My head hurts."

Jim couldn't help laughing at the vision of Randy being completely hungover. "What else do you remember?"

"I remember going to that strip club, but I lost track at some point while we were there."

"Do you remember the hot stripper who did a little teaser dance on your lap?"

Grumpily, Randy responded, "What?"

"You don't remember?"

Aghast by this news, Randy declared, "Please tell me you're kidding?"

"Nope." Jim chuckled. "I guess you were pretty wasted at that point."

Randy held his hand up to his pounding head again. "I didn't do anything inappropriate, did I?"

"No. You were a very good boy," Jim assured him.

Relieved, Randy replied, "Thank god."

Jim put his feet on the coffee table, crossing them at the ankles. "Has it hit you yet that you're gettin' married in two days?"

"I am aware of that."

"And we have to pick up our tuxes today," Jim reminded him. "You gonna be sober enough to do that?"

"I'll manage," he said. "I need to call my brother. My parents just got into town."

"Stellar." Jim hopped off the couch. "I wanted to stop by and make sure you were still alive and kickin'. I'll come back in a couple hours so we can jam and go get our tuxes."

Randy nodded in approval. "Alright. Thanks, Jim."

Jim flashed a shaka sign. "Lates, Bro."

Randy flopped back on the pillow and held his aching head in his hands.

After several cups of coffee and a shower, Randy felt slightly better. Not lightheaded anymore, but still had a horrible headache and didn't quite feel up to par. He picked up his brother from the hotel then met Jim and Bruce at the tux shop. Jim and Bruce were chatting outside when Randy pulled up with the top down. He and Robby stepped out of the car, and Randy walked over to them, removing his sunglasses. "Why is it that every time you two are together you're laughing under your breath until you see me coming? Then you abruptly stop all conversation and stare at me. You have some conspiracy going on against me or something?"

"No," Bruce said.

Jim patted Randy's shoulder. "How's your head?"

"Hurts."

Bruce laughed. "Damn, Dude. You drank a piss load last night. I have never seen you that wasted."

Robby chimed in, "What did I miss?"

"Randy had his bachelor's party last night," Jim clarified. "Probably drank at least four pitchers of beer by himself."

"Damn," Robby picked on his brother. "And you're walking around today?"

When everyone was situated and had tuxes in hand, Randy announced, "Rehearsal is at six. Dinner afterwards, and you better not be late."

"I won't," Jim replied. "I'll be there with bells on."

Randy and Robby got in the Corvette and drove back to the hotel. Once they arrived, Randy followed Robby inside to visit with his parents for a while.

He carried a sour expression, which made his mom ask, "You ok, Sweetheart?"

"Still a little hungover."

"Hungover?" Mark asked. "From what?"

"Had my bachelor's party last night. Jim poured way too much beer into me, and I've had a headache from hell all day."

Mark grinned. "Sounds like you had a good time."

"I did. But damn, my head is killing me."

Robby had a tuxedo in his hand. He hung it in the closet by the bathroom. "I see you picked up your tuxes," Mark said.

"Yup," Randy replied. "Jane called the florist, the bakery, and the photographer this morning to confirm. Everything's good to go."

"Rehearsal's at six, right?" Mark asked for clarification.

"Yes. And I made reservations for everybody for dinner tonight."

"Good," Mark said. "Glad things have been taken care of. How are you doing, Son? You nervous?"

"I'm doing ok. I'm excited about graduation tomorrow." Randy sat in a nearby chair. "I'll finally have M.D. behind my name."

"We're proud of you, Honey," his mom said. "Two Dr. Hansons in the family now."

"Yup. About to have another Mrs. Hanson in the family too." Randy smiled thinking about it. "Wow. What a wild week this has been."

Chapter Sixty-Two

During rehearsal dinner, Randy grabbed Jane and picked her up over his shoulder. She giggled and kicked her feet, trying to get loose. "I can walk, you know."

"Oh, I know. But it's more fun to watch you struggle and fight," he declared.

"Randy, put me down," she demanded.

"What do I get if I do?" he bribed her.

"A kiss."

"Come on, Janey. You can do better than that. Use your creativity."

"Ok, I'll make you breakfast in the morning and give you a massage tonight."

"Sounding better. Keep going," he probed.

"What more do you want?" she asked.

"Will you put on that sexy red lingerie for me tonight?"

"If I do, will you put me down?" she compromised.

"Yes."

"Ok. Now put me down."

He gently set her on the sidewalk. The minute her feet hit the ground she took off running toward the beach. "Come on, catch me," she challenged.

"Oh I will. I'm pacing myself." He chased her across the beach, speeding up his pace until he was able to catch her. They both tumbled to the sand, and he pulled her on top of him. "Ha! Gotcha!" Right as he was about to kiss her, it started to rain.

A water droplet dripped off Jane's nose. "We're getting wet."

"Yes, I know we're getting wet, but we are not getting out of this rain until I get a kiss." The rain poured down harder, soaking their shirts. "Close your eyes. Think about the rain hitting your body and imagine that tropical waterfall."

She closed her eyes and let her imagination run wild.

Randy interlocked his mouth to hers. It was a delicious sensation; his entire body developed chills. When he was satisfied, he opened his eyes and looked at her. Both were soaking wet, drenched from head to toe. He hopped up and offered his hand, running alongside her out of the torrential downpour.

Safely inside the building, they both laughed, which immediately drew everyone's attention. Randy turned around and, in a rather boisterous voice, addressed the group. "Ok, everyone. We have reservations at BayWolf. You can follow me if you don't know how to get there."

The entire wedding party hurried to their vehicles, trying to dodge the spring deluge.

Randy took Jane's hand and they scurried out to his car. As soon as they were seated, Randy focused his eyes on Jane. She had water dripping off her hair and nose, which made him laugh. "Honey, you're soaked." He wiped rainwater off her face then looked in the mirror on the back of his visor and combed his hair out with his fingers before he put the keys in the ignition. "This wedding doesn't sound too hard."

"It's going to be beautiful," Frantic and hoping everything was perfect, Jane rattled on, "The manager said the reception room and garden outside would be ready at 2:00. The bakery is supposed to bring the cake over in the afternoon and the florist is delivering the flowers in the morning. The photographer is scheduled to come at 3:30, the DJ is going to start setting up at 3:00, and Lisa are Stephanie are bringing the sorority over to put up decorations. Lisa said she would make sure everyone got their flowers, and…oh my god I hope we're not forgetting anything."

Randy laughed at her. "Honey, relax. Everything is going to be fine. Now let's go eat."

Immediate family members, as well as the eight person wedding party, all met at the restaurant to indulge in the pre-wedding festivities. Randy claimed their fifteen person private room and everyone took their seats.

The waiter filled all the glasses with champagne then returned a few minutes later with a vase full of long-stemmed red roses. "Where might I find the bride?"

Everyone pointed to Jane.

The waiter set the vase in front of her and handed her a card. "Congratulations on your marriage."

Randy sat with his arms folded across his chest carrying a smug grin.

"Read the card!" everyone shouted.

She carefully opened the envelope and proceeded to read aloud, "My darling Janey, Words cannot express my feelings for you. Your love has touched my life in many ways, and I am truly blessed to have you by my side. Thank you for being a part of my life. I am a better man because of you. I love you with all my heart. I always will."

The entire room awed.

Touched by his sentimental words, Jane gazed at Randy.

His eyes brimmed with adoration. "I love you, Baby."

"I love you."

The corners of his mouth raised to form a smile and they embraced in a kiss.

Randy's dad stood up with a glass of champagne in his hand. He clanged it with a fork to get everyone's attention. "I know we are all here to celebrate the wedding of my son and future daughter-in-law, but we mustn't forget the three young men here tonight who are graduating from medical school tomorrow. I know from personal experience how challenging a feat that is. It takes a lot of dedication, and I would like to take a moment to congratulate them. Jim,

Bruce, Randy, may your futures be prosperous and your careers successful."

Everyone raised their glasses to toast the young men.

"Hold on." Jim stood up. "Since we're offering toasts, I have one."

Jim was about to say something to embarrass the hell out of Randy. He had to intervene. "Sit back down, Ryan."

"I get my shot here too, Hanson, so take the pain."

This playful commentary made everyone laugh.

Jim proceeded, "This one goes out to Randy and Jane. Randy has been my best friend for nine years. We trudged through pre-med and medical school together, and I was around through his many romantic encounters." Everyone in the room who knew Randy's playboy history chuckled at this comment. "But Jane has proven to be a very special woman in his life. Their friendship blossomed into a romance that has inspired all who have witnessed it. They've shown everyone around them how precious love is. Randy and Jane are partners, companions, lovers, and have been inseparable since the day they met. It is an absolute privilege to know them both on a personal level and to witness the kind of love they share." Jim lifted his glass. "Jane, Randy, congratulations. May your marriage and your life together be blessed and may you have many babies."

Randy lifted his glass. "Thank you."

Everyone toasted.

Jim could be serious when he had to be. Amazingly, when he was in a formal or professional situation, his surfer lingo disappeared and he was quite articulate. James Ryan was one of the most interesting characters Randy had ever had the privilege to know. He was a fun-loving, kind-hearted, humorously sarcastic, notoriously cheerful, and very bright. Randy loved the man.

Driving home from dinner, Jane gazed out the window at all the stars. "I love San Francisco at night. It's so pretty."

Randy reached over and held her hand. "I think my favorite thing about this city is driving over the Bay Bridge at night with the top down. I've driven over that bridge hundreds of times, but the thrill never goes away."

"Are you gonna miss San Francisco?"

"A little. A lot of memories have accumulated in this city, at Berkeley." With a sigh, he admitted, "I'm gonna miss Jim more than anything. It's gonna be hard to say goodbye to him."

"I'm not going to miss San Francisco," Jane boldly stated.

This comment surprised him. She had lived here her whole life. How could she not miss it? "No?"

"I'll miss Daddy and Brian, but not San Francisco. I'm ready to begin my new life as your wife."

He exchanged a smile with her. "I'm ready too. I can't wait 'til Saturday."

Being a light sleeper, the sound of Mr. Fingers singing and squawking woke Randy up, but he didn't mind. He was in a good mood. It was graduation day, the culmination of his entire medical school career, a day he'd anticipated for far too long. Quietly, he slid out of bed, careful not to wake Jane. He cleaned up all the clothes that were scattered across the floor then prepared himself for an exciting day.

While Randy was finishing a cup of coffee, a knock resounded through the apartment. When he opened the door, Jim stood on his porch wearing basketball shorts and a tee-shirt. "Hey, Jim. What's up?"

"Thought we could shoot hoops this morning."

"Alright. But I need to eat first. I'm starving."

The two men grabbed breakfast together before heading to the gym. After playing for about an hour, Jim checked the time. "Yo, Randy. Thirty more hours and you'll be a married man."

Randy stood for a minute, soaking in Jim's words. "Wow! Can you believe that?"

"You nervous?" Jim tossed him the ball.

"A little." Randy dribbled down the court and fired a jump shot. "I'll tell you, though. I didn't think it was possible for one person to have so many emotions going on simultaneously. Joy, excitement, nervousness, agony. It's crazy."

"Agony? What the hell could possibly be causing you agony? You're graduating from med school in three hours, gettin' married tomorrow, and this time Sunday mornin' you'll on a plane to Bermuda to spend two luscious weeks with your new wife. This is the most righteous time of your life. You've got it made, Bro."

"You're right. I do have a lot of exciting things going on." He laid his heart out on the line. "But it occurred to me last night that I'm moving to Seattle without you."

Jim dropped the ball and it bounced away. This reality had not really dawned on him before. The two of them stood in the middle of the court staring at each other.

"I mean, hell, Jim." His eyes were bordered with tears. "We've been friends for nine years, and you're the best friend I've ever had. As excited as I am about becoming a doctor and starting my new life with Jane, I'm gonna miss you, man."

Jim's heart crumbled. He had to fight to keep his emotions in check. "Damn you, Randy. You had to bring that up, didn't you?"

"I'm sorry. It popped into my head last night." Randy's stomach knotted; the inner torment gnawed at him. "You know I love you, right?"

Jim swallowed hard, choking back the lump in his throat. "Yeah."

"I want you to know how honored I feel, not only to have you standing beside me tomorrow on that altar when I take my vows, but also to have the pleasure of walking with you at graduation today. You got me through this, you know."

"We got each other through this. And it's been a privilege, Randy. But hey," Jim said faking a smile. "It's not over. If I have my way, I'll be your sidekick 'til you either get sick of me or kill me."

He looked at Jim with a hundred percent respect for the man. "Thank you for being my friend."

"Thank *you*. By the way, Bruce and I decided that we want you to meet us at the gym tomorrow morning to help you relax your nerves."

"Alright."

"Bring your brother," Jim suggested. "He plays basketball, doesn't he?"

"Yes he does."

"Good. Meet us at ten." Jim put his hand on Randy's shoulder. "Come on. Let's go graduate."

UCSF medical students had the option during graduation to choose their hooder, an M.D. who would place the doctoral hood over the graduate's head, pause for a photo, and finally escort the new doctor off the stage. Randy choose his father to do the honors. Mark was issued a ticket for an assigned seat in the main level of the Masonic Center and would accompany Randy on stage. Randy couldn't wait to share this experience with his dad.

Prior to graduation, a class photo was taken with all the graduates in their caps and gowns, which Randy purchased. He also made plans to attend the post-graduation reception with his fellow graduates following the ceremony.

One hundred twenty-one members of the School of Medicine eagerly and excitedly walked into the Nob Hill Masonic Center. Randy carried his cap and gown on a hanger over his shoulder. Spotting a stack of programs lying on a table, he grabbed one and skimmed through it. All the graduates' names and residency matches were listed in the program. He quickly searched for his name. At the bottom of the program was a small sub-section: *During these commencement ceremonies, Bruce M. Buckman, M.D. will receive the Gold-Headed Cane, the highest honor given to a graduating UCSF medical student. Buckman, who will enter a neurosurgery residency at*

UCLA, will be honored with runners-up J. Randal Hanson, M.D., and Elizabeth L. Mahlin, M.D. Hanson will start an Obstetrics/Gynecology residency program at University of Washington in Seattle, and Mahlin will complete her residency in internal medicine at UCSF.

Reading this made Randy smile, not only because he was thrilled for Bruce, but also because this was the first time he had seen the letters M.D. after his name. He folded up the program and slipped it into his pocket.

He looked across the room and spotted Jim, Mandy, and Bruce. Bruce had that menacing look on his face, nothing out of the ordinary for him. Mandy stood close to Bruce, flirting with him as usual. Jim had his hands in his pockets with his bleach blonde hair spiked up, looking like Joe Cool. They were his three best friends, and they'd all been through hell and back together. What a group they made.

Randy took several strides toward them. "Hey, guys."

"Hanson." Bruce shook Randy's hand. "Can you believe we are actually graduating from med school today?"

"I know. This week has been insane."

"For you, yeah," Mandy stated. "How you doing?"

"I'm doing alright. Hoping Jane and I didn't forget anything in our wedding plans."

Trying to ease some of Randy's tension, Jim said, "Let other people worry about that. You shouldn't have to deal with that, especially not today."

Randy slipped on his gown and honors cords and left the hanger in a pile on the floor. Then he went with Jim, cap in hand, to find their seats.

"Are you comin' over to my place tomorrow to change into your tux before we go or what's the plan?" Jim asked.

"Probably. Jane's gonna be with her bridesmaids all day, getting her hair done, doing the manicure thing, all that fun bride stuff."

"Don't forget to bring Sabrina's basket and the pillow for the rings," Jim reminded him.

"Lisa has all that stuff. She said she'd divvy things out once everyone got there."

Graduating from medical school was one of the most emotional and moving events Randy had ever participated in. He was truly touched when his friends walked across the stage, received their hoods, then walked off as new doctors. When it was his turn, he sauntered up to the stage. Mark stood proudly, ready to hood his son. Randy's body felt heavy; he couldn't breathe. The name, Dr. Jonathan Randal Hanson, resounded throughout the entire Masonic Center. His dream had come true. All of his hard work, countless hours of studying, weeks with little sleep, and sacrificing so much of his personal life had finally paid off. He was a doctor. A bona fide practicing M.D.

When Jim was pronounced as Dr. James Edward Ryan, Randy got teary-eyed. His best friend did it. Despite the turmoil of a psychotic, heroin addicted ex-girlfriend, a very nasty break up, dealing with a pregnancy and custody battle, moving in with a new girlfriend, and trying to raise his son by himself, Jim was a doctor.

This was, without a doubt, the happiest day of Randy's life. By twenty-seven years of age, he had earned three degrees: his Public Health Bachelor's Degree, a Master's Degree in Health and Medical Sciences, and now his M.D. He had a provisional license to practice medicine…and a license to get married. Which, now that graduation was over, was his number one priority.

Following the post-graduation celebration, Randy dropped his cap and gown off at the apartment, grabbed all the bread they had left in the pantry, and clasped Jane's hand. "Come with me."

"Where are we going?" she asked.

"We need to get rid of this bread. Let's go to the park and feed the ducks."

Jane protested. "The last time I tried to feed a duck it pecked at my feet and chased after me."

Randy openly laughed. "You're bigger than that duck is. But if I have to protect you from da widdle ducky, I will," he teased. "I can't believe you're afraid of a duck."

"I'm not afraid of them," she said in her defense. "I just don't like them very much."

"I won't let the ducks get you."

At the park, they strolled along a path by the pond. The setting sun reflected off the crystal water and a cool breeze swayed the tree branches. Jane gripped his hand and directed him away from the path.

"Where are we going?" Randy asked.

"I want to show you something."

"What is it?"

"You'll see."

She led him to an open grove, where wildflowers nestled quietly on a grassy hill between the trees. The smell of lavender permeated the air, and squirrels frolicked playfully, running from tree to tree. Randy had never seen this part of the park before. "What is this place?"

"Mom, Dad, Brian and I used to come here all the time. We'd pack a picnic lunch and spread out a blanket right here." She bounded to the hilltop. "Daddy bought a kite, and Brian and I took turns flying it. We played tag and threw a Frisbee. Mom laughed when Daddy chased us around the hill. No one else was around. It was just the four of us." She sank into the grass and stared up at the sky. "I bet Mom is lying on a blanket in a warm sunlit field watching us right now."

"I bet she is."

"And you know what else? Tomorrow, when I say I do, Mom will be there," Jane said confidently. "Maybe not her physical body, but she'll be there in spirit, watching the whole thing."

Randy put his hands in his pockets, grinning at the radiant smile on Jane's face. She rarely talked about her childhood. Yet today, she embraced joyful memories. Perhaps she had finally found peace with her mother's death. Seemed like an unusual time to do it, but Randy would take it no matter when or how it came.

Chapter Sixty-Three

Unable to sleep any longer due to the excitement level, Randy decided to get up. The crazy week he'd had was more exhausting than any week of medical school or any night shift in the ER. His nerves were shot and his anxiety level had reached its peak. Since Jane was already awake, Randy straightened the sheets and comforter on the bed and repositioned the pillows. He put on a pair of shorts and a tee-shirt then slipped on his basketball shoes and headed to the kitchen to brew a pot of coffee. As he passed by the living room, he saw Jane curled up in a chair reading a book. He snuck up behind her and gently touched her arm.

She flinched and screamed. "Oh my god. You scared the bejesus out of me."

"Sorry." When he leaned forward to kiss her, he read the title of the book she was reading. "Stephen King? No wonder you're jumpy."

She marked her page with a bookmark. "You know what I want?"

"What do you want?"

"A great big bowl of mint chocolate chip ice cream," she told him.

"For breakfast? And you give me hard time about what I eat."

"Well, you harass me about eating yogurt. It's better for you than some of the crap you put in your body."

"What's wrong with what I eat?"

"You are the king of Oreos," she declared.

"I keep the company in business. Oreos are a vital element in human nutrition," he said playfully.

"They are not."

"Sure they are. Water, carbohydrates, proteins, vitamins, minerals, and Oreos."

"You're going to turn into an Oreo." She kissed him tenderly on the lips. "Aren't you playing basketball with Jim and Bruce this morning?"

"Yes I am." Randy grabbed his keys and shoved his phone in his pocket. "I think there's some ice cream in the freezer if you really want some. We need to eat it all before the move anyway." He went into the bedroom to grab his tux and a change of clothes.

Randy thought about what this day had in store for him. The rings he and Jane would exchange held a promise. A lovely promise that although they would surely encounter some stormy waters in their marriage that might instill fear in them, they would survive and outlast any challenge they faced because they would be together through it all. They'd already proven they could weather any storm, and Randy was confident that together, they could take on whatever obstacles life threw at them.

When he reemerged from the bedroom, Jane was watching Mickey Mouse cartoons with a bowl of ice cream in her hand. Moments like this made Randy fall in love with her all over again. "I'll see you in a few hours." He leaned over the back of the couch and gave her a kiss. "And the next time I kiss you, you'll be my wife."

"I can't wait."

"Bye, Baby. I love you."

"I love you too."

He closed the apartment door, carefully slipped his tux and athletic bag inside the trunk of the car, then took off to the hotel to pick up his brother.

Robby was still asleep when Randy arrived.

"What do you mean, he's not up yet?" Randy threw a pillow at his brother to wake him up. "Yo, Rob. Get up."

Robby groaned and rolled over. "Go away."

Randy tried to entice him. "Get up. We'll grab some doughnuts before we go to the gym."

Mark came out of the bathroom and spotted his son. "Well, good morning, Randal. How are you on this lovely day?" he asked, hoping his son wasn't suffering from wedding day jitters.

"Feeling pretty good actually." His brother still hadn't moved. "Robby, get your lazy ass up. We gotta go."

Once Robby joined the land of the living, he and Randy stopped at Dunkin' Donuts then headed to the gym to play basketball.

Jim and Bruce were in the middle of a game of HORSE when Randy and his brother walked in. "Good morning, gentlemen."

"Well, hello, Dr. Hanson," Jim said. "How are you this morning?"

"Very well, thank you. I brought doughnuts." He set the box on the bleachers and lifted the lid. Hungry men instantly mauled the doughnut box, scarfing up every last one.

"You're not nervous?" Bruce asked.

"No," Randy replied. "But I have a piss load of energy I need to get rid of before I lose my mind."

Grinning, Jim and Bruce looked at each other and simultaneously stated, "He's nervous."

Randy grabbed the ball and dribbled. "Come on. Let's play."

A little before three o'clock, Bruce and Robby piled into Bruce's truck and drove over to the resort.

Jim stayed with Randy.

Randy held a notecard in his hand, glancing down at it occasionally while he looked up at the ceiling mouthing words to himself.

"What are you doin'?" Jim asked him.

"Looking over my wedding vows one more time."

"Make sure you bring those with you."

"Don't need to," Randy replied. "I have them memorized."

"Bring them anyway." Jim checked his watch. It was time to transport the groom to the resort. "We have to jet, Bro. You want me to drive?"

"No. I'm good."

"Do you have your marriage license?"

"Yes."

"Then let's get you married, Dude."

They hopped in the Corvette and took off down the freeway. Randy turned the radio on to keep his mind occupied.

During the drive, the song 'White Wedding' came on. Jim found this amusing. "Fitting choice. It's like he knows," he said in an ominous voice.

Randy laughed. "How would he know?"

"Maybe he's psychic."

"And maybe you're a dumbass."

Jim gasped playfully. "I'm offended by that remark."

"Then don't say stupid shit."

Jim cranked up the radio and sat back enjoying the pleasant drive to Monterey Bay.

While Jim and Randy and the rest of his wedding party were en route, the girls were at the resort diligently working to get Jane ready. Lisa and Stephanie helped Jane slip her dress on, separating the layers and lying them flat, careful not to mess up her hair or her makeup. She put her white satin heels on her feet then clipped on the pearl and crystal earrings and necklace that belonged to her mother. Pearl-studded clips held up her classic French twist, and her nails were painted in a French manicure. She looked at her reflection in the full length mirror and started to cry.

Lisa gave her a hug. "You're going to ruin your makeup."

"Don't worry," Jane said. "I told the beautician I cry a lot and she gave me waterproof."

Lisa delicately wiped Jane's eyes with tissue. "You ok?"

"Just emotional. I'll be alright."

Randy walked into the reception hall with Jim and couldn't believe what he saw. Banquet tables covered with white linen tablecloths and full table settings surrounded a good-sized dancefloor. Each setting came complete with silver utensils and red linen napkins, which stuck out of the wine glasses. The center of every table had a round mirrored tray with a gorgeous arrangement of various sized white candles. Each centerpiece was sprinkled with loose red rose petals. Red and white flower arrangements were strategically placed around the reception hall, and every chair had a six inch red ribbon tied around the back.

A longer table against the wall had a similar setup, with the exception of the red and white rose garland that draped across the front of it. A three-tiered gourmet cheesecake covered in white frosting and decorated with red roses, small white pearls, and white ribbon sat on one end of the table. Another smaller table housed an open guestbook and a red ribbon-wrapped pen. White lights wrapped around several potted trees from the base of the trunk to the highest branch.

"Whoa," Randy said as he surveyed the scene.

"Damn, Dude. This looks badass. You guys went all out, didn't you?"

"I only plan on doing this once, and I wanted Janey to have the wedding of her dreams."

"Well, you certainly delivered."

Outside, a concrete path overlooked the beach, and a white wedding arch, decorated with red and white roses, served as the main attraction. On either side of the arch were two white marble columns, each of which held a marble pot. The pots were filled with fragrant red and white flower arrangements. Over a hundred and fifty white garden chairs lined up in rows facing the arch. The chair on the end of each row was decorated with red and white roses, tied on with white ribbon.

The DJ had set himself up at the front of the reception hall, and the photographer was getting his camera prepared. Resort workers busily buzzed around, and guests were starting to show up.

"How many people did you two invite to this shindig?" Jim asked.

"One-hundred fifty-seven," Randy answered.

"Damn."

Frantic, Lisa darted outside to Randy and Jim. "Oh my god, there you are."

Randy checked the time. "I'm not late. I'm early."

She handed each of them a red rose boutonnière to pin to their lapel. "Here. You need one of these."

Randy, concerned about his bride, asked, "How's Jane?"

"She's fine. She's in the other room. Where are Bruce and Robert?"

Randy shrugged. "I don't know. They left before we did."

Lisa hurried off to search for them.

Jim laughed. "I think she's had too much coffee."

While the two of them helped each other pin on boutonnières, Jill came outside with the kids. Sabrina had on a sparkly red dress and matching shoes. She immediately ran to Jim and hugged him.

"Hey, Princess." Jim squatted down to her level.

"Do like my dress, Daddy?" she asked, happy to show it off to him.

"I do. Look how pretty you are."

Christopher toddled out in a black suit and tie. He had a red rose bud pinned to his lapel.

Jill held the empty ring pillow in her hand. "Please tell me you have the rings, James."

Jim stood up and pulled the rings out of his pocket. "I have them right here." He took the pillow from her and tied the rings onto it. "Why the hell is everyone so damn uptight?"

"Because Lisa and Stephanie have been trying to get these flowers to everyone, but some people aren't here yet."

"Jane's here, isn't she?" Jim asked.

"Yes."

"So is Randy. We have the bride and groom. What else do we need?"

"You need to get Randy in the room," Jill said.

Randy did not like that sound of that. "The room?"

"You're the groom," Jill reminded him. "You can't be running around out here, you might see Jane."

"So what?"

"You're not supposed to see her."

"Why not?" Randy wanted to know.

"It's the rules." Jill looked over at Jim. "Please take him to his room, Jim."

Jim laughed hysterically, thinking everyone was insane for making such a spectacle of this. "Where is this dreaded room?"

"I'll show you." Jill escorted them to a citrus-scented room with a full length mirror and a couple of lounge chairs. "You need to keep him in here until someone comes and gets you."

Randy protested loudly, "I am *not* staying in here."

"You have to," Jill said. "We can't risk you seeing Jane." She gave Jim a firm directive, "Keep him in here. You can't let him leave."

Jim gave her a kiss, trying not to laugh at Randy's uncomfortable predicament. "Ok. If that's the rules, I'll oblige, Honey Bun."

Jill closed the door and left the two men alone.

Upset that he was stuck in this stupid room, Randy griped, "Ok, who the hell made this rule? I have to be trapped in here for twenty minutes just waiting? This is going to drive me nuts."

Then there was a knock on the door. "Come in," Jim said.

Stephanie walked in, in her red formal bridesmaid gown, carrying a white and red rose bouquet. "Hey, Brat."

Seeing his sister made this room slightly more tolerable. "Hey, you."

She gave her brother a hug then examined his formal attire. "Look at you all fancied up. How you doing?"

"I'm fine. Being forced to stay in this damn room sucks though."

Stephanie straightened his collar. "She looks amazing, Randy."

Randy's eyes gleamed as the topic of Jane came up. "She does?"

"Oh, yes. She is a beautiful bride."

Randy's imagination ran wild, picturing in his mind what he thought she looked like. "I wish I could see her."

"Almost. We should be starting in fifteen minutes or so."

Randy pulled an envelope out of his pocket and handed it to his sister. "Will you do me a favor and give this to her?"

"What is it?"

"Just give it to her," Randy insisted. "And see if you can find Dad around here somewhere."

"Ok." She kissed her brother on the cheek and left the room.

Stephanie walked into Jane's room, where several other women were, and handed Jane the envelope. "Randy wanted me to give this to you."

Jane took the envelope in her hand. "He's here?"

"Yes. He's with Jim."

Jane opened the envelope. Inside was a handwritten note from Randy. *Today we will become husband and wife. As we climb life's ladder together, take my love along with you, and I will bring you happiness and make your dearest dreams come true. I will always be here to understand you, to talk to you, to laugh with you, to cry with you. I will support you in all that you do, and I will help you in all that you need. I will share with you in all that you experience, and I will encourage you in all that you try. I will dream with you in all that you wish for, and I will love all that you are. There is no one else in this world who brings more joy to my life than you do. I love you, Janey. I always will.*

Tears flooded her eyes and her hands started to shake.

"What's the matter?" Lisa asked her.

"He's getting all sentimental and sappy and he's gonna make me cry again."

Lisa looked at Jane's trembling hand. "You need to move your engagement ring to the other hand so Randy can put your wedding ring on that finger."

Jane switched her engagement ring to her right hand.

Lisa inspected Jane once more. "You're ready. Now breathe and try to calm down."

Jim, Robby, and Bruce all sat with Randy in the dark chasm of hell, otherwise known as 'the room', as time crept closer. Randy jammed his hands in his pockets and paced back and forth across the floor like a tiger in a cage.

Randy's restlessness was beginning to bother Jim. "Would you sit down please? You're makin' *me* nervous."

"I'm not nervous."

"Yeah, and I'm the Prime Minister of England," Jim retorted.

"I'm not," Randy denied. "But I don't like waiting in this stupid room. They're going to have to commit me after keeping me locked in here. I need to get out of this hell hole before I go crazy."

"I can't let you leave. I've had seven people tell me that now," Jim said. "Jill bein' among them. If I let you leave, she'll kill me, so sit down."

Randy was quickly losing his patience. "I want to get this thing going."

"Be patient," Jim advised.

"I wonder what Jane is doing right now." Randy paced around again. "I need a cup of coffee."

"Dude, you don't need a cup of coffee. You're edgy enough."

Anxious and fidgety, Randy plopped into one of the chairs. He rubbed his bangs off his forehead then rested his elbows on his knees, desperately pleading to Jim. "And I thought Stephanie was going to go get my dad. Where the hell is he?" Once again, he stood up and walked from one end of the room to the other.

Jim tried to calm him down. "Lay low and relax, man."

"I don't want to," Randy snapped. "I want out of this prison cell they've put me in."

Randy was rambling and obviously nervous. And being trapped in this dreaded room was going to drive him insane. Jim wanted to come to Randy's rescue and save him from this unnecessary stress, but was told not to let him leave. He patted Randy's shoulder and stated, "Hang tight. I'll be right back." Jim exited the room and headed down the hall to see if he could find Randy's dad.

Jane's father stepped into the room and gazed at his beautiful daughter. "If your mother could see you now."

"Hi, Daddy."

Choking down tears, he said, "We're going to start soon, Honey. The men are about to take Randy out then we can line everyone up for your parade in."

She took a deep breath to calm her nerves.

"You alright?" he asked her.

"I'm a little nervous."

He gave her a huge hug. "This is your day, and you are a beautiful bride."

Not wanting to let him go, she squeezed him tightly. "I love you, Daddy."

While Jane was talking to her father, Randy finally had the chance to talk to his.

"You need to calm down, Son."

"I'm trying to." Finally admitting how he felt, Randy said, "I'm nervous."

"I know you are." Mark straightened Randy's cuffs. "You're marrying a wonderful woman today."

"I know I am, and I can't wait to see her."

"She looks beautiful."

Annoyed that he hadn't seen Jane all day, Randy complained, "You know, I think every person in this building has seen her except me. I find that unfair."

"That's the way it's supposed to be. You'll get to see her in about four minutes."

Randy exhaled deeply, releasing some tension. "I've spent all twenty-seven years of my life watching you and Mom together. If Jane and I can have even half the marriage you two have, I'll be happy."

"You and Jane are going to be fine," Mark reassured him.

"I wanted to thank you for helping me pursue my dream, for always being around to support me and listen to me."

"Your mother and I are very proud of the man you've become. I'm honored to have you as my son."

The hug between them lingered.

"I'm going to sit down with your mother now," Mark said. "You try and relax."

"Yeah." Randy released his father and straightened his coattail.

The minister walked in, in an overly bubbly mood. "Let's get the ball rolling, shall we?"

"Yes, please."

Jim put his hand on Randy's shoulder. "Ok, bud, this is it. You ready?"

Randy grinned. "Definitely." They stared at each other for a minute, then four men marched out to the altar.

Randy took in a big breath. Ah, fresh air at last. And the weather couldn't have been more perfect. The sun was shining and the sky was clear. Warm rays beamed down, and the scent of roses filled the air. Randy took his position on the altar with Jim, Bruce, and Robby by his side. He quickly scanned the area; every chair was full. And who were all of these people? Faces he had never seen before occupied some of the seats.

When the 'Wedding March' played, Randy's hands began to shake. Jim leaned forward and whispered, "Calm down. Breathe."

Sabrina paraded in carrying her basket of flowers. The bridesmaids, each holding a white and red rose bouquet, trailed behind her. Christopher followed carrying his little pillow. Then he heard it, 'Here Comes the Bride.' He stood tall and exhaled deeply; his heart pounded.

Jane paraded down the aisle grasping her father's arm with one hand and carrying a bouquet of red and white roses in the other. Everyone stood up in respect to the bride and all eyes were on her, especially Randy's. Her hair was pulled back to reveal her pretty face. Her long, flowing, white lacy gown set off a terrestrial glow. The pearls and crystals on her ears and around her neck glistened in the warm afternoon sun. She was beautiful—the most beautiful woman he had ever seen. He swallowed from the depths of his throat as Jane and her father approached the altar. Butterflies fluttered in his stomach and his hands suddenly felt clammy. Yet his eyes remained glued on his bride. Everything else around him seemed to disappear.

Jane and her father stopped at the altar, at which time Randy stepped forward and took possession of her hand. Dale took his seat, and the wedding ceremony began.

When it was time to exchange vows, Randy went first. He turned facing Jane, took both of her hands in his, and looked into her eyes. Swallowing to clear the lump in his throat, he began, "Jane, I love you, not only for what you are, but also for what I am when I am with you. I love you, not only for what you have made of yourself, but for what you are making of me. I love you for the part of me you bring out. I love you for passing over all those foolish things, weak things that are seen within me. I love you for drawing into the light all the inner belongings that no one else had looked far enough to find. I love you for helping me meet my goals and my dreams and for allowing me be a part of yours. I love you for taking all the lumber of my life and helping me build not a tavern, but a temple, and of the words of my life, a song. I love you, not only because you have done more than any creed could have done to make me good, but also because you have done more than any fate could have done to make me happy. I love you for being my friend, being yourself, and for loving me in return. I promise I will faithfully love you, I will always be here when you need me, and I will offer my support and acceptance in everything you do. I will do everything possible to make your dreams come true. I love you, Jane. I love you with all my heart."

Tears welled in Jane's eyes, and Randy felt himself tearing up as well. Several other people in the audience were also crying, including Randy's mom, his sister, and Dale Davine. Randy reached up and lovingly wiped Jane's tear away.

Now it was Jane's turn. She looked into Randy's eyes and said, "I've been trying to find the words to tell you how I feel and discovering I'm not very good at this. But here goes." And she began, "As I looked back on our relationship, there were so many things about you that made me fall in love with you. Your boyish charm, your enthusiasm for medicine, your weakness for Oreos, your excitement when the Lakers make a three pointer. I melt every time I'm in your arms, and I'm swept away every time you kiss me. You make me happy, all day, every day. I want you to know that I'll forever love you. I'll be faithful, supportive, and do my best to be a wife who can make you as happy as you've made me. I'll always be by your side, always listen to what you have to say, and forever offer you my unconditional love. I'm marrying my best friend today, and I love you with all my heart, Randal Hanson."

Randy mouthed the words, I love you, back to her.

Then the minister turned to Randy and said, "Do you, Jonathan Randal Hanson, take this woman to be your wedded wife?"

With a huge grin on his face, Randy confidently answered, "Yes, I do."

"Do you, Jane Elizabeth Davine, take this man to be your wedded husband?"

"I do."

"May we have the rings, please?"

Jill shooed Christopher up to Jim, who squatted down to untie the rings from the pillow. Once Jim secured the rings in his hand, he handed them both to Randy, who in turn handed his to Jane.

"Randy, take your bride's left hand," the minister directed.

Randy looked into Jane's eyes and took her by the hand. He held her wedding ring between his thumb and forefinger and gently slipped it onto her finger. Jane followed suit, never once turning her gaze away from him. As soon as the ring exchange was complete, the minister said, "By the power vested in me by the great state of California, I now pronounce you husband and wife. You may kiss your bride."

Randy moved his hands around Jane's waist and pulled her closer to him. He tilted his head slightly and their lips touched for the first time as husband and wife. Time seemed to cease, and he had no idea how long they'd stood up there before he pulled his lips away from her. They nuzzled forehead to forehead looking into each other's eyes. Some guests cried, some cheered.

The minister proclaimed, "Ladies and gentlemen, it is with great pleasure that I present to you Dr. Randal and Mrs. Jane Hanson."

Randy and Jane marched down the aisle together, hand in hand, away from the crowd, as everyone stood and applauded. When they were a distance away, Randy took his new wife in his arms, lifted her off the ground, and spun her around. "We did it, Baby. This is incredible." He kissed her as he set her back down. "I love you, Mrs. Hanson."

She giggled at the sound of her new name. "I love you." Jane moved her engagement ring next to her wedding band then reached for Randy's left hand. "Lemme see."

679

Proudly, Randy held out his hand to show off his ring.

"Looks good," she said.

"Feels even better." He lifted her chin and loved her with his eyes. "You are gorgeous, Babe. This dress is magnificent." He ogled over how incredibly gorgeous Jane was. "I saw you walking down that aisle, glowing white with the sun shining in your hair—you took my breath away." In one swift motion, Randy swept her into his arms and linked his mouth to hers, focusing only on her and this blissful moment they shared.

Jim ran around the corner interrupting the bride and groom's embrace. "Come on, you two, break it up. You have the rest of your lives to kiss."

Randy and Jane both turned their heads.

Jim grinned at the happy couple. "You two make a beautiful pair. I've always thought so." Jim patted Randy's shoulder. "Congratulations, Bro."

Randy beamed with excitement. "Thank you."

"The photographer is waitin' to take a few group shots. Let's get these pictures done so we can eat."

Following a brief photo shoot, the wedding party headed toward the reception hall. As they approached the door, Jim told Randy, "I'm gonna have you announced before you walk in."

"Jim, that's really not necessary."

"Come on, man. Let me relish this. It's not every day my best friend gets married."

Knowing how much Jim had been looking forward to this, Randy gave in to his request. "Alright, fine. Knock yourself out."

"Sweet. Wait 'til you hear your names before you walk in." Jim scurried away to the reception hall.

Randy shook his head and laughed at this ridiculousness of this showy entrance. "Can you believe him? He's crazy."

"I think it's sweet," Jane said.

Jim stepped up to the microphone and tapped on it. "May I have your attention please." The floor quickly cleared. "Standing right outside that door is the most remarkable couple I have ever known. Not only are they dear friends of mine, they are partners, advocates, and companions for each other. Their love is an inspiration to all. Truly these two people were made for each other. So without further ado, let's give a warm welcome to Dr. and Mrs. Randy and Jane Hanson."

When Randy and Jane entered the room, all of their guests applauded. The lights turned low and the DJ played a ballad very familiar to them both; it was their song. Randy took Jane's hand and led her onto to the dancefloor. Since the song lyrics expressed how he felt far better than he could, he sang the words to her. When he got to the line, "the hand that lifts your veil…" he chuckled in delight. Even though Jane hadn't worn a veil during the ceremony, he still fulfilled that role. As the song so perfectly stated, he had become her everything.

Surrounded by family and friends, he stole a kiss in the middle of the dancefloor. He couldn't recall a time when he felt as much joy as he did at this moment. Undeniably, this was the best day of his life.

When dinner was announced, Randy held Jane's hand and together they promenaded to the head table, joined by the wedding party. As soon as everyone was seated and had their meal in front of them, Jim stood up.

Randy grabbed his arm. "Where are you going?"

Jim smiled deceitfully. "You'll see." With a wineglass in his hand, he stepped up the DJ's station and picked up the microphone. "Excuse me, ladies and gentlemen."

The crowd quickly settled down.

Randy leaned over to Jane and whispered, "This is where he gets to embarrass the hell out of me. Listen to this load of shit."

Jim adjusted the microphone and began his speech. "As Randy's Best Man, I would like to propose a toast to my best friend and his new wife." Jim glanced over at Randy. "About four years ago, Randy and I were in Santa Cruz playing volleyball on the beach when this beautiful, spunky, fun-loving woman waltzed into his life. She touched his heart in a way that no one ever had. Randy and Jane are the true definition of love, a love deeper and more intense than any I've ever witnessed." Jim lifted his glass. "Randy, this is your day, buddy. And this toast goes out to you, my best friend in the world, and to Jane, your beautiful wife. I wish you happiness for the rest of your lives. I love you both."

Randy felt a sentimental lump in his throat. He lifted his glass and accepted Jim's toast.

Jim sat down with a smug grin on his face.

Randy leaned toward him. "You son-of-a-bitch. Don't say shit like that. You're gonna get me all emotional."

"It's your wedding," Jim said. "You're supposed to be emotional."

About ten minutes into the meal, Jane's father stood up and headed toward the microphone. "Oh no," Jane said. "Daddy's going up there."

Randy turned to look. "Good. You haven't cried in about twenty minutes."

She playfully whacked his arm. "Hush."

Everyone focused their attention on Dale and he began his speech. To no one's surprise, Jane cried the entire time.

The DJ turned down the lights and Jane and her father met on the dancefloor.

While they danced, Randy drank down his glass of wine. "I'm glad they mended whatever issues they had," he said to Jim. "It's good to see them dancing out there together."

"Yes," Jim replied. "Especially after some of the stories you told me. The way you described him, he sounded like an ass."

"He didn't want to let her go. Can't say that I blame him. I don't want to let her go either."

When the song was over, Dale escorted his daughter over to her new husband. Dale and Randy stared at each other for a few seconds. Their relationship hadn't always been the best, and they didn't always understand each other, but today, Dale Davine and Randy Hanson had a mutual respect for one another.

Dale always hoped his daughter would marry someone who would offer her unconditional love, treat her with respect, and have the means and the desire to make sure she had everything she needed. He now knew that Randy was indeed that man. "Welcome to the family, Son."

Overjoyed that his father-in-law acknowledged him as 'son', Randy said, "Thank you, Dad."

Several hours into the reception, Randy and Jane were nowhere to be found. Jim searched everywhere, but couldn't find them. He checked with Lisa, thinking maybe she knew where they were. She hadn't seen them either.

"They're hidin' somewhere I bet," Jim assumed. "And I have a hunch I know where. Come with me."

Jim and Lisa stepped outside and peered down at the beach. Low and behold, the newlyweds were right there, absorbed in a kiss, just like Jim thought they would be. With an ornery smirk, he said, "Hmm, kissing. Whatever shall we do?"

"I say we leave them alone," Lisa suggested.

"We could, but if we do, they'll stay down there all night."

"So? Let them stay down there if they want to. They'll come back inside eventually."

"But everyone is waitin' for them to cut the cake. It is my Best Man duty to find a solution to this problem." Jim cupped his hands over his mouth and attempted to gain Randy's attention. "Hanson!"

Randy pulled away from Jane and glared at Jim. "Something you want?"

"Yeah. We need you to come back inside."

"Why?"

"So you can cut the cake. The natives are getting restless."

Randy grinned at Jane. "What do you think?" he asked her. "You ready for a slice of that cake?"

"I could go for some cake."

"Alrighty." Randy put one arm around her waist and they walked back up to the reception hall together.

As soon as the cake cutting ceremony was announced, Randy picked up the knife. With a grin on his face, he offered a bit of cake cutting advice. "It's just like holding a scalpel. Nice and smooth with gentle strokes."

Jane eyeballed him, thinking he was nuts. "We're slicing a cake, Randy, not performing surgery."

He laughed and gave her a kiss.

Together, both gripping the cake knife, they sliced the first piece. Randy picked up a small slice with his fingers and fed it to Jane, smearing frosting all over her lips. She fed him an even bigger piece, shoving the whole thing in his mouth. He ended up wearing most of it.

"You kinda missed my mouth, Babe."

Jane grabbed a napkin and wiped the frosting off Randy's face. "You look adorable with a frosting mustache."

He dipped his finger into the red-tinted icing and wiped it across the tip of her nose. "Red's a good color for you."

About twenty minutes later, Jane stood in the middle of the dancefloor holding her bridal bouquet in her hand. Single women swarmed all around her. She counted to three and tossed the bouquet over her shoulder. Mandy fought off other women to gain possession of it.

Randy knelt down on one knee in front of Jane and positioned her foot on his thigh. The men in the room gathered for the show. Randy slowly and seductively lifted her silky dress, exposing the bare skin of her leg. Wolf whistles echoed through the area as Randy erotically rubbed his hands up her thigh. He reached his hand way up and, with a lustful look in his eye, slid the garter down her leg. Then he gently kissed her knee, gradually working his way down to her ankle. With the garter securely in his hand, he stood up tossed it behind his back. It landed right at Jim's feet. When Randy saw who had it, he laughed hysterically.

The celebration came to a close. One by one, guests bid the happy couple farewell until the only people left at the reception hall were Randy's family, Jane's father and brother, the wedding party, and Jill.

Randy rubbed his hand across Jane's cheek. "I'm gonna change out of this tux and load our bags in the car. That'll give you some time to say goodbye to your dad."

This was the moment she'd been dreading all night.

"It's gonna be alright." Offering reassurance, Randy kissed her forehead. "Go on."

With a forlorn sigh, Jane walked over to her father. When she saw his face, the tears came.

"Sweetheart, don't cry." Dale Davine held his daughter close.

"I can't help it. I'm going to miss you."

"I'll miss you too." he remarked. "Call me when you get to Seattle."

"We will." She gave her father a lingering hug, hesitant to let go. "I love you, Daddy."

"I love you, Honey."

She then addressed her brother. "Look after Daddy for me and be careful playing football."

"I will," Brian reassured his sister. "Maybe you'll see me in a bowl game next year."

"If you make it into a bowl game, we'll fly out and cheer you on in person."

"Love you, Sis," Brian said, squeezing Jane with his strong arms.

"I love you."

Those were the last words spoken before Dale and Brian left the room.

Twenty minutes later, Randy pranced over to Lisa with a duffle bag over his shoulder and his tux in his hand. "Where's Jane?" he asked.

"She's changing."

"Good." He set his bag down and waited. "Thank you for your help today. We couldn't have pulled this off without you."

"You're welcome," she returned. "Congratulations on graduating, by the way. With all the wedding excitement, I forgot to mention it to you yesterday."

"Thanks."

As soon as Jane was dressed, she and Randy joined his family. "Jane and I are going to take off," he said to them.

"Are you?" Mark asked.

"Yup. Thanks for getting everything situated for us." He looked at Bruce, who stood amid the Hanson family huddle. "And you, hanging out with the Hanson clan. You must be a glutton for punishment."

This comment made Bruce laugh. "Nah. I just like being backstage after the show."

Randy shook Bruce's hand, which quickly turned into a hug. "Thank you, my friend. You keep in touch, you hear me, Buckman?"

"I will. You couldn't get rid of me if you tried."

"Don't get lost in Southern California, buddy," Randy warned, offering his last words of advice. "And if I ever need a neurosurgeon, I'll call you."

"You better call me more often than that. I expect to hear from you at least once a week."

Randy directed his attention to his sister. "Did you get my apartment key from Jim?"

"Yup. Don't worry. I'll make sure the movers don't forget anything."

Mark chimed in, "I'll leave your car keys on the kitchen counter. When the movers come, Robby and I will help get everything sorted out for you. We'll have your bird at our house until you get into town."

Randy replied, "Ok, cool. I'll have his bedding and a bag of food by his cage when you come get him tomorrow. Be careful with him though. I don't want him to bite you."

"I'll be careful."

Before Jim headed home, he bid the newlyweds farewell. "Jill and I have to jet. The kids are gettin' cranky." He took Randy's tux from him so he could return it to the tux shop along with the others. "I'll come by at five o'clock tomorrow morning to take you to the airport."

Randy protested, "Damn, Dude. That's early."

"Yes, but I wouldn't want you to miss your flight, so be ready."

Randy stared at Jim, dreading the departure they would face tomorrow. "Thank you for taking care of the tuxes for me."

"No problem, Bro." Christopher started screaming, tired and cranky from the long day. "I gotta get these kids to bed," Jim said. "But I'll see you guys in the morning."

Randy and Jim embraced in a hug. "Thanks, buddy."

"Later." Jim flashed the shaka sign at his best friend before he left.

Randy wrapped his arm around Jane. "You ready?"

"Yup."

He gave one final farewell to his family. "We're gonna take off."

"Have fun in Bermuda," his father said.

"We will. And we'll see you in a couple weeks. Thanks for everything." He took Jane's hand and escorted her out to the car. As they strolled across the parking lot, Randy sighed in contentment. "Man, this week has been crazy. We have been nonstop go for the last four months. It'll to be nice to sit down and relax for a while. This vacation is just what the doctor ordered."

"I can't believe we're going to Bermuda tomorrow."

Randy popped the trunk. "I know. Warm beaches, clear waters, my beautiful wife. Pure heaven." He squished his bag into a small space between two boxes then carefully placed her wedding dress on top of all the gift bags that were back there. "As exciting as this day was, I'll be glad to get home."

"Me too."

Chapter Sixty-Four

The alarm resounded at 3:45 A.M. Objecting to the loud, shrill buzzing noise the clock emitted, Randy rolled over and slammed it off with a groan. "Shit." He flopped back down on his pillow with one arm and one leg dangling over the edge of the bed. In a daze, he rubbed his eyes and rolled over toward Jane, who was still asleep. A content, but tired smile swept over him. He would be waking up next to this woman for the rest of his life. "Jane," he whispered groggily. "Honey, wake up."

In a sleep-deprived, cantankerous voice, she protested, "Go away."

"Honey, come on." He softly kissed her. "You gotta get up."

She moaned and pulled the pillow over her ears, ignoring his request.

Randy chuckled at her grumpiness. She was definitely not a morning person. He swung his feet over the edge of the bed and stretched, trying to wake up. Jane wasn't moving. He pulled the pillow off her face and the light hit her eyes. "I know it's early, but we have a flight to catch. We're going to Bermuda, today. Remember?"

The scowl on her face was anything but enthusiastic.

Randy thought it was cute. "Good morning, Sunshine," he said, kissing her softly.

She didn't share his sentiments. In fact, she displayed an ill-tempered frown and almost seemed annoyed by his early morning ramblings. "You are way too cheerful at four in the morning."

He tried to lighten her mood. "But we're going on our honeymoon, Baby. Twelve days, just you and me."

Not feeling like conversation at the moment, she groaned.

"We are going to relax, clear our heads and enjoy each other. We'll sip on tropical drinks and make tropical love in the tropical sand on the tropical beach under the tropical sun." Lips parted, he swept her into his arms and kissed her. "Now get up," he insisted.

Jane wearily stumbled out of bed.

"Go ahead and hop in the shower, Babe," he suggested. "I'm gonna do a quick sweep to make sure we haven't forgotten anything."

Still heavy-eyed, she trudged to the bathroom.

Randy packed up the loose articles of clothing that were lying around the room before he snuck into the bathroom to join her.

When they got out of the shower, both wrapped in towels, Randy asked, "You have the tickets and our passports in your purse?"

"Yes," she assured him.

"Good." He moved his lips to her ear and whispered, "Twelve days all to ourselves. It's gonna be great. I hope you packed that red bikini."

"Yes, and the black flowered one."

"Ooh," he said lustfully, looking forward to seeing it on her. "I like that one. And I hope you packed some of those negligées your friends gave you at your bridal shower."

"I did. And the body oils."

"Excellent," he grinned playfully.

At five o'clock sharp, Jim pounded on the door. "Rise and shine."

"Hey," Randy replied.

"You ready, Freddy?"

"Yeah." Randy picked up their suitcases and carried them out to Jim's car.

Randy was barely awake. Jim had to give him a hard time about it. "Dude, you look dead."

"Up all night."

"Doin' what?" Jim wondered.

As if it wasn't obvious. "Jim, it was my wedding night. What the hell do you think I was doing?"

With a snarky grin, Jim said, "Oh. I see. The whole marriage consummation thing. So literally, you were up all night."

"Shut up, Jackass."

They needed to get moving if they were going to dodge morning traffic. "Get your wife so we can jet."

They grabbed some breakfast together then Randy and Jane checked in at the airport. The three of them browsed around the gift shop for a bit before Randy turned to Jane and said, "I'm going to grab a cup of coffee with Jim." He began to get teary-eyed, shuddering at the thought of what he was about to do.

The anguish on Randy's face broke Jane's heart. She tightly gripped his hand. "Do you want me to come with you?"

He closed his eyes, fighting back tears. "No."

"I'll be here if you need me."

"I know." He gave her a kiss then walked over to Jim. "Come get some coffee with me."

"Sure," Jim replied.

The two friends walked to Starbucks without saying a word to each other. They both knew what was about to unfold and had dreaded this moment for days. They each ordered a cup of coffee and sat down at a table, staring at their cups but not speaking. No longer able to handle the silence, Randy finally said, "Dammit, Jim. You and I have been friends for nine years and suddenly I can't think of a damn thing to say."

Jim looked up from his coffee. The agonizing expression on his face was comparable to the one Randy wore. "Look, Randy." He swallowed hard; his voice was shaky. "I wanted to thank you for givin' me the opportunity to be a part of your life, for bein' my best bud over the last nine years, for all those talks we had, for all those times in college we acted stupid together."

Randy gave a choked, desperate laugh, trying to counteract the heartrending pain he felt. "Oh, man. We did some stupid ass shit too."

Jim laughed on the outside but was dying on the inside. "Yeah, we did. I have so many memories of you that will last a lifetime. Oreos and Lakers games, late night study sessions and early mornings at the gym, Coronas and salsa during playoffs, kickin' me in the ass when I didn't feel like studyin', bein' there for me through my breakup with Trina and lettin' me crash at your place. The list goes on and on." Jim couldn't fight the tears any longer. With pain in his heart, he struggled to find the right words. "You are the best friend I've ever had or will ever have."

Randy stared at Jim, trying to maintain steady control over his emotions. "You and I have been through so much together. I couldn't have asked for a better friend."

Jim found it increasingly more difficult to even look at Randy without breaking down. He took a few sharp breaths until he was strong enough to raise his head. "You have a wife now, man. It's time to start your life with her. Just don't be a stranger, ok? Call once in a while."

Tears continued to surge, and Randy couldn't hold them back no matter how hard he tried. He swallowed hard; a suffocating sensation tightened his throat. "You send us pictures of those kids. They're our babies too you know."

"I will."

"And let me know how it's going with Jill."

They stared at each other for a minute, not saying a word. Tears still trembled in Randy's eyes. His chest rose and fell with labored breaths, and a huge, painful knot hardened his stomach. Unable to handle the painful silence, his voice broke, "I love you, man."

They embraced in a hug. "I love you too, Bro."

Jim looked Randy in the eye and said, "You have a wife out there waitin' for you."

Randy managed to crack a smile. "Yeah."

"Have a kickass time in Bermuda. Send pictures, Dude."

"I will," Randy replied with a nod. "I'll call you when we get to Seattle."

"You better." Jim inhaled deeply and stared at his best friend for a second, weighed down by the raw sores of his aching heart. "Be happy, Randy." Those were the last words he said before he threw his coffee cup in the trash and walked away.

Randy shoved his hands in his pockets, his body slumped in despair. With a frown, he leaned against the wall and watched his best friend walk out of sight.

Jane peeked out of the gift shop and saw Randy standing alone with his head slumped. His broad shoulders heaved with every breath. His expression was dark, lifeless. She knew he was upset. She walked over to him and gently touched his arm. In a kind, loving voice, she said, "Hey. How you doing?" Randy didn't have to say a word. The despair on his face told her all she needed to know. "Oh, Sweetie. I'm sorry." She felt him shudder as she drew him nearer.

He clung to her, desperately seeking comfort. Little by little, warmth crept back into his body. "I'm really gonna miss him."

"I know."

"I didn't think it was going to be this hard," he admitted. "I didn't think I'd fall apart like this." Unable to hold them back any longer, Randy let loose of the emotions that were choking his system.

Jane held him in her arms and let him cry.

Jim walked in the door of his apartment feeling more agony than he had ever felt before. With a broken heart, he closed the door and leaned against it. His trembling hand went up to his forehead. Unable to contain his misery, his body slid to the floor, giving in to the pain he felt.

When Jill heard him come in, she slipped her robe over her shoulders and joined him. His spirit was broken. Her heart ached for him. "Jim?"

He immediately stood up, brushed his tears away, and cleared his throat so she wouldn't see him blubbering like a baby.

Even though Jim tried to hide it from her, Jill knew what he had just gone through. Saying goodbye to Randy was probably the hardest thing he'd ever done. She rushed to his side and hugged him. "James. I'm so sorry."

He put his arms around her and held her, choking back tears. "I don't know if I can do this without him, Jill." He sighed heavily, his voice filled with sorrow. "It's always been me and Randy. He's always supported me and kept me going no matter what was going on in my life. Randy's always been my rock. I want him to be happy but…" Jim shook his head, shaking off tears. "I'm gonna miss him."

She held him tighter.

He gently caressed her back, thankful for the unconditional love and limitless understanding this woman always offered him. "Thank you, Babe." He kissed the top of her head. "I love you."

"I love you, too."

Jill only worked a four hour shift that day because she was covering for someone else. When she got off work, Jim took both of her hands and brought her into the bedroom with him.

Curiously, she asked, "Why are we in here?"

He closed the door. "I'm about to say somethin' that might sound crazy. Stop me if I'm jumpin' the gun or if you think I'm completely insane."

She knew he was up to no good. "What are you up to, James?"

"How would you feel if I told you I wanted to have a baby with you?"

She stood quiet for a moment. "What did you say?"

"I want to have a baby with you," he repeated. "I know you've had a bad experience with marriage, but I love you. And Sabrina is like a daughter to me. I love that little girl. I wanna get married, make this a real family, and have a baby with you."

Thinking that, yes, he was totally insane, she replied, "Are you feeling ok? I think this emotional rollercoaster you've been on lately has really worn you down."

He explained, "It dawned on me today how much I need you. I want us to share this whole pregnancy thing together, and I wanna be the man you share the rest of your life with. I want us to be a family." She didn't say anything and her facial expression gave nothing away. Jim wasn't sure what she was thinking. A bit concerned by her reaction, he tried to get her to reply. "Honey Bun, you gonna answer me or leave me hangin'?"

Finally, after a long silence, she said, "Ok."

Jim wasn't sure what that meant. "Ok?"

With a wide smile she said, "Let's do it."

"Sweet." Thrilled that she agreed to his crazy idea, he held her in his arms and kissed her.

Remembering his behavior at the wedding, she said, "Why were you snickering when Randy said his vows to Jane? I thought what he said was the sweetest thing I've ever heard."

"He's a mushy sentimental sap," Jim accused. "He's into all that lovey, starry-eyed shit. That's really not my thing."

"You prefer blood and broken bones instead. It wouldn't kill you to be romantic once in a while you know," she remarked.

Was she challenging him? "I can be romantic."

"Prove it," she exclaimed.

Fine. She wanted romance, he would deliver. "Alright. You're off Wednesday, right?"

"Yes."

"Then we will hire a babysitter and you and I are going to go out to dinner together. Not Happy Meals or pizza either. An actual sit down dinner with menus, cushioned seats, linen napkins, silverware, and ceramic plates."

"Hmm, maybe there is a bit of romance behind that sassiness of yours. There might be hope for you after all, Dr. Ryan," she teased him.

"And for your information, Florence Nightingale, I don't like blood and broken bones. Why do you think I try to fix them?"

She laughed at him. "Smartass."

He took that as a compliment. "Thank you."

Chapter Sixty-Five

Randy and Jane stepped off the plane in Bermuda positively beaming with excitement. Standing at the gate, a man held up a sign with the word *Hanson* printed on it. "Hmm, suppose that's for us?" Randy asked.

"I don't know," Jane replied.

"Won't know if we don't ask." So Randy did just that. "Excuse me, Sir."

The man looked up. "Yes?"

"That sign in your hand says Hanson. My wife and I have that name."

"Are you Dr. Randal Hanson?" the man with the sign asked.

Randy smiled in affirmation. "Yes."

"Ah, good. We've been expecting you. Come with me and I'll retrieve your bags and escort you to your resort."

Randy looked at Jane with wide eyes. "Sweet! First class plane tickets and VIP treatment. I'm liking this already."

They followed the man to the baggage claim, after which he led them outside to a white horse-drawn carriage.

Jane's jaw dropped. "Oh my god. I feel like Cinderella."

Impressed with the romantic aura this place offered, Randy said, "Ok. I have to admit. This is pretty cool."

The carriage driver held out his hand to help Jane. "Ma'am."

Jane took his hand and stepped inside the carriage. Randy followed right behind her.

They trotted through the streets of St. George. The afternoon sun in Bermuda was warm and glowing, fanned by cool sea breezes. Randy snuggled in closer to Jane and enjoyed the scenery around them while the clapping of horse's hooves and the distant chirp of birds serenaded them. Hibiscus, oleander, and flowering trees brightened the already vivid landscape. Coral pink sandy beaches, crystal clear turquoise seawaters, and rolling hills outlined the road they traveled on. The beauty and vibrant color of the picturesque terrain was breathtaking—stunning from one end to the other.

"Randy, look at this place. Have you ever seen anything so beautiful?"

"No, I can't say that I have." He kissed the top of her head and enjoyed the rest of the ride.

Cambridge Beach Luxury Resort had a romantic fairytale feeling. It was a cottage colony located on a private peninsula surrounded by incredible water views, palm trees, tropical flowers, and lush grasses. This was a luxurious destination and would be the ultimate tropical escape.

When the carriage came to a stop, Randy climbed off. He offered his hand to Jane, then they walked hand in hand through the main entrance. The carriage driver carried their bags inside.

As they entered the resort, the desk clerk joyfully greeted them. "Welcome, Dr. and Mrs. Hanson. We've been waiting for you."

Randy stepped forward, stopping at the front desk. He wasn't expecting this kind of welcome. Even though he and Jane had never been here before, they were treated like regulars.

"Your room is ready, Sir. Just need to get your keys."

"Thank you."

While the man retrieved their room keys, Randy picked up a brochure and looked over the list of amenities. This hotel had three private beaches. It also offered both a lap pool and infinity pool, a fitness center, three on-site restaurants, a full service marina, and a variety of recreational activities. "Honey, look at this." He pointed out one particular amenity that drew his attention. "This place has a spa, and as guests we'll receive free lessons in aromatherapy massage." He raised his eyebrows seductively. "That will be fun. We need to check that out."

"Yes we do," she replied.

"And every morning, we'll receive a complimentary breakfast in our cottage. We won't have to worry about transportation because the resort will provide us a horse-drawn carriage to any location on the island."

The clerk handed Randy two keycards. "Here you are, Sir. We will bring your bags out to you. If you need anything, let us know. We hope you enjoy your stay."

The hotel staff was friendly and offered them personal attention. Randy was impressed. "Thank you." He took the keycards from the clerk, handed one to Jane, then they headed out to their room.

Their cottage had a private terrace and a bird's eye view of the beach, perfect for romantic moonlight dinners. The king-sized bed in the bedroom, along with a separate dressing area and living room, provided space and comfort. The entire suite was decorated in traditional, colorful chintzs and antique furniture. The marble bathroom featured a whirlpool tub surrounded by scented candles and luscious green potted plants. There was a television in the living room, high speed Wi-Fi, and a small refrigerator which was already stocked with Pepsi, Diet Pepsi, and Coronas.

A bottle of champagne sat on the table accompanied by a large basket of fruit. A card was attached to the basket. Randy picked it up and read it. *Happy honeymoon, Jane and Randy. Have a glass on us. Enjoy the sun, the sand, and the sex. Eat some fruit, take a soak, and indulge in the joys of marital bliss. We love you guys. Jim, Bruce, and Amanda.* He set the card down and looked around as if he had lost something. "Honey, do you see a coffee pot anywhere?"

Jane searched the room with him, but neither found one.

"That won't do. I'm not staying twelve days in this room without coffee." He gave his wife a kiss and uttered, "I'm gonna call the front desk."

While Randy was on the phone, Jane unpacked their belongings.

Several minutes later, resort staff brought them a single-cup coffee machine, a bag of coffee packets, and a package of Styrofoam cups. "Now I'm in heaven," Randy said, staring out the window at the dazzling ocean view. "Got my coffee, a spectacular view, a bottle of champagne, and twelve nights of romance with my wife. This is going to be incredible." He moved his mouth to hers and kissed her. The sweetness of her lips whisked through his body like lightning, stunning him and leaving him breathless.

That night, they had a romantic candlelight dinner together on their terrace, in full view of a golden ocean sunset that beamed through the windows of their cottage. It was a spectacular, blazing affair.

Jane reached up and gently touched Randy's face. "You need to shave."

He rubbed his chin with his hand; it was a bit scratchy. "I know. I've been kind of occupied. But tell you what, I'll go do it right now." He kissed her tenderly then walked inside the room to get his overnight bag and shaving supplies. Jane followed him, closing the glass plated door behind them.

While he was in the bathroom shaving, Jane removed her clothes and leaned barebacked on the bed. A soft breeze blew in from the window, and the luminous luster of the moon reflected off the water outside. She heard the bathroom door creek and turned her head toward the noise.

Randy walked into the room naked. He eyed her soft round breasts, which were more enticing than ever. Wanting to touch her, he came closer to the bed and sat next to her. She sat up and slid her arms around his neck; his went across her back. Tilting his head, he groped with his mouth for hers, exploring her luscious lips and tongue. He felt her skin under his hands, sleekly tormenting him. Slowly, his hands moved downward, skimming either side of her hips and thighs. Her breasts and belly crushed against his chest, and he could feel his heart pounding.

Embraced together, they reclined on the bed. He looked down at her with passion-filled eyes. "You're beautiful," he said.

She wrapped her arms and legs around him, living ropes that bound him to her. As his body molded with hers, her mouth dropped open, gasping in helpless astonished pleasure. He buried his chin into her shoulder, feeling the softness of her cheek against his. Bound together, his body melted against hers, and he surrendered to the maddening, exasperated drive within him.

Randy woke early the next morning. Jane was in his arms, and the early morning sun caressed their bodies. Waking in the same bed with her—his wife—was, in a way, more intimate than the sexual act preceding it. He was supremely happy, happier than he could ever remember being. He stretched luxuriously, yawned, and cleared his throat. "Good morning, Baby."

"Good morning, Sweetie." She peeked out the window at the clear blue sky. "It's a beautiful day."

"Yes it is. But then again, any morning I wake up next to you is beautiful." He felt her smile against his chest. "If I could scrape up the energy, I'd call for breakfast."

"I'm too comfortable to get up and eat." She snuggled closer, enjoying the feel of his arms around her.

"We should go down to the beach today," he suggested. "Take a swim, lounge in the sand. Maybe make love under a coconut tree."

"That's just what you need, to be hit in the head and knocked unconscious by a coconut on our honeymoon."

This comment made him laugh. "That would be a little hard to explain, wouldn't it?" He took in a deep breath and sighed contently. "Oh man, this is the life. Hanging out with my wife with no responsibilities whatsoever, having a night of inconceivable romance under the stars, waking up to the warm sun with you in my arms. It doesn't get any better than this."

Jane softly kissed his chest.

He placed his hand behind her head, caressing every strand of her glowing hair. The closeness he felt with her at this moment was more intense than anything he had ever experienced before. With a smile permanently glued to his face, he kissed her head then swung his legs off the bed, sat up, and stretched. He slipped on a pair of shorts and walked over to the paned glass door that looked over the ocean. "This is an incredible view."

Jane lay on the bed watching him.

He opened the door and stepped out to the terrace to take in the morning air. The tide was in. The pink sand glistened in the warm sun. Little crabs and insects scattered across the beach. A cool breeze swayed the branches of the palm trees, and the sound of waves lapping against the shore filled the air. He took in a deep breath to clear his lungs. "Come out here and join me, Babe."

Jane got up, slipped on her silk robe, and joined him on the terrace.

He pulled her in front of him, embraced tightly in his arms, and they enjoyed the lush view together. "You know, I've been so wrapped up in the chaos of my life that I've never stopped to smell the roses. There are many things in life I'd taken for granted. Like those little bugs crawling around in the sand or the graceful way the waves move across the shore. I never took the time to enjoy little things like that. But the world looks different to me now. Every tiny speck of sand has a purpose and each one is beautiful in its own way. Every leaf, every petal of every flower, every drop of rain. Man, the intricate detail of it all. This world we're in is amazing. Being with you has helped me see that." He kissed her hair, taking in the sensual aroma of it.

They stood and stared at the beach, immersed in one another's arms. After several minutes, Jane claimed, "I'm hungry."

"I am too, and I'm dying for a cup of coffee." He turned her around and kissed her. "Tell you what. Why don't we take a shower and call for some breakfast. Then we'll check out what this island has to offer and find you that waterfall."

After breakfast, Randy and Jane reported to the front desk to get information about attractions in Bermuda, at which time they decided to spend the day snorkeling by the coral island. When dusk settled on the island, the sun had gone down just far enough to bloody the sea and stain the pink sand a hazy shade of orange. Randy held Jane in his arms on the beach as they watched the sun disappear into the sea. Crickets chirped and the fragrance of tropical flowers perfumed the air. Randy used the romantic atmosphere to steal a kiss.

"Let's go back to the room, take a soak in that whirlpool tub, and crack open a bottle," he suggested.

Jane loved this idea. "Sounds good."

Once inside their cottage, Randy lit the candles around the tub and uncorked a bottle of wine. He poured wine into two glasses, shut off all the lights, stripped down naked, and climbed into the tub. He placed Jane's glass on the edge and held his in his hand. "I have some wine here for us and some nice candlelight. All I need now is you."

Jane came into the bathroom wearing her silk robe. He stared at her and grinned, swishing his wine around in his glass. "Care to join me?"

She slowly untied the lace that bound her robe to her. He sized her up seductively as she stripped the silky garment off her shoulders and let it fall to the floor, exposing her delicate curvy body to him.

He took her hand and pulled her in with him. She sat on his lap, with one leg on either side of him. The soft flickering of the candlelight made her hair glow and shadowed her beautiful face with erotic luster. He took a sip of his wine then gently set his glass on the edge of the tub. His fingertips slowly moved down her wet body. The nipples of her breasts peeked out of the steaming water and barely rubbed against his chest. His breathing intensified. Just looking at his gorgeous wife made deep desire brew within him.

He handed Jane a glass of wine.

Jane took a sip and said, "That jambalaya we had for dinner tonight was good."

"It was."

"And all those creatures that live in the coral were fun to watch."

"They were." Randy didn't feel like talking. He had other ideas. His eyes fixated on Jane's lips.

"The man at the restaurant said there were some cool shops in St. George. Since we're going that way to see the lighthouse tomorrow, I thought maybe we could check them out."

"That's fine."

"Wasn't the sunset beautiful tonight?" She tried to take another sip from her glass. But before she could, Randy took the glass out of her hand and set it on the edge of the tub next to his. Protesting this action, she declared, "I was drinking that."

"I know."

Normally Randy was quite talkative. But tonight, he seemed to have a two-word sentence vocabulary, and he was staring at her with a look in his eye she'd never seen before. "You ok?" Jane asked, concerned about his odd behavior.

"Everything's great," he said with a grin.

"You're not saying much. You sure you're ok?"

His lips traced the silkiness of her sun-tanned skin. "Your sexy body is staring at me, and your lips are enticing as hell. I love the way the candlelight shadows the curves of your breasts."

Randy's sexy bedroom voice and seductive words radiated through her like a magnet. Her lips parted slightly as she gazed upon him with fevered want. "Keep talking."

"And I love the way your skin feels when it touches mine. I can feel your heat." His finger meandered across the little crevice between her breasts then down to her bellybutton.

Jane's chest heaved in excitement. She closed her eyes and lifted her chin, giving him free access to her neck, which he took full advantage of. He kissed the smooth skin at the base of her throat and slowly worked his way to her breast. Her heart pulsated wildly.

"This feels really good."

"Ssh." He held his index finger over her lips. "No talking. Just relax and let me love you."

He sank his fingertips into the flesh of her buttocks then captured her lips with his. His kiss was more persuasive than ever; it gave her chills, despite the fact that she was sitting in hot steamy water. As his tongue explored every crevice of her mouth, she felt his strong hand cup her breast. Aroused now, she drew herself closer to him, giving herself freely to the passion of his embrace.

The pleasure was pure and explosive. He moaned softly and closed his eyed, taking in every sensation. Skin to skin, they were as one. He moved slowly and steadily, quickening his breath with every motion. The flickering light in the room, the warm sensation of the water, the sweet aroma of the candles, the taste of her lips, and the sound of each other's breath made the experience more sensuous than any intimacy they had shared before. Every human sense was stimulated.

In the morning, Randy opened his eyes to full caresses of the warm sun on his and his wife's naked bodies. Jane was in his arms and her legs were intertwined with his. He removed her carefully, trying not to wake her up. Luckily she was a pretty heavy sleeper, so he was able to sneak out of bed without disturbing her. He slipped on some clothes and quickly combed his hair then headed down to the lobby to talk to the concierge.

The man at the front desk greeted him. "Good morning, Dr. Hanson. Are you enjoying your stay?"

"Yes, very much, thank you. I was wondering if you could help me out."

"What can we do for you, Sir?"

"Is there a swimming hole with a waterfall anywhere around here?"

"As a matter of fact there is. At the far end of the beach, there's some thick foliage. Hike through there about thirty yards and you'll find a hidden cove. There's a lagoon back there with a small waterfall tricking into it. Not many people know about it because it's pretty remote and well-hidden. It's a beautiful place though. Definitely worth the hike."

The corners of Randy's mouth formed an impish smile. "Perfect. Appreciate your help."

"Can we get you anything else, Sir?"

"Some breakfast brought out to our room would be nice."

Graciously, the concierge complied. "Certainly. I'll have the kitchen whip something up for you."

"Thank you."

Randy went back out to their room and quietly opened the door. Jane was still asleep. He slipped into the bathroom and took a quick shower before room service arrived with fresh fruit, bagels, scrambled eggs, freshly brewed coffee, and ice cold milk. Randy tipped the man then brought the tray inside. He brought a plate over to Jane and removed the metal warming cover. "Janey, Honey. Breakfast."

The salivating scent of eggs roused her sense of smell. She opened her eyes and began to stir.

"You hungry?" He handed her a fork.

"Thank you, Sweetie." Appreciative of the way Randy always went out of his way to do small things for her, she sat up and softly kissed him.

Randy sat in a chair next to her, and they conversed over breakfast.

Following a busy day in St. George, Jane and Randy lounged on the beach together watching the sunset as they listened to the sound of the waves. The moment the sun set,

Randy hopped off the sand and held his hands out to Jane, lifting her up. "Come with me. I wanna show you something."

Hand in hand, they strolled to the far end of the beach. They navigated through some thick trees and bushy green plants to discover a hidden tropical oasis—an open sanctuary of beautiful colorful flowers and lush greenery surrounded a clear blue lagoon. Jane's mouth dropped open in awe, admiring the splendor of it all. "Oh my god. This is beautiful."

"Listen. Can you hear that?" Randy pointed to a cliff where a small, steadily flowing waterfall emptied into the pool below. "There's your waterfall, Baby."

A blissful smile painted her pretty face. "How did you find this?"

"This morning I had a chat with the concierge and he clued me in on this little treasure." Her eyes shone bright in the pale light of the moon. "Come on." He held her hand and led her down to the water. At the edge of the lagoon, he stripped his swim trunks off and dove in. When he came up for air, he said, "Come in with me, Honey. The water's warm. It feels great."

She seductively bit her lip and stripped off her bathing suit. Randy watched in anticipation as he treaded water and waited for her. She dove in after him, and together they swam to the shallow waters behind the waterfall.

Randy felt sand under his feet. He stood up and pulled Jane into his arms. "So, what do you think?"

She was completely overwhelmed. "This is the most beautiful place I've ever seen."

"Will this work for your fantasy?"

"It's perfect. I can't believe you did this." She threw her arms around him.

He stroked his fingers through Jane's wet hair. Slowly, they moved under the waterfall, where the water sleekly ran down their bodies. Randy rubbed his fingertips across the bare skin of her back and suckled her breasts, while the cool water massaged their skin. He gradually moved his lips to hers, feeling every contour of her mouth. Under a moon glow spotlight, his body molded to hers, fulfilling Jane's long-awaited fantasy.

Everything around them was serene, from the peaceful melody of the crickets at night to the warm rays of the sun in the morning. When the sun was out, they lazed together on the beach and swam in the warm ocean waters. During the daylight hours, they explored the sights of Bermuda, including the thirty-six acre botanical garden and Devil's Hole Aquarium with over four-hundred different types of sea creatures from groupers and sharks to giant sea turtles. They followed a looping walkway and crossed a wooden pontoon bridge that led to a vast cavern one-hundred twenty feet underground. They went horseback riding along an eighteen mile trail edged with hibiscus, palm trees, and lush tropical gardens that ran the length of the island. Randy even tried his hand at fishing the Bermuda seas, showing Jane how to cast a line out.

By night, they sank their toes into the wet sand and enjoyed the stunning sunsets. They shared romantic dinners in the privacy of their terrace and lounged in the whirlpool feeding each other fruit. Giving each other massages with scented body oils was a nightly activity for them, and they often drank champagne or wine under the stars. Their time together was heavenly and truly bonding in many ways.

Their final night together in Bermuda came with the setting of the sun. Randy stood on the terrace in a white terrycloth robe and enjoyed the idyllic view in front of him, taking in every sight, every scent, every sound, making it all a permanent part of his memory.

Jane climbed out of the shower to find Randy staring off at the horizon. She slipped a robe over her navy blue negligée and tied it around her waist. Wanting to be closer to her husband, she stepped out into the night air and stood by his side.

With a content smile on his face, Randy took her hand and pulled her in into his arms. "The last twelve days with you have been the best days of my life. Look at the beauty, the enchantment, the romance of this place. We definitely need to come back here for our anniversary."

"That would be nice."

"We have so many memories to take home with us, memories I will cherish for the rest of my life."

"I know. I don't want to leave."

He kissed the top of her head. "I don't either. But reality awaits us. My residency and grad school for you, and we have to unpack and set up our new home. We have a lot to do."

Jane sighed, thinking about the tremendous amount of work awaiting them upon their return to Seattle.

"My sentiments exactly." He moved his lips to her ear. "I love you, Mrs. Hanson."

"I love you, too." Standing under the stars of a moonlit Bermuda sky, they held each other and embraced in a kiss.